From nationally acclaimed, bestselling author

MAGGIE SHAYNE

Miranda's Viking

Yesterday, Viking w~~...~~ perfectly preserved in ~~...~~ in scientist Miranda ~~...~~ all six feet seven inches of ~~...~~ the touch—except for his ice-cold heart. But Miranda knew *one* way to thaw it out....

Kiss of the Shadow Man

Her memory erased in an "accident," Caitlin Rossi discovered a husband she no longer knew—yet fuzzy images of Dylan's burning passion penetrated the darkness. Then Cait realized there had been no accident—and *someone* might try again!

Out-of-this-World Marriage

Thomas Duffy had lost his faith in everything—until Janella landed in his life. She was full of otherworldly charm and a purity that tugged at his rusty heartstrings. Though their marriage was a facade, Thomas might learn something about love from his out-of-this-world wife.

Books by Maggie Shayne

MAGGIE SHAYNE

AFTER MIDNIGHT...

Silhouette Books

Published by Silhouette Books

America's Publisher of Contemporary Romance

SILHOUETTE BOOKS

ISBN 0-373-20178-8

by Request

AFTER MIDNIGHT...

Copyright © 2000 by Harlequin Books S.A.

The publisher acknowledges the copyright holder of the individual works as follows:

MIRANDA'S VIKING
Copyright © 1994 by Margaret Benson

KISS OF THE SHADOW MAN
Copyright © 1994 by Margaret Benson

OUT-OF-THIS-WORLD MARRIAGE
Copyright © 1995 by Margaret Benson

Visit Silhouette at www.eHarlequin.com

Printed in U.S.A.

CONTENTS

Dear Reader,

Before I'd ever published a novel, I had a wild idea for a tale about a Viking warrior, frozen over time, until he was thawed out by a modern-day female archaeologist. I could clearly see this big, muscular, mostly naked man on a table in a lablike room. I could see a woman in a white lab coat frantically fiddling with controls, her back to him. And I could hear him draw his first strangled gasping breath. I saw the woman go stiff and turn slowly, her eyes wide with disbelief.

Eventually I set this story aside, thinking it might be a bit too "out there" for the market at the time. I worked on others, and sold three books. But some of my writing friends started urging me to dig out *Miranda's Viking* and do something with it. Silhouette loved this story, and decided to publish it as an Intimate Moments novel.

The second paranormal Intimate Moments title of the two, *Out-of-this-World Marriage*, is another oddball notion of mine that begins with a gorgeous female alien crash-landing in a doctor's backyard in small-town Iowa, and was inspired by the film *Starman*. Not your typical Intimate Moments story!

The one novel in this collection that does not have any paranormal element is the one that was originally published as a Silhouette Shadows title. I wondered if I could write a dark, scary tale that would fit the line without using anything supernatural. *Kiss of the Shadow Man* was my idea of a modern take on a classic Gothic plot.

Enjoy!

Maggie Shayne

MIRANDA'S VIKING

To Maria Greene,
who helped Rolf think like a true Norseman,
and to Anita Gordon, who helped him speak like one.
And to Gayle Callen and Angela Bartelotte,
who helped him hoist the sails for his ultimate voyage.

Prologue

The sting of icy spray seemed determined to peel the skin from his face, despite the heavy beard he'd grown to protect it. The long, sleek *drakkar* pitched and rolled helplessly, a toy held in the unpredictable hands of an angry sea. Frigid waves reached even to the prow, battering the fierce-looking dragon's head carved there. Men struggled to capture the tattered square sail they'd attempted to furl, but the wind proved too powerful even for their muscled arms. With one vicious gust the mass of green-and-white-striped fabric was carried away and dumped into the raging waters. A sharp crack, a slow groan and the mast came down like felled timber. Rolf lurched forward, abandoning the rudder to the fury of the sea. His arms outstretched, he launched himself from the deck toward the three men. He caught one, sending him backward to land with a jarring thud. The other man had instinctively ducked his leader's attack. Rolf had lost sight of the third.

Rolf struggled to his feet against the frantic rocking of the ship. Shielding his eyes from the slashing, sleet-filled wind he saw Svein, the man who'd avoided his running leap, lying facedown with the heavy mast across his back. He ran forward, shouting uselessly into the roaring wind for assistance. He bent to the mast and bared his teeth with the effort to raise it. But the wood was smooth and wet. Less effort to cling to a slippery eel. He chanced one downward glimpse as he steeled himself for a second assault on the burden, and saw that his efforts were all for naught. Svein's agonies had already ceased.

Rolf tilted his head back and roared his anger, his fury, his frustration. All this carnage! All due to the faithless heart of one king and the treachery of another. A curse on Knut's soul, wherever it might now reside! And a curse upon Magnus, as well! Ah, but how well he knew that the true credit for this mayhem rested in one devious woman.

Rolf lurched sideways as the ship was tossed again, and he struggled to his feet, leaning into the wind to make his way back to the rudder. When the wind threatened to down him, when the bite of the ice on his face almost forced him to turn back, he needed only think of her to regain his strength, his determination. He would not surrender easily.

Adrianna. How he'd adored her. How he'd longed to have her. Fool! He'd only been following the lustful path of every red-blooded Norseman ever to lay eyes upon her stunning beauty. How gullible he'd been not to see that her beauty was but an illusion. Her flame-colored hair and wide-set, deep gray eyes were but gifts of heredity, or fate. Her slender frame and endlessly long limbs convinced a man of her fragile nature. Her graceful and rare height only added to her allure. Truly, though, her heart was as ugly as death itself.

By the gods, he'd been taken in!

As had Knut.

A frigid wave smashed into the side of the sleek dragon ship and she rocked dangerously, righted herself only to be pummeled by another. Rolf reached out, nearly blinded by the sleet and his own bitter anger, and he gripped the ice-coated rudder. He watched in mounting fury as the chests filled with the plunder of this journey slid over the side and sank beneath the waves. The booty was the result of his rage against Adrianna and against the fates themselves. For months he'd vented that rage as a scourge on the shores of every land he'd passed. Again and again his *drakkar* had swept down upon the rich coastal villages of England, of Francia, of Normandy, of Ireland, with vengeance billowing in her sails. So great had been his plunder he'd had to hide the first of it well, before returning again for more. This latest trip had netted greater riches than the first.

All of it gone now at the whim of an angry wind.

The hurricane raged around him, rain and sleet slanting so heavily he could no longer see an arm's length ahead of him. He clung to the side as his glorious ship lurched and rolled over, but to no avail. Icy water reached for him, caught him in relentless, greedy hands, and dragged him away. He felt himself enfolded in raging, biting cold. He struggled to keep his head above the waves. He would not surrender! He was a warrior! He would die at the point of a sword, not at the hand of a storm.

He refused to allow his exile to become a death sentence. He was *úrhrak,* outcast, but he would not die as one. He went under, fought his way to the surface and was pulled beneath the waves again. His body burned with cold. His muscles tightened to such a degree they began to tear themselves from the bone. His lungs screamed for air. His head pounded as if it would crack and his heart seemed about to explode.

Once more the angry waves tossed his body higher. He was allowed only one glimpse, just enough to fill him with the bitterness of irony. The barren shores of Helluland, black water and white ice, seemed to mock him. So close, he might've been able to swim it, had not the seas been so angry, so determined to take him into their final, glacial embrace.

Nei! He would not die! He was not yet ready to ride off with the beautiful Valkyrie upon the backs of their magnificent horses. Not ready to let them carry him onward to Valhalla where he'd feast and fight with the fallen, perhaps with Odin himself. *Nei!* He forced his arms to stroke against the frigid waves, forced his legs to propel him toward the shore.

Even as his body was tossed and battered, Rolf silently vowed he would not die. When he could no longer raise an arm for even a single stroke, he closed a fist around the gilded hilt of his sword, Hefnd, still secure in its bronze-trimmed leather scabbard, still held fast to his nearly lifeless body. "We have not yet finished," he whispered, though the words were drowning as they left his lips.

The last thing Rolf glimpsed before the waters swallowed him up were the barely visible shapes of the fur-ensconced Skrælingar of the north looking on from the shore. He imagined their eyes were filled with awe, and with wonder.

Chapter 1

The wind had knives in it. Razorlike shards bit into her face and stung her nose as Miranda lifted the pickax high above her head and brought it down. Its tip cracked into the solid ice, spraying her cheeks with more shrapnel. She brushed at her face with a gloved hand and paused, glancing to the right, where her father worked furiously on the glacier. The cave was here, its mouth sealed by an icy hand. The sonar equipment had confirmed it. The cave and the secrets it had concealed for centuries lay just beyond this wall of ice—a wall left slightly less than impenetrable by the recent trend of global warming. The cave was only a few inches away. Or perhaps, Miranda's analytical mind reasoned, not *the* cave, but *a* cave.

No. *The* cave. She could feel it.

She warned herself against childish optimism. It would likely put a fissure in Russell O'Shea's stone heart if this expedition turned out to be yet another wild-goose chase. She hoped to God it wasn't. Because she knew, all too well, it would probably be his last.

Now, however, even the cool, sensible Miranda that ruled her most of the time couldn't contain the thrill of anticipation. This time, even *she* was convinced. The legend had been handed down in various forms and was still told in the remote Inuit villages of Baffin Island. The variations were wild, but the similarities were strong—strong enough for Miranda to concur with her father that a kernel of truth must be concealed in the tall tales. He believed that "kernel" to be the man buried in the hidden cave, sealed by ice.

That he was a god, who had ridden the seas upon a dragon only to be attacked by demon spirits before he could reach the shore, was, naturally, nonsense.

An unusual man, a man unlike any encountered by the early Inuit, had been pulled from the sea and buried with great honor in a cave. The gods, it was said, then sealed the cave, thus preserving their comrade for some divine future mission. Highly unlikely, of course. That his body might have been preserved by an act of nature, however, was entirely possible. It was that man they sought.

Tracking the exact location of the Ice Man had been her father's life's work and, in turn, hers. Because of that renowned devotion to this project and the sterling credentials of the Drs. O'Shea, the government of Canada had agreed to a joint expedition. They accepted the funding of the illustrious Beaumont University and the leadership of its most respected professor. Her father.

The expedition would be the culmination of his life's work. The one thing he cared about, the one thing he felt any real passion for. And it would come just in time.

She wriggled the pick free of the stubborn ice that held it, lifted it once more, and brought it down hard. And again, and again, so absorbed in the work she was barely aware of the others working similarly in other areas around her. She paused periodically to glance toward her father. Tall and far too thin, he worked a short distance from her, his long arms wielding a pickax of his own. She didn't like the slight grayness to his stern face, or the short, shallow way he breathed. She didn't like the stiff way he tended to hold his left arm and shoulder. She was certain he'd sit down and clutch his chest if he were alone. In front of her and the others, though, he'd never concede to a weakness.

She pulled her gaze from him and resumed working. With the next impact, a huge chunk of ice broke away to drop backward into a vast blackness. Miranda stiffened as a low sound, like the deep-throated howl of a wolf, filled the air. Before her eyes the hole made itself bigger. The edges crumbled and fell inward. The moaning sound grew louder as the hole grew larger, and it took a full minute for her to realize what caused it. She dropped the pickax. "Russell, I'm through!"

Her father froze in place for an instant before he rushed toward her. He paused at her side, one hand gripping her upper arm to pull her back a few steps. In moments they were surrounded by the others, all craning their necks to see and murmuring excitedly.

"It's a vacuum, Miranda." He released her arm almost at once.

She nodded, understanding as her father did, that no air had been inside the cave. A vacuum seal had been created by nature and now the fresh air was rushing in, filling the far recesses of the cave with life-giving oxygen. She stood back and watched in fascination as larger and larger chunks of ice snapped away from the hole she'd made, and the opening grew. The moan became a roar, then slowly began to fade. The rush of air eased little by little...and then it died. Swallowing hard, Miranda looked at her father.

His hard gray eyes very nearly twinkled, and the pallor of his sculpted cheeks gave way to glowing color. She wondered if he'd ever felt for another human the way he felt for his work.

"This is it, Miranda. You know it, don't you? You feel it, just as I do."

She couldn't help but smile despite the part of her that ached over his inability to show his feelings for her this way. His excitement, so rare, was contagious. "You usually call relying on feelings unscientific and foolish."

"Not when there's hard evidence to back them up." He turned from her and shouted, "Bring the lights, some rope! We're going in."

A lean, rather awkward student raced down toward one of the crop of dome tents, which seemed to have sprouted up like vegetation far below on the tundra in the glacier's shadow. It was warmer there, nearly fifty degrees unless one factored in the biting Arctic winds. This was summer on Baffin Island. Presently he returned with two huge spotlights, a length of rope looped over his shoulder and Russell's ever-present journal held to his chest. "You'll need this, Dr. O'Shea."

Russell took it and slapped the youth on the shoulder, his way of showing what little affection he was capable of feeling. "That I will, Darryl. Go on and get the cameras and other equipment. Choose five others and wait here. I'll call you when I need you." Darryl's face beamed. He shoved his round wire rims up higher on his nose, tugged his knit ski hat down over his ears, and raced away once more.

Miranda took one of the lights, flicked it on and shone the beam through the opening, now large enough to crawl through. She bit her lip and prayed silently the cave would be large and open, not cramped and suffocating. She wasn't certain she could go a step farther if it were the latter. Already her heart began to pound, her hands to shake. She chanced a quick glimpse toward her father, dreading to see that he'd noticed her hesitation. He detested weakness, and that's what her mild claustrophobia was. A weakness, but a manageable one.

The darkness within was unrelieved. The beam of her light danced over black stone walls and an equally dark floor. No dank, musty air rushed up to greet her. The place had been filled with the fresh air from outside. She smelled no hint of dampness or mildew. Best of all, the cave was huge, at least, this first section of it. Maybe she'd be all right.

"The floor's about ten feet down." She picked up a chunk of ice and dropped it, nodding when she heard it thud. "Sounds solid enough." Drawing a fortifying breath, she handed her light to her father, then scooped up one of the helmets lying nearby and flicked its light on, instead. She fastened the chin strap with care. "I'm going in." She attached the belt around her waist, giving the carabiner links an experimental tug.

Her father handed her a rope, with another carabiner attached. She snapped it to her belt and slipped over the edge. She waited until those anchoring the rope had drawn it taut before beginning to rappel down.

"I'm right behind you," Russell called out. The hiss of rope through the links was punctuated by the tap of her boots against the sheer inner wall. The distance was not great. At the bottom she disconnected, and the rope disappeared above her.

Her father dangled a flashlight a short distance above her head. She caught it, her five feet seven inches of unseemly height making it easier. His own light followed, and then he lowered himself to the floor beside her.

Miranda tucked the spare lights into a pocket, and used the one on her helmet to examine their surroundings. The light showed her a narrow, stone-lined area, like a tunnel. The ceiling arched high above it, making it a bit less likely that she'd be rendered immobile with panic as she moved through. There was only one way to go and she turned in that direction, her father right beside her.

As they moved, their steps echoed. They placed each foot

carefully, testing each bit of stone beneath for safety before putting any weight on it. Miranda fought her mind's rebellion at being in the place. She tried to think of herself as the fearless heroine in a gothic novel, traversing the hollow, chilly halls of a castle. Much more romantic than being a shivering scientist moving through a dark cave in search of a well-preserved body. She moved her head and her light…if she were that heroine, her light would come glimmering from a candelabra…scanning the black walls for writings or drawings indicating they were about to find what they'd hoped for. Surely if the Inuit had believed the man to be a god, there would be something, a shrine of some sort.

There was nothing. Perhaps the Inuit thought to protect their newfound god by secreting him here.

They rounded a curve in the passage and stepped into a large open area, its ceiling a massive stone dome. She nearly gasped with relief when the stone walls expanded so suddenly. The romantic within her fancied this would be the great hall of that castle she'd been imagining. And her fur-collared parka would be instead a white muslin nightdress.

She almost laughed at her ridiculous ponderings. Next she'd be casting a pile of bones in the role of the brooding hero, who would sweep her away on a tide of passion! She chided herself. It was okay to use foolishness to distract her from her fear of small spaces. She knew such fantasies did not occur in real life, nor would she wish them to.

This was real life. Biting cold, hard work, and piles of bones from which secrets could be learned.

Miranda turned around slowly as she stood near the center of the chamberlike area, shining her beam on the walls and rock formations around her, wondering how long it had been since a human had stood in this place, seen these things. The air was frigid, fresh, and utterly still. The silence within the cave was like a living thing, a heavy leaden force that could smother them should the idea appeal to it. She shivered, took a calming breath, and continued studying the hollowed-out room, putting aside her imaginary world in favor of the real one.

Her body stilled as a tingling sensation skittered over her nape. The tiny hairs there stood upright, and suddenly Miranda knew they were not alone. She felt the presence as surely as she felt the cold air on her face. Behind her. Directly behind her. She turned very slowly. Her legs became jelly, and as all the air escaped her lungs in a slow, involuntary rush, Miranda sank to her knees.

He lay upon a table of stone, his skin as perfectly pale and rigid as if he were carved of white marble. His hair gleamed the light's reflection, making it seem silvery, but as stiff as the rest of him. It was long, and as her eyes adjusted, she saw it was a deep golden blond, rather than the pale silver it had at first seemed. His face was all but concealed behind a bushy, reddish beard that curled wildly. He wore a brown tunic over a well-worn shirt that might once have been blue but now was gray. The long sleeves of the shirt covered his arms, and the shorter tunic sleeves came only to his elbows. A wide black belt with a tarnished buckle that might prove to be silver if it was polished encircled his middle. His legs were encased in tight-fitting black leggings that clung to his form. Miranda's throat went suddenly dry as she studied thighs like tree trunks and calves apparently banded with steel. On his feet were furry boots laced tightly with leather thongs.

Her father had heard her gasp, seen her sink to the floor, and he, too, turned to stare in wonder at the slumbering giant before them. "It's him," he said in the darkness.

Miranda forced herself to stand and look at her father. "It can't be.... Russell, look at him. He's...perfect." The last word was a whisper. She shook herself. "He can't have been lying here for nine centuries."

"It was the vacuum, Miranda." He spoke with certainty. His hand came up, his forefinger extended. "Look."

She moved her gaze to the direction he pointed and saw the weapon that lay at the giant's feet. The sword's blade was at least four feet long, and from all appearances, without rust, though the iron seemed dulled with time. The gilded hilt added another foot to its length, and was decorated with intricate patterns and engraved with shapes that might have been letters, words. She moved closer, leaned over it, somehow unable to make herself touch the beautiful piece. She frowned when she recognized the symbols. "Runes." Frowning harder, she studied the ancient writing and tested her memory, as she tried to translate. "*Hefnd. Vengeance*," she said slowly.

"Look, Miranda. The battle-ax, the shield."

She looked, and shook her head in awe, knowing what her eyes were showing her, but still not quite convinced. The fanciful Miranda within would have been alive with excitement, but that one was allowed no access to the real world. She was reserved for those times with the books, late at night when she needed to fight the loneliness.

The scientist, Miranda O'Shea, was a skeptic. "All the things you'd expect to find with a Viking," she conceded. She looked closely at the sword. "It looks genuine, but—"

"What we have here, Miranda, is the perfectly preserved remains of what was once a Viking warrior…maybe *our* Viking warrior." He shook his head. "This is the find of the century. It has to be him, Miranda. The Plague of the North. The man banished from all of Scandinavia for treason against Knut the Great, and who wreaked havoc in his vengeance." He paused. "I'd say his sword was aptly named."

She turned to face her father, amazed he would believe so easily. He set his light on a stone protrusion, opened his journal, and pulled a pencil from his coat's deep pocket.

He sat down near the man and began writing furiously, effectively shutting her out.

Miranda studied the giant again and an uneasiness crept over her. She wasn't sure why, but she suddenly felt she was committing a sacrilege by being here. Genuine Norseman or not, his appearance was that of a god. No wonder the Inuit had treated him with such reverence. His size alone would have made him appear like some supernatural being to them. With that glorious golden hair, in contrast to their naturally dark features, and the sword, he must indeed have seemed godlike.

It seemed wrong to defile the grave of such a magnificent man.

Her doubts made no sense. She'd come to terms with those kinds of feelings years ago. She knew that her work was for the benefit of mankind. Somehow, though, this was entirely different.

She moved closer to the man...*specimen,* she corrected herself, and examined his chiseled face. His eyes were closed, his frozen blond lashes touching his hard cheeks. He was huge; she guessed at least six foot seven, and well over two hundred fifty pounds. His arms and shoulders bulged beneath the material that covered them. His chest was as wide, she thought, as a small table. His hands had a span that could easily surround her throat without much effort.

Too perfect to be real, she thought.

Miranda tugged off her gloves and thrust them into a pocket. She reached forward and ran her fingertips over his cold, unresponsive, huge hand. She curled her fingers around his and squeezed. A shiver worked its way through her wrist, upward to her elbow, a tingling sensation so mild it was barely perceptible. She jerked her hand away and blinked rapidly. "I don't think we should take him." She'd blurted the words before she knew she was about to speak them.

"What?"

She shook herself and tried to give voice to the uneasiness settling more heavily upon her with each moment she spent here. "I just...I don't know, something doesn't feel right."

Russell sighed and set his journal aside. He got to his feet with an effort. "This doesn't sound at all like you, Miranda. You've never been superstitious. You're a scientist."

"It's not superstition. I'm not sure what it is. There's something wrong here. I feel it."

His face, as he searched hers, hardened. "I thought you were beyond this type of sentimental nonsense. I am aware that with a specimen that looks as...human as this one, well, it can be difficult. To an amateur. A beginner. A student. Not to a scientist of your caliber, Miranda. Shake it off and let's get on with this."

She wanted to tell him what she was feeling, to ask him to help her understand, to share with him. But she knew better. He cared little for feelings. His own, included.

"To leave the body would be to destroy it," he went on, no longer looking at her. "The seal's broken now. The air and the moisture have invaded the cave. There'd be nothing left if we came back in a few years. Nothing. Is that what you want?"

She frowned and shook her head. The idea of leaving the great warrior—if, indeed that's what he was—to the merciless elements was just as unpalatable as the thought of taking him from his sacred place and disturbing his rest. It was too late to back out now, and to be honest with herself, the guilt she was feeling made no sense. She'd do better to ignore it and get on with her mission.

She sighed, wondering where the weak sentimentalism that sometimes reared its head within her could possibly come from. She'd had no one with that type of bent in her life since her mother. "You're right. I don't know what's wrong with me." She forced a smile but it felt shaky. "Shall I call Darryl?"

"Go ahead, but warn him to take care. Nothing is to be touched or disturbed in any way until we've photographed, measured and mapped every inch of this chamber."

"Darryl knows all of that." Her voice, she thought, lacked any hint of enthusiasm for the task.

"He might need reminding. If he has any sense at all he'll be half-crazy when he sees this find." Russell shook his head, then sucked a sharp breath through his teeth.

Miranda tore her gaze from the man—the specimen—and knelt by her father's side when he sat down abruptly. "What is it?" She knew without asking that he was having chest pains again.

He grated his teeth; she could tell by the tight line of his jaw. "Nothing. It's nothing. Just go on with what you were doing. Get some measurements."

Fear streaked through her. Cold though he was, her father was the only living being left with whom she had any sort of connection, any bond. She didn't want to lose him, too. "Dammit, Daddy, tell me."

He glared at her. "You call me by my name. You want your colleagues to regard you as a scientist, or as Russell O'Shea's little girl?" He fumbled in his coat pocket, pulled out a pill bottle and attempted to remove the cover. She reached to take it from him as he struggled, but he jerked his hand away and managed to extract a pill on his own. She blinked against the tears she knew her father hated, but not before he'd glimpsed them. "You have to get over this, girl. One of these times the chest pains will come, and they won't leave until I'm dead. You know that. I know that. There's no use crying over what can't be changed."

She bit her lip. "I know."

"I've had a good life. And as of this minute, I've achieved every one of my goals. We don't live forever. It's just the way it is."

Miranda nodded.

Russell reached into her pocket and removed her gloves. He pressed them into her hand. "Put them on, your hands are freezing."

It was the most affection he'd shown her in years. It nearly made her sob. Instead though, she simply put the gloves on. "You'll be the most respected archaeologist in the field by the time you hit fifty. Take my word for it."

It wasn't praise. It was more like an order. "I know," she chanted from long habit.

He took his specs from a deep pocket and slid them up on his nose to resume making notes in the journal. His relaxed facial muscles were the only indication that the sudden spasm of pain had passed.

Miranda went to the entrance and passed along her father's orders.

With the jet chartered by the university, it was only a matter of hours until the warrior was safely installed in the climate-controlled room that took up half the basement of their huge Georgian-style home, two miles from Beaumont University in Mourning Bluffs, Maine. Under lock and key—or rather a high-tech, digital lock—he continued his peaceful slumber, undisturbed by Miranda's careful ministrations.

She unlaced the tunic's neck to apply the sensors to his broad, hairless chest. She ignored the shiver of unease that danced over her spine as her fingers moved over frigid flesh. She was a scientist. That shiver had been felt by someone else, someone who should be banished from this room. But for some reason, it was more difficult than ever to shut her out.

She pushed the tangled blond hair away from his face to attach more electrodes near his temples. In the adjoining room, a bank of control panels and monitors lined the walls. Here, in this refrigerated tomb, there was only the sheet-draped table, as hard, she thought idly, as the slab of stone on which they'd found him.

On another table, near the farthest corner of the window-less room, were his double-edged broadsword—Vengeance—his well-worn shield, his battle-ax, the heavy, gold pendant in the shape of Thor's hammer and the leather thong that had held it around his thick, corded neck. A small rawhide pouch rested there, too, and inside it, Norse coins. Some were round, some half circles, some pie-shaped wedges. The silver had been exchanged according to its weight, and coins were often cut to the proper heft for a purchase in the early eleventh century. She had all the proof she required now that it had been his time. She no longer doubted. She only marveled.

Miranda pulled her lab coat more closely around her and removed her gold-framed reading glasses. They steamed up every time she exhaled. Russell had fallen asleep in the control room, his journal open on the desk before him, his chin pillowed by his chest. No wonder. Neither of them had eaten or slept from the moment they'd discovered this wonder in the Arctic.

She paused near the table—his bed—and scrutinized the warrior's face. But the person looking through the scientist's eyes was the one the scientist wished would go away. She was the one who whispered very softly, as if he might be able to hear her, "I'm almost tempted to give you a shave, see what you look like without all that hair." She caught her hand moving nearer, as if about to stroke his whiskered face. She stopped herself, frowning. "Listen to me, talking to a frozen Viking. I'd be drummed out of my profession if word got out." She felt a foolish grin tugging at the corners of her lips. "I don't suppose you'll tell, though, will you?"

She caught herself in a firm grip and ordered her practical side to take over. She needn't waste time speculating about such trivial things as what his voice might have sounded like or what he'd looked like when he'd smiled. She focused on important matters, examining him closely for signs of deterioration. She saw none.

She shook her head in wonder. What had come over her? She was the most sedate, levelheaded person she knew. Oh, sure, she occasionally felt that little girl inside trying to get out, but it had never been a problem. Since when did she engage in one-sided conversations with one of her finds?

She felt silly. Lack of sleep, she supposed. Or maybe the high of helping to realize her father's dream. "You," she said sternly, "are nothing but a specimen. You're an experiment, and nothing more." Saying it aloud did nothing to make it seem true. "I suppose some part of me recognizes what else you are…the one man I can't scare away. Most of them find me exceedingly unappealing, you know."

Releasing a slow breath, Miranda lifted a sterilized instrument and placed it against the exposed flesh of his chest. With a single, efficient stroke, she cut a snippet of flesh the size of a saccharine tablet from him. She winced as she did it, even knowing he couldn't feel any pain. "There I go again, giving you all sorts of attributes you don't possess. I need that for the radiocarbon testing, and you certainly won't miss it. We want to know just how old you are."

She placed the sample in its prepared receptacle and frowned. "Where was I? Oh, the men who find me unappealing. Those are the ones with good eyesight, I imagine. Won't be a problem with you. I'm too tall, too thin, too clumsy. I don't suppose you notice any of that, though. My eyes are set too far apart and they're the most perfectly dull shade of dark gray." She shook her head. "Those few men bold enough to get past all my physical faults run screaming when they learn that I don't particularly enjoy sex."

She pulled a tall stool nearer the table and perched herself upon it. She studied him. "This is kind of nice. I can say just about anything to you, can't I?"

She sighed hard, wishing she were an insomniac. She wanted to do everything herself tonight—run every test conceivable before she had to share him with the world. Beaumont's agreement was to return the specimen to Canada after a year of study. So little time. But already exhaustion began to slow her. "I shouldn't be talking to you like this. I'm just overtired. You're just a specimen…not a man." She tilted her head to one side. "I've never dealt with one that seemed so…"

What? So human, so real? Yes, as if you had just lain down for a nap and might wake and smile up at me any minute. What color are your eyes, I wonder? What is your name?

She pressed her fingertips to the front of her throat in alarm. This was getting out of hand. She quickly rose to her feet, but her eyes seemed determined to remain focused on him. The rest of the testing would have to wait, she decided at once. She no longer felt sure of herself, or her abilities.

Tomorrow he'd need to be bathed in fungicide to prevent any fungus growth on the body. His clothing would be carefully, painstakingly removed. It would be studied, tested, and eventually put on display somewhere, along with his sword and other belongings. He would be CAT scanned, autopsied, DNA tested. Before the professionals were through with him they'd know what he'd eaten, where he'd lived, how he'd died, and even the names of his closest living descendants. Studying him would be the dream of every scientist in the world. The university would charge exorbitant fees for photo opportunities. Russell would probably write a book on him, and Miranda would no doubt be asked to do articles and go on lecture tours. And after a single year of study, as per their agreement, the Ice Man would be shipped back to Canada, where the process would begin all over again.

She sighed once more, wondering why she felt so incredibly sad at that thought, and forced herself to leave the room.

It was past midnight when something woke her. Some sense of unease in the house. Frowning, she shoved back her covers, knocking her paperback to the floor in her haste. She stepped over *Shadows of Love,* and pulled on her heavy, terry robe. She'd fallen asleep right after the dark, mysterious hero had pulled the defiant heroine into his arms for a desperate kiss. She shook her head, wondering why she felt the need to entertain herself by reading such nonsense. No one loved like that in real life. That kind of passion…it simply did not exist.

Then again, neither did the monsters Stephen King wrote about, and plenty of people read his books. Fantasy was fantasy. There was a place for it in life. She reached for her glasses, belatedly remembering she'd left them lying beside a large, forever-still hand in the basement.

She padded barefoot into the hall and toward Russell's room. The door hung wide. The rumpled bed lay vacant. Frowning, she switched direction and hurried downstairs. She didn't bother checking the rooms on the first floor. If Russell were up at this hour, she had little doubt where she'd find him. She walked softly. She'd just peek in to be sure he wasn't ill again. He'd be furious if he knew she was checking up on him. Her light steps took her fluidly down the basement stairs. She saw light gleaming from the slightly ajar control-room door.

As she moved through it she realized something was terribly wrong. In the space of a heartbeat, her eyes took in the disarray. Chairs were toppled, files scattered over the floor, spilling from open drawers. Then she saw Russell, crumpled on the floor, a trickle of blood spider-webbing across his forehead, over his closed eyes.

She took a step toward him, her heart leaping painfully, but whirled as she sensed the blow coming at her from behind. Her sudden movement caused the fist to miss its target and crash down on her shoulder rather than her head. The force of the blow knocked her to her knees and wrung a cry of pain from deep in her chest. She caught only a vague impression of a dark silhouette as the intruder fled. She heard heavy steps on the stairs and the door slamming hard. She blinked back tears of pain and fear, and drew a calming breath.

He was gone. She was alone now. Her gaze darted toward the still-closed door to the next room, where the Viking warrior rested. That the door remained undisturbed eased her mind. She moved clumsily nearer her father. She touched him, wincing when she tried to use her right arm. Then with her left she stroked his pale face, gently shook his shoulder. "Daddy. Wake up, Daddy, please!"

He didn't stir and she felt a cold hand grip her soul. She struggled to her feet, holding her right arm tightly to her chest to avoid the stabbing pain in her shoulder whenever she moved it in the least. She made her way back through the darkened, ordinary-looking half of the basement and mounted the stairs. She hoped her assessment that the bandit had fled was an accurate one. And she hoped to God he wouldn't try to get between her and the telephone.

Chapter 2

A siren screamed and warbled, announcing the ambulance's arrival. Miranda rushed to let them in, then led two men and a woman down to the basement where her father lay unconscious. She stood aside to let them work. Her blood pounded in her temples and her entire body trembled. She could no longer see Russell's pale skin, or his blue-tinted eyelids. She could only see the forms bent over him and hear their urgent words, spoken in clipped, choppy sentences.

"BP dropping...pulse erratic."

"Get that IV set up."

"Hustle. We need to transport stat."

"We have V-fib. Get the paddles. Clear!"

A percussion permeated the room. Her father's body stiffened and arced. Miranda forcibly held back the cry that leapt to her throat when he went limp once more. She should have heard her father get up and come downstairs, she thought. She should have been the one hit by the burglar.

"Still V-fib. Give him another shot. Clear!"

Miranda staggered backward, clinging to a control panel for support. "It's only a bump on the head…it isn't that bad…it can't be that bad—"

"Again! Clear!"

She knew, though, what was happening. It wasn't the blow to his head that threatened her father's life. It was his heart. She closed her eyes as hot tears oozed from between her lashes. She blinked them quickly away. She needed to keep her head now. Russell needed her, loath though she knew he would be to ever admit it. "He's been seeing Dr. Milton Fenmore."

"We'll alert the hospital, miss. They'll call him."

"He's been having chest pains, shortness of breath," she added, as the paramedics lifted her father's limp form onto a gurney and began to carry him away. "They told him to consider a transplant but he's…so damned stubborn." Her throat tightened and choked off her words. She would have followed them out, but several newcomers blocked her way. A man in a neat gray suit put one hand on her shoulder and she glanced into hard eyes that reminded her of her father's.

"Miss O'Shea? I'm Lieutenant Hanlon. Can you tell me what happened here?"

She shook her head, her gaze wandering past him toward the paramedics who were hurrying up the stairs. "I have to go—"

"I know. Believe me, there's nothing you can do for him right now. He's in good hands."

His words, while softly spoken, were firm. Miranda pulled herself up mentally and nodded.

Miranda knew this had been the longest day of her life. First, the seemingly endless questioning by the police, then the interminable waiting at the hospital. She'd left the house in the chill hours of predawn. As time passed like putty through a sieve, the warm, late-July sun traveled its course through the sky. She'd dressed quickly, without thought, and regretted it now, for the hospital corridors were chilly despite the warmth outside. Her lightweight khaki trousers and thin white cotton blouse did little to warm her. She hadn't even grabbed a jacket.

She'd left Lieutenant Hanlon at the house with Erwin Saunders, who'd rushed over at her phone call. As the head of Beaumont's archaeology department, he was frantic with worry over the well-being of the specimen. Miranda assured him she'd glanced at the monitors and found them all reading as they should. Hanlon wouldn't let anyone back downstairs until his men had finished. She'd taken care to firmly warn them both against opening the door to the cold room, where the specimen rested. Any contamination could spell ruin.

Finally, when Miranda had nearly paced a rut in the tiled floor of the waiting area outside ICU, a man with steel-wool hair around a shiny pate approached her. She recognized Dr. Fenmore at once. "Is my father—"

"He's alive, but I'm afraid that's the only good news I have for you. Why don't you sit down? Can I have someone bring you something? Coffee? A sandwich—"

She stopped him with a brisk shake of her head. The pins holding her unruly carrot-colored hair were coming loose, and the move only made it worse. She supposed she looked like the farthest thing from a scientist at the moment. "Just tell me about Russell. Is he going to make it?"

Dr. Fenmore sighed and slowly shook his head. "I wish I could tell you what you want to hear, but I can't. Miranda, we've discussed this before. You knew it was only a matter of time—" he paused, drew a breath "—his condition is critical. He's suffered a massive heart attack."

For the first time since she'd arrived, Miranda sat down. Her suddenly weak knees had made the decision for her. "What are his chances?"

"Not good. The next forty-eight hours will be crucial. If

we can get him stabilized and keep him going, he might recover enough to go home, but this is going to happen again.'' He took a seat beside her. ''You ought to go home, get some rest if you can.''

She looked up into sea green eyes and thought she saw genuine kindness beyond the requisite bedside manner. ''Can I see him?''

''It will have to be a brief visit. Be extremely careful what you say to him. Don't upset him in any way.''

She nodded and walked beside the doctor through the formidable doors with the crisscrossing of wire mesh between the double panes of glass. The trek through the corridor was a short one, and then she was led into a room with nearly as much equipment as Russell's control room at home. But these monitors produced spiking lines on their screens and the one that emitted a soft but steady bleat gave her a surge of reassurance, reassurance she knew to be false.

Lying in the stark white bed, Russell looked thinner than he ever had. His skin differed little in color from the sheets. Tubes ran into his nostrils. An IV line was taped to his wrist. He had more electrode wires running under his gown to his chest than the Viking warrior had taped to his much larger one. Only *he* wasn't garbed in a thin, pale blue hospital gown.

She pasted a smile on her face and approached the bed. She closed her hand over his. Even his skin felt different, she thought. Loose and tender. How could he have changed so thoroughly in a matter of hours? Or was it just her imagination?

His eyes opened. The slate hardness was gone. They were dull now. ''Miranda...''

She squeezed. ''Right here, Russell. You're going to be fine. Everything's going to be fine.''

He drew a weak breath and closed his eyes. ''The specimen—''

"Safe and sound. No one's going to get near him. Don't worry."

He released a sigh and seemed to relax. "Be careful, Miranda. Someone wants—"

"I left Professor Saunders and the police at home. They'll keep track of things and I'll be very careful. I don't want you worrying. You know I'll take care of everything. I want you to trust me. You trust me, don't you?"

"What good…are you doing here? You can't…watch over it…if you're here."

She blinked to battle the tears that gathered in her eyes, and leaned over to kiss his cheek. He stiffened. "They said I couldn't stay long, but if you need me, I'll insist. I'll stay right beside you all night, if you want."

The way she had with her mother, she thought. She'd sat up all night, and they'd talked. Her mother had held her as if she'd never let go, and told her how much she loved her, and that she would always be with her. She longed for those comforting words from Russell.

But he only shook his head. "I want you home…with the find."

"I told you, it's safe. I can stay—"

"Anything could go wrong!" The pace of the soft beeps picked up, and Russell's face tensed.

"Okay. Calm down. I'll go home right now if that's what you want."

He sighed deeply, raggedly, and nodded. "Yes. Go home. I won't worry if I know you're there." His eyelids dropped, but popped open again. She could see he was exhausted by the simple act of talking to her. "Miranda, there's something…you don't know. About the specimen. I—" he paused to catch his breath "—my journal…it's all in there. Read it, Miranda. Tonight." He gasped, breathless from the exertion of speaking. "It's up to you now."

Her eyes burned. She was glad his were closed so he wouldn't see the flood of tears that suddenly spilled over.

He would have been furious. She hadn't shed a tear in front of her father since her mother died, since that awful dawn when she'd been only twelve. But those tears had dried the instant she'd seen his reaction to them. Somehow she'd sensed his anger was only a cover for his pain. He needed her to pretend everything was fine, in order for him to be able to do so. So she had.

She'd seemed to stop being his daughter that morning. Instead she'd become his student, and then his colleague. All she'd done in her life, she'd done to please him, to gain his elusive approval...with that one brief, disastrous exception.

She brought his hand to her lips to kiss it, then thought better of it. She wasn't supposed to upset him, and physical displays of tenderness tended to drive him nuts. A hand on her shoulder interrupted her, and she turned, still clutching Russell's hand.

"He's asleep." Dr. Fenmore's voice was as soft as his touch. "It's the best thing for him right now. You ought to do as he asked and go home. I'll leave orders you're to be contacted if there's any change," he soothed. "Any change at all, or if he asks for you."

But he wouldn't ask for her. Miranda knew that without a shadow of doubt.

The house seemed abandoned, not the same one she'd left some sixteen hours ago. Her car's headlights moved over the brick exterior like trespassers violating some sacred spot. No welcoming light shone from the windows.

She turned off the ignition and killed the headlights. She murmured meaningless greetings to the two officers who stood outside the house. Apparently Professor Saunders had convinced Lieutenant Hanlon that the find needed guarding before he'd gone home.

She unlocked the house and went inside, flicking on lights as she went. Emptiness met her everywhere she looked. It was almost too much to bear. What if Russell didn't recover? What would her life be without him? She had very little except her work and her father, and the two had always gone hand in hand. They'd worked and lived together, except for that brief rebellious period, when she'd accepted Jeff Morsi's proposal of marriage just to prove to her father and herself that she could be a "normal" woman. Instead she'd only proven she couldn't be. Losing Jeff had been a narrow escape from a nightmare. Losing Russell would leave her bereft...utterly alone.

She pushed the thought aside, tossed her purse on the sofa, and walked down the basement stairs and into the control room. Russell wouldn't die, not yet. It was too soon, and he was too stubborn to go in the midst of his greatest discovery. And when he came back home, his first concern would be for that discovery. She'd care for it diligently. If anything happened to the find, it would kill her father faster than any heart attack ever could.

At first glance everything seemed just as she'd left it. Files on the floor and a small bloodstain where her father had fallen. She shivered and gave the monitors a cursory glance...then sucked in her breath.

The digital temperature panel read ninety-eight degrees Fahrenheit. Panic knocked the wind out of her as surely as a fist to the stomach would have done. The climate-control panel must have been knocked askew in the struggle. A quick glimpse at the setting confirmed her guess. Why hadn't she checked it before? Why had she satisfied herself with a glance at the readings, and not checked the settings? God, everything her father had worked for could be ruined!

She punched numbers rapidly into the panel to release the lock, threw the door open wide, and hurried inside. Only the soft glow of the minimal lighting in the window-less room guided her. The stifling heat slammed into her like a living thing. But the Viking lay as he had before.

His skin seemed less chalky, but it might be the lighting or her fear making it seem so. Maybe it wasn't too late.

She turned to go back to the control panel and readjust the climate control to lower the temperature as rapidly as possible. She froze in the doorway when her gaze locked on the monitor directly opposite. The wavering white line across the screen sent her blood to her feet. She blinked and double-checked the label on the monitor. EEG. Electroencephalogram. The meter of brain-wave activity. But it had to be malfunctioning. It couldn't be reading what was there. It wasn't possible for there to be—

The sudden, strangled gasp was drawn with harsh desperation, and it came from behind her. Then silence.

She whirled and saw the body on the table, every muscle tensed as it began to shake. The huge arms and legs trembled convulsively. The broad chest vibrated. The corded neck was arched and quivering.

She stopped seeing a specimen at that moment. What she saw was a man on the brink of suffocation. A man straining to breathe, but unable to do so. A man about to die…again.

She reacted instinctively, not taking time to dwell on the unthinkable thing that was happening. She was beside the table before she knew she'd moved. She gripped the solid shoulders, fighting to hold him still as she pressed her ear to his chest. She felt nothing there. She lifted her head, and then clasped her hands together in one balled fist. She brought them down hard on his sternum. He flinched.

Frantically she caught his whiskered face between her palms and tipped up his chin. She pinched his nose and covered his mouth with her own and she blew life into him, once, twice, again. She blew hard to fill his massive lungs, then returned to the chest, positioning her hands over his sternum to massage a long-silent heart.

A rapid thud tapped against her palm, and it seemed her own heart rate sped up until it echoed his. The fit of convulsions slowed and died. She watched in utter awe as the huge chest rose and fell, far too quickly, but regularly. Beneath her hands, now-supple flesh gradually warmed.

He was breathing.

His heart was beating.

His brain was functioning.

She stepped backward, away from him and turned in the doorway to scan the monitors. They confirmed the impossible. Not one flat line among them. Not one.

An agonized moan, so hoarse it hurt her ears, brought her around once more. His eyes were blue…the pale, silvery blue of an icy sea, and they were staring right into hers. She saw many things in those piercing blue eyes—confusion, pain and an unfocused quality that told her he wasn't seeing clearly. He remained on his back, just staring at her, silently asking her a thousand questions, most of which she was certain she couldn't answer.

She was in awe, in shock. Life's blood pulsed through the formerly dormant body, giving color to his skin. She took a step toward him, then another. Slowly, tentatively, she approached him. He moved only his eyes, keeping them locked with hers. Beside the table she stopped. In wonder, she lifted a trembling hand, and placed it with tender reverence upon his face. Her fingertips brushed over the small expanse of his cheek uncovered by beard. "You're alive." It was no more than a whisper.

His response was to slowly lift one of his large hands and thread his fingers through her hair, pulling what few strands had remained pinned in place down to join the rest in what she knew must resemble a pumpkin orange disarray. "Valkyrie." The word came in a voice hoarse from disuse.

Her words, she knew, were foreign to him. She understood his, though. It was almost laughable. If he thought her one of the legendary demigoddesses, the Valkyries, who in Norse mythology were said to greet fallen warriors at their deaths and lead them to Valhalla, he must be incredibly disappointed. Valkyries were supposed to be beautiful, strong, sensual creatures. She saw herself as none of the above.

She stifled her amused grin and met his wonder-filled gaze. "No." She shook her head. "Not Valkyrie. Miranda." She frowned hard, searching her memory for the Islensk words. "*Eg heiti* Miranda."

She wished she had a more thorough knowledge of the language. Not that it mattered. She wouldn't be able to tell him anything, anyway. She had no idea how this had happened, but she was absurdly glad it had. Her eyes burned and she had the urge to laugh out loud. "You're alive." She said it softly, a sense of wonder in her voice. She stared down at him, wondering what he was thinking, what he was feeling. Was he in pain?

His hand clasped the base of her neck to draw her nearer. He squinted, then blinked as if to focus his vision. Suddenly the curious, reverent gleam left his eyes and they narrowed in a way that made her heart jump in fear. His hand in her hair turned cruel, twisting a lock around it until she thought he'd rip it out. His mouth curled into a sneer and he gruffly ground out, "Adrianna." It was, she sensed, an accusation.

He rose slightly and with a brutal thrust pushed her away from him. His shove was so forceful she found herself on the floor. Even as she fought panic and shock and began to get to her feet again, she saw him leap from the table. He loomed over her, spewing forth a stream of Norse words so filled with anger and bitterness she could barely believe the strength of it. How had she allowed herself to forget, even with all that had happened, who this man was? The Plague of the North. He reached down for her, his huge hand menacing.

She cringed, terror-stricken, but then he stopped. His large body swayed slightly. One hand pressed to the side of his head and he wobbled on his feet like a tree about to fall. Miranda shot up, gripping his upper arm with all the strength she possessed and slipping an arm around his waist when that first effort was no longer sufficient.

"Easy. Come on. Lie down," she said in a low, firm voice. He couldn't understand her words, but he might be able to sense her intent in her tone. She trembled with fear, but refused to give in to it. "I mean you no harm," she went on as she urged him toward the table. *"Eg er... vinur pinn,"* she managed. "I'm your friend."

He scowled darkly, and she thought he called her a less than flattering name. He still remained unsteady on his feet.

"You're sick. *pið eruð veikur."*

He hesitated, but finally he sat on the edge of the table. He closed his eyes for a long moment and his voice was almost sad but tinged with bitterness when he spoke again. The words had the ring of despair and the lilt of a question. And again he used that name—Adrianna.

"No." Carefully she touched his face, tilting it upward so he would look at her more carefully, then quickly drawing her hand away so as not to offend him. It would be in her best interest to make him see she wasn't whoever he thought she was. He seemed as if he'd like to throttle Adrianna, whoever she might be. When his ice blue gaze, clearer now, fixed upon her face, she said softly, "I am Miranda." She tapped her chest with her forefinger. "Miranda."

He frowned and his eyes narrowed as he studied her more closely. Again he reached for her hair and she forced herself not to draw back in fear. He drew a lock forward and rubbed it between his fingers. He shook his head and leaned nearer, lifting the hair to his nose and inhaling its scent. His gaze traveled over her face and he seemed confused. Not convinced, though.

After a moment, he glanced at the room around him, his brow furrowed. Then he lowered his head and pressed a palm to it. When he noticed the electrodes taped to his chest, he frowned harder and lifted a hand to tear one free.

"No." She laid her hand over his, looked him in the eye and shook her head. "Let me. It will hurt if you just rip them off." He tilted his head, seemingly just realizing she spoke in a tongue he'd never heard. She clasped his hand and gently moved it away. He allowed it, then watched curiously as she caught the edge of a strip of tape and carefully peeled it back. As she pulled it away, she winced, knowing the sting he'd feel. She glanced up at his face to see if she'd hurt him.

To her amazement, he smiled at her. His eyes glittered with unmistakable amusement. His huge hand came up again, and imitating her, he picked at the edge of a strip of tape. Unlike her, once he had it, he yanked it free in one quick motion, not even blinking as he did so. He kept glancing at her as he repeated the procedure until his chest was free of wires and sensors. He was showing off, she thought, her mind reeling. He thought it funny that she'd been worried about hurting him. She smiled back at him. She couldn't help it.

Her smile instantly instigated the return of the angry glare in his eyes. He looked quickly around the room, made a sweeping gesture with his hand and murmured a hoarse question. What is this place? she imagined he wanted to know. Or where am I? How did I get here? She made a helpless, shrugging gesture. Then she touched his throat with her fingertips. Instantly his hand closed like a steel trap around her wrist.

She stiffened, but didn't turn away from him. God, but he didn't trust her. "Thirsty. You must be thirsty. That's all I was trying to say." With her free hand she made a circle of her thumb and fingers to lift an imaginary glass to her lips. "Drink," she told him. "Would you like a drink?"

Frowning, still looking skeptical, he released her wrist. "*Eg er pyrstur,*" he said hoarsely.

"Right. *pyrstur.* Thirsty." Miranda quickly left the room

and him. She paused in the control room, her hands gripping the edge of the sink as her knees began to tremble in reaction. For a moment, the enormity of what was happening hit her like a whirlwind, but she had to keep calm, not think about it too deeply or she'd lose her mind or have a fit of hysteria. Things like this did not happen. "What in God's name am I going to do with him?"

She shook her head, filled a glass with cold water, and returned to the cold room, which had now become hot. The table was empty. Startled, she swung her gaze around the room and saw him in the corner, so large she nearly reconsidered her determination not to be afraid of him. He held the massive sword by its hilt, turning it this way and that. Miranda found herself glad she'd painstakingly polished it, to ready it for viewing by the archaeological staff tomorrow.

She swallowed hard. What on earth was she going to tell the staff? And Professor Saunders? "Sorry, guys, the find came to life. I'm afraid you can't have him." She rehearsed the words silently in her mind, and her eyes widened as she realized they would still want him. He'd be the center of study by every scientist on the planet when they learned…if they learned.

He saw her and came toward her, his stride not quite steady, but extremely confident. She held the drink out and he took it. He held it up, frowning harder than ever as he examined the glass and the clear, sparkling water it held. "Glass," she said firmly, tapping the outside with one short fingernail. "Glass."

He nodded slowly and, his voice still coarse, repeated the word, "Glass."

Miranda couldn't suppress a smile. She nodded. He lifted the glass to his lips and began guzzling. When he lowered it, Miranda said, "*Vatn.* Water."

He cleared his throat, and returned the glass to her. "Water," he mimicked. When her hand closed around the glass, though, he caught it and lifted it, examining her fingers with close scrutiny. He even ran the pad of his thumb over the edges of her unpainted, neatly cropped nails. He frowned. Then he released her hand and studied her face. "Adrianna?"

She set the glass down. "No." She shook her head firmly. "Miranda." She tapped her chest hard for emphasis. "Miranda." She saw that she was at least making some headway. He now wondered. She spotted her glasses where she'd left them the night before, and automatically picked them up and slipped them on.

A second later, they were removed by amazingly gentle hands. He turned them this way and that, a frown making parentheses between his brows. He drew them close to his face and peered through the lenses.

He's like a child, she thought, watching him. Like a big, lost child in a strange new world. Except that he was a dangerous child, one she needed to handle carefully.

She took the glasses from him and slipped them into her pocket. She pointed to his chest and said, "Ulf? Svein?" So far she only knew him as The Plague of the North. "*Hvaŏ,* um, your name…*heitir pú?*"

"Rolf Magnusson." His voice was clearer now, and decidedly louder. He nodded, indicating the empty glass. "Water."

"More?" She took his wrist in her free hand and drew him carefully from the room and into the adjoining control room. He gazed curiously all around, eyes widening at the bank of monitors with their flat white lines and the rows of buttons and dials and switches. He was more amazed, though, when she turned on the faucet and water flowed into the sink. He watched her, and a second later, he moved her aside to stand where she'd been.

Setting his sword aside, he turned the knobs first one way and then the other, making the water flow, hot then cold, and finally making it stop. He studied the stream, following it to the drain. Dropping to his knees, he next examined the pipes beneath the sink.

He frowned, nodded slowly, and rose to take the glass from her hand. She willingly let it go, and watched as he filled it on his own. He held the glass beneath the faucet until it was spilling over his big hand. He reached again for the knob and turned it off. For a long moment, he regarded the glass in his hand. Finally he brought it to his lips and tilted it up as if he'd down it all in one gulp as he had before.

This time she put a hand over the one holding the glass. "Slow," she told him. She pushed her other hand in a downward sweep and repeated, "Slow." She placed a palm on his stomach by way of explaining that he'd give himself a stomachache if he drank too quickly. It was as hard as rock and warm beneath her fingers, even through the thin tunic he wore and the shirt beneath it. She looked up quickly. His eyes seemed to darken. He held her intense gaze for a long moment, and it was Miranda who finally looked away, baffled by her sudden shortness of breath and the odd tension coiling somewhere within her.

He studied her as if she'd done something unexpected, then he drank, slowly this time. It was remarkably easy to make him understand her, she thought. When he finished, he set the glass carefully on the counter. "Rolf." She tested the name. "Rolf Magnusson." What now, she wondered.

The sound of footsteps on the stairs alerted her, and when Rolf saw the way her eyes flew wide and her body went rigid, his powerful hand closed around her upper arm, jerking her behind him as he lifted his sword and sent a fierce glare through the doorway, into the darkened basement.

"No, Rolf. *Nei!*" she whispered urgently. She tugged at his arm until the sword lowered. She reached around him to close the door until it was only open a crack.

"Miss O'Shea?"

"Who is it?" She clung to Rolf's tensed biceps, praying

he wouldn't decide to behead the man with a single swipe of Vengeance before he could answer.

"Officer Phillips, miss. I was knocking for quite a while. Got worried when no one answered, since the lights are still on. Everything all right?"

Rolf emitted a low grunt and his expression told her what he thought of her restraining hand. "Fine, everything's fine. I'm afraid I can't talk to you now, though. Some of the controls got knocked out of whack earlier and I have to get them back in order. Sorry to be rude."

"No problem. Anything I can do to help?"

"No, thank you. Good night, Officer Phillips." She sighed in relief when he responded in kind and she heard his steps returning up the stairs. She listened until the door slammed. Then her entire body sagged at the close call. She hadn't realized until this very moment what she was going to do with Rolf. It shocked her now that she had. Her entire life had been devoted to science. The decision she'd made, though, was the opposite of the one the scientists of the world would wish for. It was more like the one the romantics of the world would approve. But there was only one decision she could make. She couldn't allow him to become the hottest new guinea pig in the world. She simply couldn't. She had to hide him from everyone…she didn't know how, but she had to do it.

Rolf's hand closed on her shoulder and she winced. He turned her toward him, his frown deeper than ever. His fingers closed on the collar of her blouse and he pulled it to one side, snapping the top two buttons and baring the shoulder he'd inadvertently hurt. He saw the bruise she knew had formed there, the one she'd received from the intruder. His face turned thunderous and he spewed forth a stream of words she didn't understand. As he spoke he motioned with his sword toward the stairway and the last phrase sounded as if it might have been a question.

She wondered if he were asking whether Officer Phillips

had given her the bruise, or whether she'd like the man dissected for his crime. Either way, she knew she had to disabuse him of the notion. Funny, she thought, that he would pull her hair the way he had, shove her around like that, yell at her for whatever this Adrianna had done, and then get so angry at the knowledge that someone else had harmed her. She touched his face, bringing his gaze back to hers. "*Nei*, Rolf. It wasn't him. *Nei*." She touched the hand holding the sword, putting a slight downward pressure on it, and he lowered the weapon, looking none too pleased about it.

She nodded in approval and smiled. His gaze dropped to her bruised, exposed shoulder and softened. Gently he touched the purplish skin with two fingers and murmured something low and soft.

She pulled her shirt together hastily, feeling the blood rush to her face at his show of tenderness. It was an odd feeling, having someone so angry on her behalf, one she didn't remember ever having experienced before. Of course Russell would have been upset if he'd known the intruder had harmed her, but not like this. Rolf had been ready to do battle...all over a little bruise. All right, not so little from the way it ached, but still... She shook herself and took one of Rolf's hands, or as much of it as she could grasp.

She looked up into his eyes. "I'm not going to hurt you, Rolf. I'm your friend. *Eg er vinur pinn.* You're going to have to trust me."

He watched her closely, his eyes going from hers, to her lips as she spoke, to her throat and back to her eyes again. He licked his lips after a moment, pressed two fingers to his thumb and tapped his lips three times. "*Eg er svangur.*"

"Hungry? I'm hungry, too." She touched her lips as he had. "I am hungry. Say it, Rolf. I am hungry."

"I am hungry." His mimicking ability was astounding.

She nodded encouragingly. "Now say my name. Miranda. *Endurtakið*. Repeat it, Rolf. Miranda." She had no doubt he understood what she was asking of him. He seemed keenly intelligent.

He studied her for a long moment, his eyes narrow with suspicion. At last, sneering slightly, he gestured, lifting one hand, four fingers touching the thumb. He flicked the fingers open with a sarcastic little snap and whispered, "Adrianna."

"Can't pull one over on you, can I?" She shook her head, rolled her eyes to show her displeasure, but still gripped his hand and drew him through the basement and up the stairs.

Chapter 3

Rolf's body felt oddly weak, and strange tingling sensations still radiated through his limbs, though not as severely as they had at first. His mind seemed fogged. He knew not where he was nor how he'd come to be here, let alone why he felt so peculiar.

The woman—Adrianna, he was certain—was behaving strangely, speaking in this odd language, pretending not to understand him. Without a doubt the language was of her own creation. Did she believe she could deceive him, the man known throughout the North for his gift with languages? He could learn any tongue there was in a single night of study—enough to communicate, at least. Given a week he'd be as fluent as the natives. Adrianna knew that. Everyone knew that. Before his name had been ruined by her slanderous tongue, Rolf had been summoned to England by King Knut himself to act as translator to visitors from other lands. So what game was the lovely Adrianna trying to play?

He watched her as he sat at her table and ate the cold

roast fowl she placed before him and drank the milk, wishing it were mead. He nibbled the oddly shaped, sliced bread and he studied her. There was something...something different about her. Her eyes were the same deep gray of storm clouds, set far apart and fringed in rich auburn lashes. But they were filled with some turmoil he had yet to understand. She covered them with a strange shield. Disks of what she'd called glass, though clearer and smoother than any he had ever seen, held in place by thin metal the color of tarnished gold. They seemed to distort the vision, those eye shields. Her fiery hair, wild now that he'd tugged it free, had at first been pulled tight to the back of her head as if in an attempt to tame the unruly waves.

In fact, her very mannerisms seemed to have changed. Adrianna had always dressed provocatively and moved with a sensual grace designed to tease and entice men. Her eyes forever threw sparks to her admirers, and her lingering gazes and sidelong glances had been perfected to an art.

She was different, obviously troubled about something, seemingly oblivious to her own charms. She wore strange, loose-fitting leggings and a simple white shirt without adornment or sashes. She hadn't even bothered to scent her hair with henna, though it did carry a scent all its own.

And there was more. She was treating him oddly. There was such uncommon softness in her voice, and a hesitancy in her slightest touch. She looked at him with an awe visible in her eyes, even beyond the unrest he saw there.

The strangeness of this place puzzled him, as well. Rolf rose now to examine it. Already the food seemed to be restoring his strength. He began with the water-spurting device, which he recognized, though it differed slightly from the one below. This one had a wooden box built around it to conceal the pipes beneath, with swinging doors and shelves within for storage. Other wooden storage boxes were fastened to the walls. He opened these, one after another, and found strange vessels that appeared to hold food-stuffs, and stacks of dishes made of a shiny, hard substance.

A tall metal box held more food, but this one was cold inside. There was a niche cut into its door and a lever within. Rolf closed the door and touched the lever. At once several small bits of ice spilled over his hand and onto the floor. He jumped in surprise, then swung his head around at the sound of a feminine laugh.

She hurriedly clapped a hand to her lips, but her eyes sparkled with mirth. Rolf felt a warm spiral of anger begin to curl within him. So she found him amusing, did she? As he glared at her, she rose and moved to stand beside a wall. She pointed to a small protrusion fastened to it. She moved a little appendage, and said something. The small lamps suspended above the table went out. Rolf stared in wonder, for when she moved the thing again, they lit once more. He frowned and stepped nearer the lamps. Their flames, he'd first thought, were only concealed beneath the painted shades of glass. Now he saw there were no flames at all, only oddly shaped globes which emitted a blinding white glow.

"How is such a thing accomplished?"

She only shrugged, again feigning near ignorance of the tongue he spoke. How long would she persist in this game?

He sighed in disgust and returned to the food. He needed every bit of it. He felt weaker than he could ever remember feeling. Mayhap he had been ill. Might Adrianna have nursed him through some long sickness? He glanced up at her quickly. *Nei.* Such selflessness was not in her.

There had been a moment in the rooms below when he'd forgotten her black soul. When he'd seen the ugly bruise marring her perfect, lily skin, an anger had risen within him. He'd wished to discern the name of the one respon-sible, and to make him pay for such cruelty. It made no sense. She'd done worse to him by far than bruise his flesh. She'd borne false witness against him, accused him of murder. She'd stood by and seen him banished from Norge, and as a result he'd—

Rolf dropped the leg of fowl he'd been eating. His head came up fast as he fought for the memory. A sudden shiver raced through him and he felt again the sting of ice lashing his face, but only for a moment. The sensations faded fast and he was left wondering what had become of his vaunted memory.

Then there was softness, her hand covering his, her eyes filling with concern. Her voice was plaintive as she spoke his name and asked a question. Did she wish to know what troubled him? He searched his mind again, but found only a deep well of darkness. The journey from Norge across the North Atlantic was nearly forgotten. He knew he'd embarked on that journey, but its memory was as elusive as that of a dream one tries in vain to recall.

"Rolf?"

He studied her face, so soft, and her eyes, so intensely searching his. Truly she had never seemed as beautiful as she did at this moment. How could she be here? If he'd ever completed that journey, then he should be in the wilderness of Helluland, among the Skrælingar by now, far to the north of Vinland with his crew of other outcasts.

How could she be here?

In answer to her queries, he only shook his head and returned his attention to the food. As he ate, he recalled her brief lesson below and that she had said she, too, was "hungry." He pushed the platter of fowl toward her and repeated her words as he remembered. "Adrianna...am hungry."

"No." She shook her head firmly, giving him no mistake as what her no meant. "Miranda. Miranda is hungry. Rolf is hungry."

"Adrianna is," he stubbornly repeated. "Rolf is." He frowned. "I am."

She nodded, but he could see a flare of anger in her gray eyes at his refusal to use her newly acquired name. He

sighed his relief. At least she would now give him a lesson
in her make-believe language. Did she insist on using it,
he might as well learn to speak with her.

She pointed at him with her graceful finger. He wondered
briefly why she'd cut off her nails. They had once been her
pride. "You are hungry." She made a motion with her
hand indicating them both, and went on, "We are hungry."
She picked up a piece of fowl and placed it between her
full lips. Rolf watched her eat the food. His own appetite
had vanished.

Every once in a while he looked at her in a way that sent
shivers down the back of her neck. They weren't from fear,
because she no longer saw the anger she'd seen earlier. His
gaze would simply intensify…to an unbelievable degree.

The rest of the time she could only marvel at his obvious
wonder and occasional delight with everything he encountered. He didn't pretend not to be impressed, as most of the
men she knew might have done. Especially her father.
Rolf's feelings were out in the open in full view. Especially
the sudden frustration he'd seemed to experience a few
minutes before. She wasn't certain of its cause, but she saw
that he was troubled about something.

As they shared the meal, Miranda began his English lessons in earnest. There was so much he would need to know
if she was going to pull off this charade. First and foremost,
she needed to be able to communicate with him. His ability
to learn astounded her. In a single sitting, she taught him
to conjugate the verb "to be" and to name every object in
the entire kitchen. In fact, by the end of the meal she was
pointing to things and asking "What's this?" and getting
perfect answers every time.

She'd been amused by his reaction to the fork. It was
alien to him, but he was curious, so she showed him its
use. He only shook his head, his expression telling her more
eloquently than words could, how ridiculous an instrument

it was. With elegant grace he continued picking up the fowl in his long fingers and placing it between his lips. Watching him, she nearly conceded that forks were useless.

She longed for some time to sit down and think through this crazy decision of hers. She longed to analyze and plan, to weigh the consequences of her actions, to make a list of pros and cons and to prepare for the possible results of such a deception. But she couldn't. She didn't dare leave him alone at this point. It was vital that she find a way to communicate with him as quickly as possible, and equally vital that she think of a way to hide his presence from the police and Professor Saunders. That was the only thing she knew for certain. She couldn't let anyone know. She couldn't let him fall into the hands of ambitious scientists who would see him only as the opportunity of a lifetime. They would justify his incarceration and resultant torment as being for the greater good.

With two police guards right outside the door, she realized her predicament was precarious at best. If they saw Rolf...

"Clothes," she whispered, mostly to herself. "We need to get you some clothes." She looked at him frowning at her and tilting his head to one side. Shaking her head, she picked up the telephone and dialed Darryl's number. If she could trust anyone at all it would be her father's sidekick, assistant and devout worshiper. He answered on the first ring.

"Darryl, it's Miranda O'Shea." She smiled as Rolf tilted his head and frowned again.

"How's the professor?" Darryl asked without preamble, genuine concern in his voice. "I called the hospital, but they wouldn't tell me anything."

Miranda swallowed hard. Guilt reared its head inside her. She'd actually forgotten about her father for a little while. How could she? "He's not good, Darryl. Not good at all."

She heard the young man swallow hard. "Will he—"

"The doctors don't know yet. They're doing everything possible, but…'' Her throat swelled and her words faded out.

"Man, I'm sorry. What about you, Ms. O'Shea? Are you all right?''

She sighed. "I'll be fine. But I do need a favor and you're the only person I can ask.'' Rolf was standing now, staring curiously, coming nearer.

"Sure. You know I'll do anything I can. What is it?''

Rolf positioned himself right in front of her. He reached out a hand to the phone on the wall, fingers touching the buttons and causing tones to sound in her ear. She pushed his hand away and shook her head at him. "A friend of mine just arrived from Norway, er, Iceland.''

"A friend?''

"Colleague, actually. He's a…um…'' Rolf was tugging the phone from her ear, and she had to struggle briefly to regain it. She caught his questing hand and held it in hers, trying to send him a silent message with her eyes. "…historian.'' She rushed on to cover her stammering explanation. "He didn't know about Russell, of course. Anyway, he's staying here and the airline lost his luggage.''

"You gotta be kidding me.''

"No, I'm afraid not. The thing is, he hasn't got a single thing except the clothes he's wearing—'' Rolf gripped the phone with his free hand and pulled it from her ear. He bent his head lower, listening, eyes going wider. She tugged the receiver back in time to hear the last part of Darryl's offer to take Rolf shopping.

"Actually, he speaks very little English and he's really timid about going out in public. Do you think you could just pick up a few things for him? I know it's a lot to ask, but—''

"Come on, after everything you and the professor have done for me? It's nothing. Here, let me get a pen. What size is he?''

She knew his measurements by heart, so an educated guess wasn't difficult. "You'll have to go to a big and tall shop, I imagine. Do you want to stop by for my credit card?"

"I'll just use my own and bring you the bill."

It was the answer she'd been hoping for. Time was of the essence here. God only knew when the police outside would take it into their heads to check on her again. "As long as it's okay with you," she said. "If you could just grab a couple of casual outfits and some basic necessities, I'd be grateful. And I hate to say it, but I need them in a hurry."

"No problem. I'm glad I can help out."

As soon as Miranda hung up, Rolf had the receiver in his hand, holding it to his ear and punching buttons at random to hear the tones they made. She reached up, depressed the cutoff, and motioned with her hands for him to stay where he was. She ducked into the living room and picked up the extension. "Hello, Rolf. This is Miranda." She saw him step into the doorway, receiver in his hand, and stare first at it, then at her. "*Gott kvöld,* Rolf."

His face broke into a broad smile. He spoke into the mouthpiece as she had, his voice deep and resonant, caressing her ear. "*Gott kvöld,*" he replied.

She smiled back at him and replaced the receiver. He did the same. The scientist in her was steadily shrinking. This was going to be an adventure. "Come on, Rolf. You need a bath. And a shave. If we disguise you, we can say the specimen was stolen and that you are my dear old friend from Iceland. Old Norse is still spoken there, so it ought to be believable." She looked at him and shook her head. "More believable than the truth, at least."

He frowned at her and muttered, "*Eg skil ekki.*"

She took his arm, quickly glancing into his eyes to see if he would object. He didn't seem offended by the contact. She drew him toward the stairs. "Come with me, Rolf."

He did, albeit reluctantly, as she guided him up to the second floor and along the hall. He stopped often to peer into each room they passed. In the bathroom she forced herself to take her time, to show him the tub and the basin, the hot- and cold-water settings, to teach him the words for these things. His patience seemed as boundless as his curiosity. She started the water running in the tub, and while it filled she located a pair of scissors, a razor and a can of shaving cream.

She swallowed hard and brought him to stand before the sink where he could see his reflection in the mirror. He jumped at first, but she saw that he understood what it was and gradually accepted it. In a moment he was studying his reflection with interest. Mirrors in his time had consisted of nothing more than small disks of polished steel. This one must be quite a surprising change.

"Rolf?" He looked at her, his blue eyes wary and searching. She lifted the scissors to her own face, moving the blades on an imaginary beard. Very slowly she moved them toward his face.

Rolf drew back fast and shook his head. *"Nei!"*

"All right. It's all right." She spoke softly, feeling as if she were soothing a confused, frightened child. The poor man had traveled thousands of miles and nine centuries from everything he'd ever known. He'd died and been resuscitated. The last thing on his mind would be the need to shave, but she had to force the issue.

She approached him, setting the scissors aside, lifting her hand to show him it was empty and then moving it closer, slowly, until she let it rest gently on his face. "Trust me, Rolf," she said softly. "You've got to trust me." She glanced down at the scissors, then back at him. She fingered the thick whiskers and grimaced slightly. *"Gjöriğ svo vel?* Please?"

He frowned and turned toward the mirror once more. He studied his face, threading his fingers thoughtfully through the curling reddish beard. When he looked at her again, she saw his reluctant compliance even before he sighed and said, *"Já."*

He stepped forward again and stood with unbelievable patience while she trimmed and trimmed and trimmed. It seemed to take forever to get the beard down to a manageable thickness. He watched in the mirror as she worked, but his eyes were as often on her reflection as on his own. Eventually she whittled enough hair away so that he wore only a thin coating of it on his face. He now had the look of a dangerous rebel rather than a lumbering mountain man.

He was much more attractive with the shape of his face visible. Not that she would be foolish enough to let herself actually feel an attraction to him...even if she were disposed to that type of thing, which she most certainly was not. She didn't even like men.

Finally she set the scissors aside and lifted the razor. She showed him what she intended by smearing lotion on her own face and scraping it away with the razor. Rolf glanced into the mirror, running one hand thoughtfully over what remained of his beard. He nodded once and turned to her. Miranda smeared the lotion over his face, feeling the tickle of his whiskers against the sensitive hollow of her palm. It seemed such an intimate act, rubbing her hands over his face this way. But of course it wasn't. It was simply something that needed doing, and who else was there to do it?

She could let him shave himself. He would manage. Shaving had not been unheard of, even in his day. She frowned and glanced down at the razor. No, she didn't want him cutting his face to ribbons just because she was ridiculously shy about touching him. Besides, she'd never shaved a man before.

She rinsed the scented lotion from her hands and lifted the razor to his cheek. In careful, steady strokes, she began to remove the bristles from his skin. Little by little his face was revealed to her. First the shape of his cheeks, then the wide, firm line of his jaw, then his square chin with the cleft at the center.

When she finished she took a wet cloth and dabbed the remaining cream and loose whiskers from his face. She stopped, staring mutely up at him and blinking down her shock. The man was incredible, the most undeniably handsome man she'd ever encountered, bar none. She knew she was gaping like an idiot, but she couldn't take her eyes from him.

He grinned and she caught her breath. He had dimples in his cheeks!

Okay, that's enough, she told herself firmly. *With all I have to worry about it's positively insane to be standing here, staring at him this way. So what if he's gorgeous? Lot's of men are gorgeous. What does it matter to me? I'm frigid, remember?*

He glanced into the mirror, running one hand over his now-smooth face. He looked at her once more, nodding in approval. *"þakka þér fyrir."*

"þakka þér fyrir," she repeated. "Thank you. Repeat, Rolf. *Endurtakið.* Thank you."

"Thank...you."

She smiled. She couldn't help it. He seemed so pleased with himself. "You're welcome."

"Ahh, yor welcome," he echoed. *"Verði yður að góðu. Já?"*

She was fairly certain he'd just repeated "you're welcome" in Islensk. "Yes, that's right." She couldn't contain her pleasure. He really was good at this.

His gaze intensified then as he studied her. His smile died slowly, and he searched her face. One hand rose slowly and covered her cheek. He shook his head. "Adrianna?"

"No. Miranda." She put as much emphasis as she could manage behind the words. His eyes narrowed, seemingly roving her face in search of some proof of her identity. She

knew of none she could show him, none he would understand, at least. Instead, she reached for a spare toothbrush
and proceeded to give him another lesson in modern hy-
giene. He actually seemed to enjoy brushing his teeth. But
even while he did, he kept his eye on her.

She shut off the water in the now-brimming tub, force-
fully dismissing the lingering effects of his probing stare.
She pointed. "Bath. Rolf, take a bath." He didn't move
and Miranda reached up to his already unlaced tunic and
tugged it slightly. He seemed hesitant, but he pulled the
tunic over his head. She nodded. "Good, now the shirt."
She touched the shirt as she had the tunic. "Take it off."

His eyes glittered with some secret amusement, but he
obeyed, removing the shirt and standing bare-chested before her. Her gaze fixed itself to that muscled wall of chest,
then moved downward over rippling pectorals and a tight,
flat belly. His skin was utterly hairless, with one exception.
Sparse golden hairs inches below his navel traveled a narrow path downward, disappearing into the waist of the leggings he wore.

The raw masculinity of him hit her like a solid blow to
the solar plexus. She couldn't seem to draw a deep-enough
breath for a moment, or to take her stupid, stubborn eyes
from his bare skin. With great effort, she forced herself to
meet his gaze. She saw his knowing look and perhaps a
hint of something else, as well. She was humiliated and
looked away. She pointed again to the tub and repeated her
earlier words. "Take a bath, Rolf." Her throat was tight.

Lifting one foot he very nearly stepped into the water,
leggings and all.

"No!" She gripped his arm, her discomfort momentarily
forgotten, and drew him back. She shook her head in exasperation. She knew perfectly well his people had been
fond of bathing. He must know what she asked of him.
Honestly, there was so much to be done and so little time.

She tugged at the ties that held his leggings tight at the waist.

His hand covered hers, stilling it.

She looked up slowly and gasped. His eyes blazed with some unnamed, but obviously potent, emotion. In a second he'd closed his arms around her, drawing her flush against his warm, naked chest. She brought her hands up, trying to put some space between them, but to no avail. His body forced hers to bend backward as he leaned over her. His mouth came so near to hers she could feel his every breath. He whispered, ''Adrianna...''

''No,'' she began, but too late. His mouth claimed hers with ferocity. He forced her lips open and thrust his tongue inside, ravaging her mouth the way his people had ravaged the coasts of England in his time. One hand moved upward, to cup the back of her head and hold her face more tightly to his for his brutal, punishing kiss. His other hand dropped lower, cupping one buttock and squeezing hard, painfully hard. His hips moved against her and she felt the rocklike arousal pressing into her stomach.

She forgot that he was confused and out of his time. She forgot that he was huge and could probably break her neck with one hand. She only knew a rush of panic and a need to escape. She lifted one shoe-encased foot and slammed it down hard on the top of his bare one.

His hold on her relaxed with his shock, just enough for her to avert her face from his. She tried to pull free of him, but he gripped the front of her shirt and shot a rapid stream of Norse words at her, words she was glad she couldn't understand. Anger rose to displace her fear. She brought one hand stingingly across his face and tore loose from him, her blouse ripping down the front as she did.

And then Rolf froze. For a long moment he stood stock-still as if paralyzed. When she dared glance up, she saw that he was staring at the dark, berry-colored birthmark on the upper half of her right breast. It was the size of a silver dollar, but kidney-shaped. He blinked twice, shook his head and lifted his gaze to her face. Whatever he saw there seemed to confuse or confound him. He scowled harder than ever and released her at once.

She glared at him, despite the hot tears she felt pooling in her eyes. She fought down the waves of nausea that swamped her, but to no avail. The fear had been too real, and she whirled, falling to her knees in front of the toilet, and violently emptied her stomach.

For a moment she remained there, trembling. His hands on her shoulders urged her to her feet, and then he pressed a damp cloth into her hands. She couldn't look at him. She swiped at her face and flushed the toilet. She pointed to the tub. "Take a bath." The words were bitten out. She turned and left the room without another glance at him.

She went downstairs and into her father's study. She reached up to the top bookshelf and pulled down a tiny key. It opened the top drawer of the tiger maple desk, the drawer where Russell kept a tiny, antique derringer. Miranda checked to be sure it was loaded and was about to tuck it into her pocket when she paused and thought hard. Could she really take the life of a nine-hundred-year-old, living, breathing Viking? Hiding his existence from her colleagues was bad enough, but to destroy him utterly? She slipped the gun back into the drawer and pushed it closed. She didn't think he'd attack her again. If he did, she'd drive a letter opener into his leg, or give him a dose of hair spray in the face. If he got to be too much to handle, perhaps she'd have to let someone else in on the secret. For now, though, she'd manage on her own. She wouldn't allow her nightmarish memories to drive her to act hastily.

She looked down at her torn blouse and exposed skin, and felt her stomach heave once more. She fought the sensation and this time she won. She supposed she ought to be grateful for the birthmark she'd always hated. Apparently Adrianna, whoever the hell she was, didn't have one.

* * *

Rolf bathed. Did the woman wish so badly for him to bathe, then bathe he would, no matter that it seemed a waste of his time. Bathing was the last thing he wanted to do. He was eager to learn more about this place, this land, the language...the woman.

She was not Adrianna.

At least, not the Adrianna he'd known. He imagined himself a fool to believe she might not be Adrianna at all. He suspected he might well be about to entangle himself in another web of her deceptions and lies. But even when she'd been trying to win his trust, Adrianna had never treated him as gently as this one had. She'd never looked at him as this one had.

Miranda. Adrianna's twin? Or one of her plots? Her emotions showed clearly in her eyes. When she looked at him in awe, it was clear. Equally obvious when she felt concern or worry on his behalf. And then, just before he'd mauled her like an angry bear, she'd looked at him with desire so potent it had altered her stone gray eyes to the color of molten steel. A desire so real he could feel it emanating from her.

He thought of the Adrianna he'd known, of her deceptively innocent eyes and ready supply of tears. Her true emotions, did she have any, had never been apparent. Never.

But Miranda, or whoever she was, had desired him. Unlike the woman in his past, she'd been unable to hide or alter the feelings that showed in her eyes.

No doubt he'd cured her of that malady. It wounded his pride that she would react to his kiss so violently. It stung to think he repulsed her to such a degree. But as he soaked in the hot water that eased the burning aches in all of his limbs, he gave the matter more thought.

If she were repulsed by his kiss, he had only himself to blame. For at the time he'd been certain she *was* Adrianna. He'd been certain the longing so plain in her eyes was no more than another of her tricks. He'd been angrier still that his body had felt a response to her heated gaze and trembling touch. Would he never learn? He'd thought to teach her a lesson she would not soon forget. Oh, he guessed he'd done that and more. Only the lesson had, perchance, been taught to the wrong woman.

He shook his head slowly and closed his eyes in disgust. He supposed it was well to know where he stood with the woman. She'd done nothing but show him kindness and patience, despite her fear and dislike of him. If she was Adrianna, perhaps this was her method of atoning for past wrongs. If she was not Adrianna, Rolf was deeply in her debt. True, he hadn't requested her hospitality, had no idea how he'd come to be in her house, and could not find the words to ask her.

No, not any more than he could find the words to explain his actions. Or should he feel the need to explain? For even were she not the woman he had believed her to be, she had been the cause of his lust. Did she not desire to enflame his passions, why had she looked at him as she had? Why had her eyes moved scorchingly over his body?

Rolf had never lifted a hand to a woman in his life. And now he'd done so. Twice, he reminded himself, whether she'd been deserving of it or not. He knew he'd been far more rough than was decent. Even were she Adrianna. He was far bigger than she was and had ten times her strength.

Mayhap she would order him away now. Mayhap she would summon her man to defend her honor, did she have one. He'd seen no evidence of it thus far. Was she alone in this place, then? What of Steinholf, her *faðir*? Of Kalf, her *broðir*? *Nei,* the more Rolf pondered it, the less sense it made. He'd known those men, known them well. Never would they have allowed their cherished and spoiled Adrianna to travel alone to such a strange and remote place.

For more than an hour he soaked and he considered. When the water became too cold to allow such laziness to

continue, he put an end to it. He rose slowly from the water,
stepped onto the floor and reached for the huge, soft "towels" she'd left for him. After a vigorous rubdown he conceded that he felt a good deal better. He glanced around in
search of his clothes, disconcerted to find she'd taken them.
What was he to wear?

He anchored the towel around his hips and went in
search of her, wondering how she would react to him now.
How could he make his peace with her when he knew so
few words of her language? Were he only able to locate
some writings, or find his way into a room filled with talking people. He had endless questions and he must gain
answers.

He moved over the softly padded floor of the corridor
and down the stairs. He found her in the largest room, the
one with the overly stuffed seats all around and the curious
box that seemed to be the focal point. She had several packages spread on the largest seat of all and was pulling garments from them. She looked up quickly when she sensed
him standing there.

Her eyes wavered beneath his gaze and he saw, for a
moment, the fear within them. But she averted them
quickly. She reached over to the small wooden stand in
front of her and picked up a large knife with a long, curving
blade. She studied the item for several moments then
caught his gaze again as she slowly replaced it, at her side
this time. She'd delivered her message without uttering a
single word. Did he touch her again, she fully intended to
run him through.

Rolf glared at the blade and then at the woman. She
thought to tame him with threats, did she? To frighten him?
Him? The notion infuriated him. Not that he thought her
capable of doing him harm. She could have no chance to
outwit or outfight him.

"Come here, Rolf."

He heard the words and committed them to memory, yet

still wondered at their meaning. She used her hands to explain, and repeated the words. Rolf moved nearer, spying his sword and sheath leaning against a small table. He made no move to pick them up. He could reach for them quickly enough should the need arise. That is, should some enemy burst in upon them. To deal with her, he'd need no more than his two hands. Possibly one.

She handed him a small garment, colored like cranberries, but he only stared at it, frowning. Surely she did not intend that anything so small go anywhere on his body?

Sighing, she bent over and demonstrated the way to slip one's feet through the two small openings. She handed him the garment once more, saying the word, "underwear." Rolf lifted his brows as he took them from her. She nodded. "Put them on, Rolf."

He shrugged, hooked a finger beneath the knot in the towel and jerked it free. She turned her back to him at once. He awkwardly stepped into the underwear and pulled it up. The garment fitted like a second skin, and he supposed when she turned back to face him that she must not be pleased. She could see as much of him with the garment in place as she would have been able to without it. Her eyes wandered downward only briefly before she quickly adjusted her gaze and handed him something else.

They reminded him of heavy, outdoor leggings. But they were blue and of a sturdy fabric he did not recognize. He pulled these on and learned they were called jeans. They had no string at the opening. There was only an odd metal contraption with countless tiny teeth. He peered at it.

"Zipper," she told him. She hesitated, then finally squared her shoulders and stood very close to him. Too close, for her scent filled his nostrils at once. She grasped the little piece of metal on the zipper, her hands so near to him he fought the urge to cover them with his, and to press himself against them.

Thor save him from his foolish notions! How could he continue to desire the one who'd so betrayed him?

She pulled the zipper upward. He smiled, distracted for a moment from her charms by the cleverness of the device as he watched her fasten the button at the top. Her fingers seemed to burn him as she touched his skin. When he looked into her eyes once more he saw how it disturbed her to stand so near to him, to touch him. Truly, Adrianna or not, she feared him now.

He walked away from her, trying to accustom himself to the odd feel of the snug-fitting jeans. He moved this way and that, bent at the knees and straightened. He finally came back to her, nodding. He liked them very much. But why, he wondered, was she showering him with gifts after threatening him with a blade?

She gave him little time to wonder. She handed him a shirt made of a soft, pale blue fabric with buttons down the front. He put it on and fastened the buttons, discovering more at the wrists and fastening them, as well. She fixed the collar to her liking, her touch light and fleeting upon the skin of his neck, then she quickly stepped away. "Sit down."

He did. He'd learned that particular phrase in the kitchen.

She remained standing, obviously still not wishing herself too close to him. She handed him two soft white items, and after inspecting them, he deduced their use and pulled them onto his feet.

Rolf was beginning to feel decidedly uncomfortable accepting not only food and shelter, but now bright new clothing from a woman he'd treated roughly, despite that she likely deserved it. Despite even that she'd brandished a blade large enough to eviscerate him.

He thought it over and decided he ought to offer some form of payment. At the very least as a balm to his pride. He rose, ignoring her questioning glance, and crossed the room. Through the door and down the stairs he went, to the place where he'd first awakened to find her standing over him. He hurried into the room where he'd lain, knowing she was on his heels, no doubt wondering at his intent. Rolf snatched up the pouch that held his coins and turned.

Miranda stared, curious and perhaps afraid. Rolf caught one of her hands in his and turned her palm upward. He dropped the pouch into her hand, met her gaze for one moment, then moved past her and back up the stairs.

Chapter 4

Miranda fully intended to tell him exactly what she thought of his manhandling...just as soon as she could communicate with him. She'd combed her father's library, and found a volume on runes with a page translating runic symbols to their equivalent English sounds. She also dug up an Old Norse, or Islensk/English dictionary. The language had changed little over the centuries since Rolf had spoken it.

He used the brush she'd given him, while she gathered the necessary things from the study for his lessons. She tried not to notice that he looked like he'd stepped off the pages of some bodybuilder magazine. She fought with the fool inside her, who kept picturing him garbed in the finest red satin, or worse yet, bare-chested, astride a mighty black stallion, charging into battle, his muscled arms effortlessly wielding his broadsword, his golden hair flying behind him. She managed to dismiss the vivid image just before she groaned aloud.

He no longer shot her suspicious, angry glances every

few seconds. She thought his gesture—giving her his pouch of coins—might have been as much an apology as a payment for the clothes. But she didn't want to think about it. She didn't want to think about him at all, certainly not as a man. Only as an experiment. One she was selfishly keeping all to herself. After his assault upstairs, she thought she would have gladly dropped this entire idea, but she knew she couldn't. For her father's sake, she would see this through. He would no more want to see Rolf incarcerated in a government-funded lab than she did. She had started on this insane path and she would follow it to the end.

She ardently denied that, on some primal, animal level, the memory of his tongue ravaging her mouth sent shivers up her spine.

When Rolf saw the books, his expression changed completely. His eyes rounded and he very nearly smiled. Miranda stifled a feeling of shock as she watched him pick them up, one after another, riffling pages, scanning them. For a moment she was so enthralled watching his reactions that she forgot she was supposed to be afraid of him. If she had any sense, she would be. She wondered, briefly, why she wasn't.

''Rolf?'' He looked up reluctantly. She held out the book in her hand, opened to the rune chart. That would help him with pronunciations more than anything else. When he immediately sat down, carelessly sweeping boxes and tissue paper and the rest of his new wardrobe onto the floor to clear himself a space on the sofa, she almost laughed at his enthusiasm.

She gave him time to study the chart while she busied herself writing the words for every object in the house that came to mind. She included all the words she'd taught him so far, and soon he was moving nearer to her on the sofa, peering over her shoulder, watching every stroke of her pen.

She fought the sudden surge of awareness that made her

want to move away and move closer, all at once. From the corner of her eye, she glanced up at him. He wasn't in a lecherous mood just now. He wanted to learn, wanted it desperately from what she could see. And slowly, tentatively, she began to teach him.

She no longer worried about the police officers outside. If they came in and saw him, she could cover it. At least he looked more like an ordinary man now. No, she thought vaguely as he repeated the word he'd just painstakingly written down. Ordinary, he'll never be. Suffice it to say, he might pass for someone of this century—unless he reaches for his sword and starts offing with someone's head.

She could handle the police. She knew she could. But what if they asked how he got in? What if someone wanted to see the dead Viking in the basement?

I'll handle it. Whatever comes up, I'll simply have to handle it.

He could no longer believe her language was one of her own creation.

It was nearly dawn and Rolf saw that her eyelids were heavy. She must be very tired, yet she refused to rest. She seemed as eager to teach him as he was to learn. With each stride he made it seemed a little more of her dislike of him disappeared, to be replaced by a growing excitement. Each minor goal he reached filled her with delight. She seemed amazed at the amount he'd learned in a single night.

He wished he could tell her that he'd learned many, many languages in his lifetime. Some called him the wisest man in Norge. He'd made it a point to study and learn the languages of every people he'd encountered and he'd encountered many. He hadn't been overly boastful of this knowledge. It wasn't that he was more intelligent than others that made learning new tongues come so easily to him, he knew. He'd always believed it had to do with his ability to remember things precisely after seeing or hearing them only once.

His gift with languages was legend among his people. He'd been much admired for it…until the judgment and his subsequent exile. Despite his position, Adrianna's word had not been doubted. She was the daughter of a jarl, after all. The only thing that made his exile bearable, he recalled, had been his ambition to learn the ways and the words of the elusive Skrælingar of Helluland.

That thought brought a flash of memory, men struggling with the broad-striped sails of a dragon ship. The feel of icy sea spray stinging his face. The riotous rocking of the vessel, and the hideous howl of the wind. The sudden snap of the mast, and the sound of tearing fabric. The water closing its frozen hands over his body, dragging him downward, covering his head, filling him—

Thor, help him, he wished to recall that last voyage! He remembered clearly only what preceded it—Adrianna's treachery. He remembered hoisting the sails, and setting out across the North Atlantic. He remembered his thoughts about the Skrælingar, and his burning anger toward Adrianna for her betrayal. Had not Kalf been his friend, he'd have fought her before the council. He'd have found a way to prove his innocence did he have to fabricate it, as the wench had fabricated his guilt. But to do so would have only served to transfer his sentence to his friend, for Adrianna had accused Rolf only to free her *broðir*. Besides, with Knut dead, and his sworn enemy, Magnus on the throne, proving Rolf's innocence would not have bettered Rolf's predicament. Knowing Rolf was loyal to Knut would only give Magnus more reason to banish him.

Exile would have been Kalf's death. He was strong neither in body nor spirit. And knowing how he'd been used and made a fool of, Rolf had too much pride to make the knowledge public. So he'd set out in exile, seething with anger and bitterness, and his memory faded where the open sea began. Except for these puzzling glimpses.

Her head fell softly upon his shoulder. Her hair touched his cheek, and he could smell its delicate scent. For an instant he stiffened, surprised by the intimate nature of the contact. Then her deep, steady breathing came to his ears and he knew she slept. He tilted his head slightly to the side so that he might brush his face over her satin hair, just once. Despite all of Adrianna's faults, she had been beautiful beyond compare. She still was, for surely, he thought, no woman could look so much like her and not *be* her. By Odin's justice, he wished her heart were as lovely as her body, her face.

Gently, Rolf moved her from him, easing her down to the cushions even as he rose to make way for her. She continued her slumber undisturbed. He took the decorative blanket from the back of the large seat—sofa, he revised in silence—and placed it over her. For a long moment he studied her, the way her auburn lashes rested against ivory cheeks and the peculiar pouting lips, slightly parted and moist. He reached to the back of her head and silently, carefully, removed the pins she'd replaced in her hair, one by one. When he finished, he threaded his fingers through the fiery curls and shook them softly, until they framed her face and cloaked her shoulders.

She made a very tempting offering this way, no animosity in her eyes, no fear. Rolf stood straighter and turned from her. He had much to accomplish while she slept and he would do none of it here. Did he remain in the presence of this sleeping temptress he would continue to stare at her until she woke, he knew he would…at the least. At most, he might bend nearer, gather her pliant body up to his and taste her sweet lips once again.

He pawed through the garments he'd tossed to the floor and found the odd-looking shoes made of cloth, with laces up the front. The bottoms were soled in some strange material he'd never encountered before, like leather but thicker, with an odd, elastic texture and a funny smell. He pulled these onto his feet and then gathered a selection of the books she'd brought to him.

In silence he moved through the house and located other printed works with softer covers and larger pages. Some were glossy, others larger still, unbound and all black-and-white. He used one of the sacks she'd taken his clothing from to hold the volumes, wincing at the rustling sound it made as he packed them inside. But she didn't stir. Lastly, he belted his scabbard around his waist. He would not go in peace without Vengeance at his side.

He longed to go without. He had no notion of what land this might be, with its magical speaking devices and flameless lamps. He suspected he was not in the North, for he felt warm and saw no fire to account for it. He peered through the door in this room and saw the men beyond it. Her servants, he assumed. Or guards of some sort. He felt no desire to attempt conversing with them, given his extremely sparse knowledge of their tongue. Instead he sought another exit. He found it in the lower level—a square of glass, surrounded by a frame of wood. He forced it open easily, despite its strong locks, and squeezed through its narrow space.

Miranda woke with the absolute certainty something was wrong. Terribly wrong. Her groggy suspicion was confirmed when she sat up straighter and looked around. There were still books, and page after page of notebook paper filled with her printing and Rolf's. The boxes and bags from Wilson's Big and Tall still littered the floor along with their contents. The only thing missing was Rolf. Her heart sank as her gaze moved toward the coffee table, where the sword had rested. "Oh, God!"

She leapt to her feet and rushed through the house, first into the kitchen and the formal dining room beyond, then back when she didn't find him. She checked the study, then ran up the stairs, calling his name in a hoarse, urgent whisper. She checked all the bedrooms, the bathroom, even the closets. He was nowhere to be found, and panic began to seep through her limbs like ice water.

She took the stairs two at a time and yanked open the front door, half-expecting to see the severed bodies of two police officers on her front step. Both men looked at her, startled. "Morning, Miss O'Shea," one attempted.

She smiled weakly, her gaze surreptitiously—she hoped—sweeping the length of the driveway and the front lawn. "Have you, uh, seen anyone this morning?"

"No, ma'am. You expecting someone?"

"No." She ducked back inside and slammed the door. "Where the hell are you, Rolf?"

The only place she hadn't checked was the basement, and she hurried down there now, scanning every corner. Just when she was sure he'd vanished like mist, she spotted the opened window in the control room. A cool, early-morning breeze wafted in from the sea. Miranda didn't wait to hunt for her coat. She scrambled up onto the counter and slipped through the opening.

He wasn't in sight, at least not on the back lawn. A brisk wind whipped her hair and Miranda hugged her arms and started off for the path that wound through the small patch of woods to Mourning Bay's craggy shore. Please, she thought, please, for God's sake, be here, Rolf.

The dimness of the path added to the chill, but she soon emerged at the other end into the brilliant sunlight. The cries of sea gulls, high-pitched and shrill, came in riotous chorus. Whitecapped waves rolled in toward the shore and crashed against the rocks below. The aroma of dewy grass and the ever-present fishy smell filled the gradually warming, morning air. Rolf sat with his back against a tree, facing the sea. He had an open book on his lap, and she knew from the intense concentration on his face that he wasn't just looking at it. He was reading it. His long golden hair moved now and then with the breeze.

She gaped for a moment. Then she twisted her wrist to see how long he might have been gone. Seven a.m. She'd fallen asleep about three hours ago. She moved nearer and was able to see the astonished, confused way his eyes sped over the lines of print.

She stepped on a twig and it snapped. Rolf was on his feet in a single motion, sword drawn and poised for battle. The book fell to the grassy ground, its pages fluttering in the sea breeze. Their gazes locked. Then slowly he lowered the sword, slipping it back into its sheath. Rolf bent, picked up the book and held it out to her. He shook his head. "This...not my world."

She closed her eyes slowly and opened them again. "No."

Again the book was allowed to fall from his huge hand. He took a single step forward, gripped her shoulders and searched her face. "*What* world? How I am here? Why?"

She swallowed her fear, only to have it replaced by a heartache for what he must be feeling. She knew she had to explain to him what had happened but she was still unsure she could make him understand. God, that he could speak to her at all, so soon, was nothing short of amazing. "Rolf, come back inside. I'll explain."

He released her shoulders all at once and spun away from her, his fingers pressed to his temples. "I have seen ... ships." He gestured toward the rolling sea. "Small, fast, they...roar." Again he turned, one arm extended toward the ribbon of pavement visible beyond the house. "Wagons, no horses. Move alone. The speed..." He shook his head, looking as if he'd like to scream.

Miranda's fear vanished. She put her hands to his big shoulders and turned him to face her. "It's all right, Rolf. I can explain it...all of it."

He shook his head. "I know not...ex-plain."

"To make you understand."

He closed his eyes and the pain was so apparent on his face, she felt it as well. "Make me un-der-stand. *Minn faðir? Minn broðirs?*" His eyes opened once more, scanning hers in desperation. "Tell me!"

"I will, Rolf. I will." Without thinking, she reached up and gently stroked his face, as if calming a frightened animal or reassuring a lost child. "First, know this. I am your friend. Do you understand? *Vinur pinn.* Your friend."

His eyes narrowed. "I have no…friend…" He lifted both hands palms up. "…here."

"Yes, you do." She took his hand, tugged him toward the path. "Come with me, Rolf. Please." He sighed heavily, but he followed.

They clambered back through the window. He didn't question it. Up the stairs, across the living room. She drew him into the study, all the while wondering just where to begin. She was still in shock over his ability to speak to her, to understand her.

She paced toward her father's desk and was sharply reminded of where Russell was right now, how precarious his situation. She needed to see him this morning, but they wouldn't let her in before nine, anyway. Right now Rolf was waiting for answers. He stood just inside the doorway, watching her, impatience and frustration clear in everything from his taut, drawn facial muscles to his poised-for-action stance.

"Tell me."

She sighed and looked around her, wondering how to start. She spotted the globe and went to it almost desperately. She turned it slowly with one hand. Pressing a finger on Norway, she glanced back at Rolf. "Do you know what a map is? A drawing, showing—"

"*Já.* I know this. Go on."

She blinked at his sharp reply, but made herself continue.

"This is called a globe. It's a map of the world." His brows drew together. "The world, Rolf, is round, like a ball."

He shook his head. "Round, yes. But flat. Not a ball."

"It's true. Men have traveled all the way around it."

Looking doubtful, he drew nearer and studied the globe with perplexed interest. "This world of yours...truly is ball?"

She nodded. "Look. Here is Norway...Norge." She moved her finger to Denmark, then Sweden. "Danmark," she pronounced carefully. "Svíaríki." He stared in what she thought was disbelief.

For a long moment he studied the shapes of Western Europe and Scandinavia. Then he sought her gaze. Lifting two hands to encompass the room, he whispered, "And this?"

"It's called the United States." She moved the globe, tracing a path across the Atlantic and stopping at the east coast. She pressed her fingertip to coastal Maine. "We are here." Slowly she moved her finger north, all the way up through Canada and across Hudson Strait to Baffin Island. "Here is where I found you."

"Found me?" He looked up quickly at her words.

"Yes. What were you doing there, Rolf? Why did you sail so far from your home?"

His face darkened and his eyes seemed shuttered all at once. "There was storm," he said, avoiding her question completely. "*Minn drakkar*...went down. I see Helluland..." He shook his head, pressed fingertips to his temples. "I do not..."

"Remember," Miranda supplied.

He nodded. "*Já*. I only...remember...cold, cold water, pull me down." She closed her eyes slowly, feeling the horror of what he'd been through crash over her like one of those frigid waves. "I think...*já*...I see Skrælingar on the land."

Native North Americans, all of them, be they Inuit or

not, were Skrælingar to Rolf. So the Eskimos of Baffin
Island—his Helluland—had seen the ship go down. "They
thought you were a god," Miranda said slowly. "The
Skrælingar, we call them Inuit, called you 'the god who
rode the seas upon the back of a dragon.' They'd never
seen a ship like yours, Rolf."

Rolf nodded and he gazed at her intently. It was obvious
he was listening, believing her. "They pulled you from the
water. They took you to a cave…" He frowned, obviously
not sure what the word meant. She scanned a shelf, located
a book on geology, and riffled the pages until she found an
illustration of stalactites and stalagmites. She showed it to
him and he nodded in understanding. "A cave, inside the
earth." She laid the book down. "They put you on a bed
of stone, and they left your sword, your battle-ax and shield
at your feet."

"Ax and shield? The ones below?" She nodded.

"*Nei,* not mine. Only this…" His hand closed on the
hilt of his sword.

"Maybe the ax and shield were found and thought to
belong to you."

He nodded thoughtfully. "Skrælingar take me to cave.
Why?"

She sighed and licked her lips. "They believed you were
dead."

"Fools!"

"Rolf…"

He waited, and when her gaze fell before his, he gripped
her shoulders. "Tell me all."

"I'm trying. It isn't easy." Tears welled up and blurred
her vision for no other reason than the emotional blow she
was about to deliver. "You were not breathing, Rolf." He
shook his head, and she demonstrated, inhaling loudly, ex-
haling. "Breathing." She placed her hand on his chest, just
over the pounding beat. "Your heart…was silent."

His eyes narrowed and he grimaced in disbelief. "I am not understanding. You say, I *was* dead?"

"Today we know that a person is not really dead when the heart and breathing stop."

"How one is dead, and not dead!" He whirled away from her, stalking across the room. "You make stories!"

"It's not a story, Rolf, it's the truth." She drew one hand over her eyes in frustration and moved behind the desk to sit down. "There is life in the brain. This is fact. We know it beyond doubt." He turned, looked at her from across the room. "The brain..." She tapped a forefinger on the side of her head. "A person is not dead until the brain dies, too." She struggled to find simple words to explain a complex concept. "The brain dies only a little at a time. Bit by bit, you understand?"

He walked slowly back toward her. "Go on."

"If the brain is cold, the tiny bits do not die. They are preserved. The cold water kept your brain from dying, though your heart had stopped."

He drew a long, deep breath. "You say much...difficult to believe."

"I'm just getting started." She bit her lip, knowing he hadn't caught any of that rapidly spoken comment. "There is more, Rolf, that will be even harder to believe."

"Harder than dead, yet not dead?"

She nodded. Rolf moved forward and took a seat in front of the desk. With one palm-up gesture he invited her to continue, and she did, despite the pain she saw in his eyes, the frustration.

"As you lay in the cave, a glacier—that's a large mountain of ice—moved over the cave's mouth and sealed it. Your rest was undisturbed for a very long time."

His eyes went stony and held hers prisoner in an iron grip. "How long?"

Miranda's throat went dry. She cleared it and forced herself to continue. "The Inuit who put you there have died.

They told the story to their children. When their children died, it was passed to their grandchildren, and so on. My father heard the story and decided to try to find you."

Rolf got slowly to his feet. "How long?"

"Please—" she held up both hands "—I need to explain first. My father is a scientist. So am I. We study people of long ago, how they lived. We teach the young people all that we learn. Do you understand?" He nodded, clearly impatient with her.

"There is much to be learned from the past. Things that can help the people of today. We spent years searching for you, Rolf. And then we found you, in that cave. We brought you here to study you, to learn from you. We, too, believed you dead."

Finally, it seemed, she had his interest once more. "Is not right, to bring dead man, *útlendur,* to your house."

"We didn't see you as an outsider, Rolf, only as an incredible discovery. We put you in that room below and kept it very cold to keep your body from ruin. But something went wrong. The room grew hot, and as your brain warmed, it began to work again."

"My brain began…" His eyes widened, searching her face. "Upon the hard bed, below. I…remember this. I cannot…breathe. I believed…I am in the sea." He frowned, struggling for the memory. When it came, she knew, because his gaze suddenly narrowed, growing so intense it felt as if it were piercing her. "You…your lips on mine. Your breath in my…" He pressed his fists to his chest.

"Lungs," she supplied. "Yes, I blew my breath into your lungs. I saw that you were alive and couldn't breathe. So I helped you to breathe."

He muttered in his own tongue, then confronted her angrily. "Was not it enough to give shelter, food?" He tugged at the shirt he wore with a thumb and forefinger. "The garments I wear? I owe to you my life, as well?" He slammed a fist on the desk in his anger, and she jumped to her feet.

"You asked me to tell you all of it."

He glanced at her with an impatient shake of his head. "You have my...thanks, lady. Only I like not...owing to another. To you, I loathe it."

She blinked back the effect of the stinging remarks. "Because I look like Adrianna?"

He glared at her. "I am unsure you are not Adrianna. She would much like such a game, to cause my mind to leave me."

"You know I'm not Adrianna. You saw the mark on my breast."

His smile was bitter. "You put it there...with the juice of berries, I think." He came around the desk, his anger like a burgeoning flame in his eyes. "I will see again, this...mark you give to your breast."

It was the way he reached for her that induced the panic. It was so menacing. She wouldn't allow herself to be abused that way. Not again. In one quick movement, Miranda jerked the desk drawer open, yanked out the tiny gun and brought it up between them. "If you touch me again, I will kill you."

He stopped short, staring down at the gun, head tilting slightly to one side. "What is this?"

"It is a weapon far more deadly than your sword, Rolf Magnusson. It shoots a small lead ball at such speed the human eye cannot see it. It will put a hole through your body faster than a blink of the eye."

He lifted his gaze to hers. "I do not believe."

"Take another step, and I'll give you all the proof you could ask for."

He shook his head. "You lie not so well as once you did, Adrianna." He took a step toward her, and Miranda closed her finger on the trigger.

Chapter 5

The shot blew a hole in the globe and sent a shredded mess of litter to the floor on the other side.

Rolf jerked in shock, his eyes widening when he saw the damage. He exclaimed in his own language, but Miranda was beyond paying attention to him. She heard only the two police officers shouting, then the door crashing open and her name being called. She'd panicked and maybe ruined everything in the process.

"Oh, hell. Rolf, listen to me. You have to hide, quickly. I'll explain later, but for now you have to trust me. If those men see you here I'm going to be in a lot of trouble. Please." As she spoke she hustled him toward the closet in the rear of the room. She opened the door and shoved him inside.

"Rolf Magnusson hides from no man."

"Those men have guns, too," she told him quickly. "Please, I'm begging you, just stay here and be quiet." She tried to close the door, but he held it open with arms of iron. She glared at him. "Don't forget how much you owe me, Rolf. I saved your life."

That seemed to do the trick. He stepped farther back and let his arms fall to his sides, but as she pushed the door closed he caught her wrist. She looked up fast, hearing the approaching steps of the officers. "These men…they mean you harm?"

She gaped for a moment, shocked he'd show any concern at all for her safety, as much as he seemed to despise her. "No. They're here to protect me."

He nodded and pulled the door closed himself. Miranda spun around just as the study door swung inward and the two men came in cautiously, guns leading the way.

She stepped away from the closet, praying Rolf would behave, and shrugged. She offered the men her most sheepish expression. "Honestly, I'm such a klutz. I didn't realize it was loaded." She lifted the gun as she spoke and moved toward the desk, dropping it as if it were soiled.

The officers visibly relaxed, darted each other a speaking glance and holstered their weapons. One spotted the destroyed globe and barely suppressed his laughter. He elbowed the other, who did chuckle.

"You all right, Miss O'Shea?"

She nodded. "I feel utterly foolish, but no harm done."

"I assume you hold a valid permit for that weapon?"

"Actually I don't. My father does, though. It's his gun. I was just checking on it. I felt a little nervous after the break-in."

The first officer frowned. "Ordinarily I'd have to confiscate the weapon…but under the circumstances…"

"Better let her keep it, Roy," said the other. "You never know."

"Yeah. I have to advise you, Miss O'Shea, that if you use that weapon, you'll be in violation of state law and subject to criminal charges. You understand?"

"Yes, of course. I'm sorry I scared you like that, really."

"Just lock it up and leave it alone and you'll be fine."

"Doing so as we speak," she assured them, opening the drawer and shoving the gun across the desk until it fell in with a loud thunk. She slammed the drawer shut and patted the desk's surface, looking for the key. When she came up with it, she inserted it in the lock.

The police officers nodded, apparently satisfied, and turned to leave. As soon as the outer door closed she rushed to the closet and opened it. Rolf stepped out, replacing his sword in its scabbard as he did. He'd been ready to come out fighting at a moment's notice, she realized a little shakily.

She sighed and shook her head. "That was close."

Rolf stood rigid, searching her face. "Never have I seen such weapons," he murmured.

"Things have changed. You were in that cave for a very long time, Rolf."

"I do not wish to believe this story you tell...." His gaze moved over her face. "You are so like Adrianna...yet different. Your eyes, so...hers showed only what she wished. And she...never so feared my touch."

"I don't fear it, I just don't want it."

"*Nei.* It was fear I saw in your eyes. I believe you rather would kill me, than—"

"We were talking about you."

He ignored her. "Have you had a man before me, lady?"

"Do you want to know how long you rested in that cave or not?"

His intense blue eyes probed her soul one last time before he shrugged and looked away. "You may tell me. I may choose not to believe."

"Fine. Do you know what a year is?"

"Four seasons. I read many books while you sleep."

"Do you know our numbers?"

"Numbers?"

She returned to the bookshelf, scanned it and finally

found a book with sufficient pages. She opened it, and showed him the page number in the upper right corner. "Numbers."

"Ah. Those I have begun. I will learn numbers today."

She hesitated, frowning at him. "How do you learn so fast?"

"I remember all things. Your words. Say them and they are locked forever in my…brain. I know more tongues than any man in Norge."

"Your English seems to improve by the minute."

"I do not know…minute. But I learn more with every word you speak. Now, these years, each four seasons. How many years did I rest?"

She bit her lower lip. She flipped the pages over until only the cover remained open. "If each page is a year…" She captured pages one through nine hundred between her fingers. "You slept for about this many pages."

He stared at the book, then at her. He shook his head slowly, taking a step from her. "*Nei.* You lie. You are Adrianna! You—"

"Who ruled England when you went on that last voyage, Rolf?"

He watched her warily, as if she were going to try to trick him somehow. "Knut died the year of my voyage. As I sailed, his *sonir* by Emma, Hardacnut, claimed the throne, as did his *sonir* by Ælfgifu, Harald Harefoot."

"England is now ruled by a woman, Queen Elizabeth."

"Lies!"

She shook her head, again scanning the books, grateful for her father's endless library. She found the one she wanted, and opened it to the pages listing the rulers of England and their lines of descent. She set it before him and he looked as she pointed. "Here is Knut…the year he began ruling is here. One thousand seventeen. These are the rulers who succeeded him, beginning with Harald Harefoot. Knut's wife, Emma, was exiled then. Harald died in one thousand forty—five years after you left Norway—and Hardacnut took the English throne without a fight. While he was busy in England, though, Magnus of Norway took Denmark, if my history lessons serve me. Hardacnut died after only two years on the throne, and England was then ruled by Emma's son from her first marriage, known as Edward the Confessor.''

Rolf's brows lifted. ''The *sonir* of Æthelred?''

''Yes. Look for yourself. There have been many on the English throne since then.'' She pushed the book closer toward him and Rolf took it, studying the pages solemnly for a long moment.

''*Stodva!*'' He closed the book with a bang and turned from her. ''You seek to drive me from my mind. Only Adrianna would—''

She came around the desk, putting a hand on his huge shoulder though he refused to look at her. Her throat burned as she realized what he must be suffering and she hated to add more to the burden, but she had no choice. ''You know I'm telling you the truth. You wish it wasn't so and you are angry that all of this has happened. But you know it's true. You saw the little ships without sails and the wagons without horses. These things did not exist in your time and you know it. There is still more I have to tell you, so you have to stop arguing with me and listen.'' She paused, swallowed hard. ''I'm sorry. I know this is hard for you, but we have to talk about these things now.''

He shook his head, so much dejection in his eyes she could hardly bear to look at him. ''If what you say is true, *mínn*…my *faðir*, my *broðirs*, all are gone. Therefore, it cannot be true.''

She felt a hot tear brim over and run down her cheek. Her heart constricted in her chest. She hated inflicting this kind of pain on him, would hate doing this to anyone. Given her own father's precarious hold on life, she knew too well the loss Rolf was feeling. "I'm sorry, Rolf. I'm so very sorry."

He looked up, saw that tear and spoke slowly, his gaze penetrating. "Adrianna has tears for no one. Tears to her are…were…weapons." He squeezed his own eyes tight, tilted his head back. "Odin, why? Thor…speak to me! Do you yet live or have all the gods died, as well?" She gulped back a sob that only seemed to tear further at the man's heart.

"*Nei*, you are not Adrianna, are you?" He faced her once more.

She shook her head. "No, I'm not."

He looked at the floor. "So I must believe." He walked slowly from the room, scattering bits of the globe as he went. He reached the sofa, sat down and let his head fall back so he faced the ceiling, though Miranda knew he wasn't seeing it. "Speak what you must. I will hear."

She had followed him into the living room and now stood near the sofa. Why were her instincts telling her to sit beside him, to pull his head to her breast and cradle him there? She swallowed hard and remained standing. "There are other scientists, Rolf. Many, many others. I have not let them know that you are alive. They all believe your cold body still lies below on the table. They all want a chance to look at you, to study you."

"They will be saddened, no doubt."

"They would be overjoyed if I told them. But I'm not going to. Even my father doesn't know."

He frowned and brought his gaze level with hers. "Why?"

"They would give anything to find out how you were preserved for so long, without harm done to your mind or your body. Nothing like this has ever happened before."

"I will tell them all I can."

She shook her head. "They wouldn't question you. They'd lock you up in a room like the one downstairs and they'd study you. They'd cut small pieces of your flesh to see if they were different. They'd want to look inside you, inside your brain.''

He grimaced. ''What sort of men do such things to one another?''

''They would say it was for the good of many, to learn all they could about you.''

''I will not allow it. Do they try to take me, they will know the sting of Vengeance.''

''What is Vengeance against the weapons of today?''

He looked at her for a long moment. ''Yet you think to keep me from them?''

''I *will* keep you from them.'' As she spoke she felt the firmness of her conviction. She saw his eyes narrow upon her as she went on. ''Rolf, we cannot let them know the Norseman below has been revivified. We have to say you are of this time, a friend, visiting me from Iceland.''

He released a short burst of air. ''And what tell you them do they wish to see the Norseman below?''

''That someone came here while I slept and took him away.''

''*Nei*. It is you who are losing the senses. Who would believe such a tale?''

''Rolf, before you woke, someone did come here while I slept. I don't know who it was or what they wanted, but my father was hurt as he struggled with them below. He thought they were after you. That's why the men stand guard outside right now.'' He only frowned. ''It will be easier to convince them of the lie than it would be for them to believe the truth, Rolf. They would never guess it, because they believe such a thing impossible.''

Rolf stubbornly stood his ground. ''I hide behind no woman. I will stand and I will fight.''

''No.'' She stood fast and held his gaze. ''My father spent years trying to find you, and so did I. After all that I will not allow you to simply let them take you, and make no mistake, Rolf, they would take you, or kill you."

He closed his eyes and sighed. "Better had you left me in the cave of the Skrælingar, Miranda." When he looked at her again, he seemed resigned. "I will do as you ask for a time. You have given me much, Miranda. I pay my debts."

Rolf felt as if the very life force had been drained from his body. He'd lost so much in such a short time. His exile had been disheartening enough, but at least he'd known his family had been alive and well. Now... He shook his head. It was very difficult to believe they were gone. Gone like early morning mist rising from an emerald sea with the sunrise. Gone, along with everyone and everything he'd ever known. The pain was nearly crippling.

Oddly enough, it seemed this woman, this...Miranda, shared in his pain. She seemed genuinely distressed at having to reveal so much to him all at once. The glimmering sheen covering her storm-cloud eyes had to be genuine, for she fought against it, repeatedly blinking, pressing her knuckles to tightly closed lids, and averting her gaze altogether.

She touched his shoulder, shaking him from his reverie. Her eyes had darkened to the color of deep slate as they dug their way into his. "Are you all right?"

"I am a warrior."

She frowned, making three tiny crescents appear right between her auburn brows. "That is not an answer."

"But it is," he replied. He consciously straightened his spine and sought to busy his mind with something else. "You have spoken of your *faðir*. Where is the man, that I might thank him?"

He didn't miss the flicker of agony in her eyes, though she turned from him quickly enough. "He is in the hospital. That's a place where our sick and wounded are cared for.

We have men and women called doctors. These people spend many years learning to heal and they work at the hospitals to tend the unwell.''

He nodded. She spoke slowly, carefully, as if speaking to a dull-witted child. He would not correct her just yet, however. Better that he understand every word. ''He is ill?''

Her words sounded forced through a small space. ''He was hurt the night someone broke in here. He was struck on the head, and his weak heart gave out.''

No wonder the woman seemed to be in pain. The idea of her facing some unknown intruder, alone except for a weak parent, sent a jolt through Rolf. ''You were here, then?'' Rubbing her shoulder with one hand as if unconsciously, she nodded. So, she'd got the ugly purple bruise at the hands of this intruder. He wondered at her valiance. Did she fight to protect him, though she thought him dead? No, more likely the woman fought in defense of her *faðir*. She must love the man greatly. ''We will go to this…hospee-tal. I would speak with him.''

She nodded, her mind clearly elsewhere. ''Yes, we do need to go to the hospital this morning. But it is not a good idea for you to see him just yet. It would be a shock for him to see you. Shock is not good for a weakened heart. It might kill him.''

Her words made perfect sense. Truly she was learned in many things. ''I would not wish to harm him. We go now? I am eager to see more of your world.''

She shook herself from her lingering worry and faced him. ''First, we bathe. In this time it is customary to do so every day, rather than once a week as your people preferred.''

Rolf frowned. ''I do not know 'week.' ''

''Seven days is one week. Each day has a name. Today is Tuesday.''

''Tuesday,'' he repeated slowly. ''But this 'seven…' ''

She held up the corresponding number of fingers. "Seven."

"Ahh."

She looked thoughtful for a moment. "Our biggest problem is going to be the two police guards outside."

"Dismiss them," he told her quickly. "Are they not your servants?"

Her lips curved upward into a slight smile. "No, I have no servants. They serve the public, like soldiers. Their job is to protect all who live here, and to stop the lawbreakers. They stand watch in case the intruder I told you about tries to come back. The problem is, they'll know you didn't come in from outside and they'll wonder where you did come from."

Rolf studied her as she paced and pondered. Odd it was, to have a mere woman taking such pains to ensure the safety of a powerful fighting man.

She snapped her fingers. "Okay, I have an idea. You'll have to listen carefully and do exactly as I say, or it won't work. That photographic memory of yours will come in handy."

He shook his head. He did not know "fo-to-gra-fik" but he would look it up in the large book of words. It eased his own wounded spirit to see her with color in her cheeks. He thought she might not be fully aware of it, but she was finding joy in the challenge of keeping her secret. It showed in her eyes. A glitter of excitement, a silvery sheen. "Tell me what I must do," he said.

She spoke firmly. "Not until after we shower and change. I'll use the bathroom first." She waved a hand at the chaos that surrounded them. The boxes and wrappings that had held his clothing littered the floor, along with many more garments. The books and papers they'd used in their studies last night covered every surface, along with writing implements of various types. "While I'm gone, you can clean up this mess."

Rolf felt his eyes widen. "You say you have no servants, lady. Do not think to make me your first."

She bit her lip and drew a long breath, as if exercising great restraint. Finally she spoke. "You have no servants, either, my friend. And in this century, women do not spend their time picking up after men. We each serve ourselves. Those are your clothes."

He nodded, wondering whether she spoke true, or was simply being difficult. "Those," he said, pointing, "are your books."

Her silken brows rose in two perfect arches and she seemed to chew her inner cheek. Finally she shrugged. "Fine. I'll take care of the books. You take care of the clothes...and their wrappings. There's a guest room at the top of the stairs and to the left." She turned to walk up the stairs without awaiting his answer.

"Miranda." At his voice, she stopped and faced him, one hand on the rail at her side. "Which way is this... 'left?'"

She smiled, fully this time, and came down the two steps she'd ascended. To his surprise she reached out, clasped his hand in hers and lifted it. "This is your left hand." She gripped the other, her skin supple and warm. "And this is your right. If you face this way, then that's left." She gestured as she explained. "But if you turn around, left is that way. You see? Left is always to the same side as this hand."

She still gripped both his hands and she stood close to him. Her head came to the center of his chest and she had to tilt it back to look at him as she spoke. Rolf found himself suddenly very sorry he'd made her afraid of his touch. Now that he knew she was not Adrianna, he wished for the opportunity to erase his earlier behavior. Of course, he couldn't be certain it would matter. After all, she'd vomited. Such a response certainly indicated a strong aversion to him, one that might have been there even had he not handled her roughly.

Besides, he reminded himself harshly, he could not be certain yet that her heart wasn't as corrupt and unreliable as Adrianna's had been. If he'd learned anything from her betrayal, it was not to give his trust again so easily. A beautiful face and ivory skin did not necessarily reflect the soul they hid beneath them.

But if it were true that one could see a person's soul through the eyes, then hers must be pure. Pure and complex and very, very deep, he thought as he searched the gray orbs thoroughly. He noticed for the first time the thin ribbons of jet radiating outward from the pupil, and the deep, dark blue outline surrounding the storm gray irises. Her lashes were long and thick, a sable color, but tipped with auburn like her hair, giving them the impression of radiance. He did not recall Adrianna's eyes as having been so lovely, or so deep. He felt as if he were being drawn into them, as if he were in a quagmire from which he had no desire to escape. As if...

She blinked and lowered her head and the spell was broken. She released his hands and stepped back. "I, um, we have to get going."

"Miranda," he began, with no idea what it was he wanted to say.

She glanced up at him with a plea in her eyes that silenced him at once. She gave her head an almost imperceptible shake, taking another step away from him. Her eyes were wide and smoky with confusion. He lifted one hand, palm up, a silent entreaty, for what, he knew not.

She turned and fled up the stairs. Fled, yes, it was the appropriate word. She ran from him as if he were the wolf, Fenris, or the Midgard serpent. Or the Plague of the North, he thought grimly. Which, indeed, he was.

Chapter 6

She had to push it out of her mind. Her plan to fool the police wouldn't work if she were not convincing. And she couldn't be convincing if she were distracted by that freak storm of sensation she'd felt an hour ago.

God, but it had been powerful. The way he'd stared into her eyes as if he were searching for something. Not just searching, desperately searching. For a brief, unsettling moment she'd felt herself longing to give him what he sought, though she didn't even know what that was.

But it was foolishness. She felt sorry for him, that was all, and naturally she wished she could ease his pain. Any decent person would feel the same.

She licked her lips, checking quickly over her shoulder to be certain Rolf was out of sight in Russell's study. Between the two of them, they'd restored the living room to order. No sign of his presence remained. She gripped the doorknob in a white-knuckled hold.

"Miss O'Shea?" The officer on the right bobbed his head at her. "Anything wrong?"

"It's chilly out here. Why don't you two come on in for a coffee break?" They hesitated. "The house is so empty with Russell in the hospital."

That did it. Flanders and Morgan couldn't have been more willing to share a cup of coffee with her. She led them straight to the kitchen where the machine was just gurgling its last few drops into the carafe. Miranda casually closed the door that led to the living room and proceeded to pour the coffee. She rattled the cups and silverware, walked heavily, and deliberately scraped the chairs over the kitchen floor, all to cover any noise Rolf might inadvertently make slipping outside.

She thought she'd covered everything. She'd told him step by step what to do, what to say. Knock on the door, act like a friend she hadn't seen in a long time, shake the officers' hands when she introduced him. She'd even given him one of her old suitcases, stuffed with enough towels to give it convincing weight. Nothing could go wrong. What cause would anyone have to doubt her?

Still, when his oversize paw thumped on the front door as if trying to knock it from its hinges, she came out of her chair as if it had suddenly burned her. Both officers, she noted in alarm, leapt up as well, hands on their pistol butts. A little breathlessly, Miranda attempted, "I wonder who that could be?" Weak, pathetic and ineffective.

"Whoever it is, he doesn't sound friendly," Flanders said.

"Better let us get it, ma'am," Morgan added.

They made their way cautiously toward her front door. Flanders stood to the side, while Morgan reached for the knob. They glanced once at each other. Flanders nodded and Morgan jerked the door open.

Rolf's brows arched up. He'd obviously been expecting Miranda to open the door. She quickly inserted herself between the two officers. "Rolf! Why, it's only Rolf, my dear old friend from Iceland.'' The officers looked quizzically at each other, then at her.

Meanwhile, Rolf stepped inside, dropped the suitcase and swept Miranda into his arms, lifting her off her feet so high she found herself looking down into his face with her hands braced on his shoulders. He whirled her in a circle, moving forward as he did, stopping only when they were in the center of the room. ''How good it is to see you,'' he blustered. He lowered her slightly. ''Have you no kiss for your dear old friend?''

She fumed. The officers had heard him, of course. They stood near the door, which was still wide open, wearing amused expressions. ''Damn you to hell,'' she muttered through grated teeth. She lowered her head and brushed her lips over his. He caught the back of her head with one hand and captured her lips between his, holding them there with gentle suction. His hand on her head exerted minimal pressure and she could have easily pulled away, except that it would look strange to the police. His lips moved against hers, around them, in an oddly sensual way. He sipped at them as if they expressed some succulent fluid, as if he were thirsting for it. Then he broke the contact and set her on her feet.

As she slid down the front of his hard body, Miranda felt a bit light-headed and breathless, though she wasn't sure why. Nerves, she supposed. It wasn't often she tried to pull one over on officers of the law. Rolf kept one arm around her shoulders, an act she was simultaneously angry about and grateful for. She wasn't sure she'd be too steady on her feet just now without the added support.

Facing the officers, she tried to keep her voice even. ''Officer Morgan, Officer Flanders, this is Rolf Magnusson, a friend and, uh, colleague.''

Morgan stepped forward and extended a hand. Rolf looked at it blankly for a moment and Miranda jabbed her elbow into his ribs. He held her so close to his side she was certain neither of the other two noticed. Rolf extended a hand and clasped Officer Morgan's. Morgan grated his teeth through a forced smile and his jaw went tight. After he took his hand away, he repeatedly flexed and bent his fingers. With a studious frown at Morgan, Flanders refrained from offering his own hand for similar punishment.

God, she wished this were over. "More coffee, anyone?" Oh, beautiful. That would speed things up. Why not invite them for breakfast?

"We'd better get back outside, ma'am. Thank you, anyway."

"Nice meeting you, Mr. Magnusson," Morgan added. They both nodded at Miranda before ducking out the door and closing it behind them.

She pulled herself from beneath the weight of Rolf's arm, and faced him with her fiercest scowl. "I didn't say anything about kissing me! What did you think you were doing?"

"You did not vomit this time." The man had the audacity to grin, twinkling those dimples at her until she felt like slapping him.

"Where did you learn a word like 'vomit'?"

"I looked it up," he quipped, still grinning.

The oversize jerk. "Not that it's any of your business, but I only vomit when I'm assaulted."

"I do not know 'assaulted.'"

"Mauled," she clarified. When he still frowned at her, she added, "forced."

"Forced?" His face changed. The smile died utterly. "I have no need of such methods. And you—" he stopped midsentence, his frown deepening, his gaze boring into hers "—you speak as if you—"

"It's time to go. Visiting hours begin soon." She reached for her jacket, a casual black suede one with brown leather patches at the shoulders and elbows. "I've explained to you about the car. Just follow my lead, and re-

member, act like you've been getting into cars your whole
life. All right?'' She glanced up at him, but he still had that
speculative look in his eye.

''Have you had a man before me, lady?''

Miranda stiffened, averting her gaze. She didn't like the
question and it was the second time he'd asked it. She had
no intention of answering, no matter how many times he
asked. Moreover, she'd like to know what the hell he meant
by that ''before me'' part. ''Do you want to ride in the car,
or not?''

''I wish to know the answer to my question.'' He waited,
but she turned her back and strode out the door. He followed her in silence, but she felt those piercing eyes on her
the whole time.

She leaned over to open his door, then moved around to
the driver's side. He settled himself on the small seat, dwarf-
ing the car with his size. A Toyota simply wasn't designed
with the Viking warrior in mind, she thought. He stiffened
a bit when she fired up the engine. She'd explained what
to expect, but she supposed riding in a car was still quite
an ordeal. He must feel the way she would if she traveled
by way of the space shuttle.

''Watch me,'' she told him as she reached for her seat
belt, pulled it around her and snapped it in place. ''Now
you.''

He glanced over his right shoulder, pulled the belt around
him and snapped it in easily. He lifted his brows.
''This…car. It moves so fast one needs be restrained?''

She chuckled in spite of herself. ''No, Rolf. These are
for safety, so if I have to stop fast we don't crack our heads
on the windshield.'' She tapped the windshield when she
said the word. ''Are you ready?''

He nodded, his jaw still tight, and watched her as she
shifted into gear and pulled out of the driveway. His hand
clutched the small armrest as the car began to move forward, but gradually he relaxed. By the time they reached

the hospital he was asking questions. Was the pedal what controlled the speed? Did the wheel choose the direction? What was the meaning of the numbers behind the glass on the dashboard? Why did she stop at the red light? He had extracted a promise from her before they entered the hospital corridors. That she would teach him to drive. And soon.

The Intensive Care waiting room hadn't changed overnight. She led Rolf to a padded seat and pressed him into it. "I'm going just beyond those doors." She pointed. "I won't be long." She hated leaving him alone in the waiting area while she went in to see Russell, but saw no alternative.

"Do not trouble yourself, Miranda. Go, see your *faðir*. I will wait."

She nodded her gratitude and hurried through the double doors and to her father's room. Dr. Fenmore hadn't been available for an update and she had little idea what to expect. She braced herself and walked in.

"Miranda." Her father tried to sit up when she entered, but she quickly went to his bedside, pressed her hands to his shoulders, and kept him from completing the motion. He looked terrible, his face a sickly gray, his skin drawn, bloodless.

"Easy, Russell. I'm right here."

He shook his head slowly. "Go home. Stay with the find. I told you—"

"It's under guard. Stop worrying."

He relaxed, but only slightly. "Did you do as I said... read my journal?"

She pressed her two fingers to the center of her forehead. "Actually, not just yet. I was planning to do it right after this visit."

"Not the blue one, Miranda." He spoke very slowly, taking deep, uneven breaths between the words. "The real one. The real one."

She frowned. "I didn't know you had more than one."
He only nodded.

"Russell, what are you talking about?"

"I...kept it secret. I wasn't sure. Didn't want to be...laughingstock...but I thought he might be...the one... they called...Plague. You know. We had no proof."

He stiffened and drew one arm up to his chest. Miranda's heart leapt and she reached for the call button on his pillow.

"No...listen." He touched her hand, stopping its progress. "I'm...not going to...make it. Been...like this all night. Exhausted."

"Don't you dare say something like that to me, Russell O'Shea!"

He shakily held up one hand to silence her. "Can't...talk so much. Can't breathe well." Again, he drew the deep, unsteady breaths that so frightened her. "It's all in the journal...the real one. So much more. Th-the plunder. Still hidden." He grated his teeth, seemingly forcing himself to continue despite her protests. "So much more to do, Miranda. You have to...finish. Finish it!"

She closed her hand around his and reached for the button with the other. "I'm calling a nurse. You're getting worse by the minute." She depressed the button with her thumb and released it as panic seeped into her heart.

"I waited for you," he rasped. His eyes brimmed now, watering from the force of whatever pain he must be in. He sighed, shook his head. "Wish that damned...elephant...would get off...my chest."

She thumbed the button once more, holding it down this time. "Hold on, Russell. Someone will be here any—"

He winced suddenly and the EKG monitor leapt unnaturally.

"To hell with it, I'll get them myself." She rose to go to the door, to shout the halls down until someone came to help him.

"Wait!" He gripped her hand with surprising strength.

She faced him just as the door burst open and three people in white seemed to rush through at once. One gripped her shoulder. "Daddy?" She couldn't help calling out to him like that. She did so now as his grip on her began to relax. She did so in a voice choked with emotion and with eyes suddenly blurred by tears.

"Remember..." He gasped the words now, and Miranda struggled against the hands that were pulling her from his bed. Her hand slipped from his. "Jules...Verne." His hand went limp. His eyes closed. The EKG's intermittent beep became a steady tone, and as she was pushed toward the corridor, Miranda lurched toward him, fighting the hands that held her back.

"No. Don't make me leave him," she heard herself plead. "Daddy!" None too gently, she was forced into the corridor despite her loud protests. "No! Let me go!" The door was closed in her face. Miranda cried her father's name as if she could somehow hold him to her, even though she felt him being torn away.

Chapter 7

Neither the heavy double doors nor the countless men and women in white coats stopped him when he heard her cry out. In less than a heartbeat, Rolf skidded to a stop before her. She stood beside a closed door, her back pressed to the whitewashed wall. Her eyes were dilated to an unnatural degree, the gray no more than a narrow band around the black of her distended pupils. She stared straight ahead, but he was certain she wasn't seeing. Her breaths came quickly, as if she'd just run a great distance. Her lips trembled and her skin was pale.

Confused, Rolf looked around her. He'd thought someone must be attacking her when he'd heard her scream. Now, though… He looked through the small pane of glass in the door beside her, and he became aware of the steady, high-pitched tone emanating from within that room. More of the white-garbed individuals hovered around a bed, so that the still body upon it was barely visible.

Rolf stepped closer, eyes narrowing as he watched the urgent movements of the people in the room. Then the activity slowed. One man's gaze lifted to that of his colleagues and he slowly shook his head. A woman turned, touched a button, and the irritating bleat halted, leaving silence in its wake.

Beside him, Miranda emitted a low, anguished groan, barely audible though he stood very near her. Her knees seemed to dissolve, and with her back still pressed to the wall, she began to slide downward. Rolf stooped quickly, catching her beneath the arms and hauling her up. Even that effort did little good. All of her bones seemed to have melted. Her head hung as if no longer connected to her body.

He knew without being told that the man in the bed was her *faðir* and that he had died. Despite the animosity he'd felt between them, he experienced a stabbing pain in his chest solely on her behalf. Without thinking about it, he pulled her limp body tight to his hard one, and he held her.

He felt her trembling in his arms and he wished in vain for words of comfort to spring to his lips. Instead he remained silent, for there were no words that might help her now. He understood her grief. He still felt his own, spawned by her revelations this morn. For the moment he thought the best he could do for her was to take her from this place. But as he stepped away from her, her arms shot around his waist and her face pressed once more against his chest.

His shock at her action was exceeded only by his shock at the response it stirred within him. A rush of emotion shot up from his toes to the nape of his neck, shaking him. For just an instant, he felt an instinctive urge to protect her. Normal under the circumstances, he presumed. His size and strength alone would be enough to stimulate this protective instinct. Was it not natural for the strong to defend the weak? With her in this heightened emotional state, the impulse became even stronger. But it was nature working. Nothing more.

He battled the sensation and won. He managed to hold her tightly to his chest, to press soothing hands to her trembling shoulders and back without feeling a thing in his heart. He had no intention of allowing himself to fall prey to the wiles of another Adrianna. The feminine weapons of weakness and tears, be they genuine or false, would no longer work upon Rolf's emotions.

The man he'd noticed before, doctor, he reminded himself, came through the door, his expression grim. When his hand touched Miranda's back she stiffened. Her chin rose slowly and she squared her shoulders as she turned to face him. To Rolf's surprise, her eyes remained dry. Wide, yes, and overly dilated. But dry. She had not shed a tear.

"I'm sorry, Miranda. We did everything we could."

"I know." Her voice was low, but level. "I'll make arrangements for—" she cleared her throat "—everything as soon as possible."

"Are you all right," the doctor asked. "Do you need anything? A sedative?"

Rolf didn't know what a "sedative" was, but Miranda shook her head indicating she did not require one. When she turned to start off down the corridor, her hand closed on Rolf's upper arm. She held to him tightly, though he had the impression she was not aware of doing so. She kept that rigid posture all the way through the double doors and into the waiting area he'd previously occupied. Then she froze and her grip tightened still more, as four men rose from their seats and approached them.

Without intending to, Rolf took a step that put him between her and the group. They certainly looked harmless enough. An aging gentleman with a dignified air and snowy hair and beard, a skinny youth who wore eye shields like Miranda's and an adult male, of average size, with brown hair and eyes. On second thought, that third one had a decidedly belligerent gleam in his eye. The fourth man was dark of hair and powerfully built. It was he who came forward, moving past Rolf as if he had no fear...or no sense. As Miranda stepped from behind Rolf, the man put his hands upon her arms and searched her face.

Rolf cursed himself for acting hastily and on instinct yet again. Next he'd be doing battle on her behalf.

The two other adult men eyed him warily, while the youth seemed to turn to stone in his tracks as his jaw dropped.

"It's all right, Rolf," she said in that deep, calm tone she had no business using after what she'd just witnessed. She stepped away from the dark-haired man's touch, and nodded to the one with the pointed white beard and snowy hair. The man was too thin, save a paunch at his middle. "This is Professor Erwin Saunders, head of the archaeology department at Beaumont," she told Rolf. "I've told you about him." She smiled shakily toward the youth. "And Darryl Watters, a student. He is, that is, he was..." Her voice seemed to thicken and she stopped speaking all at once.

Rolf's gaze left the youth to focus on Miranda. Despite her determination to stand tall, she was slipping. "Your father's assistant. You spoke of him, as well." Rolf nodded toward the boy, who still gaped. His skin had gone milky and he looked as if he would faint. "I am Rolf Magnusson. I am visiting from Iceland." He recited the lines Miranda had taught him, giving her time to recover her composure. This latest revelation of her character stunned Rolf. Tears and weakness he could witness and remain unmoved. But steely strength and stubborn pride? These were qualities he'd become accustomed to finding in warriors, not women.

To his surprise, the one called Saunders extended a hand to him. Rolf lifted his own hand, to find it gripped firmly and pumped twice. "Good to meet you, Mr. Magnusson."

Miranda cleared her throat and faced the man nearest her, the one who felt it his right to touch her so freely. She glanced once at Rolf before her gaze flew back to the man.

"This is Fletcher Travis, archaeologist, numismatist and all-around genius. It's been so long…" She shook her head, blinking rapidly. "Russell would have so loved to see you again, Fletch."

The man, this Travis, frowned suddenly. "Miranda? Is he—"

Rolf watched her. She met the man's gaze squarely, chin lifting still higher. A convulsive spasm moved in her throat. "He's…gone."

Travis put his arms around her and hugged her, but only briefly. Saunders lowered his head, eyes closed, while the youth, Darryl, finally snapped out of his stupor. He covered his face with one hand and turned away from the others. From the look of things, Rolf thought the boy was crying, but he couldn't be certain. The fourth man, the belligerent one whom he had yet to meet, seemed unmoved.

Saunders wrapped Miranda in a firm embrace the moment Travis released her. She hugged him in return, but, Rolf noted, she didn't bury herself in Saunders the way she had in Rolf's arms. She hadn't clung to Travis in such fashion, either, and for that he felt inexplicably glad.

"I can't believe…when? Is there anything I can… You'll take some time off, of course…and I… Oh, Miranda, I am so very sorry." The old man stammered and it was difficult for Rolf to follow his words, but the meaning was clear.

"Under the circumstances, Professor Saunders, don't you think it would be in everyone's best interests to move the find?" The angry man spoke without emotion. "Miranda isn't going to be up to having hordes of scientists and students, not to mention the press, trooping in and out at all hours."

Rolf disliked his tone. For though he attempted to sound concerned for Miranda, Rolf heard another motivation behind the words.

"Well, I hadn't thought—" Saunders began.

"You'd like that, wouldn't you?" All at once, Miranda's

eyes blazed and she took a step nearer the man. "Just where would you suggest we move him, Jeff? We all know there is only one other place with the facilities to pre-serve—"

"That's right. We have the facilities at Cryo-Life. You're going to shoot me for that?"

"You're not taking him," she said slowly. "This project was my father's life's work, and I'll be damned if I'll hand it over to you!"

"I'll be there whether you like it or not. C.L. paid dearly for the right to have access to this find, and I'm going to make sure they get their money's worth." He took a step closer, and Rolf felt sorely tempted to throttle him. He wasn't certain why. Perhaps the way the man's small brown eyes moved deliberately over her body. "If you don't mind my presence in your little basement lab for the next twelve months, then I have no objections."

She blinked, and for the second time since he'd known her, Rolf saw fear in her eyes. The first time had been when he'd brutally kissed her in the tiny bathroom. She tore her gaze from the man's and glared at Saunders. "Is this true?"

"Your father knew about it, Miranda. It was a financial decision. We needed the funds."

"So badly you were willing to sell out to a company that exists only to bilk sick people out of their life's savings?" Her voice rose as she spoke, and the fire blazed again from her eyes.

"We're scientists, just like you," the one called Jeff fairly shouted. "We offer terminal patients an option." ·

"Hand over your money and we'll freeze your body," Miranda shouted right back. "We don't know how to thaw you out yet without killing you, but don't let a little thing like that bother you. We'll figure it out while you're on ice. What kind of an option is that?"

"Their only option, at the moment. And a find like this one could give us the answers we still don't have. Saunders says it's perfectly preserved. I need to get my hands on a cell sample, see whether there's been any crystallization of the cell walls.''

"Not one cell." Miranda forcibly lowered her voice. "Not if I have to stand guard over him myself."

"You really think that would bother me…Randi?"

She turned deathly white when he called her that and one hand came flying upward. Rolf caught it deftly before she could slap the man senseless, as no doubt she'd intended to do. Gently he pulled her aside, while Fletcher Travis gripped the dog by one arm and growled at him, "Get off it, Morsi. She's been through enough. Open your mouth again and you'll lose a few teeth."

"Now, gentlemen, please. We're all on the same team here. There's no need for this bickering." Saunders's soft manner and overly flamboyant use of his hands for gesturing made his words all the more weak.

Miranda ignored them and glared at Rolf as angrily as she had at the other man. "Why did you do that?" She slid her gaze to the hand still gripping her wrist.

Rolf kept his voice low. "Miranda, I know not why you hate the man. Only that you have been dealt a terrible blow and are not thinking clearly."

"I'm thinking just fine, thank you."

"Then why do you argue the fate of a…a find which no longer exists?"

She blinked quickly, then slowly closed her eyes and kept them that way as she released all the air from her lungs. She bit her lower lip and shook her head. "God, what was I thinking?"

"Dr. O'Shea?"

She turned at the young man's call. Rolf wondered how she held on to her composure with all of this hitting her at once. He further wondered about the silent turmoil he sensed between her and the dog, Jeff Morsi, not to mention the closeness he felt sure Miranda shared with Fletcher Travis.

"Your father did know about this," Darryl went on, finally rejoining the rest of the group. His eyes were still damp and terribly red rimmed. "He hated it, but he agreed to it. Said there was no choice. He was planning to tell you about it, but…well, I guess he knew how you'd react."

"Miranda, if you want the find left where it is, I'll respect your wishes," Saunders said gently. "But you have to know we can't delay. We only have possession for one year, and there is so much to be done. The studies need to begin right away."

"Right away," she repeated in a monotone.

"Yes. It would be inhuman of me to expect you to take part at a time like this. I'll take your place, if you like. But we simply cannot delay."

"You…want to begin…today?"

He nodded, dropping a withered hand upon her shoulder. "We can do the initial exam and testing with just the three of us, if it will help. I've brought Travis in to examine the coins that were recovered. He's the best in the field. Russell would have approved. The press release can be postponed until tomorrow, but no longer, I'm afraid. And then the entire archaeology department is going to expect an opportunity to view it." He licked his lips. "You don't even have to be present if you don't want to, Miranda. But I'm afraid we have to begin today."

"Right," Jeff nearly sang. "Cryo-Life has a signed contract with Beaumont. We're to be allowed initial inspection of the find today, and today it will be. We'll follow you home, Randi."

Her head swung around and the glare in her eyes was fierce. "If you ever call me that again—"

"You'll what?"

"What *she* will do should not be your first concern, Morsi." Rolf hadn't meant to step to her defense, but he'd remained silent for as long as he cared to. Regardless of his feelings—or lack thereof—for Miranda, he instinctively disliked the swine. And Rolf's instincts about men were rarely wrong, though his record with women was far less intact.

Rolf drew Miranda with him toward the stairs they'd ascended when they'd arrived. She accompanied him without resistance and when he glanced down, he caught her studying him with a puzzled frown rippling the bit of flesh between her brows.

Chapter 8

"You are tired, Miranda."

She agreed. The pain crushing her chest was damn near unbearable. That she'd known her father's heart condition was severe, that she'd guessed it to be terminal, helped very little. Always the knowledge that he might still be with her if not for the break-in lurked in her mind. It wasn't fair.

"I...want to thank you." She glanced at Rolf as she drove the Toyota toward the house. "You were a great deal of help to me back there."

"I did nothing."

She swallowed hard, her mind going back to the moment when she'd heard that low, steady tone stop utterly and found herself held in those massive arms. He might think he'd done nothing. He would probably never know just how much he'd really done.

"You did, you just aren't aware of it."

He studied her face for a long moment. "You are grateful I stopped you from striking Morsi? Is it for this you thank me?"

She carefully pasted a stony expression over her face. "No, I'll never thank you for that."

"What is he to you?" Rolf persisted.

Face impassive, or as impassive as she could make it, Miranda forced words to her lips through a rapidly constricting throat. "Nothing. He is nothing."

"I think you lie." When she looked at him quickly, he shrugged. "Women do. I am not surprised."

"You have a low opinion of women."

"You have a low opinion of Morsi," he countered.

"I have reason." She returned her gaze to the street.

"As do I."

She didn't respond to that, but drove in silence, her mind numb, her soul empty. She felt unreal, like a shell of a person, a hollow plastic mannequin.

"You care for Fletcher Travis," he stated after a moment.

"Very much. He is one of my best friends."

"A friend only?" He looked at her and she nodded.

"A friend only. We've never been involved romantically. Why are you so curious?"

He only shrugged and was silent for a long moment. "What of the boy?"

Miranda turned again and saw the troubled look in his eyes. "Darryl?"

"He knows, Miranda."

Still numb, she struggled to speak. "What do you mean?"

"He was your father's assistant. This means 'helper'?" At her nod, he continued. "He was with you when you found me in the cave of the Skrælingar?"

"Yes." A slow trepidation made a home inside her and Miranda was shocked that she could feel it there.

"He looked upon my face?"

"Your face was covered with whiskers. Your eyes were

closed. Your skin was like a plaster sculpture. You looked nothing like you do now.''

"He knows. Watch his eyes, Miranda, and you will see it there.''

She sighed and absently pressed her fingertips into her right temple, making small, brutal circles. "Are you sure?''

He nodded. *"Já.''*

"All right. I'll talk to him, find out if he is suspicious.'' She lowered her hand, but the throbbing in her head continued. "He won't say anything if I ask him not to. He's a good person, Rolf. My father adored hi—'' The last word was cut off by a sudden sob that leapt into her throat. She choked on her effort to suppress it and bit on her lip until she drew blood. She blinked away the stinging tears before they could escape and wished her throat would stop burning and spasming.

"Why do you do this?''

"Do what?'' she asked, not comprehending.

Frowning harder, he studied her. "You do not behave like the women I have known.''

"I'm not like other women.'' Without meaning to, she'd quoted her father. She hadn't realized just how thoroughly his words had embedded themselves into her thought processes. She wasn't like other women. She swallowed hard. "I am not ashamed of it. Would you prefer it if I fell into a sobbing heap at your feet?''

Shaking his head, he replied, "I dislike tears.''

"Tears are healthy. It simply happens I prefer to shed mine in private, as I'm sure you do, as well.'' She blinked. "I imagine you're feeling the same way I am right now. Or worse. You've lost your entire family, your world.''

He averted his gaze. "I am a man. A warrior. I will withstand the loss.''

She sighed. "Men feel sadness and heartache as much as women do, Rolf.''

"Nei, this is a lie.''

"You can deny it to yourself, but not to me. Men have spent centuries denying they had emotions. Today we know better. Men have even been known to cry when they're hurting."

Rolf's face hardened. "Never will you see Rolf Magnusson spill tears like a woman!"

She shrugged. "And you ask me why I'm not crying. Sounds like you understand already."

He frowned across the space of the car's interior at her. She studied his face and saw the sadness in his eyes. She wondered how much of it was his own, and how much was there strictly for her loss. She was certain part of it was for her. She knew he must be feeling a pain nearly identical, if not more intense, than her own, whether he would admit it or not.

She'd pulled the car partially into the driveway and come to a stop as the force of his pain and her own became unbearable. "I know you're hurting, Rolf, and I'm sorry."

"Make the car move, Miranda. The others come."

She glanced into the rearview mirror and saw two bigger, sleeker cars waiting in the street with their signal lights flashing impatiently. She finished pulling into the driveway and out of the road. They pulled quickly in behind her.

As she reached for the door handle, Rolf caught her arm. She paused and looked around at him. His face grim, he spoke in a low, deep voice, slightly hoarse. "I did not say I have no pain, only that I could withstand it." He met her gaze, his own steady. "I know what you are feeling, and I, too, am sorry."

Before she could formulate a response, he was opening his door and getting out. He waited for her to join him before walking to the front entrance. Miranda watched his gaze narrow and wondered why only briefly. All at once she realized that the two officers who'd stood guard at the front door were no longer there. As her stunned eyes moved upward, she noted the pry marks on the door itself. She reached up to touch it and jumped when it swung slowly inward with a slight groan.

Rolf's hand closed on her shoulder to pull her back. He stepped past her and peered inside. "Stay here, Miranda," he whispered, before ducking into the house and vanishing from her sight.

"The hell I will," she whispered right back as she slipped in behind him.

The first sight to greet her as she walked into her living room was that of Officer Morgan's still body, and the pool of deep crimson beneath his head.

Miranda froze. Her gaze remained glued to the poor man's pale face even as the others came in behind her. In some far-off region of her consciousness, she was aware of Darryl gasping for breath, and then the sound of his inhaler. She heard Jeff swear and reach for the phone to call the police, then Fletcher shouting at him not to touch anything. She heard Erwin Saunders's shocked exclamations. Yet she only stopped staring when a pair of large hands gripped her shoulders and turned her from the sight. "No one is here now," Rolf told Fletcher. His grip on her tightened. "Miranda?"

She looked up, saw Rolf's eyes searching her face. He kept saying her name over and over, shaking her slightly. She swallowed hard and forced her mind to obey her commands. She fought the shock that wanted to take control.

"What is happening? My God, is this all a nightmare? Has the world gone completely insane?"

"Take her into the study, Magnusson." Vaguely she recognized Fletcher's confident voice. "You've already got the phone in your hand, Morsi. Go ahead and make the call. No one touch anything. There might be fingerprints, or some other evidence." Fletcher knelt beside the police officer as Rolf attempted to tug Miranda into the study.

"Police are on the way," Jeff announced, holding one hand over the mouthpiece.

"Tell them to send an ambulance, too. This cop isn't dead."

Miranda felt a whirlwind of confusion sweep through her mind. She felt Rolf's gaze capture hers. She saw something in those blue eyes, something to cling to, to keep her afloat in the sea of insanity engulfing her.

"My God, the find. Saunders, do you think..." Jeff's words trailed off as he raced through the room and into the basement. Seconds later his voice came wailing back to them. "It's gone! My God, it's gone!" Fletcher and Professor Saunders immediately bolted down the stairs to join him.

Darryl gasped deeply, hoarsely. Then again and again, wheezing more loudly with each exhalation. Miranda finally broke eye contact with Rolf to glance in the younger man's direction. He struggled to lift the inhaler, but dropped it. His wide eyes remained on Rolf as he fell to his knees, patting the carpet in search of the medication.

Rolf released Miranda and knelt beside him, closing one hand over the inhaler and handing it to Darryl. He took the shaken student's forearms and helped him stand, then eased him into a chair. "You are ill? What is it?"

The youth kept looking up into Rolf's eyes while he fitted the inhaler to his lips and sucked two spurts of medication into his lungs. Miranda forced herself to move forward. "He has asthma. It affects the breathing, Rolf. That's a drug that makes it better," she explained, calmly, she thought, given the upheaval in her mind.

Darryl's breathing eased. He glanced around him and saw that he was alone with Rolf and Miranda. His eyes still wide, he stared from one to the other and back again.

"It is the shock of finding Officer Morgan that makes you ill?" Rolf asked.

At his words, Miranda came to her senses. What on earth was the matter with her? She moved away, still listening to their conversation, but belatedly attending to the unconscious man on the floor. He probably has a family, she thought sadly, tugging a blanket from the sofa and tucking it around him. A wife. Children, perhaps. She lifted his feet and propped them up with throw pillows, then stationed herself near his head and pressed two fingers over the cut on his right temple until the flow of blood slowed to a trickle. She kept the pressure on and watched his chest rise and fall.

Darryl remained agitated, his eyes never leaving Rolf's face now. "It's you—" He began panting once more, and lifted the inhaler for another shot.

"Me? I cause this fit?" Miranda looked up to see Rolf shake his head. "There is no need, boy. Those who call themselves my friends have in me a loyal protector. Those who are my enemies die mercifully swift deaths." He eyed the youth's awestruck face. "Choose."

"Ch-choose?"

"Rolf, you're frightening him," Miranda attempted, but found her words ignored.

"Choose," Rolf repeated. "Friend or foe, young Darryl Watters?"

Darryl sat up straighter in his chair and held Rolf's gaze. "Friend. Unless—"

"You place conditions on your friendship?" Rolf growled, but so low that no one else could have heard unless they were as near to him as Miranda. "Go on, boy. Tell me of your conditions."

"Unless...you hurt Ms. O'Shea. If you do, then I'll—"

"You will what?" Rolf glared at Darryl, but the slightly built young man glared right back, though his knees were knocking together.

"Rolf, that's enough," Miranda nearly shouted.

"I'll make sure you pay, that's what. And I don't care who or what you are," Darryl whispered. "She's been through enough."

Rolf's expression eased. He nodded his approval. "On

that, at least, we agree." He cupped the back of Darryl's
head with one large hand for a moment. "I am proud to
call such a valiant one friend," he said quietly.

Darryl sighed his relief and tucked the inhaler into his
pocket. He continued staring in awe at Rolf, though. "Are
you, really—"

"He is, Darryl," Miranda managed to interject. "But
you can't say a word to anyone. Promise me. I'll do my
best to explain it all later."

Darryl swallowed hard and nodded. "Did your father
know—"

Rolf held up a hand and Darryl fell silent. Then Miranda
heard the others trotting back up the basement stairs.

"So the only things missing are the body and the
sword?" Lieutenant Hanlon paced the living room, a notepad in hand. His forensics team were combing the basement
for evidence, while he did his best to make sense of the
situation. A large car of white with flashing lights atop it
and a piercing cry had carried the wounded man away only
moments ago.

When Rolf had searched, in case the swine still lingered
here, he'd discovered that Miranda's home had been truly
ransacked. Every drawer had been opened and emptied,
along with every cupboard and closet. Beds had been
stripped, the cushions removed from every seat, the furniture overturned.

"And every file we had on the find," Miranda reminded
Hanlon.

"Which is my point exactly," Jeff Morsi snapped. When
all heads turned in his direction, he pointed at Miranda.
"You all heard her say she'd keep this find to herself if
she could. Looks like that's just what she's trying to do."

Rolf rose slowly, his gaze pinning Morsi to the spot.
Miranda must be on the verge of insanity with all of this.
She did not need this man's insults to push her still farther.

Travis was quick to grip Rolf's shoulder. Before he could pull away and lift Morsi by his throat, Miranda leapt to her own defense, surprising Rolf yet again.

"You're a fool, Jeff! The find would be ruined in a matter of hours outside that climate-controlled room and you know it."

"Suppose you have another lab somewhere, one we know nothing about?"

"And what did I use to pay for it? My incredible looks?"

Her sarcasm wasn't lost on anyone in the room, not even on Rolf. Yet he could not, for the life of him, understand it.

Jeff Morsi sneered. "Right, I forgot. You couldn't buy a ticket to Tuckahoe with the entire package, could you?"

Rolf's fist moved so rapidly no one saw it coming, until Morsi was flat on his back with blood spurting from his nose. Lieutenant Hanlon, Fletcher Travis and Darryl all gripped different parts of his body, but he gently extricated himself. Miranda stood motionless, staring wide-eyed at him. "I will not strike him again," he said to reassure them. In truth, he thought he just might.

"Obviously we're all tense here." Erwin Saunders helped Morsi to his feet, and handed him a white linen handkerchief. "I'm sure Jeff is sorry for that remark, and that Rolf is sorry for striking him. Correct?"

Morsi eyed Rolf warily. "Sure. I'm sorry, okay?"

"I am not. And do you insult the lady again you will know the full extent of my wrath, Morsi."

"I imagine Cryo-Life would have the kind of facilities to maintain a find like this one, wouldn't it, Mr. Morsi?"

Morsi, pressing the hankie to his nose where it rapidly became soaked with crimson, glared at the lieutenant. "Is that an accusation?" He spoke like an old woman with a congested nose.

"I'd need a motive, and not being a scientist, I can't think why a company trying to develop suspended animation for sale would want to steal a nine-hundred-year-old body. Maybe somebody else here can, though.''

Darryl cleared his throat. ''The body was perfectly preserved. If even one viable cell were found, it would be a boon to Cryo-Life. They'd want to take the body apart bit by bit to find what had allowed life to remain...'' His voice trailed off. He glanced at Rolf and swallowed.

''Which is precisely why my father and I have opposed allowing anyone from Cryo-Life to take part in any stage of this project, and why we adamantly insisted they should not be permitted to touch the Ice Man, even before we discovered him. It is also why I said what I said at the hospital. I'd sooner let you cut me up than him.'' As Miranda spoke those defiant words, she slipped her hand into Rolf's and her fingers closed around it. He was so shocked he nearly gasped aloud, but managed to contain himself and simply stare at her in wonder.

''Is that why you hid it, Miranda? To keep me from cutting it up?'' Jeff removed the hankie, glanced at it and pressed it back to his nose. ''Would you rather see it ruined than benefiting human beings the world over?''

''Human beings the world over would benefit from the proper study of the man, how he lived and what he did. They won't benefit from some witch doctor like you taking the life savings of cancer patients in exchange for dropping their bodies in dry ice when they die.''

''Is that a confession?''

''You know damn well it was no confession. It was a simple statement and it was the simple truth. You people at C.L. aren't scientists, you're con artists!'' Rolf's free hand came down on her shoulder, gently, but firmly enough to remind her of his presence. It seemed to have a calming effect. She drew a breath, stiffened her spine. ''You're welcome to search the house, Lieutenant. My office at the university, too, if you want.''

''Searching the house will be necessary, I'm afraid,'' he

explained. "But not because we suspect you of anything, Miss O'Shea. Just to try to ascertain how the specimen was taken out of here and when and by whom."

"You don't even *suspect* she might have done this?" Morsi all but shouted, earning him Rolf's most speaking glare.

"Why should he suspect her?" Fletcher Travis asked. "Russell and Miranda O'Shea have been members of this community and tenured university professors for a combined three decades. It isn't as if they would sell to the highest bidder and skip the country. Besides, I know the passion and the years they've given to this project. Neither of them would risk it just from pure selfishness. They knew years ago they'd be compelled to share the specimen, if they ever discovered it."

"Yes, that's true, but not with me," Morsi countered.

"And I still didn't know I'd have to share it with you, Jeff. Not until you so tactfully broke the news in the intensive care waiting room."

"It makes little sense to me to believe Miranda would wreak such havoc with her own house," Rolf began, his voice level and firm. "It would seem to me the dog was looking for more than just the...the speciman."

Professor Saunders paced the room, nodding. "He's right. Anyone who knew about the specimen would have known where to find it, without trashing the house this way, and they certainly didn't expect to find it under cushions or inside drawers. They took all the files on the find. I would assume that's what they were searching for."

"Were the files hidden, Miranda?" Fletcher Travis touched her arm as he asked the question, concern for her etched on his face.

"They were in the file cabinet. Whoever did all this was looking for something else."

Lt. Hanlon nodded. "My thoughts exactly. Now we know Miss O'Shea wasn't responsible. Witnesses place her at the hospital at the same time Officer Flanders got that bogus message saying there was an emergency at his home. The rest of you, I'm sorry to say, don't have such solid alibis."

"I told you, I was alone at home up until I left to meet Travis," Saunders stated.

"And Travis was eating alone at a crowded diner," Hanlon reminded them. "And Morsi was stuck in traffic, and Darryl was sitting by the lake, studying. Any one of you could have clubbed Morgan over the head, forced the door and dragged him inside before trashing the house. Any one of you could have taken the body, but I don't seriously suspect you did. Until I know more, I'd like you all to keep quiet about this. The fewer people who know about it the better, from my standpoint."

"I suppose it's lucky we haven't yet announced the find to the press," Saunders observed.

"You got that right." Almost offhandedly Hanlon added, "An unidentified body turns up, most likely someone's going to call it in. If they think it might be a nine-hundred-year-old body, the citizens will be cutting it up for souvenirs." He nodded when several disbelieving pairs of eyes turned his way in shock. "Oh, yeah. Wouldn't be the first time. People are sick." He cleared his throat. "Professor Saunders, you can go on home if you want. I'll keep you informed. Mr. Morsi, you can leave, too, but I'll be wanting to talk with you later, and maybe take a tour of Cryo-Life, if you can arrange that. Mr. Travis, you won't be leaving town in the near future, will you?"

Fletcher Travis shook his head.

Professor Saunders prepared to leave. "Darryl?"

"I'd like to stay, Professor Saunders. I can walk back to campus later."

Saunders nodded and left, Jeff Morsi stalking out the door close behind him. Hanlon turned to Miranda. "We'll be doing a thorough check outside first, Miss O'Shea. See if there's any evidence of a body being dragged. I doubt they carried it. According to these notes the stiff was as big as—'' he glanced around the room ''—as Magnusson, here.'' Darryl choked loudly and spun around until his back was toward Hanlon. Hanlon looked curiously at the young man, then shrugged and stepped outside.

Fletcher peered thoughtfully at Darryl, then shot a speculative gaze at Rolf. His brows crinkled deeply, and he shook his head from side to side as if dismissing some errant notion. He came forward and offered Rolf his hand. ''If you hadn't decked Morsi, I would have. He had it coming.'' He glanced at Miranda. ''I'm glad you're here for her, Rolf.'' Rolf shook Travis's hand, wishing he didn't instinctively like the man. Travis hugged Miranda once more. ''If you need anything—''

''I know,'' she said softly. ''Thanks, Fletch.''

The moment the door closed, Darryl looked at Rolf and grinned a bit uneasily, still staring at Rolf in awe. ''It's true, isn't it. It *is* you.''

Rolf nodded. ''Do not forget the men downstairs and those just outside,'' he said gently. ''Miranda asked me to keep this secret, and because I owe her my life, I agreed. Only now do I begin to see that she was right to do so.''

''Damn straight. Morsi and his bunch would do just what she said they would—cut you to ribbons.'' Rolf saw now, that in age, Darryl was man grown, but in size and in mannerisms, he still seemed little more than a boy. Darryl pushed his glasses up on his nose. ''See, usually when a body undergoes extended periods of conglaciation, there's crystallization damage to the cell walls. Despite the gelidity and the vacuity that preserved you, you must have been exposed to some chemical compound—theoretically a naturally occurring one—that kept your cell walls intact, unaltered. Might've been ingested, or maybe the contact was topical. Either way, they'd kill to know what it was.''

''Darryl, easy. Rolf is just learning English. He's not

ready for Anatomy 101.'' Despite the softness of her tone, Rolf thought her voice sounded lifeless.

"You would do well to rest in your bed, Miranda."

"I have too much to do. Arrangements to make, and—" She pressed a palm to her forehead and closed her eyes tiredly. "If I keep busy, I won't have time to think, you know what I mean?"

Rolf did. "I know," he said.

"I have some calls to make. I'll use the phone in the study."

Chapter 9

"She puzzles me."

Darryl replaced the receiver, apparently realizing that his detailed explanation of its use was being largely ignored. Rolf had watched Miranda leave the room and his gaze still lingered on the doorway to the study.

"Dr. O'Shea?"

Rolf drew his gaze back to the youth and nodded. "She has no man. This is common among your women?"

Darryl shook his head. "She's unique. Her father was always telling her so. I heard him say once that a husband would only hold her back."

"Hold her back?"

"In her career," Darryl explained. "Her work, you know?"

"And does Miranda believe this is true?"

Darryl tilted his head to one side, looking doubtful. "I don't know. If she does, she didn't always. She and Jeff Morsi... Maybe I shouldn't be telling you this."

Rolf's spine stiffened. He felt a tremor of anger rumble

deep inside him, but he knew not why. "I have eyes, Darryl. I can see there is something between them."

Darryl chewed his lower lip and nodded. "Yeah, pure hate."

"Why?" Rolf leaned forward in his chair, his elbows resting upon his knees. His gaze scanned the young man's face. He did not understand his need to know all about Miranda. No, no more than he understood the feelings she stirred within him. He wished with everything in him to take away her pain. Why?

Darryl squirmed in his seat. "They were engaged once. Planning to get married," he hurriedly clarified when Rolf only frowned. "It was two years ago, when I was just a freshman."

"She intended to wed that worm?" Rolf stood without meaning to. He shook his head in disbelief, not merely at the information, but at the rage he felt in reaction to it. "Why did she not?"

"I don't know. Half the campus had theories, but no one really knew. It was…like things changed overnight. Dr. O'Shea avoided Jeff like the plague, and he acted like he couldn't stand the sight of her." Darryl lowered his voice. "A friend of mine said that Jeff told him she was frigid. Can you believe he'd say something like that about her?" He looked up at Rolf. "I'm glad you hit him."

Rolf made a mental note to look up the word "frigid" when he had a moment later on. Right now he had to concentrate on keeping up with the conversation, and on keeping his anger in check. Why should he wish to feel the tip of Hefnd sink deeply into Morsi's throat?

Darryl coughed a little. "A lot of people believe she is. She gets jumpy if a man even looks at her, and as far as anyone knows, she hasn't had a date since she broke it off with Jeff."

"Date? What is this?"

"You know, when a woman goes somewhere with a

man. Like out to eat, or to a movie or dancing or some-thing.'' Rolf shook his head, still not quite clear on the date thing. Darryl sighed. ''Well, it's like… In your time, when you met a girl you liked, *really liked,* what did you do?''

''You mean a woman I wanted?'' Darryl's face colored slightly, but he nodded. Rolf gave his answer some thought. ''I assume you refer to a woman of some virtue, rather than a wanton. In that case, a man would first seek the permis-sion of her *faðir*. He then could visit her on occasion. Per-haps bring some golden bauble to her on returning from *i víking*. He might coax her into going walking, or perhaps take her for a short ride on one of the small ships one day.''

''That would be a date,'' Darryl said, snapping his fin-gers.

''If that is so,'' Rolf replied, ''it is difficult to believe the story you tell about Miranda. Adrianna was never with-out a half-dozen men groveling at her feet.''

''Adrianna? Was she—''

''A woman I once knew. The most sought-after woman in all of Norge, some said. Her beauty could blind a man to all of her faults. She used men, tricked them to suit her purposes and then sent them on their way. She was an artist at…I believe the word is…flirting. She dressed and acted and even spoke in ways designed to entice men, to make them crave that which they could not possess.''

''We have a few like that,'' Darryl acknowledged. ''Al-though I've always figured you couldn't hate them for it. If men are stupid enough to fall for it, then who's really to blame?''

Rolf scowled suddenly. That had to be the oddest point of view he'd ever heard, and yet in a way it made sense. He had believed himself a fool to allow Adrianna to use him, had he not? ''So Miranda does not use her beauty in such a way?''

''Use her…'' Darryl fixed Rolf with a look that made him feel he'd missed something important. ''In case you haven't noticed it yet, she doesn't seem to know she has any. I bet it would never occur to her to use her looks to get ahead. She probably believes she is completely unattractive. The way she dresses and keeps her hair all bundled up, she's managed to convince a lot of other people of it, too.''

Rolf thought for a moment. ''Yet she walks proudly, with confidence.''

''I figure that's because she's good at what she does and she knows it. That's what people see when they meet her. A plain, but keenly intelligent scientist. You don't notice her looks until you get to know her better.'' Darryl shot a wary glance toward the study, then looked back at Rolf again. ''You want to know something else? I think she likes it that way. Those rumors about her being an ice queen. Well, she hasn't said or done a thing to stop them.''

''I see.'' Rolf studied the young man, weighing his words. ''I think you, too, have this keen intelligence. You see much.''

''I minor in psychology.'' He shrugged as if that explained everything.

Hours passed. Hours in which the police finished their work and left, and in which Darryl finally ran out of questions for Rolf and went his way, as well. During all that time Miranda had emerged just once. She'd come from the study only to pass through the living room and go up the stairs. Rolf had approved, thinking she'd decided to get some rest. But as he'd patiently told tales of long ago to Darryl, Rolf had begun to feel uneasy.

When he finally was alone, he mounted the stairs and strode purposefully to Miranda's room, only to find her bed empty and undisturbed. He needed only to follow the nearly inaudible sounds of movement to find her.

He pushed open a door and stepped into her father's bedroom. Miranda stood before the bed. Suits of clothes lay spread before her. Jackets, ties for the neck, crisp white shirts, knife-creased leggings. She moved slowly, her head tilting first one way, then another, as she moved a striped tie from a blue jacket to a gray one. She nodded decisively and picked up the gray jacket.

"Miranda, you need to rest."

She didn't react to the sound of his voice. Had she known he was there? But she didn't answer. Instead she brought the jacket close to her face and inhaled its scent. "It still smells like him, you know. That specially blended pipe tobacco, and a hint of Skin Bracer after-shave."

He felt her grief and knew she ought to give it release, but not here, he thought. Not here in this room surrounded by vivid images of the man she had lost. He went to her, took the jacket gently from her hands and laid it on the bed. "Come down with me. You need food and then rest."

"I can't. I can't eat. How can I eat when my father—" She bit off her words as a sob threatened and liquid diamonds began swimming in her eyes.

"Finish it," he instructed. "When your father…"

She sniffed and shook her head, but when she lifted her gaze to meet his the tears came again. "Is dead," she said in a choked voice. "He's dead." The tears spilled over and she turned her back to Rolf. Her hands came up to cover her face, and her shoulders shook with the force of her sobs. When she could draw a breath, she spoke in broken sentences. "Go away. Leave me alone. I don't…need an audience."

"No. Whatever an audience is, I have no doubt it is not what you need." With one decisive movement he stepped next to her and swept her up into his arms. It showed him the true extent of her turmoil that she didn't yell at him or struggle. She remained all but limp, still trying to avert her tear-streaked face from his view.

This proved it. He'd been mistaken about her from the start. He saw that now. She wouldn't use tears as weapons. She was loath even to have them seen. Rolf carried her down the stairs and into the kitchen, where he lowered her into a chair. "Now, cry. It is good, I think."

She sniffed a little, her distress seemingly lessening. "I thought you hated tears."

"These ones are needed."

She blinked and swiped the moisture from her cheeks with the backs of her hands. "I can't cry with you standing there watching me."

"You wish me to leave, then?"

She looked at him for a long moment. "No. I guess I don't."

Rolf turned from her, confused by the tone of her admission, and opened the refrigerator. He removed a brick of cheese and a couple of apples and oranges. "In my village, when a warrior fell, we would join together, his comrades and his family. The women prepared much food, and all would feast the night through in the fallen man's house, telling stories of his heroic deeds until the dawn."

He closed the door and moved to the sink where he located a sharp knife. He began slicing the cheese and the fruits and stacking the wedges on a plate. "I missed the feasting for my father." He pronounced the word carefully, just as she did. "My brothers, as well." He set the filled platter before her and returned to the cold box for milk, and to the cupboard for glasses. "It is the way a warrior gives release to his grief. Mine is still within."

He turned to find her watching him, eyes red, but drier now. "I'm sorry."

Rolf eyed the platter of fruit and cheese in the center of the table and smiled sadly. "It is not much of a feast."

She sniffled and rose from her chair. In a moment she was pulling vegetables and thinly sliced meats from the refrigerator, and stacking these artfully onto what she called kaiser rolls, which she first smeared liberally with a tangy white cream she called mayonnaise. She placed the completed meal onto two small plates and placed one at her seat, one at his.

Rolf sat down when she did, noting with some satisfaction that the anguish in her eyes had subsided somewhat. When she spoke, her voice was almost normal. "You could tell me about your father," she said slowly, "if it would help."

"It would, I think. But you must tell me about yours, as well."

She closed her eyes for a long moment, then blinked them open. "I'll try."

Rolf looked pleased. "Good. And there is one other thing you need tell me, Miranda." His tone was deliberately serious. When her dark auburn brows rose in two perfect arcs, he jabbed a forefinger at the food before him. "What do you call this meal, and how does one eat it?"

Her full lips turned up at the corners. A second passed, and then she laughed very softly.

Midnight. They'd moved to the living room and Rolf had insisted on building a fire in the hearth, though she explained about central heating and argued that it was a warm night, anyway. Miranda rested in her father's favorite chair, a worn corduroy recliner. Her feet were up, her head back, and she held a cup of steaming cocoa in her hands, as Rolf went on with his tale.

"Of course the man was drunk. Had no business being on a dragon ship with that much ale in his belly. But Svein was never known for his wisdom. A fight ensued, and the fool lost his balance and plunged into the icy waters."

"That's terrible."

Rolf agreed. "Yes. Svein had a wife and seven children. My father threw himself over the side. Had I known what he intended I would have tried to stop him. When I saw him in the water I tried to go in after him, but the other men held me fast. I was but—" he hesitated, mentally counting "—twelve years. It was my first time on my father's *drakkar*."

Miranda brought the recliner down and leaned forward in the seat. "What happened?"

"Father caught hold of Svein. Nearly drowned the way Svein floundered about. Finally my father hit him and, while Svein was senseless, dragged him to the side. A rope was tossed over and both men were brought back onto the ship."

Miranda relaxed then. "You must have been very proud of him," she said softly.

Rolf smiled. "My chest was puffed up for the rest of that trip."

She tried to imagine Rolf at twelve, but failed. Twelve…it had been a painful age for her.

"I see the sadness again in your eyes, Miranda. Tell me."

She was amazed at his perceptiveness. "I was twelve when my mother died. It was ovarian cancer. By the time we learned she was ill, it had progressed too far. A month later she was gone."

"And you stepped into her place, cared for your father."

"Yes. I began working with him right away. It was as if we both needed something to focus on." She curled her legs beneath her in the chair and sipped the cocoa. "At first I just helped transcribe notes, but I became fascinated with the work. When I was fourteen I went with him to a site in England, one of your people's burial mounds. My first dig." She smiled fondly at the memory. "We sifted the dirt, Rolf, and found bits and pieces of the past."

"And you loved this…sifting?"

She nodded hard and felt another smile tugging at her lips. "I still do. The sifting, the exploring. It's been my life."

"And what of Morsi?"

"Jeff?" She blinked and averted her gaze. "If you don't

mind, I'd just as soon not discuss that with you. It's… personal.''

''You wished to wed him.'' It was a flat statement, given without inflection.

''Darryl has been talkative, hasn't he?''

Rolf shrugged. ''That you despise him is obvious. His manner toward you suggests…familiarity.''

''You *are* mastering the language in a hurry.''

''I learn more with every word I hear. What did you do to anger Morsi so much?''

''What did *I* do?'' She took a deep breath, set her cup down onto an end table and sat up straight. ''What makes you so sure it was my fault?'' She sighed and rolled her eyes. ''That's right, I forgot. You dislike women, don't you?''

''More distrust than dislike. And I did not accuse you of anything. Only asked how you angered him. He looks at you with murder in his eyes, you know.''

''Yes. Just the way you looked at me when you thought I was this Adrianna.''

The blow hit home; it was obvious in the tightening of his jaw. He was silent a long moment. ''You could be her twin,'' he finally said. ''If you resemble her so much within as without, then it is no wonder Morsi would like to wring your neck.''

Miranda flinched. ''What did she do to you, to make you so bitter?''

''Ahh, we have two questions now. No answers. Will you tell me the truth about Morsi, if I tell you of Adrianna?''

It was Miranda's turn to be silent. In her mind, for just a moment, she felt again Jeff's hands on her, tearing at her clothes, hurting her, hitting her. She blinked rapidly as tears of humiliation burned in her eyes. ''No.'' She rose and moved toward the stairs. ''I'm going to try to get some sleep.''

"Is it so shameful, then?"

She whirled on him, her face burning with anger. "Oh, yes, it is. So shameful I've never told a soul. Not even my father. But you don't want to hear it. You'd rather sit there and let your cynical mind conjure up a list of crimes to credit me with."

"If you refuse to tell the truth, I am left with little alternative. I believe you were not always the pillar of virtue Darryl sees today."

"And you can judge me for that? You, who spent your life ravaging coastal villages, murdering and robbing and raping—"

Rolf stood so suddenly that Miranda jumped backward. "You know nothing of my life. You cannot read a man's soul by sifting the dirt on which he trod. You cannot know a man by finding some trinket he left behind. And I will not defend myself, or my people, to you!"

Part of her wanted to cringe, or to turn and run. But another part, a part she hadn't realized existed, made her thrust her face upward, closer to his, as he stood towering over her. "Yet you expect me to defend myself to you."

He said nothing. Her back rigid, Miranda turned and walked calmly up to her room.

Anger. Fury. Rage.

As he slept in the guest room that night, Rolf felt them all invade his dreams. Miranda's face became Adrianna's. For the first time Rolf saw the differences. Adrianna's nose had been narrower and pointed at the end rather than turned up slightly like Miranda's. Her lips were not as full, her eyes duller and rarely showering him with sparks the way Miranda's had tonight. Miranda...insulted and fighting mad at his implications.

Adrianna. He thought of her and of the way, when faced with an accusation, she would simply concoct a lie. He recalled that she'd done exactly that to him. Accused him of murder in order to save her brother. The result had been his exile and very nearly his death. Indeed she had cost him his entire world, his family, everything he'd ever known.

Miranda assumed that, because of what he was, he'd raped and murdered innocents. It hadn't been until that final voyage that he'd—

Rolf sat up in bed, eyes flying wide, fully awake now. He'd been struggling for the memory of the last voyage to no avail. Now, suddenly, it came to him without effort. He'd sailed from Norge a condemned man, *úrhrak,* outcast, and his anger had driven him to behave like one. In a rage he'd led his crew of misfits on a rampage along the coasts of England and the Shetland Islands, along the coasts of Francia and Normandy.

As he thought of it now, Rolf wished the memory had evaded him a bit longer. He'd allowed his anger at Adrianna to completely overwhelm his mind and to command his body. He remembered and he covered his face with his hands and groaned softly.

The clash of steel on steel, the screams of terrified women, the wide-eyed children. Oh, Miranda had been wrong about the rapes and murders she'd accredited to him. Rolf's upbringing had taught him better than to force himself on a woman, or to kill a man without cause. Men had died, all the same. Those who were foolish enough to fight the Plague of the North. Rolf and his men had swept through the wealthiest villages, taking what they wanted. They'd taken spoil from peoples who had never wronged them, and Rolf's upbringing had taught him better than that, as well.

His father, had he known, would have been appalled. But Rolf had been wronged, vilely so. He'd had his vengeance. He'd plundered his riches. By the time the *drakkar* was on its way across the fickle North Atlantic for the second time, he'd amassed enough gold and silver to suit a king, enough iron to forge blades for an army.

He'd determined he would build his own village in the midst of the Skrælingar, south of the barren wilderness in which he'd secreted his first cargo. In Vinland. He'd trade for what his people needed, trade with the civilized lands within easy sailing distance. If they refused to trade, he'd raid, instead. He'd be prosperous and wealthy, and his name would once again be on the lips of kings, this time uttered with fear of his vengeance rather than with good will for his friendship. His friendship, he'd believed at the time, had meant so little to his high-placed allies that they hadn't even stooped to help him when his life was in peril.

And now, with hindsight, he saw that he'd been wrong to let his rage so fully rule him. Thor had seen that he was punished. For truly, had not the ship been so laden with chests of booty, she might have made it to the shore.

Miranda couldn't sleep. She'd known it before she'd tried but she'd tried anyway. She'd done all there was to be done—chosen the clothes, talked to the funeral director, ordered the flowers, contacted all the relatives she could think of. She'd even arranged to have Erwin Saunders give a eulogy. Her father hadn't been much for religion. Few scientists were.

Still she kept getting the feeling there was something she had forgotten. Something important. It wasn't until her eyelids grew heavy, toward dawn, when she hovered between sleep and wakefulness, that she remembered what. Her father's last words to her had been a plea. Read the journal. The real one. And then he'd said something that made no sense. Jules Verne.

Too tired to think and too wide-awake to lie still, Miranda got up. She didn't bother dressing. She wore an oversize football jersey, a gift from a student, and she figured that was enough. Darryl and Rolf had done an admirable job of picking up the ransacked house while she'd been dealing with the funeral arrangements. They'd left the study, probably so as not to disturb her while she'd been in there. She would have done it herself, but it had seemed such a poignant reminder of her father that she'd had to get out of the room all at once. Now, though, she felt able to tackle it. She wanted to smell the scent of his pipe tobacco clinging to the curtains and the carpet. She wanted to run her hands over the supple leather of his swivel chair, to hear it creak as it used to whenever he sat down or rose, or even moved.

She began by replacing the desk drawers, and sorting through the items that had been dumped from them before they'd been tossed to the floor. Reverently she picked up notepads and pencils, a favorite lighter. The antique pistol lay on the floor, its pearl-inlaid grip marred with scratches. She stroked the tiny gun, tears blurring her vision as she replaced it in the drawer.

The desk restored to order, she moved on to the bookshelves. Volume after volume had been scattered over the floor. One by one, she picked them up and slid them back onto the shelves. When she held in her hands an old edition of *Around the World in Eighty Days,* she paused, and her father's odd words came back to her. "Jules Verne," she whispered.

She yanked the leather chair closer to the desk, sat down, and opened the book. Only instead of the pages and illustrations she remembered, the book had been filled with lined sheets, each one covered in her father's spidery script.

She cursed herself for leaving her glasses upstairs, and didn't want to risk waking Rolf to go and retrieve them. Instead, she bent the desk lamp's long neck lower, and squinted as she began to read.

Chapter 10

When she finished an hour later, Miranda shivered.

Her father, never satisfied with the Inuit version of things, had longed to know more even before they'd discovered Rolf in that cave. He'd believed so completely that they would find him that he'd already begun work on the next step. He'd researched every historical account he could find until he'd found one that fit. Of that much, Miranda had already been aware.

The rest of what she found came as a complete surprise to her. The man known as the Plague of the North had not always been so, her father noted. In fact, he'd been considered one of the wisest men in his country. He'd been called upon by Knut the Great not only to fight by his side in battle, but to act as translator in sensitive discussions with other European leaders. He'd been respected and trusted implicitly.

And then he'd brutally murdered one of Knut's emissaries in Norway at a crucial time in history. The man had been beaten to death, and the information he'd been gathering for Knut came to a stop. As a direct result, Knut's archenemy, Magnus, had gained the Norwegian throne.

With his banishment, the once-honorable aid to a great king became the Plague of the North. Lawbreaker. Ruffian. Thief. Murderer.

Here Russell had noted that, despite popular belief, most Vikings did not go around raiding and plundering at random, but only in serious efforts at political and commercial expansion, or colonization of new lands, or in retribution for some serious wrong they felt they'd suffered. A few notorious renegades had broken the code, and history had recorded their deeds more thoroughly than those of their more honorable counterparts.

The exiled man, however, was ruthless. He and his band raided villages along coastal Europe. He robbed people of their stores and their valuables. Then, suddenly, he vanished.

The recorded description of the criminal shook Miranda even though she knew what it would say. From the time they'd found Rolf, she'd known he had to be the legendary Plague of the North her father sought. She simply hadn't been so enlightened as to the details of his crimes. He was described as large, much larger than most men of his time. His hair was golden and worn very long. His face was covered by a reddish gold beard, and his eyes were the blue of a winter sky. He carried with him a magnificent sword known far and wide as Vengeance, and with it, the legend went, he was invincible. He raided in the manner of the Berserkers, wearing no helmet or armor of any kind, and often barechested, as if daring his enemies to strike a killing blow.

At the end of the hand-penned notes, a notation, "C: plague," was written in red ink, followed by the word, "Biblio."

Miranda shot to her feet and ran into the basement, flicking on lights as she went. Every disk in their files had been taken in the burglary. But according to what she'd read, this information was stored in the hard drive. She switched on the computer and typed in the path: C: plague. The screen went black. In seconds it lit up once more. "This file is password protected." Miranda typed Biblio at the command prompt and tapped the Enter button.

Then she sank slowly into a chair as she scrolled through page after page of her father's words. Dazedly she realized she was reading a synopsis. He'd been working on a book—a book about the Plague of the North. A book about Rolf Magnusson. It appeared he'd been trying to delve into the past more deeply than ever before. He'd asked himself questions. Why does one of the most respected men in his country suddenly commit murder and go on a trans-Atlantic spree? What became of all the stolen goods? Her father theorized that more than one trip had been made across the Atlantic. He based that supposition on the period of peace between one raiding spree and the next. The ship had been laden with plunder, he wrote, and that plunder had been carried across the North Atlantic. It had been hidden away before Magnusson and his cohorts returned to the coasts of Europe with a vengeance.

"He was an intelligent man," Russell had written. "A genius, by all descriptions. Too intelligent to continue in this manner on the basis of a mere tantrum. I believe he had a plan, and I further believe he may not have been guilty of treason and murder to begin with. The accounts I've seen of the tale tell only of a single witness against him, the daughter of a Norwegian noble. The nobles of Norway were the ones who placed Magnus on the throne. Furthermore, if Magnusson were guilty of treason against Knut, he'd no doubt have received a pardon the moment Magnus took the throne. He did not. The why of that puzzles me."

The text of the synopsis went on for page upon page. Russell had planned to return to the site and search for the missing treasure before the agreement with Canada expired next August. He'd wanted to search for the sunken dragon ship, as well, to learn if any part of it still remained. The sword, with the word "Vengeance" carved in runic symbols upon its hilt confirmed his theory that the respected Rolf Magnusson of Norway and the feared Plague of the North were one and the same man, and he wanted to find every clue he could uncover as to why.

So did Miranda.

Was she presently living under the same roof as the crazed Berserker who'd plundered three villages in a single night, leaving forty dead men in his wake? Leader of the raiders who penetrated the most heavily guarded fortresses in all of England, and looted them to the bare walls?

"Miranda."

She leapt to her feet and spun around. No. There was more. There had to be more. Her father had sensed it. Miranda knew it. What?

Rolf's gaze narrowed, then heated as it moved down her body, tracing the shape of her lengthy, unclothed legs. She saw his lips thin and felt the force with which he lifted his gaze up again to meet hers.

And then he frowned. "Why do I see fear in your eyes? Only a few hours ago you would have fought me to the death, I believe. I angered you enough to do so, no doubt."

"What do you want?" She bit the question off too quickly, too impatiently. She didn't fear him. She'd simply managed somehow to suppress the knowledge about who he had been. The account of all the deaths and destruction attributed to him, written in her father's own words, had been a sharp reminder. It had shaken her. She'd had enough of death.

"I wish to know what I have done to frighten you. I did not take you for a woman easily frightened."

"I'm not—"

"What is this?" With a quick movement, he pushed her

aside and peered at the computer screen. Reading the words there, he scowled and whirled to face her. "Plague of the North, is it? And you, no doubt, believe every word this...machine tells you?"

"Th-they are my father's words. He—"

"He judged me by rumors, stories. He could not have known the truth."

She shook her head quickly. "He didn't judge you at all. He questioned everything he learned. It was his way. Look." Returning to the screen, but careful not to turn her back to him fully, she scrolled back to the questions she'd just read and stepped aside to allow Rolf to do the same.

When he finished, he looked away and blew an exasperated sigh.

"Well?"

He only looked at her, his expression tired. "What?"

"Is it true? Are you the same man who raided those villages?"

He met her gaze, his own unwavering. "I am."

Miranda averted her head. She'd been so hoping he would deny it. She just couldn't look him in the eye.

"You are disappointed? I thought you had already branded me as a murderer, a plunderer, a rapist."

"Are you?" She looked up quickly, wishing there could be some plausible explanation for what he had done, fearing there wasn't. Fearing that the certainty inside her was no more than wishful thinking.

He looked her up and down, and finally shook his head. "Believe what you will." He turned to go. "I will leave here in the morning."

"Wait." He faced her again. She cleared her throat. "I don't want you to leave."

His brows went up as he studied her. "You wish for the Plague of the North to remain sleeping beneath your roof, Miranda? Why, when you fear me, do you wish me to remain?"

"I told you, I'm not afraid of you." She stiffened her spine and stepped closer to him as she spoke. She couldn't let him leave; it was that simple. She sensed that if she didn't convince him she wasn't afraid, there'd be nothing she could do to make him stay.

"You are a poor liar, Miranda."

"It's not a lie. I honestly don't think you would hurt me." Oddly enough, it wasn't until she spoke the words that she realized how true they were.

His eyes narrowed. "A woman who reacts to a kiss as you did to mine is afraid."

She shook her head. "That was no kiss. It was an attack, and you're too intelligent to pretend you don't know the difference."

"Correct. I know the difference. Shall I demonstrate?"

She felt herself stiffen, and though she didn't mean to, she drew away slightly. His breath escaped him in a rush. "You fear me. I will go."

He turned from her for the second time, and Miranda felt self-disgust rise through her. Because of her ridiculous reactions she could easily lose the chance of a lifetime. Desperation made her voice louder, harsher, than necessary. "It isn't you! Dammit, Rolf, you can't assume I'm afraid of you just because I don't want you touching me."

He stopped in the doorway, but didn't turn. "What then am I to assume?"

She sighed, pushed a hand through her hair, wished for her wire rims to hide behind when he turned slowly to face her as he awaited her answer. "I just...don't like to be touched."

He pursed his lips thoughtfully, then observed, "That is untrue. You did not mind so much the embraces of Saunders or young Darryl. You found comfort in the touch of Travis. Even in my repulsive embrace you relaxed." He glanced again at the electric blue screen behind her. "But that was before you knew of my crimes, was it not?"

She closed her eyes. "Listen to what I am saying. It is not you. When you held me in the hospital, I did find comfort." She was disconcerted. She hadn't given that odd reaction much thought before now. "More even than when Fletcher hugged me. But that was different. You touched me then only to give comfort, not to—" She bit her lip and looked down.

"Not to what, Miranda?"

"Look, I just don't like men, okay? Not in *that* way."

He scowled and his head tilted to one side. The movement of his head sent his long hair sliding down over his shoulder. "You...prefer women?"

"No!" She pressed two fingertips into her forehead, grimacing. No help for it, she had to blurt the truth. Remaining in that posture, eyes tightly closed, she did just that. "I'm frigid, Rolf. I don't like sex. In fact, I adamantly *dislike* it."

He stepped closer, his expression hard. "Then, you have known men before me?" Always he had to end with that "before me" comment. It shook her to the bone. "How many, Miranda?"

"Enough to know my own mind." She turned from him back to the computer. She'd pretend she had to finish reading her father's notes. Anything.

But Rolf caught her shoulder, his hand surprisingly gentle as he turned her to face him once more. "How many?"

She swallowed the lump that came into her throat. She did not want to discuss this. It would only resurrect the memory she'd murdered and buried. "One." There, it was said. Maybe he'd leave her alone now.

"Only one? You base this certainty about yourself on the touch of one man?"

Bitterness welled up in her like the sea at high tide, and she forgot that she was going to say no more on the subject. "One was plenty, believe me."

His gaze moved rapidly over her face, as if he was trying to read every nuance of her expression at once. "Was it—"

She shook her head hard and fast. "No. I won't discuss this with you. Not anymore. I've told you I'm not afraid of you. I've asked you to stay. Will you or won't you?"

He considered her question for a long while before he answered. She knew he was debating whether to drop the subject of her problem with sex and she prayed he would. Already her stomach churned and her hands trembled slightly.

He drew a deep breath. "I cannot stay."

Miranda felt a fist tighten around her heart. "Why?"

"Because I am not of your time, Miranda. I do not think the way your people think. I cannot allow a woman to provide for me. My garments, my food, my bed. I must find a way to do for myself."

She blinked. She hadn't taken time to think about his pride, or to wonder how it might be faring in all of this. "The silver you gave me is worth more than I make in a year, Rolf."

"You no longer have it," he countered. "You gave it to Travis."

"Just to study. He is an expert in old coins. He won't keep them."

"Nor will you. Your university will put them out for the world to view. Foolish waste of good silver."

"Rolf, I'm not going to let you leave. I need you. I need your help."

"In what?" The skepticism in his voice was evident.

"In answering the questions my father asked. In finishing the book he was writing about you. I can't do it alone. You are the only one who can help me."

"That is foolish. Writing words on paper will not pay for the food you eat."

"Yes, it will. Publishers will pay a great deal for this

book when it's finished. Especially if we locate the relics to back it up. And I need your help to do that, as well.''

''Relics? I do not—''

''The treasure you and your crew amassed on that first set of raids, that you carried across the Atlantic and hid before going back for more. Do you know where it is?''

Doubt clouded his face. ''What could remain after so much time?''

''You were preserved. Why not the treasure?'' She paced across the floor, turned and retraced her steps. ''And the ship. I need to know precisely where the ship was when it went down. Can you tell me?''

Rolf watched her intently, wondering at the sudden change in her. Where before she'd seemed weary, saddened by the loss of her father and slightly afraid of him, now those feelings slipped from her countenance like ice thawing in the hot sun of summer. Her steps brought her to a stop in front of him and her eyes widened as she awaited his answer.

He cleared his throat, sensing the import of what she asked of him, not wishing to disappoint her and see the soft light fade from her eyes. ''I might.'' He scratched his head, giving the matter much thought. ''I cannot tell by using your maps, as I am unfamiliar with them. No, nor by traveling northward by land,'' he added, recalling the shape of this continent on the globe she'd so recently demolished. ''But from the sea...'' He stroked his chin and strode toward the window. He pushed it open and inhaled the familiar scents of the ocean. ''By sea I believe I could take you there.'' He faced her again, nodding firmly.

''If you can do that, Rolf, it will be worth more than you can imagine, more to me than if you gave me every bit of that treasure.'' She turned from him, staring into empty space, seemingly seeing nothing, he thought, but oh, how her eyes sparkled. ''This would make up for everything, for losing the Ice Man, even.'' She faced him again, hurrying to him until she stood so close her warm breathing bathed his chin as she tipped up her head. ''Will you stay? Will you help me finish what my father began? It would mean so much to him...and to me.''

He would. He could deny her nothing, not when she looked at him in such a way. Did her heart turn out to be as rotten as Adrianna's, no doubt Rolf would again be taken in by it. There was no helping it.

He looked down her body, his gaze moving over the unbound shapes of her breasts beneath the thin layer of cloth. He could see them so clearly there. He wished to touch them, to learn their shape, their weight...their taste. Her long, slender legs, bare from midthigh to unclothed feet, held his attention for a very long time. He wanted to press his lips to that supple skin on her thighs.

''Rolf?''

The sound of her voice made him look up again, but he only became lost in the wondrous mane of her auburn hair, which floated about her as untamed as a windstorm. How he longed to bury his face in that unruly silken mass, to inhale its scent, to feel it touching his skin. He shuddered and forced himself to speak. ''I will help you, Miranda. I owe you as much. There is one thing I would ask in return. Nothing too difficult. A token, really.''

She smiled, her excitement showing in her heightened color. Her cheeks glowed as if they'd been vigorously rubbed with rose petals. ''What is it?''

''A kiss,'' he replied.

She sighed in despair, dampening his enthusiasm. ''Rolf, I've already explained to you, I don't—''

''I understand. I do not expect you to respond or to feel any...attraction to me. I only wish to be certain you no longer fear me, Miranda. I cannot remain unless I know I am not frightening you each time I come near you. Do you allow me to kiss you, and do I not feel you recoil in utter revulsion, or see you grow pale and ill at my touch, then will I know you fear me no longer.''

A convincing reason for a kiss, he thought. Especially considering he'd made it up this very moment. In truth, he did long to feel her lips beneath his. And more, to feel her response to him, for he thought she was wrong about herself. He had seen the hint of a flame in her eyes before he'd frightened her so badly with his brutality. He'd felt the heat in her gaze as it had moved over his body. He wanted more than anything to believe his behavior hadn't extinguished that flame for good.

He looked at her face now as she struggled with unseen demons. ''I don't know,'' she said, and her voice was very soft. ''If I ask you to stop, will you stop right away?''

''On my sword, I will stop.''

Her lower lip trembled, but she nodded. ''All right, then.''

She braced herself as if preparing to be struck rather than kissed. Rolf lifted his hands to her shoulders and immediately her eyes flew wide. Damn, but she feared him, despite her words to the contrary.

''It isn't you,'' she whispered fiercely, as if sensing his thoughts. ''Could you do it...without touching me?'' Her gaze slanted to his hands resting on her shoulders as she made her request.

Rolf contained his frustration and lowered one hand to his side. With the other, he hooked only his forefinger beneath her chin and gently lifted it. He lowered his head, and as he did, he felt a new purpose. No longer was he eager only to satisfy his own inexplicable thirst for her mouth. Now he also longed to erase that haunted, wary look from her eyes. He wanted to prove to her, because his pride would not allow him to tell her, that he was not the ruthless killer she believed him to be.

His lips touched hers lightly, brushing their satin surface briefly while every fiber in his being yearned to crush them beneath his. He indulged himself only by allowing his mouth to open slightly, that he might capture her full lower lip between his lips and suckle it softly...oh, so softly, not to frighten her. His free hand began to move upward, but he stilled it with a supreme act of will. He released her lower lip only to capture its mate and taste its sweetness, as well.

She didn't move away from him. In fact, her eyes tremulously closed, her thick lashes resting upon her cheeks like frightened birds, ready to take flight at a moment's notice. With the tip of his tongue, Rolf traced the shape of her lips. When he slipped it between them, to touch the tip of hers, she did not pull away. He caressed her tongue and then the inside of her mouth. He felt himself grow uncomfortably hard. The restraint was killing him. He wanted to put his arms around her and pull her tight against him. He wanted to force her mouth open wide and plunder the sweet moistness within. He refused to allow himself anything beyond this tiny sip. And when a moan of suppressed desire leapt from his mouth into hers, her hands came up to press lightly against his chest.

Rolf lifted his head, keeping his forefinger still hooked beneath her chin so he could search her eyes. They were wide, but not with fear or revulsion. With something else...something that might almost have been...wonder.

Chapter 11

Miranda stood very still for a long moment, her hands resting lightly upon his chest, her eyes still searching his. There was so much there she hadn't seen before. The ice blue depths grew darker the deeper you looked, just like the sea itself. His lashes were not golden or honey or wheat, the three colors she saw in his hair. They were darker, a rich sable brown, as were the smooth, full brows above them. And those very eyes in which she'd allowed herself to become immersed were plunging themselves into her own just as searchingly.

She blinked, breaking the spell under which she seemed to have fallen. Never in her wildest imaginings had she believed he could be so gentle. It was a shocking contrast. He was big, with a raw power and masculinity that was almost frightening. Yet he could kiss her with the tenderness of a poet, with a touch lighter than a springtime breeze rippling the surface of the bay, far from shore. A touch so tender… She shook her head in wonder. It had been so tender she hadn't been afraid. In fact, she'd enjoyed the kiss. When her hands had planted themselves against the muscled wall of his chest, she hadn't intended to push him away. She'd been ready to pull him nearer. Only his soft groan had prevented her from doing just that.

She was surprised. She hadn't believed she could ever want a man's kiss again. She'd wanted his, she realized slowly. She'd wanted it very much. Maybe she still did. Recalling the reason for the experiment in the first place, she cleared her throat. "You see? I'm not afraid of you."

His lips curved slightly upward at the corners. "No, you are not, are you?"

She smiled her answer. "So will you stay?"

"I cannot leave now, Miranda, even do you ask me to go."

She was taken aback. He was being utterly ridiculous, of course, offering her a compliment as he no doubt thought she would expect after such a tender encounter. "You d-don't—" My God, she was stammering like an idiot! She drew a calming breath and ordered herself to be sensible. "You don't have to say things like that."

He reached out to thread his fingers through her hair. *"pu ert unaðsfögur."*

A tiny chill ran up the back of her neck at the depth and resonance of his voice as it caressed her with those foreign words.

"Wh-what?"

"You are beautiful, Miranda."

She shook her head automatically. When she did, her cheek touched his fingertips as they moved through her hair. She chided herself because she wasn't altogether certain she hadn't done it deliberately.

He responded by stroking the side of her face. "Adrianna was the most beautiful woman in Norge. Never did she doubt it, though she had only a precious disk of polished steel in which to see her reflection. You have a houseful of glass mirrors, and yet you fail to see what is there."

Again she shook her head. "If your Adrianna knew how beautiful she was, it was probably because people were constantly telling her so."

Rolf disagreed. "Might men have noted her beauty less, had she any other virtue? Might they not fail to note yours only because there is so much more in you to praise than mere beauty?" She frowned up at him, unsure what he meant. His seawater eyes narrowed. "So much more. I believe I've only begun to see it."

Rolf took a seat in the rear of the large, crowded room, leaving Miranda to move forward alone. The body of her *faðir* lay within a box of polished hardwood. He wore fine garments, though to Rolf the colors appeared dull and the fabric plain. In his time brilliant crimson and scarlet or bright blues, threaded with gold, had been favored for such solemn occasions. Cloaks of wonderful, shimmering cloth from the East were not uncommon among those able to afford them. But times had changed, he thought as he regarded the people crowded into the room, filling every chair. All of them wore somber colors—black, brown, gray, midnight blue.

Miranda was dressed in a black skirt that hugged her hips and legs, stopping just below her knees. Her legs were encased in a whisper-thin fabric she called nylon, and on her feet she wore shoes with pointed toes and spikes poking from the heels. Her shirt—blouse, she'd called it—was white, with tiny buttons of pearl and a thin border of lace at her throat and wrists. The blouse's neck was high, and she'd fastened a brooch at its center, an oval of onyx with a female face silhouetted in white. Her hair she'd gathered high and loose, so that her auburn curls spilled freely in a coppery cascade.

She was beautiful. Even with her eyes red rimmed and swollen behind their shields of glass, and her nose shiny, she was beautiful. Rolf glanced at the other women in the room and found none to compare. His glimpses were fleeting, though, for he did not wish to have his attention diverted for too long. Though he'd broken away from her side, he'd done so only to allow her to grieve privately as seemed the custom of her people. She would have the seat of honor near the finely crafted box, as was fitting. He would allow her the time to bid her father farewell in her own way. He knew well the import of the occasion.

In his time, all would gather around a pyre. The fallen warrior would be dressed in his finery and laid upon satin carpets and cushions. A great leader was ofttimes laid within his *drakkar,* and the ship itself placed upon the pyre. His weapons would be placed at his side, along with offerings of meat and fruits and mead. If a slave girl, or even a wife, wished to go with the fallen one on this final journey, she would drink the *nabid,* and submit to the ceremonial murder.

When all stood in readiness, the warriors surrounding the pyre would begin to beat their shields with clubs, as the eldest son of the fallen, stripped to his bare flesh, walked backward to the pyre to toss a torch over his shoulder upon it. As the blaze took hold, the others would light smaller torches and toss them in, as well. Even after Christianity forbade cremation, the ritual was kept by many Norsemen. In burning, the spirit of the dead man was freed at once to journey toward Valhalla and receive its final reward. Rolf had never understood the Christians' preference for tossing their dead into the earth to rot slowly.

Rolf shook off the memories, though for a moment he could smell the acrid smoke, see before his eyes the fire lighting the night, hear the pounding of the shields. He felt a pang of homesickness, but forced it away and resumed his observation of the burial customs of Miranda's people. A somber, quiet occasion, he thought. They would all die of shock to see the boisterous funerals of his time.

Miranda stood for a long time beside the body of her

father. Rolf wondered at the look of the man in the box. His skin color had not altered in the least, nor had he swelled as the dead are wont to do, especially in warm weather. The man looked to be in better health now than he had upon his deathbed in the hospital.

Miranda leaned over, and her soft hand covered the still one within the box. She whispered something no one else could hear, then pressed a kiss to her fingertips, and her fingertips to his unmoving lips. Rolf felt a hard blockage take form in his throat and a hot stinging at the back of his eyes. She straightened and moved toward the chair that had been placed near the box. Before she sat, though, she turned and quickly scanned the room. In a moment her gaze found his and she came toward him.

She said not a word as she reached him, only extended her hand. Rolf took it, rising and following where she led. She drew a chair from the rest and placed it beside hers. She sat down now, still clutching his hand so that Rolf had no alternative but to sit beside her.

As Erwin Saunders took his spot near the front and began to speak in slow, measured tones about the fallen man, Rolf felt Miranda's grip on him tighten. He squeezed her hand in return, glancing down to see the fresh moisture gathering on her lashes. The lump returned to Rolf's throat. Truly she honored him, by allowing him to sit beside her, to be the one with whom she shared her grief.

The only one, he noted a short time later, as the ceremony ended and the mourners filed past her. Each one touched her, either pressing a hand to her shoulder, hugging her, kissing her or simply taking her hand. She dried her eyes for them. For them she forced a false smile and spoke brave words. Even for Fletcher Travis, though he hugged her harder and longer than most others, she kept her sadness hidden.

Only when they were alone, in her small car, did she succumb to her grief. Rolf sensed it building inside her as she drove. When she pulled the machine to a stop on the path that led to her home, she trembled visibly, then lowered her head onto her arms, resting across the steering device.

He touched her shoulder. "Miranda—"

"I'm sorry," she said, her voice shaking and weak. "I don't know what's the matter with me. I never cried like this when my mother died."

"Because you sensed your father needed your strength." She lifted her head, looking at him through rivers of tears. "You cry now, perhaps, for both of them. You cry because you know you can."

She sniffed and nodded. "You see so much." She wiped her tears away. "I'm just sorry you had to see me like this."

"Do not be sorry, Miranda. Perhaps it is you who are in need of strength now. Do you wish it, I would give of my own."

She glanced at him through dewy lashes, her lips trembling. "Didn't you know? You already have. I couldn't have survived this day without you."

He slipped his arms around her slender frame, pulling her across the seat and against his chest. He held her hard, willing her pain to leave her. "The day has not yet ended, *astín mín.* Give your grief to me."

Her arms curled around his neck and she clung. Her tears soon soaked the front of his shirt, but he cared not. He would cry them for her, were it possible. His body absorbed the trembling of hers as she wept. And it seemed only natural, when he cupped her head in his hand to tilt it back and lowered his mouth to hers, to capture her sobs, as well.

She didn't compress her lips when his mouth covered hers. She let them remain parted, as if she wanted his gentle invasion. Her hot tears dampened his face as Rolf complied. He drank from her lips and then from the honeyed recesses beyond. He tasted her tongue hungrily as his compassion became only passion. The flames ignited within him, and he forgot that he'd been holding her to give comfort. He licked at the silken interior of her mouth, and with a low groan, he tightened his hold on her body. He shifted slightly in his seat, pressing her backward and leaning over her in his eagerness to quench the thirst raging within.

Miranda's eyes flew open. She drew a ragged breath and twisted her head from beneath his demanding mouth. Her hands, formerly clutched around his neck, became fists that pummeled his chest. "Get off me!" she cried in a hoarse, panic-filled voice. "I can't…breathe. Get off me!"

Frustrated and confused, but seeing the sudden fear in her eyes, Rolf quickly straightened. She flew from his arms, collapsing against the opposite door, breathing as rapidly as he was, though he doubted hers was a result of arousal.

He watched her for a moment. Her shoulders were trembling uncontrollably. "Forgive me, Miranda. I did not mean…" He groaned. "I am sorry."

"No." She faced forward as if forcing herself to do so. She drew several deep breaths and it was as if she measured them, forced them to calm her. "I'm the one who should be apologizing. I'm a fool to think you would ever…" She shook her head, not finishing the thought. Instead she said simply, "Thank you…for stopping when I asked you to."

Rolf felt a fury slowly begin to stir to life deep within him. So, she had been afraid he wouldn't. She'd suddenly realized she was in the arms of a murdering, raping villain and she'd panicked, thinking her fate sealed. No doubt his restraint surprised her. She hadn't expected the Plague of the North to respect a woman's wishes when she said no.

She turned her back on him and shoved the door open. Her unsteady steps took her away from the car, but she did not go into the house. Instead she veered around it and vanished from his sight.

Rolf swore loudly, slamming a fist into the seat. He'd been a fool yet again. He'd begun to allow himself tender feelings toward another beauty with a heart of stone. He'd let himself believe her lies, when she'd so cleverly convinced him she had no fear of him. In truth, she wished only to use him to find what she sought.

He wrenched his door open and took the same path she had. She would soon learn that Rolf Magnusson was not a man to be used. His steps broad and quick with his anger, he followed the path to the rocky bluff above the sea. And there he found her, seated upon the ground, her knees drawn to her chest. She faced the sea, and the sun was slowly sinking behind her. He heard her sobs as he drew closer, and in spite of his anger, his heart twisted in his chest. Seabirds sang in loud discord as he approached her. But when he parted his lips to condemn her, he found no sound would emerge.

"I'm sorry, Rolf."

He grated his teeth. Sorry, was she? For lying to him? For using him to reach her own goals? Or for her frightened reactions to his touch? "You needn't fear I will kiss you again, Miranda. You've made your feelings known to me, though you deny them with your lips."

She shook her head, not turning to face him. "You're wrong about that. It wasn't you—"

"No more lies."

She did face him then. "Rolf, it isn't—"

"*Stodva.* You need not continue in your charade. You fear me. It is clear. I will find your precious treasure for you, since I have given my word. And when it is found, I will take my leave of you, your house, your very life. I will make my own way in this world of yours. Have no doubt, Miranda."

She rose to her feet. "It was the car, Rolf. That damned tiny car, and—"

"Do you continue to speak falsely, my leave will come sooner."

She closed her eyes slowly. "You're not going to believe me, no matter what I say, are you?"

He said nothing. It pained him to know her heart, when he'd wished so much to believe she found solace in his arms. A small sound from far above drew his gaze upward, and he saw a silvery bird, the likes of which he'd never seen.

Her voice was hoarse when she spoke. "It's an airplane. A ship that sails in the skies."

Rolf shook his head in wonder. "Your people travel by such ships?"

"Yes. It is faster than any other way. And safer than the car, believe it or not."

Rolf lowered his gaze to hers as the bird ship vanished from sight. "Your world is filled with wonders, lady. Still, I believe I would rather sail in my own sort of ship." As he spoke, he looked out toward the sea.

"You love it, don't you?"

He nodded. Then stiffened as her hand closed on his upper arm.

"You have to let me explain, Rolf."

"*Nei.* I do not." He allowed his gaze to travel once more over her lovely, tear-stained face before he turned and walked to the house alone.

Two days after the funeral, Miranda sat beside Rolf in front of Erwin Saunders's desk at Beaumont.

She leaned forward in her seat, forgetting for the moment the things that had been troubling her. Rolf had treated her coldly, had been distant toward her, since her stupid reactions to him in the car. He honestly believed she was afraid of him, and he refused to allow her to explain. But she had to push those thoughts aside. She needed to make her points clearly and forcibly. "Don't you get it, Erwin? That is what the person who broke in was after. Not the Ice Man, but whatever clues we might have gleaned from him. He must have known what Russell knew, who the man was, what he was accused of doing. He knew there was a massive treasure involved, and he wants it.''

Saunders shook his head. "How could anyone have known? You said the information was in a coded file in the computer. Russell was obviously keeping it to himself.''

"Anyone could have figured it out the same way my father did, by following leads and tracking down records. And the very fact that he had the information so well hidden proves to me that he suspected someone else might be after it.''

Saunders stroked his goatee thoughtfully. "You might very well be right.''

"I know I'm right. Furthermore, we don't have any idea how much more this person knows. We have to locate the two sites involved before he does, or we'll lose any chance we ever had to complete the work my father began.''

"Miranda, what makes you think we can find either the shipwreck, or the missing booty? We don't have a clue … unless there was something in that hidden file.'' He stood quickly, coming around the desk with a light in his eyes. "Miranda, did your father think he knew where—''

"No.'' The man seemed to sag before her eyes, but he straightened quickly when Miranda added, "But Rolf thinks he can locate both of them.''

Saunders's gaze met Rolf's, and there was no doubting the skepticism there, or the hope. "How?''

"I am not certain of finding the lost treasure,'' Rolf said slowly. "Landscapes change.'' Saunders opened his mouth to interrupt, but Rolf quickly continued, "Of the *drakkar,* I have no doubt I can show you precisely where she rests, though I wonder whether anything remains.''

Again, Saunders uttered the one-word question. "How?''

Rolf shrugged. "It is only a matter of being familiar with

the old methods of navigation, of knowing the most likely landings, of studying the currents, the winds.''

"It would be best if you could simply show me the site, mark it on a map or—''

"Impossible. I will not know it until we are there.''

"We'll have to go by ship," Miranda observed. "It doesn't have to be a large one. But we are going to need a RCV and sonar equipment. It isn't going to come cheaply.''

"That's an understatement, Miranda. Do you know what a submersible remote cam-video costs?" Saunders drummed his fingers on the desk thoughtfully. "Of course, we might be able to borrow one from another university. I hate to, though. The fewer people who know about this the better.''

"Do you think the board will approve funding?" Miranda sounded apprehensive.

"The board." Saunders breathed the words on a rush of air. "Time is of the essence here, isn't it? No, I don't think we can wait for Harry Kirk and his board to mull this over. We need to act now, before the agreement with Canada expires in August and we're forced to get permission all over again.''

"Does that agreement cover offshore explorations, Erwin?''

Saunders shrugged. "It doesn't say 'land only.' That's as good as an okay in my book. I could get outside backing. Just proceed with the project and get permission later.''

Miranda stood slowly, shaking her head. "Erwin, you could get into a lot of trouble—''

"You think they're going to care, once we find it?" Saunders's face glowed with heightened color. "Are you sure you can do this, Magnusson? What experience do you have? I don't even know your credentials.''

Miranda spoke before Rolf could so much as part his lips. "Rolf's an expert, Erwin. He's mostly self-taught, but there is no denying his abilities, I guarantee it. If you want to waste time checking his background, I suppose—"

"No. We need to act right away. If you vouch for him, Miranda, then I'm sure he's legitimate." Saunders rose, again stroking his beard, apparently lost in his own thoughts. "You go on now. I'll take care of everything." He seemed to snap out of his reverie for a moment as they moved toward the door. "Remember, not a word to anyone. We have no way of knowing whom we can trust."

Miranda looked at him doubtfully. "Erwin, I don't know about doing this without consulting Harrison. He's the dean, after all, and I don't want—"

"There'll be no risk to you, my dear. I'll take full responsibility for any repercussions, I promise you. We have to do this." He studied her face. "For your father," he added quickly.

Miranda became certain all at once and she nodded firmly. "Yes, you're right. Call me as soon as the arrangements are made."

One week later, Miranda stood on the deck of *Mermaid,* a former minesweeper built for the British Royal Navy in 1942. She'd been acquired by an oil company in '67, and fitted with sonar transmitters and receivers, as well as two submersible remote camera videos for use in monitoring underwater pipelines.

Mermaid was now the property of Cryo-Life Industries. It galled Miranda that once again Saunders had gone to the company for funding, and it baffled her that they had agreed. He must have dangled before them the hope of finding another Ice Man, or perhaps suggested they might still locate the original one, to gain their cooperation so readily. It galled her still further that Jeff Morsi would accompany them as Cryo-Life's representative.

Still, she had other worries besides Jeff Morsi's infuriating presence. She turned to look at Rolf standing at the rail. The sea wind blew his golden hair back off his shoulders, and he leaned into it as if in ecstasy.

Miranda frowned. He hadn't so much as touched her since that time in the car. She hated herself for panicking the way she had. It was ridiculous for her to think, even for one uncontrollable moment, that Rolf could hurt her, could force her the way— She stopped the thought. That was in the past, and she had to find a way to leave it there. She'd discovered something about herself since Rolf had come into her life. She was not as immune to the touch of a man as she had once thought. When he touched her, when he kissed her, she felt things she'd never felt before. Longings, desires, tiny flames igniting throughout her body. She was sure no one else could inspire those wonderful feelings in her. No one ever had. But Rolf could. And now he was angry or hurt, and mistrustful of everything she told him. She was afraid she'd lost the only chance she would ever have to feel like a woman.

Of course, she couldn't blame him. She'd reacted like an idiot. God, if it had been anywhere else, she might have been all right. Why the car? Why did it have to be in that tiny damned car?

For a moment she wondered just why she felt so certain he wouldn't hurt her, knowing what she did about him. He'd admitted to being the dreaded Plague of the North, to ruthlessly raiding coastal villages, to robbing and quite probably raping and killing.

No. She felt a sudden conviction that it wasn't so. No man capable of such atrocities could caress her as tenderly as Rolf had. She tried to recall every word her father had written on the subject, to trace in her mind the source of the rage which had driven him to violence so long ago.

He'd been a trusted friend of Knut…right up until the charge of treason and murder, and then the exile. There'd been only a single witness against him, she recalled reading. The daughter of a nobleman. And, as her father had noted, it had been the nobles who usurped the throne of Norway, and handed it to Magnus.

That was all in the past. The needs of the present demanded her attention now. The preparations were complete. The equipment had been checked and double-checked, the plans gone over. They only awaited the last few members of Erwin's handpicked crewmen and then they could depart. There was nothing pressing to be done at the moment, except talk to Rolf. She could think of no excuse to put it off, though his attitude this past week had been discouraging in itself.

She came up behind him, entranced by the waves of his wind-whipped hair. He knew she was there before she said a word, and he turned slowly, leaning back against the rail and eyeing her. "There is something on your mind?"

She stood near him, head tipped back. "I want to talk."

He shrugged lazily. "Talk, then."

"You're angry with me."

His gaze was hooded. She found herself sorely missing the changing colors she'd seen in the depths of his eyes before he'd chosen to hide them away. "You are mistaken. I have no anger toward you, lady."

"I think you do. And I know it's because of the way I reacted that time in the car, when you kissed me. But it isn't fair of you to refuse to let me explain. I just want a chance to make you understand."

He shrugged again, refusing to answer her.

"Would it matter if I told you that my reaction had nothing to do with you? It's me. I have certain…problems, things in my past that I haven't dealt with. I can see I need to face them now, and I will."

The veil over Rolf's emotions lifted a little to reveal the heat of anger in his eyes. "You thought I would rape you. You were so afraid that your heart thundered in your chest." He stared hard at her. "You deny this?"

She bit her lip. "It was a brief panic, that's all. It would have happened no matter who had been kissing me. It wasn't you.''

He shook his head. ''You found yourself in the passionate embrace of a barbarian. It is little wonder you felt fear.''

''You aren't listening.'' She sighed deeply. ''It isn't you. Something happened to me once, and—''

''Will you tell me of this thing that so troubles you?''

Footsteps approached, then passed, and Miranda glanced over her shoulder to see Jeff Morsi striding across the deck. She could easily imagine what Rolf might do to him if he ever found out. Swallowing hard, she faced Rolf again. ''I can't. I'm sorry. You'll just have to trust me. I'm telling you the truth.''

''Trusting you is difficult, Miranda. I once trusted a woman so like you as to be your twin. My reward was betrayal, and nearly death.''

''Adrianna,'' she whispered. He said nothing, but she turned his words over and over in her mind. ''Was she the one who accused you of murder?''

He pursed his lips, and finally gave a curt nod. ''Her *broðir,* my friend, stood accused. She betrayed me to clear him.''

''Did he do it?''

''Are you so sure I did not?''

''It isn't impossible, you know,'' she went on, ignoring his comment. ''The nobles put Magnus on the throne. They could have been plotting to frame you from the start.''

Rolf released a laugh that sounded more like a bark. ''Then I am twice the fool. I never suspected—''

''Were you in love with her?''

He shrugged again, averting his gaze. ''Half the men in Norge were in love with Adrianna.''

''That is no answer.''

''It is the only answer you will get, lady.''

She felt mulish the way she pressed on. ''Why was your exile carried out even when Magnus took the throne? I would think he'd have approved of your supposed treason against Knut.''

''Magnus was no fool. He knew where my loyalties lay.'' Rolf turned as he spoke, staring once again out to sea.

''Then the charges were false. You just said it. You were loyal to Knut.''

''*Stodva.*'' He uttered the word without inflection. ''Cease this interrogation, Miranda, and come to the point. What is it you wish to know?''

''Only the truth, Rolf. What made you do what you did? Which of the crimes attributed to the Plague of the North are true, and which are embellishments added by generations of storytellers?''

He sighed, nodding as if he suddenly understood something previously beyond his grasp. ''I am *útlendur maður,* an outsider, unproven. You wish to hear me defend myself against the charges, to listen as I confess my crimes or attempt to explain them away. I will not do it, lady. Believe of me what you will. Judge me by whatever evidence you choose, be it the words of those who are now ashes in the wind, or the man you see before you. Do not ask me to convince you of the one or the other.'' His gaze remained on the horizon and his last words sounded like a dismissal.

Miranda sighed hopelessly. He didn't need to convince her of anything. She already believed him innocent of the murder, and incapable of the brutalities of which he'd been accused. She'd only wanted the details and... All right, she admitted to herself, perhaps she'd wanted a little reassurance, as well. She'd wanted confirmation that she wasn't letting her growing fondness of him interfere with her common sense. Why couldn't he grant her that much, at least?

She lifted a hand toward him, but let it fall when she heard her name shouted. She turned to see Fletcher Travis jump from the small gangplank and trot toward her, and she couldn't stop the smile that leapt to her lips. "Fletch! What on earth are you doing here?"

He grinned in return, coming toward her and leaning on the rail as Rolf did. "Hey, you didn't think you were going to sneak off on some grand adventure without inviting me, did you?"

She gave him a teasing look. "Since when do shipwrecks interest the famed numismatist?"

"Since his favorite archaeologist is sneaking off to locate one, that's when," he quipped. "Besides, I'm an archaeologist, too, and furthermore, there are liable to be some pretty interesting coins if you find the site."

"Oh, we'll find it," she said softly, glancing toward Rolf. "Make no mistake about that."

Rolf saw the emotion in her eyes as she expressed her faith in him. Would that it were genuine. He knew too well it was not. She feared and quite possibly despised him. She believed him capable of heinous crimes, and even of violence against her. It tore at his gut that she could think it of him even now. It tore at his pride that she'd asked him to defend himself against her assumptions. He wouldn't. Let her think what she wished. It mattered not to him.

Oh, but it did. How very well he knew that it did!

"Hello, Rolf, how are you?"

Travis's arm was resting around Miranda's shoulder when Rolf reluctantly faced the man. Rolf's glare must have penetrated, for the man lowered that arm all at once and offered a friendly smile that seemed genuine.

"*Gott kvöld*, Travis. I am eager to be away," he answered honestly. "Will you be accompanying us?"

"Unless you have objections," Travis said. His tone of voice conveyed little meaning, but in his steely eyes Rolf saw more. Something the man was not saying.

"You are welcome to join us, do you wish."

"Good. I, uh, have my luggage to bring aboard. Mind giving me a hand, Rolf?"

Travis wished more than Rolf's aid in carrying, and Rolf knew it. He nodded, and the two men walked away toward the gangplank, leaving Miranda behind at the rail. At a small car near the dock, Fletcher picked up two suitcases and handed one to Rolf. "I wanted a word with you, away from Miranda."

Rolf nodded. "*Já*, I discerned as much."

"I might be overreacting, but I'm worried." He slammed shut the trunk from which he'd taken the cases, turned, and set his case on the ground. "This entire expedition is being kept very quiet."

"With reason. How did you learn of it?"

"I overheard Jeff Morsi and Erwin Saunders discussing it as I entered Erwin's office yesterday. You know, it's highly unusual to keep something like this under wraps."

"There is a possibility of great wealth to be found. Miranda believes the one who broke into her home was seeking information about the missing treasure, as she calls it. The secrecy was to keep that one from learning of the trip and attempting to sabotage it, or to steal the treasure for himself."

Travis nodded. "That's all just fine, but suppose he already knows about it?"

Rolf frowned. "Explain yourself."

"I'm just saying, what if the guy already knows about this trip? What if he's just waiting for you to lead him to the site? What then? With so few people knowing what you're up to... Do you see what I'm saying?"

Rolf considered this possibility. "If the man wishes to steal the plunder, he might wait until it is recovered and take it from us. It would sorely aggrieve Miranda."

"And what if it isn't the treasure itself he wants? What if it is only the credit for locating it he's after?"

"I do not understand," Rolf admitted.

"If Miranda pulls this off she'll be in demand by every university from here to Alaska. She'll gain the respect and standing in the scientific community that most people work their whole lives to achieve. That kind of acclaim is worth more than the plunder."

Tilting his head, Rolf studied Travis. He needed to look down only slightly. The man was nearly his height, and solidly built. A worthy opponent, but a valuable ally. "You are saying there may be one who wishes to claim it was he who located the *drakkar,* and the treasure it holds? But to do that, he would need to silence—" Rolf stopped suddenly, now understanding Travis's alarm. To claim the credit, all who knew the truth must needs be silenced. Rolf feared not for himself, but for Miranda.

"Now you see why I've decided to come along," Fletcher said, bending to pick up his case once more. "It's a farfetched scenario, but not impossible."

"The villain would likely follow by sea," Rolf said, turning the possibilities over in his mind. "He would need stop us before we could tell anyone of the find. Perchance he has implanted a spy among us, to keep him abreast by means of that magical box Miranda calls radio."

"Magi—" Travis glanced up, frowning, but let the matter drop. "You're right, there might be a rat on board. We'll keep a sharp eye on those crewmen Erwin hired."

Rolf nodded his approval. "It is good that you wish to protect Miranda. I accept your help with gratefulness."

"Protect her," Travis said thoughtfully. "Yeah, and maybe I ought to add that it's *all* I want. She's my friend, Rolf. That's all. I love her, but like a sister. You got that?"

Rolf shot the man a suspicious glance. "Why think you I care?"

Travis's dark brows went up. "You're kidding, right?"

Chapter 12

Rolf stood once more in the prow, leaning into the night wind. He felt as if it were his body knifing through the deep blue waters, his breath stirring the air. This time no sails. No oarsmen. Only the dull throb of the ship's heart, pulsing with energy, moving them along like a great living thing, kind enough to carry them all in her embrace. He felt as if he'd come home. Here, in the chill air, in the dark of night, he forgot, for a few precious moments, about Miranda and what she thought of him.

His respite was all too brief. For in the fickle way of the sea breeze, voices carried in odd patterns. "Looking for me?" Jeff Morsi's words were laden with suggestion.

"What do you think?" Miranda's voice trembled, though it seemed she sought to make it biting.

Rolf straightened from his position on the rail and turned slowly. They were not in sight. Probably somewhere on the starboard side.

"I'm not an idiot, Miranda. I think you're looking for your muscle-bound boyfriend."

Rolf listened for her ardent denial, but heard none.

"Does he know what a cold little bitch you are, I wonder?"

"Jeff..." It was little more than a whimper. Rolf frowned hard and started toward the sound of their voices.

"Or have you changed?" Morsi went on. "I wonder—"

"Jeff, don't—"

"Oh, come on. Just a little experiment. I'm dying to find out what he sees in you."

Rolf came upon them. Miranda's back was pressed to the rail. Morsi's arms entrapped her there. As he leaned over her, his face drawing nearer to hers with each second, she arched backward until it must have been painful. Rolf almost smiled, waiting for her to deliver a little pain of her own. Surely she would kick the bastard in his vulnerable groin, or stomp his foot, or pummel his chest. Any moment now she would coolly threaten to rip his heart out, did he not desist.

She didn't. Her face went white and Rolf heard her strangled efforts to breathe combine with her choking sobs. Even from where he stood, he saw her body tremble. What was wrong with the woman? Was she going to stand there and allow this? Apparently she was, for Morsi leaned closer and caught her mouth beneath his. He quickly moved his arms from the rail on either side of her to capture her head in his hands as he cruelly kissed her.

Rolf lunged forward, gripped Morsi by one shoulder and whirled the man around.

"Rolf." Miranda had time only to gasp his name before she spun, lowered her head over the rail and retched violently.

"This is a private conversation, Magnusson. Do you mind?"

"I mind a great deal." Rolf swung a fist at the bastard's face, but Jeff was ready. He ducked quickly and as he rose drove a fist into Rolf's stomach. Rolf took the blow admirably well, he thought. He clenched his stomach muscles in the instant before the fist landed, and though it hurt, he managed not to flinch. The reaction, or lack thereof, had the desired effect. Morsi paused to peer slowly up into Rolf's face, a stunned look in his eyes.

Rolf hammered him with one blow. Jeff Morsi crumpled to the wooden deck.

Rolf began to reach down to him, but before he could, Miranda launched herself from the rail and into his arms. His anger abated slightly as he closed his arms around her. She was shaking, her entire body rippling like the water's choppy surface. "If you touch her again, I will kill you, Morsi. Make no mistake." Rolf scooped Miranda up into his arms.

"No, Rolf. D-don't say—" She hugged his neck, burying her face there, stammering as she tried to speak. By Thor's justice, why did she react this way?

"It is said." Rolf turned away from the beaten man, unsure whether his promise had been heard or not. Morsi lay very still, blood trailing down his neck.

Rolf carried her to his cabin, closed the door and turned the lock. The light still burned, just as he'd left it, filling the small cabin with an amber glow. He laid her upon his bed as gently as he could manage, then straightened and took a step backward. For a moment he only stared at her, trying to fathom the reason for her failure to act in her own defense. He wondered what might have happened had he not heard her voice. How far might that villain have taken his demented game? Rolf's anger simmered anew.

"Explain yourself, woman."

Miranda's gray eyes widened and she blinked away the tears that had begun to coat them. "Wh-what?"

"Why do you allow Morsi so much?"

She shook her head, bewildered and wounded by the look in her eyes. "Allow him? Rolf, he didn't ask. He had me cornered. You saw him. How can you—"

Rolf shook his head and blew a loud sigh. He walked away from her across the cabin and back. Standing close to her again with hands on hips, he searched her eyes for an explanation. "You recall the time I first kissed you? Despite my size, my strength, you crushed my unclothed foot and wrenched yourself from my arms. The next time I made a move toward you, you threatened me with a blade large enough to eviscerate me. The time after that, you offered to make a large hole in me with your little gun, and proceeded to demonstrate that you could carry out the threat. In your car you pounded my chest with your fists. I do not—" He stopped suddenly as some odd constriction formed in his throat.

He found he could scarcely force the words from his lips, but he made himself. He hadn't been aware how much more he wanted from her than simply to bed her. He wanted to have her as his exclusively, he realized now, to have the *right* to kill Morsi for touching her.

"Is it that you prefer his touch to mine? Am I so much more detestable to you that—"

She sat up quickly. "Is that what you think? Did it look to you like I *wanted* his filthy hands on me?"

"You did not seem to fight his touch, Miranda. Not the way you do mine, at least."

"If you thought I was enjoying myself so much, why did you interrupt?"

The bitterness and the anger in her voice stunned him. He knew full well she hadn't welcomed Morsi's touch. He was only reacting to his unfounded jealousy. Yet he couldn't seem to stop himself. "I'll not trouble myself again, lady." She lowered her head, such sadness in her expression that he wished he could recall his impulsive words. She rose from his bed, her gaze on the floor as she moved toward the door. When she reached for it, Rolf's hand shot out to grip her wrist. "Wait."

Her head came up, eyes glittering with anger. She

wrenched her wrist from his grasp, slamming her other palm into his chest with such force he actually staggered backward. He stood there, searching her face.

"You see why I am confused, Miranda? I am twice Morsi's size. Where was this ferocity when he was mauling you?"

The anger faded. Her face became softer, her eyes seeming to search inwardly. "I...was too afraid. I wanted to fight him, but I—" She stopped, slowly shaking her head.

"Are you not afraid to strike out at me? Miranda, I am a powerful man. I could do you a good deal more harm than that puny dog could."

Her eyes met his and she denied his words quickly. "No, you couldn't. You wouldn't. Maybe that's the key to my reactions. I lash out at you because I feel safe in doing so. I know you won't hurt me."

Rolf drew his brows together in bewilderment. "He is a civilized man of your time. I am a murdering barbarian from the past. How is it you feel safe with me?"

She lifted her gaze, her eyes haunted. "Every age has its barbarians, Rolf. Even mine."

"Do I see him touch you again, Miranda, I do not believe I can stop myself killing him."

She almost smiled at the warmth that spread within her at the ferocity in his tone. Surely this was what every woman must crave—a man like this one, ready to kill for her at a moment's notice, even though she prayed he wouldn't take it that far. "Then you didn't mean what you said...that you wouldn't bother helping me next time."

"I meant none of what I said to you. I was angry."

"Why?"

He turned from her, pushing both hands through his golden hair, lifting it from his shoulders as his fingertips raked his scalp. "I dislike the notion that you might prefer another man's touch. Or even that you might loathe the touch of another less than you loathe mine.''

Miranda was stunned by his admission. ''Really?''

He nodded, facing her again with a grin that was slightly sheepish. ''I was not aware you honored me by feeling safe in battering me.''

She swallowed hard, licked her lips. ''I don't loathe your touch, Rolf.''

His brows rose in disbelief. ''No?''

''No,'' she said, shaking her head.

''But in your car—''

''It wasn't your touch that frightened me,'' she forced herself to say.

''I do not understand.''

''I know.'' She wished she could explain, but she couldn't. Not unless she wanted to see Jeff tossed overboard and Rolf behind bars. Reluctantly she gripped the door handle. ''I should go.''

''Nei.'' Rolf placed his hand over hers. ''You will sleep here tonight.''

As propositions went, she thought, it wasn't exactly poetic. ''I'm not sure I'm ready for—''

''It matters not. You say you trust that I will not harm you. I know it to be true. Of Morsi, I am not so certain. He looks at you with anger, with rage.'' He stared so intensely into her eyes she shuddered with the force of his gaze. ''Will you tell me yet what went between you?''

''Between...Jeff and me?''

He nodded curtly. ''You intended once to wed him. Why did you not?''

She looked away. ''Marrying Jeff would have been the worst mistake of my life.''

''On this we agree.'' Rolf cupped her cheek, turning her to face him. ''You did not part as friends.''

''No. The truth is, we were engaged for six months. During that time we...well, we slept together. I never...I didn't—'' She broke off lamely. It was difficult to speak so frankly about something she'd never discussed with anyone.

"Morsi was not able to pleasure you," Rolf filled in with uncanny insight.

She nodded, feeling the blood rush to her cheeks. "I was ashamed, so I hid it. I...I pretended."

"Ashamed? Why, Miranda?"

"I thought I must be frigid. My father was constantly telling me that I wasn't like other women. That a career was all I needed in my life. That a husband and a family could never make me happy. My time with Jeff was...was my last-ditch effort to prove him wrong. Instead it seemed like I'd only confirmed what my father had been saying all along." Miranda crossed the room, sinking onto the edge of the bed. "I got tired of pretending and decided to tell Jeff the truth." She averted her face from Rolf's all-seeing gaze. "He didn't take it well."

With an expression of deep concern, Rolf came to her. He caught her chin, tilting her head up as he searched her eyes. "Miranda, what—"

"Would you mind if we didn't talk about it anymore right now? Please, Rolf?"

Eyes narrowing, he nodded at last. "I do not trust Morsi. Will you stay here tonight, under my protection?" She hesitated, not because she was thinking it over, but because he'd asked her, rather than ordered her to stay. Mistaking her pause, he hurried on. "I'll not rest do you return alone to your cabin, Miranda. You may rest upon my bed. By my sword, I will not touch you. Only watch over you."

"Yes, all right. I should go to my cabin for a nightgown, though." She rose as she spoke, but found her legs oddly watery. Whether from reaction to Jeff's assault or nervousness, she didn't know.

"Your knees wobble too much to walk, and I've no desire to leave you unguarded while I fetch the garment for

you. Here." He handed her the oversize robe she had
bought for him, and promptly turned his back to her.

She began unbuttoning her blouse, but her fingers trembled and she swore softly at her clumsiness. He faced her
at once. In two steps he stood before her. His hands closed
on the front of her blouse and he gently released each button. His gaze dropped to the swell of her breasts, now visible above the lace-edged cups of her bra. He cleared his
throat and turned away once more. "You may wish to consider making me sleep beyond the door, lady. Plague of the
North or not, a man would have difficulty remaining honor-
orable when you lie so close."

She peeled off the blouse, shimmied out of her slacks
and pulled on the robe. Tying the belt around her waist,
she said simply, "I trust you." She slipped into the bed
and pulled up the covers.

Rolf faced her again. "It amazes me that you do. I am
still unsure I believe it." He took an extra blanket from the
foot of the bed and threw it over his shoulders like a cape.
When he'd settled down directly in front of the door, Miranda studied him, feeling guilty for making him sleep on
the hard floor.

"Well, it's true. I trust you. If you want to share the bed,
I won't object."

He closed his eyes as if in pain. "Think before you
speak, woman. Have you not yet realized how much I want
you?"

She sat up, tilted her head to one side. "You do? I can't
understand it."

He laughed very deep in his throat. "That you have no
idea how desirable you are only makes you more so, Miranda. Do you allow me in that bed, you'd do well to sleep
with your gun beneath the pillow. The blade, as well, perhaps."

She smiled a little. "You underestimate yourself. You
wouldn't touch me if I objected."

His blue eyes raked her. "There is much about yourself you do not know."

"Like what?"

"There is a fire that burns inside you, lady. I have felt its heat. I think, perchance, you would not object at all."

Chapter 13

She studied his face, feeling the warmth of his gaze and sensing the desire behind it. "Do you really believe that?" she asked, shaken by his observation.

"I do."

She shook her head quickly. "Rolf, some women simply don't respond—"

"This I know. You are not one of those women, Miranda."

"How can you know that? I told you, I'm not inexperienced. I never felt anything with Jeff."

"When Morsi kissed you, you felt nothing?"

Her gaze fell to her hands clenched in her lap. "No. Nothing."

"And when I kissed you?"

Her gaze rose slowly then and locked with his. "I...I felt..."

"You see, lady? The problem before was in him, not in you."

She took that in with silent wonder. Could he be right?

For so long she'd considered herself immune to desires of the flesh. It boggled her mind to think she might not be. But she had begun thinking it, and to know he thought it, as well, gave added credence to the idea. When Rolf had held her, had touched her, she realized that she *had* felt something...something powerful. A tingling awareness throughout her body, a tight ball of longing deep within her. She drew a deep breath and held it. She wanted to explore these new feelings. She wanted Rolf to be the one to guide her. No one else would do, for no one else made her feel this way.

"Rolf?" His head lifted once more. "I want you to kiss me again."

He rose to his feet, the blanket falling from his shoulders like a cascade. Slowly he came to the bed and lowered himself onto its edge. She waited, sitting straighter as he leaned forward, his arms braced on either side of her. His lips came to hers lightly, teasingly. He nibbled the lower one, suckled it softly. Then his arms closed around her and he kissed her deeply. His tongue swept into her mouth as it had done before, and it elicited the same response.

Miranda considered the sensations crashing through her, trying to analyze each one. Her arms crept around his neck and she pressed herself closer. When his head lifted from hers, his eyes glittered with unmistakable passion. Her voice hoarse, she whispered, "My God, you're right. I do feel it."

"It is only a whisper of what you could feel, Miranda. Do you allow me, I would show you."

She licked her lips tasting him on them. She nodded once, and closed her eyes as she waited. His strong hands slipped beneath the covers, tugged the belt loose. They returned to her shoulders and pushed the fabric down over her arms. Her eyes fluttered open to find his hooded and focused on her breasts.

"You are beautiful, Miranda." He slid the back of his

fingers downward over her breasts. When the roughened
skin skimmed her nipples she sucked in a breath. She felt
them harden as he turned his hands over to cup her in his
palms. Then, so gently she marveled, he rolled the taut
crests between his thumbs and forefingers. A shudder
rocked her, and as her head tilted backward, his moved
lower. His lips closed over one nipple and she gasped
again. Tenderly he suckled her, and in a moment Miranda
realized that her hands had gone to the back of his head to
hold him closer. Rolf lifted his head, a look of wonder in
his eyes. "You wish me to stop, Miranda? Speak it now,
if you do."

Too breathless to speak, she shook her head from side
to side.

He pressed her gently back until she was lying flat.
Slowly, giving her time to object, she thought, he pulled
the covers from her. She wore nothing now, and she
squirmed inwardly as his heated gaze moved over her from
head to toe with agonizing deliberation. "How did I ever
mistake you for Adrianna?" he whispered. "Her beauty
pales beside yours."

Again he leaned over her, suckling her breasts, nibbling
them, flicking his tongue over her nipples until she was
panting with a longing she'd never felt before. One hand
slid lower, his palm flat on her belly. His fingers tangled
in her soft curls, then circled down, until they parted her.
He touched a hidden spot with his forefinger and her eyes
flew wide at the surge of sensation.

Slowly he lay down beside her, his right hand still sending spirals of heat through her. His lips lingered over her
throat; his tongue laved her skin. He caught her earlobe in
his teeth and worried it softly. His fingers moved lower,
leaving that magical place he'd discovered to slip easily
inside her. She felt the dampness there and wondered at it.
But as his fingers probed more deeply, she tensed with the
anticipation of what was to come.

"Relax, my lady. I only seek to show you pleasure, hmm? Relax and allow it. Do not think or worry. Only feel. Feel my touch. Never would I harm you. You need only tell me to stop, and I will."

She closed her eyes and his mouth traced a path along her jawline to find her lips again. He kissed her harder this time, demanding greater access, thrusting his tongue deep within her and touching off fires all through her.

When he moved again to her breasts, she writhed with pleasure and yet she felt fear. He must have sensed it, for he stopped and searched her face. "Miranda...let me pleasure you. By the gods, I will not harm you. I will not remove a stitch of my clothing unless you ask it. I swear by Thor's hammer."

She had no clue how he could continue making love to her without removing his clothes, but she consented with a brisk nod. He was pushing her to a realm beyond the one she knew. Her body was taking over, sending urgent messages to her brain.

Again he resumed his exquisite torture of her breasts until her nipples throbbed with longing. But his mouth left them to the chill air and moved downward. His tongue traced wet paths over her belly and probed her navel. She whimpered with suppressed desire as he persisted, licking a hot trail over her abdomen.

Her hips moved against her will, and then his hands were gripping them, pulling her around sideways and toward the bed's edge. Vaguely she realized he'd shifted position until he was on the floor, kneeling. He gently spread her thighs open and bowed his head between them.

She felt his mouth, his hot breath caressing her most intimate spot. Then his fingers parted her and his tongue touched her in ways she'd never dreamed of. He pressed his face to her, as if he, too, were deriving the same exquisite pleasure he was giving to her. He drank from her, like a man dying of thirst, desperately. Her fingers tangled in his hair. His hand moved upward, arms reaching until he caught her nipples again in his merciless fingers.

Moving his mouth away only slightly, he spoke with an air of command. "Give me your sweetness, Miranda. Let it go, for I must have it." When his tongue dipped again, fiercely thrusting and swirling and tasting her, Miranda felt something inside her give way. She cried out as myriad explosions went off in the core of her. The final drafts he drank from her brought convulsive spasms of ecstasy. She shook from head to toe with the force of her release.

She was still trembling when he lifted himself to lie beside her. She curled into his arms and felt their warmth and strength surround her. As she cuddled nearer, she felt, too, his arousal pressing against her. He'd shown her pleasure, given her release like nothing she'd ever known, revealed to her a knowledge about herself that would change her entire life. He'd asked nothing in return. More than before, she knew she could trust this man. He had kept his word to her, despite the obvious difficulties. It was so opposite what Jeff had done to her.

She focused on Rolf, instead of on the ripples of reaction still shuddering through her body. She felt the thundering of his heart, heard his ragged, shallow breathing. He held her tightly, almost desperately. He was in a thoroughly aroused state, she realized. She could give him release. She could give to him as unselfishly as he'd given to her. She marveled as the truth hit her. She wasn't afraid anymore.

He rolled away from her suddenly, sitting up and thrusting one hand through his hair. She gripped his shoulder when he started to rise. When he glanced down at her, she shook her head. "No, Rolf. Don't go yet."

"I must. I'm a man, Miranda. Not a god. Do I not leave you now, I will be unable to—"

"Stay."

He searched her face. "You are grateful for this lesson I have taught you."

"Yes." She reached up to his bare chest and ran her hand over it. "And eager for another lesson."

His eyes closed briefly. "Speak plainly, woman. Do I touch you again, I may not stop so easily."

"I don't want you to stop." She met his gaze without flinching. "Make love to me, Rolf."

He studied her face for a long moment. "As you wish it, lady." He stood, still holding her gaze. He removed his jeans carefully, then the briefs beneath them. He hesitated as her gaze moved lower. The state of his arousal alarmed her, but only momentarily. "Are you certain?" he asked, still standing, exercising obvious restraint.

She swallowed hard. "You would never hurt me."

"I would die first," he told her. He lowered himself onto the bed beside her. He rested on his side, facing her. She believed him.

Shyly she slipped one hand lower to touch him. His soft moan told her how this affected him. A moment later, his arms were around her. His mouth possessed hers with a new urgency and he rolled her onto her back, covering her body with his own.

Miranda's hands moved over his back as she returned his kiss. She traced the hard contours of him, felt the heat of his tight skin. At the heart of her she felt him nudge her moistness and she parted her thighs for him. Already the fires were burning brightly. She found herself more than ready for him when he entered her.

Carefully he moved deeper. She arched her hips upward. Rather than discomfort she felt excitement as her body stretched to fit him. He withdrew slowly and began again, inching inward. His hands slipped beneath her to cup her buttocks, holding her to him so he filled her more completely this time.

His gentle rhythm held, though she sensed the effort it cost him. His body shook with it. As the ship rocked gently beneath them, Miranda felt the recurrence of the pattern she now recognized. The tightening within her, the heat searing her wherever they touched. His pace increased, his movements growing quicker, less delicate. She caught her breath when she knew she was once again on the brink of ecstasy. Her gasp reached him even now, and he paused. "Miranda?"

She tightened her grip on his shoulders and moved her hips, sheathing him heatedly within her. "Please, Rolf," she muttered. And when he responded with more urgent movements of his own she moaned softly, "Yes. Oh, yes."

She felt the tension mount in him even as she sensed the same within herself. They moved in unison, seemingly anticipating each other's needs with psychic perception. Finally he thrust more deeply than before and she knew he'd found release for the throbbing inside her. That knowledge pushed her over the brink, as well, and she clung to him with every part of her. His lips found hers, and when he moaned with pleasure, it was into her mouth.

He collapsed on top of her then, his weight a warm burden, one she wouldn't willingly relinquish. "Miranda." He lifted his head and his eyes widened. His hand came up, and with his thumb he stroked a tear from her cheek. "I hurt you!"

"No." She shook her head quickly. "No, you didn't hurt me, Rolf. Not at all." She smiled and raised her head off the pillow to press her lips to his.

"But you cry." He obviously didn't understand.

"How can I explain?" She sniffed and tried to stifle the urge to shed more tears. "It's as if part of me was dead, or asleep as you were for so long. You've awakened that part. I feel truly alive, more than I've ever felt before." She gazed at him in wonder. "How can I ever thank you?"

He smiled, the concern leaving his face. "Let me hold you in my arms until the dawn, *ástin mín*. It will be all the thanks I need."

She snuggled nearer, silently rejoicing as his arms tightened around her and his shoulder pillowed her head. "What does that mean?"

"What?"

"*Ástin mín?*" She repeated the phrase he'd used, and felt him stiffen beside her.

"I said that?"

"Mmm-hmm." A sweet lethargy was stealing over her, a peace such as she'd never known before. "What's it mean?"

"If it has an English equivalent, I am not aware of it."

"Oh." Her eyes closed.

She slept curled in his embrace, every so often snuggling closer. Rolf didn't sleep at all. He held her, constantly aware of every aspect of her. The touch of her skin against his, the deep, steady pattern of her breathing, the scent of her. It was not her thanks he wanted, he acknowledged at last. It was her heart. And while he had given her physical pleasure, he knew he did not have that.

All he'd really accomplished, he realized grimly as night moved toward dawn, was to awaken the sleeping temptress inside her. Now that she knew her own desires, she would feel free to explore them with other men. Hadn't young Darryl explained that today's women were free to give themselves to any man they chose? Miranda herself had said that a husband would interfere with her career.

A husband? Had he really been fool enough, even for a moment, to let that thought enter his mind? What could he give to a woman like Miranda? He possessed nothing of value, save his sword. And why would she want a man like him, ignorant of this world, uncertain how to make his own way within it?

No. He must keep in mind always that the night they had shared meant little to her, apart from the things she'd learned about herself. She would place little importance on it. For Rolf, it seemed, the matter was quite different. The experience for him had been a revelation, too. For he had not known the depth of his feelings for her. Now that he did, he nearly wished he'd remained on the floor.

He glanced down at the woman in his arms, her face resting on his chest, her hand gripping his upper arm as if to keep him by her side. No, he couldn't regret bedding her. Though she was aware only of her own sexual awakening, Rolf knew he'd experienced one of his own, for never had sex been as moving or as potent as it had been tonight.

As they continued north, it became necessary for them to wear their heavy overcoats on the open deck, even though the sun burned bright and long into the night. It set only briefly, sinking only slightly below the horizon, still casting a glow in the sky. As the *Mermaid* charged steadily through the waters between Greenland and Helluland, or Baffin Island as it was now called, Rolf remained in the prow almost constantly. Icebergs here were common, and deadly. A man must be alert for them, always. They harbored a fondness for slipping out of the mists and into a ship's path.

They'd just crossed the invisible wonder Miranda called the Arctic Circle, when Rolf saw the familiar shape of the coast—ice mountains sloping sharply downward, then stretching into flat vast tundra as far as one could hope to see. The cool wind bit his face, despite it being summer, and Rolf imagined himself momentarily transported back in time. He felt again the pitch and roll of his *drakkar,* once more heard the harsh cries of his men and shivered in the sea spray.

A sharp crack sounded behind him, and he whirled, half-expecting to see the mast crashing down upon his helpless crewmen. He realized the sound had just been in his mind when he saw only Miranda, looking concerned, and Fletcher Travis, at her side as always.

"Rolf?"

He turned back to face the rail, unwilling to let her see the weakness in his eyes. The memories were too fresh. For him, the horror had occurred only a matter of days ago. He had no real sense that nine hundred and fifty-nine years had come and gone. "Tell your friend to drop anchor, Miranda."

He heard quick steps leaving the deck. But when he turned she remained, alone now. "Fletch went to tell Paul."

Paul. The man who piloted this vessel was now as friendly with Miranda as every other male in her reach apparently wanted to be. To the others, the man was Captain Potter. To Miranda, he was Paul.

She touched his arm. "Are you all right?"

It was not her fault she treated everyone with such kindness, Rolf thought in self-reproach. He had no right to become jealous of every man she knew. He had no right to become jealous at all. Not having that right made him jealous all the more. "Why do you think I would not be?"

She blinked and stepped to the rail. Her gaze moved over the pale blue waters, over the chunks of blue-white ice floating everywhere. "Growlers," Captain Potter called them. She looked beyond to the jagged shores, as Rolf watched her. "You were this close?"

Rolf stood right next to her. He couldn't help wishing to be as near to her as possible, whenever he could manage it. "Nearer. See that small finger of ice? That is near the place where my *drakkar* went down."

She gripped his arm and stared, her expression pained. "That's only about five hundred yards from shore."

He nodded. "That ridge, see it?"

She looked where he pointed, and nodded.

"It was there the Skrælingar stood."

"The *Inuit*, Rolf. Skrælingar is a derogatory term. To use it is to insult them. They are not weaklings, by any means."

"They must not be, to have survived so long here in this wilderness. What does Inuit mean?"

"It means 'the people.'"

He continued his tale. "The People stood there. Their dark-colored fur clothing showed clearly against the snow beyond them."

"Were you blown off course by the storm?"

He shook his head. "*Nei.* We chose this place for its remoteness. Our plunder could be transported south easily enough when we'd established a defensible fortress. We planned to build in Vinland."

Her head snapped around suddenly. "Leif Eriksson's Vinland?"

"*Já.* Eriksson was there."

"And you?"

"Of course. I wouldn't have chosen it without first seeing for myself. Until we built there, we saw this as the safest place for our bounty."

Her brow creased in thought. "The cave where we found you isn't far from here." She pointed south, toward the craggy, treeless hills. "The expedition there is still going on. There's a little village of dome tents and scientists." She licked her lips. "Is there any chance of them finding it?"

"My plunder? No, they will never find it, Miranda." He took her arm. "Come, we will instruct your Captain Potter to ease us in nearer the shore, and show him where dangerous reefs and fingers of ice lie just beneath the surface. I know them all."

Paul knew his stuff, she had to give him that. He manipulated the remote camera skillfully, keeping his eyes on the video monitor. Miranda stood crowded against him, with Fletcher at her side, and Erwin and Jeff crammed on Paul's opposite side, all craning their necks to see.

They'd been here for hours. It was a painfully slow process. Rolf rarely left the ship's rail. He stood there, staring down into that icy water as if time didn't exist. It pained Miranda to see him so tormented. But he wasn't accepting any comforting just now. Respecting his need to be alone, she'd come back in here. She'd monitored the sonar receiver, but her lack of experience left her with little idea which blips were hunks of ice, stone formations or sunken dragon ships.

"Bing-go." Paul said it softly, and it took a moment for her to realize his meaning. Her gaze moved back to the screen.

The dark shape protruding from the murky bottom of the sea on the monitor's screen was completely encrusted with sediment. Still, there was no mistaking that shape, not when one knew what one was looking for. It was the carved dragon's head, the *drakkar*'s daunting prow.

"We've found it," she whispered. Then louder. Then everyone was speaking at once and Fletcher folded her in a crushing embrace and kissed her face repeatedly in his excitement. When he released her, she was whirled around and into Paul's arms for a similar celebratory hug.

Chapter 14

Fletcher Travis slapped Rolf's shoulder. "Good job, damn good. I still don't know how the hell you did it, but—" He broke off at Rolf's quelling glance, then Rolf sensed Travis's gaze following his own. Miranda stood amid the others, being hugged first by Erwin Saunders and then various members of the crew.

Travis smiled rather uneasily and shook his head. He stepped nearer Rolf and kept his voice low. "Look, no one's doing anything improper here. Don't look so glum. Go hug her yourself if you want to. It doesn't mean anything."

"It matters not to me," Rolf lied. "I am only glad she's overcome her aversion to physical contact with men."

Travis seemed not the least shocked by Rolf's remark. "It's the excitement, Magnusson. Don't read more into it than that. Miranda isn't that kind of woman." His tone was no longer so kind.

"Perhaps she wasn't. People change."

"What is that supposed to mean?"

"Only that Miranda seems to be thoroughly enjoying the attentions of those men."

Travis shouldered Rolf out of the doorway where they'd been standing and onto the open deck. "You bastard," he said in a still, even voice. "Make another remark like that one and I'll knock you on your oversized backside."

"Are you certain you're able?"

"You care to find out?"

Rolf watched the man for a long moment, tempted to break his neck just to teach him a lesson. But he couldn't. He liked Travis, despite the man's blindness where Miranda was concerned. "As it happens, I do not. Take me at my word, Travis. Do not attempt to bed her. I won't allow it."

"Bed her?" The man's dark brows rose in shocked surprise. "Bed her? Where the hell did you get a phrase like that? Look, I told you before, I have no romantic feelings for Miranda. I don't have the least interest in taking her to bed."

"You don't?" Rolf shook his head, confusion beginning to whirl in his brain. "Why not?" From what Rolf could see, every man aboard the *Mermaid* was biding his time to mount Miranda's newly awakened body.

"What kind of a question is that?"

"A logical one, I think. Look at her. The way she glances up from the corners of her eyes. The way she moves. She is beautiful."

"Son of a—" Travis chuckled with delight. "You're in love with her. You big jerk, you're in love with her. Why didn't you say so?"

Rolf looked away grimly. "You know nothing."

"I know Miranda. And believe me, she isn't the least bit interested in Paul Potter or Erwin Saunders or any of those others. Anyone with two eyes in his head ought to be able to see she despises Jeff Morsi. I've already told you, she and I are only friends. There's never been a hint of anything romantic between us. To tell you the truth, I never thought of Miranda along those lines. I see her as a scientist, a colleague.''

''If she has no interest in them, then why does she embrace them that way?'' Rolf glumly eyed the still-celebrating group in the corner.

''Look, now Paul has his arms around Erwin. See how hard Erwin just squeezed him?''

Rolf's face began to clear. ''Like men celebrating victory after a hard won battle.''

''Exactly. They're excited. This find is a major one, especially after the disappointment of losing the Ice Man.''

Rolf felt like a fool. Why was such a simple explanation so obvious to everyone but him? The woman was driving him from his senses without doubt.

She chose that moment to join them, and the smile she'd been wearing died slowly as she approached. She touched Rolf's shoulder so gently it was painful. What was happening to him? Where was his warrior's strength now? How could the simple sight of a woman in the arms of another cause him such agony?

In self-disgust, he jerked from her touch. Her eyes clouded as she searched his face. ''Leave us alone, would you, Fletch?'' She spoke without looking away. Travis muttered something about forests and trees and then he was gone.

''Rolf, what is it?''

Such innocence in her eyes. Might Travis have been right? But again, what if he wasn't? Rolf's feelings for Miranda had rapidly grown deeper than he'd realized. Her betrayal would cause him considerable pain, more even than Adrianna's had. So much more it didn't bear comparison. He needed to distance himself, to somehow convince himself that he could get along without her. For he knew, beyond any doubt, that he would have to do just that. Hadn't she told him there was no room in her life for a man?

"Talk to me," she said softly. "Is it something I've done?"

The goal for the moment, he decided at once, was to hide from her his pathetic weakness. Surely if she, a mere woman, could share what they'd shared and walk away unscathed, then he, the Plague of the North, could do the same.

"It's this place, isn't it? The memories... This must be hell for you." She slipped her arms around his waist and lowered her head to his chest.

He ordered his arms to remain at his sides. They disobeyed, closing around her as if commanded by some greater force. He bowed his head and immediately the cool sea wind brought the scent of her hair to his nostrils. Yes, he thought grimly. He did, indeed, feel as if he were a prisoner in Hel.

The sky was gray, but not dark; for a short time in July, the sun here never sank completely below the horizon. Fletcher was assisting Miranda in lowering the small motorboat from its hoist and into the calm, cold waters.

"Miranda, it is a mistake to go ashore." Erwin Saunders shook his head and gestured with his hands. "We all agreed it was best to keep this undertaking a secret until we have it secured."

"I really don't see the need for secrecy now that we've found it," Miranda countered, her tone as patient and reasonable as she could make it. This would be the biggest find Erwin had ever been personally involved in, and she could understand his concern. His lack of hands-on participation in recent expeditions had been commented about more than once in her presence. She imagined he was worried about job security. "The more people who know about it, the less likely someone else will be bold enough to try to take it from us."

"That's your opinion. I believe the opposite is true. This

person has already committed violence twice in his quest for this very site. He won't hesitate simply because of public opinion. Miranda, please.'' His voice was harsh, nearly desperate.

''I agree with Erwin,'' Jeff Morsi put in. ''Cryo-Life would be furious if someone decided to try something. I say we keep quiet until we have the retrieval operation well underway, and a lot more bodies around for security.''

Miranda sighed her exasperation. She caught the glance that went between Rolf and Fletcher, and she wondered at it. ''All right, Erwin, I won't breathe a word to anyone about what we're doing out here. That wasn't my purpose in going ashore, anyway. I just wanted to show Rolf the cave where we found hi—the Ice Man. That's all.''

She saw Fletcher's deep frown and the way he glanced sharply at Rolf all of a sudden. Had he caught her slip? No. That was ridiculous. Who would even consider such a farfetched notion?

Saunders still stubbornly shook his head. ''There are too many people camped around that site. There'll be a lot of questions and you're the worst liar I know.''

''Come with us if you don't trust me.'' She knew her words were short. All she'd wanted was to give Rolf some time away from the ship and from all the eyes aboard. He needed time to deal with the memories that must be attacking him even now. And time to open up and share some of his turmoil with her. She wanted to know exactly what was bothering him. He seemed as tense as the still summer air before a thunderstorm.

Saunders looked at her for a long moment, apparently trying to reach a decision. ''I guess I have no choice,'' he finally muttered.

They headed for shore in the small boat—Rolf, Miranda, Jeff and Saunders. Miranda heard Fletcher tell Rolf that he intended to stay aboard the *Mermaid* to ''keep an eye on things.'' Miranda wondered about the secret the two of them seemed to be sharing, but dismissed the notion as the boat neared the shore. Jeff handled the helm, angling southward slightly to bring them to land as near as possible to the site. He had to negotiate the waters slowly, to avoid the countless blue-white ice chunks that dotted the surface.

Miranda had no idea why Jeff had insisted on coming along. He seemed loath to let any of them out of his sight. Maybe he was as concerned about theft as Erwin was, but Miranda suspected he had an ulterior motive.

She was sorely disappointed that the two had come along. She'd wanted it to be just her and Rolf, alone together. There were so many things she wanted to say to him. She wasn't even sure what things exactly, but she knew they had to talk. Their relationship had changed now. At least on her part it had. What they'd shared last night had been far more than sexual...unless he didn't see it that way. Maybe that was why he seemed so distant today. Maybe he didn't want her reading more into it than a simple one-night stand.

At the shore, Rolf tugged the boat up out of the water without aid and then looped the rope around an outcropping of rock. There were no trees to tie to. They were north of the tree line. Nothing much grew here. There were only the craggy, glacier-formed hills to their left and the endless, flat tundra to their right.

Saunders glanced uneasily toward the rocky hills and the crop of dome tents nestled nearby. "I'll remind you again, Miranda, not a word about our mission."

"Don't worry yourself," she snapped. "Rolf and I are going straight to the cave. You two can do what you want." She snatched up the backpack beside her and slung it over her shoulder.

She hiked away, skirting the tents and heading up a sharp incline toward the cave's entrance. She knew Rolf followed, but she was in no state to walk in companionable silence with him just now. She was unsure of his feelings, confused by his apparent hostility toward her and more than a little hurt by it. Erwin's attitude had nettled her still further until now she felt like swearing at someone.

Still, all of her disquiet faded when she stood at the opening in the ice. The crew left behind had widened it, so it was a much simpler matter to step in than before. Even so, her heart quickened its pace and so did her breathing. Her palms, despite a temperature below thirty degrees, began to dampen with sweat inside her heavy-duty gloves.

An archaeologist with claustrophobia was like a pilot with acrophobia, the way Miranda saw it. She clenched her teeth and slipped the pack from her back. She bent over it, unlacing the flap and removing the items they'd need. Two helmets with lamps attached, a length of rope and a pair of carabiner links, to go with the ones on the belts they both wore at their waists, and an extra flashlight just in case. She plopped on her helmet and fastened its chin strap. She slipped the flashlight into one of the deep pockets of her overalls and looped the rope, carabiners attached, over her shoulder. By the time she finished, Rolf was standing behind her, scanning the cave entrance with narrowed eyes.

"What is it? Do you know this place?"

He shrugged. "I am unsure. The ice—"

"The glacier moved in after the shipwreck, Rolf. It might not have looked like this the last time you saw it." She handed him a hard hat and he scowled. "Put it on," she said firmly, "or we don't go in. And be sure and fasten the chin strap, or the entire helmet is useless."

Rolf nodded and obeyed. Miranda reached up to the top of his hat and flicked on the light, then did the same with her own. Drawing a deep breath, she slipped over the lip of ice and jumped lightly to the floor below.

She stepped aside and in a moment Rolf landed beside her. He straightened and turned slowly, the light of his helmet moving over the stalactite-covered ceiling, pausing on the glasslike needles sprouting like vegetation from one of them.

"Helictites," Miranda said softly, some of her irritation with him fading as the familiar thrill of discovery began coursing through her. "They're formed by seeping water. Look." She turned her light on another of the crystalline bushes growing upward from one sloped wall, seemingly in defiance of gravity.

Rolf remained silent, nodding as she spoke, but making no comment. She led him through the passage, reminding herself that she'd been here before and hadn't suffered a single bout of panic. It was not a small, cramped crawl space, but a wide, arching passage, with plenty of room to breathe. She'd be fine.

After entering the massive room, Miranda paused, and pointed to the flat stone table. "That's where we found you."

When Rolf glanced around the room his eyes widened as if in recognition. "This? This is where they put me to rest?" He sounded incredulous.

"Yes. Right there, on that flat stone." She couldn't help but recall her odd reactions to her first glimpse of him. "I stood at this spot, only facing the other way," she told him.

"This is not credible."

Miranda shivered, and prickles ran along the back of her neck as they had once before. "I got this weird feeling all of a sudden, as if someone was standing right behind me. And I turned and saw you lying there." Her voice softened as the memory came flooding back.

"Miranda, are you certain it was this cave—"

"I fell to my knees when I saw you." She took a deep breath and sighed. "It was as if they just turned to water. And I think even then I had the most profound sense of sadness that you were not alive."

Rolf stood perfectly still, his gaze narrowed, raking the cave's interior. "How could they have known?"

"I think I was meant to find you here. I know it isn't scientific or logical, but I honestly believe it. I think that somehow all my father's work was truly just to lead me here, to you, though he never knew it."

At last Rolf drew his gaze from the room around them and met hers. He lifted a hand toward her face. "Miranda, do you mean to say—"

At that moment a violent explosion rocked the ground beneath their feet. It felt like the entire world was quaking and Miranda fell to her knees much as she had the first time she'd set foot in this cave. Fear gripped her with fists of ice as the roar ripped through her eardrums, to be followed by a low, ominous thunder that matched the racing of her heart. Beneath her knees the uneven stone floor clawed at her through the heavy overalls and wool underwear. Her palms vibrated where they were pressed to the ground. Fragments of stone rained down onto her back and the rumble grew louder.

Buried. She was going to be buried alive, here and now. All of a sudden she couldn't catch her breath. She gulped desperately, dragging little but dust into her lungs.

Then strong hands gripped her shoulders and hauled her to her feet. Rolf put his arm around her shoulders and, bending them both low, ran with her. She thought he spoke, but she couldn't hear. She was only aware of her fear, of the grim certainty that she was about to be smothered by the earth that surrounded her, and the knowledge that she didn't want to die so young. Not when she'd just begun to come alive.

Dirt and dust rained so thickly it was impossible to see even with the headlamps still glowing. The showering stones grew steadily larger and she sensed that in seconds the entire cave would fall down upon them. Her panic overcame her and she would have frozen in fear had Rolf not propelled her along at his side. He released her, pushing her down as he shoved with all his might at the stone table

which had once been his bier. She couldn't make sense of
his actions, not until the stone moved. Rolf's face tensed
with the strain, and he bared his teeth as he pushed, and
without thinking at all about it, Miranda rose and pressed
her hands to the stone, as well, shoving with all of her
strength.

It moved a bit farther. Rolf pointed and Miranda obeyed
without question, slipping down into the opening the rock
had concealed. Her fear of this small, dark area was sec-
ondary to the fear of remaining where she was and being
buried.

She felt a stone ledge under her feet, and then she ducked
her head beneath the huge table above. Waiting for Rolf to
join her, she fought a fit of violent shaking that engulfed
her body. She screamed aloud when he disappeared, instead. A moment passed, a moment in which she felt certain
she'd lost him. But then he returned, carrying the length of
rope in one hand. He must have gone to get it from the
floor where she'd fallen with the first jolt. He squeezed
through the small opening to join her.

"Rolf, what—"

"No," he shouted above the roar, swinging one arm out
to snag her around the waist. "Do not move. There is no
floor. I must lower you down." He aimed the beam of his
light downward. She gasped when she saw how near she
stood to the edge of the small protrusion of stone that held
her. He pressed the carabiners linked to the rope into her
hand. The air was thickening with dust and a lot of rubble
was falling on him through the small opening. "Get down,
Miranda. We'll be buried soon."

She snapped the locking carabiner to the link on the belt
at her waist. Rolf didn't anchor his end of the rope. He
only braced himself and held it in his hands. Miranda
trusted him. She pushed off from the side and quickly rap-
pelled down the sheer stone. She tried not to imagine what
kind of debris was pounding Rolf's body from above. She

moved as fast as possible, and the second her feet were on solid ground, she cupped her hands and shouted up at him, "Rolf! Come on, hurry!"

His form came hurtling down from the darkness above. He landed with a terrible impact, tumbling forward and then lying still. He made no move to get up. Miranda rushed forward, falling to her knees beside him, her heart in her throat. She gripped his shoulders and shook him hard. "Rolf, come on. Get up. Get up!"

He opened his eyes. "Can you never stop giving orders, woman?" Slowly he maneuvered himself up onto his knees, a difficult thing to do, she imagined, since her arms were wrapped tightly around his neck as he attempted it.

She pulled back just enough to scan his face by the light of her helmet. "Are you all right? Please tell me you're all right."

"I am, but are you?" His hands cupped her head, molding her hair to it, he held her so tightly.

"Yes. Fine." She hugged him and he cradled her to his chest.

"Thank the gods, Odin and Thor and Tyr for their mercy. I feared they would punish my foolishness by taking you from me, Miranda."

"What—"

"Later. We will speak of these things later. Now we must not." He stood slowly, lifting her with him.

Miranda began to get her bearings and to believe that, perhaps, she wasn't going to die just yet, after all. It was cooler in the cave where the temperature remained steady year round. She put it at twenty degrees Fahrenheit or a little less. Still, with the absence of the cruel Arctic wind, it wasn't the same chilling cold as outside. The stone walls were smooth and black, much like the ones above. They were rough and uneven, with otherworldly columns protruding down from the arching stone above, narrowing at their middles, widening again as they stretched to the floor like sentries standing guard. But there were newer speleo-thems, as well. Unlike the ones at the entrance above, which had been formed long before the glacier had rendered the cave airless, many of these appeared to be in the process of formation. Which meant this was a well-ventilated area…which in turn meant there must be an opening somewhere.

Finally, she thought, her brain seemed to be functioning on all eight cylinders again. "Rolf, how did you know about this place?"

"The better question would be, how did the Skr—the Inuit know?"

She could hear him much more clearly now. Apparently the falling rubble had sealed the hole through which they'd descended, and maybe the avalanche above was nearly over, as well. "Are you telling me you've been here before," she asked. "Before the shipwreck?"

"Yes. Miranda, the secrets of this cave were to fund my village, and then my city. They were to make me a respected leader, or at least a feared one. It was to be my revenge."

She studied him, her mind jumping far ahead of his words. "Go on. Are you saying this is the place…"

"*Já*"

She swallowed hard. "This is where you stashed all the plunder? My God."

"Miranda, the sound I heard before the cave fell in, it was not natural. Not the sound of falling rock or the splitting of ice."

She nodded, recalling the initial roar and the violent shock wave. "I think it might have been some sort of explosive."

"Another of your modern weapons?"

"They can be."

"We were not far from the entrance, Miranda. Someone has decided to kill us both." Rolf touched her face again, then moved his hand to stroke her jawline, then her neck. "I have never been so afraid...afraid you would be hurt or..." He shook his head. "Never have I had such a weakness, Miranda."

Miranda covered his hand with her own, then wished she wasn't wearing gloves. "I would have been killed if you hadn't been here." She swallowed hard and looked around her, her light moving with her head. "Then again, we're not out of here yet."

"Do not be afraid," he assured her. "I will see you to safety, Miranda, do I need dig us out with my hands."

She smiled at him, taking some comfort from his words, but not nearly enough. A shudder went through her. "This was deliberate. I guess Erwin was right."

Rolf tilted his head. "Your Fletcher Travis believes someone may wish to steal not the treasure itself, but the credit for locating it. Does this theory make sense to you?"

Miranda considered for a moment, then sucked in a sharp breath. "If Fletch is right, they'd have to get rid of everyone who knew better. Including Fletch and Erwin."

Rolf nodded. "And who knew precisely when we entered this cave, Miranda?"

"Only Erwin...and Jeff. Jeff!" She bit her lip. "He lost all credibility in the scientific community when he went to work for Cryo-Life. He didn't care then. He only wanted the money they were willing to pay him. But it began to gall him after a while, the lack of respect. If he could claim credit for this find..."

"You'll not prevent me from killing him this time, Miranda." Rolf picked up the rope that lay coiled at his feet. He must have tossed it down just before he'd jumped. He wound it up quickly as Miranda released the carabiner from her belt. He looped it over his shoulder, clasped her hand in his, and started forward.

For some time he didn't speak, only guided her farther along the uneven rocky floor. They were shrouded in absolute darkness. The only areas visible at all were those where the beams of light from their hard hats cut through the pitch-black cave as they moved along. Directly ahead of them she heard the sound of rushing water. She stiffened, the proximity of the fickle sea leaping into her mind, but Rolf inexorably pulled her onward, never slowing his pace.

They rounded a bend, and immediately ahead of them a waterfall tumbled and splashed into a dark frothy pool at their feet. Breathless, Miranda could only stare, awed by the simple beauty of the spectacle. She strained to see through the dark, and thought the pool was actually a stream, which wound and twisted its way down another passage to the left.

Rolf shone his beam downward, then leapt easily over the water to land on the other side. There seemed no obvious reason to be there. He stood with his back to a wall, upon a narrow ridge of black stone, beside the waterfall. Trusting him nonetheless, Miranda leapt across to join him.

She caught her breath as he drew her back until she was pressed flat to the cool stone wall, then slowly he side-stepped and took them right behind the cascade. Miranda watched the curtain of water flowing down in front of her and felt the oddest sensation of having just stepped through the looking glass. Her surprise increased when Rolf seemed to disappear through the wall at his back. Her breath caught in her throat, for his hand still clutched hers and he was pulling her through with him.

It wasn't a wall, after all, but a hidden fissure within the wall. Beyond it, Miranda thought, was the treasure of Ali Baba. As Rolf moved the beam of light around the chamber she saw the remains of what were once trunks and chests. The iron bands on most had rusted to nothing, with bits and pieces here and there still showing their original shape. The wood, too, had rotted, leaving little but black piles of mulch where it had been. Amid these remains were heaps of tarnished silver, piles of gold, relics of every imaginable

kind. There were chalices and goblets, necklaces and jeweled bracelets, headdresses with— Miranda moved closer,
leaning over one piece in question —yes, diamonds, rubies,
sapphires. Daggers with jeweled hilts and mounds of ancient coins littered the floor. Brooches of gold, silver
combs, strands of pearls and golden chains. Silver bowls,
rings, belt buckles, golden plates and bronze sculptures.
And those were only the few things she could identify from
the light of the beam. There were many more, oh, so many
more. The piles of treasure, their chests long gone, lined
the entire chamber.

She was nearly speechless with wonder. To a person in
her profession, this was a dream come true. She glanced at
Rolf, suddenly aware that, from his point of view, this all
belonged to him. "If we tell the authorities, they'll take
this all away from you, Rolf. This will be considered the
property of the government of Canada. Beaumont University might get to study it for a time, but then it would have
to be returned. Do you understand that?"

"You speak as if there is another choice," he said in a
low, steady voice.

She blinked. "Well, I suppose you could try to smuggle
some pieces out of the country. Sell them to an unscrupu-
lous dealer or collector somewhere. Believe me, just a few
of these treasures would give you all the money you could
hope to spend in a lifetime."

"And you would not reveal my actions?"

She answered thoughtfully. "No. Of course I wouldn't.
It's just that we can't tell anyone your role in this discovery
without admitting who you are, and we can't do that."

He searched her face, seemingly trying to see through to
her soul. "And if it were learned that you helped me in
this way?"

She averted her gaze quickly. "It...wouldn't be good."

"I believe, Miranda, that your...career...would be at an

end. Would it not?'' She shrugged. ''And yet, you would still allow me to take what I wanted?''

''It's yours,'' she said quickly, though she knew it wasn't true.

He shook his head slowly. ''*Nei*. It never was.'' She glanced up at his odd words, but he showed no inclination to speak any further on that subject. ''Morsi had no idea what he gave up by sealing us in here.''

''No. But I guess he must have decided he had to get rid of us before we announced finding the ship,'' Miranda said as her mind began working to find a way out of their predicament.

''The Inuit must have seen my men and me as we left this place that first time. They returned my body here, since it was the only place they connected with me.''

''Why do you assume they saw you leaving, and not entering?''

''Entering, we carried the chests. Had they seen them, no doubt they'd have searched until they found them.''

She swallowed hard before asking the next question. ''Is there a-another way out?''

He met her gaze squarely, his eyes glittering in the darkness. ''There once was.'' He turned his head so that the beam of light danced on the opposite wall, then slid lower.

Miranda gasped when she saw the tiny tunnel, black and small, only large enough to crawl through on hands and knees. Her hands began to shake and she averted her gaze. Rolf gripped her trembling hand and pulled her toward the little hole.

She stiffened, planting her feet as a full blown panic attack swept over her like a hurricane. ''I can't go through that.''

''Miranda, there is no other—''

''I can't!'' Already her lungs felt as if they were constricting. ''I'd rather stay here.''

His hands closed on her shoulders. "Miranda, if you stay, you will die."

Faster and faster came her breaths. Yet she wasn't inhaling deeply enough to sustain her. Her heart raced. She could feel the pulse pounding in her temples. "I...can't. I can't, Rolf. Please...you go. Just leave me. I can't...."

"Why?"

His voice didn't just ask for an answer. It demanded. She pressed her palms to either side of her head and spun away from him, removing her hard hat as if that would ease her breathing. *I'm not going in there. I'm not. I won't do it and nothing he says or does can make me do it.*

Chapter 15

"Why, Miranda?" he repeated, more gently this time. "Where does this fear come from?"

She shook her head. It wasn't as if she could talk about it, especially not to him. The question itself was eliciting the memories, though she fought to block them out. "We were in his car when…" she heard herself blurt. She forced herself to continue. "We—we were in his car when I told him I couldn't marry him. That damned tiny car."

"Morsi," Rolf uttered in a low voice.

She moved on shaking legs toward a stone outcropping, and sank onto it. She stared straight ahead into the dark, the images of that long-ago night flashing inside her mind. Why did she have to recall it all so vividly? Why now? "He asked me why. I told him. That was my mistake. I shouldn't have told him."

She heard Rolf moving nearer. He stood behind her and his hands closed over her shoulders. "You told him his touch left you unmoved."

She swallowed hard and lowered her head. Her eyes

closed tightly. "He was angry." She recalled his expression, illuminated only by the car's dashboard lights when she'd admitted she'd been faking her response to him from the start. He'd looked murderous. He'd *been* murderous. "And then he stopped the car."

"Miranda—"

"And…and he locked the doors," she whispered, but she was barely audible. Her throat convulsed painfully. Forcing the words out hurt her. "And then…he hit me." Her fists clenched until her nails nearly pricked her palms right through the gloves. If she hadn't been wearing them, she would have drawn blood. "I couldn't get away from him. The front seat under me, the locked door at my back, my shoulders jammed between the dashboard and the back of the seat. Him on top of me, raping me. I couldn't move. I couldn't breathe." As she spoke her breathing began to quicken again with the memory. "I honestly thought he was going to kill me."

She wrapped her arms around herself and bowed nearly double. It seemed to Rolf as if she was trying to protect herself from the memory.

He would kill Jeff Morsi. The dog would die slowly and painfully. Rolf knew that beyond any doubt. He wished in vain he had not left his sword behind at Miranda's home. But that would come later. For now, he had to bring Miranda into the present once more. He had to make her see that the danger was past. His arms went around her shuddering body and he pulled her into his lap as he sat on the cool stone floor in front of her. He held her hard, to be sure she knew he was there.

"I was so afraid, Rolf. So afraid and repulsed, and so ashamed."

"The shame belongs to him, Miranda. Not you."

"No. I shouldn't have let it happen. I should have tried harder to stop him, fight him. But he hurt me. God, how he hurt me. When it was over, I was sick. I couldn't stop throwing up. I could barely walk." She sobbed in his arms, and Rolf held her more tightly.

"Miranda, I understand now why you questioned me. Will you listen while I give you the answers you sought?"

She sniffed and nodded, her head still resting weakly against his chest.

"I was a boy of ten when a neighboring village was besieged by an enemy of the local Jarl. The sister of my mother, a woman still in the prime of her beauty and only recently wed, was raped by the marauders. Her husband, my uncle, was murdered before her eyes. She came to us, no longer the happy, lovely woman I knew, but a hollow-eyed ghost. All of my mother's comforting did little good. She took her own life less than a week later."

She shuddered in his arms. "Why do men do it?"

"No *man* takes a woman by force. Only a cowardly dog would act in such a way. This lesson I learned at a youthful age, and never did I forget. Later, in my rage, I put aside many of my father's words, but the lesson of my aunt Helga I remembered always. I have never forced myself on a woman, Miranda. I am sorry I did not assure you of that sooner."

She swallowed hard. "Why didn't you?"

He thought her shaking was subsiding a bit. He held her harder. "Because it wounded my pride to be asked to defend myself against such a charge. Perhaps I wished you to believe in me without my explanations."

Her head lifted, and in the glow of the light beams her tears glittered like diamonds. "I did, you know," she whispered. "If I hadn't, I never would've been able to let you make love to me."

"I ask too much of you, Miranda, to believe in my innocence when I refuse to explain. I was enraged after my exile. My king and my friend, Knut the Great, turned his back on me. My country banished me. I felt I had no more to lose. I was determined to build a great city to show them all my worth. For that, I needed gold and silver, iron and steel. So I put aside the ways of my father. I raided every coastal village I came upon. Yet my men knew that rape and murder were forbidden on pain of death. The only blood to stain our swords was the blood of those foolish enough to defy us. For those few brave men, Valhalla awaited.'' He paused to allow her time to consider. ''I was not guilty of the crime for which I was banished.''

''I know that,'' she said.

He lowered his head and pressed his lips into her hair. ''Do you also know that I would die before I would let harm come to you, Miranda? Do you know that I would use my sword to remove the fingers from my hands before I would cause you pain?''

She lifted her head and stared into his eyes, shadowed now in the dim light. ''Do you mean that?''

''I can prove it to you, lady. For do you choose to remain here, I will remain, as well. I will die at your side, rather than take the path to escape and leave you behind.''

She shook her head and he thought her eyes widened. ''I can't let you do that.''

''Nor can you stop me.''

She drew a long, slow breath and squared her shoulders. ''How long is the passage?''

''Not long. But I must warn you it becomes smaller before it grows larger again.''

She closed her eyes tightly and he saw her catch her lower lip in her teeth.

Stroking her silken cheek, he whispered, ''Nothing will hurt you, Miranda. I will be close to you all the time.''

''I know.''

''Are you ready, then?''

She nodded, but he felt her body trembling. The merciful thing to do, he thought, would be to knock her unconscious and drag her to safety before she awoke. The very thought of raising a hand to Miranda caused Rolf's stomach to heave. He couldn't do it. Did her life depend upon it, he could not harm her deliberately.

Questions raced in his mind, but he held them back. Now was not the time to ask her the things he longed to know. Why, for instance, she had not taken steps to see that Morsi was punished for his acts? Surely her society had laws providing for the protection of its women. He simply could not fathom the reasons a woman like Miranda, a woman intelligent, capable and respected by all who knew her, would allow herself to be wronged in such a way without seeking retribution. It baffled him. It seemed so foreign to her character.

Rather than question her in her agitated state, he rose, setting her easily on her feet. He retrieved her helmet from the floor and placed it upon her head, fastening the chin strap securely. Taking a firm hold on her hand, he drew her to the small oval opening in the stone wall. He released her hand and slipped his legs into the tunnel. Once inside, he rolled over onto hands and knees. Facing her, he extended a hand. When she took it, he moved farther back into the darkness. The cold stone touched his sides. Only inches of space separated him from the stone above. "Come, Miranda. Come to me now."

He heard her movements, and saw the approach of her light. Her grip on his hand tightened as she crawled toward him. "Look only at me," he instructed. "Nothing else." She said nothing, but he heard the quickened pace of her breathing. He touched her face. "Come with me, Miranda. It will be over within a few moments, I promise you." Awkwardly he crawled backward, keeping his senses attuned to her, feeling the heat of her body, hearing the brush of her knees over the stone as she crawled toward him. He moved slowly enough so she was never beyond his reach.

The tunnel sloped downward, then leveled off. The passage narrowed until Rolf had to stretch his legs behind him and push himself backward lying flat on the stone. Miranda could still crawl, but he knew the ceiling must be pressing down on her back, the walls against her sides when she moved slightly off center. Her breathing became harsher and she stopped moving. Panting, she fought to speak. "I…can't. I can't go—"

Rolf reached out to cup her face in his hands. He brought his head close to hers, touched her lips with his. "No harm will come to you, Miranda. Nothing here can hurt you. There is only you and me. Nothing else."

"I—" she fought for air "—I want to go back!" He heard the tears in her voice, the overwhelming fear.

"It is farther back than it is to the outside now, Miranda. Trust in me, if you can. Here. Hold my hand." He gripped her hand in his again and pushed himself backward with the other. Her hand felt as cold as the stone, even through the glove. It trembled violently, but she came with him all the same. He thought there could be no measure of the courage it took for her to forge ahead when she was nearly paralyzed with fear. He wished for greater strength, for unnatural speed, as he kept pushing himself backward. He spoke to her constantly as they struggled on.

Finally the tunnel widened again. A few yards more and its breadth was enough to accommodate them both, side by side. Rolf turned himself around and drew her up beside him. He was able to get up on his hands and knees again. "It is not much farther," he assured her. He wondered that she didn't faint with the rapid pattern of her breathing. He felt icy moisture dotting her face when he touched it again, and wished he knew a way to ease her torment.

At last they rounded the final bend in the passage. His light beam found the half circle of the tunnel entrance and then the snow and ice beyond. He heard her gasp deeply, and her pace increased. Rolf stayed at her side until they crawled out into the biting wind.

He stood then and helped Miranda to her feet. Instead of

standing on her own, she collapsed against him without warning. His arms encircled her to hold her upright. The hammering of her heart alarmed him. He flicked the button to extinguish his light, then hers. Easily he scooped her up and began trudging down a snowy slope toward the village of tents and scientists that seemed so out of place in this barren land.

The place was oddly silent and seemingly abandoned. Rolf crouched low to enter the first tent he came to, and once inside, he lowered Miranda to the folding cot near the back. The tent was warm, a little heating device eliminating the chill. He tugged a blanket over her and knelt beside her, searching her face in the light of a lantern someone had left ablaze. "Are you all right, lady?"

She nodded, pressing a hand to her chest and forcibly, he thought, regulating her breaths. "I'm sorry, I'm such a coward."

"No, Miranda. You have the courage of a warrior. I've known few men in my life who could face such a powerful fear and conquer it."

"I couldn't have…if you hadn't been there. You saved my life, Rolf."

"If I did, then it is no more than you did for me." He watched her face for a long moment, feeling an unnatural tightness in his chest. He hadn't realized the might of the feelings for this woman until tonight. When he recalled his thought to curb his fondness for her, to avoid the pain she would cause him in the end, he nearly laughed at his own ignorance. It was too late for him to hope for mercy. It would kill him when she told him to go, when she continued with her life without him.

Miranda sat up slowly, one hand pressed to her forehead. "Rolf, we have to stop Jeff. Erwin and Fletch are both in danger now."

"I will go. You remain here, warm and dry. Rest here. Where are the others you spoke of?"

"Probably heard the explosion and are all at the original entrance trying to determine the cause." She threw back the cover. "I'm not staying here. We have to go. Quickly, Rolf. I pray we're not already too late." She got to her feet and came toward him. "My God, if I'd come forward about what he did to me two years ago, Jeff might be in jail right now. If anything happens to the others…"

Rolf's questions leapt to mind again. "Why did you not, Miranda?"

She shook her head, her eyes focused on the floor. "I was afraid."

"Of Morsi?"

"Yes, and of the stigma that would be attached to my name. No matter how much evidence there is in a rape, Rolf, there are always those who refuse to believe the victim, or who somehow find a way to claim it was her fault. I didn't think I could bear that." She bit her lip. "I was wrong. But I kept silent. He hadn't hit me in the face, and the other bruises were easy to hide." She looked up at him quickly. "I can't back down in fear of him this time, Rolf. I have to come with you."

"Please, Miranda, stay. I will not allow you to put yourself at risk again."

She lifted one hand to his face. "I'm going with you. I'm afraid—" She broke off, and shook her head.

"Afraid of what?" he prompted.

She lifted her gaze to his. "Afraid that if I let you go, I'll lose you. That's not something I can allow to happen."

He stared at her concerned face, trying hard to see the meaning behind her words, but failing. She couldn't mean that she had come to care for him. He knew he was unworthy of such a magnificent woman. Before he could argue with her further, she slipped past him out of the tent, and trudged determinedly over the frozen ground toward the sea. "Fletch is alone on that ship, and God knows where Jeff is."

Rolf caught up with her only as she was climbing into a small and battered-looking metal canoe. "They've got to have already gone back to the *Mermaid*," she said breathlessly. "The boat is gone." He knew her fondness for Erwin Saunders, and her greater love for Fletcher Travis. He felt a sharp concern of his own for Travis, for he'd grown to like and respect the man.

Rolf shoved the small craft into the sea. He stepped into it, sitting quickly as it wobbled. Miranda handed him a short, stubby paddle. She sat with her back to him holding a similar one. "Like this," she told him, lifting the paddle to demonstrate the proper grip. "You paddle on that side, and I on this. Ready?"

Rolf dipped his paddle as she did hers and pushed the water away behind them. He had to adjust his stroke right away, for his was so much more powerful than hers that the craft began to veer to the right. He soon mastered the rhythm. The sleek little craft knifed quickly through the mercifully calm sea. Soon they bumped against the hull of the *Mermaid*.

Rolf had no idea what Jeff Morsi's reaction would be to see them both alive when, no doubt, he'd thought them dead and buried. He only knew that he would not allow the dog to harm Miranda, or to draw another breath now that he knew how much harm he'd already done.

The rope ladder still hung over the side of the *Mermaid*. Rolf easily scaled it, then stood watch as Miranda climbed up to join him on the deck. He held her waist in his large hands as she clambered aboard. He tied no line to keep the little craft from drifting. Better to let it go and not announce their presence, Miranda guessed.

Miranda's heart leapt into her throat when she heard footsteps. Rolf's arm came around her fast and sure and he drew her into the shadows. The steps passed. Rolf held on to her hand, and together they moved down the shallow stairs to the area housing the cabins.

Rolf moved steadily, silently, in the direction of Jeff's cabin. Miranda tried to swallow her fear. Rolf stopped outside the door. He pressed her back against the wall and signaled her to stay there. Then he slammed open the door and leapt inside with murder in his eyes.

Miranda braced herself. Nothing happened. Only silence came from the room, and she turned, unable to stay still another second, and went inside. Jeff Morsi's body lay crumpled on the floor, a neat round bullet hole between his eyes. She screamed. She couldn't help it. She turned into Rolf's ready embrace and sobbed uncontrollably.

"What the hell—"

At the sound of Erwin Saunders's voice, Miranda tugged free of Rolf's grip. Relief washed over her when she saw him. "Thank God," she breathed, moving forward automatically to embrace him. "Thank God you're all right," she sobbed. "We were afraid Jeff had killed you."

"Jeff had—" Saunders tensed and held her away from him, searching her face. His hard expression eased at once, and he hugged her once again. "And I was certain he'd killed you, Miranda. I tried to go for help, but he forced me back here at gunpoint."

She sniffed, and wiped her tears away with a finger. "He wanted the credit for everything," she concluded. "Oh, Erwin, what happened here?"

"There, there, child. Calm yourself. Everything is fine now. Come, both of you. To your cabin. I'll fix you a warm drink and explain everything. The authorities have already been notified. They're on the way."

She walked beside Rolf, his arm firmly around her. In her cabin, she slipped out of her overalls and damp clothing, and donned fresh woolen underwear, a heavy sweater, sturdy denim jeans and a warm coat. Rolf changed, as well, and by the time they'd both finished, Saunders had returned with mugs of hot buttered rum for each of them.

Miranda sipped hers gratefully, feeling its warmth sing through her veins. Rolf's drink was half-gone with his first swallow. Then he faced Saunders. "How did Morsi expect to achieve this without help, Saunders?"

Saunders waved them both into seats, while he continued standing, watching them, his face seemingly concerned. "He had help. I've learned of the entire plot. It's all very involved."

Miranda sipped her drink again. Rolf downed his. "Who killed him?" Rolf asked.

"His partner. Guess the selfish bastard wanted all the credit for himself." He stroked his beard, his gaze glued to Rolf's face.

"Who?" Rolf pressed a hand to his forehead, blinked a few times, and shook his head as if to clear it.

"Would you believe...Fletcher Travis?"

"*Nei.*" Rolf began to stand. As he did, Miranda saw two of him all at once, and her head was swimming. Odd. Probably shock.

"Not Fletch," she mumbled, her tongue feeling thick and awkward.

"No, not Fletch," Saunders agreed. "Did I tell you about his accident? He took a blow to the head and fell overboard a little while ago. Damn shame he was so clumsy."

"No!" Miranda leapt to her feet, and instantly sagged to her knees.

Rolf leaned over to help her, but sank instead to the floor beside her. He turned an angry glare on Saunders. "You...poisoned the...drinks."

"No, not quite, but close enough. You might have also guessed the identity of Morsi's partner by now, or I should say, ex-partner." He stepped back as Rolf's arm swung out toward him. He reached for the door, stepped through it.

"Morsi wouldn't admit to stealing the Ice Man, Miranda, so I can only assume you did it. Care to tell me where it's hidden while you still can?" She didn't answer. "Ah, well, no matter. I'll find it. Have a nice nap, you two. I'll be taking steps quite soon to insure it is a permanent one."

Miranda saw Rolf's head fall forward, his eyes droop closed, just before her mind went blank and her body limp.

Chapter 16

When she opened her eyes, Miranda knew something was different. She felt the cool air and the constant spray of water on her skin. She felt the sun's heat gradually warming her chilled flesh.

She sat up suddenly, rocking the small boat. She gripped its sides and looked around her, eyes wide. "Oh, my God," she whispered hoarsely.

Everywhere, in any direction she looked—water. Deep, dark blue, ice-cold water. Its surface was a study in ripples and lines, and gentle, ever-moving swells lifted and lapped at the small craft. Far, far away, the brilliant orange ball of fire seemed to rest on the water's surface. There was nothing else in sight. No land, no ice. She didn't even see a seabird circling in the distance. She had time to be grateful for the overcoats they still wore before panic took root, colder than the sea that surrounded her.

A low groan brought her head around. Rolf stirred, but didn't open his eyes. He lay slumped in the rear of the boat, near the motor, his head cocked at an impossible angle, one arm bent beneath him. Carefully, so as not to tilt the little boat, she crawled to him, gripped his shoulders and attempted to make him more comfortable. When she tugged his arm out from under him, he grunted. It must have hurt. His eyes flew open and slowly he seemed to focus, first on her, then on the small boat and the limitless sea surrounding them.

He sat up slowly, his gaze returning to Miranda. He rubbed his left temple with his fingertips. "He put something into the drinks," he said finally. "A sleeping powder." Miranda shook her head in denial as the truth hit home. "It was not Morsi alone who tried to kill us, Miranda." Rolf shifted, lifting himself onto the soft padded seat in the stern. "It was Erwin Saunders, as well."

Again she shook her head. "But why? He was my friend, my father's friend—"

"*Nei.* He is a man with much greed and a great hunger for glory. He wished to retain all credit for the discovery of the *drakkar.* And perhaps he meant to find the treasure, as well, to take a goodly share of it for himself. You yourself told me what a simple matter it would be to sell a few pieces, and acquire more wealth than one could spend in a lifetime." As she desperately sought for another explanation, he touched her face. "Travis said it would have been the greatest achievement in your father's career, or in yours. He said you would be in such great demand by universities, you would be able to name your own price."

She nodded, and studied his face. "I just can't believe money and acclaim would be so important to him that he would try to kill—" She stopped short and glanced out to sea once more. "Is he going to succeed this time?"

Rolf laughed. It began as a low rumble deep in his chest and gained momentum until he fairly bellowed. Finally he wrapped his arms around her and hugged her hard. "My sweet lady, your friend picked a poor method to execute the Plague of the North."

He turned toward the stern again, touched the motor. "No doubt this contraption was the first thing to be disabled." To give proof to his theory, he attempted several times to start the thing, but found it uncooperative. He then found the bolts that held it in place and twisted them free with his fingers. Gently he eased the motor up and, with a shove, tossed it into the freezing waves where it disappeared.

Miranda choked back a sob, but too late not to have him notice the small sound. He turned, frowning at the tears that shimmered in her eyes. He eased her up onto the seat at the bow and knelt beside her. "No tears, Miranda. Not only do they cause me unspeakable pain, but they rob you of precious water. You need to conserve what you have in your body." He put his hand on hers. "Have you so little faith in me?"

She sniffed and blinked away her tears. "It hurts me to be so betrayed by someone I once cared for. That's why I was crying."

He nodded. "I know that pain, lady. I've had much experience in that pain." He was silent for a long moment. Then he took the seat beside her, one hand gripping hers tightly. "But he never truly felt anything for you, you know. Or for your father."

"No. He must not have."

"He was pretending all along, even earlier, when he funded the expedition to find me."

"He must have been laughing at us then. He thought it was all madness. But when we found you, he couldn't wait to cash in. I wonder how much of Cryo-Life's backing went into the budget, and how much went into Erwin's pockets."

"He used your father, Miranda. He used you."

She felt her spine grow tense. "He caused Russell's heart attack. He broke in that night, searching for the true journal, the one we found in the computer."

"No doubt." Rolf studied her face as Miranda felt her

heart begin to pound, pumping the blood that no doubt colored her cheeks right now. Anger burned a hot path through her veins. Her hands clenched with it. "Although I am sure he didn't intend for your father to die," Rolf added.

"He might as well have. He killed my father and now he's trying to kill us. Damn him, Rolf. Damn him, he'll pay for this!"

When she turned toward him he was smiling very slightly. "Much better. Your eyes glitter like silver when you are angry, Miranda. I much prefer silver to the diamonds in your eyes when you cry."

Her anger was unabated but she filled with warmth toward him. "I think I know how you must have felt after your exile. I don't know what stings more than betrayal. Especially when the traitor is someone you loved."

"In my case, it was little more than a young man's lust. At the time, though, it was the nearest thing to love I had known." He shook his head. "There is no excuse for what I did. Since the object of my wrath was not available, I sought my vengeance upon the innocent coastal villages of Europe."

"I feel angry enough to raid a village or two myself at the moment."

He chuckled, obviously amused at the image. Then he looked around. "We are drifting at the whim of the currents. Not a safe prospect. We need power, and direction." He grabbed one of the two oars from under the seat. "Behold, a mast." He dragged out the other oar and then set them both down beside him, and rummaged beneath the seats for more tools. He emerged at last with a length of rope and a first-aid kit. He tossed the latter to her. "See if there is anything of use in this box." Then, with the oars crossing over one another in his lap, he began wrapping the rope around them in an X pattern.

He took his time and worked carefully, sometimes unwrapping and rewrapping when he felt it hadn't gone just right. "I will need your shirt. You can keep the coat, but your shirt and mine will be our sail."

Miranda caught her breath. He was truly amazing, her Viking. "You won't need the shirts, Rolf. You can use this." She held up the folded square of impossibly shiny material. At Rolf's frown, she explained. "It's supposed to be very warm. You wrap it around you in case of emergency. It's a sort of blanket." As she spoke she unfolded it, but clutched it to her chest when the wind threatened to rip it from her hands.

Rolf nodded in approval. "Very good, Miranda. Have you any ideas for a rudder?" As he spoke, he painstakingly tied the corners of the blanket to the crosspiece and the main mast. This finished, he laid the newly formed sail to rest, instructing Miranda to hold it lest the wind blow it away.

She watched in wonder as Rolf tore the cushions from the rear seat and pulled a small dagger from his boot. Slowly, steadily, he chipped away at the wooden board. It took the better part of an hour for him to carve a small jagged hole in the seat. He thrust the bottom of the oar-mast into this, tested its stability, and added two lengths of rope to anchor it in place.

No sooner had he raised the sail than Miranda felt the wind pushing them rapidly through the water. She felt the thrill of success sing through her veins, but not for long. Only a moment after she squinted directly into the rising sun, she caught her breath. "Rolf, we're heading east. Shouldn't we be going the other way?"

"You'd have made a fine oarsman, woman." He hurriedly disconnected the rope anchoring one side of the sail. Then he slowly turned the sail until it angled to one side. When the boat rocked dangerously, the wind pushing it sideways, he pushed the outermost edges of the sail closer together, until the thing was pointed, rather similar to the

triangle-shaped sails of today's sailboats. Their direction
changed gradually, until they moved away from the sun.
Rolf anchored the sail and relaxed for a moment. "We
travel west by southwest," he told her. "And we still need
a rudder."

Miranda dumped the contents from the first-aid box.
"This is plastic. You could cut it to the right shape with
your knife."

Rolf took the box from her hands, turned it over slowly.
He nodded. "Yes, it might work. He retrieved the dagger
and went to work once more, stopping periodically to leap
to his feet and readjust the sail. Miranda realized it would
be frightfully easy to tip over, especially sailing against the
wind as they were, and having to cut the boat in and out
of it.

Yet she wasn't afraid. Instead she felt an odd excitement
stirring within her. She silently thrilled with each demon-
stration of Rolf's skill and her blood churned with the adventure of it all. The challenge.

All day they skimmed over the waves. Rolf used the
position of the sun to gauge them, sailing toward it rather
than away once it passed its zenith. Rolf sat on the floor
of the boat, behind the sail, so he could maneuver the sail
and the rudder simultaneously. They spoke little.

Miranda was cold and her head ached with the afteref-
fects of whatever Erwin Saunders had drugged them with.
She was hungry and before the day waned, terribly thirsty.
She spoke of none of this, though, since she knew Rolf
must be feeling the same things she was. She racked her
brain to think of a way she could boil the water and capture
the purified steam.

They sailed past huge icebergs, and once Miranda spotted the dorsal fin of what she swore was a whale, far off
in the distance. The day seemed to last forever, but finally,
after what must have been eighteen hours, the sun dipped
below the horizon. Her eyes widened. "Rolf—"

"*Já,* we have moved to the south. The current pulls us rapidly southward. We will find the warmth as well as the shore, Miranda. I'll not have you dying of the cold." As the sun sank just out of sight, Rolf lowered the sail, and dropped the anchor over the side. He came to the fore where she huddled in her coat, and sat down beside her.

"Are we stopping for the night?"

"No. Only until the stars appear to guide us. The anchor should keep us from drifting too far, though it will not hold us steady. At the moment we are in a southwesterly bound current, so if we drift, we drift in the right direction."

She snuggled closer. "Put your arms around me, Rolf. Hold me."

He did, and she immediately felt warmer. "Are you afraid, Miranda?"

"No. Strange, isn't it? But I'm not. Aside from a few minor discomforts, I'm enjoying this."

"You are a woman of odd tastes. You enjoy being cold, hungry, thirsty?"

"I enjoy facing insurmountable odds and beating them, although today you've done most of the beating." She shifted her position so she could look up into his face. She ran a hand over his stubble-coated cheeks and chin. "Ahh, your beard is coming back. Soon you'll look like you did when I first saw you."

"You change the subject. You wish to take part in beating these odds you speak of?"

She thought about it a moment. "Yes. Ever since you convinced me to crawl through that mouse hole I've begun to feel differently. Not like myself. More...I don't know...confident, stronger. You know?"

"When once a man conquers his strongest foe and yearns to repeat the battle, this is the mark of a true hero." He looked at her intently. "It was one of my father's favorite proverbs. The fear of that tunnel was your strongest foe, my lady heroine, and now you are eager to conquer all others. I think you like adventure."

She shrugged. "Maybe I do."

"Then you will learn to man the sail and the rudder, and give my tired arms some time to rest."

She tensed in his embrace. "I'd better not. I might get us both killed."

"It isn't so bad. I've died before, remember?" At her look of absolute shock, he smiled, his amused face clearly visible in the pale sub-Arctic night. There would only be a very short period of real darkness. "I was kidding, as you say, Miranda. You have not enough faith in your own abilities. You are a strong, intelligent woman, with more courage than some warriors I have known. You will manage."

She did. He'd known she would. Rolf sat behind her, his arms around her, guiding her hands as she got a feel for the wind in the sail and the rush of the sea on the handmade rudder. He pointed out the stars they would follow, and told her their names in his native tongue.

She was nervous at first, but as she relaxed the knack of handling the boat came to her, as he had sensed it would. "Feel the wind caress the sail, Miranda? There, that gentle change, feel it?" She nodded and easily adjusted the sail to accommodate the shift in the wind.

"This is incredible," she whispered. Her hood blew back and her hair whipped around Rolf's neck. He took his hands away from hers to replace it but she put a hand on his arm. "No, leave it. I want to feel the wind."

He looked into her eyes with understanding. Had he not stood upon the deck amid raging storms simply to feel the power? Instead of replacing his hands on hers, he lowered them, encircling her narrow waist. She was doing well, sensing instinctively what was needed and when. Rolf would know if she made a mistake and he would right it before any harm was done. For now, he'd let her maneuver the boat in the gentle wind and easy current. He leaned over and whispered in her ear, "You are not *in* the boat Miranda, you *are* the boat. You are one with the wind and the water and the wood. You see?"

She nodded. "Yes. And with you."

Rolf blinked in astonishment, but realized at once she was right. He was feeling it—too, this union of spirits. The sense of uniting with nature was a familiar one to him. That of uniting with another soul was foreign, and for a second it shook him. Then he thought it over more carefully and he knew that was exactly what he'd felt when he'd made love to her. Union. He hadn't been inside her; he'd been a part of her. They'd been as one mind, one body. He'd sensed her pleasure, her needs, much as she'd seemed to sense his. It had been beyond any experience he'd had in lovemaking, and he knew it had been the same for her, as well. Just like sailing. Just like becoming one with the sea and the wind and the ship. Blessed union. Consummate understanding. He hadn't believed such a thing was possible between two human souls.

His hands rose higher, and he slipped them beneath her coat and then her blouse, cupping her breasts, squeezing them, stilling when her tender nipples blossomed to his touch. They pressed to his fingertips as if pleading for attention and he gave it without hesitation. He bent his head to nuzzle her neck with his lips.

"Your hands are cold," she whispered, tilting her head backward to ease the way for his mouth.

"You wish me to stop?"

"Never."

He angled his head around farther, so he could taste her lips. They were dry, but he moistened them for her. The sweetness they protected was as succulent as ever and he drank deeply of her for a long time. "I want you very badly, Miranda."

"But..." She struggled for words against her rapid breathing. "The sail..."

"Trust me," he muttered, nibbling her earlobe like an exotic fruit. He moved his hands to the snap of her jeans, and in a moment he was shoving them down over her hips, underwear and all. He ran his palms over the warm, bare curve of her buttocks, then threaded his fingers forward, finding her hot center already open and moist.

She made a sound deep in her throat when he probed her. "Do not close your mind, Miranda. Keep it open to everything. Not just me, but the sea and the wind, as well. Feel it all." She nodded, and Rolf removed one of his hands so he could free himself of the constraints of denim and zipper. He throbbed for her, and in a moment he lifted her slightly and lowered her over him. He knelt, sitting back on his heels, her lovely rounded buttocks pressed tight to his lap, her sweet, narrow passage tight around him. Her thighs parted and her knees supported most of her weight, a situation Rolf wished to remedy. He did, slipping his hands beneath her thighs and lifting her.

Immediately her weight shifted. He lifted his hips until her entire body was supported only by his manhood. He gripped her waist and pulled her down harder, feeling himself penetrate more deeply inside her. When she would have fallen forward, he lifted his hands, holding her and cupping her breasts at the same time. He moved his hips rapidly, plunging into her again and again.

At the first hint of his growing aggression, she stiffened and lifted her body as if to move away from the intruding shaft of heat that invaded her. But he held her to him with gentle firmness and plunged as deeply as was possible. "Surrender, Miranda," he growled deep in his throat. "Feel." Again he thrusted himself into her. "Tell me, is it pain you feel, or pleasure?"

Breathing ragged, she replied, "It's just...so tight, and...and so deep."

Her words drove him to the brink of madness, and he quickened the pace of his thrusts. He was not surprised when she joined in his efforts to increase the depth to which he could caress her, slamming her body harder and harder down onto him. When she neared release, he knew. He felt the way her body tightened around him, the sudden rush of her honeyed fluids coating him, the fit of trembling that engulfed her. He held her harder, giving himself over to every sensation. To the rocking of the boat beneath them, to the breeze caressing their bodies.

She cried out as her body began to convulse around him in a rhythmic massage. Rolf exploded into a million searing bits of sensation as he poured his essence into her. He remained within her for a long time as the desperate throbbing eased in both of them, slowed, and cooled. Finally he eased her from his lap and righted her denims before his own. As soon as he settled back once more, she snuggled into his embrace, her body nestled between his legs, her back pressed to his chest. Her head came to rest just beneath his chin and he bent his own to kiss her hair.

She tilted her head up a little to see him. "I'm in love with you, Rolf."

He blinked rapidly. In love with him. He knew the significance of her declaration, yet he doubted the truth of her words. "You believe there is a chance we will not survive this voyage, Miranda, so you say things you would not say otherwise."

She shook her head, but he only smiled softly and continued. "It flatters me that you might think yourself in love with me, but we both know it is only the situation. You will soon be the most respected, sought-after scientist in your field. You will have achieved the goal you have worked your entire life to reach. There is no room in your life for a barbarian from the past."

She opened her mouth to speak, then bit her lip. Her head moved very slightly from side to side. "You're wrong, but I can see I won't convince you of it with mere words. I suppose it can wait.''

The wind shifted abruptly, and Miranda sat up fast, moving the sail to the right and reaching for the rudder almost from instinct. Truly Rolf could almost believe they were one. A shame that she would never be able to devote herself to him above her career, her science. For only that would do. He couldn't have her if she placed more import upon the work than upon the two of them together. He felt too strongly for her to settle for that. And anything else, he knew, was not possible.

For now, though, he would revel in her nearness, her closeness to him, body and soul. He held her to his chest, breathed her scent, and gazed upward into the growing darkness. Truly he felt content here with her like this, he felt. As if, after a very long voyage, one fraught with confusion and loss, he'd come home to her welcoming embrace.

He almost wished to prolong their voyage together, for when it ended, so would this closeness between them. At the thought of that, a warm tear escaped from Rolf's eye and rolled in silence down his face.

Chapter 17

Miranda slept, though she wasn't sure exactly when. As she slowly opened her eyes, a cold dawn greeted her and the sea rolled less gently than it had before. Frigid waves lapped at the sides of the small boat and rocked it frighteningly. Rolf manned the crude sail with expert hands, but his face seemed drawn and tired.

She'd told him she loved him last night. She recalled his tender caresses, his soft-spoken Norse words, his fevered lovemaking. He hadn't said he returned her feelings. Far from it. He'd argued that she would have no room in her life for him. He was wrong.

She straightened and stretched her arms above her head to work the kink from her spine. Shuffling into position, she removed his hands from the sail and replaced them with her own. As his blue eyes scanned her face, she forced a tremulous smile. "Rest for a while, Rolf. I'll take over."

He smiled tiredly. His hands came up to cup her face and he leaned over to press his lips tenderly to hers. Without a word he settled back and closed his eyes. In minutes his deep, steady breathing told her he slept. That he trusted her enough to pilot the tiny vessel while he slept sent a wave of warmth through her, and she took great care to keep them on course, checking often to see that the sun remained behind her right shoulder.

Hunger pangs stabbed at her. She shivered constantly now, unable to get warm even in the folds of her heavy coat, dampened as it was with sea spray. Her throat cried out for water and she was sorely tempted to scoop a handful of seawater to her lips. She resisted that impulse, knowing it would do her more harm than good. She forcibly closed her mind to the physical discomforts and focused only on the boat, the sail, the sea, striving to experience again that oneness she had felt last night. More and more, though, she felt only despair. She truly began to wonder if she'd ever set her feet on solid earth again.

Rolf rested only an hour by Miranda's guess. He stirred awake too soon, she thought, and again took the sail. Miranda wrapped her arms around his waist and rested her face against his broad shoulder. ''You should sleep more, Rolf. You've been awake all night.''

He released the rudder long enough to stroke her hair. ''There will be time for sleep later, *astín mín,* when we reach the shore.

Her head came up quickly. ''What shore?''

''The same one I found many times in the past. The place I planned to build my city, Vinland, with its forests and sweet grasses, lies farther to the south. And a great distance still farther, in the land you call Maine, is another place Leif Eriksson visited, and I after him. We will find land before then, I know. I know not how far, but I think we will see it by nightfall.''

His certainty bewildered her and he must have seen the doubt in her eyes. ''You forget, Miranda, I have sailed these waters many times, with no aid from your compasses and maps. The stars last night showed me the way. The skies are fair. We will soon see land again.''

"Rolf, we have no idea how far Erwin took us. It could be hundreds of miles to land, any kind of land, let alone some that's inhabited.''

"We are with the *straumr,* the current, now, Miranda. By nightfall, I promise.''

That assurance was all that got her through the day. She kept scanning the horizon until her eyes ached. It was nearly full dark when she felt his hand grip her shoulder and followed the direction of his gaze. A seabird swooped down, emitting its piercing cry like a welcome, and ascended again to the skies with a small fish clamped in its oversize bill. Her heart raced, adrenaline giving her newfound energy.

An hour later they sighted a beautiful shape of land protruding from the sea. Another hour after that, Rolf skillfully guided the small boat around two densely forested and apparently uninhabited islands, and into shallow waters along the coast, which swelled in a gentle green mound up from the sea. At an Inuit fishing village, with its clusters of neat houses and occasional house trailers and its rows of bobbing fishing boats, Rolf dragged their small craft out of the water. The place smelled of conifers and fish entrails.

Someone spotted them and then several men rushed toward them, exclaiming in accented French and something that sounded like Inuktitut. Miranda stepped from the boat unaided, trying to judge exactly where they were, staring at the hills and forests in the distance. Then Rolf turned to help her. The moment his strong hands closed on her arms, darkness descended and she slumped into his embrace.

If he'd thought the journey had been difficult to this point, Rolf now saw their time in the little boat as a fond memory. The Inuit—and he was certain that is who these people were, by their sun-darkened skin and exotic almond eyes—had definite ideas about how to care for Miranda, though Rolf had refused to let them take her from his arms. He'd been guided to a sled, which was pulled by another, one with a motor like a car. The ride was gut-wrenching and cold despite the friendly sun and the blankets they'd both been draped with. But at the end of that ride, there had been another, far more harrowing journey.

Tensed to the breaking point, Rolf had clung to Miranda in the silvery-winged bird-ship as it carried them right into the skies. At least this time the man at his side spoke in Miranda's tongue, though his words were strangely accented. Rolf was fairly certain they were being taken to a hospital where Miranda could be cared for properly, and for that he was grateful.

At last he'd been forced to surrender her. Only two hours after tugging the boat onto the shore, Rolf watched helplessly as Miranda was placed upon a table with wheels and pushed down a corridor and through a set of doors. This place had the same pungent aroma and white-coated people filling its halls as the first hospital Rolf had visited. The place where Miranda's *faðir* had died. It had the same hushed quality and the same clean, orderly appearance. Rolf slumped into a chair to wait, only to find himself approached by a stranger.

The man introduced himself as Le Blanc and held up a badge, which meant very little to Rolf. "Can you tell me what happened?" Unlike the others he'd spoken to so far, Rolf found this man's speech easy to understand.

Rolf nodded, supposing this Le Blanc must be in some position of authority here. "There is a group of scientists at the place you call Baffin."

"Baffin Island? You mean the expedition team that uncovered that Ice Man?"

"*Já,*" Rolf said, nodding hard. "The woman, Miranda, is one of them. She located the sunken *drakkar*...the dragon ship of the man she called Viking, and the place where his treasures were hidden." He recalled again Miranda's courage in the cave, and his heart twisted painfully in his chest. His gaze turned toward the place they had taken her. "Will she live?"

"I'm sure she'll be all right. I heard the doctors say it was a mild case of exposure...too much time in the cold." The man pulled a notepad from his shirt and printed words upon it with a pencil. "You said her name is Miranda?"

"Miranda O'Shea," Rolf told him, his voice flat. "And the man who attempted to kill her is called Erwin Saunders."

The man's head came up slowly. "Tried to kill her?"

"*Já*, and me, as well. We were given a beverage with some kind of sleeping powder. We woke upon the small boat, far away from shore. The boat's...motor...had been disabled."

Le Blanc narrowed his eyes. "Why do you think this man wanted to murder you?"

"He wished to claim it was he who discovered the ship and the treasures it held. He was, I believe, envious of Miranda's wisdom, and fearful she would replace him in his position at the university."

"Do you have any proof of all this?"

"My word. Miranda's, when she wakes. Saunders killed Jeff Morsi with a gun, but has likely put the body into the sea by now. And Fletcher Travis..." Rolf shook his head, pressing his fingertips to his brow and closing his eyes. "I fear he has killed Travis, as well." Rolf got to his feet. "I have told you all I know. I will go to her now."

Le Blanc stood, as well. "Maybe you ought to let them have a look at you."

"I am well." Rolf turned and started down the hall.

"They're not going to let you in there," the man warned.

"They will not keep me out." Rolf strode away, and pushed the doors open.

"Damned if I don't believe you," he heard the man mutter before the doors swung closed again.

Hours later, as he held on to her hand, Miranda's eyes opened, and Rolf's throat tightened painfully as his limbs turned weak with relief. He leaned nearer her, only to have her arms encircle his neck and her lips press to his face. No words passed between them as they embraced. Rolf held her hard to his chest, buried his face in her silken hair, breathed her scent. Would that he could remain just so for all time.

When she finally straightened, she searched his face, her own eyes dark with concern. "What's happening?"

"The authorities of this…Canada…were unable to find Saunders. The *Mermaid* has gone. I am told, Miranda, that Saunders is expected at Beaumont today. He has scheduled something called a…press con-fer—"

"A press conference." Her eyes narrowed and Rolf saw the tightening in her jaw that boded not well for the one who had caused it. "No doubt he's going to announce his discovery. I wonder how he'll explain our deaths?"

"Your police will be there, Miranda. He will be taken, though I would much prefer to inflict my own justice this time."

She started to smile, but it died utterly all at once and her eyes swam beneath an onslaught of moisture. "What about…Fletch?"

Rolf stood and moved away from the bed. He heard the sob that caught in her throat as he reached for the door. He pulled it open, then turned to watch Miranda's eyes light up when Travis entered. He had a white bandage wrapped around his head and one hand was heavily bandaged, as well. He held a wooden walking stick as he limped into the room.

"Fletch!" Miranda leapt from the bed and threw her arms around him. For once, Rolf felt no jealousy. His own reaction to the man's appearance had been much the same. "What did you...how did—"

"Easy, Miranda. I'm not exactly myself." As she stepped away, she seemed to note his injuries for the first time. Travis only smiled crookedly. "When I heard the explosion I was half-crazy to get to that cave. Someone hit me from behind and tossed me overboard. I should've been watching my back."

"Are you all right now?" Her concerned eyes moved over his bandaged head and hand, then lit on the cane.

"A little frostbite, a few stitches in the noggin. Nothing serious. I was about to leave the hospital in St. Anthony when your Canadian cop, Le Blanc, tracked me down. I caught the first flight down here."

She frowned. "Where are we, Rolf?"

"A hospital in a place called St. John's in Newfoundland. They brought you here because it is the best hospital in the area. We came by way of one of your wondrous bird-ships, Miranda. I wish you had been awake."

She smiled at him, her eyes brimming with emotion. "You flew? You must have been scared to death."

"More afraid of losing you than of sailing in the bird-ship."

She stepped up to him and slid her arms around him. He held her tight for a long moment. Then she turned, still in his embrace, to face Travis once more. He was looking very strangely from one to the other. Miranda stiffened, "It's just that he's never flown."

"No doubt," Fletcher replied, one brow lifting higher than the other.

"How did you end up in St. Anthony?" Rolf sensed she was trying to change the subject.

"I swam for the shore, passed out at some point, but I must have made it. The Inuit inhabitants pulled me out of the surf." Travis slanted a sly glance at Rolf. "Seems to me they're making a habit of doing that. First Rolf, now me.''

Rolf froze, Fletcher's meaning clear. Miranda's grip around his waist tightened.

''I'm just glad they took me to the nearest dome tent and turned me over to the Beaumont expedition. Sure beats the hell out of being dragged into some cave and left for dead for the next nine centuries, huh, Rolf?''

''Fletcher…'' Miranda began.

''Hey, don't look like that. I'm not saying a word to anybody.'' He glanced at Rolf once again. ''Who the hell would believe it? No, I'd probably end up in a psychiatric ward wearing a brand-new jacket.'' He smiled at the two of them and turned to go.

''Thank you, Travis,'' Rolf said softly.

''Don't think I won't expect some form of compensation, big guy. I'll be bugging you to tell me stories until you're ready to throw me back in the sea.''

''No chance of that, my friend,'' Rolf replied with a wide grin.

Again, Rolf flew. This time holding Miranda's hand and enjoying the novel adventure, rather than clinging to her limp form and fearing for her life.

She'd insisted they leave at once to be present for Saunders's press conference. It seemed she did not trust in the police to see justice done. Or perhaps she simply wished to witness the event firsthand.

Either way, a short time later they found themselves in a crowded room, which was slowly being lined with police officers. A crowd of men and women holding flashing lights and odd devices of all sorts milled around a platform where Erwin Saunders stood speaking. Rolf, Miranda and Travis lingered unseen at the rear and listened to the lies he spewed so easily.

''I had no choice but to shoot Jeff Morsi. He would have

killed me just as he did my peers, numismatist Fletcher Travis, our own archaeologist Miranda O'Shea and her friend, an Icelandic historian called Rolf Magnusson. Their bodies, I fear, may never be found since he tossed them into the sea. And he did all of this from simple greed, I'm afraid. They knew that it was I who tracked down the exact locale of the sunken ship, and Morsi was determined to take the credit.''

Miranda lunged forward then, despite the hand Rolf reached out to stop her. "If you're finished, Professor Saunders, perhaps the press would like to hear the truth now.''

A rumble went up from the people around her. Her name was whispered, then shouted, and the blinding lights flashed like explosions. Saunders turned white. His mouth gaped and he sought words but found none. A second later, he bolted, but was easily grabbed by the police officers who had been silently waiting. Miranda watched his capture, rage visible in her eyes. She stepped up to the podium and addressed the crowd.

"It was Rolf Magnusson who located the ship. Fletcher Travis and I knew it, and that is why Erwin Saunders tried to kill us all. Jeff Morsi was Erwin's accomplice in all of this. Erwin shot him because he didn't want to share the credit...or the spoils."

"She's lying!" Saunders's hoarse cry was so obviously desperate that few in the room gave it heed. Instead, questions were shouted at Miranda, who waved them aside.

"I'm sorry. No questions. I promise the details will be forthcoming.''

She stepped down amid shouted questions and made her way toward Rolf, who waited to fold her into his arms. He swelled with pride for her strength and her courage, and yet as he saw the way the people in the room sought her attention, his heart grew heavy.

Truly his time with Miranda had come to an end. No longer would she need his strength, for it seemed she had

found her own. Her goal would be reached with this latest
adventure. She would be as sought after as Saunders had
hoped to become due to this discovery. Rolf had remained
long enough to assist her in finding the ship and the treasure. She didn't need him any longer. It was time, past time,
for Rolf to make his own way in this world.

"Which offer will you accept?"

Miranda replaced the receiver and faced Rolf. He carried
two cups of steaming cocoa. He really did have a weakness
for chocolate, she thought idly. He'd been oddly distant
since they'd returned three days ago. Not that there had
been much chance to be otherwise. Reporters had hounded
their steps. The telephone had rung off the hook, one call
with word that Paul Potter and the rest of the shiftless crew
Saunders had hired had been located and were in custody.
Offers from the most prestigious universities in the country
had been pouring in steadily. And not just for her. Many
sought the expertise of Rolf Magnusson, the man who'd
used some sixth sense, as far as they could tell, to find the
sunken ship and then the treasure within the cave. He'd
volunteered that information, observing the treasure had
never really been his to hold.

"What do you think I should do?"

He shrugged, handed her a cup and took a seat opposite
her. He stared into the crackling fire on the hearth. "You
have reached your goal. You are the most sought after, the
best, as you said you wished to be. The choice is yours,
astín mín."

She shook her head. He was her choice. But how could
she make him see that? "Those were more my father's
dreams than my own." She drew a deep breath and sighed.
"I don't want to be the head of any department. I don't
want to be tied down to a classroom and a university and
a desk. It would bore me, after all we've been through."
He studied her in silence. "Rolf, you've had offers, too.

You have a great deal of knowledge, and people would like for you to share it.''

"*Nei.* I, too, would soon grow bored with it. Fear not for me, *astín mín.* I will find my way in this world of yours. These jobs they offer, there are too many complications. They wish to know where I came upon my knowledge of the past.''

"You are self-taught. You've proven your abilities. No one will make too much fuss.''

"I am not a citizen of your country. There are laws. How will I explain my past, or seeming lack of one? No, it will be easier to find a simple job, to earn my way with my hands. I am strong. I will manage.''

"There are ways around the laws, Rolf." She straightened her spine and lifted her chin as she gathered her courage. "We could—" She broke off as the doorbell sounded. Angrily she set her mug aside and went to answer it. She was growing more frustrated by the minute. The man seemed determined to leave her, and that was not something she thought she could bear.

Harrison Kirk, Beaumont's Dean, came in slowly and patted Miranda's shoulder with one hand as he shook the other. He approached Rolf and greeted him warmly. "Sorry to intrude. I know it's been hectic.''

"It's all right, Harry. Come in. Cocoa?''

He held up a hand. "No, thank you. I just wanted to check in, see if you've decided what to do.''

She turned, studied Rolf's expectant face. *Astín mín,* the words he used more and more often when he addressed her, echoed in her ears. Last night she'd looked them up in her Islensk dictionary. My love. Did he toss such endearments around lightly, or did he mean it?

Time to find out.

"Yes, as a matter of fact, I have. I'm turning down all offers, yours included.''

Rolf frowned until his pale golden brows met over his Arctic blue eyes.

"Turning... Miranda, dear, what are you saying?"

"I don't want to tie myself down, Harry. I can't be head of anyone's department. I want to be in the field, with my hands in the dirt and the excitement in my heart." She tore her gaze from Rolf's surprised one and faced Harry squarely. "If Beaumont will continue funding my expeditions, I'll stay on for now. But on a project-by-project basis."

Harry looked shocked. "You can't be serious. Do you know what you're turning down?"

"I'll manage. My father had begun work on a book, you know. The life story of the man they called the Plague of the North. I think I'll finish it." She glanced up at the stunned dean and smiled, feeling free and unfettered for the first time since... since that night she'd spent with Rolf in the little boat with nothing between the two of them and the sea and the wind. "Well, Harry? What do you say? We could begin with an excavation of a site right here in Maine, proving Leif Eriksson's explorations extended much farther south than previously believed."

Harrison's eyes widened and took on an excited gleam. "You... you are serious, aren't you? You want to... to freelance?" He said the word as if it were distasteful, then bit his lip. "You really think you can find evidence of Norsemen in Maine?"

"Rolf can. Of course you realize we're a team now. I can't work without him."

"You can't?" Harrison seemed confused, but Miranda ignored him, her gaze returning to Rolf's.

"No, I can't. I can't work without him... I don't think... I could live without him."

Rolf rose slowly, his eyes never leaving hers. "Miranda, consider your words. I cannot take second place to your work, much as I would like to do so."

Miranda stepped forward until she could reach up and run her palm down the side of his face. "I would never ask you to, my love," she replied softly. "I love my work, but it's only a shadow compared to the way I love you."

Harrison Kirk stepped awkwardly back, gripped the doorknob, cleared his throat, shook his head. "I'll, um, come back another…" He gave it up and ducked outside, closing the door behind him.

"You are giving up a great deal, Miranda."

"No. I'm trying to keep what I want most in the world. Don't leave me, Rolf. Stay with me always. Be my…" She bit her lip and forced her gaze to hold his as she said it. "Be my husband."

His smile was quick and brilliant. "This world of yours puzzles me always. Is this another new bit of progress, that a woman might propose marriage to a man?"

She shrugged. "It's done, though not often." She slipped her arms around his neck. "What is your answer?"

He stroked her hair away from her face with gentle fingers. "*pu ert unaðfödur, astín mín,* Miranda. Lovely Miranda with the courage of ten warriors and the beauty of a Valkyrie. I will care for you, cherish you, love you always. I am a fortunate man, truly blessed by the gods, to have you as my wife."

He bowed his head to kiss her deeply, with a fierce possessiveness in which she reveled. In his embrace, in his love, Miranda found that part of herself that had so long eluded her. She clung to it and silently vowed she would never let go.

* * * * *

KISS OF THE SHADOW MAN

For my own Katie, a heroine as feisty and tough
as any I've ever written.
And as smart and beautiful, too.
I love you.

Chapter 1

Some there be that shadows kiss; Such have but a
shadow's bliss.

—William Shakespeare

The pain lanced her head like a dull blade, sawing, cutting,
ripping its way through. It was all-encompassing. At first,
that was all she felt. Then, slowly, as if the lights were
coming up in a darkened theater, she became aware of other
sensations. The hard, irregular shape of her pillow. Her fists
clenched around it, and the words "steering wheel" surfaced in her brain. She wasn't even certain what that meant.
Then it came to her.

Next, the warm, steady trickle along her neck. She lifted
her hand to touch the skin above the pulse point, only to
find it soaked and sticky. Her fingers moved upward to
trace the source, and located the gash at her temple. She
pressed against it and a sharp pain made her wince. Still,
she held the pressure there. It would stop the bleeding. She
didn't know how she knew that, but she did.

Sounds filtered through the dense fog surrounding her
mind. Sizzling...like bacon in a frying pan. No. Rain. It
was rain. She lifted her head slowly, fighting the rush of
dizziness the action brought, and peered through the darkness. Rainwater cascaded in sheets over the shattered windshield. She could see nothing beyond the spiderweb pattern
of the broken glass, and the rain. Only darkness, filled with
the howl of a vicious wind.

At first, she thought the wound to her head was what
made her feel off center, out of balance. But when she tried

to sit straight, she realized the car was at a strange angle, tilted with the driver's door pointing downward.

"I've been in an accident." She said it aloud, trying to take stock and finding it difficult. But the sound of her own voice made her gasp and jerk herself rigid. It wasn't her voice. It couldn't have been. It was the voice of a stranger, a voice she'd never heard before in her life. She blinked rapidly, looking around the car's interior, though she could see little detail in the darkness.

Then there was a flicker of light, a snapping sound, an acrid aroma.

Fire!

Her hand closed on the door handle, and she shoved desperately, again and again. It wouldn't budge. Panic giving her strength, she clambered up the sloping seat toward the opposite door. Her knee banged against something, a stick shift on the floor. Her skirt caught on it when she tried to move. She tore it free, and the sound of ripping fabric somehow added to the fear exploding inside her.

Her body shaking, she groped for the door. The latch gave when she wrenched at it. But the door wouldn't open. No. It would, it was just gravity making it difficult. The car was tipped on its side. The door, nearly horizontal above her. She pushed with all her might, bracing her feet against the hump in the center of the floor. The door lifted, and she growled deep in her throat and pushed harder. It wouldn't swing far enough to remain open on its own. She could only hold it up, her arms straining above her head, as she inched her way up and out. She braced one foot on the dashboard, the other on the seat's headrest and shoved herself upward, still holding the door. Another step. She pushed and shoved and hauled herself inch by inch through the opening, then out into the punishing rain and brutal wind.

Her legs gave way as soon as she hit the slick, muddy ground. She fell, curling into a small ball in the mud. Pain screamed through her brain. She could barely tell up from down, she was so dizzy. Her entire body throbbed with pains she couldn't isolate. She was cold, and afraid. So very afraid.

She only struggled to her feet again when the flames began to spread. Brilliant tongues of fire licked a path from the front of the vehicle toward the rear. The sharp scent of gasoline burned her nostrils. She pulled her mesmerized gaze from the hungry flames and bolted, only to skid to a halt in the mud. To her right, a sheer drop stretched endlessly into blackness and pouring rain. To her left, a steep, muddy embankment angled sharply upward.

Cold rain beating against her face, pummeling her body, frigid wind buffeting her every step of the way, she started up the bank. She clawed with her fingers and dug with her toes. She wore no shoes. She had no idea what had happened to them.

Countless times she slipped, losing more distance than she'd gained as the cold, wet soil scoured her palms, her knees, her chin. Each time, she grated her teeth and began once more. She'd be damned if she'd die here in this mud and misery. She gripped every protruding twig or outcropping of rock that she was fortunate enough to encounter. Slowly, agonizingly, with blood spilling over her neck and dampening her shoulder, she made her way to the top...to the twisting, narrow and utterly empty road.

An explosion rocked the ground beneath her, and she nearly fell from the force of its percussion. Bits of metal and glass rained around her and she shielded her face with her arms, frightened beyond rational thought. The car from which she'd escaped became a blinding ball of flame, and she had to turn her eyes away. The pounding in her head and the pressure against her temples grew stronger with every ragged breath she drew.

She heard the sirens then. In the road ahead of her, vehicles with flashing lights and flapping wipers screeched to

a halt. Men emerged, and several hurried toward her, shouting.

Again she felt an inexplicable fear. She whirled from
them and ran headlong in the other direction, bare feet slapping on cold wet pavement, raindrops ricocheting in front
of her, lashing her face and legs. Headlights rounded a
curve. The car swerved to miss her, skidding to a stop on
the shoulder. She went rigid as the door opened.

She could only see his outline. He stepped around the
car, the headlights at his back, rain pounding his body, and
came toward her. He was no more than a powerful, menacing, black silhouette. A shadow.

Her heart hammered and she couldn't draw a breath. It
was more than fear she felt. It was stark terror. He would
hurt her, she was sure of it. He would kill her. He kept
coming, closer, closer.

She screamed. It was a shriek of unbridled horror, and it
froze the big, dark shadow-man in his tracks. Again, she
turned to run blindly. The paramedics were in her path,
hands held out as if to gentle a frightened pony, voices soft.
"Easy now, just calm down. We're here to help you.
Easy."

She shook her head, pressing her hands to the sides of
it. One came away dripping crimson and her throat closed
off. She backed away from them, turning again only to find
the shadow-man there, so close she could smell the rain on
his skin.

She screamed again when his arms closed around her
like a steel trap. She fought, thrashing in his grip, kicking,
pounding him with her fists.

"Dammit, Caitlin, that's enough!"

His voice was deep, loud, frightening. But it wasn't his
voice that made her stop her struggling. She blinked, and
shook her head, looking up into a face that was no more
than a grouping of angles and planes in various shades of

gray. A square, wide jaw. High, defined cheeks. Full lips. Prominent eyebrows.

Her voice a croak, she whispered, "What did you call me?"

His grip on her eased. She felt, rather than saw, the shock that rippled through him. "Caitlin." His arms freed her, but his large, hard hands gripped her shoulders. "Caitlin," he said again.

She was aware of the others closing in behind her. She shook her head, and dizziness swamped her like a small boat in a hurricane. "No...that's not my name." Her legs seemed to dissolve and her upper body sagged. She fought the sensation, leaned into the hands that supported her and managed to remain standing.

"Then what is?" It was nearly whispered, but there was a coarseness to the words that rubbed at all her nerve endings.

She closed her eyes, searched her mind. It was a simple enough question. What was her name? She squeezed her eyes tighter, trying to extract the information from her mind like juice from an orange. Nothing came. Her answer was an empty hole. A dark, empty hole in her mind where her identity should have been.

"I...I don't know."

"You don't know?" He seemed to be searching her face but she could barely see his. All crags and harsh lines, and beaded droplets of rain. Deep-set eyes. Wet hair that looked like a windstorm. No colors. Only shades of gray.

She felt the fear well up in her throat. She didn't know who she was. She didn't know where she was. But she did know that she was afraid, terribly, paralyzingly afraid. Of what, or whom, she had no clue. Right now, it was of everyone, everything. Most of all, this broad, hard-faced shadow man. She tried to pull free of him, but he wouldn't release her.

"Let me go!" She twisted her shoulders back and forth,

heedless now of the icy rain pelting her, the streams of it running between her shoulder blades and soaking her clothes. "Let me go!" Again and again she screamed the words until the dizziness returned. The varying grays around her lost their form and blended into one cold, dark color. And then, even the pain in her head drowned in the gray sea.

Dylan Rossi stared through the double-paneled glass with the wire mesh between the panes into the room where they'd just wheeled his wife. He couldn't see her now. He only saw the backs of doctors and nurses in their pale green scrubs, with the white strings tied in neat little bows up their backs. He saw the dome of chromium steel above her, the blinding light it gave. And he saw the monitors. Their waving white lines coming erratically, the beeps without rhythm. The white sheets on the table that held her were spattered with crimson.

He couldn't see her. Not now. But he'd seen her less than an hour ago, when she'd struggled against his brutal grip in the pouring rain. In the glow of his headlights, he'd been able to see just fine. The gaping wound in her head, the blood pulsing from it, soaking her hair, her face, mingling with the rain on her neck.

And he remembered her eyes, the fear in them. It had been real. She'd been afraid...of him. And he couldn't say he blamed her. She had every reason in the world to be afraid of him.

Dylan paced away from the double doors marked Sterile Area, No Admittance. His wet shoes creaked over the polished tiles. The scent of the place turned his stomach.

No, no, it wasn't the damned scent that was making him sick. It was *him*. It was what he was thinking, what he was feeling right now that made him want to puke his insides out. But that didn't stop him from feeling it, and nothing could stop him from admitting it, at least to himself.

And he shouldn't hate himself for acknowledging what the rest of Eden, Connecticut, already knew. It would be best for everyone concerned if his coldhearted bitch of a wife never came out of that room.

Thirsty.
There had never been a desert dryer than her throat was right now. She forced her eyes open, but the room was blurry, dim. She licked her lips and tried to sit up. Her body responded with little more than a twitch of several muscle groups. And even that small effort left her limp with exhaustion. God, what was the matter with her?

"Caitlin?"
That voice sent a shiver up her spine. She tried to turn her head toward it, even as she felt herself instinctively cringe farther into the stiff sheets.

The form, dark as before, and blurred by her errant vision, rose from a chair to lean over the bed. "You're awake." His finger jammed repeatedly at a button on the side of her bed. "How do you feel?"

She twisted away from his touch, frightened to have him so near. Her back pressed against a cool metal rail at the far side of the bed. She turned fast, startled. Her head throbbed with pain.

"Take it easy. Caitlin, you're in a hospital. You're going to be fine."

She swung her head around to face him again, though the movement increased the pain abominably. "Who are you?"

He frowned. Her vision was steadily clearing, and while the room was only dimly lit, she could now see his features. His eyebrows were dense and dark. His hair a jumble of deep brown satin waves, mussed as though he'd run his hands through it.

In a flash, she saw him doing just that. Not here and now, but somewhere else...before. He was tall, solidly built and he looked as if he were trying to see through her eyes, into her mind as he stared at her.

The door was very wide and made of wood. She noticed that as it swung open and a miniature nurse came through, took one look at her and whirled to run out again.

The man never moved. He only continued staring at her, eyes like melted chocolate, glistening, probing. ''You don't know who I am?''

She shook her head, then closed her eyes because the action hurt her.

''Do you know who you are?''

Tears stung her eyes, so she squeezed them tighter. She felt droplets work their way through to moisten her lashes and roll over her cheeks. He swore, low harsh words that made her spine stiffen.

She heard the door again, the shuffling of feet and a feminine voice, very low. ''You'll have to wait outside, Mr. Rossi.''

Rossi. The name meant something. Bells sounded in her mind, but there was no more. Nothing but the vague feeling that she ought to know the name.

''You told me there was no sign of brain damage.'' The deep, rumbling tenor voice, Rossi's voice, came to her as he was urged toward the door.

''I told you we couldn't be sure until she regained consciousness.''

''She says she doesn't know who she is,'' he growled. He sounded as if he doubted it to be true. ''So run your damned tests and tell me if this is legitimate, pronto.''

''Please, try to be patient. I know you want your questions answered, but right now we need to examine your wife.''

An electric shock zapped through her body at that word. ''No!'' The denial flew from her lips, riding her coarse voice to fill the sterile-smelling room. ''No! I'm not his wife. I'm not. I don't know that man. I don't know him, I swear it! I—''

"Calm down, Mrs. Rossi." Cool hands on her shoulders, then her forehead.

"Don't call me that!" she shrieked. She sat up, flinging the covers from her. She had to get out of here. Everyone here was crazy. She swung her legs to the floor, only to feel her arm grabbed firmly and jabbed with something sharp. She caught her breath. By the time she drew another, her head was swimming, and someone was pushing her back onto the bed.

She looked toward the door. He still stood there, staring at her. She met his gaze and moved her lips, forcing words with an effort. "Keep him...away from me."

He shook his head, yanked the door open and left as quickly as possible.

Night again.

God, why was it dark whenever she opened her eyes? Was she to live in darkness from now on?

"You're sure she's not faking this?"

It was his voice. The man they'd said was her husband. And it was filled with contempt.

"Mr. Rossi, why on earth would she want to?" The feminine voice paused, awaiting an answer. There was none. "Amnesia is rare," she said at last. "But it does happen, and I'm convinced it has happened to her. She needs patience and understanding right now. Not suspicion and mistrust."

The shadow man's head turned toward her in the darkened room. Caitlin closed her eyes again, and lay utterly still, waiting.

"She's been through a terrible trauma, Mr. Rossi."

"All the more reason not to tell her. Not anything. If she's faking, I'll know soon enough. If not..." He let the sentence hang for a moment. "If not, then telling her would only do more harm.'' It wasn't, Caitlin thought, the ending he'd intended to tack on to the sentence.

"Quite frankly, I'm inclined to agree with you. She's better off not knowing too much. Yet. She'll have to be told, though."

"Yeah, well, I'm her husband, so I'm calling the shots. I decide when and how much."

"*I* am her doctor, Mr. Rossi. And as soon as she shows me that she is on stable mental ground, you'll no longer be in a position to decide anything about her care. If you haven't told her by that time, then I will. Make no mistake about that."

"Fine."

The door opened, closed again.

A sense of solitude slowly invaded the room. She was alone again. With no more answers than she'd had before. God, could she really have lost her memory so completely? Could that big, frightening shadow man really be her husband? And what was it they intended to keep from her?

Caitlin rolled over, very slowly so as not to aggravate the dull throbbing in her head. There was something else, something that was missing, something precious. She couldn't put her finger on what, exactly. She only knew a ball of loneliness rested in the pit of her stomach. She felt empty inside, aching for something she couldn't identify. Not her memory. Not the man who claimed to be her husband. Something else, something she missed so terribly that it was a gnawing pain in her heart.

A teardrop worked its way from between her lashes, and she closed her eyes tight before a flood of them could follow. She wrapped her arms around her pillow, hugged it tight to her chest. When the floodgates finally broke, the sounds of her sobs were muffled in the fabric.

"I've dimmed the lights, Caitlin. The brightness will aggravate the headache, and hurt your eyes. It's better this way."

She turned toward the woman's voice. The tall, blond doctor sat in a chair beside the bed. She wore a white coat, and the tag pinned to it read Dr. Judith Stone, M.D., Ph.D. She had a pretty face, but hid it behind oversize, black-rimmed glasses. Her hair was pinned to the back of her head.

"My name is Judith. Yours is Caitlin. Do you mind if I call you that?"

"How do you know?"

"Your name? Well, your husband told us, for one thing."

"He's not my husband. I don't know him."

Dr. Stone tilted her head to one side. "Caitlin, we're not just taking his word. He had photos of you. We checked your fingerprints, too. We'll bring your brother in to confirm it, if you like."

"I don't have a brother."

"Well, there is a man running around claiming to be your brother, with a birth certificate that has your parents' names on it. It's all a matter of public record." Dr. Stone paused for a moment, to let that sink in, she thought. Then she added, "Come to think of it, there is a marriage license that says you're married to Dylan Rossi. Also a matter of record."

Why did the name feel so...important? Unless it was true. He was her husband.

"If I have a brother, why hasn't he been in to see me by now?" No one had come to see her, she added in silence. Not her professed husband, or her parents, if she had any. No friends, no one at all.

"I thought it would be best not to allow visitors, Caitlin. Seeing a lot of strangers who claim they know you would only add to the stress."

She probably had a point. "Why can't I remember anything?"

Judith leaned forward in the chair, her eyes attentive. "How much *do* you remember, Caitlin?"

She shook her head slowly. The name still felt odd, like a pair of shoes broken in by someone else. It must be hers, though. The doctors were certain, had been insisting on it for days now. You couldn't argue with a birth certificate.

"Nothing. I woke up in a car, in the rain. Before that, there's just…nothing." She opened her eyes and faced Dr. Stone. "I've answered these questions before. Every doctor that comes in here asks me the same things. I'd like some of my questions answered now."

Dr. Stone blinked, but smiled gently and nodded. "All right."

All right. Just like that. She didn't know where to begin, there were so many things she wanted to know. Where she'd lived, what she'd done for a living, who her friends had been.

"Am I ever going to get better?"

Narrow fingers closed on the black-framed glasses and removed them. "Caitlin, you were in a serious accident. You saw firsthand the distance your car fell, and how much farther it could have gone. If you'd been unconscious another few minutes, you'd have died. If the car had landed differently, you could have been paralyzed, or worse. I want you to keep all of that in mind."

Caitlin—she was finally trying to think of herself by that name—braced herself. "As things stand," Judith Stone continued, "you escaped almost unscathed. The head injury was serious. You already know you spent a week in a state of coma before you woke up three days ago. Many times, patients who experience that never regain consciousness, or when they do, they're—"

"Please, stop preparing me and just say it. I'm not going to get my memory back, am I?"

She sighed. "I'm afraid I can't answer that. Not yet."

Caitlin sunk back against the pillows as tears threatened. She blinked against them.

"Only time will tell, Caitlin. There's just no medical way to predict whether you'll regain some or all of your memory. But in the meantime, you have to begin again. You have to start right now, today."

"Start what?"

Hands gripped hers and squeezed. "Learning who you are."

"I don't remember who I am." She wanted to wail the words, but she only whispered them.

"Not who you were, Caitlin. Who you are. Who you will be from this day on. That's the most important thing for you to accept. You aren't that woman anymore, and if you spend too much time trying to find her, to become her again, you'll drive yourself crazy. I want you to remember that." She tilted her head again, as if trying to read Caitlin's reactions on her face. "Anymore questions?"

She licked her lips. "My full name?"

"Caitlin Amanda O'Brien Rossi."

She turned that over in her mind. "So I'm Irish?"

"Sure sounds Irish to me."

Caitlin nodded. "It does, doesn't it. What about my family?"

"Parents are deceased. You have...no children. There's your brother, Thomas, and your husband, Dylan."

She nodded, glancing down at the rings on the third finger of her left hand. "How long have I been...married?" The word didn't come easily.

"Five years. You're thirty-three. Your brother is twenty-nine."

She met Judith's brilliant green gaze. "And Dylan?"

Pale brows rose. "I never asked him. Why don't you?"

"He hasn't been here since I woke up."

"No, that's not quite true. He's been a fixture around

here. He only doesn't come into the room because you made it clear you didn't want to see him, and because I thought it would only upset you if he did.''

"Oh.''

"Do you want to see him now?''

She bit her lip. "I don't know.''

"Caitlin, there's something else I need to let you know. Your stay in the hospital is no longer necessary. Physically, you're fine now. You need to start thinking about where you'll go when you leave here.''

A cold finger of panic traced a path around her heart. Where could she go? "My b-brother?''

"He and his wife live with you and your husband.''

The fear she'd felt right after the accident resurfaced, and she searched in vain for its source. "Doctor—''

"Judith,'' she gently insisted.

"Judith,'' Caitlin said. "What do you know about the accident? Where was I going? How did I end up going off the road?''

Judith licked her lips, and for the first time, she didn't meet Caitlin's eyes as she answered. "The police department would know more about that than I.''

Caitlin sighed. The answer was no answer at all. She had a feeling the accident was important, somehow. Almost as important as that wellspring of sorrow she felt inside her. More pressing, though, was her situation now. It looked as if she would have no choice but to return to her former home, if Dylan Rossi would even have her.

And there was another thing bothering her. "Why are there no mirrors in here?''

Judith rose slowly. "I asked that they be removed. I wanted to be sure you were ready to see your reflection. It'll be kind of shocking at first. Like looking at someone else's face.''

Caitlin drew a deep breath. She knew her hair was a deep, dark shade of auburn. She'd pulled a lock of it around her face to stare at it. It was very long, and she felt curly bangs on her forehead. "I'd like to have a mirror. I think I'm ready now."

"There's one in the room next door. Feel up to a walk?"

Caitlin nodded. Judith opened a closet and pulled a pretty, red satin dressing gown from it. "Here, put this on."

She got to her feet and let Judith help her slip the robe up over her arms. "Whose—"

"Yours. Your husband brought some things when you were still in the coma."

At the mention of her husband, Caitlin stiffened, and her nerves jumped. "When do I have to leave?"

Judith walked with her to the door, and held it open. "Tomorrow."

Chapter 2

Dylan went rigid when she scuffed out of her hospital room, Dr. Stone at her side. He'd been at the desk only ten minutes, just getting the full report of how she'd passed the day and what progress had been made. He hadn't set foot in her room since she'd screamed that he be kept away from her. Seeing her now brought a sickening twist to his stomach and a jolt of memory to his mind. Again, he saw her caught in the beam of his headlights, frightened as a startled doe, as he moved toward her. Again, he saw her fear of him when he called her name, heard her scream, watched her turn and run away as if he were Satan himself.

Later, he'd wondered if she'd really had sense enough to think she might finally have pushed him too far, or if her fear had all been an act. One more scene in the never-ending play where she was always at center stage. One more bid to tear him apart a little more. He couldn't imagine what more damage she could hope to exact. But if there was anything, if she even imagined there was anything left that could hurt him, she would do her damnedest to use it. Cold, spoiled Caitlin. She would never change.

But she hadn't faked the injury, or the coma. And now this amnesia. Real, or a ploy? She had the doctors fooled, there was no doubt about that.

Dr. Stone opened the door to the room beside Caitlin's. "Do you want me to come with you?"

"No." Caitlin seemed to hesitate before answering, but when she did, her voice was firm. "No, I want to do this by myself."

"Okay. I'll be just down the hall if you need me. And I'll come back for you in five minutes."

Caitlin nodded and Judith Stone walked away. Dylan watched as Caitlin seemed to brace her shoulders, and stepped into the room, shoving the wide, brown door farther, and allowing it to swing slowly shut behind her. He was curious, and no one seemed to be paying much attention at the moment. He walked with deliberate casualness across the pale gray tiles of the hall, toward the door she'd entered. He pressed it open, just a little, and he peered inside.

She stood as if transfixed, staring into a full-length mirror on the inside of an open closet door. Dylan looked at her reflection, seeing everything she saw. The soft, ivory-toned skin, the high sculpted cheekbones that gave her a regal look. Her long, wavy hair, the color of an old penny. Her eyes, huge and round, wide-set and penetrating. They were wider right now than he thought he'd ever seen them, and greener. Like emeralds. Shocking, glittering green. Too green to belong to her.

Her hand rose slowly, and her fingers touched her cheek, then slipped slowly downward, over its hollow, tracing her jawline to her small, proud chin.

Her fingers were trembling.

Her gaze moved downward, over her slender frame, her endlessly long legs. When her eyes met those of her reflection again, there were tears brimming in both.

Dylan retreated in silence.

If she was acting, she was doing a hell of a job.

She was silent in the car, head turned away, eyes pretending to scan the roadside as they passed. Dylan kept a steady pressure on the accelerator as he negotiated the narrow, twisting strip of pavement that passed for a road.

She'd fastened her seat belt the second she'd slammed her door. It surprised him. Caitlin never used a seat belt. Oh, but he was forgetting Dr. Stone's lecture, wasn't he? This was not the same woman he remembered, not the woman he'd married, not the woman he'd known. This Caitlin was a new woman, a perfect stranger.

But that was the punch line, wasn't it? He and his wife had been strangers for a very long time now.

She certainly didn't look any different. At least, not now that she was dressed up in one of her chic, designer label skirts, with its brilliant yellow color. The matching jacket was cropped at the waist to show off its minuscule size, and flared at the hips to accentuate the way they would sway when she walked. The pumps were the precise shade of the suit. She did tug at the hem of the jacket once or twice, though. And she shifted in the seat as though uncomfortable with the amount of slender, long thigh exposed by the skirt. And she hadn't put her hair up. She hadn't gone out in public in more than a year without a classy French braid or a twisting chignon. Today, she just sat there with her coppery curls spilling all over the place.

So she'd forgotten how to braid her hair. So what? She hadn't changed in any way that mattered. It was still painfully obvious that she wished she were somewhere else, anywhere but with him. Not that the feeling wasn't one hundred percent mutual. So where was this big change he'd been told to expect?

He sighed and returned his attention to the pale gray ribbon that stretched ahead of him. In a way, it was good she'd continue being distant and cold. It would be easier to keep his secrets that way. There were some things she was far better off not remembering. He'd had a hell of a time convincing Dr. Stone of that, but in the end she'd agreed. If the amnesia was real—he glanced toward Caitlin, and felt a resurgence of doubt—she was better off.

She ran one hand over the supple leather seat. The car was an Infiniti Q-45. She knew, somewhere in the tangled jungle of her memory banks, that it was a luxury car. It seemed to have all the extras. The air conditioner silently cooled the interior, while the sun outside made heat waves dance above the pavement ahead. It smelled new, good. She tried to remember what the other car had looked like, the one she'd seen go up in a ball of white hot flame. She frowned, searching her mind, but nothing came.

"What is it?"

She jumped, startled by the suddenness and resonance of his deep voice. She was still afraid of him. Just being in the same car with him had her nerves standing on end, and seemed somehow to intensify that emptiness inside her. "I was trying to remember the car. The one that burned."

He slanted her a skeptical glance. "You don't remember your car?"

"Only that it was small, and there was a stick shift. I remember banging my knee on it when I was trying to climb out."

He shook his head. "It was a red Porsche." He released a low chuckle. "Figures that would be your first question. You thought more of that car than…" He shook his head, leaving the sentence unfinished. His face darkened, and his lips tightened.

His answer made her hesitate to ask any further questions. She sensed his disapproval. Still, there were things she needed to know. "What…what do I do?"

"What do you mean, what do you do?"

"For a living."

His eyebrows shot up and he stared at her for so long, he had to jerk the wheel when he finally glanced back at the road. He gave his head a quick shake. "For a living? You? Give me a break."

Caitlin felt a prickle of knowledge make its way into her brain. Dylan Rossi didn't like her. Not at all. In fact, she was feeling the touch of his intense dislike right across the space between them. She tried to find some patience for him. After all, he had lost a wife and gotten back a perfect stranger. He had reason to be short-tempered. "Look, it would help if you could put a damper on the sarcasm and simply answer me. Do I have a job or not?''

He glanced at her from the corners of his eyes. ''Not.''

She nodded. ''Can you tell me why not?''

He shrugged noncommittally, flipped down the visor, and pulled a pair of black sunglasses from it. When he slipped them on, his eyes were completely hidden.

She shook her head, exasperation growing with every minute. ''I need to know. You were her husband—'' She bit her lip. ''I mean, my husband. If you don't know, then who does?''

''You don't work because you were born rich. You don't need to exert yourself any more than it takes to sign a check and you have all the money you could want. Happy?''

His words stung her. ''No, I'm not.''

''No,'' he repeated. ''You never were.''

He turned the car onto a long, winding driveway. She felt the crunch of the tires over gravel, but didn't hear it in the silent interior, as the car moved beneath a tunnel of overhanging trees. It was shadowy, and darker. He could easily have removed the sunglasses, she thought. He didn't.

They rounded a bend, and the house towered before her. Old red brick, everywhere, most of it covered with clinging, creeping vines that seemed to Caitlin as if they were trying to smother the place. The windows, narrow and arched at the tops, were surrounded with bricks in fan patterns. The entire place was a harsh combination of severe corners and dull colors. It frightened her, this house.

In an upper window, a curtain parted, and the shadow of a face peered out. Caitlin caught her breath, but before she could say anything, the curtain fell once more.

Dylan was already getting out of the car. He glanced in at her, as he replaced his sunglasses on the visor. He frowned when he saw she wasn't moving. ''Something wrong?''

Yes. God, everything was wrong. Why would she feel

such terror at the prospect of entering her own home? Why was there a gnawing sadness digging a pit into her soul? Why was she so uncomfortable with the man she'd married...perhaps even loved...once? She shook her head, and instead of asking any of the questions that truly troubled her, she asked a safe one. "Who else lives here, besides us?"

"Your brother and his wife, and..." He stopped, cleared his throat. His gaze moved away from hers for just a moment. A quick flicker of those dark eyes, and then he faced her again. "And my great-aunt, Ellen Rossi. Other than that, there are only Genevieve and Henri Dupres." He pronounced both names with a perfect French accent.

"Who are they?"

He sighed as if running low on patience. "The French siblings you insisted on hiring last year. Genevieve worked for your family once, but your old man let her go right after your parents' divorce. You always liked her."

As he spoke, he moved around the car to her side. His hand gripped her arm to urge her to her feet and draw her along beside him, an automatic gesture, she was sure. But the warmth of his touch, the pressure of each finger on her skin disturbed her. It sent her nerves skittering in a hundred directions, and a shiver over her nape.

"So when she showed up with her brother to answer your ad for hired help, you gave them the jobs. She's our maid and he's our cook."

Caitlin stopped walking, vaguely aware she'd missed most of what he'd said. Something tickled her consciousness, teased her senses, tugged at her. A scent. *His* scent, clean and pleasantly spicy...and familiar.

She frowned as an image flickered in her mind. His face, very close to hers. His eyes filled with dark fire, staring intensely into hers, as his strong hands held her to him. She felt his skin, hot and damp against hers, felt his warm breath on her face as his lips came nearer.

"Are you coming in or not?"

She gasped and blinked up at him. His brows drew close, and he reached out a hand. She instinctively took a step backward. Strong hands caught her shoulders, preventing her from going any farther.

"Caitlin, what in hell's the matter?"

She closed her eyes slowly, willing herself not to pull away from his touch. The image had shaken her, but she didn't want him to know. A heat spread up through her cheeks. Her skin seemed to burn where his hands rested, though that was all in her mind, of course.

"Nothing. I'm fine." She drew a steadying breath, and began walking at his side again, trying to act as if nothing had happened. Her feet sunk into the hot gravel. The humid, stifling air bathed her. Perspiration broke out on her forehead in the seconds it took to reach the steps. She felt her skin growing damp and her clothes sticking to her. And she smelled the Atlantic.

She frowned, tilting her head to listen to the sounds she hadn't noticed before. Waves crashing against rock in the distance, and the discordant harmony of sea gulls.

There seemed little lawn. Mostly the place was surrounded by shrubs and trees and plants of every size and variety. It was like a miniature jungle here, with the humid, heavy air to match. Not a single breeze stirred a single leaf. But she imagined that on the back side of the house, closer to the shore, there would always be a breeze. The idea was appealing at that moment.

"Caitlin?"

"Hmm?" She tore her mind away from the ocean and the gulls and the imaginary breeze, and glanced at him.

"Coming?"

She'd stopped again, at the base of the steps this time. She nodded, and made herself move. Already, the gravel she stood in was heating her feet right through the soles of her stylish, torturous pumps. Dylan walked beside her up the wide, stone stairs to the front door with the oval window of frosted glass through which one couldn't see. He opened it, held it and waited. Knees trembling for no reason she could name, Caitlin stepped inside.

The house had the chill of a meat cooler.

Her footsteps echoed over the deep blue, marble floor, floating up to the high, vaulted ceiling and vanishing there. A twisting stairway of darkly polished hardwood began at one end and writhed upward, out of sight. A tooled, gleaming banister supported by elegant spindles wound its way alongside the stairs. The place smelled of oil soap and old wood.

She absorbed it all, shuddering at the darkness of the decor, and at the cold. A woman descended the stairs, very slowly, one gnarled hand gripping the banister for support. Snow white hair was twisted into a smooth bun at the top of her head. She wore silver-rimmed glasses, Coke-bottle thick. And as she reached the bottom of the stairs and came nearer, Caitlin saw that her eyes were as brown as Dylan's.

Dylan rushed forward, extending a hand to help her. She waved him away. "Leave me be, boy. I'm not crippled."

Dylan's lips curved into a crooked smile, and he stepped back. Caitlin caught her breath. He was looking at the old woman with tenderness and a sort of indulgent smile. Real affection lit his eyes, and for some reason, it made her feel more alone than she could remember feeling.

"I've brought Caitlin home, Aunt Ellen." He walked beside his aunt, watchful, ready to reach out if she stumbled.

The old woman moved slowly, her feet scuffing the floor. "I can see that. I'm not blind, either." When she was standing six inches from Caitlin, she peered into her face. "So, you're back, are you?"

Caitlin smiled at the woman. "Yes. It feels good to be out of that hospital."

The woman sniffed. "Been better if you'd stayed there. For all of us."

"Ellen." Dylan's voice held a warning.

"What? She might as well know my feelings on the subject, or is that supposed to be a secret, too?" Caitlin shot Dylan a questioning glance. He averted his eyes. "You never liked me, girl. No more than I liked you. They tell me you've forgot all that, but I imagine it'll come back to you soon enough. Old habits die hard, you know."

Caitlin opened her mouth to deny it, then closed it again. How could she? She remembered nothing.

"Ellen, where is everyone?"

She faced her nephew, squinting. "How would I know? No one around here ever tells me anything."

Caitlin almost smiled. Despite Ellen's frosty attitude toward her, she was like a petulant child. And at least she was up-front with her feelings, not brooding and sending her veiled glances, the way Dylan had been doing.

Another woman entered the room then, coming through an arched doorway. She was tiny, with her jet hair cut in pixie style, and huge, dark, Liza Minelli eyes. She wore the regulation uniform of a maid, black dress with white collar and cuffs. Stiff white apron.

She came forward, smiling nervously when Caitlin's eyes met hers. "Madame Rossi, I am so glad to see you home. You look well." Her speech was laced with a silky French accent. She stretched both hands to clasp Caitlin's, and squeezed softly. A gesture that suggested familiarity, yet Caitlin felt none.

"I'm sorry. I don't—"

"I know," she said softly. "It is all right, you will be well soon, *non?* I am Genevieve—"

"Our maid," Caitlin filled in, more to solidify the information in her own mind than anything else.

Genevieve's hands fell away, and Caitlin noticed her nails. They were immaculate, not excessively long, but far from cropped. They were hot-pink at their bases, with a black diagonal line bisecting them. The top portions were white, with tiny black dots.

"More than your maid," Genevieve was saying. Her voice had dropped an octave, and was softer than before. "We are friends, as well."

Caitlin looked up, saw the expectancy in the woman's eyes, and offered her a smile that was far from genuine. "That's good to know, Genevieve. I could use a friend, right now."

Dylan cleared his throat, drawing both gazes toward him. Ellen had settled herself in a broad rocking chair that looked ancient, and was rocking back and forth rapidly.

"*Monsieur?*" Genevieve inquired. "Is there something I can get for you?"

"A cold drink would be terrific." Dylan all but ignored Caitlin, though the old woman's eyes never left her as she rocked.

"Ice tea?" the maid asked.

"Fine. It's pushing ninety again today. Air's so heavy you can barely breathe outside." He slanted a glance toward Caitlin. She felt his eyes on her face and knew it was beaded with perspiration, though not from the stifling heat he'd mentioned. The house was as cold as a tomb. "One for Mrs. Rossi, too. Ellen?"

"I'll get it myself. Haven't had any servants waiting on me in ninety-two years and damned if I need 'em now."

Dylan's mouth pulled upward at one corner, but he quickly remedied that twitch, and nodded toward Genevieve. She left, and Ellen stopped rocking all at once. "That gal's bucking for a raise, mark my words. Friends. Bah! I never did like her."

"You don't like anyone, Ellen," Dylan gently reminded her.

Caitlin shook her head, confused. "I don't understand. Am I friends with Genevieve, or not?"

Dylan shrugged. "Like I said before, you always liked her."

Ellen sniffed, pulled herself from the rocker and scuffed out through the arched doorway, taking the same path the maid had. Dylan was watchful of her every step until she moved through the doorway and out of sight.

"I guess your aunt and I didn't get along."

He faced her again, his eyes skeptical. He sighed, shook his head and walked to an elegant eggshell sofa, with scrolled wooden arms and clawed feet. He sat down, reaching for a newspaper on the matching end table. "She's my great aunt. And no, you never got along."

Caitlin remained standing, watching him as he shook the paper twice, then began scanning the headlines. "Why not?"

He lifted his head, his gaze meeting hers, still packing thinly veiled distrust. He opened his mouth, but snapped it shut again when Genevieve reappeared carrying a tray and two tall, dewy glasses. Caitlin moved forward and took one. "Thank you." Her throat was suddenly parched. She sipped the beverage gratefully.

Genevieve handed Dylan's glass to him, sent Caitlin an encouraging smile and vanished again. Dylan took a long drink. Caitlin's gaze affixed itself to him, the way his lips parted around the glass's rim, the rippling motions of his throat as he swallowed repeatedly.

A sound floated to her ears then, breaking the tense silence between her and her husband. A soft, demanding cry. It pierced Caitlin's nerves like a blade. She stiffened, and a second later heard the glass shattering at her feet. She didn't look down, only stepped past it, vaguely aware of the crunching beneath her shoes, and moved toward the staircase. Dylan jumped to his feet, then stood motionless, poised.

Again and again the tiny wail came. Caitlin felt her eyes moisten, and her heart twist. She turned to face Dylan. "My

God, no wonder I've felt so empty... Why didn't you tell me?''

"Caitlin, wait—"

She ignored him, whirling once more and racing up the stairs. She had a child. A baby! No wonder she'd felt so utterly bereft since she awoke in that hospital. It made perfect sense now. She'd been aching for her child.

She ran as fast as she could along the maze of corridors, following the sound of the baby's cries, paying no attention to the countless rooms she passed on the way. She didn't even pause when she came to the closed door of what had to be the nursery. She flung it open and hurried inside.

The infant lay on its back, eyes pinched tight, mouth round. Tiny arms and legs stretched out and trembled with every wail, then relaxed in between. Dark, thick hair swirled over a small head, and chubby fists clenched with frustration.

Without hesitation, Caitlin bent over the crib and scooped the small, wriggling bundle up into her arms. The child wore only a diaper and a tiny white T-shirt. Caitlin rescued the receiving blanket that had been kicked into a wad at one corner of the crib, and wrapped it around the baby, holding the child close to her chest, resting her cheek against the silken hair.

The crying stopped at once, and Caitlin looked down into huge eyes that were so blue the whites of them seemed tinted blue, and thick, long lashes and chubby cheeks. So soft, the skin on the pudgy arms and legs. And the baby smell that filled her senses was like pure heaven. Caitlin ran her hand over the baby's fuzzy dark hair, and bent to press her lips to a soft cheek. She closed her eyes as they filled with tears, and held the baby against her once more, rocking it slowly in her arms.

"God, I don't even know if you're a boy or a girl. But you're beautiful. You're beautiful, and Mommy is home now.''

She heard his steps stop in the doorway, but she didn't turn. She just held that child to her breast and let the tears of joy and relief fall unchecked over her face. "Everything is all right now, little one." She felt as if her heart would explode, it was so full. That emptiness inside her was filled. She had the part of her that had been lacking. Everything *would* be all right.

"Caitlin." His voice was hoarse.

She turned slowly, smiling though her lips trembled. "You should have told me, Dylan. If I'd known we had a—"

"She's not ours."

Those three words spread a blanket of ice over her heart. She shook her head in denial and held the baby closer.

"Caitlin, that is not our child." He took a step closer, and she backed away.

"No."

His face was tight, his eyes glittering with something. Anger? "She's your brother's little girl, Caitlin. She's Thomas and Sandra's baby."

Again, she shook her head. "But...but—"

A young woman with a towel wrapped like a turban around her head joined them in the room then. She stopped when she saw them there, her wide blue eyes on the baby in Caitlin's arms. She wore a jade dressing gown, tied with a sash, but it gaped at the neck, giving a more than ample view of her swollen breasts.

"Cait." She shook her head, in self-deprecation, perhaps. "First day home an' here I've got you baby-sittin' already. Sorry," she said with a sexy southern drawl. She tipped her head back, fixing Dylan with a potent stare, her eyes huge and jewel-like. "I thought sure she'd sleep long enough for me to take a shower." She came forward, and took the baby from Caitlin's suddenly numb arms. "Come on, Lizzie, come to Mama."

Caitlin felt colder than ever all at once. She shivered,

and tried to blink back a new rush of tears. This couldn't be true. Holding the baby had felt so right, so natural. How could she not be her child?

"Caitlin, this is Sandra—" He broke off, his gaze leaving Caitlin's face when the narrow-faced woman sat down in a rocker near the crib, baring one plump breast as if she did so with an audience every day. Lizzie nuzzled, found her target and latched on with vigor.

Caitlin turned away, and pushed past Dylan into the hall.

Dylan braced one hand against the door frame, and watched her run away. She disappeared into one of the guest rooms, and he heard her lock the door after she'd slammed it.

"Gee, what's wrong with her?"

Dylan didn't answer. He couldn't, just then.

"What's wrong, little one? Not hungry?" She sighed. "I swear, she must have a tiny tummy. Eats just a little, and twenty times a day."

He heard the brush of fabric against skin as Sandra righted her robe, and then rose. "I'm taking Lizzie back to my room with me while I change. Then we're going out for a walk, aren't we, Lizzie?"

He ignored her artificially pitched voice as she murmured to her daughter all the way down the hall and out of sight. Dylan stepped back into the nursery and closed the door. He stared for a long time at the crib, and the litter of stuffed animals inside it. Mindlessly, he reached down, and stroked the silky fur of a teddy bear with a big red bow at its throat. When he'd walked in here, when he'd seen the way Caitlin held Lizzie in her arms, the ecstasy on her face, the relief, the tears of sheer joy...

It was like getting hit between the eyes with a two-by-four.

His hands clutched the brown fur until the bear was twisted into a grotesque blob, his chin fell to his chest and Dylan Rossi cried.

She had no idea how long she huddled on the bed in the obviously unused room. She cried, but she didn't know why. It was ridiculous to feel such devastation over a simple misunderstanding.

Then why was she devastated? Why did it hurt so much to have believed she was a mother for a few precious seconds, and then to learn that she wasn't? Why?

When the knock came, she sat up, and swiped at her tear-stained face with the backs of her hands. It would be Dylan, she had no doubt of that. She got to her feet, and pushed a nervous hand through her hair. She wanted it to be Dylan, she realized slowly. She wanted him to explain what she was feeling, and she wanted him to comfort her, perhaps even hold her, the way a husband would hold a wife. His arms were big, strong, his chest wide and firm. It would feel good to be cradled there, even if it was only a gesture. Even if it meant nothing at all.

She opened the door and frowned at Genevieve's curious, dark gaze.

"You are ill?" she inquired, scanning Caitlin's tear-stained face.

"No. I'm fine."

Genevieve shook her head slowly. "You do not look at all fine. Something troubles you, *non?*"

Caitlin only shook her head. "Really, it's just a headache. I'll be all right." Friend or not in the past, Genevieve was no more than a polite stranger in the present.

The maid looked Caitlin over with a narrow eye, and finally nodded sharply, just once. "Fine, then. Your husband asked me to show you to your rooms. You'll want to

change for dinner.'' She shook her head in that way she
had, that made it seem as if she were scolding herself. ''I
don't know why I did not think that you might not remember the way. My head is not, as you say, screwed straight,
I think.''

Caitlin smiled a little, looking down at the rumpled yellow suit she wore and nodding. Yes, she would like to
change, into something that didn't look like an ad from
some fashion magazine. But when the maid led her to her
rooms, she began to wish she'd stayed where she was. She
stood in the doorway for a moment, blinking. Crimson
chintz draperies with blousoned valances adorned the tall
windows like debs at a Southern ball. The bedspread was
satin, as vividly red as the drapes. The wallpaper's soft
ivory tone was splotched with huge scarlet roses.

For an instant, she saw that shattered windshield,
splashed with blood. Her blood. She shivered.

''Is something wrong?'' Genevieve's hand touched Caitlin's shoulder from behind. ''It is beautiful, *non?*''

She turned slowly, tearing her eyes from the decor to
stare at Genevieve. She blinked twice at the woman, who
was glancing admiringly into the bedroom, then turned to
look at it once more herself.

Beautiful? Maybe, to anyone but her. Maybe the colors
seemed vibrant, and alive to the casual viewer. But all Caitlin could see was the red, and she could almost smell the
blood, and beyond it, the sharp odor of gasoline, and the
pungent smell of fire. The room might have seemed beautiful to her once, but, God, not anymore.

''I'll send Monsieur Rossi for you when dinner is served.
If you have no memory, you won't find your way.'' She
stepped back, and closed the door.

Caitlin drew a bracing breath and made herself walk
through the bedroom. She peered into the adjoining bathroom and found it just as troublesome. Red curtains, even
the shower curtain, with a frilly ruffle bordering it. The

carpet was the same plush ivory tone as that in the bedroom, and that was a welcome relief. There were even red towels, huge and plush, hanging from the racks. She shook her head in disappointment. She hadn't needed one more bothersome thing to add to her list. She'd hoped for a haven, something familiar in her rooms, something that might jar her memory. The only memory this room jarred was that of the accident.

She returned to the bedroom and tugged open a closet. At least she could get rid of this expensive outfit now. But as she sorted through the items hung in neat rows, she found the clothes were all the same. Cropped and tight, in vibrant shades and noisy prints. All expensive, chic and sporting designer labels.

She sighed her disappointment—she'd been longing for something casual and comfortable—and turned to the bureau, already half-sure of what she'd find inside. One drawer spilled over with silken lingerie. Another was filled with spandex leotards, leggings and tops that looked as if they'd never been worn. Finally, buried in the bottom drawer, she uncovered a pair of designer jeans. She was so relieved, she could have cried as she pulled them on.

They were too tight to be comfortable, even though she'd lost weight. They must be old, she thought. Everything else was conspicuously loose on her, though obviously designed to fit like a second skin. She took a green silk, sleeveless blouse from one of the suits in the closet, buttoned it and tucked it in. She added a belt, from the fifty or so she found hanging on a special rack all their own, and knelt to search for footwear. The pumps that lined the closet floor were all alike, except in color. There seemed to be a pair to match every suit that hung above them. At last, she located a pair of running shoes, no doubt top of the line. It seemed the old Caitlin had never settled for anything less. They were as white as if they'd just come off the shelf, and she saw not a crumb of dirt in their tread.

She pulled them on, wondering if Caitlin had been the type who wanted to look great when she exercised, but rarely did so.

She was on the edge of the burgundy-cushioned Queen Anne chair, bending to tie the shoes, when she heard the door open. Dinner was served, then. And her hostile husband was here to fetch her. She felt again that emptiness inside her, and didn't turn to face him. She told herself not to be disappointed that her homecoming wasn't what she'd hoped for. What had she expected? For that hard-faced shadow man to take her in his strong arms and shower her with kisses? That he'd be so glad his wife was alive, he'd overlook the rest? Had she really expected this family to welcome a stranger into its midst?

Strong hands came to rest on her shoulders. She stilled utterly, shocked at the tenderness of that touch after his earlier coldness.

A second later, his head came downward, and lips nuzzled the crook of her neck. She closed her eyes.

They sprung open again when she felt the tickle of a moustache against her skin. She flew to her feet, whirling to face him at the same time. The man who stood there smiling at her was not Dylan. She'd never seen him before. He was shorter than Dylan, but just as powerfully built. His swarthy complexion and blue eyes were unfamiliar, as was the thick black mustache.

"Who are you!" She was breathing hard and fast in her anger.

The man looked stricken. "Surely, you have not forgotten me, *ma chérie?*" He studied her face for a long moment, then shook his head sadly. "Ah, but you have. It is I, Henri. Do you not remember the man who has begged at your feet for so long?"

Henri. Their cook, she recalled. My God, what on earth was going on in this house? She shook her head quickly and fought to find strength to put him straight. She stiffened her spine, and made herself meet his suggestive gaze head-on. "If you ever touch me again, Henri, I'll...I'll tell my husband, and he'll probably fire you on the spot. Is that understood?"

He smiled, one side of the moustache tilting upward. "Do you really believe he would care so much, *ma petite?*" He shook his head. "*Oui,* I dare much in saying so, but it is so clear to me, he does not know how to love a woman like you, he does not know what a treasure he holds. He is a fool—"

"That's enough!"

He stopped speaking, eyes downcast, lips tight. "My apologies. I forget myself in my joy to see you safe and sound once more. It is only that, I assure you, nothing more." His head came up, and his eyes, black and full of mystery, met hers. "Know that *someone,* at least, is happy to see you home again, and *alive* as well, *chérie.*"

His eyes were filled with meaning, and Caitlin felt a chill snake over her spine. "Maybe you'd better go, now." The words were spoken firmly, despite the tremor that shuddered through her body.

He nodded once. "Forgive me if I have upset you. It was not my intent." He turned and left the room.

Caitlin found herself slamming the door behind him, and throwing the lock. Stupid, senseless behavior, she told herself. He hadn't harmed her, or threatened to. And his affection would probably have been flattering, under any other circumstances. But, God, there was enough of a rift between her and Dylan without this added burden. Was Henri in the habit of flirting with Caitlin? Had she allowed such behavior in the past? Or was he truly only reacting to her close brush with death, as he'd implied?

She leaned her forehead against the cool, dark wood and closed her eyes. He'd implied that not everyone was glad to have her back, and the emphasis he'd placed on the word "alive" still rung in her ears. What had he meant by that?

Was he giving her some cryptic warning? She'd felt sheer terror at her first sight of this house. Might there be a reason for that reaction?

She straightened and paced away from the door. They were keeping things from her. She already knew that. Part of her had agreed to come back here just to unravel the questions of her past, to learn what secrets Dylan was keeping from her and why. But another part, the part that had trembled at first sight of this house, and still trembled, in something other than fear, whenever she was close to her husband, wanted to leave. To go someplace where no one knew her and start fresh, and forget she'd ever had a past that had been erased from her mind.

She shook her head slowly, knowing even as the thought occurred to her that she wouldn't run away. She had to learn about her life before. Something inside was insisting on it. She might never be whole again, until she did.

Dinner was like a wake. A wake in a cold mausoleum filled with false smiles and stilted conversation. It was difficult for all of them, she realized dully. Sitting with a woman they'd once known well, a woman who was now a stranger. Knowing she didn't remember a thing about any of them.

The glasses were crystal, and the table shone with polished silver and the muted glow of the candelabra on the sideboard.

Caitlin wished she'd never come out of her room when the timid maid had found her there. But she had. She'd dried her eyes and tried to squelch the devastation she felt tearing her in two, and followed Genevieve to the formal dining room, achingly aware that Dylan hadn't wanted to come for her himself.

She picked at her food, eating little. She had no appetite tonight. The entire room was filled to the breaking point with tension, and she knew too well that she was the cause.

Dylan sat at the head of the glossy, dark wood table, eyes sharp and always moving. He paid close attention to every move she made, every bite she took. His features were tight, drawn as if he was in pain. He wasn't, though. She imagined he was just disgusted at having her in his house, in his elegant dining room with its dark-stained woodwork and its immaculate stucco ceiling. She certainly didn't feel she belonged here, beneath the muted glow of an antique brass chandelier.

"It would be a welcome relief if this weather would break," Dylan observed, spearing a bit of the succulent roast beef with his fork. "It isn't usually this bad here, Caitlin."

"I hardly notice the heat," she said. No, what she noticed was the lighted candles spilling their warm glow on his face, softening it in a way that was utterly false. "The house is so cool, and I haven't been outside at all."

"You used to..." Thomas stopped before he finished the sentence. He was just as tall and solidly built as Dylan, but his hair was brilliantly carrot-colored and wildly curly. Freckles spattered his face, and his eyes were troubled. "Sorry. You don't want to hear about what you used to do."

"Yes, I do," Caitlin told him. "What were you going to say?"

He met her gaze, a look of uncertainty in his. "You used to love to walk along the cliffs at night. Said you could hear the wind singing with the sea."

Caitlin closed her eyes, wishing she could recall that feeling.

"That was before. It wouldn't be a good idea to indulge in that habit now, Caitlin. You're not familiar with the cliffs, and there are some dangerous spots out there."

She frowned at Dylan, at the tone of command she heard in his forbidding voice. And then she stilled utterly, just staring into his dark eyes, glittering in the candlelight.

She'd seen them glitter before...but in moonlight...and the strong emotion in their dark brown depths had been passion, not anger.

From somewhere far away, she heard an echoing whisper, a masculine voice, his voice. *Always, Caity. No matter what.*

"He's right, Cait." Thomas's voice intruded on her dream-state. "Better stay clear of the cliffs until...unless—until you're better." Her brother's lips thinned, and he broke eye contact with her to stare without much interest at his food.

Caitlin's stare was drawn back to Dylan. To the muscled column of his neck, the taut forearms revealed by his rolled-back sleeves. Her stomach twisted into a knot.

Across from Thomas, Sandra lifted her pale golden eyebrows. "It's not like she's crippled, you guys." She shook her head, and sent Caitlin a glance. "Don't let them start bossin' you around, or you'll never leave the house again. Believe me, I know 'em. Not just Tommy, but Dylan, too," she drawled sweetly. "Matter of fact, now that you lost your memory, I prob'ly know him better than anybody."

She glanced up at Dylan as she said it. He sat at her elbow, and returned her quick glance. His might have been slightly amused, but it was too short for Caitlin to be sure. She felt a sudden, swift jab of jealousy. It was ridiculous. After all, Thomas was only twenty-nine, and if Caitlin was any judge of ages, Sandra couldn't be more than twenty-two. She was practically a child, for God's sake.

Still, she was beautiful, her long, silvery blond hair hanging over one shoulder, her rounded breasts straining against the clingy fabric of her skintight black dress. It was short, exposing most of her shapely thighs to anyone who cared to look. Her voice, laced with that delicate Southern accent, made every sentence she spoke like a caress. Besides all that, she was the mother of the child Caitlin had thought was her own.

"We're in for a storm," Ellen remarked. "Been building up to it all week. I feel it in my joints."

"And your joints are usually right," Dylan returned, his gaze softening when it lit on Ellen's.

Caitlin picked at her food, and told herself not to feel animosity toward her sister-in-law. Sandra had done nothing to deserve it. She turned her attention to Thomas, who sat beside her. Her brother. How could her own brother seem like a perfect stranger to her? There was a strong resemblance between them, she noticed. His green eyes looked a lot like her own.

"Something wrong, Caitlin?"

He'd caught her staring at him. She shook her head. "No, I ...I was just trying to remember."

"To remember what?"

She shrugged. "Anything. What it was like growing up together. Whether you were a jock in high school, whether I..." She sighed and shook her head.

Thomas set his fork down with exaggerated care. "Our parents divorced while we were in high school. You stayed with Dad, I went with Mom."

She licked her lips. He seemed uncomfortable with the subject, but her curiosity was pestering her. "Why did they break up?"

"Because he was a bastard."

The sentence was clipped, and Thomas's eyes became hooded. "You never believed that, though."

"Is that why I stayed with him?"

He shook his head. "You were his princess, Caitlin. You blamed Mom for the breakup. No one really expected you to leave the lap of luxury and live the way we did."

Her eyes widened as he spoke, and she searched his reddening face, then glanced toward Dylan.

"That's enough, Thomas. What happened wasn't her fault."

"It's all right," Caitlin said quickly. "I want to know—"

"No, Cait." Thomas lowered his head, pushed one large hand through his curls and sighed hard. "Dylan's right. I'm sorry. It gets to me sometimes, that's all." He met her puzzled stare. "It was a mess. A big, ugly mess." He shoved his plate away from him, pushed his chair back and stalked out of the opulent dining room.

"Why'd you have to bring all that up? Dammit, Caitlin, he'll be ornery for the rest of the night, now."

Caitlin blinked rapidly at the woman who was her sister-in-law. "I'm sorry. I didn't mean—"

"Don't apologize, Caitlin." Dylan's gaze met hers for the first time that evening. "Your brother is still angry—"

"With good reason," Sandra cut in.

"Sandra O'Brien, it's time someone taught you some manners!" The declaration came loudly from Ellen, who sat across from Caitlin, and was accompanied by a wrinkled fist banging the table.

"Oh, hell, you're all treatin' her like she'll break in a strong wind!" She glanced at Caitlin. "If Thomas is still mad at you, it's no wonder, and I don't blame him!"

Dylan stood slowly, purposefully. "Go and see to your family, Sandra." His words were not shouted, but their tone carried the same impact as if they had been. And suddenly, the tall, powerful form of Caitlin's husband seemed terrifying. "Now."

Sandra rose, glaring at all of the them in turn. Dylan sat down slowly, saying nothing.

"Fine. That's just fine." She threw her linen napkin down on her plate, and hurried from the room.

Caitlin sighed, and leaned her head into her hands, elbows propped on the table. "I'm sorry. I didn't mean to spoil everyone's dinner."

A low, rasping chuckle brought her head up, and she met Ellen's glazed brown eyes, which were crinkled at the outer corners. "Didn't spoil mine, girl. I'd much rather eat without that kind of comp'ny."

Caitlin shook her head. She looked across the table to Dylan. "Why is my brother so angry with me?"

"He's not angry with you. Only at what happened. Your parents' divorce is ancient history now, Caitlin. He got over it a long time ago."

"But he was so—"

"It bothers him to talk about it, that's all. He was a kid, his family split up. It's understandable, isn't it?"

She bit her inner cheek, and finally nodded. "I suppose so."

"He doesn't resent you, Caitlin. When Sandra got pregnant, he didn't have two dimes to rub together. You're the one who offered to let them move in here—"

"And nagged Dylan until he gave the worthless bum a job," Ellen cut in.

"I did?" Caitlin shook her head. It was difficult to picture herself nagging Dylan. His very presence shook her to the marrow.

She looked up then, curious, scanning his handsome face with sudden interest. "What kind of job? God, do you realize, I don't even know what you do?"

He licked his lips, his eyes narrowing as if he wasn't sure she spoke the truth. "I'm an architect."

"Best architect in the state," Ellen added. "Owns his own firm, a whole office building's worth."

Caitlin nodded, looking around the richly furnished room. "That explains this place. You must make a lot of money."

His head came up, eyes alert. "You want to talk money now, Caitlin?"

She frowned, not understanding the sudden bitterness in his tone. Had she said something wrong?

"It's your house, not mine. I never wanted it. I still don't."

Caitlin was stunned. She sent a glance toward Ellen, who only nodded her affirmation. She shook her head. "I don't understand." She felt sick to her stomach. The more she learned about the past, the more confused she became. But she had to know, didn't she?

"Water under the bridge," Ellen declared all at once. "And here's dessert. You both better dig in, 'cause I hate to eat alone."

Genevieve crossed the room with a tray of dessert plates, laden with chocolate cake and whipped cream. She set one in front of Caitlin. Caitlin closed her eyes. "I don't think I can—"

"Sure you can. Barely touched your dinner, girl. You're already thin as a rake. Eat up."

Ellen lifted a forkful to her lips, and sighed as though she'd found ecstasy. Caitlin couldn't help but smile at the older woman. Ellen might dislike her, but Caitlin was beginning to wonder if she might have good reason. There had obviously been a lot of animosity in this marriage. Ellen pretty clearly adored her nephew.

"You really must try to eat," Genevieve put in. "I can see how much weight you have lost since the accident. You'll get well sooner if you eat."

She felt Dylan's eyes on her, and knew Genevieve was right. She had lost weight. The designer clothes hung looser than they should. Her curves didn't strain the seams the way Sandra's did. She dipped her fork, and lifted it. She'd force herself.

The fork was slapped out of her hand with stunning force just before it reached her lips. It clattered to the floor, smearing cake and cream all over the marbled black tiles.

"Ellen, what the hell—"

"It's carob!" was her shouted answer to her nephew's unfinished question. "Did you eat any, girl?"

Ellen was shoving her own water glass into Caitlin's

hands as she spoke. Dylan was on his feet, shouting at Genevieve. "What in God's name were you thinking?"

"I didn't know! I swear, Monsieur Rossi, I had no idea."

He brushed past the trembling maid and stood beside Caitlin. "Are you all right?"

She set the water glass down and stared up at him in shock. Was that concern or fury she heard in his tight voice? She nodded. "Yes, fine, but I don't understand. What in the world is carob?"

Dylan sighed hard and pushed a hand through his hair. "A bean from some Mediterranean evergreen. It's used as a chocolate substitute, among other things. You have violent reaction to carob, Caitlin. Rare, but potentially lethal. This damned dessert could have killed you."

His gaze met Ellen's, and there was some hidden knowledge that passed between them. "How did you know?"

Ellen shook her head. "I know real chocolate, boy. This stuff has a bitter aftertaste to it." She made a face.

Dylan glared at the maid, who was crying loudly. "Get Henri in here. I want to get to the bottom of this."

She nodded jerkily and hurried out of the room.

"You're sure you're all right?" Ellen asked. "You didn't eat any of it?"

"No, not a crumb." Caitlin felt the trembling in her hands, and she tried to force it to stop. First the accident, and then this, an inner voice whispered. Almost as if someone were deliberately out to get her. She gripped herself mentally, and shook. It was ridiculous. She was only being paranoid.

The dark look that passed between Ellen and Dylan just then made Caitlin's heart skip a beat.

She turned toward Dylan, certain there was something he wasn't telling her. She opened her mouth to demand an explanation, then closed it again. She was tired, upset. It was her first day home after a serious accident, a week in coma and a total loss of her own identity. Her judgment was far from what it should be. She was overreacting to what surely must have been an accident. Dylan disliked her enough without her shouting accusations of conspiracy at him over dinner. Her head throbbed. She rose slowly, closed her eyes at the increased pain in her skull.

"Caitlin?"

She opened her eyes and faced him. "I'm just going upstairs to lie down. It's...been a long day."

Genevieve reentered the dining room, with Henri at her side. His eyes met Caitlin's with a silent reminder of his earlier, veiled warning glowing from their onyx-black depths. Dylan moved toward Caitlin, one hand on her arm telling her to stay where she was.

"Henri, I want an explanation for this dessert. And it had better be a good one." Dylan's voice was dangerous, and its depth made her tremble. He shot her a brief, side-long glance. He must have felt the vibrations shuddering through her arm, where his hand still rested. He took it away.

"Monsieur Rossi, I promise you, I had no idea the cake was made with carob. It was delivered this afternoon."

"*Oui,*" Genevieve added quickly. "I answered the door."

"Delivered from where?" Dylan demanded.

"The box said Alyce's Bakery. There...there was a card." Genevieve's voice trembled.

"Get it."

As she scurried out of the room once more, Caitlin looked up at the towering, angry form of her husband. "Dylan, I'm sure it was an honest mistake. Please don't—" She broke off at his quelling glance.

"The *madame* is right," Henri put in. "She must know *I* would never do anything to hurt her. This was simply a tragic error."

"I'll be the judge of that." Dylan snatched the small envelope from Genevieve's hand when she returned. He pulled out the card and read, "Wishing you a speedy recovery. It's signed, the Andersons."

"Who are they?"

He frowned down at the card, answering Caitlin's question without looking at her. "Our nearest neighbors. They live a mile farther down the road." He shook his head. "I'd better call them, just to be sure—"

"No chance of that, boy. They left for Europe yesterday. An extended vacation. Mahalia Anderson called to say goodbye just before they left." As she spoke, Ellen got up from the table.

Dylan sighed hard. "From now on, Henri, no food comes to this table unless it's prepared by you. This might have been a fluke, but it could happen again."

"Of course." Henri turned those knowing eyes on Caitlin. "I am terribly sorry, *madame*. I hope you believe that."

Caitlin only nodded. "Of course. It wasn't your fault." She glanced up at Dylan. "I really would like to go up and lie down now."

"Fine."

She licked her lips. "I'm not sure I remember the way. Genevieve brought me down and I wasn't paying much attention. This place is so big…"

His gaze slid past her to Genevieve and for an instant she thought he would abandon her to the maid's care. The Frenchwoman's eyes were wide, nervous, before she averted them. Poor thing. Caitlin knew *she'd* hate to be on the receiving end of Dylan's anger.

After a moment's hesitation, Dylan sighed, took her arm and turned her toward the doorway.

She felt three pairs of eyes on her all the way out, and she suppressed a shudder. Dylan led her up the stairs, through a number of tall, narrow corridors, all lined in that same gleaming, dark wood. The grim paintings all looked alike, abstract displays of dull colors that meant nothing.

She was sure she'd never learn how to find her way around this mausoleum that was supposedly *her* house.

Finally, he paused and opened a door. Caitlin stepped inside and stopped, glancing around. The deep red decor stared back at her. Her feet sunk, but refused to move, in the plush carpet.

She shook her head and took a step backward into the hall. All that red. God, why couldn't she shut out the image of the blood-spattered windshield? She felt the sticky, warm flow on her neck again, and she closed her eyes tightly to block out the vision.

"You don't like it? Caitlin, you decorated it yourself."

She turned away from him, and drew several deep breaths. "It'll be fine."

He caught her shoulders and turned her to face him. "Look, Caitlin, if you don't want this room, say so. There are plenty of others." His hands stilled on her outer arms. He'd only need to bend his elbows to pull her against him. She almost wished he would. She almost longed for his hard chest as a pillow, his muscled arms as blankets, closing out the confusion, the pain.

She shook her head. And then she felt the phantom sensations like whispers on her body. Friction. Skin against skin. Hot, wet, frantic. Something skittered through her midsection. A tensing, a longing. Why didn't he pull her into his arms?

"I—um—" She fought to pull her thoughts into order. "I don't want to be difficult—"

"Since when?"

Her chin rose at the cynicism in his voice. It had hit her like a bucket of ice water, shocking her back to reality. She met his gaze and saw the censure in his eyes. Had she thought he might harbor a single spark of feeling for her? Was she insane?

"The room is fine. Thank you for bringing me up." She

forced herself to step back inside, refusing to look at the stifling, dramatic red that surrounded her. She closed the door behind her.

Chapter 4

The disappointment was like some living force, draining the energy from her body. But then, what kind of homecoming had she expected? One where her loving family members would hug her hard, one by one, their eyes filled with genuine joy that she was alive and back with them, instead of suspicions and secrets?

And it wasn't only the anticlimactic first day home that was getting to her. It was compounded by the still unidentifiable sense of loss, the gnawing ache for something she couldn't identify, the feeling that she was on the brink of tears all the time. Not being able to remember the reason did nothing to dull the pain.

Then there was this other feeling, the invisible threat, the menace of this cold, echoing house. The way the circular knots in the wood's dark grain seemed like evil eyes, always watching, waiting.

God, waiting for what?

It was ridiculous to feel so vulnerable, so much at risk, and she knew it was more a result of the trauma she'd been through than any real danger. She was in *her* house, with *her* family. There was no reason for this insane feeling that she was being stalked, or that the carob-laced dessert had been a deliberate attempt to hurt her.

It had been a gift.

But Caitlin couldn't help but wonder if it was more than just a coincidence, as she recalled again the speaking glances Dylan had exchanged with his aunt, and Henri's earlier words, laden with meaning.

She hadn't lied when she'd said she was tired, but instead of resting, she paced like a condemned prisoner. Again and again she moved past the foot of the tall, four-poster bed, its wood nearly charcoal, gleaming, its posts rising as high as gallows.

Gallows? What made me think that?

Finally, when she knew she wouldn't close her eyes until she did so, she picked up the phone on her bedside stand, dialed information and got the number for Alyce's Bakery, in Eden. She dialed that number, and waited.

"'lyce's. What can I do for you?'' The feminine voice was one that sounded as though it answered the phone in the same way many times each day, even dropping the "A" in "Alyce's."

Caitlin licked her lips. "My name is Caitlin Rossi. A cake was delivered to me today, but, uh, the card was missing. I wanted to thank whoever sent it to me, if I could."

"Just a minute." The answer was quick and brief. Not even a pause, as if Caitlin's story sounded fishy. "You said Rossi?"

"Yes."

"That cake was sent by Mr. and Mrs. Jacob Anderson."

"Oh."

"You have a nice—"

"Wait!" Caitlin drew a steadying breath. "Can I ask... how it was paid for? I mean, credit card, check or—"

"Sure, just a sec." Pages riffled in the background. "Cash, Mrs. Rossi. Was there a problem with the cake? Is someone looking for a refund, or—"

"No, nothing like that. There was just a question as to who sent it. The Andersons are in Europe, you see, so..."

"Hmm. Well, maybe they asked someone to take care of this for them. The order was waiting when we opened up this morning."

"Waiting?"

"Yup. Cash and instructions in an envelope, slipped through the mail slot in the door. We get those all the time, 'course they're not usually cash, but once in a while..."

"I see. And the instructions, did they specify carob instead of chocolate cake?"

"That's right."

No one actually saw the person who placed the order.

A tree branch scraped across the window glass, like fingernails on a chalkboard.

"Thank you for your help."

"Anytime, Mrs. Rossi."

And they paid in cash, so there's no way to trace the source.

Caitlin hung up the phone, an antique replica, gleaming black with brass trim and a bell-shaped mouthpiece. It was just coincidence. There was no reason to see diabolical plots around every corner. She could well imagine Mr. and Mrs. Anderson, whoever they were, hurrying to the airport to catch their flight early this morning before the shops opened, and remembering at the last minute that today was the day their critically injured neighbor was to come home from the hospital. So they'd improvised, stuffed some cash and some instructions in an envelope, and dropped it off at the bakery, barely breaking stride in their rush to catch their flight.

It was possible.

But not very likely.

She shook herself, vowing to put the entire incident out of her mind, and went into the adjoining bathroom. A long, hot soak might help her rest.

She'd only peeked in here briefly before. She was unprepared for a spigot in the shape of a lion's head. She shuddered, and adjusted the knobs until steamy water spewed from the gaping maw. The tub had clawed feet. She'd missed that before, too. She'd been too busy noticing the blood-red decor. She looked around a bit more now, while the tub filled. A spider wriggled its legs, in a high corner, while a fly struggled to free itself from the web.

She bit her lip, trying not to liken herself to the fly. She was being ridiculous, melodramatic, overly afraid.

She forced grim thoughts aside and left the tub to fill while she searched for a comfortable nightgown. She had in mind an oversize football jersey or a dorm shirt. What she found, instead, were long and flowing, softly feminine nightgowns. Every fabric from cotton and soft white linen, to silk, and sheer gauze. Every color from one end of the spectrum to the other.

Apparently, the old Caitlin had a touch of a romantic inside her. Had she bought so many attractive nightgowns with her husband in mind? Or was it just that she'd been fond of pretty things?

Caitlin stilled, holding a white muslin gown held up by its spaghetti straps. One thing about this room was obvious. It was hers, and hers alone. There wasn't a single thing in it that suggested the presence of a man. Not a bit of masculine clothing anywhere. No men's colognes or shaving implements in the bathroom. Only one toothbrush, standing alone in a cup on the edge of the basin.

How long had they used separate bedrooms? she wondered. Had Dylan moved his things out since the accident, in an effort to make things easier on her? Or had it been this way far longer?

Another unanswered question to add to her growing list. Sighing, she took the nightgown with her into the bathroom, and twisted the knobs to stop the flow of steaming water. It brimmed near the overflow drain, and already the mirror and small window were coated in mist. Clouds of it rolled off the surface of the water, invitingly. Caitlin stripped off the designer jeans and silk blouse. She wasn't overly fond of either of them. They looked like the clothes of a rich, well-placed, confident woman.

Maybe that was why she felt so uncomfortable in them now. She didn't feel rich or well-placed, and she was anything but confident. She felt alone and afraid, unsure of herself and everyone around her. Putting on the expensive clothes was like putting on a disguise. They belonged to another woman. A woman she no longer knew.

The long, steaming bath she indulged in did little to settle her nerves, though she did her best not to look at the spigot, or the spider.

Her skin damp, she pulled on the nightgown, and slid beneath her satin sheets, but was unable to sleep for hours. Countless questions and myriad possible answers flooded her brain each time she closed her eyes. Finally, though, exhaustion took over, and she did sleep, only to be tormented by vivid, disturbing dreams.

She was standing in warm, wet sand. There was rain pelting her skin. Her wet hair clung to her neck and shoulders, until large, strong hands pushed it away, and moist lips moved over her skin where it had been.

There was a chilly wind. Goose bumps rose on her arms and naked thighs. Those hands moved down over the curve of her spine, long, graceful fingers kneaded her buttocks, pulled her close to hardness and heat, held her there.

She couldn't see, in the dream. Her head was tipped back and her eyes were closed. She could only *feel,* and what she felt made her breath come in short little gasps, and her heart beat faster.

A mouth covered hers, and she parted her lips in silent welcome. A tongue probed, thrust, suggesting things that heated her blood to boiling. She reveled in the feel of it and curled her arms around his neck, threaded her fingers in his hair, pressed her hips harder against his.

Then the mouth lifted just slightly, lips still brushing hers as they moved to form words. "I love you, Caity. I always will. No matter what."

"Dylan…"

She'd spoken his name aloud in her sleep, and the sound of her own voice roused her, broke the seductive spell the dream had wrapped around her, brought her back to cold, harsh, lonely reality.

She sat up in the bed, blinking in the darkness. Her fingers rose of their own volition to touch her lips, which seemed to burn with the memory of those phantom kisses, then brushed over her breasts to find their nipples taut and yearning. She shuddered. Had it been a dream, or a buried memory? Had Dylan ever held her, touched her like that? Had he ever whispered those words against her lips with such passion? Or had it all been a figment of her imagination?

She pressed a hot palm to her sweat-slick forehead and lay back down. Would she ever know? God, had she really had something that intense once, only to let it slip away?

It was 5:00 a.m. when the baby began crying. Caitlin was wide-awake, curled into a ball on her own bed, still shaken from her dream of making love with Dylan, still dreading its return...and longing for it. She lifted her head, listening, waiting for Lizzie's cries to be answered. But they went on and on. No one seemed to be in any hurry to check on the poor little thing.

Caitlin flung back her covers and got out of bed. She chewed her thumbnail and began to pace the room. Surely, someone would pick Lizzie up soon. They had to. She felt it wasn't her place to step in and care for the child herself. Sandra might resent the intrusion, and so might Thomas. She didn't want to do anything else to alienate her family.

"I'm being utterly ridiculous," she said firmly. "I'm her aunt, and no one else is bothering to take care of her."

Caitlin pulled her door open and strode out into the hall. Darkness greeted her. No light spilled through the drawn draperies, which stood between the night beyond the towering windows and the darker halls within. No lamp had been left aglow to show her the way. She glanced up and down, all the same, as a chill assaulted her body, and the hairs on her nape prickled with electricity. She narrowed her eyes, gazing into utter blackness as if by doing so she'd somehow sense if anyone was there, watching. There was only the scent of rich wood and oil polish, and the sound of Lizzie's cries. She told herself there was no reason to think anyone would be, but the shiver up her spine argued that point, so she looked, anyway. She felt nothing but emptiness. Utter isolation. She was alone, right to the soul of her.

The baby still cried and Caitlin turned in that direction, stepping softly, her bare feet making no sound on the plush carpet. She strained her ears to hear if anyone else was up, moving around, maybe answering the baby's demands already. She heard nothing. Or did she?

She halted, glancing over her shoulder, puckering her face in concentration as her heart was slowly filled with ice water. There was a sound. Not footsteps. No, something much more menacing than that.

Breathing, all but silent; slow inhales, deliberately quiet exhales came to her in steady rhythm. It seemed to grow louder as she listened. Or was it in her mind? Was the stalker coming nearer? Was that his heart she heard pounding, or her own?

She whirled and ran the rest of the way. The baby's cries still guided her, drawing her in as surely as a lighthouse guides a ship among the rocks and reefs, to shore.

She didn't slow down at the nursery door, only gripped it and flung it open, ducking inside and closing it behind her; turning the lock by sheer instinct.

She leaned back against the cool wood, fighting to catch her breath, and calm her rapid pulse as the baby kept crying in an odd sort of cadence that worked to ease her panic. She got her breathing under control. As jumpy as she was, it might well have been her own slow breaths she'd heard out there just now. Or even the rhythmic respirations of

someone sleeping with the door open, in one of the bedrooms she'd passed.

It was neither of those and you know it.

She ignored the voice of her fears and moved toward the
crib. There was a fluttering, then a clenching of Caitlin's
abdominal muscles, a heavy sort of ache in her breasts.

She leaned over and scooped Lizzie up. "Hush, little
one," she murmured, cuddling her close. "Ooh, you're
wet, aren't you? No wonder you're so grouchy."

Her attention was only half-focused on Lizzie as she laid
the child on the changing table, stripped her down and
washed her pink bottom. The other half was busy glancing
every few seconds at the locked door. Despite her silent
rationalization, she almost expected to see the handle move
as someone tried to get in. It didn't, and in a few more
moments, Caitlin shook her head slowly, wondering if she
were losing her mind.

Naked, Lizzie kicked her feet and waved her hands, cooing and chirping like a little bird on the first day of spring.
As Caitlin taped a fresh diaper in place, Lizzie grinned
broadly, dimples in her cheeks and her chin, toothless gums
fully exposed.

Caitlin found herself smiling back. "Your auntie is a
little bit paranoid, Lizzie. Must have been that bump on the
head." She struggled to capture Lizzie's flying feet, one at
a time, and fit them into the legs of a soft sleeper. Then
her arms. "Anyone could have been out there in the hallway tonight. Right? You were crying loudly enough to
wake the dead. Just because no one around here is overly
fond of me, doesn't mean they spend their nights following
me around this gloomy old place. Does it, Lizzie?" She
fastened the snaps, and scooped the baby up once more,
heading for the rocking chair near the window.

Her explanation wasn't very convincing. Sure, someone
might have been on their way to see to the baby, but if so,
why hadn't they spoken? Why try so hard to keep their

presence behind her a secret? And even if she could make herself believe it was just a coincidence, it didn't erase the earlier incident. Somehow or other, a cake that was poison to her had wound up on her dessert plate tonight. She'd tried to explain it away as she lay in bed, but combined with the presence in the pitch-dark hallway just now, she wondered. The "accidents" and "coincidences" were beginning to pile high.

"I cannot find her, Monsieur Rossi."

Dylan frowned over the morning paper and his coffee cup at the maid. "What do you mean, you can't find her?"

"She is not in her room."

Dylan glanced at his watch, and shook his head. He had to be in the office today. He didn't have time to play Caitlin's games.

"Not thinkin' of going off to work without even seeing her, are you, boy?"

He tossed the newspaper down none too gently. "As a matter of fact, Ellen—"

A crooked finger was waggled near his nose. "Head injury like that, no tellin' what's become of her. Might have gone for a walk and taken a fall. Might be lost, maybe passed out somewhere. Can't just leave, Dylan Rossi, no matter how you feel about her. That explosive temper of yours makes you forget things. She's still your wife, your responsibility. I taught you better than that."

Dylan drew a deep breath, to keep his "explosive temper" from raining down on Ellen. "I'm not going anywhere until I know what she's up to."

"You're not worried?" Ellen demanded. "After the accident, and that close call last night?"

"Ellen, there was no proof that accident was anything but accidental."

"The brake line—"

"Was torn, not cut." He spoke slowly, carefully.

"You might try saying so without sounding so defensive, boy. And what about that cake last night?" Ellen squinted at him through her thick-lensed glasses.

"Are you sure she didn't send it herself, Ellen? Just another ploy, though God knows what she could hope to get out of it. Attention? Or maybe she's trying to set me up for attempted murder, so she can take the whole shebang."

Ellen looked stunned. She stopped eating and blinked down at the plate in front of her. "Well, I never heard of such a thing," she muttered.

"I'm not saying it's a fact, just that it's something to keep in mind. Don't get taken in by her acts. I don't intend to."

"Dylan!"

He looked up at Sandra's shout and saw her coming toward the table, wringing her hands. "What is it now, Sandra?"

"I can't get in the nursery. Door's locked from the inside, and I—" She broke off, glancing around the table. "Where is she?"

Dylan felt a small fist poke him in the gut. "Where is who?"

"Oh, Lord, she's in there with Lizzie, isn't she? That knock on the head was more serious than anyone thought. She's gone off the deep end and now she's holed up with my baby. Dylan, do somethin'!"

Dylan was on his feet before she finished her tirade, gripping Sandra's shoulders to calm her down. "Did you try knocking?"

"N-no. I didn't want to wake the baby. We can't just go up there and knock, Dylan, it might set 'er off." The more agitated Sandra became, the thicker her twang grew. "Git the key. Please, for God's sake, git the key."

"All right. All right, just calm down." She pressed herself to his chest, clinging to his shoulders as if she would fall down without his support. Dylan rolled his eyes. Sandra was nothing if not overly dramatic. "Caitlin would never do anything to hurt a baby, for God's sake."

"How do you know," she moaned. "She's different now. Like a stranger."

Dylan shook his head.

Ellen stood, slapping a hand to Sandra's shoulder from behind. "You want to blubber, girl, go find your own husband to hang all over and let Dylan get that door opened up."

She gave a rather ungentle tug and tore Sandra from Dylan's chest. Leave it to Aunt Ellen not to pull punches. Dylan knew damned well Thomas was still in bed, sleeping. Thomas had been up pacing the halls half the night. Dylan knew, because he'd been restless last night, too. After he'd called the bakery the cake had come from, only to be told his wife had already called, after he'd demanded they tell him, word for word, what they'd told her, he'd been too keyed up to sleep.

He turned toward the kitchen, and located the right key on the rack. Then he went back through the dining room, and on to the foyer and the stairway, with Sandra right on his heels. Thomas's young wife had one valid point. Caitlin was acting differently, strangely. Quiet, almost timid. Her usual assertiveness seemed to have disappeared along with her memory.

As he stopped outside the nursery door, a little ripple of apprehension went through him. Suppose Sandra wasn't overreacting? Suppose there *was* some lingering aftereffect of the accident that had left Caitlin less than sane, and suppose that baby in there was just the shove it took to push her over the edge? Maybe his problems would be solved in a way he hadn't even considered. If she were dangerous, maybe Caitlin would have to be institutionalized. Hadn't he wondered about her mental state all along? It was why he hadn't told her the secret he was keeping. She might know, though. She might have remembered. She might have some kernel of subconscious awareness buried in her mind, and it might be just a little more than her injured brain could take.

He turned the key in the lock, twisted the doorknob, and pushed it silently open.

Caitlin sat in the rocker, with her head leaning to one side, eyes closed, her long lashes just touching her sculpted cheekbones. Her hair was a wild tangle of auburn curls and there wasn't a trace of makeup anywhere to be seen. She wore a thin white nightgown, and her arms, thinner than he remembered, and bare to the shoulders, pale from being hidden from the sun for too long, were wrapped protectively around Lizzie. The baby was cradled to her chest, sleeping just as soundly as Caitlin. The relaxed little cherub-face was nestled in the crook of Caitlin's neck.

A searing hot blade sliced cleanly through Dylan's heart, and he grated his teeth against the flood of pain that would have liked to cripple him. He blinked twice, cleared his throat and made himself move forward as Sandra stood in the doorway, sighing in relief.

He leaned over, lifted a hand toward his wife's face, then lowered it. "Caitlin," he said.

Her eyes flew wide, and she stiffened.

"It's all right, it's only me." He searched her emerald eyes for any sign of insanity and found none. She calmed at once, drawing a breath, shaking her head self-deprecatingly. She lowered her gaze to the baby in her arms, and the most tender smile he'd ever seen whispered across her lips. She slowly got up, walked to the crib and lowered the baby into it, careful not to wake her, then tucked a tiny blanket over Lizzie and turned.

A finger to her lips for silence, she tiptoed into the hallway, past Sandra. Dylan followed, and pulled the door closed behind him.

Sandra turned on Caitlin the second the door was

closed. "Do you mind tellin' me just what the hell you think you're doin'?"

"Ssh, you'll wake her." Caitlin frowned at the door, then at Sandra.

"She's my baby, Caitlin. I'll wake her if I want to."

Caitlin shook her head. "I know whose baby she is." She frowned until her auburn brows touched. "What I don't know is why you're so upset. Last night she cried for a half hour before I got up and went to her. She was soaking wet and probably hoarse from all that yelling. You didn't get up so I did. What's the problem?"

Sandra closed her eyes slowly. "Oh, God, it must have been the antihistamine I took last night. I never heard her." She opened her eyes again, and in an instant the anger and worry that had clouded them was replaced by regret. A second after that, her blue eyes narrowed again, searching Caitlin's face. "But that doesn't explain why you locked yourself in the nursery with Lizzie. I was scared half to death when I couldn't git that door open."

Dylan put a hand on Caitlin's shoulder, firm, not comforting. "Caitlin, why did you lock the door?"

She whirled to face him, blinking twice before she seemed to understand. "Oh…so that's what…" She lowered her head and pressed one palm to it. When she looked up again, it was to face Sandra. "God, no wonder you're ready to strangle me. I'm sorry I worried you, Sandra, really, I didn't mean to." She lifted her hands, palms up, and shook her head. "I did it without thinking. I was scared half to death, and I—"

"Scared of what?" Dylan caught her arm and turned her to face him again.

She licked her lips, and met his gaze only briefly, before looking away. "I don't know. It was probably nothing but a case of nerves."

Dylan frowned. "Tell me what happened." His hand still clasped her upper arm.

"Really, Caitlin. If somethin' scared you that bad—"

Caitlin shook her head slowly. "I didn't sleep well."

He nodded. He'd already noted the puffy eyes, the beginnings of dark circles forming beneath them. She was pale, too, and on edge. "Bad dreams?" he asked.

Her green eyes pierced his like arrows, and for just a second, he glimpsed a raw longing in their depths; a longing that shook him right to his frozen core. "Dreams. Not bad ones, though." Her cheeks flushed with color, and she turned away, facing Sandra instead of him. "I woke when I heard Lizzie, about 5:00 a.m. The halls were pitch-black, and I don't really know this place well enough to find light switches in the dark. I just followed the cries."

Her lips thinned, and Dylan saw her throat move as she swallowed. He jerked his gaze upward again. "Go on, Caitlin."

She shook her head. "I thought I heard something… behind me. Someone…breathing. It seemed to get louder, as if they were coming closer, and when I moved, it kept pace." She sighed. "I panicked, and ran the rest of the way. When I got to the nursery, it was a reflex to slam the door and throw the lock. I didn't even think about it, just did it." She lifted her gaze to Sandra's. "I'm really sorry I scared you, Sandra."

Sandra drew a deep breath, then let it out as she nodded. "It's okay." She shifted from one foot to the other. "Look, next time, why don't you just wake me up, all right? I'd really rather see to her myself."

Caitlin nodded. "If that's what you want." She couldn't keep the hurt from her voice, or hide it from her eyes.

Sandra nodded and turned to leave them. Dylan took Caitlin's arm and began walking. She tugged it free.

"We need to talk, Caitlin, and we can't do it here. Come on." He resumed walking, not touching her this time, and she followed. He stopped at her bedroom, opened the door and held it as she preceded him in.

She moved slowly toward the bed, then turned to face him. "What is it we need to talk about?"

"What happened last night? Did you see anyone?"

She looked down at the floor, closed her eyes slowly, shook her head from one side to the other. "This is like walking blind through a maze."

"*What?*"

She bit her lip, met his gaze again. "What kind of a marriage did we have, anyway?"

He opened his mouth to answer, but she hurried on. "I feel like I've just stepped into another woman's life, without a clue how she lived it. I've been handed this part to play, but the roles aren't what they're supposed to be, and the lines keep changing, and..." She turned, strode to the walk-in closet and whipped open the door. "Look at these things."

Dylan frowned. "Your clothes? What's wrong with your clothes?"

"Not *my* clothes, not anymore. There's nothing wrong with them, they're just wrong for me. Wrong for the *me* I am now, not the *her* that I was then." She reached in and began yanking tailored suits, narrow skirts, cropped jackets off hangers, and tossing them onto the bed. "They're bright, and expensive, and chic, and they're just not me."

He caught her shoulders, stopping her from emptying the closet entirely. He stood behind her, and her shoulders slumped forward, her chin touched her chest. "Didn't she even own a pair of jeans without a designer label? A sweatshirt?"

Dylan couldn't allow himself to fall for the act. This vulnerability, this confusion, was just a mask she'd put on. "Not in a long time," he said softly.

She turned toward him, searching his face. "You hated her and now you hate me."

"I never said I hated you, Caitlin—"

"Were the separate bedrooms your idea?"

He shook his head.

"No, I didn't think so." She closed her eyes, and the tensing of her throat muscles made him think she was fighting tears. Or at least, that was what she *wanted* it to make him think. "How long...how long since we made love?"

He licked his lips. "Eight months. Except..."

"Except?"

"There was one time."

Her face pinched tighter as he spoke the words. "One time. Why in God's name did you stay with her?"

He shook his head, fighting the image she was trying to project, angry that her apparent pain was so convincing. "You, Caitlin. Not *her*. You. Why did I stay with *you*." He said it as much to remind him as her.

Her brows lifted, green eyes meeting his, clear and direct. "Well?"

"I didn't have a choice."

She shook her head. "I don't know what that means."

He shrugged. "Doesn't matter. We've veered way off the subject here. You said someone was in the hall last night, following you."

She waited a long moment, and he thought she might insist on an explanation from him. It wouldn't matter if she did. He damned well wasn't going to say anymore. He wasn't even sure who she was anymore.

She stared at him for a long moment, searching his soul, it seemed. Finally, she sighed, long and low. "I've told you everything I can. I didn't hear anything except breathing. I saw nothing. No one touched me or said a word. I have no idea who it was, or even if I imagined the whole thing, and I wouldn't even have mentioned it, except to explain why I locked the nursery door. Okay?"

He examined her face with skepticism he didn't bother disguising. "Okay."

"I didn't mean to send Sandra into hysterics." She

looked at the floor for a long moment, then shook her head slowly. "Maybe I just ought to leave."

Dylan was stunned. "Leave?"

She nodded and glanced again toward the closet. "I don't even need to pack. There's not a damned thing here I want."

"Caity, you love this place. You'd never leave—"

"What did you call me?" Her head had come up all at once, those sharp eyes probing again.

He shook his head, still confused by his own reaction to her suggestion. He'd known the end was at hand. He'd been eager to get it the hell over with. "Sorry. I know you hate it. It just slipped out."

"Caity," she said once, then again. A rush of air came through her lips even as they pulled upward at the corners. "God, all this time everyone's been calling me Caitlin, and I've felt like it was someone else's name. Not mine. But Caity…" She smiled fully. "That's who I am." She hugged herself and laughed softly as her eyes fell closed. "Oh, God, that's who I am."

Dylan saw a single tear work its way from beneath her lashes, and travel a slow path down her face. His gut twisted into a hard knot, and he had to clench his hands into fists to keep from reaching out. Whether to wring her slender neck for blatant deception, or to brush that tear away, he couldn't have said.

Chapter 5

Caitlin dashed the tear from her face with the back of her hand, nearly limp with relief at having found a shred of her identity to cling to.

Dylan shifted his stance. "Why don't you get dressed, come downstairs and get something to eat. You'll feel better."

She shook her head. She didn't want to put on the other woman's clothes, or eat at her table. She wasn't even sure she liked her. "No. I really think I need to get out of here."

"And go where?"

"I don't know. Anywhere. A hotel, a—"

His loud sigh stopped her from completing the sentence. "You're *not going* to any hotel. I've told you, this is your house."

"*Her* house. *I* don't want it."

Dylan turned from her, pushing one hand through his hair and pacing slowly away. "Look, you're two days out of the hospital. This is no time for you to be on your own."

"I don't care."

"Well, I do." He blinked fast after he said it.

"The hell you do," she said very softly.

He lurched forward, gripping her upper arms hard. "You're still my wife."

"Your wife is dead."

He stared hard into her eyes, and she felt his searching, probing, and doubting. She kept her gaze level with his, staring right back. She noticed for the first time how dark his eyes were, like melted chocolate. She felt the contained strength in the hands that held her, and glanced downward, at the corded muscles of his forearms extending from rolled up sleeves. Again, she felt herself wishing he'd fold her into those strong arms. That instead of digging his fingers into her flesh and despising her, he'd rock her against him and tell her that everything would be all right. She closed her eyes at the image, and battled back new tears.

His hands fell away, but when he spoke, his voice had not gentled. "Get dressed. You want out, I'll take you out. You can buy some clothes that meet your latest set of standards."

"I—I don't have any money."

His eyebrows rose slightly. "Caitlin, you're *rich*. When your daddy died, he left you every dime he had."

She shook her head. "Don't you understand? That isn't my money. It was hers. I'm not her, Dylan." She stepped nearer to him, and in her desperation to make someone understand, she caught his face between her palms and tipped it downward. "Look at me. She is gone. I'm not her. I'm not sure I even want to be."

For a long moment, he said nothing. Then slowly, one hand came up to stroke a slow, crooked path over her hair. For a fleeting moment, she saw his eyes lose their glittering harshness. "God, I wish I could believe that." Then his face hardened into the stone sculpture that was becoming familiar. "You'd like me to believe that, wouldn't you?"

Her hands fell to her sides, and she bit her lip. "But you don't, do you?"

"I can't."

"Why?"

He took a step away from her and shook his head slowly as she lifted her gaze to his face once more. "Sheer self-preservation, Caitlin. Go on and get dressed. If you feel you can't spend your own money, then consider it a loan."

She swallowed the lump that tried to choke her. She frowned, then, recalling what he'd just told her. "You said I inherited everything from my father. What about Thomas?"

Dylan's face went still. "Thomas was excluded from the will. He and your father never got along, and when he took your mother's side in the divorce, the old man disinherited him."

Caitlin blinked rapidly. "No wonder Thomas resents me."

"He doesn't resent you. Let's not rehash all this now. I haven't got the time or the inclination. I'll meet you out front in an hour."

She looked up briefly. "I'll only need twenty minutes."

Aside from a brief frown, he said nothing. Then he was gone.

She saw that frown again and again that morning. Dylan drove in silence to the bank and helped her through the process of claiming the replacement bank credit cards they'd been holding for her. Hers had all burned with her car. He was quick, efficient and seemingly emotionless. She felt oddly guilty accepting a new card from the teller, but she took it, silently vowing she'd find a way to replace every dime she had to spend. She'd repay the woman she considered dead, the woman Dylan Rossi distrusted so openly.

Back in the front seat of his plush car, he turned to her. "I'll drop you at Eden Mists."

"What's that?"

"Your favorite boutique. Very chic."

She grimaced and shook her head quickly. Then her stomach rumbled loudly enough to be heard.

"Maybe we ought to start with breakfast. I forgot you hadn't eaten this morning. We'll swing by Milford's?"

"Another chic spot?"

"Four-star cuisine." His tone was deep, level, unfriendly.

"Don't we get enough of that at home? What about that?" She pointed to the golden arches in the distance.

"You're kidding, right?"

She shook her head and opened the car door, leaping to her feet. The gloom of the drafty house and its hostile atmosphere were wearing off fast. Even Dylan's grim face couldn't keep her mood from soaring, with the brilliant sun spilling all over the neat little city. There was so much to do, so much she must have done once, but couldn't remember. The small city of Eden was bustling, even this early in the morning. Cars buzzed up and down the broad lanes, people walked in groups of two and three, in and out of shops and businesses.

Dylan caught up with her, and they walked side by side to the fast-food restaurant, and through the double doors. Caitlin inhaled the delicious aromas, but hesitated at the crowd standing in front of the counter. She was suddenly uncertain of what to do. She didn't like the large number of strangers around her. She pressed closer to Dylan, not even fully aware she was doing it until he frowned down at her, and his arm came around her shoulders. It was like an automatic act. His face said he regretted it, but when she felt his arm begin to move away, she scrunched closer, and he let it remain.

"You want to leave?"

She gazed up at him, feeling the warmth of that arm around her, seeing the real concern in his black-fringed eyes. His strength seemed to flow into her. She wanted to turn into his embrace, feel his arms surround her...the way they had in her dream.

"No. I'll be fine." *As long as you hold me.*

Dylan's hand rested nervously on her shoulder, and he propelled her along beside him. "What'll you have," he asked, leaning closer as he spoke above the noise. His warm breath fanned her ear.

She shrugged, glancing at the menu high on the facing wall, then at the pastries under a clear cover on the counter. "Those look good."

"Cheese Danish?" He stared down at her for a moment, an odd look in his eyes, then he blinked it away and strode to the vacant spot near a cash register. "Two cheese Danish and two coffees."

A moment later, his arm was no longer around her, because he was carrying their meal on a cardboard tray as he made his way to an empty table. Caitlin sat across from him, unwrapped her pastry and took a bite, then closed her eyes in ecstasy. "Oh, this is terrific."

He only watched her and shook his head.

"What is it? Have I done something wrong, or—"

"We used to come here a lot," he said slowly, carefully, as if he was afraid something would slip through his lips against his will if he didn't watch every word. "You always ordered those."

She set the Danish down and studied his face. It seemed taut, as if he were in physical pain. "When?"

He averted his eyes. "A long time ago, Caitlin."

"Caity," she said quickly. "Can you please call me Caity?"

He lifted his Danish and met her gaze briefly over it. "I don't think so."

She was doing a hell of a number on him, and the worst part was, he felt himself starting to fall for it. First the fast food, then choosing K mart over all the stylish dress shops in the city, and now—

Dylan had to blink down his gut-wrenching memories when she came out of the fitting room in a pair of five-pocket Levi's jeans and a T-shirt. She had the T-shirt tucked in, and the jeans hugged her slender hips and buttocks just the way they had all those years ago, when she'd blown him away every time he looked at her. So long ago, before her mother's suicide, before she'd inherited all that money from her old man. Before she'd started to change, to close herself off from him, to change into the unfeeling woman she'd become.

They'd been something then. Like a live flame and gasoline. When they were together... He closed his eyes, remembering the way Caitlin used to make love to him. She'd put everything into it, heart, soul and body. But he'd soon begun to sense her slipping farther and farther from him, disappearing inside herself, drawing away. He'd responded by drawing back a little, himself. He'd poured even more time and attention into the business, stung by her coolness. And that had only seemed to make her build more walls. And eventually, what they'd had had died. He'd lost her. He'd finally accepted the facts, and resigned himself to ending his farce of a marriage.

And now, she was coming off like the girl she'd been before all that. She acted innocent, trusting and naive, and so damned vulnerable. Afraid, nervous. Pretending to enjoy his company. It was all an act. It was impossible for her to have changed so completely, virtually overnight. Impossible.

She picked out three more pairs of jeans, a half-dozen tops and a couple of simple sundresses, then added a pair of flat summer shoes to her collection. When they left the store, she balled up the bag that held the designer suit she'd arrived in, and stuffed it into a trash can.

She faced him smiling, her eyes glittering with pleasure, the wind whipping her long auburn tresses into mass chaos. "What next?"

Ah, damn, she looked like a teenager.

"We'd better call it a day. I need to go into the office so—"

"I'd love to see where you work!" She slung the shopping bag over her shoulder and started for the car.

He stood where he was, stunned into motionlessness. When she glanced back over her shoulder and saw him there, she stopped beside the car and turned. "What did I do now?"

Dylan shook his head. "You've never given a damn about the business." He made his legs carry him to the car, and slid in behind the wheel. "You sure you want to do this?"

She got in beside him, carelessly tossing her purchases onto the back seat, before studiously fastening her safety belt. "Of course I am." She looked up at him and her smile died. "Unless...you'd rather I didn't. I really didn't mean to monopolize your entire morning like this. I wasn't thinking—"

"It's all right, Caitlin."

She sighed and sat back in her seat. "You can take me back to the house if you want to."

He started the car, and backed out of the parking space. What the hell was she up to? She wasn't genuinely interested in the business all of the sudden. She couldn't be. She'd always seen it as a bother, a drain on his time and attention. She'd had enough money for them both, so why waste time on such a difficult project? She was just pretending, because she was up to something. He hadn't figured out what yet, but she was definitely up to something.

Or was she?

Doubts about his sanity pestered him, but he drove toward the office just the same. He'd give her enough rope to hang herself, and then he'd know for sure.

Caitlin stood just outside the glass-paneled office building, blinking. In gold letters across the front door were the words, Rossi Architectural Firm. Then his hand was on her arm again, and he marched her through the doors, into an elevator that whisked them up to the fifth floor.

The place even smelled successful, like new carpet and leather. He led her down a corridor, nodding to people who passed. They all greeted him with deference, "Hello, Mr.

Rossi." "Good afternoon, Mr. Rossi." "Good to see you, Mr. Rossi." None smiled, though. They all looked rather pious when they looked at Dylan.

He took her through a door marked Dylan Rossi, CEO, into an office that would have suited the president of IBM. His desk was huge, his carpet, plush silvery gray. A drafting table stood near the windows with a stool in front of it. A computer terminal held court on the desk, with notepads and pencils and books piled around it.

"This is incredible."

He glanced at her once, and once only. He took the thronelike chair behind the desk, and began rummaging through file folders.

It didn't bother Caitlin. She moved around the office, impressed beyond comment at the place. And it was his. She wandered to the drafting table, and looked at the drawing there. The lines and angles, numbers and codes jotted all over the thing meant little to her.

She paid scant attention to Dylan as he spoke on the phone, and made notes in several files. When he finally took her on the promised tour, she felt a little guilty. He obviously had a lot more pressing things to do. Still, it was pleasant, and he seemed to swell a bit with pride as he showed her the various offices and storage rooms in the building, and introduced her to several young architects who worked with him. All the while, he was watching her, studying her reactions. What was he waiting for?

He showed her the small office her brother occupied, but Thomas seemed elbow-deep in something pressing, and only muttered a greeting.

Hours later, as Dylan led her back through the lobby and to the car, she looked back once more and shook her head.

"What?"

She glanced at him, seeing more of him than she had before. He was talented, successful, determined, capable. The people who worked for him respected him, and when he spoke to them, it wasn't with the same coolness in his eyes that always seemed directed at her. "Caitlin must have been proud to be your wife," she said, and her voice was strangely hoarse and soft.

He shook his head. "Not exactly."

Caitlin frowned hard. She couldn't believe the woman she'd once been had been indifferent to her husband's abilities. "She must have been. Maybe she just...never said so."

He looked at her for a long moment. "No, she never did."

"Then she was a fool." She swallowed hard, cleared her throat and made herself continue. She had to begin somewhere. She had to try to right some of the wrongs her old self had wrought. But first she had to find out what they were. She'd alienated her husband, somehow. She touched his arm as he leaned over to open the car door for her. He straightened. "She must have been a fool, Dylan, but for what it's worth, I'm not."

He searched her eyes so deeply, she felt his burn into her soul. Then he broke eye contact, leaving her feeling cold and alone. He jerked the car door open. "Get in, Caitlin. It's going to pour any minute."

Caitlin glanced up at the darkening sky. The sun was rapidly setting, and ominous black clouds roiled in masses overhead. She got in without another word, and they drove in silence.

By the time they approached the looming house, rain poured over the windshield in sheets. The headlights did little to pierce the wall of water, and Dylan drove slowly, braking with care as the drive came into view.

Caitlin sighed, drawing his attention.

"Something wrong?"

She shook her head. "I was just thinking...wishing..." She bit her lip and looked at him. "Wouldn't it be wonderful to just keep on going?"

He frowned, pulling to a stop at the end of the drive. "What?"

"Just keep driving," she rushed on. "Right past this house and on to...I don't know, someplace cozy and warm, and...and kind."

He looked at her strangely, then pulled the car into the long, curving drive and up to the house. A chill raced up the back of her neck when the house came into view. So grim, towering there with it's dark red bricks and masses of clinging vines. It seemed even more spectral in the middle of the night, with the rain pouring down. She fought to suppress it, but felt herself shiver, all the same.

"Running away wouldn't solve anything, Caitlin."

"Wouldn't it?" She faced him in the darkness of the car.

"You can't just walk away from your life, you know. It's not that simple."

She shook her head. "I know I can't. Not yet, anyway." She hurried on before he could ask what she meant by that. "I don't want to go inside yet. You know, all I've seen of this place is the front...all I can remember, anyway."

"Cait, it's raining."

She sighed long and low. "Feels good, doesn't it? It's been so hot." She opened the car door and got out. For a moment, she just stood still and let the rain pour over her. She tipped her face up and let the downpour bathe it.

She didn't hear him come toward her, only the sounds of the wind and the rain battering the ground, pinging and ricocheting on the car roof. His arm came around her shoulders and he urged her toward the house.

She pulled free. "No. I want to walk out back, by the ocean."

"The cliffs are dangerous at night, Caitlin, especially when it's raining. You could slip—"

"I'll be careful." They stood facing each other. His hair

was already drenched, plastered to his head. His jaw was set and rigid.

"Cait, this is crazy." He pitched his voice loudly to fight the storm, and again it carried that tone of command that made her tremble.

"I'll be fine. Go on to the house, Dylan."

"That's exactly what I'm doing." In a second, he'd scooped her up into his arms and was striding toward the front door. He flung it wide, carried her through and kicked it closed behind him. The light in the foyer was too bright after the murky darkness outside. A shiver moved through her and his arms seemed to tighten just a little. He looked down, into her eyes. She stared back into his. Her arms had linked themselves around his neck, and their faces were close. She could feel the heat of his body through her wet clothes. And all at once, she wanted to kiss him. She wanted to know if it could be the way she imagined it...or had she remembered it?

Her fingers slid upward, into the dripping sable waves, and she brought her face closer to his. Her heart pounded harder. She closed her eyes, and eliminated the last inch of space between their mouths. She pressed her parted lips to his, felt them move in response, felt her mouth captured by his gentle suction. Then everything changed. His arms clutched her tighter, so tight she could barely breath. His mouth took hers in a frantic, desperate assault. His tongue plunged and dove, as if he couldn't taste enough of her. She kissed him back just as eagerly. Her body strained against his, her tongue twined with his in a sensual dance...

...that stopped all too soon.

He pulled away and abruptly set her on her feet. He looked at her once, his gaze narrow, almost wary. Then he shook his head and strode away.

Chapter 6

She got turned around in the labyrinth of corridors on her way down to dinner. She knew she was on the ground floor, but she'd somehow taken a wrong turn from the foyer, and wound up in a part of the house she hadn't seen. The towering ceilings and darkly stained wood, the parquet floors and tall, arched windows, were the same as the rest of the place. The house was gloomy, unwelcoming, even with all the lights blazing. The rain slashing against the windows and the wind howling through the trees outside, only made it seem worse.

She walked over cold, hard ceramic tiles of the strange hallway, peering through one darkly stained door after another to try to get her bearings. She found a cluttered office, with wall-to-wall file cabinets, a desk full of computer equipment, and a fax machine. Maybe Dylan worked at home sometimes, she mused. She drew back, closed the door and moved along the hall to the next. She was just reaching for it when she heard soft voices farther down. She hurried toward them. Then stopped at the low, throaty laughter.

"Of course, I love you, *mon cher,* but I cannot wait forever." The voice was Genevieve's.

The one she heard whisper a reply startled her. It belonged to her brother. "It'll all be yours, baby. You just have to be patient."

"I run out of patience, playing servant to these people. And your wife, she treats me like a dog. How much longer, Thomas?"

"I need a little more time. I promise you, we'll be on

top...and Dylan Rossi will be sorry he ever underestimated me. I'll show him. It'll be a lesson he won't forget.''

Caitlin drew a sudden gasp and her brother's words stopped. A second later, he appeared in front of her, stepping out of the room—a cozy, private parlor, from what she could glimpse—where he'd been having his little chat with her maid.

"What are you doing here?" The words had the ring of an accusation, but the expression on his face was one of pure guilt—and something tugged at her mind.

"I, uh, got lost on my way to dinner." She fought to keep what she'd heard, and what she was feeling, from showing on her face. "I'm glad I ran into you. I was afraid I'd never get back on track."

Thomas's hooded green eyes tried to hide his offense, but at the same time he stole quick glances at her face to see if she knew. He took her arm and started off in the direction from which she'd come.

The image came to her then. The pudgy red-haired boy, in a grimy Little League uniform, looking up at her just the way he was right now, as he tried to wipe the white foam from his shirt.

She squinted, trying to fine-tune the memory, then clapped a hand to her mouth to stifle the burst of laughter when it all came clear. "Tommy, *you* were the one who shaved Mrs. Petrie's poodle!''

He stopped walking, faced her, blinking. "Mrs. Pe—" He grabbed her shoulders, smiling broadly. "You *remember* that?"

She grinned back, nodding hard, mentally hugging the memory to her, wanting never to let it go. "I covered for you. Helped you ditch the razor and cleaned the foam off you before anyone saw."

"Damned dog had it coming." He shook his head, and laughed. "Stole my lunch at practice. I thought I'd starve before I got home."

"I think you went overboard in your retaliation," she teased.

"I only shaved the puff from the top of the mutt's head." He turned, and began walking again. After a few moments, he said, "So, um, how long were you standing out there?"

She frowned up at him. She wanted very much to get close to her brother again, especially now, having regained such a cherished memory of him as a child. But she'd just heard him threaten her husband, unless she'd completely misunderstood. She couldn't trust him. Not yet. "Not standing, walking. I was just wandering aimlessly and you stepped right into my path."

"Oh." He looked relieved.

He guided her through the maze of corridors until things began to seem familiar to her. It seemed to take a long time, though. She realized why when she finally entered the dining room to find Genevieve had managed to get there before them. She was already setting covered platters on the formally set table. Dylan rose when Caitlin came in.

"There you are. I was getting ready to send out a search party." His voice was level, controlled, but there was tension in his eyes.

Caitlin sat down just as Ellen entered the room behind her, and did likewise. "Enjoy your day out, Caitlin?"

Caitlin glanced up at the older woman and nodded. "Very much."

"I see you got some new clothes." Ellen looked down at Caitlin's jeans and shook her head. "Not your usual style."

"It is now."

Platters were passed, and Caitlin frowned across the long table at her husband. "Shouldn't we wait for Sandra?"

Dylan shrugged. "You've always insisted on promptness at dinner. She knows that it's one of your favorite rules."

"It's a stupid rule."

Genevieve stopped halfway across the room with a bowl

in her hand. Dylan paused in filling his plate. Thomas stared at her.

Ellen chuckled. "I always said so. Still, I think we may as well get on with it. Baby was fussing. Sandra probably won't be down for a while."

"Is Lizzie sick?" She directed the question toward her brother.

"I don't know. Just cranky, I think."

"Don't worry about it, Caitlin," Ellen said. "Tell me about your trip. What did you do?"

Caitlin was worried, and vowed to check on the baby after dinner. In the meantime, though, Ellen seemed genuinely interested, and Caitlin wanted to build some bridges with the woman.

"Dylan took me on a tour of his offices."

Ellen frowned, her silvery brows bunching behind those thick glasses.

"I had no idea how successful he was until I saw for myself. I was very impressed."

"Did he tell you he started in one room, and not a big room, either. Built everything from the ground up. Designed that building himself."

"No, he didn't."

Ellen nodded. "That's his, girl. I won't stand still to watch anybody try to take it from him, and that includes you." Her bony finger poked into Caitlin's shoulder as she spoke.

Caitlin only shook her head. "Why would you think I—"

"I know what you're up to. You just remember that."

"That's enough, Ellen."

Ellen shot her nephew an impatient glare, and returned her attention to her plate. Caitlin let her chin fall to her chest. She'd honestly believed she might be making some progress with the woman.

Sandra's hasty entrance brought her head back up, and

then she shot to her feet. Sandra held little Lizzie in her arms. The child's eyes were heavy-lidded and dull. She lay limply, as if exhausted, her head resting against her mother's shoulder.

"She's burnin' up!" Sandra drawled thickly. "I cain't get the fever down."

Caitlin raced forward, instinctively placing her palm across Lizzie's forehead, feeling the unnatural heat and the clamminess of the baby's skin. Sandra's eyes were pleading as they met hers.

Thomas stood, but didn't make a move to approach his daughter. Ellen rose with effort, moving slowly forward.

"Landsakes, you're shaking like a leaf, girl. Give her here, before you drop her."

Sandra surrendered the child to Ellen, who, in turn, placed Lizzie in Dylan's arms, obviously unaware, or unconcerned that Dylan would prefer the child were anywhere other than in his grasp. He held her stiffly. The veins in his neck bulged.

"Take her upstairs," Ellen ordered. "Sandra, call the doctor if you think you can talk straight. I imagine by the time you get done on the phone, the fever will be down, but call anyway."

Dylan left the room with the baby clutched awkwardly to his chest. Ellen hobbled behind him. Sandra went to the living room and picked up the phone. Thomas, to Caitlin's amazement, sat back down to his dinner, but he didn't really eat any of it.

"Aren't you going to go up there?"

He shook his head. "It's not that I'm not worried. I am, I just…she's so tiny. I feel like a giant when I hold her. I'm…not comfortable, you know?"

Caitlin frowned at him and shook her head. "No, I really don't." She followed Ellen up the stairs, knowing she wasn't wanted or needed, but too afraid for Lizzie to stay behind. In the nursery, Ellen gave calm instructions.

"Dylan, just sit and hold her. Caitlin, make yourself useful and run some water in here." She handed Caitlin a
small plastic tub. "Make it cool. Not cold, but cool to the
touch. Go on, hurry it up."

Caitlin nodded and took the tub into the adjoining bathroom to fill it. She carried it back into the nursery, and
placed it atop the changing table.

Dylan had the baby in his lap. He was peeling the little
sleeper off the child, then removing the diaper. His lips
were drawn into a thin line, brows furrowed.

As she watched, Caitlin felt her eyes fill. Ellen dipped a
gnarled hand into the tub. "Just right. Set her in here, Dylan, but keep hold of her." Dylan rose. "Better get those
sleeves rolled up first."

He looked down at his white shirt, then glanced at Caitlin. She hurried to him without a minute's hesitation, un-
buttoned his sleeves and rolled them to his elbows. Her
fingers moved over the curling hairs on his forearms and
she felt a pain twist inside her.

Dylan stepped away from her, and haltingly lowered
Lizzie into the tiny tub. The water just covered her chubby
legs. "There now, Lizzie," he said softly, falteringly,
clutching the infant under the arms as if afraid she'd dissolve in the water. "You like baths, don't you? Sure you
do. There we go."

"Now cup your hand, Dylan, and just pour the water
over her chest. That's it."

Dylan followed Ellen's instructions, bathing the hot little
body in cool water as Lizzie stared trustingly up at him,
looking sleepy. After a few minutes, Dylan leaned Lizzie
forward, over his arm, and bathed her back in the same
manner. He even managed to wet her head and neck, all
without upsetting the baby at all, though his hands shook
visibly.

Sandra burst into the room then. "What's happenin'? Is
she all right?"

"What did the doctor say?" Caitlin asked.

Sandra glanced at Caitlin, then frowned. "You shouldn't be here, Caitlin. You can go now. *I'm* her mama."

God, was Sandra threatened by Caitlin's presence, her fondness for Lizzie? Was she jealous?

"Answer the question, Sandra, 'fore I cuff you upside the head for ignorance," Ellen scolded.

Sandra shot Ellen a nearly blank glance, before she answered. "He said to put her in a cool bath and keep her there until the Children's Tylenol has a chance to work."

"When did you give her the medicine?" Ellen asked.

"I—I couldn't get it down her. She was fussin' so much, and then she got so hot, I just—"

"Well, she isn't fussing now. Get that medicine in here."

Sandra went into the bathroom and returned with the little bottle, and a baby-size medicine spoon. She poured the dose and handed the spoon to Dylan.

"Uh...hey, Lizzie, look what Uncle Dylan has for you." He spoke as if he were talking to an adult. He slipped the spoon between Lizzie's lips and she took the medicine without a fight. Then he returned to his messy, nervous bathing of her heated body. His shirt was soaked, as were the fronts of his trousers and a good deal of the floor.

Sandra paced, Ellen sat in the rocker and Caitlin just stood and watched Dylan with the baby, a lump in her throat making it difficult to breathe. After twenty minutes, Ellen ordered the baby removed from the bath. Dylan scooped her out and wrapped her in a towel. As he patted her dry, she fell asleep in his arms. Dylan stared down at her, some secret turmoil in his eyes. He blinked it away at once.

"She feels cooler now." He placed her in the crib.

Ellen got up and touched the sleeping child's forehead. "Put a diaper on her, Sandra. Nothing else. Get that medicine down her every four hours. If you can't, or if that fever shoots up again, you come and get me."

"Yeah, okay. And I'll take her to the doctor in the mornin'. He said he'd see her first thing."

Ellen nodded and left the room. Caitlin turned to go, as well, but stopped cold when Sandra slipped her arms around Dylan's neck and pressed herself close to him. "I was so scared," she whispered. "Thank God you were here."

Caitlin saw Dylan's arms creep around Sandra's waist. Dylan's back was to Caitlin. But not Sandra's, and that blond head lifted from Dylan's shoulder just long enough to send Caitlin a look of unmistakable meaning.

Biting her lower lip to fight the tide of burning jealousy, pure and bitter, that rinsed through her heart, she turned and fled the room. It was obvious that Thomas's young wife had designs on Caitlin's husband. And from the looks of things, Dylan wasn't putting up too much of a fight. Not that Caitlin could blame him. After all, he hadn't slept in her bed in months and months. What had the old Caitlin expected him to do?

She raced past her bedroom, tears threatening. She felt more an outsider than she thought possible. Seeing Sandra in Dylan's arms, seeing the truth at last, in the other woman's eyes. God, she needed to get out of here!

She took the stairs at top speed, and went right out the front door into the rain-filled night. And then she stopped, and stood, tilting her head up into the black rains, razor winds and the night's bracing, icy hands.

It was almost as if the rain could wash away the person she'd been before, leaving her clean and free to begin again. She closed her eyes and let the drops roll over her heated lids, drenching her lashes, rinsing the hot tears from them, cooling the burn.

Almost without thinking, she began placing one foot ahead of the other, as her clothes slowly soaked through and began clinging to her skin. She followed a worn path in the grass that took her around to the rear of the house, down a mild slope, and through a small wood.

The sounds of waves hurling themselves against jagged rock were like a siren's call, luring her onward, until she stood at the very lip of a cliff. The wind blew in off the sea, razing her face with the stinging, chilled droplets it carried. It smelled of the ocean, and of the rain. Freshness and freedom. It sent her wet hair snapping behind her, and she closed her eyes and just felt its touch. She forced everything else from her mind, and lived only for the moment, for this experience.

God, it felt good.

She opened her eyes, but ahead there was only darkness, roiling clouds and curtains of rain. She edged closer to the granite lip, and let her gaze fall downward. White foam seethed from the surface around glittering fingers of rock, far below. More white exploded from each black wave that battered the shore.

She was as wet as if she'd been swimming, fully clothed, but she didn't care. She needed to think, and here was the best place to do it. She couldn't keep a clear head in that house.

The woman she'd been had left behind as much devastation as a hurricane. All of it, it seemed, was now hers to clean up. She had to begin somewhere.

But how?

She obviously couldn't mend any fences with Sandra. The woman was after her husband, there was no way around that. Sandra had declared her intentions in no uncertain terms.

The question was, what did Caitlin intend to do about it?

Would she surrender? Give up without a fight? Stand quietly by while the sleek little blonde seduced Dylan?

That the first option rubbed her wrong told her something about her personality. Whether it was the old Caitlin or the

new one, she wasn't sure. But she knew that having something that belonged to her stolen while she watched was
not a plausible answer. She couldn't do it.

And the only other option was to keep him for herself.
And of course, she had no idea if she wanted that, either...or even if he'd have her.

She turned and walked along the edge for a time, letting
the wind buffet her right side. When she came to an oblong
boulder, she sat down upon its slick surface, and turned to
face the sea again, her feet dangling over the rain-filled
space between her and the shore.

"You should have died in the accident, Caitlin."

The voice rasped near her ear, just as she felt the gloved
hands settle around her throat. She tried to turn around, but
one fist closed in her hair, and she couldn't move her head.
The voice went on, throaty and gruff, neither masculine nor
feminine, unidentifiable.

"But you're about to have another one."

Even as the hands at her neck loosened, she felt the impact of a foot at the small of her back. Her body arched
forward, pain slicing her spine. Her hands grappled for
something, but only slid from the wet rock.

She was going over the edge. There was nothing to stop
her. The cry she released was one of pure fear, and it split
the night, pierced the walls of rain and drowned out the
wind as she tumbled and twisted and grabbed for salvation.

Somehow, her fist closed on a jagged outcropping. Ra-
zor-edged stone cut into her palm, but she clung tighter,
even as her body twisted and slammed into the sheer stone
face. Frantically, she moved her toes and her other hand,
in search of more support. One foot found a niche in the
rock, and dug into it.

She was panting, breathless with fear. The rain battered
her back and the sounds of the waves crashing to shore
below were louder, echoing through her consciousness. She
lifted her head, to look above at her assailant, but saw noth-

ing. Only the jagged edge from which she'd fallen, and the inky sky above. She hadn't fallen far. Surely she could climb back up.

But what if he's still there, waiting? What if he pushes me again? She closed her eyes and prayed for courage, and strength to hold on. She dared not try to scale the wet, sheer wall. If she let go, she would fall, there was no question in her mind, but she couldn't remain where she was, either.

"Caitlin..."

The howling wind seemed to cry her name, then again, louder this time. It wasn't the wind. Someone was there, looking for her. The call came again, and she recognized Dylan's voice. She parted her lips to answer, then bit the cry off before it left her throat. What if Dylan was the one who had pushed her? What if he were only calling out now to ascertain whether his mission had been a success?

Seconds ticked by. Then other voices joined the first, calling her name. Thomas's, Henri's, even Sandra's.

"This way," Dylan's voice shouted into the wind. "I heard a scream."

"*Mon Dieu,* do you think she has fallen—" Henri began.

"Here," Caitlin cried out with every ounce of strength left in her. Whoever had pushed her, they wouldn't try again, not with all of them there to bear witness. "Down here. Help me!"

There were footsteps, then lights above her, glaring down into her eyes. She averted her face. "Hold on, Cait. Don't move, just hold on!" The light moved away, and she heard Dylan's voice once again, gruff and unsteady. "I can reach her, hold my legs, Thomas." There was shuffling, movements of bodies on the wet stone. She looked up again to see Dylan's dark shape. He lay facedown above her, and bent at the waist until his upper body hung over the edge. His arms stretched down for her, his strong hands closed like vises around her wrists.

"Let go of the rock, Cait. Hold onto my arms."

She didn't. She couldn't. What if he just let her go?

"Let go," he said again. She tilted her head up, and looked at him. "Trust me for once, dammit! I won't let you fall."

She had no choice. She couldn't hang on much longer, anyway. Trusting Dylan with her life right now was her only option. She released her precarious hold on the stone, and gripped his wrists just as he was gripping hers.

"I have her," he shouted. "Pull me up."

Slowly, she was dragged up the wet, cold, washboard face of stone, and onto the blessedly level ground again. She lay facedown on the uneven stone, head buried in her arms. Dylan's hands on her shoulders urged her to her feet. His eyes scanned her face, her body, as the fear enveloped her all over again. With a strangled cry, she threw herself against him, and his arms closed around her. He held her against him with all the strength she'd known his arms would possess, and as she shook violently, she noticed that he was trembling, too.

His hands stroked her wet hair, her back and shoulders. "It's all right, Cait. It's over. You're safe now. It's all right."

She couldn't make the tears stop flowing. She couldn't let go of him. So she was glad when he scooped her up into his arms as if she weighed nothing at all, and turned to begin back toward the house. She kept her arms tight around his neck, her face pressed to the warm, wet skin of it. She knew the others walked with them. She felt their curious eyes on her, but she didn't care. She'd experienced raw terror in the last few minutes. She was clinging to her sanity by clinging to her husband. It didn't matter what they thought.

She knew he'd mounted the front steps. She heard the door open and felt the rain stop lashing her as he carried her inside. Then he was lowering her onto the sofa, leaning her head back against the armrest, sitting right beside her.

Caitlin couldn't take her eyes from his face, as he looked her up and down. His hands moved anxiously over her arms, then her legs. "Are you all right? Were you hurt?"

She shook her head as someone handed him a blanket, and he tucked it around her. Then he stared at her face, and shook his head, and the hardness crept over his features, little by little, until the ice sculpture was complete. "Dammit, Caitlin, I told you not to go out there tonight. I told you how dangerous it was, that you could fall—"

"I didn't fall." She blurted the words quickly, and everyone in the room stilled, looking toward her.

Dylan's face contorted then. He shook his head slowly as if in disbelief. "You didn't...my God, are you saying you..."

"Can't say it, Dylan?" Thomas's voice was laced with bitterness. "She jumped. Tried to take the same cowardly way out our mother did." Caitlin caught her breath, but Thomas went right on. "We all could've been killed trying to pull you up, big sister. Next time, try something a little smarter."

Dylan whirled on Thomas, fists clenched. Caitlin threw back the blanket and leapt to her feet, only to sway on weak knees. She gripped Dylan's arm, both to keep from falling at his feet, and to keep him from hitting her brother. "Stop it! For God's sake—"

"Caitlin, don't do this." Thomas's voice cracked and changed pitch. The next sentence was an octave higher, a plea. "I'll never forgive you if you do what she did—"

Caitlin released Dylan's arm, only to grip both of Thomas's. "My mother...are you saying...suicide?"

"It was cruel, Caitlin, and I hate her for it! Damn you, for trying—"

"I didn't!" she shrieked. Thomas went silent, and she saw actual tears swimming in his eyes as he searched her face. More calmly, she went on. "I didn't jump off that cliff. I was pushed."

"Pushed?" Dylan gripped her shoulders from behind, turned her to face him. He'd paled, and his eyes were wider than she'd seen them yet. "Who—"

"Did you say 'pushed'?" Caitlin turned her head to see Ellen, scuffing into the room, followed by Genevieve.

"Oh, *mon Dieu!* Are you all right?"

Caitlin's eyes met Dylan's, and she nodded. "For now I am." Silently, she heard her heart begging him, *Please don't be the one.*

Chapter 7

The room went utterly silent. Dylan only stared at Caitlin, and said nothing.

"*I* think Caitlin ought to pay another visit to that shrink of hers."

She glanced toward Sandra's doubting eyes and shivered. Was the woman that desperate to latch on to Caitlin's husband? Desperate enough to kill?

Caitlin shivered. Dylan's gaze narrowed on her. "You need to get into some dry clothes before you get sick."

She turned toward him. "Is that all you have to say? Dylan, someone tried to kill me tonight!"

He searched her face, and she saw the skepticism in his eyes. "You don't believe me."

"I didn't say that."

"You didn't have to." She pulled free of the tempting warmth she could feel emanating from his body, turned and walked calmly toward the staircase and up it. She focused on the cool, smooth feel of the banister as her hand glided over it, on the number of steps her feet climbed, on the pattern of the wood grain on them. Anything but the feeling of their eyes on her back, and the fear that still made her heart thunder.

No one followed, only the grim specter of fear that seemed to grow larger with every minute she spent here. She closed the bedroom door, and flicked on the lights. Her nerves tingling, she moved slowly through the room. The closet loomed ahead of her like a dare, and she answered, stepping forward, flinging it wide and scanning the dim interior.

Nothing inside except the mounds of clothing she detested, and the few things she'd chosen for herself. But a chill raced up her spine, and she whirled. The bathroom door was closed. Hadn't she left it ajar?

She stood for an eternity, barely breathing as she listened. She heard only the howl of the wind and the hands of the rain slapping her windows. She moved forward, slowly, mindlessly closing her fingers around something cold and hard and heavy as she passed the nightstand. She gripped the doorknob, turned it and holding her breath, flung it wide.

When she saw only the dark shapes of the fixtures, she stiffened her spine, reached in for the light switch and snapped it on. Oh, God, the shower curtain was pulled tight.

She swallowed hard, snagged the curtain in one hand and lifted her makeshift weapon in the other. She tore it open. The porcelain tub stood gleaming, empty.

"Caitlin."

She spun at the sound of his voice, again lifting the weapon instinctively. Dylan stood near the bedroom door. It was closed behind him, and Caitlin's darting gaze quickly noted that it was locked, as well.

"What do you want?"

He frowned, his eyes focused on the object in her hand. "You won't need that, Cait. Put it down." As he spoke, he moved forward.

Caitlin blinked as her hand lowered. She studied her weapon, a shiny onyx-colored vase with a scarlet rose painted on the front. A thin rim of gold encircled the lip. It would be about as useful against a would-be killer as the pillow on her bed. She closed her eyes and stepped into the bedroom, replacing the vase on the stand.

She heard his sigh as he stepped closer. "You're still shaking."

She rubbed her arms and shrugged.

"Tell me you didn't try to jump, Cait."

She lifted her head, met his eyes. He stood very close to her now. "I didn't jump. I told you, I was pushed."

"By whom?"

She tipped her head up and studied the planes and angles of his face. It was a strong face, with deep brown eyes filled with emotions she couldn't begin to fathom. "I didn't see. He came up behind me."

"He? It was a man, then?"

She shrugged. "It could've been. I'm not sure, the voice was deliberately disguised."

"He spoke to you?"

She nodded. Dylan's hands came to her shoulders and her heart beat a little faster. It was a stupid reaction. For all she knew, it could've been him.

"Cait, what did he say to you?"

She swallowed hard. "That I should've died in the accident. That I'd die tonight, instead."

"And you still didn't get a look—"

"His hands were on my throat. I couldn't turn my head."

Brows bunching together, Dylan's glance dipped to her neck. His warm hands touched her skin there, and tilted her chin upward. His head lowered. An onlooker would have thought he was about to kiss her, she thought, and a shudder rippled through her at the vision. His long fingers touched her throat and she wished they'd explore lower. She knew those fingers had teased her breasts, had taunted her center to throbbing readiness.

How can I want a man who may have just tried to kill me?

"He left marks. There'll be bruises tomorrow."

"So now you have to believe me."

Dylan's hands fell away. "I believed you in the first place."

"Then why—"

"I thought it would be best if we discussed this alone."

Her eyes darted once again toward the locked door. She shivered.

"You're still soaking wet." He reached to the bedpost, where her red satin robe hung, and picked it up. "Here, get into this."

Cait took it from him and stepped into the bathroom, closing the door. She quickly shimmied out of her clothes, and wiped her skin dry with a towel. She scanned the room for something besides the robe to put on, but saw nothing. Not even underwear. Sighing in resignation, she pulled the robe on, and tied the sash tight.

When she stepped back into the bedroom, Dylan was pacing. He faced her and stopped, his eyes narrowing as his gaze moved briefly down her body. He snapped it upward again.

Caitlin felt the touch of his eyes as if they were hands, and she fought the wave of heat that rose to engulf her, even as goose bumps dotted her arms.

"So, what do you want me to do?"

She saw his eyes widen slightly. "What?"

"About tonight," she clarified. "Shouldn't I call the police?"

"I'll talk to them in the morning," he said.

Caitlin's heart skipped once, just once. "Why?"

"Because I'd like to keep this quiet if I can." He took a step toward her. "Cait, we have to handle this carefully." At his second step in her direction, she took one backward.

He froze where he was, his eyes narrowing. "What is it?"

She shook her head. "Nothing. Nothing, this is all just a lot to deal with. I just want to go to bed, and—"

"You're afraid of me, aren't you." It was a simple statement of fact. "You think it was me."

She licked her lips and forced herself to meet his gaze. "I don't know what to think."

He shook his head in disbelief. "You put down the vase."

"Maybe I ought to pick it back up."

"You think it would do any good?" He took another step forward, his hands closing on the outsides of her arms.

"I think you're trying to scare me."

"Am I succeeding?"

She felt her lips begin to tremble. "Yes," she whispered.

His eyes moved over her face in rapid, searching patterns. "Good. I hope you're scared enough to use some sense from here on in. Walking into that storm, going out to the cliffs on a night like this was insane, Caitlin. What on earth were you thinking?"

He still held her arms, and the angry sparks in his eyes were real. "I was upset. I just had to get out of this house."

"Why?"

She closed her eyes, shook her head quickly. "You don't know when to quit, do you?"

"I don't know the word 'quit,' lady. Tell me why you took off like that."

"Because I saw the way you were holding Sandra, all right?"

"The way I—"

"She was pressed so close, I couldn't have fit a matchstick between you."

Understanding seemed to dawn on his face. "In the nursery—"

"And you didn't seem to mind it at all, Dylan. And forgive me for being human, but seeing that hurt."

He shook his head slowly. "Hurt?" He repeated her own word as if trying to remember its meaning.

"She wants you, you know." She turned and paced away from him, relieved that she'd released the tension burning inside her. "And she intends to have you."

"How do you know?"

"She told me. No, not in words. Women can communicate without parting their lips sometimes, and she made her intentions perfectly clear to me. She wants you.'' Her back was still to him.

He came to stand close behind her. "And what do *you* want?''

A sob tried to escape, and she choked on it. "I don't know. I only know I want to believe you aren't trying to kill me. I want to believe it very much.''

His hands crept up to her shoulders. "But you don't, do you?''

She sniffed, and shook her head. "No.''

"What's my motive, Cait? You think I want your money? I've never given a tinker's damn about money. I could've let you fall out there if I'd wanted to get rid of you so badly. Have you thought of that?''

She laughed, though it came out as a short release of air. "What do you think?''

He turned her to face him, brows furrowed. "My God, you were thinking it at the cliff, weren't you? You were hanging over the side, clinging to nothing but my hands, half convinced I was going to let you go.''

She nodded. There was no sense in being dishonest about it, no sense lying.

He shook his head hard and blew an angry sigh. "Believe what you want, Caitlin. Go to the police yourself if you don't trust me. Do whatever you have to do.''

He turned toward the door, but her next words stopped him. "Have you slept with her, Dylan?''

He shook his head without turning to face her. He stood poised, his hand on the doorknob. "Do me a favor and stop worrying about my relationship with Sandra. It's none of your business...unless you'd care to make me a better offer.''

He stormed out and slammed the door behind him.

She took a long, hot bath to soak the chill from her bones, but it did little to soothe her frayed nerves. There was just too much she didn't know. Had her car accident been another attempt on her life? It seemed more than likely, given the assailant's words at the cliff. And the carob-laced dessert now looked like yet another. Someone wanted her dead, and badly.

But who? She knew so little about her life, it was difficult to judge who had a motive to want it to end. Did she have enough money to give Dylan a motive? Why wouldn't he simply divorce her if he wanted out of the marriage? And what about Thomas? She already knew he'd been disinherited. And she'd gotten everything. He'd sided with their mother in the divorce, and she'd apparently taken her father's side. What she hadn't known before tonight, was the manner in which her mother had died.

Suicide.

Had Caitlin been to blame for that? Had her decision to remain with her father added to her mother's depression in any way? And how could it not have? Maybe Thomas was resentful of the part she'd played in their mother's death, and maybe he was striking out against her, as a result.

Could she make amends with him now? And should she? She could offer him half of what she'd inherited from their father. It was only fair. He should have gotten it to begin with.

Snippets of the conversation she'd overheard between Thomas and Genevieve floated through her memory and she bit her lip. Thomas had said he would teach Dylan a lesson he'd never forget. Whatever he was planning, she couldn't very well help him along by giving him what he needed to carry it out. No, nor could she tell Dylan about what she'd overheard. She felt an instinctive urge to protect her brother, and sensed it was just the way she'd felt when they were growing up together. If she'd misunderstood, she might cost Thomas his job, and his wife and child their home, all without cause. That would only make him hate her.

God, she had so little to go on! If she had any sense at all, she'd probably pack her things and get out of here while there was still time. But something kept her from making that decision right now. Tomorrow, she decided. Tomorrow she would do some digging into her past, and decide how best to proceed. Tomorrow.

She dried her hair, and tried to get some sleep, but every time she began to drift off, she would hear footsteps outside her bedroom door, or the wind moaning at the window, and her eyes would fly wide once more.

She drifted off to sleep eventually, but the entire time, she tossed and turned in the throes of a nightmare she couldn't later recall.

A soft wail stroked at the edges of her consciousness, tugging her out of the dream. In the nick of time, it seemed, she emerged into the soft folds of her covers. The baby was crying.

Caitlin wiped the sweat from her forehead, and tried to settle her breathing into a normal pattern. It was just a dream. Nothing more. She was safe.

It was then she felt the presence in her room. She froze and held her breath, listening. There was no sound or movement. Just a feeling that she wasn't alone.

She tried to shake it. It was silly, she told herself. Of course no one was in her room. She was shaken, from the dream and from her close call on the cliffs, tonight.

The baby cried again, and Caitlin felt answering tears well up in her own eyes. She wished, with everything in her, that Lizzie was her own. During those few, brief times when she'd held the baby, she'd felt as if everything would be fine. It had seemed so perfect. She'd had an identity. She'd found something to cling to in this sea of unanswered questions. It hurt too much to hear that child cry, and then stop as someone, probably Sandra, picked her up. Why the hell did it hurt so much?

She rolled to her stomach and buried her face in the pillow, clutching it tightly. It absorbed her stinging tears, but gave no comfort.

Then she heard the audible click of the door closing, and sat bolt upright in the bed. Someone had just exited the room, she was sure of it. She shot to her feet, switching on the lamp. Its glaring light made her blink, and showed her nothing. The room was exactly as it had been before.

Caitlin went to the door and yanked it open, her eyes scanning the dim length of the hallway in both directions. There was no one in sight, but she heard, just for an instant, the soft padding of feet on the carpet.

Terror gripped her, and she backed into her room, closed the door and turned the lock. Someone had been in here, standing over her while she tossed in the throes of her nightmare. Someone had stood, silently, just watching her.

Why?

What would have happened if she hadn't awoke?

She sat on the bed, with her back to the headboard, and her knees drawn up to her chest. She didn't close her eyes again.

In fear and desperation, she finally got up, determined to find the guest room where she'd taken refuge that first day back. She would sleep there tonight. Not only would she feel better, but it would make finding her more difficult for the killer, if he decided to try again.

Dylan poured another shot and tossed it back in a single swallow. It did nothing to erase from his memory the feel of his wife in his arms. When he'd pulled her up from the cliff face and she'd thrown herself against him, he'd experienced a longing that was like an addict's craving for his drug of choice. He'd wanted her.

Wet. She'd been soaking wet, and shivering with cold,

and her nipples had pressed against his chest so hard, he could feel them right through his shirt. And her face was damp, and her throat, and he'd wanted to lick the rainwater from her skin. God, how could he want any woman as badly as he wanted her, let alone one who'd caused him so much pain?

But she was different now. No longer the haughty princess of the manor, but unsure of herself, and softer-spoken, and—

Damn straight she's soft-spoken. She's scared to death I'm going to kill her and if I had half a brain I'd probably oblige her. Hell, I should *have dropped her out there at the cliff.*

His hand closed around the neck of the bottle and he splashed more scotch into the shot glass. Damn her for coming back when he'd thought he'd finally been rid of her for good. Damn her for changing everything just when he'd finally broken the grip she'd had for so long. Damn her for pretending she'd changed when he knew it was impossible. He'd waited five years for Caitlin to change. It hadn't happened. Why would a bump on the head do what all his arguing and pleading with her hadn't?

He poured the searing liquor down his throat and closed his eyes as it hit his stomach. He couldn't let her go now. He needed to watch her night and day until he settled this thing. And knowing that made him angry. And the anger made him reach for the bottle again. It was a night for anesthesia. Because as much as he'd vowed to set himself free of her, Caitlin was slowly drawing him in again.

And she wanted him to call her Caity.

For just a second, he let the image of her when she'd been Caity to him, rinse through his mind like a spring breeze. Then, she'd been as happy in tattered cutoffs as she was in a designer dress. She'd turned her nose up at her father's fancy meals to sneak out for pizza with him. God, if he could have that girl back again...

Ah, but that was idiocy! She didn't even remember those times. That Caity was dead and buried. So, she'd like him to believe, was the cold and distant woman she'd become.

But he wasn't so sure.

He drank and he paced, until his pacing became an unsteady weave and his head floated far above his shoulders. And then he mounted the stairs, thinking he ought to be drunk enough to sleep. As he climbed, clutching the banister for guidance, he recalled the conversation they'd had in her bedroom. She'd admitted that seeing him holding Sandra had hurt her. The old Cait never would have done that. And she'd looked at him like...like she wanted him. But he might have been seeing things that weren't there. And then he'd challenged her to make him a better offer. Like she would. And pigs would fly, too.

He forced himself farther along the hall, groped for the door handle and leaned heavily on it as it swung open. He stepped through, swaying slightly, but catching himself. He closed the door behind him and stood in complete darkness. He knew he was drunk. He didn't mind admitting it. The way he saw it, he had reason to get good and drunk tonight. Besides, he doubted he'd have been able to close his eyes sober. There was too much going on in his mind. Too many painful memories churning to life from the enforced death he'd imposed on them. Not memories of Caitlin. Memories of Caity.

He fumbled with his buttons, his fingers feeling too big. He dropped the shirt to the floor.

Hot, eager Caity. Her skin warm and coated in sweat, her body shuddering at his every touch, her soft whimpers as he played her. He knew how. He knew her every secret, knew her scent and her taste...

He groaned, and lurched forward, dragging the belt out of his pants and clumsily peeling them off. He kicked free of the rest of his clothes, amazed he managed to do so without falling on his butt.

Naked, he stood still a minute. The nearly frigid chill from the blasting central air unit felt good on his tormented flesh. It shot a little sanity back into his fevered mind. He pulled back the covers and crawled beneath them.

Warm, soft flesh was there to greet him. Long, silken tresses brushed against his unclothed chest. A curvy, bare backside rubbed over his groin, and he knew it was his wife. Naked, warm and waiting for him.

He released an anguished sigh and let his eyes fall closed. Finally, he thought in relief so great it was painful. Finally, the estrangement was at an end. She wanted him again.

His throat oddly tight, he rolled her onto her back, slipped his arms around her slender waist, and pressed his chest to hers as his mouth sought her lips. He found them and kissed her, and as long-denied passion hit him full force, his body grew fervent with need. He felt her slack, willing mouth tighten as she came fully awake, but he chose to ignore it. He forced his tongue inside, and he jammed his knee between her thighs to press them open. Already, he was hard and ready. He nudged against her opening, and felt it moisten in readiness. Oh, God, it had been so damned long.

He felt her hands pushing at his chest, and he was afraid she was changing her mind. Aided in his decision by the scotch, he gripped them both in one of his and pinned them above her head to the mattress. Her frantic twisting beneath him only served to heighten his lust. He kissed a hot trail from her lips to her jaw, and she immediately let out the beginning of a piercing shriek. His free hand clamped over her mouth.

"Baby, don't tell me to stop now," he said, panting with longing. "Please, don't tell me to stop. You don't know what I've gone through, night after night, always knowing you were just down the hall, always wanting you. God, how much I've wanted you."

He moved his mouth lower, captured one impudent breast between his teeth and worried it roughly, biting and tugging the hard little nipple until he felt it pulsate against his tongue. Muffled whimpering sounds escaped from beneath his palm, inflaming him beyond rational thought. Her nipple stood stiffer, hardened to a throbbing nub and he licked and sucked it before turning to the other one, and giving it equal attention.

Her opening wept for him, her juices coating his head where he pressed it against her. She was ready. So was he. He pulled back slightly. This first sheathing of him inside her would be to the hilt. It would be sheer ecstasy.

Her teeth closed on his hand so hard, he was certain she drew blood, and when he relaxed his hold on her in response to the pain, she yanked one hand free, and slammed it across his face.

"Get off me, you drunken lunatic! Get off me now or I swear I will scream until the windows rattle. I'll call a cop. Get off, get the hell off!"

He rolled to one side, swearing a blue streak and trying to figure out what the hell had happened. His arousal throbbed with need. His brain, with frustration. He felt her leave the bed on one side. He quickly left on the other, and unerringly found the light switch. As soon as the room was flooded with brilliance, he saw her. She'd been looking for something to put on, and apparently hadn't found it. She stood there, facing him, not a stitch covering her. Her lower lip was bleeding slightly. There were teeth marks on her dampened breasts, tiny little ridges around the nipples. Angry, red rings encircled her wrists.

But her nipples still stood in quivering hardness, gleaming with the moisture put there by his mouth, and he knew she'd been as aroused as he had been.

"Stop looking at me," she cried, snatching the comforter from the bed and tugging it up to her chin.

"If you didn't want me looking at you, why the hell were you naked, and waiting in my bed?"

"You're drunk," she cried. "This isn't your bed!" She gulped, blinked at tears that might have been manufactured, and shook her head.

Dylan frowned, and glanced around the room, now flooded with light. It was a guest room, the one right next door to his own. The furniture was situated in an almost identical pattern, and he had come in during utter darkness, not to mention falling-down drunk.

"You...said I could find another room if I didn't like the one I had. I—this was the only one I felt comfortable in."

He moved toward her, around the foot of the bed. She backed away until she was touching the wall. "And you didn't notice that it was right next door to my room? That didn't have anything to do with your choice?"

"As a matter of fact, it did. Someone was in my room tonight, watching me. I was terrified, and for some idiotic reason, I wanted to be closer to you." Her face fell, contorted with pain. "God, I'm a fool!"

Her words made their way through the scotch-induced haze of his brain, and he felt like groaning aloud. He looked at her again, at her dilated pupils, her tear-stained cheeks, her goose bump-dotted flesh. Then he glimpsed the corner of a dressing gown sticking out from under the bed. He reached for it and she jumped. Very slowly, he pulled it out and held it up to her.

She snatched it from his hands, held the blanket in her teeth and slipped the robe on. When she dropped the comforter at last, she lunged past him for the door.

He caught her arm. "This wasn't my fault, Caitlin. Not entirely. I stumbled into the wrong room by accident. What the hell was I supposed to think when I found you in what I mistook for my own bed, like this?"

She faced him, hair tousled, eyes blazing. "You damned near raped me, Dylan."

"If I were the kind of man to take a woman by force, you'd still be on your back under me, lady."

"If that—" she pointed an accusing finger at the rumpled sheets "—was an example of your technique, I'm not surprised your wife requested separate bedrooms."

His gaze lowered, and he ran the backs of his fingers over her still-distended nipple, where it poked through the material of the robe. "Oh, yeah. I can see how turned off *my wife* is."

"You're right," she shouted. "That's the worst part, Dylan. I thought I wanted you. I've stayed awake nights, wishing... Oh, God, I'm going to be sick!" Her face crumpled. She pushed her way blindly past him, and stumbled down the hall toward her own bedroom.

Chapter 8

It was morning, but not yet dawn. And despite her night-long expenditure of energy, she was still thinking about him. Dylan.

Tears blurred her vision, and she sank onto the bed's edge, amid the piles of clothes, drained of all ambition. She'd wanted so badly to trust him, to believe he was the one person in this house she could turn to in the midst of this chaos. He was her husband. She should be able to trust him.

Then why didn't she?

Though she'd been determined not to, she recalled the events of last night with brutal clarity. His hands, holding her wrists to the bed. His mouth claiming hers with punishing force, his hardened groin digging into her. She'd felt the anger inside him, all of it, seemingly focused on her. She'd felt his contempt in his touch.

And his desire.

His throaty declaration haunted her, even now, ringing in her ears until she pressed her hands to them to stop it. But still she heard his gruff voice, the pain and frustration palpable in its timbre. "...night after night, always knowing you were just down the hall, always wanting you. God, how much I've wanted you..."

She closed her eyes as the tears spilled over her face. So many emotions assailed her, it was difficult to know what she was feeling.

So she told herself to stop analyzing and reliving it, and she stood up, and got back to work. She tightened the sash of her red satin robe, recalling as she did the coldness in Dylan's eyes as he'd held it toward her in one outstretched hand. She shuddered. She'd have to add it to the pile of clothes to be discarded, just as soon as she returned to her room with some boxes.

Sleep, of course, had not been an option last night. She'd left the guest room devastated, and angry, and confused, and too full of emotions to rest. She tried to count the nights since she'd actually slept decently, and realized there'd been none. Not since she'd come back here.

She picked her way through the mounds of clothes, all separated into piles on the floor, and on the bed, and left the bedroom, stepping silently into the hall, flicking on every light switch she came to along the way. She'd memorized their locations since her last scare out here.

The house was cold, as always, and quiet as a tomb, which was fitting, she thought bitterly, since someone was trying so hard to make it hers. She wouldn't run into Dylan. No chance of that. As drunk as he'd been, he'd probably passed out right after she'd left him. He might not even remember... She almost hoped he didn't.

She padded softly down the stairs, barefoot, and made her way to the kitchen without interruption. She hoped to find Genevieve and ask for a box to pack the clothes in, or maybe just find the boxes herself.

But the kitchen was empty, spotless and dark. She didn't know where the light switch was in here. She stood for a moment, in the doorway, her eyes moving slowly over the shapes of gleaming pots and pans hanging from racks, the cabinets, the range. With a sigh of resignation, she slipped farther inside. She pressed her palm to the wall and walked sideways, feeling for the light switch. As soon as she let it go, the door swung closed, and Caitlin found herself surrounded by utter blackness.

Panic welled up in her throat until she almost choked on it. She walked faster, both hands racing over the wall now, in search of the switch. She'd been stupid to come down here. What was she thinking of, groping her way through a darkened room where a killer might very well be waiting?

Her fingers touched a switch. Limp with relief, her pulse thundering in her temples, she moved it, and the room filled with brilliant light.

A hand dropped to her shoulder. Caitlin whirled, a scream of terror catching in her throat.

"Do not be afraid, *chérie*."

She took a step away from Henri, but her back touched the wall. "I...I was looking for Genevieve." Caitlin tried not to squirm at the notion of being alone with him, and standing so close. He hadn't lifted a finger to so much as touch her. And just because his eyes were so intense, it didn't really mean anything. So, he found her attractive. So what?

With her back to the wall, and him standing so close, she couldn't really move without shoving him aside, and looking like a total idiot. "Tell me what it is you need, what it is you want. I will take care of it."

Was it only admiration she was seeing in those dark eyes? Or was there more? A suggestion...a meaning she didn't get because she didn't remember. My God, had there ever been something going on between her and Henri? The thought shocked and shook her. Had the old Caitlin cheated on her husband? Was that why Dylan was so hostile toward her now?

She looked up, into the now-smiling face, and shook her head. No. If Dylan thought that, Henri certainly wouldn't still be employed here. Dylan wasn't the kind of man who'd take something like that lightly.

"*Chérie?*"

He was awaiting an answer. "Boxes. I, um, I need to pack some clothes I don't want, and I need boxes."

"Ah." He stepped back just slightly, pinching his chin. Then he snapped his fingers. "*Oui*, I have it. There are some in the storage room. Wait here."

And just like that, he was briskly walking across the kitchen, and out another door, beyond it. Caitlin slowly released all the air from her lungs. She knew she was simply overreacting to everything everyone said or did, because she knew that someone in this house hated her enough to kill her. She forced herself to calm down, and recalled that Henri tended to call every woman in the house *chérie,* even Ellen, on occasion. She shouldn't start reading a history of illicit liaisons into his friendliness.

He was back in seconds, with three boxes, each one fitted neatly inside another. She took them. "Thank you, Henri."

"It is nothing."

The sun never really rose. It was there, but you couldn't see it beyond the black clouds and pouring rain. Caitlin showered, hanging a washcloth over the ugly, lion-faced spigot, then slipped into jeans and a sweatshirt. She dried her hair and pulled it into a ponytail to keep it out of her face. When she stepped out of her bathroom, she folded the red robe over her forearm and dropped it into one of the boxes she'd filled with clothes.

And then she reached for the delicate antique-look phone. She'd come to only one conclusion all night long— that she needed to talk with Dr. Judith Stone. And then the police. She'd be damned if she'd sit here and wait for the next attempt on her life without taking some kind of action. The thought of just walking away from all of this pirouetted through her mind, but vanished just as quickly. She couldn't leave until she'd made some kind of sense of her life, found some shred of her identity. It wasn't even an option. This was her home; these people, her family. She'd never know peace until she solved this thing.

She brought the receiver from its elevated cradle to her ear. She was surprised to hear voices on the line.

"Just do it. Withdraw the bid."

The voice was low, resolute, and Dylan's. Caitlin was

about to replace the receiver, but the answer came, and it caught her attention.

''Dylan, we need this contract. We're going to be in the red if we don't land it. Dammit, there are only two competitors, and one of the company's CEO is involved in that child molestation case. The state won't award a guy with so much scandal attached to him any kind of contract, so we—''

''We withdraw the bid.''

Caitlin frowned, recognizing the young male voice on the other end as one of the architects she'd met at the office yesterday.

''We're about to have some scandals of our own come to light, Patrick. I'm on my way to the police right now, and you know how things leak from one government agency to another. Just pull out and maybe we can salvage our reputation.''

''What scandal?''

''Not on the phone.''

''It's a private line, Dylan. What scandal?''

Dylan sighed loudly into the mouthpiece. ''Within the next hour, I will probably become the chief suspect in the attempted murder of my wife. Scandalous enough for you?''

There was a moment of stunned silence, then, ''I don't need to ask if you did it.''

''No?''

''No.'' There was a long sigh. ''I'll pull the bid, Dylan. Call if you need anything.''

''Right.''

Two clicks sounded in Caitlin's ear, and she blinked down her shock. A second later, she placed her own call.

His idiotic boozing last night and the hangover it left him with had not in any way dulled his memory. Dylan almost wished it had. For the briefest of moments, he'd thought...hell, it didn't matter what he'd thought. He lifted his fist and pounded on her bedroom door harder than he needed to.

"Who's there?"

He closed his eyes and willed the throbbing that encompassed his skull to lessen. It didn't. She sounded scared and he imagined she was. Her fear wouldn't lessen when she knew he stood on this side of the door, either. Perhaps it would increase. He was madder than hell right now and rationalization didn't help. He hadn't hurt her last night. If anything, she'd been just as aroused as he was, but she'd never admit it. She'd hold his cavemanlike behavior over his head and make him squirm with guilt. Hell, she already had. The hurt in her eyes last night haunted him, even now. He felt like a bastard, and he was good and angry at her for that, even though it was his own fault. Not only that, but she was afraid of him. And that angered him still further.

"It's me," he said belatedly, in answer to her question.

He expected her to stand on her side of the door and speak through it. He was surprised when the handle turned and the door opened widely. Even more surprised at her murmured, "Come in."

He entered, and she closed the door behind him. She didn't meet his gaze as he looked her over. There were dark circles under her eyes that told of the sleepless night she'd spent. He might have been prone to insomnia last night, as well, if he hadn't been too drunk to stay conscious. Not too drunk to dream, though. And looking at her now, in the snug-fitting jeans, her face free of makeup, her eyes wide and wary, brought those dreams back to him full force. Dreams in which she hadn't stopped him, where he'd finished what he'd so clumsily begun last night.

He was aware of the stirring in his groin, and it only added to the discomfort he already felt. And that added to his irrational anger at her.

"You look like hell," she said, when she finally made her eyes move over his face.

"Good. I'd hate to feel this bad and not have it show."

"Hangover?"

"Mother of them all," he answered.

She nodded.

"You don't look too good yourself." He noticed the boxes of clothes stacked around the room, and the open, nearly empty closet.

She shrugged. "Couldn't sleep."

Here it came, he thought. The guilt trip. "Stay awake all night waiting for an apology?"

Her head came up and her gaze narrowed. "I was afraid if I closed my eyes, someone might sneak in and slit my throat."

"Me?"

"Maybe."

He sighed, and broke eye contact, turning to pace away from her. "I'm not going to apologize, Cait."

"I didn't ask you to."

"There's only so much deprivation a man can take."

"Then you *haven't* been sleeping with my brother's wife?"

He spun around to face her. "Show up naked in my bed again, Cait, and you're liable to get the same reaction."

"It wasn't your bed," she reminded him. "Or do you intend to get so falling-down drunk, you can't tell the difference often?"

She was so damned calm, so detached. He wanted to wring her neck. God, he couldn't get the image of her unclothed body out of his mind, or the feel of her moistened opening against his throbbing need, or the taste of her mouth, her skin, her tongue, her nipples.

"It won't matter if I'm drunk or sober."

Her fine auburn brows arched. "Thanks for the warning.

I can't say much for your brand of lovemaking, so I'll avoid it from now on.''

"That wasn't lovemaking. Just plain lust. And you can argue all you want, but it was mutual.''

Finally, a hint of something flickered beneath the cool green waters of her eyes. She lowered them, and cleared her throat. "Was there some point to this visit, or did you just come here to harass me?''

"There's a point. I'm on my way to the police station, to report the unfortunate attempt on your life last night.''

She released a short burst of air that might have been intended as a laugh. "What do you consider unfortunate, Dylan? That someone tried to kill me, or that he failed?''

He glared at her. "I came to ask if you want to come along. You're so convinced I might be the guilty party, I know you'll want to share that suspicion with the police.''

She turned her back on him, walked toward the bed and sunk onto it as if too exhausted to stand up any longer. She closed her eyes.

Dylan carefully kept any hint of concern out of his voice. "Are you sick?''

She shook her head slowly. "Just tired. Mostly of you and your hostility. You're a real bastard, you know that?''

"And you're Sweet Mary Sunlight, babe. Are you coming with me, or not?''

"Yeah.''

She didn't move, or look at him. She was pale this morning, he noted. Her cheeks hollow. She'd lost weight while she was in the coma, not that she'd had any to spare. And she didn't look as if she were putting any of it back on since coming home.

"Get something to eat. I'll wait in the foyer.''

She shook her head, and rose slowly, like an old woman with aching joints. "No, let's just go.''

She ought to eat. He ought to insist on it. Then again,

she was a grown woman with a mind of her own. She didn't need a keeper.

"There's no hurry. We have time—"

"If I eat this morning, I'll probably puke in your fancy car. Let's just go, okay? And will you send Genevieve up for these clothes? I don't want them."

"What do you want her to do with them?"

"I don't care. Wear them, give them away, burn them, for all I care."

He was glumly silent on the short ride into Eden, and Caitlin felt nauseated, even though she hadn't eaten. It was fear gnawing at her gut, fear and confusion. As angry and afraid of him as she'd been last night, she now harbored a slight doubt he'd tried to hurt her. The phone call she'd overheard was strong evidence of that. He wouldn't risk his business by reporting this to the police unless he was innocent. He'd have tried to talk her out of going to the authorities.

Or was this his way of covering his tracks? Did he simply know she would report the incident either way, and want to be there when she did? She almost asked him to forget about it, or delay the visit, but she was too afraid he'd agree readily. She was also afraid the killer would try again, and the police were the only people she was sure would try to help her stay alive.

And there was something else...something she'd not been fully aware of in her fury over his rough treatment of her last night. Something that had only begun to dawn on her in the cold light of day, with his childish refusal to apologize, and his obvious guilt about his actions.

When she'd left him last night, there had been pain in his eyes. Stark, black agony. Loneliness as acute as her own. He had wanted her, had thought she was there waiting. And the truth had been like salt in an old wound. She'd hurt him. Again. She'd obviously done the same in the past.

Enough to make him hate her? she wondered. Enough to make him want her dead? He wanted her. She could feel it. Passion ricocheted between them in waves so thick, they were all but visible. But murder was a crime of passion. Wasn't it?

Police Detective Jack Barnes was a big man, with a voice to match. He sat behind his cluttered desk in a brilliant, touristy button-down shirt, leaned back in his chair and removed his rectangular bifocals, staring at Caitlin in the same distracted manner he'd had when she'd first walked into the beehive of activity.

"I'll have to come to the house, interview everyone who was there last night." His voice was deep, booming, as if it echoed back and forth in some cavern behind his barrel chest before floating out to her ears. "We'll send a forensics team to the scene, but with all this rain, I doubt there's any evidence left. Probably not even a footprint." He eyed Dylan for a long moment. "Might have been last night, if we'd been called right away."

"I don't think so, Detective. The cliffs are solid rock, not a very good receptacle for footprints."

Barnes nodded slowly. "So, you went to your wife's room, to check on her, found she wasn't there and got worried?"

Dylan nodded.

"Any particular reason you would worry so quick, Rossi?"

"Hell, Barnes, you're the detective. You figure it out. I've already told you about her condition. It was late at night, not to mention pouring rain."

Barnes's gaze narrowed, then softened just as quickly when he looked at Caitlin. "Why'd you go outside, Mrs. Ros—"

"Caity, please." She instinctively liked Detective Barnes, except for his gruff, suspicious manner with Dylan. Then again, she couldn't blame him for that. She was suspicious of Dylan, herself. "I was told I used to love to walk along the cliffs at night. I wanted to try it…see if I could remember." There was no sense telling him about how upset she'd been, or about the way Sandra had thrown herself into Dylan's arms. It was irrelevant.

"And who told you that?"

She frowned. "My…brother. Thomas." *Who happens to resent me for inheriting when he didn't, and who's having an affair with my maid, and who I overheard plotting against my husband.*

Thomas? Is he the one?

Barnes made a note. "Okay." He looked at Dylan again. "So, you found she wasn't in her room. Then what?"

Dylan glanced at her, and she thought he was uncomfortable having her hear him retell the story. "I searched the house, and then I realized she must have gone out to the cliffs. She'd mentioned earlier that she wanted to—"

"And Dylan warned me not to go out there alone," she put in quickly, then wondered why she'd defended him.

Dylan sent her a strange look, before returning his attention to Barnes. "Then I went out to look for her."

"Alone?"

Dylan shook his head. "I took Thomas, his wife, Sandra, and our chef, Henri, out with me. Genevieve and Ellen stayed in the house to look after the baby."

Barnes pulled a tissue from a box on his desk, and casually wiped the lenses of his glasses. He looked as if his full attention was focused on the rectangular specs. "You all left the house together?"

"Yes. We walked out to the cliffs, and then we split up."

"Who was closest to her when you heard her scream, Rossi?"

Dylan shook his head. "It's impossible to say. We all sort of ran in that direction from where we were."

Barnes replaced his glasses on his nose. "You have a will, Caity?"

She blinked. "I, um, I don't know." She looked at Dylan.

"Yes, she has a will. Last I knew, I was in it. So was her brother."

Barnes licked his lips. "Who's your lawyer, hon?"

She shook her head, not a bit put out by the endearment. He was at least fifteen years older than she, and he seemed to have some genuine concern for her. "I don't know."

Barnes shook his head, and glared at Dylan. "Done a good job of keeping her in the dark, haven't you, Rossi?"

"She's barely been home three days, Barnes. It hasn't come up in casual conversation." Dylan took his wallet from his pocket, pawed through it for a minute and extracted a business card. He snapped it down on the desk, and pushed it toward Detective Barnes. "Here's his card."

Barnes examined it, and nodded, slipping it into his shirt pocket. "You have any plans to leave Eden in the next few days, Rossi?"

Dylan opened his mouth, but Caitlin cut him off. "My husband makes a poor suspect, Detective Barnes."

The man's smile was obviously forced. "It's Jack, and I wish you'd let me decide who the suspects are."

She licked her lips and swallowed, refusing to glance Dylan's way as she spoke. "When this comes out, his business is going to suffer. He's already had to withdraw a bid on a government contract because of it. This whole thing is costing him money." She bit her lip, only now realizing how vehement she'd sounded. But she'd only spoken the truth, and Jack Barnes ought to have all the facts before he came to any conclusions.

Barnes pursed his lips and rose from his seat. He moved to the file cabinet across the room with measured strides, while Caitlin remained in her hard little chair beside Dylan. She felt her husband's eyes on her. She didn't look back.

Barnes returned, and slapped a file folder onto his desk. "This is the report on the accident you had, Mrs. Rossi. We were suspicious then, but there wasn't enough evidence to warrant an investigation. The brake line was torn, not cut. But I can tell you, it wouldn't be too difficult for someone to have done it deliberately. I suspected it then." He tapped the folder with his glasses for emphasis. "Now I'm certain of it." He slanted a glance at Dylan as he spoke. "You and your husband had a loud argument just before that accident, Caity. You left the house, driving like a bat out of hell, from what witnesses say. He went after you a few minutes later."

Caitlin wasn't aware of slowly shaking her head from side to side, or of rising to her feet. Her gaze turned inward, and when she spoke, she was addressing herself more than she was Jack Barnes. "But he pulled me up the side of that cliff last night. I wasn't holding on to anything but him, and if he'd wanted to drop me, he could have done it right then. No one would have believed it wasn't an accident. Not when he was hanging half over the side himself just to reach me."

Barnes sighed and got to his feet. "That doesn't prove anything," he said gently. "Caity, you're a nice girl. I don't want to see your name cross this desk in a homicide report. Take my advice. Move out for a while. Go stay with a relative—"

"I don't have any, except the ones who live with us."

"Then a hotel. You're somebody's target. You ought to get out of the line of fire."

She sighed hard, shaking her head. "I'll give it some thought." She already had given it thought, though. She just couldn't bring herself to leave. Not yet.

"I think there's another side to that argument, Barnes," Dylan said. She looked at him as he spoke, tried to read his motives in his fathomless, dark eyes. "In the house, there's one person who wants her dead—maybe—and four who don't. In a hotel, she'd be alone, and the killer wouldn't have much trouble tracking her down."

Did Dylan want her to stay, then? Why? To keep her from being killed...or to keep her within his reach?

The detective shook his head, ignoring Dylan. He addressed Caitlin. "Don't trust any of them. I'll be checking up on you."

She nodded. "Thank you."

"Stay in touch. Let me know if you decide to leave." His gaze sharpened when he turned it on Dylan. "Don't let anything happen to her, Rossi." His tone held a warning that couldn't be missed.

Dylan took her arm and walked her out to the car. Once he'd pulled out of the lot, he spoke without looking at her. "Since when are you my staunch defender?"

She shook her head at the sarcasm in his voice. "I was going to make a call this morning. I heard your conversation with Patrick Callen."

"So?"

"So it doesn't make sense that you would risk the business just to get rid of me. It would be simpler just to file for divorce."

"Oh, yeah. That would be a real simple solution, wouldn't it?"

She slammed her fists on the dashboard, and his head swung toward her. "Damn you!" She grated her teeth, squeezed her eyes tight, but the tears came, anyway. "You won't even deny it was you, will you? You can't even give me that much! Did it ever occur to you that I *need* to trust someone? That I need someone on my side right now? I can't..." She bit her lips to stop the endless flow of words that wanted to tumble through them.

"And you want that someone to be me, is that it? You want me to come to you on my knees and swear I'm innocent, beg you to believe me, vow to protect my loving little wife, no matter what?"

"Go to hell, Dylan."

"I'm already there. Don't expect me to come to you, swearing my innocence. If you can't trust me now, you have no one to blame but yourself."

"I don't even have that, Dylan. Because I wasn't around when some woman I don't remember was making you hate her. I was dropped into the middle of her life, not even knowing her name."

"Maybe *you* don't remember her, Caitlin. But *I do*." He braked to a stop at an intersection and waited for the light to change. "So are you going home, or to a hotel?"

She shook her head. "I don't have a home."

"How about a straight answer for once?"

She nodded, and swallowed the lump in her throat. "Take me to Dr. Stone's office. I have an appointment."

The light changed and he pressed the accelerator. "And then?"

"And then leave. When I decide where I'm going, I'll call a cab."

Chapter 9

"I have to agree with Detective Barnes, Caity. It seems to me, you'd be safer somewhere else."

Caitlin continued pacing the length of Judith Stone's office. The knotty-pine walls and gas jet fireplace were supposed to be cozy, comforting, she supposed. But there was nothing comfortable about the way she felt.

"You're probably right."

"But?"

"I'm not sure I can leave yet. There are still too many things I don't understand about…about her."

"Caitlin Rossi?"

Caitlin nodded.

"You told me you considered her a stranger, one who's dead and buried. Someone you didn't know."

"I *don't* know her. But I feel I *have* to. I feel as if I'll never understand myself unless I come to grips with who I was."

Judith shifted in her chair, reaching for the cup of tea on her desk. "Is there one specific thing you want to know about, or just her life in general?"

Caitlin stopped, and faced the psychiatrist. "I need to know how she could have been so cold to her husband. How she managed to alienate him so completely, and why."

Judith calmly sipped her tea. She held up the mug. "Are you sure you won't have some? It's chamomile."

Caitlin only shook her head.

"Caity, are you developing feelings for Dylan?"

"I don't know. He acts like he can't stand to be near me most of the time."

"And the rest of the time?"

Caitlin walked to the huge window and looked down at the street. "When he took me shopping, there were moments when he let me glimpse the man behind the mask. But every time I started to feel some sort of closeness starting to develop between us, he pulled back."

"And you didn't want him to."

"No. I guess I didn't."

Judith lifted the tea bag from the mug with the spoon, wrapped the string around the spoon three times and gave the bag a dainty squeeze. "What do you want from him?"

Caitlin drew a slow breath and held it. She closed her eyes. "When he pulled me up from the cliff..."

Judith leaned forward in her chair. "Go on."

Caitlin swallowed hard. "He held me so tightly I could barely breathe." She closed her eyes and replayed the incident in her mind. Not the terror, but the crushing strength of his arms around her. The way his heart had thundered beneath her head, and the way his body had been shaking almost as much as hers. "For those few minutes, I didn't feel so alone. He told me everything was all right, and I believed him. He held me like he'd never let me go."

"You felt close to him then?"

Caitlin sighed. "Yes, I guess that's what I want. I want to be able to turn to him when I'm afraid, when I feel so alone I want to die. I want all that strength to be with me, not against me. I want to have someone I can depend on, trust in, and I want so much for it to be him."

"But it isn't?"

Caitlin faced Judith levelly. "How can it be? He won't even deny that he's the one who wants me dead."

"If he were the one, he'd probably deny it loudly. Sounds to me like his pride's been wounded."

"If it has, then it's because of the woman I was. I just don't know how to fix the damage she did." Caitlin began her pacing again. "He wants me."

"Physically?"

Caitlin nodded. "I went looking for another room last night, and chose the one nearest his. He came in later, drunk, and—"

"And what?" Judith rose from her seat.

"Things got a bit rough. He thought I was there waiting for him."

"Caity, are you telling me this man raped you?"

"No. It didn't go that far. But it was close."

Judith shook her head. "And how did you feel about that?"

"I don't know. I was afraid. There was so much anger in him, and it scared me. But I can't deny that there was a part of me that responded to him."

"You wanted to make love with him?"

"I did. I do." She turned in a small circle, pushing one hand through her hair. "I keep getting these flashes of us together, and it's...it's incredible."

"The sex?"

Caitlin nodded. "It's so frustrating. I don't know if they're memories or fantasies. I only know I want him. Madly. But not like that. God, how can I be attracted to a man who seems to despise me? Am I that sick?" She walked to a chair and slammed herself into it. "I disgust myself."

She closed her eyes, bit her lip. "But then, I look him in the eye, and I think he isn't being honest. I think he might not hate me as much as he pretends to. Dammit, if I could just go back and find out what went wrong, I might stand a chance of making amends." She lowered her head, then lifted it again as an idea occurred to her. "What about hypnosis? Could you put me under and make me remember my past?"

Judith crossed the room and knelt in front of Caitlin's chair. "It could work, Caitlin. But there is a very high risk factor involved in your case. The trauma of remembering might be more than your mind could take. You could end up worse off than you are now.''

''It might be worth the risk.''

Judith straightened, looked down at Caitlin and sighed. ''That will be your decision. But I want you to give it careful thought. And I want you to try to work things out in the present, before you go delving into the past. If these flashes you've described *are* memories, hypnosis might not be necessary at all. Let's save it for a last resort, all right?''

Caitlin nodded.

''In the meantime, Caity, why don't you try to get him into an honest, open conversation. He might be as confused about your feelings as you are about his.''

''How's Lizzie?''

Sandra looked up from the book she was engrossed in, when Dylan crossed the room toward her. ''She's gonna be just fine. The doctor put her on antibiotics. She's got a slight chest cold, is all.'' Her gaze swept the room behind him. ''So where's the lady Caitlin?''

Dylan shrugged and said nothing. He had no idea where Cait was right now, and he told himself he didn't give a damn. The police had been roaming the place all afternoon. Detective Barnes in his loud shirt and khaki trousers, with his suspicion in his eyes every time he glanced Dylan's way had been almost too much. They'd questioned everyone, even Ellen. And their forensics crew had only just packed up and driven off, having found nothing on the cliffs.

Sandra rose and stood near him. Her hands rested lightly on his shoulders. ''I don't know what I'd have done without you last night.''

''I care about Lizzie.'' The glint in her eyes made him uncomfortable.

''More than her own daddy does.''

''That's not true, Sandra. Thomas just—''

"Just what?" She shook her head. "He don't want her. Or me, either. You treat us better than he ever has."

"He needs time to adjust to the idea of being a father." Dylan went to step backward, but her hands slid around to the base of his neck.

"Lizzie's three months old. How much time you s'pose it's gonna take?" She sighed and a slight smile touched her full lips. "It doesn't matter. I don't want him either." Her grip tightened, pulling her body closer, until it pressed tight to his. "You know who I want."

"Sandra, for—"

Footsteps behind him made his spine stiffen. He knew without turning that Caitlin had come in. He caught the smug glance Sandra threw over his shoulder, before she lowered her head to it.

Dylan caught her hands, unwound them from his neck, pressing them to her sides, and stepped away from her. He turned, but only in time to see Caitlin's rigid back as she marched up the stairs. He swung his gaze back to Sandra. She was smiling.

"Dammit, Sandra! Do you know what she's probably thinking?

She shrugged. "I really don't care *what* she thinks."

"It was deliberate, wasn't it?" Dylan's voice was far louder than necessary, but he did nothing about it. He had enough trouble right now, without Sandra adding to it with her theatrics.

"She might as well know where things stand," Sandra yelled back. "You don't want her. I'd be so much better for you than she's ever been, can't you see that?" She lunged toward him again, throwing her arms around him.

Dylan shoved her roughly away. She staggered backward, tripped on the book she'd dropped and fell to the floor.

"What the hell is going on in here?" Thomas strode into the room, with Genevieve at his side. When Dylan glanced up, he saw Caitlin standing halfway up the stairs, staring downward. All of them had seen him shove Sandra. Cait must have heard the entire exchange.

Thomas crossed the room and reached down to take his wife's hand and pull her to her feet. "What are you two arguing about? We could hear you yelling all the way in the kitchen."

Sandra glared at Dylan. He pushed a hand through his hair and moved past them all, not saying a word. Let Sandra explain the fight. He had no doubt she could come up with a lie right on cue.

Dylan went to the library and reached for the bottle of scotch in the cabinet. Then he stopped himself. It had been stupid getting drunk last night. He needed a clear head, not anesthetic.

Caitlin's voice coming from behind him brought him around, still holding the bottle by its neck.

"I wish you wouldn't."

He glanced at the bottle, then at her. "Why not?"

"I want to talk to you. I'd prefer you sober."

He shrugged, and replaced the bottle. "So talk."

She came the rest of the way into the room, and turned to close the double doors behind her. Then she crossed the carpet to the sofa, and sat down. She pinned him to the spot with her eyes glittering like polished emeralds. "How do you feel about me, Dylan?"

He said nothing, but moved to the sofa, and sat on its opposite end.

"Do you hate me as much as you seem to?"

He shook his head. "I don't hate you."

"Dislike, then?"

He closed his eyes. "Why don't you just ask the question you came to ask. You want to know if I'm planning your murder, don't you?"

She shook her head. "No." She sighed, and averted her eyes. "You turned Sandra down. Thank you for that."

"I didn't do it for you. Contrary to what you might think, I'm not the kind of man who gets his kicks by sleeping with his sister-in-law."

"I know. More and more I'm seeing just what kind of man you are." She cleared her throat, licked her lips. She was nervous. "I want you to tell me…tell me about us. Our past. I want to know what went wrong. I need you to give me this one chance…"

"Chance to do what?"

She brought one knee up onto the sofa and leaned toward him. "To show you who I am. I'm not the woman who hurt you, Dylan. You can't keep hating me for the things *she* did. You don't even know me. I'm a stranger that looks like your wife, that's all."

"No, that's not true. You're a lot like her. The way she was when…" He stopped, blinking fast, averting his eyes. God, she was getting to him. He hated his weakness.

Caitlin frowned. "When what?" She slid nearer, placed her hands on his shoulders. "Please, tell me. Turn on a light so I can find my way through this maze. Give me a candle."

Dylan felt the heat of her hands through his shirt. He fought with the ridiculous arousal her touch brought, and he fought with the equally ludicrous hope that kept leaping up when she was like this. But he lost the battle. Her voice was almost a plea, and in her eyes he saw nothing but confusion.

"Fine. Fine, you want to hear a bedtime story, I'll give you one. But I warn you, the ending isn't happily-ever-after."

She sighed and gave him a soft smile that he couldn't keep looking at. He glanced away, toward the massive bookcase opposite the sofa. "We met in college. You were nineteen. We started dating the day we met, and stayed together right through your graduation. By then, I'd already started the business."

"What was I like then?"

He looked at her. He couldn't help himself. She was the image of the girl he'd known then, right now, and the pain of seeing her and knowing she wasn't *his* Caity was almost paralyzing.

"You were different." He fought to keep the emotions from his voice, his face, as he spoke. "You lived in a mansion, had more money than you could count, but never wore anything but jeans. And your hair was consistently in one of two styles. Either long and loose, or up in a ponytail. You hated what you called snobs. You treated your father's household staff like guests instead of employees. Genevieve was one of your favorites. And you never gave a damn if I couldn't afford to take you to the best restaurants or the hot concerts in town. You were just as happy to go for a walk, or a fast-food joint."

She turned to lean back on the cushions, and the act brought her side right up to his. She tipped her head backward and closed her eyes. "And what about you?"

Dylan wanted to recite the facts without getting caught up in the memories, but it was difficult. Her pale arching neck was right under his nose, and he had the ridiculous urge to run his lips and tongue over that satin skin.

He cleared his throat, and his mind. "I was struggling to get a new business going. I spent most of my time working. All I wanted was to be a success, so I could give you what your father could. You said it didn't matter. Maybe I knew, even then, that it really did."

"What kind of grades did I get?"

"Strictly Bs. You could have done better. You had this philosophy that spending too much time studying was unhealthy and a waste of your youth. You liked cutting classes now and then, dragging me away from my shabby little office to the beach." He licked his lips, remembering. "We used to strip down to our skin and swim. Then we'd get out of the water and make love in the sand." Even now, after all this time, Dylan could recall the feel of her warm, wet skin beneath his hands, the grate of the sand coating her damp body, taste her hungry mouth beneath his.

Her head tilted sideways until it rested on his shoulder. Part of him wanted to pull away, but most of him didn't. Against his better judgment, he kept on talking. "I remember once, a couple of the guys who worked for me followed us and stole our clothes. We drove back to my little apartment in nothing but our towels." He caught himself smiling at the memory. "I ran a red light and got pulled over. I'll never forget the expression on that cop's face."

She laughed aloud and the sound was like a knife in his heart, like a ghost from the past sneaking up on him to implant the blade. His smile died.

"When did we get married?"

The blade twisted.

"After you graduated. Your father insisted on throwing us a huge wedding, and you insisted we let him. I didn't like that he was footing the bill, but I wanted to make you happy, so I went along. By then, your parents had been divorced for years."

She turned her head, and when she spoke her breath fanned his neck. "What happened to them?"

"I don't know. It was one of those things you refused to talk about. Your mother and brother moved away, and you stayed with your father. I think that was when you started to change."

"In what way?"

Dylan shook his head. How many times had he cursed himself for missing the warning signs? "You kept things from me. You used to go and visit your mother, but you would never let me come along, even after we were married. You'd come home depressed and short-tempered, but you wouldn't tell me why. I do know that your mother took nothing when she left your dad. So I imagine she had it pretty rough."

She frowned, but in a moment went on with her questions. "Where did we live?"

"With Aunt Ellen. She had a big old house that was practically falling down around her. She wouldn't let us pay rent, but I chipped in what I could toward repairs. It wasn't much. Those first years were lean. And then your mother died."

She nodded, her hair brushing his neck with the action. "She killed herself."

Dylan nodded. "I was working that night, so I wasn't there when you got the news. You wouldn't talk about it at all, just said you wanted to forget. And the next thing I knew, you'd decided to buy a house. I wanted to wait until I could afford to do it, but you were adamant, almost obsessed with the idea. You picked this place, and just dipped into your trust fund to pay for it. It's all in your name. One big investment. You hired decorators and went crazy with remodeling it, and then we moved in. The one concession you made was to let Aunt Ellen move in, as well. I refused to leave her alone."

She gasped, and straightened to stare into his eyes. "I didn't want her?"

"She raised me. My parents were killed in a car crash when I was ten, and she was there for me. I wanted to return the favor. You didn't argue about it. You never really voiced an opinion at all. I have no idea how you felt."

She closed her eyes and gave her head a quick shake. "I don't know why I would have disagreed with you."

"It nearly killed her to leave her old house, but she couldn't afford to keep it up on her own. And I knew she shouldn't be by herself at her age."

"You were right."

He shrugged. "I couldn't seem to talk to you about anything then, Cait. You were so closed off from me. After a while, I stopped trying. I just poured everything I had into the business, while you worried about investments and stock options and whether our property value was increasing. You became so involved in making sure your money was gaining top interest, there was no room for me anymore. Things just went downhill from there.''

"And then Thomas and Sandra moved in.''

"Yeah. Your brother thought he'd be all set when your father died, but he was cut completely out of the will. I was surprised when you didn't offer to split your inheritance with him. But I guess I shouldn't have been. That money meant everything to you. By then, the business was on solid ground, so you pressured me into hiring him. About the same time, you hired Henri and Genevieve. We ended up with the life you'd always scoffed at. Our house was as big as your father's.''

She shook her head slowly. "Dylan, why did you stay with me?''

He searched her face. It was as innocent and vulnerable as he'd ever seen it. Her sparkling green eyes wide and trusting. He couldn't tell her the rest. He couldn't cause her that kind of pain, not again, no matter what had happened between them. He wasn't looking at the woman he'd known a few months ago. He was looking at the image of the girl he'd fallen in love with. Even if she was no longer that girl on the inside.

"I can't answer that.''

"Can you at least tell me why...why we slept apart?''

"You were afraid you'd get pregnant.'' That, at least, was true.

"But there are so many—''

"You didn't trust birth control, Cait. There's always a slight chance of failure and you just couldn't stand the idea of it. That's why you were so upset the night of the accident. We'd both had a few drinks that night. And we wound up in your bed, together.'' He shook his head, remembering how he'd thought then that maybe things were going to turn around. "When you woke later, found yourself naked, in my arms, you freaked. Accused me of taking advantage of you when you were drunk, said you'd never have allowed it sober. We had a hell of a row, and you threw on some clothes and stormed out, terrified I'd gotten you pregnant.''

"And you came after me."

"I knew you shouldn't be driving."

She licked her lips. "I wish we did have a baby."

The blade ran right through him, and turned hot. Searing. Dylan had to close his eyes to hide the pain those words brought. "So do I." Suddenly, he felt her fingertips brush gently over his damp eyes, and he opened them. Hers were wet, too.

"Last night, in your room, I—"

He shook his head, and silenced her with a finger to her lips. "That's not the way it was with us, Caitlin. I was drunk and I was frustrated—"

"I know." She smiled, but it was shaky, watery. "How was it, before things went wrong? What was it like when we made love?"

He shook his head. He wouldn't feel anything. He *wouldn't*. "Explosive. Mindless." He closed his eyes, and thought of the nights they'd had together, despite his vow that he wouldn't. She knew him so well, knew how to touch him and make him tremble. And he was keenly aware of every sensitive spot on her body. He could reduce her to a trembling, whimpering mass of longing in minutes. Seconds.

She touched his face, her palm drifting over his cheek, until her fingertips traced his jaw, and his chin. He looked at her. "I want to start new, Dylan. I want to get to know you, to find out if it can be like that for us again."

He shook his head. She wanted him to trust her again, to let himself care again. And just when he was out of his mind in love with her, she'd get her memory back. She'd become the old Caitlin. She'd shut him out. "Not on your life, lady. I wouldn't go through that hell again for anything." It would kill him this time.

"It won't happen, I swear it." She looked at him intently as she spoke. "Dylan, I need you so much. I can't face all of this alone, please..."

"Ah, Caity..." He couldn't resist the plea in her eyes, the little cry in her voice. He wrapped his arms around her, cradling her head in one hand, and pulling her face close. He caught her mouth with his and her lips parted instantly. He licked her mouth inside and out, and her tongue responded. Her fingers curled in his hair and he kissed her, tasted her, held her close and wished she were closer.

He was in danger. He knew it, and only a supreme act of will made him draw away. Panting with need, he searched her face. Her breathing was just as ragged, her eyes glazed and damp.

"I want you, Cait. I want you so much it hurts, but that's all. I'll try to be your friend. I'll even be your lover, but I'm not going to love you again. Don't hope for that. Don't even consider it a possibility. It isn't going to happen."

She stiffened her spine and met his gaze. The light in her eyes faded slowly and her breaths, by sheer force, it seemed, grew more regular.

"My friend?"

He nodded. "I'll try not to hold the past against you, at least until it starts repeating itself."

"It will never repeat itself."

"I can't be sure of that. It's all I have to offer, Cait. Take it or leave it."

She nodded, but didn't look him in the eye. "Friends, then. I suppose it's better than enemies." She stood and turned toward the doors. "Thank you, Dylan." She moved forward, opened the doors and walked out, leaving him alone and painfully aroused. Apparently, friends was okay. Lovers was not.

Chapter 10

She couldn't sleep. She wasn't surprised. She'd probably never have a good night's sleep in this house. But tonight, her reasons were different.

It was Dylan's kiss that kept her awake. The way he'd plundered her mouth, and the way she'd responded to the invasion. It hadn't been anger she'd felt emanating from him in waves this time. It had been desire. A desperate, long-denied desire that wouldn't be put off much longer. An answering need had flooded her body from the first touch of his lips on hers.

She wanted him. God, how she wanted him. And she still wasn't completely sure that was wise. She wanted to believe he could never hurt her. But the sight of him shoving Sandra to the floor haunted her. He was like two men in one body. He had a streak of brutality in him. She'd seen it when he'd pushed Sandra, felt it when he'd assaulted her in his bedroom so recently.

His passion was fierce, frightening. Especially where she was concerned. She'd felt its intensity when he'd pulled her from that cliff, been alternately touched by its warmth and burned by its heat. Then, last night, in the library, she'd seen the injured side of him as he'd told her things that obviously hurt him to talk about.

He'd said he could never love her again. Why, then, was there some fool inside her saying that he could? That he might?

She wondered which was the real Dylan Rossi. Which one would make love to her if she were to go to him, right now? Would she feel the violent side of his passion? Or the side that wanted her as badly as she wanted him? Or would she encounter the wounded, wary man who was afraid she'd hurt him again?

"Hell, it doesn't matter, because I'm not going to him." She kicked her covers aside and rose, marching across the room and back again in her silky-soft green nightgown, her arms and shoulders bare. "He made it clear he doesn't want to try again to make our marriage work. Why on earth would I even consider sleeping with him under those conditions? Am I insane?"

He said he'd be my lover. All I have to do is go to his room.

She could have kicked herself for thinking about it. Even up and out of the bed, she kept envisioning erotic images of her and Dylan, their bodies wet and coated in warm sand, making frantic love on a deserted beach. She closed her eyes and willed the image away, but instead, it only intensified. She could feel his hot lips on her throat. She could feel the heat of the sun on his back as her hands moved urgently over it, and the cool spray of the surf as it showered them. She could taste the drying salt the sea had left on his skin.

Her eyes flew wide, and she gasped. She remembered! The images were too vivid, too real to have been imagined. Her breathing quickened and she fought for more. She scanned her mind in search of some other tidbit, something of her past to cling to. She saw the beach for just an instant, in her mind's eye. A horseshoe-shaped patch of sand, surrounded by craggy boulders. He was there, on her, inside her, thrusting, possessing. His lips whispered across hers, the words as soft as his breath. "I love you, Caity. I always will. No matter what."

And on one of the ragged stone faces that stood like protectors around them, someone had scratched a heart, with their initials inside. D.D.R. loves C.A.O.

She bit her lip as tears blurred her vision. In another brief flash, she saw Dylan, wearing cutoff denim shorts, barefoot, his hair longer, damp and tangled, painstakingly chiseling the stone with a pocket knife.

She searched for more, but there was nothing.

Oh, but it wasn't nothing, was it? She remembered. And in that one precious moment of remembering, she'd felt more than the physical sensations his touch evoked. She'd felt the warmth of his love surrounding her like invisible armor, and the strength of her own love pounding back to him.

How could she have had something so sweet, and let it slip away? Why? God, if she could only go back to that place, have that kind of love again, she'd cling to it with everything in her. She'd never let it die.

She brushed the tears away with a swipe of her hand. It was too late to try to change the past. The most she could hope for was to alter the present. Dylan had told her he'd never love her again. But that might change. Maybe with time, he'd see that she wasn't going to revert to the woman who'd hurt him so much. Maybe he'd believe in her, someday.

Exhaustion swamped her as she paced the room, wishing for memories, finding none. God, fate was cruel, giving her just that snippet and nothing more. Just enough to realize what she'd lost. Just enough to make her want it back.

Maybe she should go to Dylan right now, and tell him. She gripped the bedroom door, pulled it open and stepped into the hall before she stopped herself.

Tell him what? That she had a tidbit of their past and that it was killing her? That she wanted a time machine so she could go back there? That she wanted—now, more than ever—to believe he hadn't tried to kill her?

She shook her head sadly. Wanting things didn't make them true. Painful as it was to admit that, she had to force herself to accept it. She turned and stepped back into her room. Just before she closed the door, a strange sound caught her attention. A sort of rattling wheeze. Almost a choke. And it came from the foyer, or the stairway. She paused, one hand on the door, listening.

There was only silence, and the dull moan of the dying wind as the storm blew out to sea.

"Is someone there?"

No voice replied. The dark hallway loomed off in both directions, daring her to brave its blackness. She didn't want to take it up on that dare. But something was wrong. She felt it as surely as she felt the shiver of apprehension dance over her spine. She stepped into the hall, and turned toward the stairway.

The wall switch was at the top of the stairs. Just as soon as she reached it and filled the darkness with light, her fear, this *feeling,* would vanish right along with the shadows.

The house was utterly silent. The wind and rain of the past few days had finally died, the clouds were dispersing, and as she approached the stairway, she saw the full moon's glow filtering through its coat of clouds to streak the floor below.

She reached for the light switch, but her hand missed its mark, and fear tiptoed over her soul. A thrill of dread raced up her spine, and yet she felt some sense of urgency drawing her toward the stairs. She fought it, but took one step down, then another. A tingling sensation raced over her spine, and she stiffened. God, here she was wandering the darkened house alone, at night, knowing full well someone under this very roof wanted her dead. Should she go down, and try to locate the other light switch, or go back to her room?

She took a step backward, but couldn't seem to turn around. There was something tugging her gaze downward. Something down there wasn't right.

She took another step back, bringing her to the top of the stairs. The clouds shifted slowly. Moonlight streamed through the tall, tapering windows that lined the foyer below, and moved across the floor. Its soft glow spilled over

the parquet, spreading like melted butter that coated everything in its path. Finally, it slowed to a crawl, having found
its target. Like a spotlight, moonglow illuminated a mound
of scarlet satin at the foot of the stairs.

Caitlin frowned. That looked like...

"My robe," she whispered. The light spread slower, as
if it were congealing and could barely move, until it
touched the pale skin of a still hand. And there it remained,
motionless. Caitlin screamed at the top of her lungs.

She raced down the stairs, propelled by panic, her palm
burning with friction as she clutched the banister too
tightly. She fell to her knees at the bottom of the stairs, her
hands gripping satin-clad shoulders, turning the woman
onto her back.

The moon's light bathed the still face, and glinted on the
crimson strand that trickled down one side from her ear,
across her cheek. "Sandra!" Caitlin touched her face, and
her voice was a shriek. "Sandra, wake up! For God's sake,
wake up!"

There was no response and Caitlin's heart, once thudding
wildly, seemed to skid to a painful stop in her breast. She
was frantic, pressing her fingers into the warm skin of Sandra's throat in search of a pulse, when light flooded the
room. She heard Henri's curse and Genevieve's sob, as
both rushed in from the archway on the other side of the
foyer. Caitlin felt no pulse beneath her fingers, and she rose
slowly, moving toward them, dazed. "I think...I think
she's dead."

Henri lurched forward, rushing to the body. Genevieve
turned to lean against the wall, folding her arms to cradle
her head. Caitlin kept walking, to the telephone on the other
end of the room. She picked it up and dialed 911.

Vaguely, she heard steps in the hallway above, then Dylan's voice, hoarse and too loud. "Caity!" His steps
pounded down the stairs, and she turned in time to see him
stop short of the body on the floor, blink down at it and

draw three openmouthed breaths that were ragged and deep. His gaze rose, and when he saw her, he closed his eyes. He looked down at Henri where the man knelt beside Sandra. Henri only shook his head.

"I need an ambulance, and the police." Caitlin's voice sounded dead as she spoke into the mouthpiece. "A woman's been killed." She muttered the address as Dylan crossed the floor toward her. He was barefoot, like her, and wore only a pair of briefs beneath a knee-length, terry robe that gaped open. His hair was wild, his eyes wide, and moving over her rapidly as she put the phone down.

For a long moment, he said nothing. Not a word. Then, very slowly, he lifted his arms, and she fell into them, clinging to his shoulders, shaking violently. He held her hard, his hands threading through her hair.

"Caity...I thought it was you."

She stiffened in his arms. *"What?"*

"The robe. It's yours. When I saw it from the top of the stairs, I thought..." He drew a deep breath and crushed her closer. "Doesn't matter. You're all right."

But the trembling that had begun in her from the moment she'd seen Sandra's body assaulted her anew, and fear made her dizzy. His words brought the truth to her with sickening clarity. "Someone else thought it was me, too," she whispered. "The person who killed her."

She heard an oath and looked up to see her brother on the floor beside his wife. His chalky face contorted, he pulled her upper body to his chest, and murmured her name. From above, she heard the baby crying, and tears filled her eyes. "Oh, God, Lizzie. Poor Lizzie."

Ellen appeared at the top of the stairs then and made her way slowly downward, stopping short of the bottom, clutching the banister until her knuckles whitened, sending a fear-filled glance toward Dylan and Caitlin on the other side of the foyer.

Dylan only held Caitlin tighter. She felt his heart hammering beneath her head, heard his ragged breaths. If he didn't care at all about her, he was certainly doing a good impression of someone who did. She closed her eyes, twined her arms around his neck and clung to him, her one anchor in a world gone crazy.

Dylan paced the library floor, feeling like a caged animal. He'd be arrested this time. There was no doubt in his mind of that as Thomas sat still as a stone, and told Detective Barnes about the argument he'd witnessed between Dylan and Sandra the day before.

"He was yelling at her. Loud enough to be heard in the kitchen."

"What was he saying?" Barnes wasn't bothering with his notepad this time. He had a tape recorder running. Henri was being questioned in another room. Genevieve had already given her statement, and was in the dining room, watching over Ellen, who was badly shaken. And Cait...Cait was upstairs with Lizzie. Thank God. Thank God it hadn't been her at the foot of those damned stairs.

But if he let himself get arrested, it might well be her next time. Damn, he felt helpless.

"I couldn't hear clearly," Thomas was saying. "I went to see what was going on, just as he pushed her."

"Pushed her," Barnes repeated. "Pushed her, how?" He walked right up to the overstuffed chair Thomas occupied. "Get up and show me."

Thomas rose as if his legs were too weak to hold him. He brought his hands upward to Barnes's shoulders and gave him a shove. "It was harder than that, though. She fell to the floor."

"It *wasn't* harder than that, and she only fell because she tripped over something."

Dylan stopped pacing to whirl around. Caitlin stood in the doorway. She hadn't bothered to change. She still wore the floor length, emerald green nightgown that shimmered like silk. Her auburn hair was as tousled as a lion's mane, and hanging down to the middle of her back. Her eyes were no longer frightened, or confused, though. They were glittering and angry.

Dylan crossed the room to stand beside her, ignoring the others. "How's the baby?"

"I managed to get her back to sleep. I didn't want to bring her down here with…" She didn't finish, only glanced in the general direction of the living room, where Dylan knew Sandra's body still rested. Barnes's faithful forensics team were as busy as ants in autumn. He could still hear the whir of the camera as the police photographer snapped pictures at the medical examiner's direction. He thought they'd have at least covered Sandra's face by now.

"Caity, if you don't mind…you witnessed this argument, too?"

"Yes."

"Then maybe you can tell me what it was about."

Her gaze shifted to Dylan. "Sandra had been doing her best to alienate me since I came back. I guess she didn't like me very much. I assumed Dylan was angry about that, but I'm not sure, since I came in at the tail end of the discussion. You ought to ask my husband if you want more details. Not that I think it's relevant. The killer obviously mistook Sandra for me in the dark."

Barnes looked skeptical, but turned to Dylan. "I suppose you're going to tell me you were alone in your room all night, and didn't hear a thing, right?"

"I—"

"Not quite alone, Detective," Caitlin said.

Dylan frowned at her.

"Before you go on, Caity, I ought to tell you I've already interviewed your employees. They said you and your husband haven't shared a bedroom in months."

"That was true, until last night."

"You telling me you two slept together last night?"

Her chin tilted upward. "I was afraid and alone. I needed someone with me last night, so I went to my husband. That isn't so farfetched, is it?"

"What time?"

"Early. Around nine, I guess."

Barnes cleared his throat, and he kept glancing at Dylan. Dylan fought to keep his surprise from showing on his face. He couldn't believe Caitlin was lying to a cop just to cover for him.

"But you slept sometime. He could have gotten up, and—"

"I didn't *sleep* at all." She sidled nearer Dylan and slipped her arm around his waist. "Dylan dozed off around midnight. I was still restless, so I got up to get a book from the library. That's when I found Sandra."

"Uh-huh." Barnes's gaze narrowed, and Dylan stiffened. If he caught on to Caitlin's lie, he'd be more suspicious than ever. "So what you're telling me is, that you and your husband have reconciled."

"Reconciled?"

"The divorce is off, right?"

Dylan felt the shock that jolted through Caitlin's body. He closed his eyes, and put his arm around her shoulders, squeezing her to his side. If she faltered now, he'd be behind bars before dawn. "Nothing's been decided, Barnes."

Caitlin pulled free of him, turned her back on Barnes and walked, on shaking legs, across the library. She reached into the liquor cabinet and pulled out a shot glass, and the same whiskey bottle Dylan had been holding earlier. Her back still to them, she unscrewed the cap, set it aside and poured a healthy splash into the glass.

"If that divorce is still on, Caity, your husband has a huge motive to try to kill you. I'm sure you're already aware of that, but I just want to remind you. The settlement you and your lawyers hammered out have you keeping everything you own, the house, too."

She downed the shot, and sucked air through her teeth. She cleared her throat, but didn't turn. "Of course I'm aware of it."

"Then you also know that your husband fought this settlement tooth and nail for months. Then, suddenly, agreed to everything without a hitch. Right before your accident."

She said nothing. Instead, she only tipped the bottle again, then calmly replaced the cap and put it away.

"It wasn't the settlement I was fighting, Barnes. It was the divorce. I didn't want it." Dylan felt like wringing the bastard's neck for spilling everything that way. And he seemed to be enjoying it, too. He had to know Caitlin hadn't been aware of their pending divorce, just from her reactions. "I'd have nothing to gain by her death."

"What you'd gain, Rossi, is half of everything she was planning to take in the settlement. What's hers is willed to her brother, and to you, in equal portions, more or less. Your share alone is a small fortune."

Caitlin turned to face them, her face expressionless. She glanced toward Thomas, and downed half of the whiskey. "I'm being rude. Would anyone else like a drink? I could make coffee."

"No, thanks anyway." Barnes frowned at her. "Will you reconsider what I said about getting out of here for a while?"

Dylan stiffened, waiting for her to say yes, and leave with the detective. If she walked out now, knowing what she knew, knowing he'd deliberately kept the truth about the divorce from her, she'd never come back. He was as sure of that as he was of his own name. He was equally sure he didn't want that to happen. Not like this. He hadn't realized it until he'd looked down those stairs at her satin robe, surrounding a dead woman's body, and thought for one heart-stopping second that it was her. But since then, he'd come to some damned painful conclusions.

She simply shook her head. "My niece needs me now,

Detective Barnes. I can't leave her.'' She finished the drink and set the glass down. Her hands were shaking, but her face betrayed nothing.

"I'll need statements from each of you." He looked at Caitlin. "Caity, can you tell me why the victim was wearing your robe?''

She nodded. "I packed up some old clothes and asked Genevieve to get rid of them for me.''

Thomas nodded. ''Yeah, Genevieve brought them to our room, told Sandra to pick out anything she wanted, before the stuff went to charity.''

"Did the maid go through the clothes herself?''

Caitlin shook her head. "I doubt she bothered. I'm so much taller than her, nothing would have fit.''

Barnes nodded. "All right. You can go see to the kid, if you want. I'll get your statement later.'' She nodded, and started toward the door.

"You watch your back, Cait Rossi. This isn't over yet," Barnes added in a low voice.

She only nodded, and before she left the room, her gaze met Dylan's. There was a wounded look in her emerald eyes, a look of betrayal, and a shimmer of tears she refused to shed. She walked out with her back rigid, her shoulders so stiff, they shook with it. And all Dylan wanted to do was run after her.

Chapter 11

She felt his presence even before the bedroom door opened. It was like an energy, an awareness of him that preceded him into the room. She stayed where she was, lying on her side on the bed. She'd been wishing for sleep, even while knowing she'd find none.

Dylan stood in the doorway. She felt him there, and without looking up, she felt his gaze on her.

"I'm glad Lizzie's too young to know what's happening." Caitlin kept her voice very low. The entire house had the air of a funeral home, even though Sandra's body had finally been removed. "If I'd died in that accident, she might still have a mother."

"Caity—"

"When were you going to tell me about the divorce?" She blinked, and finally turned to face him.

His face was tight, and his eyes revealed nothing. "When I thought you could handle it."

Or maybe not at all. Maybe you weren't going to say anything, Dylan. Maybe you figured I'd be dead long before you had to.

"You think I did it, don't you?"

She stiffened a bit. Was her face so transparent? Or was he reading her mind? "I don't know what I think." She rolled over and sat up, with her legs dangling over the side of the bed.

"Last night, you believed I was innocent."

"Last night, I thought you didn't have a motive. But you did. And you kept it from me."

He stepped farther into the room and closed the door. He leaned back against the wall, his arms crossing over his chest. Her gaze followed his movements. He wore a snug-fitting black T-shirt that strained to contain his muscular shoulders. His forearms were hard, tight. His biceps, in this position, bulged. A soft stirring in her stomach troubled her. Was it because he was so attractive, because she still wanted him so badly? Or because she knew he could break her neck without working up a sweat?

"Why'd you lie to Barnes?"

His liquid brown eyes searched her face, but they were cold, without feeling. Or maybe he was deliberately hiding what he felt.

She got to her feet, walked to the window and gazed out. The sky was as brilliant as the meat of an orange. The sun's huge upper curve was just visible in the distance; neon fire. On impulse, she released the latch and pushed the windows open. Warm, sea-moistened wind bathed her face, blew through her hair. She tipped her head back and inhaled.

"It was like this that time on the beach," she said. "Early morning. Everything so fresh and new,...like we were." She leaned out a little, wishing she could see the shore from here. She could hear it. Waves pounding stone. Foaming surf. Crying gulls. And she could smell the tang of saltwater in the air. She could even feel the sea. The breeze that caressed her face was wet with it. "That was the time you carved our initials into the rock."

She turned to gauge his reaction to that. He'd moved. He was standing nearer the bed now, stopped in the act of coming toward her. His gaze locked with hers over the bed.

"You remember."

She only nodded.

"When—"

"Last night. We were so happy together. What we had...it was so real, I wanted to believe it could be that way again, wanted to believe in us...in you." She sighed, and turned to the window once more. "That's why I lied to Barnes. I didn't want him locking you up when I was trying so hard to believe someone else was responsible.''

She heard him coming toward her. She stiffened, but didn't turn. If he wanted to shove her out the window, here was his chance. She closed her eyes and bit her lip when his hands closed on her shoulders from behind. Then he turned her to face him, his eyes, for once, windows to the turmoil inside him. Emotion roiled in their melted-chocolate depths. But what kind of emotion? Regret? Longing? Anger? Hatred? God, how she wanted to believe in him! Would he tell her now that it wasn't him? That she'd been right to believe he could never hurt her? That he—

"How...much do you remember?"

Disappointment hit her with the force of a wrecking ball. She blinked as if she'd been slapped, and let her gaze fall to the floor. "Only that. Whatever other secrets you're keeping from me are still safe."

He frowned.

"There are others, aren't there, Dylan?"

"You can't expect me to tell you your life story within a few days, Cait. You'll know everything, in time."

"Unless I don't have time."

"You really *do* think it was me." He caught her face between two hands, tipping it up until his eyes could drill into hers. "So which theory are you buying? That I killed Sandra because she wanted to jump my bones, and I wasn't as hot for her? Or did I mistake her for you in the darkness?"

She felt her lips tighten, and tried not to let her features twist in misery. Despite her efforts, a tear slipped through, and trailed slowly down her face.

"Damn you, Caitlin." His palms on either side of her face holding her still, he brought his lips to hers. He kissed her hard, his lips moving against hers in an assault as his hands tilted and tipped her head to fit her mouth to his.

She hated it, and she loved it, and she'd craved it for

what seemed like always. In spite of herself, her arms twined around his neck, tightening until they ached. Her body pressed itself to his, and her mouth moved rapidly. When his tongue thrust, she suckled it with a vicious hunger, then dipped her own into his mouth, until his joined hers in a desperate, urgent battle. His hands lowered, wrapped around her, held her tight. They pressed to the small of her back, and then her shoulders, and then her buttocks, and then her thighs. Her fingers clawed and twisted in his hair, and her breaths came in ragged, violent spasms.

His hands came between them, forced their way up to the neck of her gown, gripped and tugged and tore, and all the while he was feeding on her mouth, her tongue. But then his attention altered, and his lips dragged hotly down over her chin, across her throat. He took her breast like a madman, a starving man devouring his first crumb of food in days. He sucked hard, making her whimper with mindless need. Making her clutch at his hair as he bit and tugged just until she felt pain, then licked and sucked until she writhed with pleasure again. Small sounds escaped her throat, begging sounds, that only enraged him further.

Holding her to him, his hands at her back, his mouth at her breast, he began moving backward, dragging her with him. Then he was turning her, pushing her. Her back sunk into the mattress. His body pressed it deeper. His hands twisted and yanked at her panties, while his mouth moved back to hers. She moved her legs, lifted her hips, to help him, and the scrap of nylon slipped to the floor. She snagged the hem of the tight black T-shirt he wore, and tugged it upward, her hands skimming his muscled back, his shoulders, before pulling the shirt over his head.

His flesh was hot against hers. *She* was hot. Burning up with mindless, senseless need. His big arms encircled her waist, holding her tight to him, making her feel small and delicate as he ruthlessly plundered her mouth.

Then he tore himself away. All at once, she lay alone, completely exposed to him, and he stood beside the bed, yanking at the button of his jeans, his blazing eyes moving up and down over her body. She instinctively tried to pull the tattered edges of her nightgown together, but he lunged, gripping her wrists, stopping her.

"Don't."

She met his heated gaze, held it. He pushed the soft gown from her shoulders, pulling her up a little as he did. Then he let her lie back, and he tossed the garment to the floor. He knelt on the bed, and he pressed her thighs apart. His gaze burned her there, and then his fingers parted, and probed and pinched, all as he watched.

She moaned. It was too much. He still wore his jeans, though the fly gaped open, and she could see the curling, dark hairs there. She was fully exposed, more fully exposed than she could remember ever having been. He was kneeling over her, staring at her so intently, it burned as his fingers tormented her without mercy. He spread her folds, sunk his fingers into her. Against her will, her hips rose to meet them. His gaze seemed to darken, and he groaned deep and gruffly.

His fingers pulled back, but he still held her open, spread wide to his probing eyes. Then, suddenly, he bent over her, swooping down like a hawk diving on its prey. She gasped when his mouth touched her, his lips, his tongue. His mouth attacked her until she whimpered with passion, until her entire body trembled like a leaf in a strong wind, and until she'd have done anything he asked of her.

Then he stopped, leaving her completely insane. He stood only long enough to shed the jeans, and then he was back. He knelt, straddling her waist, staring down at her as she panted and twisted with agonizing need. His hands gripped her head, lifted her. His arousal stood before her, thick and hard. His hands were shaking as his fingers moved in her hair, urging her closer.

She opened her mouth and took him into it. He growled her name and his hips moved slightly. She sucked, and tugged him, and wanted to take in more than she possibly could. Then he withdrew, and pressed her back down to the bed.

His hard body lowered on top of hers. His arousal nested between her thighs, nudging her, testing her. She bent her knees and opened herself to him. Her hands glided down his back to grip his hard buttocks and pull him to her.

He answered her unspoken request with a single, powerful thrust. He sunk himself inside her so deep and so hard that she cried out. And then he drew back and stabbed into her again, and again, until her mind spun out of control. On and on he took her, until she clung to him, cried his name and exploded in sensation.

He thrust into her once more, and stiffened, holding himself there, pulsing inside her. She shuddered, and closed her eyes. Dylan slowly relaxed, the bunched muscles in his shoulders lost their tension, the air spilled from his lungs. He slipped off her, onto his side, and he searched her face.

Caitlin felt like crying. It hadn't been a fantasy. His touch held the same magic she'd felt in her mind. It was real, the passion that sizzled between them. She swallowed hard, closed her eyes and rolled away from him. She felt the morning sun slanting through her window, warming her face.

"You'd better go now," she said softly.

"Why?"

She said nothing, only bit her lip and prayed he'd leave before she cried in front of him.

"Are you having regrets, Caitlin? Are you going to pretend you didn't want this just as badly as I did?"

She shook her head. "I wanted it. The same way I wanted to walk along the cliffs the other night. The same way a drug addict craves his poison."

He was silent for a moment. Then she felt the bed move

as he rolled over and sat up. "So, I'm your poison. Is that what you believe?"

"It doesn't matter what I believe, Dylan. I'm stupid where you're concerned, like a moth battering my wings against clear glass to get to the light on the other side. Only I'm going to beat myself to death, and the light is just an illusion."

"I still want you, Caitlin. That's no illusion."

"Physically." She sat up, too. Then stood, her back to him. "It's not enough." She reached for the bathroom door, unconsciously stiffening her spine. "I need to shower. I'm going out this morning."

She heard him turn toward her. "Out where?"

She lifted her chin, opened the door, stepped onto the threshold. "I want to have a talk...with my lawyer." She licked her lips. "I think it's about time, don't you?"

Before he could answer, she took another step, and closed the door behind her. She turned the lock, then twisted the knobs until rushing water drowned out the sounds of her sobs.

Sandra's body had been taken to the medical examiner's office. She had to be autopsied, it was required when someone was murdered.

Dylan would have liked to think she'd just fallen down the stairs. Barring that, he'd like to believe her killer had known who she was before he'd pushed her. But she'd been wearing Caitlin's unmistakable scarlet robe, and the halls at night were pitch-black.

Dylan wasn't blind. He knew there was something going on between Thomas and Genevieve. He also knew Henri had the hots for Caitlin, and he was equally certain, no matter what else Caitlin might have done in the past, that she'd never reciprocated the feeling.

Could Henri be acting out of anger over her rejection of him? Or was it Thomas? He could have had a motive to kill either Sandra or Cait. Sandra, to free himself so he could pursue Genevieve. Cait, to avail himself of the money in her will. And Genevieve...she was such a secretive little thing. Might she have pushed Sandra, knowing full well who the victim was, just to get Thomas all to herself?

Dylan pushed a hand through his hair. This was getting him nowhere. What he'd like to do, what he ought to do, was to take Caitlin the hell out of here. Get her somewhere safe until he could figure this out.

As if she'd go anywhere with him. She thought he was the one out to murder her. And right now, his wife was at her lawyer's office, putting the final touches on their pending divorce. And there wasn't a damned thing he could do about it. He'd already signed everything that needed signing.

But that was before, dammit!

He stalked into the living room, and found Ellen there, rocking Lizzie. He sent his aunt a smile that was forced and tight. "How's she doing?"

"Just fine, boy. No more signs of that fever. I've taken care of babies before, you know."

He nodded distractedly, and paced past her to gaze out the window, into the driveway. His car was there, as well as the old pickup he sometimes used for business, hauling lumber and supplies to smaller job sites. Cait must have taken a cab.

"She hadn't ought to be wandering around town on her own, Dylan."

He blinked and let the curtain fall over the glass.

"Somebody wants to hurt her." She shifted Lizzie from one knee to the other, and rocked a little faster as the baby started to fuss. "You're letting your emotions cloud your judgment, boy. Get on the ball."

He gave himself a mental shake, realizing she was right. Despite what his wife thought of him, and what that did to his insides, Cait was out there, alone and unprotected. A walking target.

He bent low to kiss his aunt's wrinkled cheek on his way out.

Cait sat in the cab, clutching the sheaf of papers in a white-knuckled grip. The visit to the lawyer had gone roughly. He'd been furious at what she wanted to do, considering all the time and effort he'd spent on her case. Caitlin had drawn herself up to her full height and stared down her nose at the man behind the desk. In a voice she thought the old Caitlin had probably used often, she'd reminded him that he worked for her, and would be paid the same fee, no matter what the results. He'd grumbled, but accepted her decision.

She glanced up at the back of the driver's head. "You know this area pretty well?"

"Born and raised. What do you need to know?"

She warmed to his smile and friendly eyes. "There's a little bit of beach, completely surrounded by craggy rocks in sort of a horseshoe pattern. Very private. You know it?"

Glancing over his shoulder, his smile grew wider. "Sure. It's only ten minutes away."

True to his promise, the cabby pulled off to the side of the road beside a steep drop, a short time later. He pointed. "Right down there. There's a path, see it?"

She looked where he was pointing, and spotted a worn track through the tall grass. "Yeah. Thanks." She fished in her pocket for a twenty, and handed it to him.

"Don't you want me to wait?"

She shook her head. "Eden's not far, and it's a perfect day for a walk, don't you think?" She'd call another cab when she was finished here. She wanted solitude, time to think.

"If you're sure." He took her money, and she got out of the car. She stood for just a second as he pulled away, then started down the path. At it's end, she found the little cove she'd remembered, just as she remembered it.

Waves lapped gently at the white sand. Caitlin toed off her shoes, peeled off her socks and tossed both aside. She dug her toes into the warm sand and closed her eyes. It felt good here.

She stripped off her jeans, feeling no embarrassment at doing so. Her T-shirt came to her thighs, so she was decently covered. She wanted to feel the sun on her legs. She wanted to feel warmth, to counteract the coldness she'd felt emanating in waves from that house. And the coldness that seemed now to have spread over her, through her, until her very soul was encrusted in ice.

She'd had what she'd been driving herself crazy longing for, so why was she still so frustrated? She'd had sex with Dylan. It had been hot, frantic, almost violently intense sex. But it hadn't been lovemaking. She'd wanted to make love with him. She'd wanted it slow, and languid, and emotional. The way it used to be between them. The way her snippets of memory told her it had always been.

Unable to resist the lure of the water, she moved toward it. She stepped into the cool, frothy sea and it lapped over her ankles. She walked out farther and the waves licked higher, embracing her shins, her knees, her thighs. She dove into the bracing cold, the shimmering blue, and swam beneath the surface, farther from shore. She broke the surface when she ran out of air, flipping her head backward so the sun blazed on her face. She stroked away, exerting herself full force, swimming hard, as if she were being chased by sharks, then turning and starting back again, just as fiercely.

Her lungs burned and her heart thundered in her chest. The muscles in her arms and legs burned with the effort after a while, but it felt good. Just pouring everything she had into physical exertion, forgetting everything else. Just for a tiny, safe space in time, losing herself in the burn, the effort.

But it couldn't last. She knew she had to get back to the house, back to the husband who didn't love her, and never would. Back to the elderly aunt who thought she'd ruined her nephew's life, and to the brother who resented her. Back to Lizzie. The poor little thing didn't have anyone now, except for Thomas, and he was awkward and uncomfortable with her.

And me. She has me.

Just thinking of the baby made her ache inside. How could she come to care so much for a child she'd only known a few days, a child that wasn't even hers?

She paused in her mindless stroking and tread water. It didn't matter how, it only mattered that she loved Lizzie. She knew she ought to leave that house, but she wasn't going to. She missed the baby, even after only a few hours of separation.

She stroked toward shore and emerged dripping, panting, her body heated despite the cold water dripping from it. Rivulets ran down her legs and she belatedly wished she'd brought a towel. But how could she have? This hadn't been planned. She'd come here on impulse to see…

The half circle of ragged stone rose up before her and she stopped. Then, slowly, she moved toward it. She didn't even have to look for the spot. She found it as if by sheer instinct. She walked right to the stone face and ran her fingers over its warm surface, feeling the deep ridges carved there. The heart. Her initials. Dylan's.

As she stood there, her fingers caressing the spot, she recalled the warmth; the protected, loved feeling that had flashed through her memory each time she'd envisioned their lovemaking. And the lack of it during their encounter this morning. A pain like nothing she'd dreamed of reached out to grab her and held her in its grip. She lowered her head. Tears burned her eyes, and her throat tightened until she could barely breathe.

Give in to it. You're alone here. No one to see you.

She nodded her agreement with the voice of her own reason. She *was* alone. God, she was so alone.

She sank slowly to the sand at the base of the rock, and drew her knees to her chest. The flood of emotion came the instant she'd locked her arms around her knees. Not silent tears. There was no dignity in the way she cried. No pride, no control. She sobbed out loud and moaned as the pain knifed through her. Her tears ran like endless fountains and her entire body trembled violently. Spasms ripped through her chest, as if they'd split her breastbone in half.

"Caity…"

She looked up fast at the hoarse voice. Dylan stood between her and the sea, between her and the path. She cleared her throat. "What are you—"

"I followed you."

Fear rippled over her spine, jelling the tears that remained in her eyes. She remained sitting there in the sand, looking up at him. "Why?"

Through her blurred eyes, she saw the brief flash of pain in his face, but it was just as quickly concealed. "Not to murder you, Cait. I got worried. I just wanted to make sure…" He sighed hard, shook his head. "I waited outside the law office and followed the cab."

So he'd been here the whole time, watching her?

She brushed her fingertips over her eyes and fought the lingering sobs that tore through her sporadically, against her will. "Why did you wait so long to come down here?"

"I wasn't going to come down at all." He moved forward, dropping to his knees in the sand. His hands reached out to cup her face, but she pulled free, and turned her head.

"Leave me alone."

"I can't. Not like this. Cait, I didn't tell you about the divorce because I didn't want to confuse you any more than you already were. I'm not the one who pushed Sandra down those stairs. I'm not the one who tried to kill you."

She faced him then, searching his eyes with hers. "Why

now? You wouldn't deny anything before. Why are you bothering now?''

"It's important now."

She shook her head. "You're wrong. You have it all backward. It might have mattered before. It doesn't matter at all now." She stood and brushed the wet sand from her thighs and backside. She moved past him, to where she'd tossed her purse on the sand. She bent to pick it up, then pulled the folded papers from inside it. When she turned, he was behind her. She handed them to him. "It's over, Dylan."

He frowned down at the papers in his hand. She thought his lower lip trembled once, but she couldn't be sure. "No matter what's written here, it's not over. Not until you understand—"

"You're the one who doesn't understand. Read them, Dylan. Sign them, and you're free."

"I already signed—"

"Not this agreement. Look at it, will you?"

He nodded, unfolded the sheets and studied them for a long time. She stood and watched the emotions crossing his face, and tried to identify each one. Surprise? Shock? Sadness? Anger?

When he looked up again, his eyes were carefully blank. "You don't want anything?"

She shook her head. "Nothing. Not a dime. And I had the deed to the house transferred to you, too. I don't want it. I don't want anything that was hers—mine—before. I want to start over. And I hate that place."

"The old agreement?"

She reached into her bag and pulled out the official-looking envelope with the original divorce papers inside. All contained Dylan's signature. "I have both copies. Mine, and my lawyer's, right here. I knew you wouldn't trust me enough to take my word for it." She pushed the envelope into his hand. "Tear it up. Burn it. I don't care. It's up to you. I'm sure your lawyer will be happy to add his copies and yours to the bonfire.''

Dylan shook his head. ''Why?''

She shrugged and shook her head. The finality of handing those papers to him hit her and she felt tears threatening again.

''It was wrong. That first settlement was the act of another woman. Not me. It was just never my money. It was hers. It just felt…wrong.''

''No.'' Dylan grabbed her purse and shoved both sets of documents inside, then tossed it to the sand. ''You're taking away my motive. You're afraid I'm going to kill you, so you're taking away my motive.'' He stalked away from her, pushing a hand through his hair.

''I'm trying to make things right,'' she called after him. ''I just want to cut my ties with the woman I was. I want to start over, try to build some kind of a life. Dammit, Dylan, I'm giving you what you wanted!''

He whirled to face her. ''It was never what I wanted.''

''Don't…'' God, she couldn't stand for him to give her even a hint of false hope, not now. ''Look, at least this way, if the killer succeeds, you won't be a suspect.''

''Oh, thank you all to hell.'' He approached her, gripped her shoulders. ''And what if the attempts just stop now, Caitlin? What are you going to believe then?''

''Does it really matter? Do you really care what I believe?''

He did. He knew it right then, and it hit him like a mallet between the eyes. He cared a lot what she believed; too much.

He saw the strain in her eyes when they met his, but she only bent to pick up her jeans and shoes, and her purse. She thumbed the strap of her bag over her shoulder, and carried her shoes dangling from one hand. The T-shirt she wore was soaked, clinging. It molded to her shape, and despite everything else he was feeling, he was aroused. He wanted her. He always had. It had been the one constant in their ever-changing relationship.

She walked in silence up the steep incline, over the path. He glanced back down the path, at the spot where they'd first made love, and wondered how much of it she recalled. Did she know how good it was, even then? How explosive? Did she realize yet, that she could bring him to his knees with a touch of her lips? Of her hands? That she'd driven him to the brink of insanity this morning? Had it been as good for her? He needed to know.

"Caity?"

She looked at him, eyes wide, searching.

"This morning—"

"I don't want to talk about this morning." She averted her eyes.

"You going to try to pretend it never happened?"

"It shouldn't have happened. It can't happen again. It won't." She closed her eyes, shook her head slowly.

He gripped her arm, pulled her around to face him. "It could. It could happen right now."

She opened her eyes. He saw moisture gathering there.

"It could," he insisted. He gripped her other arm, and drew her closer. She planted her feet, held herself away. "You want it, too, Cait. What are you so afraid of?"

"That you'll destroy me." She closed her eyes as the tears spilled over. "It wouldn't take much more, Dylan." The last sentence was a whisper, and a plea.

He let her go.

She was on her back, with the most horrible pains trying to crush her, like steel bands around her abdomen and back, tightening, crushing, squeezing. Her head swung back and forth on the pillows and someone ran a cool cloth over it. She wanted to cry out, but couldn't catch her breath to do so. And the pain that took her breath away went on and on and on.

And then it was gone.

She sat up, gasping. Her face damp with sweat, her hair clinging to it, her eyes wide and unfocused as she scanned the blurry room. Dylan was there. Standing in the shadows, grim-faced. He held the baby in his arms, wrapped in a white receiving blanket. Caitlin lifted her arms toward him. And slowly, he moved forward.

He lowered the bundle into her arms. Caitlin cradled the child close, but frowned at its minuscule size. So small, so feather-light. And not moving. Not moving at all.

She parted the folds of the soft blanket, and looked down. The baby's skin was thin, translucent, and tinted a ghastly blue. Caitlin's hand touched the tiny cheek, and she recoiled at its feel. Unreal, unresponsive, dead.

Another pair of hands came—not Dylan's—to take the child from her arms. She clung, but they pried until her weak grasp gave way. "No," she begged, her voice choked, desperate. "No, please, don't take him away... No!"

But the stranger's hands, holding the lifeless infant, vanished into the mist. And Caitlin screamed aloud, her grief a living force in her soul.

She sat up in bed and reached for the lamp, knocking it over in her haste. It crashed to the floor, shattering, but she barely heard the sound. The panic ran like ice water in her veins as she staggered from the bed, lunged for the door. Glass razed her bare feet, but she was beyond caring.

She wrenched the door wide and ran through the hall to the nursery. She tore that door open and left it gaping as she reached for the crib, clutched it with trembling hands, leaned over it and willed the thundering in her heart to quiet.

Her hands shook, but she found Lizzie's rounded form beneath a light cover. She touched the warm, plump cheek with a forefinger, and Lizzie instinctively turned her head toward that touch, her lips smacking in her sleep.

Relief washed through her, transforming her muscles from tautly stretched wire to quivering, useless jelly. She sank in a heap to the floor at the side of the crib.

She heard the footsteps in the hall, her name being called. She saw the light spilling in from the nursery's open door. And then she was lifted in Dylan's strong arms, cradled close to his hard chest, held tight, her face pressed to the crook of his neck where his scent enfolded her.

"All right. It's all right, I have you. You're safe."

Her arms slipped around his neck, and she clung to him, crying harder, recalling the silent devastation she'd seen on his handsome face in the dream.

"What happened?"

She shook her head, but it moved very little. "Nothing." Her throat was painfully tight, too tight to speak more than a word or two at a time. "Bad dream."

But it wasn't a dream, was it? It hurts too bad to have been just a dream.

"You scared the hell out of me, Cait. The lamp in your room is smashed all to hell. There's blood in the hall all the way from your room to the nursery. Tell me what happened."

He was carrying her the wrong way, and she realized he was heading not to her bedroom, but to his. The light there was blazing, and he lowered her to the bed. He stood over her, wearing only his brief underwear that fit him like a second skin. "You sure you're okay?"

She closed her eyes. He looked so worried, as though he'd really been afraid for her. How could he look like that and not love her? How could he look like that and want her dead?

"I...cut my foot, I think. That's all."

"The lamp?"

She nodded as he bent to examine her foot. It was beginning to throb, and she could feel the blood that coated it now. She fought to control her breathing, to stop the sobs that sporadically rocked through her. She brushed her face dry with palms that were sweaty, and too warm. ''I knocked it over.''

He swore softly, left her there and walked into his bathroom, returning in a moment with his hands full of paraphernalia that he dumped on the foot of his bed. She saw tweezers, a roll of gauze and a tube of ointment, some tape. Without a word, Dylan sat on the bed's edge, and pulled her foot into his lap. Slowly, painfully, he began removing bits of the broken lamp from the sole of her foot.

When she winced, he stiffened. ''Sorry. I think I got it all.'' He smeared ointment over her cuts, his fingers so gentle on her skin, they could have been caressing her instead of ministering to an injury. He wrapped her foot in gauze, taped the dressing in place and stood again, pushing a hand through his hair.

She sat up. ''Thanks. I was clumsy—''

''You were terrified. Are you sure no one—''

''It was just a bad dream.''

He nodded, searching her face with eyes so intense, she felt them cutting through her. ''So you said. You want to tell me about it?''

She bit her lower lip. She couldn't tell him. Not now, not yet. Not until she was sure. She couldn't say the words out loud that would make that heartache real. God, but it already was real, wasn't it? It was tearing her apart inside, even now, with that one, devastating image. The baby, *her* baby. Her son, and Dylan's, lying lifeless in her arms.

She shook her head, stifling a new flood of tears. ''I don't remember.''

His eyes narrowed, but he nodded. She knew he didn't believe that, but he wasn't going to push. She started to get up, but Dylan's hands came to her shoulders. His touch wasn't firm, but tentative, light as a whispered promise, ready to lift away from her at a moment's notice. "Stay, Cait?"

The look in his dark, glittering eyes made her shudder inside. "Stay?"

Chapter 12

"Yeah. Not so I can murder you in your sleep, and not so I can ravage you, either. I won't touch you unless... unless you ask me to. I just want to know you're safe. Stay here tonight."

Here. In his bed. In his arms? She closed her eyes and nodded once. It did no good to question his motives. She wanted to be here with him, wanted it badly. Too badly to ignore, or even to deny.

She was grieving, suffering from a loss they must have shared, if her suspicion that it was more memory than dream was an accurate one. She needed to be held, to be comforted. As he pulled back the covers, peeled them from beneath her so she could slip under them, then slid in beside her, she knew she wanted this. Just to sleep in his arms, feel his heart beating close to hers. She wanted to lie close to him all night, with his scent filling her nostrils. She was stupid to put herself through it, stupid to let herself wallow in his presence. It only hurt her more deeply than ever. But she lay down beside him, anyway. She'd lie close to him tonight. Just that.

Not just that. More. Much more.

He reached for the lamp and snapped it off, plunging them into darkness. Then he lay still, on his back, not touching her. Drawing a breath, Cait rolled onto her side. She rested her head on his chest, and let her arm fall around him.

He stiffened. "Caity..."

"Hold me, Dylan." Her voice broke when she said his name.

His arms came around her, hard and fast. She felt his

strength. His smooth, broad chest beneath her head, the taut heated skin touching her cool cheek. She turned her head slightly and pressed her lips to it, not caring that it might not be wise, only knowing that she wanted this man, even more than she had before. He wanted her, too.

He had the divorce papers. She'd given him his freedom, and she sensed it would only be a matter of time until he took it and ran with it. He'd be out of her life soon, leaving her with nothing but a single, vibrant memory of his passion, his touch. It wasn't enough.

She slid her leg over both of his, bending her knee, lifting it up over his body. She kissed his chest again, her lips brushing his nipple, and she heard him swear hoarsely. He gripped her shoulders and lifted her from his chest. "What the hell are you doing?"

There was anger in his voice, but desire in his eyes, glittering up at her even in the darkness. She felt its proof, pressing hard and insistent against her thigh. She moved her leg over him, gently. "Make it like it was, Dylan." She bit her lip when tears threatened. "Make it like it used to be."

His hands tightened on her shoulders. There was a moment of hesitation, a moment when she was terrified he was about to turn away from her. Then he drew her downward until his lips could reach hers. He kissed her long and slow, suckling her lips, tracing their shape with his tongue, nipping them. She opened her mouth to him and his tongue plunged inside her mouth to taste every part of it. Deepening the invasion with every second, he took from her, and he gave to her. His hands threaded in her hair, then danced down the column of her neck. His thumbs pressed little circles under her jaw, then his lips replaced them, so gently her throat tightened.

He moaned deep in his throat, and she moved over him more completely, until she straddled his powerful hips, bringing his hardness against her burning need. She rocked against him, and he trembled. She let her hands roam his body. She pressed her palms to the muscled wall of his chest, kneaded his shoulders, learned his shape all over again. She ran her hands up and down his arms, back and forth across his back. She kissed his face, his chin, his neck.

His hand left her back and she heard the snap of the bedside lamp. She opened her eyes to see the light falling on his face. She searched his burning yes.

"I want to see you, Caity. I love the way you look."

She nodded. She understood his need. She wanted to see him, too. To see the sensations pass over his face, through his eyes, to see the beautiful shape of him. To burn his image as she held him inside her one last time, into her heart, her soul, her memory. She'd never forget this night. Never.

She sat up, still straddling him, and the covers fell away behind her. He wanted to look at her.

She caught the hem of the nightshirt she wore, and lifted it, tugging it over her head, tossing it to the floor, keeping her gaze on his face all the while. His eyes darkened, slid slowly away from hers, downward, and fixed their attention on her breasts. His hands moved up over her back to her shoulders, and he drew her forward, lifting his head from the pillows at the same time. He captured one yearning peak in his mouth, and he sucked her hard, hungrily, using his teeth, worrying her flesh, nipping it until her head fell backward and her loins ached with wanting him. He released her only to move to the other breast, laving it with his tongue until it responded, then punishing it for the offense with his teeth and lips.

He caught her hips in his hands and lifted her from him. She braced her knees on the mattress as he shoved her panties down. One hand dove between her thighs, cupping the mound of curls. Then fingers parted, explored, pleasured her. He found the tiny nub that was the center of her desire, and ran the pad of his thumb over it. She shuddered and caught her breath. He pinched it between thumb and forefinger, squeezing, rolling, torturing her. She whimpered and all at once his free hand caught her chin, tipping her head down.

"Open your eyes, Caity. Look at me, let me watch you."

She did as he asked. She'd do anything he asked at that moment. And his deep, dark eyes stabbed into hers just as his fingers stabbed into her center. He slid them in deeper, then pulled them out again, watching the responses in her eyes.

She reached down between them, finding the waistband of his briefs, thrusting one hand beyond it. She held him, her grip tight, but trembling. He was like iron coated in silk. She squeezed and moved her hand up and down his turgid length, then up again until her fingers teased at his tip.

"Oh, yeah," he moaned.

She lowered her head to his chest, and worried his nipples just the way he'd done to hers. And then he was gripping her again, rolling her over, peeling her panties away and kicking free of his briefs all at once. He settled himself on top of her, nudging her thighs apart with his, positioning his need at her moist opening.

He entered her hard and fast and deep, groaning as he did. He gripped her buttocks in both hands, and drove himself to the very hilt, holding her hard against him, refusing to back down even when she stiffened, pressing harder, forcing her to take all of him.

He watched her face as she slowly relaxed, adjusting to her body's fullness, to the feel of him stretching her to his shape and size again. And as soon as she did, he knew, and he withdrew, slowly, until she was all but empty, before thrusting himself into her again. He set the pattern, and the pace continued. Deep, hard thrusts. Slow, mind-altering withdrawals. He kissed her hands, her fingers, one by one. His lips traced a path over her forearms, making her tremble. Then his mouth dampened her shoulders, then her neck, and her ears. It was as though he wanted to taste every inch of her.

The force behind the thrusts grew stronger, harder, and faster with each stroke.

Her hips rose to meet his, her fingers dug into his shoulders. It was as if she were riding a hurricane, she thought vaguely. She felt possessed by him, filled with him and surrounded in him, all at once, and she moved without pause or forethought or planning. She moved according to her body's demands and the ones she could sense from his. And then he drove every thought from her mind as her entire body tightened until her muscles tried to tear from the bones.

Release pummeled her, exploding inside her. She clung to him as her body convulsed around his, and she cried out his name on a voice ragged and broken. He stiffened, plunging again, holding her hips to his. "Caity," he whispered, and then he collapsed atop her, panting, damp with sweat.

He lay there for a long time, his heart rumbling against her chest, his sweat dampening her body, mingling with her own, his breaths heating her skin as they slowed. He lifted his head after a long moment, when their lungs were functioning normally and their bodies began to cool. He searched her eyes, utter longing in his. He started to say something, then shook his head and rolled off her. He cradled her to his chest, held her in arms banded with steel, held her close, and warm and safe against him.

She cried softly, and silently, so he wouldn't know. This was what she'd wanted. She felt cherished, just as she had in her memory flashes. The sad part was, it wasn't real. But she could pretend. Just for tonight, she could pretend.

When she awoke, he was gone.
Dawn hadn't yet painted the horizon. But she was too

restless to lie in bed. There was so much to say. She needed to find Dylan, to beg him, if necessary, to give their marriage one more try. She wanted to tear up all of the divorce papers and start over. She wanted the cherished feeling he'd given her last night to live on and on. She wanted it to be real. She was determined to *make it* real.

She threw back the covers, got up and found her nightgown and panties on the floor. She pulled them on, then smiled as she spotted the roll of gauze and tube of ointment on the floor, recalling the tender way he'd cared for her wounded foot. She bent to pick them up, and reached for the tweezers, too. Then she carried the lot into the bathroom and opened the medicine cabinet to replace the items inside.

She set the gauze on a shelf, then froze as her gaze fell on a small, brown glass jar. She blinked at the words on the label, not willing to believe what she saw there.

"Pure ground carob."

"No." She stared at the bottle as though it might leap up and grab her, and backed away from the cabinet. "No, it can't be..."

God, the tenderness she'd felt in his touch last night, the sweet anguish in his eyes, the yearning...had it all been an act? One big performance to convince her once and for all that he was innocent? Could he have faked the passion, the affection, that she'd felt surrounding her all night long? She didn't want to believe it.

Maybe it's time you stopped believing what you want to believe, and start seeing what's staring you in the face.

Tears blurred her vision as she closed the cabinet and walked back into the bedroom. He hadn't returned. She stole in silence into the hallway, tiptoed along its dim length until she heard him, crooning a soft song, his voice deep, trembling, beautiful. "Good night, Sweetheart." She caught back a sob that leapt into her throat, and slipped nearer, peering through the open doorway into the nursery.

He walked slowly, barefoot, his calves naked beneath the

hem of a terry robe. He cradled the tiny baby on his shoulder, patting her back with his huge hand. He sang very softly, and Lizzie, wide-eyed, seemed to be hanging on every note. He turned to pace the other way and Cait saw his face. His eyes were red, and there were marks on one cheek that looked like the tracks of hot tears.

She backed away slowly, bit her lips as her own eyes filled. How could she make sense of him? Of the tender man she saw holding Lizzie, of the man with the powder that was poison to her hidden in his medicine cabinet?

Blinded by tears, she made her way back to his bedroom. What other secrets was he hiding here? The keys to her past? His hidden motive for wanting her dead? She was tired of waiting to find the answers. She couldn't wait anymore.

He wouldn't come back any time soon. Lizzie was wide-awake, and it would take a while to get her back to sleep. Caitlin went to the dresser, opened the drawers, pawed their contents. She found nothing but clothes. She turned to the closet, and rummaged inside it. Nothing. Just more clothes, shoes, suits. A briefcase.

She drew it out, and lay it on the bed. She tried the snaps, half expecting it to be locked. It wasn't, and inside she found only papers pertaining to the business. Drawings. Blueprints. Invoices. Nothing to do with her.

She closed it and slipped it back into the closet. Then she spotted the fireproof security box on the top shelf. She reached for it, glancing over her shoulder toward the door as she did.

What if he returned, caught her snooping? What would he do then?

It didn't matter. She had to try. She drew the heavy box down, set it on the floor near enough the bed that she could shove it underneath if she heard him coming. She closed the closet.

The box was locked and she felt deflated. Then she saw

his jeans from the day before hanging over the back of a chair. She went to them, searched the pockets and found a key ring. There were many keys on it, but it didn't take long to spot the small one that fit the lock. She sat on the floor, and opened the box.

There were photos. Dozens of them. Snapshots of her, in her youth. Pictures of the two of them together, mugging for the camera. She looked at all of them, blinking constantly to keep her eyes clear enough to see. They seemed so happy. So in love.

She found their marriage license. A large manila envelope held it, along with more photos, encased in a leather-bound album. Their wedding pictures. Her dress was off-the-shoulder, ivory-toned, spilling over with lace and pearls. She'd worn a sprig of baby's breath and yellow roses in her hair, carried a bouquet of the same in her hands.

She flipped through the album slowly, her heart aching for what they'd had, what they'd lost. There was a fat man in a dark suit, nearly bald, with hard, glassy blue eyes. He must have been her father, but she found no sense of recognition stirring inside her. Then she found the one of the woman. She looked just like Caitlin. Same auburn hair, only shorter, and permed in kinky curls to frame her petite face. Her green eyes held some secret pain, some deep sadness that belied the smile that curved her full lips. She didn't look old enough to be Caitlin's mother. But she knew that's who she was seeing right now. And her fingertips brushed over the troubled face.

God, she didn't remember her own mother! But she felt something, a pull, a heartache. A longing.

She closed her eyes, and then the album. There would be time to learn about her mother later. It was too late to mend the break she sensed in their relationship. Her mother was gone, dead and buried.

She set the album aside and continued pawing through the contents of the box. Her hand froze, her fingers tingling, when she picked up the envelope buried at the bottom, beneath titles to cars, and countless other documents.

Trembling for no reason, she opened it, and found inside the very item she'd most dreaded seeing. Across the top of the document, she read the words, Certificate of Fetal Death.

She caught her breath in her throat and tears stung her eyes. She swiped them away and forced herself to read all of it, the clinical, cold facts that told her she and Dylan had had a son. A tiny son, who'd weighed just over two pounds. Cause of death was listed as extreme prematurity. She blinked at the date. January 8th. Just over eight months ago. Her heart twisting, she scanned the page, and found the child's name. David Dylan Rossi.

So they'd named him. And if they had, then they'd probably buried him, as well. Where? Desperately, she reread the lines, but found no clue. Oh, God. She fought her shaking hands and replaced the paper in its envelope. But it wasn't empty. She shook out the folded card that was still inside. It read, In Memoriam. David Dylan Rossi. She found the name of the cemetery there, along with the date of his stillbirth and burial.

"My baby," she whispered, holding the card to her chest. And this was all she had of him. This, and the memory. It had been a memory, not a dream. A nightmare memory of the day she'd lost her child. And she knew, as surely as she knew anything, that losing the child had devastated her, that she'd been sure she could never survive going through it again. And that was why she'd been so afraid of getting pregnant. God, she'd been a fool.

She replaced everything else in the security box, but kept the card. She locked it, replaced it in the closet and returned the key ring to Dylan's pocket. Then she paused and took the keys back out. She needed to go there, she realized. She needed to see where her son rested. Yes, there were other things that must be done. She had to confront Dylan about this, and about the carob powder she'd found in his medicine cabinet. But first—before she could even think of anything else—she had to find her baby.

And she had to do it alone.

She found a pad and pen on the dresser and scrawled a note to Dylan. "I need to be by myself, to think. Please understand." She signed her name at the bottom, and left the note on the bed, then crept through the halls to her room, not making a sound, still clinging to the card that bore her son's name.

She set the card and the keys on the nightstand, avoiding the broken glass from the lamp while she dressed in jeans and a sweatshirt. She tugged a brush through her hair and snapped it into a rubber band.

She slipped on her shoes, quickly grabbed the keys and tiptoed out, locking the bedroom door from the inside and pulling it shut after her.

She paused at the top of the stairs, recalling the horror of seeing Sandra's broken body at the bottom. But she forced herself to move down them, through the foyer and then out the front door.

She got into Dylan's car, inserted the key, but didn't start the engine. She only turned the key enough to release the steering wheel, then shifted into neutral and coasted as far as she could down the drive. Only then did she start the car, and put it in gear. She flicked the headlights on when she reached the road.

She drove slowly, feeling her way. She hadn't driven a car since the accident, and it was terrifying to do so now. But she had to. She had to see…

She knew where the cemetery was. She'd passed it yesterday in the taxi. And she found it again with no trouble, despite the darkness. She pulled the car to the side of the road and shut off the engine. She left the keys in the switch, in her hurry to find her son.

The wrought-iron gate stood slightly crooked, like an

aged sentry who put duty before comfort. It was closed, and a chain was wrapped around the bars with a padlock for a pendant. To prevent vandalism, she assumed. It had been open when she'd passed it by day. She moved through the damp, scraggly grass, along the short brick wall that surrounded the place, and easily climbed over it. It was really rather silly to have a padlocked gate when the wall was so easily scaled. She dropped to the ground on the other side, then just stood amid rows and rows of markers.

The night wind ruffled her hair. It smelled of fresh flowers, and old ones, and of the sea. Crickets chirped incessantly. The moon's whispered glow slanted into the place, making odd-shaped shadows around the stones. But the moon hung low in the sky, and soon it would disappear entirely. There were a few huge trees, looming like guardians of the dead.

She belatedly wished she'd brought along a flashlight. How would she ever find little David here?

But she began at the first row of markers, barely able to discern the names engraved in the stone in the pale moonlight. And she moved quickly, from stone to stone, searching, her heart breaking into millions of tiny bits. And when she finished with one row, she moved to the next.

It took the better part of an hour to find it. The marker was longer than it was high. The front was adorned with a tiny, sweet-faced angel, kneeling with hands folded in prayer. It read, Our Beloved Son, David Dylan Rossi. Fresh flowers covered the grave. Lilies, pale blue carnations, baby's breath for the baby who'd never drawn one. And yellow roses.

Caitlin ran her hand over the face of the cold stone, her fingers tracing the letters of his name. The pain was too much for anyone to bear and still live. Too much. She sank to her knees, pressing her face to the stone, giving way to the tears she'd cried too often lately. And then she sank lower, until her body was pressed to the fine, new grass that covered her child. She pushed her face into the moist, green blades, and sobbed as she never had before.

When the tears finally began to subside, she sat up again, shakily. She gathered the yellow roses to her breast and bent to inhale their scent. Who'd put them here? Dylan? God, was this as painful to him as it was to her? Why hadn't he told her? Why keep something so vital a secret?

Thinking of Dylan reminded her how long she'd been here. Though time had passed without her awareness, she knew she'd been gone a long while. The moon was gone now. Soon the sky would begin to lighten with the approaching dawn. She wanted to get back before anyone realized she'd gone.

She got to her feet, surprised at the weakness her crying had left in her. She shouldn't be surprised, she supposed. She hadn't been eating right, or getting much sleep at all. Her body needed some TLC, or she'd end up in worse shape than she'd been before.

She walked, dragging her feet, back to the short wall. Then stopped, turning abruptly. She'd heard something, some sound or movement behind her.

She scanned the darkness, senses alert, her pulse accelerating to a constant thrum in her ears. But every shadow could have concealed some waiting evil. There was nothing distinct. Fear shivered up her spine and she climbed over the wall, and hurried to the car. She got in, locked all the doors and reached for the switch, to turn the key.

Only the keys weren't there.

She frowned hard. *I know I left them in the switch. Didn't I?*

Maybe not. She'd been upset, not thinking clearly. She checked the pockets of her jeans and felt nothing. Oh, hell, could she have dropped them when she'd climbed the wall? Or when she'd lain prostrate on the ground, sobbing for her lost baby?

She glanced uneasily through the windshield, eyes strain-

ing. She saw no one. She was alone with her grief and her
fears. She unlocked the door and got out, starting back for
the cemetery. She stooped near the wall where she'd gone
in and felt around in the grass, to no avail. Then she
climbed over and repeated the vain process on the other
side. Nothing. Sighing, she made her way back to the head-
stone. If she didn't find the keys there, she'd have to retrace
her steps through the entire place as she'd searched for the
grave. But as she approached her child's grave site, a slow,
smooth motion caught her eye. She squinted in the darkness.

A length of rope dangled from a huge tree, a hangman's
noose at its end. She froze, stark terror rinsing her in icy
water. She screamed in horror and turned to run back the
way she'd come.

Something came around her throat, something smooth
and firm, and tight, growing tighter with every second,
choking off her airway. She grasped at it with both hands,
clawing her own skin, trying to get her fingers behind the
leather. But the tightening only went on.

She couldn't breathe! She kicked backward with one
foot, but connected with nothing. She was dying! God,
someone was killing her and she was helpless to fight.

She was dizzy. Huge black spots danced in and out of
her vision, followed by bright red ones that seemed like
little explosions in her brain. And then utter blackness swallowed her up.

Dylan had tucked Lizzie in and returned to the bedroom to find Cait gone, and the note on his bed. That she wanted him to leave her alone was clear, but he was uncomfortable with the notion. He told himself it wasn't because he'd so looked forward to making love to her again, or because he'd dreamed for so long of holding her all night long and waking with her in his arms, snuggled against him. He told himself it was just that he was worried about her. She hadn't told him about her nightmare, but he didn't believe for a minute that she'd forgotten it. It was something she was keeping to herself. He tried to respect that, along with her need for privacy, but after an hour of tossing restlessly, he gave in to his greater need to know she was all right.

He pulled on jeans and a T-shirt, and went to her room, only to find the door locked from the inside. So he knocked, and waited.

No answer.

He knocked again, harder this time. "Caity. Come on, answer me. I'll go away if you want, I just want to know you're okay."

Still no answer, and panic began to spread through him. He pounded again. "Caity! Dammit, answer me! Caity!"

When he only heard silence, visions of her lying in a pool of blood on the floor assaulted him. He took two steps backward and kicked the door open.

She wasn't there. The room looked the same as it had earlier. The lamp shattered on the floor. The bloody footprints on the carpet. Then he spotted the little card on the nightstand and his heart flipped over. He picked it up, knowing already what it was.

He closed his eyes tightly. "Oh, God, she knows. But she wouldn't have gone there. Not at night, not alone…"

With dawning dread, he realized that his keys were no longer in his pocket, and when he raced down the stairs to the front door, he saw that his car wasn't out front, either.

But the battered pickup was. He ran to it, jumped in and found the extra key he kept in the ashtray, just in case. The engine roared to life, and Dylan shifted into gear and pressed the accelerator to the floor with his bare foot.

He was driving too fast. He knew he was, but he couldn't slow down. The feeling of impending doom assaulted him with killing force, and the pickup rocked up on two wheels as he rounded sharp curves without letting up. The headlights barely cut through the gloom enough to guide his way as he careered over the writhing roads toward Eden, toward the cemetery where he and Cait had buried their tiny child months ago…the cemetery where she'd fainted in his arms from sheer grief. He couldn't stand the thought of her there, alone, slowly regaining the memory of her most gut-wrenching experience. She couldn't handle it. Not yet, not alone. God, it still twisted *his* insides into knots to go there every week with fresh flowers.

He skidded to a stop when the pickup's headlights glinted off the metallic surface of his car, parked near the cemetery gates. He leapt out, and vaulted the wall.

He saw a flashlight moving through the darkness from the other side of the graveyard. Heard a gruff, male voice call, "What's goin' on out here? Who's there?"

He ran toward that voice, even as he heard the sound of running feet, retreating in another direction. He moved forward, tripping twice, falling down on hands and knees and lunging to his feet just as fast.

The third time he tripped, it was over a woman's still body.

"My God, Caity!" He gripped her shoulders, shook her gently. Then he saw the belt wrapped around her slender throat, and his heart tripped to a stop in his chest. He snatched the damned thing away and pulled her to him, holding her gently, rocking her, murmuring her name over and over. "Don't die, Caity, not now. Please, not now."

"Let go of that woman, mister."

He lifted his head, only to be blinded by the beam of a flashlight aimed directly at his face.

"She's my wife. Call an ambulance for God's sake, she's dying!"

"Already did that, when I heard the screams. Po-lice, too. So why don't you just stand up, nice and easy, and leave her be till they get here."

Dylan only shook his head and clutched her more tightly.

"Leave her be, mister. I got a twelve-gauge pointed at yer head, and I'd hate to have to use it."

Dylan stiffened, but he lowered her to the cool grass, and looked up, squinting in the beam of light. The light moved then, and caught a noose swaying slowly in the breeze, hanging from a tree right above him.

"Yer one sick son of a bitch, you know that?"

She was lying on a hard surface, in a small, enclosed place. Strangers hovered over her. A mask covered her face, bathing her nose and mouth in cold, sterile-smelling air. Her throat hurt. Her lungs burned. Her head throbbed.

"She's coming around."

"Mrs. Rossi. Mrs. Rossi, can you hear me?"

She nodded at the fresh-faced young man who leaned over her. He wore white, and beyond the open doors at her feet, she saw flashing lights, breaking the dawn with color. She tried to sit up, only to have the young man hold her shoulders in place. "Take it easy, now. You're going to be okay."

"Pulse is stronger. BP's gaining," another, older man said.

In the flashing light through the open doors, she saw

Dylan looking rumpled, in jeans and a T-shirt. He was barefoot, and he stood nose to nose with Detective Barnes. It
looked as if they were arguing.

Dimly, she recalled what had happened. The darkness,
the noose, the grim certainty that she was going to die when
her life was being choked out of her.

Dylan was here. What the hell was he doing here? Oh,
God, it hadn't been him. It *couldn't have been* him.

The doors swung closed, and the vehicle lurched into
motion.

Broad daylight filtered into her hospital room. She'd
been examined, X-rayed, poked and prodded until the doctors were certain she was going to be all right.

Now she lay in the bed, sipping ice cola through a straw,
letting it soothe her throat, and watching Detective Barnes
pace the room.

"I need to get out of here."

He cocked one eyebrow at her, and stopped pacing. "I
was told you'd have to stay overnight for observation."

"No."

He frowned at her, then shrugged. "Up to you, I guess.
But not until you tell me everything. And don't leave any-
thing out, Mrs. Rossi. Don't try to protect him anymore.
We have him cold this time."

Her heart skipped a beat. "Have you arrested Dylan?"

His lips thinned. "He's being held for formal questioning. His answers at the scene didn't cut it."

"I want to be there."

"What?"

"When you question him. I want to be there. I want to
hear the answers." She caught Barnes's gaze and held it.
"I *need* to be there."

He was silent for a long time. Finally, he nodded. "Need
to hear it for yourself, is that it? I can arrange it."

She sighed her relief, and leaned back on the pillows.

"So what happened last night?"

She closed her eyes. "I found out I'd had a child. He was stillborn, in January."

"Your husband hadn't told you about it?"

She shook her head.

"Then how did you find out?"

She licked her lips. "I found the fetal death certificate."

"Ah."

"I wanted to see the grave. I don't know why, I just felt this need to be there, close to him."

"Understandable." He paced again, nearer the bed, then sat in the chair beside it.

"But I wanted to be alone. I left Dylan a note, telling him not to bother me, and then took his car keys. I locked my bedroom from the inside. Then I took the car and drove to the cemetery."

"Anyone follow you?"

She shrugged. "I probably wouldn't have noticed if they had. I was pretty upset."

"I'll bet you were." He leaned forward in his chair. "So you found the place."

"Yes."

"See any other cars there? Anyone hanging around?"

"No."

"So?"

"I visited the grave for a while. I'm not sure how long. Then I went back to the car. Only the keys were gone. I thought I'd left them in the switch, but they weren't there." She sighed, pressing her hand to her pounding head. "I thought I might have dropped them, so I went back to the grave to look for them." She shuddered and closed her eyes tight. "There was a noose, hanging from a tree. I think I screamed, and I turned to run back to the car. But something came around my throat from behind." The horror of that feeling, of not being able to breathe, of certain death looming right in front of her, brought new tears to her eyes. She covered her face with both hands.

"It's all right." A heavy hand closed on her shoulder. "It's all right, you're fine."

She sniffed, lowered her hands and nodded. "That's all I remember. I couldn't breathe. I passed out."

He nodded. "You didn't get a sense of who it was? Did he say anything? Maybe you caught a whiff of cologne, or—"

"No. Nothing." She met his concerned gaze, searched it. "What stopped him from killing me? Why was that awful noose hanging there?"

Barnes shook his head. "My best guess is that the killer planned to make it look like a suicide. Leave you..." He didn't finish.

He didn't have to. "Leave me hanging from the tree above my son's grave. Oh, God..." A sob choked her.

"The caretaker lives right next door. He heard your screams. He had his wife call 911 while he grabbed his shotgun and headed out to see what was happening. I figure that your...that the killer stopped what he was doing when the old man called out."

"Thank God," she whispered.

"Mrs. Rossi, when he got there, he found your husband crouching over you. He didn't see or hear anyone else."

A cold feeling chilled her to the bone. "What did Dylan say?"

Barnes frowned and shook his head. "Let's go find out."

The mirror was two-way, he had no doubt about it. But he didn't really give a damn. "I want to know how she is."

"You answer my questions, and then we'll discuss your wife, Rossi."

Dylan clenched his fists on the surface of the table. "Is she alive?"

Barnes pursed his lips and Dylan felt like bloodying them for him. "Questions first. You want a lawyer present?"

"I don't need a freaking lawyer."

"Good. Sign here." He shoved a form across the table, then took a pen from his pocket and tossed it down. Dylan scratched his name across the bottom, and shoved it back.

Barnes took a long look at it, nodded and leaned back in the chair opposite Dylan's. "So tell me what happened last night."

"I told you at the cemetery."

"Take it from the top, Rossi. I have all day."

Dylan's glare did nothing to erase the smug expression Barnes wore. He'd get this over with so he could find out about Caity. The sooner the better. Dammit, if she'd died...he bit his lip at the thought. She couldn't have died. Not now.

"She had a bad dream. I found her crying in the nursery, took her to my room. I wanted her where I could be sure she was okay. Later, the baby was crying, so I got up to check on her. Cait was sound asleep when I left her."

"So far, so good. Keep going."

Dylan sighed hard and fought to keep a rein on his temper. "When I came back, she was gone. She left a note. I'm sure your guys have found that by now."

"Hell, yes. Found a few other goodies in your room, too." He took a plastic zipper bag from his huge manila envelope and dangled it like bait from a hook. "Ever seen this before?"

Dylan frowned and looked at the bottle encased in the plastic bag. "Carob powder?" He felt a chill pass over his spine.

"Have you seen it before?" Barnes repeated, his voice booming.

"No. Where did you—"

"Your medicine cabinet, Rossi."

Dylan nodded. "So, someone's trying to frame me. Isn't that pretty obvious, *Detective?*

Barnes only eyed him as though Dylan was something bad, as though he were a hunk of rotten meat on a platter. "So you found the note. Then what?"

"I lay in bed for a while. An hour or so. I couldn't sleep without knowing she was okay, so I went to check on her."

"Waited a whole hour, huh?"

"She made it clear she didn't want to be bothered." Dylan shook his head. "You aren't buying a word of this. It's bull, a waste of time. You've already decided I'm guilty."

"That's not my job, Rossi. You went to check on her…"

"The door was locked. She didn't answer. I got worried, kicked it in. Found the card on the dresser and guessed she'd gone to the grave. When I found the car gone, I was sure of it, so I took the pickup and went after her." He shook off the chill of precognition that had swept over him when he'd seen his car parked at the cemetery gate, and eyed Barnes. "How am I doing so far?"

"Word for word what you told me at the scene. Well rehearsed. You're smooth. I've seen smoother."

"Go to hell, Barnes."

"Been there for a long time now, Rossi. Finish the fairy tale, will you?"

Dylan shook his head. "I jumped the wall. Heard the old man call out, saw his light. I heard someone running away, and then I found her."

Barnes nodded. "You said that before, that you heard someone running away. Old man Crandall didn't hear a thing."

"He was running, too, toward me, ready to give me both barrels of that shotgun he was lugging. He might not have heard the other guy's steps over his own. But I did. Someone ran, toward the east side of the cemetery."

Barnes's eyes were still skeptical. He reached into the

envelope again. A bigger plastic bag emerged this time, with a leather belt inside. "Reco'nize this?"

Dylan's neck prickled. He took the bag and examined the belt. There was no sense lying about it. His initials were engraved in the leather. "It's mine."

"Your fingerprints are on it, Rossi. And hers. No one else's."

"I took it off her neck, you bastard."

"How?"

The guy wasn't ruffled, not in the least. Dylan imagined he had lots of experience trying to make people sweat like this. "I don't know. I was scared. My wife was lying there as good as dead. I just yanked it off her, okay?"

"Your prints were here," Barnes pointed to one end of the belt. "And here," he added pointing to the other end. "Hers were only in the center, where she struggled to pull the thing away as she was being strangled." He stood and walked slowly away, then back again. "Your prints were where the killer would have been holding the belt, Rossi. Where you held it as you choked the life out of your wife."

Dylan felt a fist pummel his gut. "Are you saying…she's dead?"

Barnes only continued staring at him. Waiting for him to break?

Dylan came out of the chair like a shot, reached across the table and gripped Barnes by the front of his splashy print shirt. "Tell me, you bastard!"

The door burst open and two uniformed cops ran through, each gripping one of Dylan's arms and jerking him away from Barnes.

"Cuff him," Barnes ordered, straightening his shirt as if he hadn't a care in the world.

Then a soft cry from the still-open door drew Dylan's gaze. Caitlin stood there in the doorway. Her eyes huge, round, her pupils too dilated to be normal. She stood there, just staring at him, as handcuffs were snapped around his wrists, pulled behind his back.

"Caity…"

She blinked, but kept looking at him from those hollow, haunted eyes.

God, the relief that coursed through him almost made his legs give out. She was okay. He wanted to hold her, to run his hands through her wild hair, to kiss her. But his relief at seeing her on her feet, breathing, was short-lived. Her expressionless face, the hurt and fear he saw etched into it, were like daggers in his heart.

He saw the red marks at her throat, the purplish bruises that were already forming. There were garish scratches on her neck, and he shuddered as he envisioned her clawing at the belt, trying to pull it away. She was pale, too pale, and dark circles under her eyes made her look as if she'd been in a fight and lost.

The cops moved him forward until he stood right in front of her, at the doorway. He wanted to reach out, to pull her into his arms and hold her until that turmoil in her eyes calmed. But he couldn't with his hands cuffed behind him. He wished to hell she would say something. Anything. "Caity—"

"You'll have to step aside, Mrs. Rossi," Barnes ordered, tugging gently at her shoulders until she obeyed. But her eyes remained on Dylan, and his on her. "Dylan Rossi, I'm placing you under arrest for the attempted murder of your wife."

Caitlin's eyes fell closed, not softly or gently. They slammed shut like the doors of a prison, and squeezed themselves together hard. And then the two cops shoved him through the door.

"Don't go home, Caity!" Dylan shouted over his shoulder. "Don't go back there. It isn't safe!" He heard no answer as he was pushed through a hallway toward the back of the building.

Barnes opened a cell, and unceremoniously shoved him through. He closed the door. "Turn around and stick your hands through the bars so I can take the cuffs off."

Dylan did, putting his desperate hurt and paralyzing fear for his wife aside, converting it to anger, which he vented on the man who twisted a key in the manacles at his wrists. "You haven't Mirandaized me, Barnes. Slipping up in your old age?"

The cuffs fell free and Dylan turned to face the man. Barnes slipped a little card from his shirt pocket and stuck it through. "Read that."

Dylan took the card, glanced at it and read the first line. "You have the right to remain silent." He'd shot that one to hell already, hadn't he? And it had probably been a stupid mistake, but dammit, he'd had to know about Caity. He shook his head and slipped the card back to Barnes.

"Understand?"

Dylan looked at him, lifting his eyebrows. "What?"

"Your rights, do you understand them?"

"Oh, hell, yes, Barnes. You really have a knack for communication." Dylan won the stare-down. Barnes's gaze flicked away. Dylan's searched the man for a weak spot. "You don't have enough to indict me."

"I think I do." He shrugged. "Either way, you won't be offing your wife today. I'll sleep better knowing that."

"Don't sleep too soundly, Barnes. She still isn't safe. Dammit, it wasn't me, but someone sure as hell tried to kill her. She needs protection."

Barnes's gaze narrowed. "Nice try, Rossi."

"Dammit, I'm begging you. Give her some kind of protection. She's just stubborn enough to go back there today."

Barnes nodded. "Especially if she believes her attacker is safely behind bars. Looked to me like she was finally convinced, Rossi. How'd she look to you?"

"You're enjoying this, aren't you?"

Barnes shrugged again. "Can't help it. I honestly like the lady. She's got that innocent, trusting quality, makes a guy want to look out for her." He shook his head. "Makes a slug like you want to take her for everything she's got and throw her away. You're a fool, you know that?"

Dylan frowned, wondering at the softening in Barnes's voice, the slightly tormented look in his eyes. "You feel like protecting her, then go for it, Barnes. Look out for her, 'cause you've got me caged up and I can't. She still needs watching over. I swear it."

"You know, you almost have me convinced."

"Did she tell you about the divorce?" Dylan knew he was grasping at straws, but he had to try. "She canceled the old settlement. Had a new one drawn up. She doesn't get a damn thing, now. I have no motive to kill her."

"What, you think greed is the only motive that drives a man to murder his wife?"

"If she dies while I'm stuck here, Barnes, I'll make sure you pay."

"You don't scare me, Rossi."

"I'm the one that's scared here. Dammit, she's a walking target. Will you think about that? What if you're wrong, huh? What the hell is going to happen to her then?"

Barnes frowned through the bars. "You're damned convincing, I'll give you that." He turned to walk away from the cell, handcuffs dangling from his fingers.

"Assign a man to watch her, Barnes. If you have one decent cell in your body, protect her!" Dylan shouted after him as he got farther away. "Suppose you have the wrong man, Barnes! Suppose the real killer gets to her while I'm here. You gonna be able to live with that? Are you? Barnes!"

Barnes didn't answer, only kept strolling down the hall as though he were taking a walk through the park.

Chapter 14

"Cait, God, I'm glad you're back." Thomas hugged her hard, but Caitlin remained stiff in his arms, feeling shell-shocked.

"Police have been here, snoopin' all over the place. That Barnes, he's a corker," Ellen snapped. "Said you were in the hospital, but wouldn't say why. Time we called, you'd checked out."

Caitlin freed herself from her brother's grip, and faced the older woman. How on earth was she going to tell her that Dylan had been arrested?

"You look ill, so pale and weak. You need to eat and rest, *non?*" Genevieve hovered with a worried expression. "I can get something for you—"

"No, Genevieve. I'll be fine, really." Her gaze moved around the living room, where they'd all gathered, but she didn't see Lizzie. Henri lurked in the arched doorway that led to the library, just watching, silent.

"What happened last night? There was another attempt on your life, wasn't there, Cait?"

She met her brother's concerned eyes, thinking his fear for her sounded genuine, and simply nodded. She hated suspecting he—or any of them—could be capable of murder. But if Dylan wasn't guilty, then someone else was. She'd only come back here to find out who...and for Lizzie.

His gaze narrowed, moving over her body as if in search of her injuries, then stopped on her vividly bruised throat, and widened. "Oh, my God."

"It isn't as bad as it looks."

"Where's Dylan?" Ellen demanded. "He took off outta

here last night like his tail was afire, just a short while after that other car roared away. Made enough racket to wake the dead, that one did.''

Caitlin closed her eyes tight. ''They've arrested him.''

Thomas froze, his eyes the only part of him that moved at all, and then, only to widen.

Caitlin dragged her feet as she made her way to the sofa, and sat down. ''I went to the cemetery last night, to see my son. I guess Dylan came after me.'' She bit her lip hard, tasting blood on her tongue. ''Someone tried to strangle me there, and then the caretaker came out to find Dylan bending over me.''

''Did he do it, Cait?'' Thomas sat beside her, gripped her hand in both of his.

''I was unconscious. I never saw—''

''But what do you *feel?*''

She shook her head slowly. ''His fingerprints were on the belt that was twisted around my throat,'' she whispered, her voice straining painfully just to do that much. ''The caretaker didn't see anyone else.''

''But did he do it?''

She broke then. Sobs racked her frame, jerking her body with each assault, and she bent nearly double, covering her face with both hands. ''I...I don't know.''

''Damn fool girl!'' Ellen's voice sounded close to Caitlin, and she felt her head jerked up by a cruel hand in her hair.

Thomas leapt to his feet, gripping Ellen's shoulders in a firm, but gentle hold. ''Let her go! I know this is tough for you to take, Ellen, but—''

''The man's so in love with you, he doesn't know which way is up! And what does it get him? You're poison to him, Caitlin O'Brien. I always said you'd ruin him someday and now you've gone and done it!''

''Ellen, I—''

"And you're bound to stand by and watch him prosecuted for this. It's gonna kill him."

"Better him than my sister, Ellen."

"It wasn't Dylan who tried to wring your neck, girl, but it should'a been. He'd have left you long ago if it hadn't been for that baby. Him and his pipe dreams that it would change things, that you two could start over. He should have left then."

But he hadn't, Caitlin whispered to herself. He hadn't, and there were eight months between the stillbirth and the car accident. Why? She swallowed hard. No one could answer that question but Dylan.

"I won't see him tried for this, Caitlin," Ellen shouted, though she was standing so close, Caitlin could see the depth of each wrinkle in her face and the deep brown of her eyes. It was a little surprising to realize how very beautiful her eyes were, even now. So dark and deep. So like Dylan's. "I won't stand for it. I'll kill you myself first!"

The older woman turned to stalk out of the room, toward the stairs.

"Ellen, wait. You can't just condemn me like this when I—" Caitlin got to her feet and followed on Ellen's heels as the old woman kept on going. "Ellen, I'm the victim here. I'm the one who—oh, for God's sake. Where are you going?"

"Upstairs. Got some calls to make. A lawyer, and then my nephew, if they'll even let me talk to him. If not, I have a few things to say to that Barnes character." She struck off up the wide stairway, and disappeared into the hall.

Caitlin let her chin fall to her chest as all the air left her lungs. Thomas's hand on her shoulder gave little comfort. "You'll be okay, sis. I'll help you through this. I gotta say, I can't believe that Dylan…" His voice trailed off, and he shook his head. "I just can't believe it."

Caitlin was having trouble believing it herself. "Where's Lizzie?"

"The nursery. Having a nap, last time I checked."

Caitlin nodded, and gripped the banister in one hand. "I have to be with her for a little while. I need..."

"It's okay. I know."

She blinked fresh tears away as she stared up at her brother. "Don't ever forget how precious she is, Thomas." Then she turned and dragged one foot after the other, up the stairs. Part of her wanted to go to Ellen's room, to try to convince the woman that she wasn't out to destroy Dylan. But she knew it would be of little use.

She brought the baby into her room, and spread a blanket on the floor for her to lie on. Lizzie kicked her feet, and thrashed her arms, cooing and spitting and sticking out her tongue, as her wide eyes fixed first on one strange object, then another. Caitlin spread toys all around the baby, then got down on the blanket herself to play.

And as she did, shaking rattles to capture Lizzie's attention, letting the baby reach for them, seeing her huge blue eyes reflect joy and innocence and acceptance, Caitlin recalled the way Dylan had looked as he'd held Lizzie last night. Patiently, he'd paced the nursery's length, rubbing and patting her little back, snuggling her close to him. And singing.

"You wouldn't believe it, would you, Lizzie?" Cait lay on her side, her head close enough so Lizzie could catch handfuls of her aunt's hair and tug and twist it. "If you could talk, you'd swear your Uncle Dylan was the most gentle man on the planet. You'd never doubt him..."

A small hand smacked against Caitlin's cheek repeatedly as Lizzie made gurgling sounds.

"...the way I have."

She sat up slowly, wrapping the baby up in her arms and holding her close. Lizzie chewed on Caitlin's chin. "It wasn't him, was it, Lizzie? It couldn't have been. And if it wasn't, then it had to be someone else. Someone else left

this house last night after I did, followed me to the cemetery and…''

Her face fell, and she held Lizzie at arm's length, as the
baby laughed out loud and kicked wildly. ''Oh, but they
couldn't have. Ellen was awake, and she said she only
heard two vehicles leave, last night. First mine, and
then—''

Cait blinked. ''No. She *heard* two vehicles, but three
drove out of here last night. She never heard me. Remember? I coasted the car all the way to the end of the driveway
before I started it up, and then eased my way onto the road.
No one could have heard me leave. There was someone
else.''

She lowered Lizzie to the blanket again. Lying beside
her, with her head pillowed by a silky brown teddy bear.
''Dylan is innocent,'' she whispered. ''The question is,
what can we do to prove it?''

Barnes led a team through the cemetery as soon as he'd
closed the cell door on Rossi. There was something about
this case that was bothering him. From day one, he'd been
half-convinced Rossi was trying to kill his wife. But now
that he'd locked the guy up, he wasn't so sure. He shook
his head, and told himself not to lose his objectivity. It was
tough, though. He wanted to protect Caitlin Rossi, and to
catch the slug that was trying to hurt her more than he'd
wanted anything in a long, long time.

He wanted Rossi to turn out to be innocent, because he
could see how much Caitlin wanted it. The way she felt
about the guy just about glared from those green eyes of
hers. He knew she'd be devastated to find out her husband
was capable of killing her. Now, he was probably letting
that wishful thinking cloud his judgment, because there was
no evidence that Rossi was anything *but* guilty.

Still, there'd been something in Rossi's eyes when he'd
begged him to put a tail on his wife, to protect her. Fear.

Desperation. Sincerity. Frustration. All of it. Not a hint of cunning, or the whisper of deceit.

And that was why Barnes had dragged the forensics boys back here again. Rossi had said he heard someone running away, toward the east side of the boneyard. When Barnes thought about that, he realized that if another vehicle *had* been parked on that side, neither the victim, the suspect nor the witness would have been in a position to see it there. So he'd sent a car out to keep an eye on the Rossi house, and on Caitlin Rossi in particular. And he'd brought the crew to look for evidence of a fourth person here last night.

But after an hour of combing the place, they had little more to go on. The roadside was gravel, not a good receptacle for tire tracks. And the grass in the cemetery itself was too dense and close-cropped to pick up footprints.

Barnes was about to give up. He didn't want to believe Rossi was lying, but there was no evidence here to suggest he was telling the truth. Then one of his men yelled, and Barnes jogged toward him.

When Barnes reached him, Melbourne was picking the scrap of material from the brick wall with a pair of tweezers. He held it up for inspection, then dropped it into an evidence bag.

"What do you make of it?" Barnes asked.

Melbourne straightened his glasses, holding the bag in front of them and squinting at it as if he could read words written across the material inside. "It hasn't been here long. Two days at the most. A few hours at the least. The sun and rain would've faded some of this color if it had been out here longer. See? It's really vivid red."

"What'd it come from?"

Melbourne shrugged. "Could be just about anything. We'll run some tests on it, see if there's a hair, or a skin cell or a drop of blood, maybe sweat or saliva if we're lucky."

The square of cloth was uneven, and not more than three

by four inches in size. Barnes wasn't hopeful. Then again, Rossi hadn't been wearing anything red last night. Neither had his wife, nor Stanley Crandall, the caretaker.

She woke with a start, ashamed to have been sleeping so deeply when Dylan was sitting in a jail cell somewhere. Still, she supposed she'd be able to think more clearly now than she could have before. She'd been exhausted, and from the looks of the dim sky, she'd slept several hours.

Lizzie was still snoozing peacefully. The baby had a habit of sleeping the afternoon away. Storing up her energy to keep every adult in the house up all night, Caitlin theorized.

She got up, realized she was still wearing the jeans and sweatshirt from the night before, and thought longingly of a long bath and a hot meal. She conceded to the bath, and put a clean white muslin nightgown on. She intended to go down to the kitchen, fix herself a snack and plot her next move.

She tiptoed past Lizzie, stepped quietly into the hallway and then to the stairs. She was barefoot, and made little sound as she traversed the hall, and descended the stairs. The chill house was quiet, and the living room dim. Light spilled from the library door, though it was opened only a crack. She heard muted voices, padded footsteps, a clink of ice against glass. Caitlin stopped in her tracks. Her lack of sleep these past few nights, or the past few missed meals, must be dulling her senses. She'd come down here wondering how she could prove Dylan innocent. It followed then, that someone else was guilty of trying to kill her. Of murdering Sandra. Someone in this very house. That hadn't changed with Dylan's arrest.

A chill snaked up her spine. Part of her wanted to turn and run, but she refused to heed that part. She needed to know the truth.

Slowly, Caitlin moved toward the doorway.

She heard Genevieve softly whisper, "Thomas, why? I love you, you know that."

"I just can't live with the guilt anymore, Genevieve. This is wrong. It's always been wrong."

Genevieve, assuming he'd meant guilt about cheating on his wife, Caitlin surmised, sighed loudly. "How can it be wrong, when we love each other, Thomas? When is love wrong?"

"What I did to Sandra was wrong, dammit!"

Caitlin shivered violently.

"You never meant—"

"No, Genevieve. It's over. Don't make this any harder on me than it already is. Please. Just accept it. I have to focus on Lizzie now, try to be a good father to her, try to atone—"

"You are a fool to throw me away, Thomas O'Brien!"

Genevieve exited the room, slamming the door behind her, and came face-to-face with Caitlin. Caitlin swallowed her shock, and her fear. She felt a wave of pity for Genevieve. She was so quiet, so delicate-looking. It was awful that she'd been hurt. But God, she should have known better than to involve herself with a married man.

Caitlin put a hand on Genevieve's shoulder. "I'm sorry, Genevieve. If you want to take some time off, you know, think things through, I won't mind a bit."

Genevieve dipped her head, focusing on the little red cloak draped over her arm, rather than looking Caitlin in the eye, now that Caitlin obviously knew about the affair. "That is very kind of you, *madame*."

Genevieve sniffed. "I think I would like to lie down for a while, if you don't need me."

"Go ahead. Oh, and Genevieve, if you hear Lizzie crying, would you just give me a call? I hate to leave her alone in my room, but I need to talk to my brother."

Genevieve nodded, and smiled softly. "Do not worry. I will watch over little Lizzie for you."

Caitlin watched Genevieve ascend the stairs, then faced the library door again, biting her lip. Aside from Dylan, Thomas was the one person with the most to gain by Caitlin's death. He'd inherit half of her estate, which he probably felt he was entitled to, anyway. He'd also had a motive to kill his wife: his affair with Genevieve. Besides that, it seemed pretty clear that the guilty party not only wanted Caitlin dead, but Dylan convicted of the crime. And she'd heard with her own ears her brother's words about "showing" Dylan, teaching him a lesson.

But she'd never dreamed he'd meant anything like this. Her own brother! She'd just been beginning to feel some kind of bond with him. Could he really want her dead?

She looked up at the library door again, and suppressed a shiver. Was it wise to confront him now?

She licked her lips, stiffened her resolve. She couldn't let cowardice keep her from learning the truth. Henri and Genevieve were both within shouting distance. And there was the police cruiser, passing out front every few minutes like a shark circling its next meal.

Thomas was pouring whiskey into a shot glass when she entered, and she was painfully reminded of the night she'd walked in to see Dylan holding that same bottle. She missed him, she realized slowly. Missed him, hell, she ached for him.

But first things first. "Hello, Thomas."

He turned, startled, slopping a few drops from the shot-glass onto the back of the hand that held it. "Caitlin."

She stayed a good distance away from him. She was still afraid, and not even her own mental reassurances that she was safe, dulled that fear. He wouldn't hurt her with witnesses so close, or with the police keeping such a close eye on the house.

"I think it's about time we had a talk. Don't you?" She tried to sound calm, but her voice trembled slightly.

He nodded, took a deep swig of whiskey and smacked his lips. "I'm not going to deny it. It's pretty obvious you overheard the whole thing. I've been a real bastard, Cait. I wanted so much…" He looked at the floor and shook his head.

"You wanted it all. With me dead, you'd inherit half of my money. With Dylan in jail for killing me, you'd probably end up with his share, as well."

She watched his face as she delivered her accusation. His head came up, his eyes widened and his skin paled. "You really believe all that?"

"What else am I supposed to believe?"

He frowned, shook his head. "Cait, I don't want to believe it was Dylan any more than you do, but for God's sake—"

"It wasn't him, Thomas. He wouldn't hurt me. He wouldn't hurt anybody."

"And you think *I would?*" He slugged back the rest of his drink, slammed the glass on a stand, and the sound reverberated through her nerve endings like an electric shock. "I'm your *brother!*"

"And you resent me for inheriting from our father when you didn't." She forced herself to go on, to carry this thing through and learn the truth. "You resent that I selfishly refused to share what I got from him, and to tell you the truth, I don't blame you for that." A lump leapt into her throat. "But it wasn't worth killing for, Thomas. My God, your own wife—"

"I didn't kill Sandra!"

"You thought she was me!"

"No!"

"Thomas, I just stood outside this door and heard you say you felt guilty for what you'd done to her."

He lifted his hands, palms up, and gaped, shaking his

head in confusion. "I *do* feel guilty. For having an affair. For being a lousy father to Lizzie and a worse husband. I feel guilty for what I've been planning..."

"To murder me and frame my husband and take everything we own? Is that what you've been planning, Thomas?"

His eyes turned accusatory and he lunged at her, gripping her wrists before she could back away. Her heart skidded to a stop and she prepared to cut loose with a scream that would bring someone running.

"I can't believe what I'm hearing! Dammit, Cait, all I was planning was to buy enough stock to force Dylan to make me his partner."

She blinked, and closed her gaping mouth. "Wh-what?"

Thomas eased his grip on her forearms and shook his head sadly. "Hell, I can't blame you for thinking the worst of me. I've been acting like an idiot. Blaming you for our father's rejection of me, hating you for having money when I didn't. Just like I blamed Sandra for making me marry her when she got pregnant. I felt trapped. I only wanted to get free. I didn't know how good I had it until she was gone." He lowered his eyes, turned and sunk onto the sofa as tears shimmered in them. "She deserved better than me, better than what I gave her."

Caitlin was shocked. She moved to the sofa, sat down beside her brother, touched his shoulder lightly, still uncertain. "Go on, Thomas. Explain this to me."

He sniffed, met her eyes. "Dylan only hired me because of you. He resented it, and for a long time, he never noticed I was actually doing a good job. I think he expected me to be a freeloader. I really do. I worked my butt off for him, Cait. I wanted more than I had and I was willing to pay for it."

He shook his head. "He promoted me a couple of times, sure. But never let me show him what I could really do. I thought if I bought enough stock to put me in a position of authority, he'd have to see. So I've been putting money aside, buying small chunks of stock whenever I can afford it. I knew he'd resent it at first, but I thought…hell, I don't know. I thought we'd end up working together, as equals, mutual respect and all that bull.'' He shook his head.

He stared into her eyes, and she felt him willing her to believe. "Cait, I was planning to divorce Sandra. I thought I wanted to be with Genevieve. I even told Genevieve about my buying the stock, and becoming Dylan's partner some day.''

She didn't say a word, just sat there, wishing she could believe him.

"God, I can't believe you think I could actually try to kill you. Cait, we haven't been close in a long time. And I may have resented you and let myself become filled with bitterness and jealousy, but I never hated you. I swear it.''

She wanted to believe him, but…

"If it wasn't you, Thomas…then who?''

He shook his head. "I don't know. I wish I did.''

Caitlin didn't know what to believe, or whom. It was late. She wanted to be alone, to think through everything he'd told her, to come up with an alternative suspect, rather than believe one of the men she loved wanted to kill her. She just couldn't believe it of either of them. Beyond the library windows, night had fallen. Caitlin glanced out, then faced her brother. "I'm going to bed. I have a raging headache.''

"For what it's worth, Cait, I don't think it was Dylan. Not really. At first, I was just too shocked to think about anything, but now—'' He shook his head. "You're right. He wouldn't hurt you.''

"Thanks for that, but it isn't exactly a relief. It means that the real killer is still free to try again.''

She hugged her brother, felt his shoulders tremble beneath her light touch. Then she rose and walked on suddenly leaden legs out of the library. She wanted to get back upstairs to her room. She'd imposed on Genevieve long enough. The woman was heartbroken, she didn't need to watch a baby on top of all that.

But when she entered her bedroom, Lizzie wasn't there. Nor was Genevieve. Caitlin frowned for just a moment, then shrugged. Genevieve probably took her to the nursery for a fresh diaper or a clean outfit. She bent to pick up the little toys from the blanket on the floor. Then the pillows, and the blanket itself. She gathered her own discarded clothes from earlier last night, as well. Someone, probably Genevieve, had long since cleaned up the broken lamp. Other than that, though, the room was really in a clutter.

She frowned as she reached for the last item on the floor, and as she picked it up, she recognized Genevieve's hooded cloak. She smiled and still held it in her hands when she heard the shrill ring of the telephone on the stand beside her bed.

Thomas would get it, she thought, folding the cloak over one arm and heading for the door. But it shrilled again, and then again. Why wasn't her brother answering on the library extension?

Frowning, Caitlin picked up the receiver. "Hello?"

"Dammit, I knew you'd go back there. Why didn't you listen to me, Cait?"

"Dylan?" She was shocked, and glad to hear his voice. God, there was so much she wanted to say to him. She had to tell him that she believed in him, had to tell him that—

"Lock yourself in your room and wait for me. Don't let anyone else in. You hear me?"

"Dylan, what—"

"They found something, a scrap of red cloth at the cemetery, that proves someone else was there last night. They're releasing me. Look, it's complicated. I'll explain it all later, just do as I say. Are you in your bedroom now?"

"Yes, but—"

"Go right now and lock your door. Please, Caity."

"But Dylan, I don't under—"

"Will you try trusting me just this once, for God's sake? You want to hear it from Barnes? It wasn't me, Cait, and you have to—"

"I kn—"

"Go and lock yourself in. Now, Cait."

"All right." She set the receiver on the stand, and turned to go the door. Dylan was scaring her, and she wanted to know why. The urgency she heard in his voice had her hands trembling as she reached for the door, and she inadvertently let Genevieve's cloak slip to the floor. Shaking her head at her own nervousness, she bent to pick it up.

And then her blood slowed to a thick, jelled stop in her veins and her head swam. A tiny square with jagged edges gaped in the red material.

They found something, a scrap of red cloth...

"My God. She has Lizzie!"

Chapter 15

She never returned to the phone. Dylan couldn't help but fear the worst as he and Jack Barnes sped through the night.

"That red scrap of cloth has three pieces of vital evidence on it, Rossi."

Dylan had demanded a detailed explanation of the evidence that had cleared him, even as Barnes's car roared through the night away from Eden, and toward Caitlin.

"One was a hair, and the boys in the lab have already determined that it came from your wife's head. That proves that the person who left the scrap of cloth there had contact with her. The second was a microscopic droplet of blood, and the type doesn't match yours, or old man Crandall's, or Caity's. That proves the person wasn't you. There was a fourth person in the cemetery last night, Rossi."

"You said three pieces of evidence," Dylan said softly, to fill the silence with something besides this gnawing fear for Cait. "What was the third?"

"A partial fingerprint. Slightly smudged, but we might still be able to use it."

"What about the blood? Can't you do DNA testing, or something, to identify the killer?"

"That would only work if we had a suspect to compare it to. DNA fingerprinting takes two weeks, Rossi. The ball's rolling, but I'm sure as hell hoping we have the bastard behind bars long before the results come in."

"And what do we do now?"

"We make sure Caity's okay. Then we work our tails off. I'm not planning to sleep until we get to the bottom of this."

Dylan's eyes narrowed. "Why?"

Barnes shrugged. "She's special. If you haven't figured that out yet, then you need some serious help."

Caitlin tore through the corridors to the nursery, knowing already that she wouldn't find Lizzie there. From there, she moved to Ellen's room, but no one was inside.

She raced down the stairs, shrieking for Thomas, running to the library and skidding to a stop in the doorway when she saw him, lying facedown on the floor, a gaping cut in the back of his head, thick, crimson blood coating his neck. She took a single step toward him when she heard Ellen's hoarse cry. "Damned if I'll let you— No!" And then a yelp like that of a wounded animal.

Caitlin forced herself to leave Thomas there, silently praying he'd be all right, and turned to race toward the front door where Ellen's cry had originated. She held the white nightgown up to her knees as she ran.

The door yawned wide. Ellen was pulling herself to her feet, staggering forward, and a car stood running, doors open, in the driveway.

Cait caught up to Ellen, saw the way she was limping. "Ellen, are you—"

"Stop 'em! Caitlin, they've got Lizzie!"

Caitlin gasped, and looked toward the car. Henri was just getting into the front seat. In the glowing panel lights, Caitlin saw Genevieve, with a wriggling bundle on her lap. She had no idea what was going on, but it didn't matter. She launched herself toward the car, bare feet bruising as each running step landed on loose stones. She gripped the open driver's door even as Henri began to pull away, reaching to shut it as he did. She was forced down into the gravel, but her hands gripped the handle tighter. Stones tore through the nightgown, clawed her flesh as she was dragged over the driveway.

And then, abruptly, the car stopped. She heard feet crunching gravel and looked up to see Henri standing over her, and in his hand, a black, evil-looking handgun. It was over, she realized. The smell of exhaust fumes, the sounds of the engine, and of the crickets chirping in chorus would be the last things she'd ever experience.

"Get up."

She blinked and struggled to her feet, shaking all over, her gaze darting past him into the car where Genevieve sat holding Lizzie in the passenger seat. The night wind cooled her sweat-dampened face, and made the muslin gown ripple. Her knees screamed in pain where the gravel had scraped them raw.

"Go on back inside, Caitlin."

She frowned. His French accent was gone. "Where—where are you taking the baby?"

"She's gonna be just fine, long as you and your husband pay what we'll ask for her. If not..." He shrugged, leaving the implication clear in her fevered mind.

"But why?"

"After all this work, you don't expect us to walk away empty-handed, now, do you?"

She didn't understand. She had no idea what he was talking about. She only knew she couldn't let them leave here with Lizzie. She wouldn't. "Dylan won't pay for someone else's child." She shook her head hard. "He won't, I swear it. This is all useless."

"You will, though."

She shook her head. "I won't. I can't. I lost my money, all of it. I signed a new divorce agreement, leaving Dylan everything, even the house. I was going to go away, start fresh." She sought Genevieve's gaze in the car's dimly lit interior. "You heard me say I didn't want the money, or anything that was hers...mine...before."

Henri, or whoever he really was, frowned, and shot a glance toward Genevieve.

"She might be telling the truth." Genevieve's cold glare raked her. "But I doubt it."

"It's true, I swear it. Look, take me, instead. Dylan would pay to get me back."

"Nice try," Henri said. "But why would he? He only wants to get rid of you."

"No, that's not true. He'd have to pay to get me back, it would ruin his reputation if he didn't. Besides, he doesn't hate me. He wouldn't want to see me dead." She saw that they were considering her words, and she rushed on. "It won't be easy to hide with a baby. She'll be so much trouble. She's been sick, remember? So fussy. Keeping everyone awake nights, crying every couple of hours. And there are diapers and feedings, and bottles to wash. If you take me, it'll be easier. Hell, I can wait on you. Think of the irony. The mistress serving the servants. Just leave her here. I'll come with you."

Right on cue, Lizzie began to squall. She twisted and writhed in Genevieve's lap, and made enough racket to wake the dead.

The car bounded over the driveway, headlights cutting through the darkness. They illuminated a hunched form, and the car skidded to a stop. Barnes jumped out, gun in his hand. Dylan ran forward as Ellen scooped the screaming baby up from the gravel. Ellen was crying, as well, when Dylan reached her.

"Ellen, are you—"

"Fine. And so's the little one." She shook her head. "Thomas needs an ambulance, though." Barnes was instantly reaching back into the car, gripping the mike mounted to the dashboard, barking orders.

"What about Caity?" Dylan felt himself tense as he awaited the answer.

Ellen chewed her lip. "They took her, boy. Henri and Genevieve. They were trying to take off with Lizzie, and Caitlin...she stopped them." Ellen bounced the baby up and down in her arms to soothe her crying. "I never saw anything like it. She grabbed on to the car door and they dragged her right down the driveway. Then they stopped and that Frenchman pointed a gun at her. But she got up and started arguin' and beggin' them to leave the baby. She told 'em to take her, instead. And that's what they did.''

Dylan swore, and Ellen looked at her nephew intently. "I couldn't have stopped 'em. I was wrong about Caitlin, Dylan. She's got guts like a lion's got teeth. I'm sorry.''

The paramedics tended Thomas on the library floor, while Dylan paced. Thomas refused to be taken to the hospital, despite the fact that his head could use a dozen stitches. Someone had clobbered him from behind with a heavy brass lamp. He was lucky to be breathing. Barnes had set up roadblocks, but he'd grimly predicted they would do little good. He said he had a feeling these people were pros. Cold-blooded criminals who'd done this kind of thing before. Otherwise, they'd never have managed to avoid the squad car that had been patrolling the area. He had men working on that angle back at the station. Doing something he called "profiling" and comparing the facts in this case with others like it via the NCIC computer network. But finding a match would take time.

He'd also predicted the pair hadn't just taken Caitlin on a lark. They would want something, probably demand something, for her return. And he was right.

The call came at midnight. Dylan waited for Barnes's signal before picking up. He was to keep them on the line for the tracers. But they were one step ahead.

"We have her. We'll kill her. One million, Rossi. By this time tomorrow night, or she's dead.''

Barnes had told Dylan what to expect, but hearing the words was like a knife in his heart. He swore he felt his blood cool to a frigid chill. The man on the phone sounded nothing like Henri. "Let me talk to her.''

"Just get the money.''

"Not until I hear her voice," Dylan insisted. "How do I know she's not already dead?"

"Listen close, then."

Dylan closed his eyes as Caitlin's scream filled the phone line. They'd hurt her. His fear, his sick worry changed form and solidified into rage. The bastards were going to pay for this.

"Good enough?" The voice he barely recognized came back. He could still hear Caitlin sobbing in the background.

"Don't hurt her. I'll get the money."

"Good."

Barnes was making a stretching motion with his hands. He had to keep them on the line longer. He couldn't fail Caity now. "Uh, where should I bring it?"

"I'll call you tomorrow night. Same time. And tell the cops they're wasting their time. I know how long it takes to trace a call." The loud click in his ear told Dylan they'd hung up. He shot a glance to Barnes, who only shook his head.

"Damn!"

Henri turned off the cellular phone, glanced menacingly at the stubby black stun gun in his hand and then smiled at Caitlin. She couldn't move. She lay on the tilting, swaying floor, where she'd hit hard, every muscle limp, trembling. If he came at her again with that snapping, crackling menace, she wouldn't be able to get away.

But he didn't. He flicked a button and put the thing in his shirt pocket. Then he bent, gripped her shoulders and hauled her to her feet. "Sorry. But your hubby wanted to hear your voice. Think you yelled loud enough for him? Hmm? I do. He sounded damned frantic before I hung up. Guess you were telling the truth about that much, anyway. He doesn't hate you."

She closed her eyes as he shoved her into a padded seat. She heard his footsteps retreating. He trotted up the shallow steps, through the open hatch and onto the deck. Then the hatch slammed down.

He wasn't Henri. It was as though a different being had come in and taken over Henri's body. Not only had his accent vanished, his entire manner was altered. The way he walked, moved, his facial expressions. He was no longer the devoted servant, or the hopeful admirer. He was mean, angry and ruthless.

But why? My God, why had he changed so drastically? And Genevieve. She seemed like a street thug now, instead of the sweet, timid woman Caitlin remembered. Why was she doing this? She'd worked for Caitlin's parents...

"I'm leaving, Scott. I know all about you and our maid..."

Her mother's voice, twisted with pain, came to her like a ghost from the past. Caitlin was eighteen, and had left for school, but had forgotten her American history text-book, and returned for it. Only to hear things she wasn't meant to hear. Learn things she'd never wanted to know.

"...and the other women, too. I know about all of them. I'm leaving today."

Caitlin burst into the den, where her parents were talk-ing. Daddy stood, pacing the gray pile carpet, his face tor-mented. He turned abruptly at her sudden appearance. Mother remained sitting, stiff-backed, in the Queen Anne chair.

"It isn't true, Mom. Daddy would never—"

"Caity, what are you doing here? This wasn't meant for you to —"

"It's a lie!" Caitlin screamed the words at her mother. "You're making it up—or, or, someone else is telling you things that aren't true. It's a lie, isn't it, Daddy?"

She turned her tear-filled eyes toward her father whom she adored beyond reason. He moved toward her slowly, not easily, due to his rounded middle. "Of course it isn't true. Your mother is just upset, Cait. Go on to school now, and all this will be settled by the time you get home—''

''No, it won't.'' Sarah O'Brien rose with liquid grace. *''You're practically an adult now, Caity. You're old enough to draw your own conclusions. I won't beg you to believe me. I'm leaving. I'll be gone when you get home today. If you want to come with me, you're welcome…''* She paused there, huge brown eyes searching Caitlin's, with no trace of hope in them. *''But I don't imagine you do.''*

''How can you do this? How can you break up our family this way?'' Caitlin wailed and cried and threw a fit, but her mother only shook her head slowly.

''It wasn't my decision, it was his. I have no choice about it. I love you, Caity.''

Caitlin blinked at the sudden onslaught of memory. It was like a riptide, dragging her out to sea. There was so much going on, so much she ought to be thinking about, doing, planning. But all she could do was remember that final confrontation between her parents, feel incredible remorse over her own choice to believe her lying father. God, she'd worshiped that man.

She turned her mother's accusations over in her mind now. She knew they'd been true. She wasn't certain how she knew it or when she'd learned it. It must have been later, because she'd certainly been in denial then.

I know about you and our maid.

Genevieve had worked for them then. But so had a half-dozen other women, most of them young and attractive. And even if Caitlin had believed her father had been sleeping with one of them, she would never have suspected Genevieve. Genevieve was her friend, even though she only remained with them for a few months. She'd moved to another job shortly after the divorce. Caitlin hadn't seen her again until years later, when she'd been looking for domestic help in her own household, and Genevieve had shown up at her door with her charismatic brother in tow.

"How do I know all this?" She shook herself, shook off the lingering effects of the paralyzing jolt of electricity that had so recently hammered through her body, and tried to analyze her newfound knowledge. She didn't remember the pertinent facts in a flashback or a visual image playing in her mind, the way she did that conversation between her father and her mother. No, she just *knew*. The information simply surfaced in her mind like a buoyant object released from underwater. Suddenly, it was just there.

And what else?

She searched her mind for more of the jigsaw pieces of her past. They were there. She could *feel* them there, just out of reach. Their familiar auras reaching out to her, teasing her, luring her, taunting her. God, she wanted her life to be whole again.

But first and foremost, she needed to be sure she would *have* a life. And that meant putting her past out of her mind, and concentrating on survival in the present. Regardless of what was motivating Genevieve and Henri, the dilemma was the same. She was their prisoner, their captive, and she had serious doubts they intended for her to leave their imprisonment alive.

Especially when Dylan refused to come across with the money. Because he wouldn't pay it. He couldn't. He didn't have that much money, and there was no way he could come up with it in time. The only way Dylan could get that much cash would be to put the business up as collateral.

And that was out of the question. He'd built that company from the ground up, and he wouldn't risk losing it to save the life of a woman he hated. Oh, he'd try to get her back. Caitlin had no doubt about that. He'd have every cop and private investigator he could get on her trail. He'd agree to pay the ransom, and he'd try to get her out alive. Because he was her husband, and he seemed to take that role seriously. He was a man of honor. He wouldn't let his worst enemy die if he could do something to prevent it.

The problem was, she didn't think he could prevent it. Not this time.

And she wouldn't want him to lose his business to save her. It was too great a price to pay for a woman who'd hurt him the way she had. She wouldn't allow it.

She wanted to get away on her own, just to be sure Dylan wouldn't do something foolish. She got to her feet. They hadn't tied her up. She was only locked into the cramped living quarters of a boat. It was a small space, lined on one side with a pair of wooden cupboards, above a two-burner propane cooking center, and a minuscule sink that could have been straight out of a child's playhouse. Below that, more cupboards. On the port side, a high bunk that was now folded to lie flat to the wall. Below was a table and two bench-type seats. Toward the bow, two more bunks, and in the stern, a tiny door that led to a bathroom smaller than a bread box.

She explored the entire area in a matter of minutes. In the bathroom, no hair spray or razors she might use to defend herself. Damn. She searched the galley and found the barest food supply in the cupboards and a little more in the twenty-four-square-inch refrigerator. She checked cupboards, then the two drawers that slid open after a bit of tugging. She found a small, sharp steak knife with a serrated edge. Her fist clenched around its plastic, fake wood-grain handle.

The hatch was flung open with a loud bang that seemed to rip through her nerves with an edge more jagged than the blade in her hand. She whirled, closing the drawer and slipping the knife into the folds of her nightgown, still holding it as inconspicuously as she could manage, just as Genevieve reached the lowest step and met her gaze with a curious, suspicious stare.

"What're you doing?"

458   Kiss of the Shadow Man

Without the French accent, her voice wasn't sultry, it was coarse. She sounded rougher than sandpaper. "Nothing. I...I was hungry."

Genevieve's eyes narrowed, scanning the cupboards behind Caitlin. "Si'down. You eat when we do."

Caitlin nodded, and hurried back to her former chair. Genevieve passed her on her way to the cupboards, to whip them open and scan the contents. Caitlin stiffened when Genevieve opened the drawers. Would she miss the knife? God, what would she do if she knew Caitlin had taken it?

Genevieve closed the drawer at last, and turned toward Caitlin. The suspicion was gone from her eyes. She hadn't missed the knife.

"Your hubby is going to pay up. You won't be here long."

"How long?"

Genevieve shrugged. "Thirty-six hours at the outside."

"And if he doesn't get the cash?"

"He will. They always get the cash, honey. He's scared out of his mind right now. He'll come through, don't you worry."

Caitlin frowned. "You talk like you've done this before."

Rather than ashamed, she looked proud. Her chin rose a little. "That's 'cause I have."

"How many times?"

Her delicate brows rose. "You really wanna know? You talkin' kidnappings?" Caitlin nodded, feeling as if she were talking to a stranger, a street thug in tight black jeans and a skimpy purple bustier. Her accent sounded like Brooklyn. "You're the fourth."

"And all the others paid?"

"Every nickel. An' we got away clean every time. I tol' you, we're pros."

"And the other...hostages. You released them unharmed?"

Her lids lowered to half mast. "Yeah. Sure we did." She poked a hand into a high cupboard and retrieved a pack of cigarettes. She shook one loose, caught it from the pack in her lips and pulled it slowly out. She held the pack toward Caitlin, but Caitlin shook her head. Shrugging, Genevieve tossed the pack down, and twisted a knob on the stove. She turned, putting her back fully to Caitlin, and bending low to light the cigarette from the burner.

Now, Caitlin thought. Just get up, take the knife and jam it into her back. The thought made her stomach turn. She didn't move, and then Genevieve was facing her again, sucking on the filter, holding the slender white cylinder between two fingers tipped in elaborately decorated nails, and blowing the smoke slowly out.

"Why were you trying so hard to kill me?"

She wasn't aware she was going to ask the question. When it came out, it surprised her, and apparently, it surprised Genevieve, as well.

"You sure it was me? What makes you so certain it wasn't your lovin' man all along, hmm?"

"It wasn't Dylan."

Genevieve tilted her head, and shrugged. "Bigger payoff. You underground, him in jail and your brother wrapped around me like a clinging vine. We could have had it all."

"You and Henri?"

Genevieve threw back her head and laughed, a guttural, throaty sound. "It's Hank. And I'm Jen. I have about as much French in me as a two-dollar bottle of wine, Madame Rossi." She affected her old accent with the last two words, and laughed as if she hadn't had such a good joke in a long time.

Caitlin just shook her head. "That's quite a leap, from kidnapping to murder. And such a convoluted plan. What made you think it would work?"

Genevieve—Jen—narrowed her eyes and sent Caitlin a silent message.

"My God, you've done that before, too?"

She drew again on the cigarette, blew smoke rings and shrugged. "Didn't say that."

Caitlin frowned, the scope of their plotting hitting her hard. "How long have you been…" She didn't know what word to put at the end of the sentence. "Were you…even when you worked for my father?"

"Your parents' marriage was in trouble. It was all over the social grapevine."

"And those are the kinds of households you like to get into, where the marriage is in trouble?"

"You're putting words in my mouth, honey."

"And you were planning the same kind of thing with my parents?"

"I managed to get your old man in the sack when it looked like they might patch things up. It was easy to make sure she found out about it. The stupid bitch walked out without a fuss, though. Didn't demand even a nickel. That screwed things up big-time. I mean, your old man had no motive. Who'd believe he'd done it? And then the old bastard fired me before I could think of an alternate plan. He didn't want his little girl to ever know about our fun and games. God, you were blind to that sleaze-bag. Thought he made the world and everything in it just so you'd have a nice place to live, didn't you?"

Cait swallowed hard. "For a while."

"Yeah. The sweet little princess found out what a bastard her old man really was…and then she turned into a frog."

Caitlin frowned and searched the woman's face. "What do you mean by that?"

Jen shook her head, her short, slick hair not moving. "Nothin'. I wasn't around then. I'm just repeating what I heard. When I left your daddy's house, you were a nice kid. I even liked you, as much as I like anybody. When I met you later, in your own house, you were an arrogant bitch. I guess after your mother offed herself and your idol got knocked off his pedestal, you lost your innocence, hmm?''

Caitlin shook her head, eyes wide, searching inwardly to make sense of all this. "I don't know.''

Jen glanced down at the glowing end of the stub she held, dropped it into the sink and rinsed it down the drain. "Yeah well, neither do I.'' She nodded toward the bunks in the stern. "You might as well get some sleep. Nothing's happening tonight.''

Cait shook her head. "I'll never sleep.''

And she didn't. She was sure they were going to kill her, anyway, when they got the ransom, no matter what they said. Jen wouldn't have admitted to so many other crimes if she planned to leave her alive to testify against them.

Jen went above and Caitlin laid on the hard little bunk, and tried not to listen to the sounds overhead, a short time later. Sounds that made her sure they were not brother and sister.

Dawn. All night they'd worked, staying in touch with the station by phone, and using the fax in Dylan's home office to send files back and forth. Dylan slugged back so much coffee he was practically floating in it. He drank it mindlessly, just to have something to do with his hands.

And then he heard Barnes say softly, "We have a hit.''

Dylan spun to see Barnes scanning the sheets that had just come through the fax. "Tell me.''

"Nine years ago, a couple name Hank and Jennifer Korbett were employed in the Garner household, in Bangor, Maine. They'd been working there for a little over a year, when Mrs. Garner was murdered. Hit and run. Her husband's car. They were in the middle of a divorce at the time. She'd been pushing for a big settlement, and that was his motive. He was tried and convicted in the death of his wife.''

"But it wasn't him, was it, Barnes?"

Barnes shook his head. "Before his mother's body was cold, the surviving son, and heir to everything, Preston Garner, married Jenny Korbett, the family maid. A week later, his body was found in a ravine. All his accounts had been drained, and Jenny and Hank had disappeared. The partial print we found on that scrap of cloth belonged to Jenny Korbett, alias—"

"Genevieve Dupres," Dylan muttered.

"She's not even French. They're both from Brooklyn."

"So they've been planning to murder Cait, and pin it on me."

"Looks like," Barnes replied. "Then Jenny would marry Thomas, get him to put her name on his accounts, which by then ought to have included all of your wife's money. Then he probably would've suffered the same fate as the Garner kid."

"But it didn't work. Cait didn't die."

"Don't feel too relieved, there's no doubt in my mind that they have an alternate plan. They have a list of priors as long as my arm. Lots of cons, three kidnapping charges—Maine, Boston, Jersey. Their mugs have been on display in every post office in the Northeast. But they were both blond and from Brooklyn. No one was looking for a dark-haired pair of French siblings. They've never been brought to trial. They're wanted in eight states for various crimes. Three of them are murder charges."

"Which three?" Dylan knew just by the way Barnes's gaze fell. "The kidnappings, right? They killed their hostages, whether the ransom was paid or not, didn't they, Barnes?"

His lips tightening to a thin line, Barnes nodded once.

Dylan couldn't stay at home, restless, powerless. Guilt-ridden. The thought that he'd ever believed he could be better off without Caity in his life kept haunting him. Was some greater force trying to show him exactly what hell that would be, or was it one of those cases where you got what you wished for, and regretted it for the rest of your life? It didn't matter that she didn't love him, didn't trust him, didn't want to be with him. All that mattered was that she live. She deserved to live. If he had to lose her, if he'd already lost her, he'd find a way to deal with it. But not like this. He wouldn't lose her like this.

He huddled with Detective Barnes—Jack, now—in front of his desk at the station, and together they pored over the histories of Jenny and Hank Korbett, charge by charge, case by case, hour after hour, amid the strong aromas of coffee, and correction fluid and pencil shavings.

Dylan swilled his fourth cup of strong, mudlike coffee, and went over the list of assets Jenny had wound up with after Preston Garner's death. She'd managed to liquidate $1.5 million in stocks right after the heir's murder. An estimated $250,000 in cash, once she'd closed out all the accounts. A Mercedes and a Vette, both brand-new. A cabin cruiser, and a half-dozen pieces of art worth a cool 500 grand if she could hawk them.

"You suppose they sold all this stuff?"

"What?"

"Paintings, cars, boat. If they did, they should have been rolling in money. Why risk it all for more?"

Jack shrugged and sipped his cold coffee, grimacing.

"Greed. The cars turned up in Jersey. A few of the paintings have been recovered, as well, but not all."

"And the boat?"

Jack shook his head. "Nope, not a sign of it."

Dylan's lips thinned. He closed the folder, and reached for another, hoping to find some clue that would help him get Caity out of the Korbetts' hands and back home, safe, with him.

Instead, he found only a grim trail of death behind the two, littering their path like bread crumbs. In all three kidnappings—the little girl in Cape May, New Jersey, the old man stricken with Alzheimer's they'd taken from his rich family in Bar Harbor, and the new young bride of a business tycoon in Boston—the hostages had been killed. All in the same horribly efficient manner, even though the ransom demanded had been paid. A single bullet, fired at close range, dead center of their foreheads. The thought of Caity, looking down the barrel of that gun, knowing she was about to die, gave him anger, fury that knew no bounds. He'd kill them if they hurt her. He'd kill them.

"Rossi?"

Dylan blinked and faced Barnes.

"You okay?"

He shook his head. "Far from it."

"Well, it's almost nine. You ought to get to the bank, see about raising the ransom."

Dylan nodded, but his eyes strayed back to the folder on the desk. "They killed the others. The families paid and they killed them, anyway. We both know that."

"I know, Rossi. But knowing that, maybe we can strike a better deal. Get them to bring her to us, and trade even up, instead of arranging a drop."

Dylan shook his head. "You don't believe that any more than I do."

The look in Jack's cornflower blue eyes was enough to confirm it without words, but there was something else there, too. A determined stubbornness that wouldn't be banked by the fear. "We'll get her back alive."

"I wish I could be as sure of that as you are."

"I'm not sure, just damned determined. I like your wife, Rossi. She reminds me of someone...someone I knew once. I've been a cop a long time, but I've never wanted to protect a victim the way I want to protect her. And I've never wanted to collar any two-bit slug the way I want to collar these two. It's gonna happen. Count on it."

Dylan tried to believe in the light he saw in Jack Barnes's eyes, but found it difficult. He shook his head. "I don't know. It's like—" His throat closed off. "Dammit." He blinked and averted his face.

"I know what you're going through, Rossi."

"The hell you do."

A heavy hand fell on his shoulder. "My wife...I lost her two years ago. I *know*."

Dylan looked up slowly, saw the brittle, sad smile of encouragement. "Maybe you do." He sighed, a short, shallow rasp. "Dammit, Jack, for the past two years, all I've wanted was another chance with her. I prayed and fought and groped for the old Caity, the one I loved. The one I still love. Only I gave up too soon, and when the chance finally came, I was too freaking blind and bitter to see it. Now she's gone. I had her back and didn't even know it, and now she's gone."

His eyes burned. Oddly enough, he felt no shame at that. Jack slapped his shoulder hard. "Come on, I'll drive you to the bank. We'll talk this through, brainstorm, maybe come up with something. And on the way back, we'll stop for a good solid belt, hmm? I think we both could use one."

"It isn't a belt I need, Jack. It's a miracle."

"Get up." The hands that shook her shoulders were soft, small and brutal. "Get up, Caitlin. It's time for breakfast."

Caitlin blinked reality into focus. She'd been engrossed in a dream so vivid, it was hard to believe it hadn't been real. She'd been with Dylan, on that beach in the cove, with nothing between their heated bodies but gritty sand and saltwater. And he'd told her that he loved her. That he'd always love her, no matter what.

A tight fist squeezed her heart, and the tears wrung from that organ leaked into her eyes, filling them. She shook herself, and sat up. She was still wearing her torn, dirty nightgown. The knife tucked in the waistband of her panties had made for a restless night. But she'd have slept little, anyway. Barefoot, she got up, and moved toward the table.

"Not there," Jen said, her voice sharp and too loud. "The stove's on the other side. There are eggs and cheese in the fridge. Get to it. We're starved."

She glanced at the woman, saw the hardness in her eyes and understood. She recalled her own words about the mistress serving the maid. Genevieve must have liked the idea. Seen it as poetic justice. Well, okay. She could deal with that. "Can I use the bathroom first?"

"Make it quick."

Caitlin nodded and closed herself in the tiny cubicle. She quickly searched the inside of the minuscule medicine cabinet there, but found only aspirin tablets, sun block and an antiseptic ointment. No sleeping pills. Nothing that she might slip into their damned breakfast to render them harmless while she tried to escape. She emerged frowning, disappointed, grimly certain her time on this planet was nearing its end.

She couldn't remember the last time she'd told Dylan she loved him. She'd wanted to say it when they'd made love, when he'd held her so tenderly in his arms. But she hadn't. God, why hadn't she? She might never get the chance again.

She moved to the fridge and found the eggs and the cheese. She cracked the fragile shells one by one, and dropped their contents into a bowl. Her heart sinking lower with every stroke, she stirred.

"I'm willing to put the business up as collateral."

The banker, Frederick R. Pembroke, leaned back in his chair. "You don't own the entire company, Mr. Rossi."

"Fifty-one percent is well worth what I need."

Pembroke nodded, and fingered the few threads of oiled-down, dark hair that were combed to cover the bald spot in the middle of his head. "I'm aware of that. And I'm sure the loan can be approved, but to get you this amount of cash by the end of the day is nearly impossible."

Dylan shot to his feet. "Listen, you pompous little twit, my wife—"

Jack gripped Dylan's arms just as he would have reached across the desk to choke the man. Pembroke had jerked backward, slamming the chair and the back of his greasy head into the wall behind him.

"Mr. Pembroke, a woman's life is at stake here. I'm willing to personally guarantee this bank that the money will be repaid, if that's what it takes, but we need the cash today."

"Or they'll kill her," Dylan said. The words were low, soft and steady. "Make no mistake, Pembroke, they'll kill her."

"Surely that's an exaggeration."

"These people are wanted in connection with several other murders," Jack said calmly. "They have nothing to lose."

"And if she dies because you refuse the money, I'll come back here, Pembroke," Dylan told him, standing straighter, shaking Jack's restraining hands from his shoulders.

"Easy, Rossi." Jack glanced across the desk. "Can you

do it or not? There are other banks in town, and we don't have all day.''

Pembroke drew a series of short breaths, his eyes darting around the office, anywhere but on Dylan's face. "I'll try. We have two other branches in nearby towns. I ought to be able to get the cash between the three.''

"How soon?'' Dylan wanted to walk out of here with the money right now.

Pembroke glanced at his watch. "Before closing, certainly. I'll call you when you can pick it up.''

Dylan nodded, yanked a business card from his wallet and tossed it onto the desk. It had his home and office numbers. "If I'm not there, you can reach me at the police station.''

He turned and stalked out of the banker's plush office. He wanted to kick something, or slam the door so hard, the bastard's false teeth would rattle. But he didn't. He stalked all the way to Jack's car, and got in.

"How 'bout that drink?'' Jack asked when he slid behind the wheel.

"How 'bout a couple?''

"You want to run home first. Change, shower? You look like hell.''

"Screw it. I don't really give a damn how I look right now.''

Jack sighed and pulled into traffic. Two blocks down, he turned again, into the parking lot of an apartment building. Dylan had expected a bar, but said nothing. He got out and followed Jack through a foyer, to an elevator. They got off at the sixth floor, and the detective opened a door and ushered him in.

"It's a shack compared to your place, but...''

Dylan walked in, barely noticing the decor, caring even less. He heard the ice chinking into the glasses, the gurgle of liquid. He smelled the whiskey. He saw none of it, though. He'd paused in front of a framed 8x10 color photo of a woman. A beautiful woman with shining emerald green eyes and long, wildly curling auburn hair. Her chin was pointy, rather than blunt like Caity's, and her nose was slightly larger. Her cheekbones were nowhere near as high, or regal, but there was no mistaking the similarities.

"She was tiny, too. Not short, but just…delicate, slender. I always loved that about her." Jack pressed a cool glass into Dylan's hand.

"Your wife?"

"Yeah. Holly. Perfect name, don't you think? Red and green?"

Dylan nodded. He tore his gaze away from the beautiful face and saw the stark agony in Barnes's gaze. "What happened?"

"Boating accident." He didn't elaborate.

"Here?"

Barnes shook his head. "We were visiting her family in Boston. Got plugged by a yacht full of drunken idiots driving on the wrong side, no lights. The bastards."

Dylan said nothing. Barnes tossed back a healthy slug of whiskey, licked his lips and went on. "I tried to find her. I knew she couldn't swim. Still, with the life jacket, I figured…" He closed his eyes. "It wasn't the water, though. She took a blow to the head on the way in. There wasn't a damn thing I could do for her."

"God." Dylan tilted his own glass to his lips, closing his eyes as the burn moved down his throat, spread heat in his belly. "I'm sorry, Jack." There was something tickling the fringes of his consciousness. Something Jack had said, setting little bells off in his mind, but he couldn't put his finger on it.

"Wish to hell we'd never gone to Boston that summer."

Boston.

"One of the kidnappings happened in Boston, didn't it?" Mentally, Dylan recounted the cases, the scams, the murders. "Boston, Bar Harbor. Where was the other one? Some cape or other. Dammit, Jack, do you see the pattern?"

The detective blinked and faced Dylan, his gaze no longer blank and stark, but sharp, piercing. "The northeast?"

"The coast. They were all on the Atlantic coast. Everything since the rich couple and their son were murdered has been on the coast. And you said Hank and Jen got a boat out of that one."

Jack whistled, and his nod was quick and decisive. "Ten to one that's where they're holding her. Off the coast on that boat. You ever think of goin' into police work, Rossi?"

Dylan shook his head. "Not on your life. What do we do now?"

The storm hit with a vengeance. The wind moaned and howled around the boat, and the waves tossed it with a violence Caitlin was certain would be the end of all of them. She clung to the bunk, facedown, and tried not to feel the nausea, the dizziness, the stark fear. But she felt it all the same.

"Don't look so damned terror-stricken. We've seen worse."

Hank's words didn't even put a dent in the haze surrounding her mind. She was sick. She was scared. God, she wanted Dylan. Needed him.

Waves slapped the boat, battered it until it shuddered with the force. Thunder rolled over the sea toward them, reverberating through the wood and into her soul.

"Look, maybe we oughta take it in. Tie up somewhere till it passes."

"For God's sake, Jen—"

"It's getting worse," she said in a firm, authoritative voice. "Let's just take it in."

"We weather it. We'll be fine. We get near shore, Jen, and we might be spotted. It isn't worth the risk."

"She's sick."

Hank's gaze moved to Caitlin, and she felt him staring in disdain. "So what?"

Caitlin lurched to her feet, groping for things to hold on to as she made her way to the toilet with the floor pitching beneath her feet. She pulled the door shut and fell to her knees, retching. God, what a time to be seasick. How could she plan or maneuver to keep herself alive when she felt this badly?

When she could stand again, she found a cloth and washed her face. She reached for the door.

"Whadda you care how sick she is? It isn't like she's gonna get better."

"She could."

"Dammit, Jen—"

"She *could!* We don't have to do it that way. Not this time, Hank."

"She knows us."

"So does everybody else in that family. They don't need her to tell 'em who did this. We don't have to do it this time, Hank."

"We do if I say we do. She knows about the boat. They'd be one step ahead of us next time."

"We don't need any next time. We have enough. God, can't we just quit this crap? Settle down somewhere? Rio, like we always planned."

"No. Just a couple more jobs, and then—"

"It's always just a couple more!" The words were shrieked at him, and Caitlin stiffened when she heard the ringing slap of a hand on skin, and Jen's startled cry. "You know what I think?" She was whispering now, harshly, loudly, but the words were punctuated by sobs. "I think you like the killing. I think you enjoy it and I think you only want her dead 'cause you couldn't get her into bed. That thing with the rope and the noose in the cemetery, when you know that's how her mother checked out—that was just to torture her. Just so you could get your kicks. You're sick, Hank, and gettin' worse all the time.''

"Think what you want, bitch. I'm callin' the shots, and you better not forget it again. Or maybe I'll be flying to Rio alone.'' There was a short pause. "We stick out the storm, and then we kill her. Enough said.''

Jen didn't answer.

"Another damned storm. I hate when it blows up like this."

Her mother's voice seemed to echo from the depths of her memory as Caitlin huddled on the bunk again later, feigning sleep amid the tossing waves and howling wind, waiting for Hank to place the call, praying he'd let her talk to Dylan before he killed her.

"But I won't see another one. Thank God for that at least. I'm through with storms."

Caitlin frowned as the memory solidified in her mind. She'd held the telephone receiver in her hand, felt the sweat of her palm making it slick. She'd slowly gone cold all over as it clicked and went silent. There'd been something in her mother's voice.

Caitlin had never believed her, never accepted that what her mother claimed had been true. Her adored father couldn't have, wouldn't have done the things she claimed. And if he was tightfisted after the divorce, it was only because he was hurt. Mom had ruined their family, torn them apart. Daddy was angry. That was all.

Still, visions of the squalor in which her mother lived had haunted her. And now the sound of despair in her voice. She was alone, in that little apartment. And Caitlin knew she had to go to her, make amends, try to mend the break in their mother/daughter bond.

And Dylan was at work, just like always. Aunt Ellen was already in bed, asleep. So she had to face it alone. She climbed into her modest car, a Mustang with one black door and one blue one, and rust spots everywhere, and drove through the deluge, wipers beating helplessly, to her mother.

Caitlin blinked as the memories rushed through her. Something told her she didn't want to know any more, some secret dread that lived in her soul. But she saw all of it, anyway. The dingy hallway, the peeling wallpaper, chipped plaster. She even smelled the mildew, the damp plaster, the rotting wood, as she climbed the dim stairs and knocked on the door of her mother's apartment.

But there was no answer, so she tried the knob. And it gave, and she went inside.

And there was a creaking sound, and she turned. Her mother's body swung very slowly from the end of a rope. Her head hung limp, chin to chest, auburn hair veiling her face. Plaster dust sprinkled from the ceiling into her hair. The light fixture she'd tied the rope to wasn't going to hold much longer.

Caitlin moved forward, slowly, as if in a trance. She reached up only slightly, and touched her mother's hand. It was cool. Not cold. Not yet. The two-hour drive had taken too long. Caitlin should've called the police. She should've called a neighbor. Anything. She could have prevented this.

She backed away, her chest heaving, wanting only to find Dylan, to feel his arms holding her tight, to feel his love surround and comfort her.

But there was something else, a small white envelope with her name scrawled across the front. She picked it up, opened it, and read with tear-blurred eyes.

It was all true, Caity. Oh, I don't blame you for not believing me. I know you love your father. I loved him, too. Don't blame yourself for this. You couldn't have known. It's him. He brought me to this. And I'm only writing to warn you, baby, because they're all the same. No matter how much they claim to love you at first, in the end it's always the same. I see the signs already, for you, my poor, trusting Caity. The late hours, the missed dinners, the nights he doesn't come home at all. He'll take everything you have to give him, Caity, and then you'll end up just like me. Alone. And in too much pain for a human to bear. You'll see.

Prepare yourself, Caity. Don't depend on him for your happiness. Find a way to make your own. Don't give your entire soul to him the way I did to your father. He'll only throw it away. Please, don't let this happen to you.

Don't trust that man with your heart.

The letter hadn't been signed. But it had stamped itself on her heart. And in the morning, when Dylan had returned home after a long night at the office, she found she no longer craved the feel of the comfort his arms would offer. She never even told him about her midnight trip, or that she'd found her mother's body. Or about the note.

Because from that day on, it had become fairly obvious that her mother had been right. The late hours, the all-nighters. He was lying to her. She knew it, and she withdrew from him as much as she could manage. And the coldness she gave began to filter back to her, and the distance between them grew.

And then Daddy died, she thought in silence, and I had his money to cling to instead of my husband. Oh, God, how could I have been so stupid?

"Hank, it's twelve-thirty."

"I know what time it is. I want the bastard to squirm a little before I talk to him. You got a problem with that?"

Cait opened her eyes in time to see Jen shake her head quickly.

"You know, bitch, you're starting to be more trouble than you're worth."

Chapter 17

"They're late." Dylan slammed a fist into the wall beside the window. He'd been staring pensively into the storm-ravaged night, conjuring images of a splintered ship, of Caity's slender hands clinging to a jagged bit of wood until she couldn't hang on any longer. Of her face, pale and nearly lifeless, slipping away beneath the angry sea.

He forced the images away and whirled on Jack. "What the hell does it mean?"

"It means they want to make you crazy. Looks like it's working, isn't it, Rossi?"

"Damn straight it is."

Thomas paced. He'd been pacing for an hour now, and it didn't look as if he planned to stop anytime soon. His path was precise and repetitive and it was driving Dylan nuts.

"Calm down, Rossi. We have their coordinates. They're anchored less that ten minutes out. The Coast Guard's ready to move out the second this storm breaks, and when Hank calls, you're going to buy us enough time to last that long."

Ellen came in, carrying a pot of fresh coffee. She scuffed over the tiled floor looking weary, her housecoat floating just above her stretchy slippers. Jack held up his cup, and Ellen filled it. "Any word yet?"

"Nothing. This brew of yours sure puts mine to sha—" He broke off as the telephone bleated like a lost lamb calling for its mother.

Thomas jerked as if electrocuted, and finally stood in one spot. Dylan lurched for the phone, jerking it out of its cradle hard enough to hurt his arm.

476 Kiss of the Shadow Man

"You have the money?"

"Yes. All of it."

"Very good. Now listen. Here's what I want you to do—"

"No, Hank. You listen. I know who you are, and I know what happened to your last three hostages. There's no way in hell I'm dropping this money anywhere, knowing you'll kill her, anyway."

"You don't have much choice, Rossi."

"I have one choice. I'll hang this phone up here and now. I'm not going to pay you to kill my wife."

There was a long moment of tense silence, and Dylan was terrified Hank would slam the phone down in his ear. Finally, his strange voice came back. "Talk."

Dylan's eyes met Jack's steady gaze. Jack shoved a scrap of paper at him. *Get them out of the water.*

"I want you to meet me...in the parking garage below my offices in Eden. And I want you to bring Caitlin. If I don't see her there, alive and well, then the deal's off. You hear me? We'll trade then. The money for Caity. You can take the cash and go, I won't try to stop you just as long as she's all right."

"Sounds like you have this all figured out."

Dylan licked his lips, swallowed the sand in his throat. "Unless you've already..." He couldn't say it. And he couldn't demand to talk to her, because he was afraid Hank would hurt her again. Make her scream in pain as he'd done last time.

"She's still alive." Hank muttered something, but had his hand over the mouthpiece, from the sound of it. When he came back, Dylan's hopes plummeted. "No deal. Forget it, Rossi. You can do this my way, or I'll off her as soon as I hang up the phone. What's it gonna be?"

"If you don't want to meet there, pick your own place. It doesn't matter where, as long as she's with you." Dylan felt desperation making his palms itch, his hands sweat.

"Bring the money to the cliffs, at dawn. I'll be watching you, so don't bring any cops with you. The first badge I see will be your wife's death warrant. Leave it in that little hollow the tide's made in the stone. You know where I mean?"

"Yes."

"Good. After I have it, after I've counted it, and I'm well out of reach, I'll call and tell you where to find your lady. All right?"

"No, it's not all right, you bastard. How do I know you won't kill her, anyway?"

"You don't. You only know that if the money isn't there, I will definitely kill her. Sweet dreams, Rossi."

He hung up. Dylan growled deep in his throat, tore the phone from the table and smashed it onto the floor. Pieces flew in a hundred directions.

"My God," Thomas muttered.

"They're gonna kill her. Dammit, Jack, they're gonna do it. We have to move now."

"Rossi, the storm—"

"They're out in it. They're still afloat. Dammit, Jack, we can't wait. You know it as well as I do. We have their location. It's time to move in. You can either come with me or I'll go by myself, but I'm going out there."

Hank slung the cellular phone across the table, and rubbed his hands together. "He'll do it. He'll pay. I could hear the fear in his voice. He's already figured it out, you know. He knows about the others. Practically begged me not to…" His voice trailed off, but he inclined his head toward Caitlin.

Jen looked at the floor. "Then don't. We don't have to—"

"We don't need her anymore. The money will be waiting in the morning, and we can take it and go. We don't need her for a damn thing."

"Hank—"

He pulled out his gun, and turned toward the bunk to waggle it at Caitlin. "Come on. We're going up on deck. Get some air."

"No...please, I—"

"Hank, stop it! I've had it with your sick games. I can't do it anymore."

He stood stock-still for a long moment. Caitlin clung to the knife hidden in the waistband of her panties, trembling inside because she knew the time had come and she was sure she wouldn't survive this.

Hank turned to face Jen. "So it's over, is it? You can't do it anymore?"

"I just...I hate the killing. I hate it, Hank. I can't— Hank?"

His arm lifted, and without a second's hesitation, he pulled the trigger. The blast was deafening in the closed-in area. Jen's head slammed backward as if she'd been punched, and then she was on the floor. Caitlin lunged from the bed, no longer thinking her actions through as terror took over. She would be next, she knew. She lifted the knife over her head, and brought it down in a deadly arc. The blade sunk into flesh, scraped against bone, and Hank twisted away from her with the steak knife embedded between his shoulder blades, as the gun clattered to the floor.

"You filthy little bitch!" He reached behind him in a feeble attempt to pull the knife free, but couldn't do it. "You're dead..."

Cait dodged his long reach, her gaze darting from the woman on the floor with the small round hole in her forehead and the unseeing stare in her slowly glazing eyes, and the widening pool of dark red spreading beneath her, to the closed hatch at the top of the steps. She ran toward it, flung it open and emerged into the darkness. Sheets of icy water lashed her body, tore at her face, carried by brutal winds. Waves slammed the boat, rocking it crazily.

There was nowhere to go. She glanced frantically behind her, to see Hank making his way up the steps, hunched over, his white T-shirt soaked in blood, the small woodlike handle protruding from his back. She reached for the hatch, and as she did, he brought up one hand. God, he had the gun again.

The shot echoed through her psyche as she slammed the hatch. Pain sliced into her midriff like a white-hot iron. Falling to the side, she grappled with the latches, hooking them to keep him where he was. Then she dragged herself away, toward the rail, her hand pressed to her side.

She felt the warmth of the blood, saw its dark stain spreading over the nightgown, felt it running down her body, coating one leg as it soaked through the muslin, dripping to the deck. She was going to die.

She clung to the rail, leaning out over the rioting sea as if in search of some trace of hope. Something. Someone. *Dylan.*

A muffled crash brought her head around. Then another, and the hatch jumped from the force of it. Then another. He was battering the door with something. It wouldn't hold long. God, what could she do?

Again he hit the door, and again. The wood splintered. She cringed against the rail, moving backward farther from him, knowing there was no shelter, nowhere to hide.

One more crash and the hatch was swinging open. Panting, cursing, Hank emerged. He looked around as the vicious wind pummeled him. He couldn't see her. She crouched in the shadows near the bow, watching, water streaming over her, waves reaching for her as if to pull her into their frigid embrace.

Hank started forward, lifting the gun, his gaze narrow, searching, murderous. He'd find her sooner or later. And then he'd kill her.

Caitlin's hands clenched into fists, one against her bleeding side, the other on the watery deck. She bumped against something. A flotation device attached to the side. Her fingers fumbled to free it, careful not to make a sound. When she had the thing loose, she gripped it in shaking hands, whispered a prayer and threw it toward the starboard side.

The instant the ring landed, Hank fired a shot. She saw the flare of the gun in the inky, watery night. Silently, she crept backward, back against the rail, curving along the port side until she bumped another ring. She threw it, as well, drawing another shot.

"That's four," she whispered under cover of the wind. She'd had a good look at the gun. A better look than she'd ever wanted. A big revolver. And she assumed that meant it only held six bullets. "Two more. God, let me find two more." She scurried backward again, her side pulsing with pain, shivering from the cold wind and the brutal rain. He was coming toward her. She wasn't moving fast enough.

Turning, she gripped the rail and pulled herself upright. Clinging to it, she walked, but something hard tripped her and she fell facefirst onto the soaking deck. A shot rang out at the instant of impact, but she didn't think it had hit her. A swell smashed into the boat, lapping over onto the deck, dumping all over her body before fleeing back into the sea. She heard him coming closer, and dragged herself away. But she couldn't keep this up. The blood leaving her body so rapidly was weakening her, making her dizzy. Her movements slowed, and grew more clumsy and noisy with every inch of progress she made. And her killer was closing in.

"All right, hit the spotlight!"

The sudden illumination of the small boat just ahead caught Dylan completely off guard. He hadn't even known it was there. The Coast Guard cutter's crew knew it, though.

Dylan stood in the bow, wearing a dark blue rain slicker with the hood thrown back, heedless of the water cascading over his face, running down his neck, soaking his hair. Thomas stood beside him. He squinted in concentration as the spotlight swept over the deck of the smaller boat. Then Dylan saw her, lying facedown on the deck, and he saw Hank, lifting a gun, pointing at the woman the light had just illuminated for him.

Dylan's agonized scream pierced the night, even above Thomas's coarse cry, and the bullhorn-enhanced voice that ordered Hank to drop the weapon or be shot. But Hank didn't, and as the cutter charged the boat as if to split it in half, a shot rang out. Dylan wasn't sure if it came from Hank's gun or one of the officers. He feared the worst, because Hank didn't falter, or collapse, or even drop his gun. He looked at it, then tucked it into his waistband and advanced on Caitlin.

Dylan's heart leapt when he saw her move. She gripped the rail and pulled herself to her feet. She staggered forward, and the spotlight danced on the blood-soaked nightgown, as Hank grabbed her.

"Shoot the bastard!" Dylan shouted, but no shots rang out. They couldn't risk hitting Caitlin. Hank held her from behind. He whirled her around in a slow-motion dance even as he was ordered to let her go.

Dylan gaped in horror as he watched Caitlin being wrenched off her feet, then cried out in stark agony as her body hurtled over the rail and into the angry sea. Hank pulled out the gun again, lifted it toward the cutter and then his body jerked like a marionette on a twitching string, as countless rounds hammered into him. Slowly, he sank to his knees.

Dylan didn't know if he sank any farther, because he was ripping off the slicker he wore, and diving through the space between the deck and the raging sea below.

He heard Jack shouting his name just before his body knifed into the angry waters. He stroked under the surface, propelling himself onward with every ounce of power he possessed. When he broke surface, saltwater streaming down his face, into his eyes, he was near the smaller boat. He looked around him, seeing only swelling whitecaps, pelting rain, darkness.

"Caity!" He tread water, scanning the sea in all directions. "Caity, where are you?"

The spotlight moved until he was caught in its glow, then swept slowly past him, searching the water for her. Dylan followed it, stroking swiftly, pausing at intervals to search. He had to find her. She couldn't die. He couldn't lose her. Not again. It would kill him.

He heard the difference in the sounds of sluicing water, and turned to see the lifeboat that was fighting its way toward him. As it drew nearer, he recognized the man in the bow.

Jack leaned out, over the water, pointing, shouting. "Near the stern, Rossi. Over your left shoulder!"

Dylan turned and swam in that direction, but he didn't see her. The swells blocked his view of anything, being down in the water. "She's going down!" Jack roared. "Get that light on her! Can't this thing move—dammit, Rossi..."

Dylan crested a huge swell just in time to see her limp hand let go of the rope it had been clutching, and disappear beneath the black water.

"No!" He drew a deep breath and dove under, angling toward her, and seconds later, his outstretched hands bumped something soft and limp, something that was sinking past them, and they gripped, clung, lifted. He pulled her to his chest as his feet propelled them upward. When he broke surface, dragging air into his burning lungs, it was with Caitlin crushed to his chest as he held her head out of reach of the angry waters.

He searched her face, pale, milky white in the harsh and erratic glow of the spotlights. Her eyes were closed, her lips, blue-tinted. Strands of her wet hair, dark with seawater, stuck to her face and neck, and she remained motionless, perfectly limp in his arms.

Frantically, he pushed his forefingers to her throat in search of a pulse. But he couldn't be certain the hammering in his fingertips came from the rush of her blood, or the current of his own. He brought her face to his with one hand, fighting to keep them both afloat with the other. He covered her lips with his open mouth, parting them with his tongue. He blew life into her again and again, praying desperately for a response, dying a little with each second that passed without one.

The shouts of men, Jack's louder than any other, grew louder in those nightmarish seconds, and then there were hands groping, and a pair of other bodies in the water. Caitlin was lifted by the three men in the water. Jack and Thomas pulled her gently into the lifeboat, and by the time Dylan hauled himself over the side, the cop was already kneeling beside her, pumping her heart with two hands, counting aloud, blowing air into her lungs. And crying. As he worked, twin rivers formed on Jack's face, and he didn't even try to swipe them away. Maybe he wasn't even aware of them.

He worked frantically, and when Thomas, rain-soaked and utterly silent, moved forward to assist him, Jack waved him away with a short bark of a command.

The lifeboat headed back toward the cutter, slicing the rolling sea. Dylan slumped down beside his still, pale wife. He clutched one of her hands in both of his as a puddle formed around him. ''Don't die, Caity. Don't leave me like this.''

Thomas sat near her, too, but only stared at her, as though he couldn't believe what he was seeing.

Jack sat back on his heels, his fingers pressing into the soft skin of her throat, his eyes intent. Then he looked across her body, and met Dylan's desperate gaze. ''There's a pulse.'' The words were whispered so softly, Dylan wasn't sure he'd actually heard them. But then Jack cracked a wavering smile and said it again, louder. "There's a pulse!"

She drew a ragged, hoarse breath then, one loud enough for them both to hear. Dylan shook his head in silent wonder. Thomas bent until his head lay flat to Caitlin's chest, to hear her heart for himself. Jack blinked rapidly, seemingly aware all at once of his tear-stained face. He averted his gaze and barked at the men to get their butts into overdrive. Someone began packing the wound at her side, and the lifeboat picked up speed.

She was warm. Wet, but warm. And vaguely aware of motion, as if she were being carried at a high rate of speed by a vehicle that repeatedly *bumped*.

She opened her eyes. Dylan was pacing the little room. Thomas was sitting right at the bedside, and it took her a moment to connect the warm pressure on her hand with the fact that he was holding it in his.

He squeezed it suddenly tighter, looking at her face, and she winced.

"It's okay," he soothed. "We'll be at the hospital soon."

"Oh, God, not again."

Her voice seemed to have magically zapped Dylan from where she'd first glimpsed him, to her opposite side. She turned when he leaned over, gripping her shoulders so firmly, it hurt.

"You're awake. Caity, are you all right? How do you feel?" His dark eyes scanned hers with more fear than she'd ever seen in them.

"I'm hurting," she whispered.

His eyes fell closed and his lips thinned.

"Thomas is crushing my hand to sawdust, and your fingers are digging pits in my shoulders." Both grips immediately eased, and Dylan's eyes flew open. "You guys don't have to hold on so tight. I'm not going anywhere."

Dylan sat gingerly on the edge of the bed. His hands slid beneath her shoulders, and he lifted her gently, slowly, until her head was cradled on his chest, his fingers gently threading through her hair. "Damn straight, you're not going anywhere, baby."

She brought her arms around him, and held him as tightly as her pitiful amount of strength would allow. "I have so much to tell you."

"Maybe…maybe I ought to leave—"

"No, Thomas. You need to hear this, too." She released Dylan, though reluctantly, and slid herself higher on the bed, stopping in midmotion at the stabbing pain in her side. The gunshot wound. She'd forgotten. Dylan stacked pillows behind her and eased her upper body onto them. His touch was so tender, so careful, it nearly brought tears to her eyes.

Thomas touched her face. "You're pale."

"Lost a lot of blood," Dylan added.

"I'm fine. My side aches like hell, but—"

"You were shot," Thomas explained.

"I know I was shot. You think I'd forget something like that?" She made the words teasing. "What about Henri…I mean, Hank?"

"Dead."

She closed her eyes and shook her head. "Genevieve, too. He shot her. They've done this before, you know—"

"I know, honey. I know. Jack Barnes filled me in. But all of that is over now. It's over. All I'm worried about now is you."

She lifted a hand to his face. "Don't be. I'm going to be fine, I can feel it. And…and I remember now."

Dylan's brows rose. Thomas leaned forward. "Your memory is back? All of it?"

She smiled at her brother. "Most of it. There are less gaps, and I think they'll get smaller as time goes on. But even if they don't, it doesn't matter. I know what I need to know. I know why I became what I was, why I treated you—'' she looked from Thomas to Dylan ''—both of you, the way I did.''

Thomas nodded. ''I already know. It was because of our father.'' His face tightened as he spoke. His eyes filled with pain, and anger. ''You worshiped him, Cait. When you were finally forced to realize that everything Mom said about him was true, you were so disillusioned, you couldn't trust anyone again. Especially not men.''

''That's a lot of it, but not all of it.'' She closed her eyes as the horrible memory threatened to engulf her as it had before. ''That night, when our mother…'' She shook her head. ''She'd called me, and sounded so strange that I was worried, so I drove over there.''

She opened her eyes to see Dylan's widen with concern. ''It was storming, and you were at the office. I went alone. And when I got there, she was…it was already…done.''

''*You* found your mother?''

''Hanging from the ceiling,'' she finished for him. ''And right at her feet, there was a note with my name on it. A note telling me that all men were like my father, and that if I wasn't careful, I'd end up alone, just like her. She said that you'd start spending more and more time away from home, with work as your excuse…''

''And I'd already started doing just that,'' Dylan whispered. ''But Caity, it *was* work. I swear it to you—''

''Shh. I know that…now. Then, I…'' She grasped his hand. ''We were so new, Dylan. I was still insecure, and you were so wrapped up in the business. I guess I started to believe her.''

''And I knew you were keeping something from me. I sensed the walls you were putting between us, and I retreated even more.''

She nodded, and turned toward her brother. ''I wasn't right, Thomas. My mind just…*wasn't right*. Seeing Mom like that did something to me. It was like I started clinging to the money and the things it could buy, because it was the only thing I trusted, the only thing I dared to hold on to. Can you understand that?''

He nodded. ''It's okay, sis. Honestly, I was an idiot to let the inheritance come between us—''

''I was the one who let it come between us. But that's over now. Everything I have, I want to share with you. It's only right, the way Daddy should have done it in the first place.''

Thomas's face clouded. ''He never really cared about me. I don't want anything that was his. I might have resented that he left it all to you, but I never wanted it. Can *you* understand *that?*''

She bit her lower lip, thinking. ''Then it's Lizzie's. I'll put your share into a trust fund for her. Is that an acceptable solution?''

He smiled and nodded. ''As long as you'll stay in her life…hers and mine. You're a lot more important to her…to both of us…than your money is.''

She leaned forward and hugged him, tears blurring her vision. ''My brother…I love you, Thomas.''

''Me, too,'' he returned, hugging her back a little too hard. When he straightened, he brushed at his eyes with his knuckles. ''*Now* I'll get out. You two need some time.''

She met Dylan's gaze and held it as Thomas left them alone. ''I'm sorry,'' she said softly.

''For what?'' He seemed truly puzzled.

''Not loving you enough, not trusting you enough back then. If I'd come to you, told you what I was going through… God, all of this could've been so different.''

''It doesn't matter.''

She bit her lips, her eyes filling. ''Yes, it does. Because you loved me once. I remember that, too, and I remember how wonderful it made me feel. But I ruined that love with

my fears and distrust. I killed it, and now, you can't bring
it back, even though I love you with everything in me.''

"You do?''

She searched his face, misery gripping her heart. ''I do.
More, even, than I did then. It's not a little-girl love anymore, Dylan. It's real, and deep, and old, and ageless. And
even if we have to be apart...'' Her words stopped on a
sob.

"Caity, I—''

"No, let me finish because this might be important, later.
I hope...those precious times we had together...I hope
there's a baby. And not because I want to replace the one
I lost, or because I want to try to use it to cling to you.
But because I want at least one part of you that I will
always have near me. Your child, and I'd give it all the
love I have for you inside...because it has to go somewhere. There's too much of it to hold back. And I—''

"Caity, let a guy get a word in, will you?''

She went quiet, sat utterly still while his fingers slipped
into her hair, lifted it away from her head, sifted it. ''I hope
you have a baby, too.''

"You do?''

He nodded. ''But don't be too disappointed if you're not
pregnant. Because if it didn't happen last time, it will next
time, or the time after that, or...'' He smiled down at her.
"You get the idea. Because I'm not letting you go, Caity
O'Brien Rossi. I love you. I never really stopped, that's
why it hurt so much to think you didn't love me back.''

She closed her eyes as all the air left her lungs and the
weight of the world seemed suddenly to lift from her shoulders. ''Say it again, Dylan.''

"I love you, Caity. I always will. No matter what.''

*   *   *   *   *

OUT-OF-THIS-WORLD MARRIAGE

Prologue

Thomas always knew when they would come. He didn't know *how* he knew. He just did. It was like some buzzing kind of feeling inside his head. He'd wake from a sound sleep, knowing they were there. He was never afraid of them. And he never told anyone. He was certain that no one would believe him anyway, and doubly certain that if he did say anything he'd be sure to get a long lecture on his overactive imagination and the difference between lies and make-believe from his dad. Dad hated lies. He didn't want to tell his dad anything that might even sound like a lie. But there was something else, too. Something inside him that made him keep quiet. He thought maybe they didn't want him to tell. So he didn't.

They were his own special secret. And on dark summer nights, when that buzzing sensation rang in his ears, Thomas would get out of bed and climb through the window and down the trellis in his pajamas. He'd run as fast as he could, around back through the tall, damp grass in his bare feet. Past the barn and through the wheat fields and up the little hill near the stream beyond them. And he'd sit there with the wind blowing his hair and the wheat dancing in the breeze and the stars twinkling overhead. And he'd watch them pass, blazing greenish lights in the sky, igniting the whole world for just a second. He'd wave his hands, always having the odd feeling that they knew. That they could see him there. That someone was waving back at him. And he'd go back to bed feeling good.

But this night was different. Tonight there was something else ringing in his ears, and the buzzing was louder, deeper. More urgent. The sounds beyond the buzzing worried him. They sounded like crying. Someone small and frightened, crying. He puzzled over that for a second or two. It wasn't like he could really *hear* it. More like he *felt* it. Soft sobs tearing at his chest, only they weren't his.

He had the oddest feeling that something was wrong.

Thomas pulled open the drawer of the desk beside his bed and took out his slingshot. He stroked the smooth, gleaming handle where he'd carved his initials. He'd better take it along, just in case.

When he pushed open the window cool air rushed in to chill him, so he grabbed his jacket off the bedpost and slipped it on, dropping the slingshot in the pocket. Then he climbed out the window, down the trellis just like always, and he started off over the back lawn and through the wheat fields. He ran a little faster than usual. That sense that something was wrong got stronger the farther he went.

For some reason, he didn't stop at the little knoll near the stream tonight. Something told him that wasn't far enough. Whatever was wrong wasn't here. It was in the woods just beyond.

He muttered his only cuss word, wishing he'd for once remembered his dad's reminders to wear shoes when he went outside. The ground was cold, and in the woods it was rough and uneven, with gnarled roots reaching up to trip him. Too late to go back for shoes now, though. He didn't know where he was going. He didn't know why; he just knew he had to, so he went.

The woods grew thicker. He shouldn't feel nervous. He played here all the time. But it sure was different at night, darker, of course, and so quiet. Usually there were birds making so much racket you could barely hear yourself think. Not tonight, though. Even the wind seemed to have decided not to come into these woods tonight. He shrugged a little deeper into his jacket. At least it was warmer here in the trees without that chilly wind.

And there was a *little* light. Moonlight, but it only came through the thick branches here and there, and it wasn't much help. It made odd, out-of-shape shadows that tried to scare him. Like that one just now. Looked just like a man walking, just beyond a stand of berry briars. But that was stupid. It was gone a second later. Just a shadow, that's all it was.

But now he saw an eerie green glow spilling into the woods. Seemed to be coming from the clearing right near the center, an open, grassy spot where he liked to go. He called it the secret meadow because it was so well hidden by the trees all around it. Thomas moved a little closer, trying to be as quiet as he could, though he didn't really know why he ought to.

Then he caught his breath and tried to stop his heart from hammering as he ducked behind a tree. Something very big and very bright sat in the secret meadow. It resembled a fat, green, glowing spider. He thought he knew what it was, but he didn't really want to know. He didn't even want to stay here and watch it, but he couldn't seem to look away.

Then that crying sound in his head got louder, and he turned. It was like some kind of superpowered magnet was pulling at him. But it was no magnet. It was that crying that drew him onward, deeper into the trees, farther than he'd ever been from his farm before.

He walked for quite a ways. He ought to be worried

about getting lost out here, since he wasn't real familiar with this part of the woods. But he wasn't. The farther he went, the quicker he walked, and the crying sounds in his head got louder and louder.

And then they got all soft again. Only they were not in his head anymore. They were real, and he was hearing them with his ears. He followed the sounds and only muttered "Holy cow" when he finally found where they were coming from.

She sat huddled against a big oak tree with her knees drawn to her chest and a mass of black hair hiding her face. There was a pool of moonlight shining down on the spot where she sat, like some spotlight pointing her out to him. The poor little thing must be terrified out here all alone. She was shaking all over, and sobbing so hard it made his throat kind of swell up just to hear her. He started toward her, then froze in his tracks when he heard the growl from just beyond her.

He spotted the dog. She must have heard it, too, 'cause her head came up fast, eyes huge and scared looking, and she uttered a little shriek when she turned to see it behind her. The dog looked like a stray, skinny and mean, crouched and snarling a few feet from her. Thomas's young shoulders straightened a little and he felt a rush of anger as he bent to scoop up a stone with one hand, yanking out his slingshot with the other. He took careful aim and let fly.

The stone pinged off the dog's head. It turned its ugly gaze on him, teeth bared. Thomas grabbed another rock, a bigger one, and this time he pegged the animal right on the snout. The dog gave a soft yelp.

"Go on, get out of here!" Thomas fitted another rock into the sling, but the dog was already turning tail and loping off when he released it.

Thomas smiled and looked at the girl. She stared back at him, wide-eyed, still afraid. He had to blink twice when he got a good look at her. She was the prettiest girl he'd ever seen, even in the pale moonlight. He figured she was about his age, maybe nine or ten. And without even asking her, he knew she was lost. He held out his hand. She only stared at it and bit her lip.

"It's okay," he told her. He wiggled his hand at her. "Really, it's okay. That dog won't come back."

She blinked, but didn't move. Maybe she didn't understand. He moved closer and bent a little, clasping her hand with his. He gave a gentle tug and she got to her feet, staring at the ground and brushing the leaves from her funny clothes with her free hand. Looked like a pair of coveralls, only they were black, and tight fitting, and he couldn't see a button or a zipper anywhere.

The small hand he held was cold and still shaking. He'd never seen anyone so scared before. He squeezed it a little and smiled at her so she'd know he was only trying to help. "I'm Thomas," he said softly. She frowned and tilted her head. "Thomas," he repeated. He dropped the slingshot into his pocket and pointed to his chest with his free hand when he said it this time.

Her lips moved a little. Not a smile, but almost. "Thom—us."

"Yeah, that's right. Thomas."

She dipped her head. Pointing to herself as he'd done, she said softly, "Janella."

"Janella." He nodded. "That's a real pretty name, Janella." He stared at her for a moment, amazed by her eyes. They were slanted a little and dark around the edges as if she were wearing makeup, only he knew she wasn't. With her dark hair and huge dark eyes she reminded him of some exotic princess. He shrugged out of his jacket, releasing her hand to do it. Then he settled it around her shoulders. Dad would be pleased with his good manners.

"Come on, Janella. Come with me." He started forward, and she snatched his hand again, holding on tight. She came with him, but he knew she was uncertain and still scared. "It's okay. Come on."

He kept talking to her that way, urging her along through the woods back the way he'd come. She clung to his hand the whole time. He'd never really thought it was much of a thrill to hold a girl's hand before, but he held hers anyhow. She was scared, and if it made her feel better, then he figured it was worth it. Besides, she was holding on so tight, he didn't think he could pull his away if he'd wanted to.

He walked slowly, so she could keep up, and it took quite a while to get back to the clearing. But as soon as that green glow spilled onto them, he knew he'd done the right thing. Her eyes got even bigger, and she smiled fully for the first time. He stood still for a second. Gosh, she was even prettier in the bright light. And before he knew what she was thinking, she threw her arms around his neck and hugged him so hard he could barely breathe.

When she released him, he looked at the ground, embarrassed. She took something from around her neck and put it around his. A charm of some sort, hanging from a light chain. Well, if that didn't beat everything. All he'd done was show her the way back. His spine got a little straighter, and for the first time in his life, Thomas Duffy felt like a real live hero.

She handed him his jacket, even as he was racking his brain to think of something to give her in return. He ought to give her *something*, hadn't he? He pulled his jacket on and stuffed his hands into the pockets. He'd forgotten all about the cold until now. The smooth wood of his slingshot touched his palm, and he nodded, pulling it out. It would make a good present. He'd carved it himself from an old beech tree, and he'd coated it in pretty brown stain and polyurethane so it gleamed. He'd worked for weeks on it. If anyone had told him a week ago that he'd willingly give it away to some strange, pretty girl, he'd have said they were nuts. But for some reason, he didn't mind parting with it now. He pressed it into her hand.

She looked at it, tilting her head one way and another. Then her head came up, as if she'd heard something, though Thomas hadn't heard a sound. She looked into his eyes once more, smiled gently at him, and for the first time in history, Thomas wondered what it would be like to kiss a girl. Really weird, since he didn't even like girls.

So why was his mind stuck on Janella's lips like this? He frowned a little, working up his nerve. But she turned and ran away, down into the clearing, disappearing into that blinding green light.

Thomas sighed long and hard. He ought to get home. But instead, he sat down on the cool, hard ground, and he waited.

A few seconds passed. No more. Then the light rose without a single sound. It flashed brighter, so bright he had to cover his eyes, and then it was gone.

Thomas sat there for a long time before he finally made himself get up and start back home. He felt good, really good. He'd done a good thing tonight, and he figured that if his dad knew about it, he'd be darned proud.

But his dad couldn't know. No one could. Thomas knew he had to keep the secret, the same way he'd known he had to come out here tonight. He vowed he'd do just that, even if it killed him. Besides, who'd believe him anyway?

The next morning, Dad showed him the article on the front page of the *Sumac Daily Star*. UFO Seen By Over 100! Dad said it was the silliest thing he'd ever heard. Thomas didn't say a word. Even when a carload of strangers in dark suits came around town asking questions about it, Thomas stuck to his promise.

For months and months after that strange night, he went out to the knoll and watched and waited, but he never saw

them again. He never heard that buzzing sound that told
him they were near. And he never saw that beautiful princess, except once or twice in his dreams.

Chapter 1

"Dr. Duffy!" The shout was accompanied by the front door of the big farmhouse slamming open. Thomas stopped with a forkful of Eugenia Overton's tuna casserole halfway to his mouth to glance up at the disheveled boy in the doorway. Grimacing, he dropped the fork and stood up. Damn women had a knack for going into labor just as he sat down to eat. It had happened every time on Karicau, that war-ravaged Third World island in the South Pacific where he'd spent the past eight years of his life. Thomas didn't know why he'd expected it to be any different here. Matthew Connor's pretty young mother wasn't going to be an exception. Except that she was strong and healthy, hadn't been suffering malnutrition through the entire pregnancy. And Thomas wouldn't have to dodge snipers' bullets in order to get to her.

Thomas reached to the shelf beside the front door for his bag and glanced back down at Matt. "So how far apart are they?"

The twelve-year-old only shook his head, his jaw working soundlessly, his pupils too dilated.

A skittery feeling crawled over Thomas's spine. Humphrey sensed it, too. The shaggy border collie had come from his customary spot under the table to stand beside Thomas, his ears pricked, the hair on his back bristling.

Gripping a skinny shoulder and giving it a firm shake, Thomas prodded the boy. "Snap out of it, Matthew. What's happened?"

The boy blinked, cornflower-blue eyes finally focusing on Thomas. "It's Dad...the tractor flipped...he's pinned, Doc. You gotta hurry."

Thomas felt the kid's hand gripping his arm, saw the desperation in the young eyes, and blocked both from his mind before there was time for a single emotion to surface there. An iron wall descended between him and this boy. It had to. This was a job. He was a doctor. He'd do what he could do, and that was that. If he'd learned anything on Karicau, that was it. You either kept your distance or lost your mind.

Matt was already running back down the driveway with Thomas on his heels. Hurrying because it was part of the job, not because he felt fear or worry. He didn't *feel* anything. Nothing at all.

The boy veered toward the battered pickup he'd left running. Thomas's hand closed on his shoulder, stopping him. "My Jeep, Matt." No twelve-year-old ought to be driving at all, let alone in the state Matthew was in now. "We'll get the pickup later."

Matt didn't argue. He ran to shut the truck off and was beside Thomas in the Jeep in a flash. Then they were bounding over the rutted Iowa roads, turning off into a partially harvested wheat field.

It was minutes, but it seemed longer. It always seemed longer. Thomas crouched beside Hugh Connor, felt his thready pulse, knew his chest was crushed. Damn fool man was pushing sixty. Had no business being on a tractor in the first place.

The neighbors had gathered, but Thomas closed his mind to their concerned murmuring until it was only a soft, distant drone. It was a little harder not to hear Shelly's quiet crying. She was too close, kneeling right beside Thomas, one arm protectively wrapped around her ballooning belly, the other, clutching Hugh's limp hand. She spoke to the husband who was nearly twice her age, though he couldn't hear her. "Thomas is here now, hon. He'll get you through this—you know he will. You'll be okay now. Thomas will take care—"

"Back off a little, Shelly."

She looked up, blinking at him, sky-blue eyes shimmering under a layer of tears, maybe a little startled at his tone of voice. But she nodded and shuffled backward. Then she reached out, touched Thomas's hand. "Don't you let him die, Thomas Duffy. Don't let him go."

He closed his eyes and tried to blot the plea from his memory. Filed it away with the thousands of others he'd heard, the wails of the mothers and wives, the cries of the children, the agonized screams of the wounded and the dying.

There wasn't time to wait for the volunteer fire department to arrive with the equipment that would make this safe. He'd already called for a chopper from the Jeep. ETA was ten minutes. The rest was up to him. Two other tractors backed up to the far side of the toppled machine. Men attached sturdy chains. They all knew what needed doing without being told. It wasn't the first time something like this had happened in Sumac. Farming was a treacherous profession. But at least everyone here had plenty to eat. There'd be no complications brought on by malnutrition and disease, and no danger of tripping a land mine if he put a foot down in the wrong spot. Hell, this was a breeze compared with where he'd spent most of the past decade.

Other men took their places, ready to brace the tractor to keep it from falling back onto Hugh once it was lifted. Thomas took the backboard from the Jeep's rear seat and returned to his position beside Hugh. Reluctantly, he inclined his head at Shelly, now standing with both arms around the son who looked more like her younger brother.

"Get over here, you two. Shelly, I need you to hold his head, just like this. Matthew, help her. Put your hands here and here. Don't let his neck twist at all. Okay?" The two took their positions, while Thomas tried once more to lower that iron wall. It seemed pretty shaky right now. He tried not to look at the stillness of Hugh Connor's face. Tried not to remember being six years old and feeling all grown up because Dad and Hugh had decided he was big enough to go trout fishing with them.

A trickle of sweat ran from his brow and stung his eye. Thomas blinked it away, wriggled a neck brace beneath Hugh, fastened it tight. Steadied his control, distanced himself.

He gave the signal. Men braced their shoulders and tractors growled with effort. The burden lifted. "Hold it there!" Thomas had to shout over the bellowing motors. He worked the backboard under Hugh, careful not to twist the man's body or move his spine. He had to be careful, take his time, do it right. Right out of the textbook. It was part of the job, and the fact that he knew old Hugh would rather be dead than paralyzed didn't even enter into it. The stubborn old goat. He still went fishing in the spring. Thomas had gone with him this year. Dad, too, Hugh had quietly insisted. If only in spirit.

Fastening the straps, focusing on each move he made in order to block the human side of him from interfering, Thomas carefully pulled Hugh away from the tractor that hovered above him. By the time he'd done it, the chopper was settling noisily into the field.

"Someone drive Shelly and the boys to the hospital. And

go and get their pickup from my house," Thomas called over his shoulder as he helped move Hugh on board. He knew the neighbors would take care of things. Sumac, Iowa, was that kind of place. Hugh Connor's wheat would get harvested. His family would have plenty of support, a little too much company and probably a half dozen of Eugenia Overton's casseroles before tomorrow was out. They were a close-knit community, a family. A member of which Thomas steadfastly refused to become.

It was midnight by the time he got back home. One of the neighbors—he didn't know which one—had driven his Jeep to the hospital and left the keys at the nurses' station. He wasn't sure why. Not out of friendly feelings for him, that much was certain. The residents of Sumac didn't much like Thomas these days. Oh, they'd liked him well enough before...before he'd gone away and served his time in hell. He supposed they'd expected the starry-eyed kid who'd left here, not the cold stranger who'd returned. But that was their problem, not his. And if they didn't like him, at least they had a healthy respect for him. Maybe even a little fear. The man they saw as unfriendly and intimidating was in fact only keeping true to the lessons of Karicau. How many of those sweet people had he let himself care about, only to see them die? Father Elton, the village priest, picked off by a sniper while helping to distribute the latest shipment from the Red Cross. Young, pregnant Maria, blown to unrecognizable bits after stepping on a land mine. Little Alena. He closed his eyes when he thought of her huge brown ones and her bright smile. She'd been the first baby Thomas had ever delivered solo. Alena lived to the ripe old age of eight before she was peppered with shrapnel by guerrillas intent on destroying supply trucks that had just rolled into the village.

There had been more, many more Karicauans whom Thomas had become close to, hell, even loved, and who had died at the hands of the bloody revolt. And with every one who'd passed, he'd fought the despair, the sense of having failed in his mission, the horrible, gut-wrenching guilt that he—a doctor—had been unable to help them. Until, gradually, the truth had been driven into his brain like a fence post into the soft Iowa ground, being hammered down deep with a twenty-pound maul. You couldn't allow yourself to care.

Here, though, it was different.

Hugh had a cracked sternum, eight broken ribs, a punctured lung and quite a bit of internal bleeding, but he was stable now. He was going to be all right. Thomas had been relieved and glad to let Dr. Monroe handle the surgery. He never operated anymore if he could help it. It was a little harder to be distant with a patient's vital organs literally in the palms of your hands. So he just bowed out of the OR, and so far, that seemed just fine with the staff at St. Luke's.

Thomas was exhausted. Not just from the work, but from the effort of keeping his distance. It hadn't been an effort in a very long time. Closing himself off emotionally had not been a luxury on Karicau, it had been a damned necessity. Like breathing. You either learned to go cold as ice and stay that way, or you ended up in a rubber room somewhere, weaving baskets for a living. And doing it hadn't been easy. Hell, for a while he'd mourned every dead child, grieved every young mother's burial. But it hadn't gone on. He couldn't have let it go on.

So why, if he'd been able to close off his emotions in the face of the most senseless mayhem imaginable, was it so difficult to do the same here now?

Maybe because *here* was where the emotional side of him was born and raised. Hell, he sometimes thought the right half of his brain had stayed behind when he'd gone overseas. That part of him that had dreamed of castles and dragons, believed in Santa Claus, imagined beautiful princesses from distant galaxies. It was that same part of him that seemed to have been waiting in ambush when he'd returned six months ago. Every breath of Sumac air seemed to instigate a memory, a rush of feeling, nostalgia, something. He'd been fighting it ever since he'd come back here, and it was difficult.

Difficult, not impossible. He'd just have to try harder.

He slammed the door behind him, tossed the bag into its customary spot and eyed his latest missed meal with regret. The plate sat on the table where he'd left it, but it was devoid of any sign of tuna casserole. He crooked an eyebrow, lowering his gaze to the dog under the table. Humphrey just wagged his shaggy tail and tried to look innocent.

"Didn't matter. I wasn't hungry anyway."

Humphrey barked once and lowered his head to rest on his outstretched paws, pretending to close his eyes. Only he kept peering out as Thomas cleared the dishes from the table and stacked them in the dishwasher. The dog knew he could be in big trouble for eating from the table. Lucky for Humphrey, his master was too tired to worry about it.

Thomas dragged himself upstairs for a quick shower and fell into bed. But even as tired as he was, sleep didn't come easily. The damned house was too big for one man and a dog. Too empty, too quiet. Especially at night, without a single sound other than the boisterous crickets outside. He told himself for the hundredth time that he ought to sell it, move into the vacant rooms above the clinic in town. Right between the John Deere dealer and the feed store. It wasn't as if he needed all this room or ever would. He had about as much intention of settling down with a woman and raising a family as he did of running for president. Of course, he'd change his mind in a hurry if the single ladies of Sumac had their way. It was a shame he had to disappoint them. But he had nothing inside him to give to a woman. He might have had once. But whatever there had been had died in the middle of a bloody revolution. It had died just a little bit with every small child, no matter how thoroughly he'd closed off his heart. It had died of starvation and disease and war. There was no resurrecting it.

So he ought to sell. He didn't run the farm anymore. His practice kept him too busy for that, but he didn't let the land sit idle, either. He rented the fields to neighboring farmers, who grew bumper crops on it. One of them would be more than happy to own the whole place.

It was that emotional part of him that kept him from going ahead and selling the place. He might have managed to exorcise the boy inside him, to be rid of him the entire time he'd spent away from here in hell. But the kid still lived in this house. Everywhere on this damned farm. And *he* was the one who kept Thomas from selling out. To that boy, this place was magic. It spurred the kinds of dreams and fantasies that seemed too real not to believe in. Made a kid feel like a hero, rescuing strange and beautiful damsels on Iowa summer nights.

God, had he ever been that young? That naive and gullible? Believed in such utter nonsense? Had such crazy dreams? Didn't seem possible when he thought about it now.

He closed his eyes, knowing good and well there'd be no dreams, no childish fantasies. He never dreamed anymore, with the exception of a few occasional nightmares.

It was 5:45 when the odd buzzing sensation woke him up. His eyes opened, bleary and unfocused. But it grew louder, and he sat up in bed as his head cleared, reaching for the light. It was still there. Buzzing, like a hive of bees, only it was coming from inside. Inside *him.* He thought of tinnitus and smacked the side of his head with his palm, but the sound didn't go away. For just a moment, he remembered what that sensation had signified in his youth.

"Ah, bull. That wasn't real...."

But something drew him and he got up. He pulled on his jeans and went to the window.

"This is stupid. This is utterly—" The buzzing grew louder. "Stupid." He pushed the window open and stood for a minute staring up at the sky. He shook his head at the insane urge to climb out, the way he used to do. He glanced down at the trellis, knowing damn well that such a ridiculous effort would probably be good for one big laugh and several broken bones.

There was a simple explanation for the sound. And he would sure as hell find out what it was and put a stop to it so he could get a few hours' sleep. He glanced down, and realized that his hand was absently rubbing the oval-shaped charm he wore on a chain around his neck. He forced his hand down.

But the buzzing sound grew still louder.

He snapped his jeans, tugging the zipper up as he trotted down the stairs. Then he stopped at another sound, a growl. Humphrey stood poised as if for attack near the door. His upper lip curled away from his teeth; his tail pointed straight in the air, nearly vibrating.

Thomas frowned. "What is it, boy? Somebody out there who shouldn't be?" Humphrey didn't change position until Thomas caught him by the collar and tugged him away from the door. Then Thomas opened it, slipped outside and closed it again before his wannabe-rottweiller could escape and do someone bodily harm.

His bare feet hit the cool damp grass, and memories rushed over him. Running through the wheat fields, warm summer breezes in his hair, eager young eyes scanning the night sky for...

Hell, he'd been a little kid with a big imagination. And the charm around his neck...well, he'd probably found it in the woods on one of his excursions. His mind had concocted a fantasy around it. Or his subconscious had woven a dream to explain its presence. He'd had a notoriously vivid dream life as a kid.

So why have you been wearing it ever since, then? Huh?

Thomas scowled at the childlike voice inside his head, forcibly ignoring its sarcastic question. Walking a little ways in the dewy grass, he looked around. The buzzing still sounded in his ears, but he saw no explanation for it. Maybe he was dreaming now. He couldn't be sure. And just because he'd stopped dreaming didn't mean his mind couldn't have decided to start up again. It didn't *feel* like a dream, though. The night breeze was real. The muscles in his shoulders and back ached from tension and his head throbbed a little. He wouldn't feel that in a dream, would he? His stomach growled and he remembered that he hadn't eaten.

"Okay, maybe it's not a dream. I'm out here like an idiot, in the middle of the night. Something is buzzing, and my dog doesn't like it any better than I do. So what the hell is going on?"

A little thrill of excitement raced up the back of his neck, the way it used to when he was a kid. He caught it, balled it up in a mental fist and tossed it away. There was no reason for it. He wasn't a kid anymore. And this wasn't one of his childhood fantasies.

He stood there a minute, staring up at the empty sky, wondering what sane man would be out here shirtless and shoeless in the middle of the night after the day he'd put in. Why the hell had he come outside, anyway? And why hadn't that buzzing in his head faded in the least now that the cool night air was slapping his face, bringing him more awake and alert than ever?

A blinding green glow cut a swath through the sky. It arced from somewhere high and east, curving downward like a big green rainbow, only to disappear just beyond the treeline in the distance. Thomas felt the ground rock with a soundless impact.

''Holy...'' He stared for a second, shocked motionless.

Something seemed to slam into him from behind, some invisible force, propelling him forward. Stupid to run like this! Stupid, foolish, utterly senseless. He hadn't seen anything. Not really. Maybe the stress from his time on Karicau had finally caught up to him. Maybe this was some sort of breakdown. He told himself all those things, but still his legs strained, air burned in and out of his lungs, his feet hammered the ground in rhythm with his pulse.

It wasn't as far for a grown man as it had seemed to a ten-year-old boy. He crossed the field, the stubble of recently cut wheat stabbing at the soles of his feet. A grown man ought to know enough to wear shoes. How many times had Dad told him that? *Thomas Allan, you're gonna lose a foot if you don't start wearing shoes when you go out.*

For a second he'd heard that deep, booming voice speaking close to his ears. But it hadn't been real. Just those damned memories sneaking up on him again, trying to claim him.

The field behind him, he splashed across the stream, soaking his jeans up to his calves. He ran through the knee-high grass, up onto the little knoll and right on over. His heart pounding so hard he could hear it, he loped into the woods, over the uneven, damp ground, toward the clearing he remembered so well. That magical, secret meadow.

He saw a silent explosion when he got there. The shape—that same glowing green spider shape he remembered—simply glowed bright white and vanished. Nothing remained. Nothing. He briefly imagined the headline in the tiny *Sumac Daily Star.* ''Local Doctor Suffers Mental Breakdown In Woods.''

But something *had been* there. The ground was charred black, completely barren. Not a single blade of grass stood in the steaming circle of earth. And the buzzing in his head was gone.

He heard a groan, and his spine went rigid. He turned

very slowly, walked without seeing, still blinded by that brilliant *imaginary* flash of light.

She lay on the ground, her black hair covering her face. She wasn't moving. Thomas knelt beside her. Maybe "knelt" wasn't the right word. His knees sort of buckled under him, landing him on the ground. He reached out, touched her, as if to be sure she was real.

And then the wall slammed down, saving his sanity yet again. His hands moved automatically, checking for broken bones, slipping under her to feel her spine, touching her neck, feeling the soft beat of her pulse beneath warm skin. He pushed the hair away from her face.

Her huge, slanted eyes opened, and she stared at him. She blinked, one hand rising weakly, touching the amulet he wore. Her lips parted. "Thom...us..." The beautiful eyes closed again, and she lay still.

He stared down at her, unable to believe what he was seeing as his vision slowly came back. Around her neck, suspended on a thin, silvery chain, hung a slingshot. He touched it, felt his initials carved into the handle. "Janella," he whispered. "My God, Janella...."

Chapter 2

She was light. Too light, maybe. Or maybe his imagination was kicking in.

Oh, yeah, start worrying about your imagination, Doc. You're carrying a semiconscious alien woman away from the spot where her frigging mothership just vaporized. I'd say that's as good a time as any to worry about the old imagination. Maybe ought to give a thought to the sanity while you're at it, don't you think?

It was too ridiculous even to contemplate. Impossible. Things like this happened in childhood fantasies, not in the real adult world. So it wasn't happening. It couldn't be. He'd probably wake up in bed and laugh about it.

The silky material of her blouse rubbing against his bare chest was too real to be a dream, though. The heat of her body suffusing his. That soft cheek resting on his shoulder. Hair like black satin, trailing down his arm. Her soft breath, whispering near his neck.

Ah, hell, it was all real. He knew damned well it was, no matter how little sense it made. He figured if he was going to fantasize, he'd have had her awake and healthy, not suffering from God knows what kinds of injuries. He wasn't even sure he could help her.

That thought brought him up short. He swore under his breath as he searched her face. Then he averted his gaze, but a little too late. That bronzed skin, bathed in moonlight, the turned-up nose, those long black lashes had already imbedded themselves in his mind. She was small, delicate, helpless, depending on him to get her through this. He closed his eyes for a second, trying to tug down that iron wall that kept him emotionally removed. But it wasn't easy. Always before he'd felt sure of himself, competent. He'd known he could do what needed doing, help any patient who wasn't beyond helping. But he didn't *know how* to help her. He couldn't check her vitals, because he didn't know what they ought to be. He couldn't administer medication without knowing what reactions it might cause in her. She looked human, but—if this wasn't a dream—she wasn't. Was she?

This was beyond his area of expertise. He ought to call someone. Somewhere in the world there must be someone who'd know what to do for her.

You can't tell anyone, and you know it.

He opened his eyes and exhaled slowly. Damn, that was the voice of a little boy lecturing him, not one of reason. He ought to call someone—

You promised!

"I never promised anything." Great. Now he was whispering to himself as he carried her back through the woods toward home.

You did so. In your mind, your heart, you swore you'd never tell.

The irritating young voice had a point there. He had sort of promised. But at the time he'd considered it more a vow to himself than to anyone else. And he still wasn't sure why he'd felt so strongly about it, especially since the secret he'd sworn to keep had only existed inside his own mind.

Or maybe not.

You have to help her. She's depending on you.

What was so new about that? People were always depending on him, pinning their hopes on him as if he were some kind of god instead of just a man with a medical degree. But that's all he was. And he didn't have any more saintly qualities, any more compassion or caring, than the next guy did. Maybe less. Show me a doctor who cares and I'll show you a basket case waiting to happen. That had always been his philosophy.

But this is different. You have to care this time. Look at her!

"Shut up," he muttered to the boyish voice in his mind. But it was too late. He was already looking at her, remembering the lost little girl, the fear in her eyes, the tears.

Those same eyes opened now, blinked up at him, and he stopped walking for a second. She smiled slightly, lifted a hand to touch his face. "I knew you'd come, Thomas. I knew..." The hand fell again as her eyes fluttered closed.

"Ah, hell," Thomas murmured, resuming the brisk pace.

He emerged from the woods onto the grassy slope and picked up his pace a little more. He splashed through the stream and crossed the stubble-covered wheat field, no longer noticing the pokes in his feet. She stirred a little, moaned softly. One hand came up to clasp his neck and his hold on her tightened automatically.

He crossed the lawn, kicked the front door opened and came face-to-face with Eugenia Overton and her endlessly curious eyes. Hands on her slender hips, she gaped at him, then at the woman in his arms.

"Thomas Allan Duffy, what in the name of heaven are you up to?"

Humphrey lunged out from under the table, barking and snarling in a way Thomas had never seen him do. The black-and-white fur on his haunches bristled and his teeth were bared. Janella's eyes flew wide and she screamed loudly enough to wake a coma patient. Her arms snagged Thomas's neck. She cringed closer to him, damn near cutting off his airway. She screamed again, louder.

"It's all right!" He turned, putting his back to Humphrey, but the dog kept barking and Janella kept screaming. "Dammit, Eugenia, grab the dog!"

Eugenia had already done just that. She had Humphrey by his collar, smacking him repeatedly on the nose with her other hand, as she tugged him into the small pantry and shut the door. When she turned to face Thomas again she was breathless. One strand of copper-red hair hung down over her pinkened face.

She blew the hair away with an exasperated puff. "Well? You going to tell me what's going on?"

Janella still clung to him, shaking all over. Hot tears dampened his neck where her face was buried. So what? he asked himself. Hell, it wasn't as if he hadn't seen patients cry before.

Yeah. You've seen her cry before. And it made your stomach churn then, too.

Shut the hell up!

But his hold on Janella tightened a little more, and one of his hands had apparently decided it was necessary to stroke her hair. He stopped it, glanced at Eugenia. "No, as a matter of fact, I'm not. So go home."

Pushing past Eugenia, he carried Janella through the kitchen, into the living room and upstairs into his bedroom. He wondered briefly whether her clothes had given her away to his neighbor. Outside, he hadn't really noticed what she was wearing.

Thank God, he thought, no silver lamé. The blouse looked like silk, but felt a lot heavier, sturdier. It didn't appear all that unusual, full sleeves with tighter cuffs. A fitted waist. High, snug collar. The pants reminded him of spandex, and both were black. She wore ankle-high boots of buttery-soft, leatherlike material.

He tugged the covers back with one hand, then bent to lower her into the bed. She stared into his eyes, hers huge and frightened, her hands still clasped tight at the base of his neck. He reached behind him and gently tugged her hands away so he could straighten. She blinked in apparent confusion, but lay back on his pillows.

A bang made her go stiff. Thomas whirled to see Eugenia standing by the window.

"What the heck did you leave that open for? It's not exactly warm outside. And on a similar note, where's your shirt? You're a doctor, for crying out loud. Don't you know better than—"

"Eugenia, what the hell are you doing in my bedroom at six in the morning?"

That shut her up. She pursed her pretty lips and frowned, and he took a second to notice that no matter when you saw Eugenia she was perfectly made up and beautiful. Single, too. Sumac's own Miss Kitty. All she needed was some big strong Marshal Dillon to come along and sweep her off her feet. Then she'd stop worrying so much about his chronic bachelorhood. Maybe.

"So?" He prodded, wishing like hell she'd take her good intentions and leave. "What did you bring this time? A carrot cake or another prospective wife for me?"

She pulled herself up taller, obviously insulted. "I saw an explosion. Or at least it looked like one. There didn't seem to be any noise along with it. It seemed to be coming from this way, so naturally I had to come over and make sure you were all right."

"Naturally."

"Don't try that nasty attitude on me, Thomas. You know I'm the only one in town who doesn't buy it."

"Are you, now?" He turned back to his patient, pushed

her hair away from her face and saw the swollen, rapidly bruising spot just above her temple.

"You know I am. Everyone else shakes in their boots when you glower at them that way. But I'm not scared of you. Not one bit."

"Maybe you ought to be." He leaned closer to Janella, touched the spot gently, decided she might have a slight concussion at the most. It ought to be all right.

"Don't you forget, Thomas, I knew you before you went away. You weren't so intimidating when you were in my ninth-grade English class."

"People change." He turned, intending to go downstairs for his medical bag. But Eugenia had apparently grabbed it on the way up. She slung it hard into his chest.

"Not really," she muttered.

Thomas snapped open the bag, took out a cold pack and crushed it in his hand to activate it. When he felt the chill working into his palm, he laid the pack carefully over the lump on Janella's head. She only watched him, wide-eyed, glancing every few seconds at Eugenia. Thomas reached down, clasping her wrist in gentle fingers, feeling her pulse, glancing at the second hand on the clock beside the bed, wondering why the hell he bothered when he had no idea what would be normal for her. Still, the strong, steady thrum against his fingers reassured him.

"This lady was in some kind of accident, I take it. That must have been what I saw."

Damn woman wouldn't be put off easily. "I guess so," he agreed.

"What about her car? Did you find that?"

"No sign of it." Thomas licked his lips. "She said she was alone, though, so we don't need to be in a big rush to go looking for it. No chance of any other victims."

"Couldn't be much left of it anyway, after an explosion like that," Eugenia added. She tilted her head, perusing the woman on the bed as she circled it, stopping on the opposite side. "Well, someone ought to call her folks. She must have family." She leaned over Janella, who seemed to cringe deeper into the sheets. "What's your name, hon? Where are you from?"

Janella's eyes widened, her gaze darting from Eugenia back to Thomas.

"Look, Eugenia, you came to check things out. You've done that. Now, if you don't mind, I have a patient to tend to. One who's not in any shape for the third degree. Okay?"

Eugenia sniffed indignantly, tossed her coppery head. "You don't scare me, Thomas Duffy." Her gaze moved back to Janella, and softened. "I'll come back tomorrow. Maybe she'll want some company by then." She turned and hurried out the door, down the stairs. He heard her car start up and move away a few seconds later, and sighed in relief.

"Thomas…"

He turned quickly, scanning Janella's face. She touched her forearm lightly. "I have pain," she whispered.

Ah, hell. The wall, dammit. Bring down the wall.

He schooled his expression to remain blank and dipped into the bag for a pair of scissors. Sitting on the edge of the bed, he lifted her arm, his touch utterly impersonal, while she watched him, eyes wide, curious, but not frightened. Holding the cuff of her sleeve, he slipped the scissor blade inside and began to cut it away. Only, the stuff didn't cut. Frowning, he tried again, until her hand closed over his, and she shook her head. "Very strong." She touched the blouse as she said it. "It will not tear."

Right. Okay, so I'm treating an alien with an injured arm, and she's wearing some material that can't be cut. No big deal. Just quit thinking about it and concentrate on the job.

She sat up, lifting one hand to the front of the blouse where there was no visible seam or button or zipper. She hooked a forefinger inside the neck and easily pulled the blouse open down the front.

Thomas knew he ought to be really amazed at this new, invisible fastener that seemed to seal the material together like magic. But he was too busy noticing the creamy swell of her breasts where the shirt fell open. He was a doctor, for crying out loud. He did not notice breasts unless there was something wrong with them.

She shrugged out of the blouse, completely unembarrassed, it seemed. She very carefully peeled it from her injured arm and lay back, fully revealed from the waist up. No, there was definitely nothing wrong with them. And he was noticing them anyway, and wondering where the hell his damned professional disinterest had hidden itself.

She frowned and held up her injured arm. "It *hurts*."

Her voice had an air of command he didn't much like. Ah, terrific, something about her he *didn't* like. Aside from her being from outer space, of course. He closed his eyes and gave his head a shake. He'd just about given up the idea that he'd wake up in the morning to find none of this had been real. Maybe he ought to try to wake up now, though, just for the hell of it. He focused on lucidity, on full awareness, and popped his eyes open.

No good. She still lay on his bed, and her breasts were still perfect and firm and entirely exposed, right to their dark centers and puckering nipples.

Thomas swallowed hard and pulled the covers over her distractions for the time being. He took the slingshot from around her neck and put it in its old spot—the drawer beside the bed. "I can't believe you kept it all this time."

She blinked at him. "Why? You kept the amulet, didn't you?"

"Yeah, but—"

"I knew we'd meet again. It was fate, Thomas."

Wondering what she meant by that pronouncement made

him uncomfortable, so he changed the subject back to the matter at hand. He examined the forearm. "It's broken. I'll have to put a cast on it."

She tilted her head. "Cast?"

"It's all right. It will feel better when I'm finished." He reached for his bag, fished out the soft gauze and then the plaster bandages, setting them on the nightstand. Then he went to the bathroom and ran a basin of hot water. He brought it back to the bedside, dropped the plaster rolls into it.

He had to set the bone first. He took her arm in both hands, met her gaze, and his stomach clenched a little at the thought of hurting her. That shouldn't have happened. He shouldn't have *let* it happen. "This is going to hurt, Janella. But only for a second."

"Pain is not good, Thomas. I do not like it."

"I have to do it, or the arm won't heal."

She frowned. "You are a healer?"

"Yes."

"You are certain?"

For crying out loud. Did she want to see his license to practice? "I'm certain."

She stared at him for a moment, some kind of wonder in her eyes. Then her jaw firmed up, and she repeated, "I dislike pain." Nonetheless she closed her eyes, braced herself.

Thomas snapped the bone into place and she screamed. Her eyes squeezed tighter and moisture seeped onto her thick lashes. He grated his teeth and refused to look at her face. "I'm sorry. It'll be better soon, I promise." She opened her eyes, glared at him for a second, then relaxed against the pillows as if resigned.

He began wrapping the soft cotton around her forearm, then the gauze. "Can you tell me where you come from, Janella?" He finished with the gauze and fished a roll of plaster out of the warm water.

She glanced toward his window, toward the sky. "Far away. I do not know how to say the name in your language." Her eyes seemed so sad.

"How do you even know my language?"

She brought her gaze back to his. "We know *all* your languages." She had to think about it before she finished. "We've always known."

Thomas nodded, deciding all of a sudden he didn't really want to hear this. His brain had taken in enough insanity tonight to put it on overload.

"I couldn't stay there," she muttered, as if to herself.

He frowned, pausing in his ministrations to search her face, then wished he hadn't. She was hurting, and not just physically.

"Why not?" Ah, hell, hadn't he just decided he didn't want to know?

She only shook her head.

Okay, so she got into some kind of trouble up there on Krypton or wherever the hell she came from, and she'd swiped a handy UFO—the glowing green model was hot this season—and made a getaway to planet Earth.

Yup, and the moon is made of green cheese, too. Come on, next do you suppose she'll ask you to take her to your leader?

"Earth is better for me."

Uh-huh, makes perfect sense. You're having a breakdown, Duffy. A major one.

Thomas began winding the warm, wet plaster around her arm, smoothing it very slowly. She closed her eyes, and he knew the warmth was soothing her pain a little.

"But my ship failed, and I could not regain control."

"And you crashed. You must have been thrown clear before—"

"The ship is gone." Her eyes squeezed tighter and she cleared her throat. "I can not change my mind now. I can never go back."

."Was there anyone else with you?" He immediately thought of going back out, searching the area for other survivors. It was ludicrous, but...

"I'm alone," she whispered.

His heart twisted a little in his chest. Thomas ordered it to freeze in place and stay the hell out of this. "You're not alone, Janella. You have a friend, hmm? One from your childhood."

She sniffed, and stared at him, smiling just a little. "Yes. One friend. One trusted friend who will keep our secret." Her eyes took on a determined gleam. "No one must know about me, Thomas. Not ever." Again that air of command.

He finished the cast. "Hell, no one would believe me if I told them." He rinsed his hands in the water. It felt real, wet the way water should. Wouldn't things be more distorted if this were a mental crisis of some kind? "But don't worry, I'm not going to. You can trust me." He took her chin in his hand, fought a brief battle with his own eyes, which seemed inclined to linger on her mouth, and turned her head slightly. "Now, let me take a look at your head."

In the secret air base in Groom Lake, Nevada, alarms went off and lights flashed. An alien vessel had entered Earth's atmosphere, and apparently crashed in the U.S.A. The tracking systems went into action, putting the crash site somewhere in the state of Iowa. That was all they got before the vessel apparently disintegrated. Still, the team was dispatched. UFO sightings from that area would get immediate attention, and they'd track down and recover any bodies or wreckage before too many people asked too many questions. They'd put the locals' minds to rest with cover stories of weather balloons or air-force test flights. They'd bring any evidence that was to be found back to Groom Lake, where it would be analyzed, studied and then stored under armed guard in hangar thirty-five. The entire inves-

tigation and the cover-up would go off like clockwork.
    They always did.

    Thomas's hands were soothing and gentle on her arm,
as he administered the ancient remedy for a broken bone.
And soft again when he examined the painful bump on her
head. He remained bare chested, and she studied him
openly and well, not nearly as afraid now as she had been
earlier.
    She cringed inwardly when she thought of the fear she'd
displayed so openly in front of him. What must he think
of her, giving vent to her emotions that way? But then she
reminded herself that things were different here. And that
this was why she'd come. She wasn't worthy of the life
laid out for her at home. And she'd often wondered if the
blood of the ruling class truly ran in her veins, or if there
had been some mix-up to explain her parentage. She was
nothing like them. Nothing. She *felt* things. Many things.
So many, she envisioned a cauldron somewhere inside her,
one bubbling over with emotions and passions. All the
things forbidden to her, the things no true ruler was supposed to feel.
    "Emotions make you weak, Janella." How many times
had her mother whispered those words to her. "They interfere with one's ability to think clearly, make practical
decisions. Look at the wars and turmoil on Earth. *That* is
where emotions will get you."
    Janella shook her head, remembering. Her father had
traces of emotion—to her mother's constant chagrin. Nothing like Janella's explosive feelings, of course. But when
his own father had grown feeble and old, and the women
of the ruling house had added the old man's name to the
list of those to be euthanized at the annual ceremony, he'd
defied them all. Janella was secretly proud of that. Her father, Matalin, had smuggled Grandfather aboard what was
supposed to be a routine reconnaissance ship. And Janella,

the only person who knew his plans, had sneaked aboard, as well.

It had been a wonderful adventure, orbiting Earth, searching for the perfect place for Grandfather to live out his waning years. Until he'd died. He'd succumbed just as they'd landed in the woods behind this place. And as Matalin had buried him there, Janella, overcome with grief, had run off into the trees. When her grief was spent, she'd been unable to find her way back to her father and the ship.

And then Thomas had found her.

She closed her eyes, remembering that night as clearly as if it had been yesterday. Thomas had been young, but so strong and confident. He'd reminded her of the heroes in the old stories, the men from days gone by. Men of courage and honor, in the times before the ruling house had taken control of the planet. She'd fallen in love with Thomas that night. She'd known then that she would hold his image in her heart forever.

She'd secretly despised the ruling house since her return, and had always intended to flee them before her time to serve as one of them came to pass. For the crime of trying to rescue his father, Matalin had been sentenced to spend the rest of his life in prison. Her father must have known what his fate would be, but he'd returned all the same. He'd been determined to use his trial as a forum, to speak out against the system and the ruling house. Janella had only seen him once after his judgment had been passed, just before he'd been taken to the ship bound for the prison planet. And his words to her still rang in her ears.

"You don't belong here, Janella. No more than I do. You're not like them. You never can be. When you're grown, leave them. Go to Earth, as I should have done long ago. Go there and find happiness. You will. I know you will."

Well, she'd heeded her father's words. She'd come here. She'd made it safely, only to find a woman who seemed far too interested in her business, and a noisy creature with far too many sharp teeth. And Thomas. A healer. Of all things, he'd become a healer. There'd been no healers at home, excepting for the few who practiced illegally in darkened, hidden rooms. If caught practicing, they would pay with their lives. The ruling house had determined there was no longer a need for healers. It was impractical to spend time and resources on illness. Simple injuries were healed with no more than an injection. The seriously ill, those born with abnormalities or disease, the old and infirm, were gathered together once a year for the ritual euthanasia. This way only the strong and healthy survived, to bear more strong and healthy offspring.

It was a system Janella had never accepted, and her explosive temper and impulsive nature had landed her in trouble over it more than once.

Her father had been right. She was never meant to live among them. She'd long ago decided she was meant to be here. With Thomas.

Thomas put the cold square back on her head, leaning over her as he pressed the frigid thing gently to her bump. His chest was smooth and rippled with strength. She'd never seen its like. The men of her world were dim reflections of him. Soft, flabby. But then, they were of little importance, anyway. No one much cared what they looked like.

She'd thought of Thomas often since he'd rescued her so long ago. She'd known he was trustworthy even then. Rare for a male. Even more odd that she should be here depending on one to help her. But even in adulthood, he didn't seem like the conquered men from her world.

She'd been right about Thomas. He'd rescued her again, tonight. Somehow, she'd known he'd be here for her. And her likening of him to one of the legendary heroes had been correct, as well. His skin bore the kiss of the sun, and the body that skin covered was broad and hard.

She lifted one hand and laid her palm against his chest. Warm, firm. She liked it, and ran her hand over it from side to side and down over his rippled abdomen. He looked down at her, frowning.

"You're very hard," she observed, letting her hand fall away for the moment.

"If you only knew," he said, and he was smiling.

She liked his smile, also. But it vanished all too quickly, to be replaced by the harsh, hardened expression he seemed to favor.

"Are all men here that way?"

He shook his head. "It comes from hard work."

She nodded. So men here still acted as laborers. No doubt their primitive technology left much that still needed physical strength to accomplish.

She tilted her head. "We have writings...stories of the heroes of old. They are described much like you. Hard and strong." She reached up, ran her hand over his chest again and nodded. "I approve of it."

The corners of his lips turned upward, as if he would like to smile again, but he resisted the urge. His mouth took on a thin line and his jaw seemed to clamp firmly.

That creature with the sharp teeth and angry voice bellowed from below, and she gasped. She barely restrained herself from huddling under the covers. Instead, she drowned her fear in righteous indignation, and then anger. If that beast came near her again she'd send it flying into the nearest wall!

Thomas's hand closed around hers, removing it from his chest as if her touch disturbed him. That made her still angrier. "It's all right, Janella. It's just my dog."

"I do *not* like *dog*. You will take it away from here."

"No, I don't think I will."

Thomas studied her face, replacing the fallen cold thing on her head. His gaze was hard and she blinked in surprise. Was he defying her?

"The dog must go," she repeated.

"Look, honey, in case you haven't noticed yet, this is *my* house. And that is *my* dog. He's not going anywhere." He pursed his lips, as if considering something. Then he muttered a few angry words she didn't recognize and went on. "I know you're scared. But Humphrey won't hurt you. He's just afraid of you because he doesn't know you."

"*He's* afraid of *me?*"

Thomas nodded. "I won't let him near you until you're ready, but believe me, he's a good dog."

She sat up a little. The thing on her arm was getting hard and heavy, but the soreness had eased a little. She met Thomas's eyes, a bit confused at his refusal to comply with her command. Still, she supposed, she could give him a bit of leeway, since he'd rescued her twice in her lifetime and since he was destined to be her mate, as she'd known for many years.

She lifted her chin, though, and made her words very firm and clear. "If he bites me with those teeth, I will pull them all out."

"He won't bite you."

She sulked, but settled back on the bed. She was very tired, which surprised her. She should be too curious about this strange place and this man to think of sleep. She supposed the effort of traveling so far and her injuries were draining her energy.

She blinked, recalling for a moment all those she'd left behind. People, family, friends whom she'd loved. But they hadn't wanted her love, anyway. And they allowed themselves to feel none for her in return. She couldn't have lived there much longer. She felt she'd have withered and died in the attempt. It will be better here, she told herself. Then, glancing at the hard, emotionless eyes of the man at her side, she wondered. Would it be better here? Or had she simply exchanged one unbearable life for another?

Her eyelids drooped. Janella yawned and rested her head on the pillows.

"That's good. You get some sleep. I'll be just down the hall if you need anything." He started to move toward the door. She sat up and slammed it shut.

Thomas stood very still near the door, just staring at it. Then he turned to stare at her. "How in the hell did you do that?"

She frowned, uncertain what was confusing him so much. "I will rest better if you stay with me, Thomas." She used a smile to soften the harsh, commanding tone of her words.

He gave his head a shake, scowling darkly for a second. He looked from her to the door and back again. Then shrugged as his expression softened, just slightly. "Yeah, okay. I can do that. I suppose you're afraid to be alone right now." He came back to her, sat down in the chair beside the bed.

She shook her head and threw back the covers with her good arm. "Here, with me. I will sleep very well with my head upon your hard chest, I think."

He seemed so surprised. His gaze affixed itself to her breasts and remained there for a very long time. So long she wondered if he saw something wrong with them.

She looked down, puzzled. "What is it, Thomas? Are they not as beautiful as the breasts of your women?" She glanced up at him again, thoroughly confused.

His gaze rose to meet hers and he opened his mouth, but only stammered for a moment. Finally he pushed a hand through his lovely brown hair. So soft and long. She liked that, too.

"Around here, women tend to keep them covered up. Especially in front of men."

She puckered her brows harder. "That is archaic." She looked at her breasts again. "But they aren't lacking in any way?"

He pursed his lips and looked at her chest for a long moment. "No, they're not lacking."

She smiled, relieved at that. She couldn't have the females of this planet thinking her inferior. Then she looked at his hair-sprinkled chest, at the smoky quartz stone he still wore, and chewed her lip. "Yours are not covered."

"Well…that's different."

"In what way?"

He closed his eyes and let his chin fall until it touched his chest. "It just is. You'll understand once you've been here awhile." He turned from her, dug through a basket and emerged with a soft shirt. He handed it to her. "Here. If I'm spending what's left of the night with you, you'd better put this T-shirt on."

She licked her lips. "I think you will have to put it on for me." She glanced down at her useless arm, weighed down by the heavy cast he'd put on it. He nodded and stepped forward, stretched the shirt over her head and eased her injured arm through. She noticed he took great care not to touch her skin any more than was necessary. Was he afraid she carried some kind of disease?

When he finished, she lay back on the bed. "I do not usually wear clothing to bed," she complained.

"Yeah, well, neither do I. Guess we'll both have to make an exception tonight. And I'll stay in the chair."

He sat back down where he'd been and she scowled at him. He'd defied her, and for the second time tonight. He was taking his role as legendary hero a bit too literally. Those men, she'd heard, had been free thinkers, independent, too strong to be ruled by their women. Could he be more like them than she'd imagined?

She wondered about that as she settled back in the bed. She found she was quite disgusted with him a second later when, instead of undressing, he pulled a blanket over himself, covering that wonderful chest. She'd been very eager to see what he looked like completely uncovered. She rolled over and punched the pillow. When he chuckled softly, she only got angrier.

Chapter 3

It was a clean break. And the head injury wasn't serious. Her physical injuries no longer worried him. It was her lack of shyness that he was concerned about now. Okay, so maybe her society didn't impose the same conventions as his did. So what the hell was his moral obligation? He'd have loved to crawl into bed with her half-naked. But he knew better. Maybe she didn't have moral burdens to carry. Hell, he didn't, either. Not really.

But he didn't want any entanglements with any women. Physical needs were easily satisfied. A woman who knew just what she was doing and expected nothing in return was pretty much his method, and it worked just fine. But not some strange woman with no sense of shyness and a head injury. And certainly not a patient. No way.

So he'd just suffer the rest of the night in this chair with a hard-on a cat couldn't scratch down. Served him right, he supposed, for failing to keep himself removed.

He'd stop thinking about her luscious little body, he decided. But when he did, it was only to focus in on her huge, dark eyes and the fear that showed in them every time he looked at her, even when she was angry. When he gazed into those eyes, he saw the frightened little girl he'd found in the woods so long ago. And that made him feel like the little boy who'd rescued her and who'd wondered for the first time in his life what it would feel like to kiss a girl. But he couldn't let himself dwell on all that, either. That kid had been driving him nuts trying to get back into his head ever since he'd come home again. He didn't need to give the little pest an opening. He had a feeling his professional distance would suffer a horrendous setback if he did.

That little kid had been the one who'd decided he had to become a doctor. That little kid—the one who'd found some kind of joy beyond measure in mending the broken wings of robins and taking in every injured animal, tame or otherwise, that he came across. He'd had a knack for healing. And he'd fallen in love with the idea that helping people get well, taking care of them, was some kind of magical gift. He'd wanted a medical degree more than he'd ever wanted anything. So badly he'd traded eight years of his life away to the U.S. Army in exchange for his education. He'd seen being a doctor as something sacred, almost a calling.

He'd been wrong. It was a job just like any other job. He refused to think of it in any other terms.

Despite the look in Janella's eyes when he'd told her he was what she called a healer. She'd seemed awed, admiration gleaming from her mysterious dark eyes as she'd stared at him. She had to be the most beautiful female he'd ever come across in his life, bar none.

Damn, he was thinking about her again. Okay, he'd distract himself by considering the telekinesis.

She'd slammed that door. There'd been no draft, no sudden shift in air pressure. She'd slammed it, and she'd done it without lifting a finger. He wondered what else she could do. It was a damned good thing she hadn't exhibited that talent in front of Eugenia.

He stared at her as she fell asleep. Odd having a woman sleeping under this old roof. Hadn't been one here overnight since Dad had tossed Mother, her belongings and her booze out the door almost thirty-eight years ago. He'd been a baby then, too young to remember any of it. But he'd heard the stories. Sumac was a small town, after all.

The improbability of a woman sleeping in his bed, in his house, was exceeded only by that of a spaceship crashing in the woods and of an *alien* woman—who liked his body—sleeping in here. He decided not to think about those things, either. It wasn't an easy task. And he never did fall asleep.

She stirred just as he entered the bedroom with the trayful of food. She sat up, blinking at him, first in confusion and then in recognition. And then a deep sadness filled her eyes. She'd remembered everything she'd left behind. He knew it without her saying so, and wished he didn't. It wouldn't do to start feeling anything for her, not even sympathy.

He went into the room, sat on the edge of the bed and refused to look at her eyes.

"My arm hurts," she snapped. "Have you nothing to eliminate pain?"

He faced her then, bolstered by her bitchiness. *That* he could handle. "We have drugs, Janella, but I have no way of knowing their effects on you. They might make you sick, might even be fatal to you. You understand?"

She frowned at him. "We are the same species, Thomas. What is good for you is good for me."

He gave his head a shake. "The same species?"

She rolled her eyes as if he were stupid. "Do you think two separate species would evolve as similarly as we have? Look at me."

He did *not* want to look at her. Especially when she sat up, her breasts jiggling beneath his thin white T-shirt. So why was he looking anyway?

"We colonized Earth thousands of years ago, Thomas, when our planet became overpopulated. We all have the same ancestors somewhere along the line. Now, give me something for this pain."

"You know, for a guest in my home, you're one bossy, demanding, *rude* woman."

"Give me something!"

"No."

She blinked and he knew she was shocked speechless.

"But—"

"Janella, even if we started out the same, we may have evolved differently. There are environmental factors, things we've been exposed to that you haven't, a million other things that could lead to differences. Ones that don't show. I'll be damned if I'll give you something that could kill you."

Her anger faded from her eyes very slowly. She sighed, nodded. "You're very wise...for a male."

He didn't even ask what the hell that was supposed to mean.

"Are you hungry?"

She lifted her face, a slight smile playing with her lips. "Yes." Then she frowned and added, "But I have heard of the way your people feed, and I will not eat that dog."

He bit his lips. Damn, it was tough to keep a cold, wide, preferably impassable gulf between them when she kept making him want to laugh out loud. "We don't eat our dogs, Janella."

"No?"

"No."

"Other creatures, though?"

"Well, yeah, we eat meat."

"Barbaric." She eyed the tray suspiciously.

"It's just pancakes with blueberry syrup." He pointed to the steaming stack as he spoke. "This is an orange, and this is coffee. No meat. I promise."

He set the tray on her lap and she picked up a wedge of the orange. "It is fruit?"

"Yeah. Try it. But be careful, and pay attention to the way you feel. If you eat just a little of things, and slowly, we can determine whether you're going to have a reaction to any of them."

She tilted her head, studying his face. "You are being very careful with my health."

"Yeah, well, it's part of the job. Try the damned orange, will you? I don't have time to sit here all morning."

She popped the wedge of fruit into her mouth, frowning and chewing. She nodded and licked the juice from her lips. His gaze riveted itself to her mouth for a long moment before he cleared his throat and averted his eyes.

She finished the orange and sat back, waiting for a few minutes, apparently paying attention to her body for signs the fruit had not agreed with it. When she ran out of patience, she tried some of the pancakes, again nodding in approval.

"It is good. Thank you." She sipped the coffee, grimaced and set the cup down. "This I do not like."

"It's an acquired taste."

She nodded and studied him for a moment. "The female, the one you call Oogena, she will come back."

"It's Eugenia, and you're right. She'll be back. She always comes back."

"Are you her man?"

The idea surprised him so much he almost laughed again. "Hell no. Just a friend. She was close to my father, and now she thinks it's her job to keep tabs on me. She's harmless. A pain in the backside, but harmless."

Janella sighed in apparent relief. Then frowned. "Harmless. That remains to be seen. What will you tell her about me?''

"She thinks you were in a car accident. Granted, that's gonna look a little suspicious when no car is found, but I'll think of something. I'll explain that to you later. For now, Janella, we need to talk about your, uh, your powers.''

"I do not understand.''

"The way you slammed the door last night. Without touching it. It isn't—''

"Thomas? You home?'' Eugenia's quick, light steps followed her voice up the stairs. Then she poked her perfectly made-up face through the bedroom door. "There you are. How's our patient this morning? Are you feeling better, hon?'' She came right to the bed and perched on its opposite side. Gripping Janella's good hand in hers, she smiled. "Does it hurt much?''

Janella studied the pretty face. "Yes.'' The woman's hand was warm and soft on hers. Her face and voice were pleasant, and there was no threatening air about her. Janella shot Thomas a glance. "Thomas helped me.''

"Well, sure he did. And I'm gonna help you, too. Has anyone called your family yet?''

Janella averted her face, trying not to show a hint of sadness. If this Eugenia saw it, she might assume Janella was weak and of little consequence. She might try to use that weakness against her, perhaps even try to steal Thomas away from her. Well, Janella thought, stiffening her shoulders, the woman would get a surprise if she put that theory to the test.

Janella sat straighter and kept her voice cool. "I have no family.''

Eugenia's eyes widened. Then she was leaning over, her arm sliding around Janella's shoulders, gently cradling her head. "I didn't know. I'm sorry, hon. But surely there must be someone we can—''

"No. There is no one."

"Janella is on her own, 'Genia. She was just passing through last night, and—"

"Well, she's not on her own anymore." Eugenia straightened, and Janella saw a gleam of determination in her eyes, but no hint of malicious intent. She clasped Janella's hand in both of hers and looked right into her eyes. "You've got someone now, hon. You've got me. And Thomas, too. Sumac is a wonderful town. You're gonna like it here—you just wait and see."

Janella smiled, a little of the wariness leaving her. This woman practically bubbled over with uncensored emotions, unlike Thomas. Obviously she was the one of no consequence and of little strength. Either that, or things truly were different here. Just as her father had told her. Now that she saw Eugenia was no threat, Janella felt a bit more comfortable with her. "You are very kind."

Eugenia stood and pointed at the tray. "You eat your breakfast now, Janella. Such a pretty name, isn't it, Thomas? When can she get up and around, anyway? I can get the spare bedroom all ready for her, and—"

"You can stop right there, Eugenia. She's staying here."

Janella blinked at the censure in Thomas's voice. He was quite firm with this Eugenia. Would she put up with that? Janella was still certain she wanted him for her own, but he would need a lot of lessons in deferring to feminine authority. The man seemed to have no respect for his superiors.

Eugenia tilted her coppery crowned head, studying him. Then she looked at Janella again. "Well, Thomas Allan Duffy, can it be your stone heart's finally softening up?" Her brows rose and she nodded thoughtfully.

"Don't start with that crap, will you? I just want her where I can keep an eye on her...for the time being, anyway."

Eugenia frowned. "For the time being, then. But

Thomas, you know how it will look. People will talk. As soon as she's able, she ought to come and stay with me.''

Janella felt her eyes widen, but she fought not to let her touch of panic show in them. He could be as haughty and cold as he wanted, but Thomas was the only person she knew here. The only one she trusted. Male or otherwise. She most certainly wasn't going to leave him to go off with this stranger. And it would be silly to leave him, anyway, since he was going to be hers very soon.

He touched her shoulder, sent her a speaking look that seemed to tell her not to worry. It was the first hint of feeling she'd glimpsed in his hard eyes.

Staring hard at Eugenia, he said, ''Since when have I given a damn if people talk?''

Eugenia shrugged. ''*She* might care about her reputation, even if you don't,'' she said. ''Meantime, Janella, is there anything you need?''

Janella thought for a minute. Then nodded. ''I need a dog, I think.''

Thomas blinked. Eugenia's brows lifted in surprise. ''A dog?''

''Not to eat,'' she assured them quickly, thinking that might be the cause of their surprise. ''Thomas says your people keep them as friends. I would like a big one as my friend. Bigger than Hum-phrey. Big enough to bite Humphrey's head off if he makes those loud noises at me again.'' She nodded, sending a smug glance at Thomas to tell him she'd prevail over this dog issue, one way or another. Once explained, they must see that her request made perfect sense.

Eugenia looked at Thomas. Thomas shrugged. ''The head injury. She's still a little...disoriented.''

''Oh.'' Eugenia reached down and patted Janella's hand. ''Don't worry about Humphrey, hon. He wouldn't hurt a fly.'' She smiled and sighed. ''Wish I could stay, but I have to open up the shop. I'll check on you later, though.''

Eugenia turned toward the door, and Thomas rose to walk her out.

"You left your container," Janella said. The small article the woman had carried was still on the bed at Janella's side. She sent it to Eugenia. Thomas turned first, his eyes widening as Eugenia's bag rose from the bed and moved toward her. He lunged as Eugenia turned, snatching the bag in midair. Janella frowned, wondering why he'd done that.

He held the bag out to Eugenia as Janella calmly picked up another orange wedge.

Eugenia frowned, but took it from him. "Thank you. I'd forget my head if it wasn't screwed on. Tootleloo, Janella."

"Tootleloo?" Janella frowned at the fruit in her hand. "I thought it was called orange?"

Eugenia blinked and her smile wavered. "Are you sure she doesn't need a hospital?" she whispered as Thomas took her elbow and escorted her out of the bedroom.

"Questioning my medical opinion, Eugenia?"

Janella heard no more. They moved into the hallway, and she concentrated on eating her breakfast.

He walked beside Eugenia down the stairs. As they moved through the kitchen, she paused at the table, pointing.

"There's a fresh coffee cake in the fridge, and I brought the morning paper in for you. Oddest things going on last night, Thomas. Reminds me of that time about thirty years ago or so...." She shook her head. "Ah, but listen to me rattling on. I have to get on into town. Haven't been late opening the shop since I retired from teaching. Wouldn't want to start now. You just call if you need anything."

She hurried out the door. Her '89 Cadillac roared like a frustrated bull as it shot out the driveway, spitting gravel in its wake.

Thomas stood in the doorway until she was out of sight. Humphrey nudged him hard, apparently disliking being ignored. Thomas scratched his head and Humphrey whined and bunted the screen door. "Yeah, okay, go on outside for awhile." Thomas pushed it open and Humphrey bounded out. Then he closed the door and shook his head slowly. This was not going to be easy. He passed the table on his way back through the kitchen and automatically grabbed the paper. His gaze caught one corner of the two-inch headline and he froze at the three letters he saw there. He unfolded the paper and stared down at it, swearing under his breath. Hundreds Report UFO Over Sumac.

"Ah, damn..."

What's the big deal, he asked himself as he sat down and began scanning the article. Hell, it had made the papers before, too, but no one had really believed it.

Someone did.

Thomas groaned at that young voice invading his psyche yet again. He tried to ignore it, but the persistent little brat kept after him.

You know someone did. Those men in the dark suits who showed up the next day, asking questions around town. They even came to school. Remember?

Yeah, he remembered. He hadn't known what to make of the "men-in-black" at the time. He'd read since that, whoever they were, they showed up with some regularity in towns where UFO sightings were reported. Seemed the alien watchers had formed some kind of group. Had their own magazines, complete with blurred photos of what looked like Frisbees or hats tossed into the air and snapped "in flight." According to most of those members, the men-in-black—or MIB—were alien agents trying to keep witnesses silent. Thomas figured they were more likely government or military types.

Whoever they were, they could be a threat to Janella if they found out about her.

Thomas smirked and shook his head. "Right. Now, get

real. They wouldn't believe me about Janella if I told them.''

He dropped the paper when he heard her scream. Sprinting up the stairs with his heart trying to pound a hole through his rib cage, he battled nightmare images of her convulsing in reaction to something she'd eaten. He flung the bedroom door open so hard it crashed into the wall, but she wasn't in the rumpled bed.

The bathroom. The door was open, and he ran through it, then skidded to a stop. She stood in the shower stall, T-shirt and leggings still in place, dripping wet, coughing and spluttering and reaching blindly for the knobs to turn the cold water off.

He couldn't help it. He burst out laughing, even as he leaned over to twist the knob and stop the flow.

''It is not funny!'' She pushed dark, dripping straggles off her face, rubbed water from her eyes.

''Oh, yeah, it is, Janella. It's funnier than hell.''

She glared at him. ''You...you dog! I only wanted to see what the dial controlled.''

He laughed a little harder, but managed to grab a towel from the shelf and hold it out to her. She didn't take it, nor did she stop glaring at him.

He flung the towel at her, leaving her little choice but to catch it. She muttered as she wiped the water from her face and neck, and began rubbing her hair.

''No man laughs at Janella,'' she stated flatly.

''This one does,'' he returned. She was an arrogant little thing—he could say that much. It was good that her attitude rubbed him the wrong way. It would help him stay aloof. He refused to think about just how long it had been since anything had made him laugh out loud. Instead, he glanced downward once, and regretted it instantly. He suddenly understood the popularity of those infamous wet T-shirt contests. The soaked, all-but-transparent material molded to her like a second skin. The shapes of her full, round breasts, chilled peaks and all, were as fully revealed as they would be were she stark naked. Which was just as well, since she angrily stripped the shirt over her head and began rubbing herself vigorously.

Thomas wouldn't have been human if he hadn't looked just a little. But he quickly ordered his eyes to focus elsewhere, and turned his back.

"That's what we call a shower. It's got hot water as well as cold. It's for bathing." He heard her slipping the tight-fitting pants off, stepping out of them.

"I wish you had told me sooner." She tapped his shoulder and he turned slightly. "I've covered myself. You will not burn your eyes out if you look at me."

Seemed to irritate her that he wouldn't gawk at her naked. Well, he couldn't help it. It was tough enough looking at her with clothes on. He turned around, smiling in spite of himself at the awkward way she held the towel against her.

"Come on, I'll find you something to wear. Then we'll check to see just how thoroughly you ruined the cast." He returned to his bedroom, yanked open a drawer and managed to dig out a pair of shorts with an elastic waist and another T-shirt. He handed them to her. "I'll get you some better things today. Shouldn't be too much of a problem. Eugenia owns a clothing store in town."

She took the clothes from him, and when he saw the towel slipping away he quickly turned his back again. What, did the women up on Krypton run around naked all the time? She certainly acted it.

"You are kind to me," she told him, as she dressed. And it sounded as if she hated having to say it. As if every word were being forced through grated teeth. But maybe she was through being angry with him for laughing. "I hope you will not expect me to go to the woman Eugenia. I want to stay with you."

It was half heartfelt admission, half command. But there had been no kind of request to her words. As if she didn't expect him to refuse her. He would have liked to disagree, just to show her who was in charge around here, but he'd already decided she'd be better off with him. Still, just agreeing with her was a little too much to ask of him.

"Well, it's a good thing. 'Cause you're staying here whether you like it or not."

Her brows drew together, chin coming up a little higher. "I'll stay here with you because it is what I want."

He turned, ready to do battle. Who the hell did she think she was, anyway?

But the sight of her in his baggy shorts dissolved his irritation with her. He damned near laughed again. Then his amusement died when a hairbrush rose from the dresser and floated right into her waiting hand.

"Will she be angry that I refuse her offer?"

"No, she'll be fine." It still gave him the willies to see her do that. "Janella, I need to point something out to you."

She faced him, continuing to brush her hair and waiting for him to speak.

"You know the way you just made that hairbrush come to you, without actually touching it?"

She tilted her head to one side, frowning.

"We can't do that."

"I do not understand."

"Okay, say I want that book over there." He pointed to the Louis L'Amour paperback on the dresser. "The only way I can get it is to walk over there, put my hands on it and pick it up."

Her brows rose in fine arches. "You cannot bring it to you?"

"Nope."

"How bothersome that must be!"

He closed his eyes for a second, opened them again.

"The point is, Janella, that if you go around moving things without touching them, people are going to know you're different. You want to keep your little secret, you're gonna have to try to remember not to do that."

She nodded slowly. "Yes. I see. It will not be easy, Thomas. I've been moving things that way since I was born. I do it without really thinking first."

"Yeah, well, if you do it around here, it's going to lead to trouble."

She nodded. "I will try. There is so much to remember. Keep my breasts covered, do not move things, dogs are not for meat." She rolled her eyes.

He chewed his inner cheek and wished she'd turn bitchy again so he could try to remember how to dislike her. "How are you feeling?" As he spoke, he moved closer, took the plaster-heavy arm in his hands and tested the dampness. It wasn't too bad. She'd had sense enough to hold it out away from the spray.

"Much better than before, Thomas." She glanced down at the cast as he ran his hands over it. "But this is heavy and uncomfortable. How long will it stay?"

"Six weeks."

She closed her eyes, counted on her fingers. "Six... That is forty-two of your days, Thomas!"

He nodded. "'Fraid so."

"But a bone takes only two of your days to heal. Why must I wear it so long?"

Thomas blinked in shock. "A bone takes..." He shook his head. "Ours take six weeks. Maybe you heal faster. Tell you what, after two days we'll have it x-rayed, and..." He sighed hard, pushing a hand through his hair. "Damn, I can't do that, either. A mild dose of radiation might kill you." He frowned and thought about it. "We can take the cast off and see how the arm feels, how much use you have. That ought to tell us all we need to know."

"I could heal in an hour at home by injecting a drug that

reconstructs the cells. But not here. I will simply have to wait, as you suggest.''

He tilted his head to one side, studying her. ''You gave up a lot coming here. Your planet must be light-years ahead of us technologically.''

She licked her lips, nodded. ''There is more to life than technology, Thomas.''

He wanted to ask what the drug was, how it was developed and whether it could be duplicated on Earth. But all of that fled his mind at the intense sadness that glimmered in her eyes all of the sudden. Hell, he could almost feel her throat closing up, the burning behind her eyes, the tightness in her chest. When she bit her lip, averting her face and blinking her eyes dry, he realized his arms were moving, rising, reaching toward her. He slammed them down to his sides, balled fists probably bruising his own thighs.

''So, other than the arm, how do you feel?''

''Fine. The pain is less now than last night. I imagine it will not hurt at all by the end of the day.''

Her voice was a little rougher than normal, softer. Damn, what had she been thinking about that made her so sad? What the hell had she run away from?

''I need to go into town. I work there, at the clinic. You remember, I told you I was a doctor.''

''Doctor.'' She faced him again, shocking him with the sudden transformation. Her smile damn near blinded him, and her still-damp eyes gleamed. ''Healer. You are needed in this...*clinic*...to heal your people?''

''Yes.''

She closed her eyes slowly. ''You do this every day?''

He tilted his head, knowing she was curious about everything, but still a little thrown by the emotion in her eyes. It made him decidedly uncomfortable. ''I take weekends off, unless there's an emergency. Thing is, you can't stay here alone. You ought to come along with me. I'm just wondering if you're up to it.''

She lifted her chin a little higher, put her good hand on her hip and struck a stance. "I am strong, Thomas. As strong as you." Her gaze lowered to his upper arms, narrowed. "Well, nearly as strong. And I want to come with you, to watch you heal them. More than that, I want to help you. Will you teach me how?"

For crying out loud! Would wonders never cease? He studied her and shook his head. "It'll take more than one day in the clinic to teach you anything."

Her lower lip pushed out just a little, and she looked so disappointed he had to swallow another healthy dose of surprise. "But I suppose you could help some. As long as you feel well enough."

"Yes!"

He nodded, studying her, wondering. "What did you do back there, Janella?"

Her lips thinned a little. That proud chin lowered. "I was in training."

"Training for what?"

She sighed, not meeting his eyes. "To take my place in the ruling house."

Thomas frowned. It sounded like something she ought to be proud of. But she didn't seem proud. It might explain her attitude, though. Maybe she was used to having her every command obeyed. "So, why'd you leave?"

She met his eyes, hers dark and distant. "I couldn't stay."

It was all she was going to say, he sensed. She didn't feel comfortable enough with him yet to tell him her most troubling secrets. Okay, he could wait.

Damn! What the hell was he thinking? He didn't *want* to know her secrets, didn't care one ounce what caused the sadness he saw lurking like a shadow on her soul. And he wasn't going to.

Turning away from her, he busied himself digging into the dresser for some clean clothes. "I'll just shower and then we'll be on our way," he told her.

Chapter 4

He put her into a primitive vehicle that bounded and growled over bumpy paths, amid beautiful lands. She couldn't take her gaze from the scene outside the noisy vehicle. Wide, vivid green fields, and golden ones, their crops swaying like a dance with every touch of the breeze. All beneath a sky so blue and cloudless it nearly brought tears to her eyes. So different here. At home the crops were grown in special buildings, without benefit of natural soil. Only chemical mineral solutions and artificial sunlight. And with the population problem, there were no more open spaces like this. Just cities, sterile immaculate cities, everywhere. And the only animals were those on display in a few scattered facilities. Trapped behind fences with man-made rocks and streams, fake trees and grass.

His vehicle bumped along onto a paved path, between neat rows of small buildings. Sumac Feed and Grain, she read, and inhaled the sweet scents coming from the place. Sumac Farm Supply. Sumac John Deere, whatever that was. Sumac Health Center.

"There's a combination grocery store, pharmacy and gas station a little farther on this road. The post office and a used-car dealership are down that road on the right. Across from those there's a restaurant, a hardware store and a bar. And that's about it."

She didn't know what he meant by all those things, but she would learn. He pulled the vehicle to a stop in front of a small brick building, which had been painted garishly pink. The sign above the door read The Pink Petunia, and had a flower surrounding the words. In the big front window forms stood, probably to display the clothing the forms wore.

He got out first, then came around and opened her door. She smiled, glad to see he was finally showing some deference to her gender. He took her hand and led her inside, again holding the door for her. Some of the people passing by turned to stare openly at her, and Janella squirmed a bit, wondering what they were thinking.

"Well, look who's come to call." Eugenia eyed Janella, the clothes she wore. "Oh, my, no wonder I'm your first stop."

There were others in the shop, as well. An older woman, who peered curiously over her antiquated eyeglasses. A young, attractive one, who watched Janella with raised brows. A teenager who wore paint on her face and ornaments in her ears.

"Well, come on, hon, we've got no time to lose." Janella only stared at Thomas as Eugenia took her by the hand. "You can go on to the clinic, Thomas," Eugenia told him. "I'll bring her over when we finish up here."

Janella stiffened, not wanting to be left alone here with these strangers. Fear twisted to life in her stomach, and she shot Thomas a pleading look.

He met her gaze, then glanced down at the band around his wrist. "I've still got some time before my first appointment. Think I'll hang around."

Relief flooded her, and Janella sighed with it. Eugenia only looked from her to Thomas and back again, then shrugged and led her into a back room.

Then, one by one, Eugenia brought articles of clothing for her to try on. The tops and bottoms—she called them jeans—were self-evident, but the torturous-looking white scraps of material that could only be made to harness the breasts were ludicrous. Janella refused even to consider them. There were pretty things, though. Soft, lacy under-garments, and blouses of something she called silk. The jeans were comfortable, and she liked them at once. She kept a pair of them on, along with a silk blouse of vivid green.

It took over an hour to choose, and when she finished, she paused a moment to consider that this primitive culture likely still used some form of currency. She had none, didn't even know what value might be placed on the clothing Eugenia was packing into bags right now. She stepped into the front room again to ask about it, when she saw Thomas hand the woman several green-colored slips of paper.

Eugenia took only a portion and gave him back the rest. "You handle half, Thomas, and I'll eat the other half. It's the least I can do." She winked at him and smiled.

"Not thinking of adopting her like you do every stray thing that comes along, are you, Eugenia?"

She shrugged. "What's the harm? Unless you plan to keep her all to yourself?"

"Dream on, lady."

Janella frowned, wondering again if this female planned to choose Thomas as her mate. In fact, several females in the store seemed to be looking at him with some degree of speculation in their eyes. Janella found she did not like the idea. In fact, she hated it. No doubt any wife of his would make it her first order of business to sweep Janella out of her household like unwanted dust. And that just wouldn't do.

Besides, she thought as she studied him from behind, she had decided to keep him for herself. She'd known he would be hers almost from the day she'd met him so long ago. And despite his coolness toward her, she hadn't changed her mind. He had as many good qualities as bad. He'd have to learn to take orders a bit better, but all in all, he wouldn't make a bad mate. He was certainly nice enough to look at, and Janella imagined coupling with him would be extremely pleasant.

She stood closer to him and slipped her arm through his as a broad hint the other women couldn't help but take. She doubted any of them would be willing to fight for the right to claim him. But if they did, then Janella was more than up for the challenge.

When he turned and looked at her in those tight-fitting jeans, with the thin silk whispering over her breasts and no bra underneath, Thomas almost choked. And when she stood so close, her body pressed to his from thigh to shoulder, and gripped his arm, he felt himself squirm. Every woman in that shop was gawking, and he knew damned well the whole town would start speculating about her before the day was out. What the hell was she up to, clinging to his arm like that?

He sidled away from her, scooped up the packages and carried them out the door, feeling too many female eyes on his back as he left. 'Lisbeth Crabtree had been in there. And God knows there wasn't a bigger gossip in Sumac than 'Lisbeth. Besides which, she'd been actively trying to rope and brand him for one of four daughters. He didn't think she much cared which one, either.

He loaded the back of the Jeep with the things she'd bought and left it parked where it was, in the small square lot in front of The Pink Petunia. Taking Janella's hand, he led her across the road to the clinic.

Opening the door with a flourish, he held it for her and she went in before him.

"This is where I work."

"Where you heal," she said, nodding. Her gaze scanned the carpeted room, the rack of magazines and the chairs lining the walls. She walked over to the toy box and peeked inside, glanced up at the television mounted on a pole in the corner.

"This is a waiting room, Janella. I can only see one person at a time. The others sit here and wait their turn." He pointed to the desk, on the other side of a partition. "And this is Rosa, my receptionist. Rosa, meet Janella...uh, Smith. She's going to be working with us for a while."

Rosa stood, eyeing Janella curiously, muttering a rather unwelcoming hello. He glanced at Janella and saw a distasteful look on her face. The two seemed to be sizing each other up like a couple of boxers in opposite corners of a ring, waiting for the bell.

"Working with us?" Rosa glanced back at him, dark brows lifted, brown eyes more than curious.

"That's right. She's a friend of mine, visiting from out of town. I've been telling her what a *friendly* little town we have here."

Rosa's lips thinned a little. "Doing what?"

Seemed she was choosing to ignore his hint.

"Assisting me with patients."

"She's a nurse?"

"Is there any coffee made, Rosa?" He was damned if he'd put up with the third degree from an employee.

Rosa turned to the fresh pot on the counter behind her, poured him a cup and handed it to him. She glanced at Janella. "Feel free to help yourself."

Janella's glare heated a bit. "I do not like coffee."

Thomas sighed hard. "Come on, Janella. I'll show you around."

As they walked past her, Rosa went to the desk, pulled the chair out and started to sit. Thomas saw the mischievous gleam in Janella's eyes just before the chair suddenly scooted a foot backward. Rosa was on the floor, spitting mad, before he could even shout a warning. And Janella smiled with contentment.

He pulled her into the first treatment room they came to and closed the door. "Dammit Janella, just what the hell do you think you're doing?"

She blinked up at him, ebony eyes all innocence.

"You moved that chair, didn't you?"

She bit her lip, but it didn't prevent her contented smile. "She made me angry."

"That's no excuse."

A little frown appeared between her brows. "I wasn't aware I needed an excuse."

Thomas closed his eyes, praying for mercy. Just what the hell had he gotten himself into? He gripped Janella's shoulders for emphasis. "Don't *ever* do *anything* like that again. Understand?"

"Thomas? Are *you* telling *me* what to do? Giving *me* an order?"

"Damn straight, I am. You might have been some kind of despot-in-training back in Nowhere Land, but here, you're no better than anybody else."

"But I'm a *woman!*"

"So what? You want a medal?"

She blinked as if in shock.

Thomas shook his head, trying to stay angry with her. He knew damned well, though, that Rosa had been just as rude as was humanly possible, and probably deserved what she got. And there was part of him that wanted to laugh out loud about it. That part that never took any crap from anybody. He couldn't help but admire Janella's spunk. Not only that, but when her eyes sparkled with mischief they damn near blinded him.

And now they were clouded and puzzled and she looked like that lost, frightened little girl again. Hell, how was he going to keep the cold, unemotional moat he'd built around himself intact with someone like Janella? Especially if he kept noticing those almond-shaped eyes, and the feelings they expressed so plainly. Wasn't it bad enough that his body was rapidly developing a strong hankering to get to know hers...intimately? Did he have to *like* the damned woman, as well?

Sighing, he yanked the door open. "Rosa, bring me the file on the Meyers kid. And call Saint Luke's for a report on Hugh Connor, will you?"

When Rosa arrived with the file folder, Thomas knew Janella was staring. Her eyes registered something between confusion and disbelief. Rosa left to make the call, and Thomas closed the door again.

"What's the matter now?"

Janella only shook her head, blinking. "She...she *obeyed* you."

The way she'd said the word "obeyed" made it sound like something obscene. "She works for me, Janella. I pay her to *obey* me."

There wasn't time to delve into whatever was making her look so thunderstruck. The first patient arrived, and Rosa led mother and son into the room.

Eugenia didn't like the looks of the three strangers who waltzed into the shop. Not one bit. City folks, she could tell at a glance. They wore nearly identical dark-colored suits, and long black coats that were too heavy for early autumn.

Still, she pasted a smile on her face and set her paperback on the counter. "What can I do for you gentlemen? You lost?"

Only the tall blond one came forward, leaving the other two lingering behind him like shadows. His smile was toothy, big and, she thought, probably false. He was handsome. Dangerously so.

He thrust a hand at her. She shook it, just to be polite. "I'm Jack Halloway, ma'am. I'm with the U.S. Air Force."

She lifted her brows. "Oh, yeah? Where's your uniform?"

He smiled again. "Don't wear them in my line of work. Are you Ms. Overton?"

She nodded, feeling more uneasy by the second. The bell over the door jangled. Sylvie Grayson peeked in, frowned hard and backed right out again.

"Maybe you ought to tell me what you want and be on your way, Mr. Halloway. You're scaring off my customers."

He nodded a little sheepishly. "We're investigating that reported UFO sighting. You must have seen it in this morning's paper."

She nodded, wary. "Didn't see any UFO, though. Don't tell me my tax dollars pay you guys to chase flying saucers around Iowa."

"Now, Ms. Overton, no one said anything about a flying saucer."

Eugenia tilted her head. "Some government test thing, wasn't it? Lord, I hope you nuts haven't decided to use Sumac skies to try out some nuclear-powered war machine. This is a farming town, mister. We don't need your experiments crashing in our woods, spreading whatever kinds of contaminants that power 'em into our water supply."

His brows went up. "You don't have to worry about that. I'm here to prevent any such thing from happening." He laid a well-manicured hand on the counter. "Now, you say something crashed in the woods?"

"I didn't say that."

"You alluded to it." He pinned her with his pale-blue

gaze. "Come on, Ms. Overton. Why don't you tell me what you saw?"

"Well...I, it's just that I..." She felt trapped. She wasn't sure she should tell him about that funny glow that had briefly lit up the night sky out toward Thomas's place. He sure wouldn't want these men poking around over there. Besides, that flash of light was caused by Janella's car accident. Wasn't it?

"What did you see, Ms. Overton?"

A form stopped outside, drawing Eugenia's gaze. A tall man stood there, near the display window. She blinked as she stared at his close-cropped sable beard peppered with white here and there and those warm sapphire eyes. He looked at her, right at her, with those eyes and gave his head a nearly imperceptible shake.

"Ms. Overton?" Halloway prompted.

She licked her lips nervously, tugging her gaze free of the grip the newcomers had on it. What in the world was going on here? Who were all these strangers, anyway?

Stiffening her spine, she made herself answer him. "I didn't see anything, Mr. Halloway. Not a thing. And I really don't think anyone else did, either. Sumac's a nice town, but it can get kind of dull for some tastes. We have a few overactive imaginations around just to keep things interesting."

The bearded man gave her a heart-stopping smile, and then he winked. Eugenia caught her breath as he walked out of sight.

"You sure about that?" Halloway was asking.

"What? Oh, yes, of course I'm sure. I'd certainly remember if I'd seen a UFO, now, wouldn't I?"

Janella battled tears all day as she watched Thomas work. She didn't do much other than hand him things, quickly learning the names of various tools and medicines and bandages. But her emotions kept her from thinking as clearly as she might have been able to do. There had been an elderly man with a heart condition, who'd regaled her with one funny story after another as Thomas examined him. Then a little girl in a wheelchair, who'd gazed up at him with trusting eyes as he worked. And later, the sweetest six-year-old boy with what Thomas called Down's syndrome. He'd been nervous, and Janella had held his hand throughout his visit. Before the boy left, he'd hugged her neck and planted a wet kiss on her cheek. That was when her tears finally spilled over. She averted her face in time to hide them from the boy and his mother, but not from Thomas.

He frowned at her after they'd gone. "What's wrong?"

She shook her head, brushing her face dry with the back of one hand. She couldn't tell him that at home, none of those people would have been given a chance at survival. No one there would care for them the way Thomas had done. If he knew, he'd probably think her as barbaric and cold as the rest of her people. But she wasn't. And for so long, she'd wondered if she was weak, somehow flawed because of her feelings.

Seeing him with those special, wonderful people today had proved to her that she'd been right all along. It wasn't she who was flawed; it was the society she'd been born into. She only wished she could make them see it.

"Janella?"

She bit her lip. "Nothing is wrong, Thomas. I am just...just very happy to be here." She couldn't stop looking at him and thinking that she'd never in her life known a man like him. "You're a special man, Thomas. A good man."

The concern left his face then. He appeared wary, instead. "Not really."

"Yes, you are. The way you care for these people, it—"

"No, Janella. Don't get confused about it. I don't care for them. I just take care of them."

She frowned. "I don't understand."

Thomas lowered his head, his breath escaping in a rush. "First rule of medicine, Janella. Keep an emotional distance. It's necessary." His voice a little softer, he added, "Believe me, I *know*."

Janella tried to see his meaning in his eyes, but they were carefully blank, as they had been for most of the day. In fact, now that she thought about it, she realized that *he* hadn't held the little boy's hand or hugged him. He hadn't laughed at any of the old man's stories. He'd just gone about his examination, almost pretending not to hear them.

"Emotional distance" was the term he'd used. But in the time she'd known him, she hadn't seen him show much emotion at all. Except when he'd laughed at her in the shower.

It was so confusing. Why would a man spend his life helping people unless he cared? And if he didn't care, then was he just like the people she'd left behind? Unfeeling? Cold?

Somehow she just couldn't believe that. She decided to watch him more closely from now on. Maybe she'd figure it out. Maybe she'd figure a lot of things out. Like why he didn't seem to have any deference to women, and why Rosa had rushed all day to obey his every request. This Earth was a puzzling place.

Chapter 5

She watched television with an intensity that would have been laughable. Except that she kept looking at him with the same studious, curious expression every few seconds. And he got the sneaking suspicion she was comparing him with the men she saw on the screen, and he wouldn't have been human if he hadn't wondered how he measured up. Not that he cared.

The movie was *Casablanca*. When it ended, she was blinking away tears. Thomas smiled a little. Seemed he had a softhearted little alien on his hands.

"Did you like the movie?"

She nodded hard, brushing her cheeks dry with one hand. "It was wonderful, but so sad."

Thomas thumbed the rewind button on the VCR. She was staring at him again. Her almond-shaped eyes narrow, probing. "I think I understand better now."

"Understand what?"

She only shrugged, rose from the sofa and went to the shelf that was lined with videocassettes. Humphrey lay in her path, oblivious to the world. She skirted him warily. He lifted his head, eyeing her, watching her every move. The two didn't much like each other, but Thomas thought Humphrey had gotten over his initial hostility. Now he was only suspicious and watchful.

Janella studied the tapes. "Can we watch another?"

"Sure. Watch them all night if you want. Best way I can think of to learn about life on Earth. Just don't take them too literally, Janella. Reality is a lot more mundane than the movies."

"I don't know about that," she said softly, not looking at him, pulling out one tape after another. "Rick seemed a good example of human behavior."

Thomas shifted on the couch, trying not to focus solely on her perfect bottom filling out those jeans. And failing. "In what way?"

"He appeared cold at first. Unfeeling, without emotion. But it was only his way of protecting himself from being hurt again." She decided on a tape and turned toward him, holding it in her hand. "It makes sense, don't you think? I would think that might be a common reaction to pain."

He pursed his lips, nodded. "I guess it might be. I don't know, I'm not a psychologist."

She smiled, lifting the tape. "What is this one about?"

He grinned at her selection. Disney's *Beauty and the Beast.* "It's a children's movie. But you'll probably like it." He got up, ejected the tape that was in the VCR and took the one she held.

"Why do you have children's movies, Thomas? You have no children."

He shrugged, fast-forwarding through the previews. "No, but I have a lot of young patients. They get bored when they have to stay in the hospital for any length of time, so I buy videos and take them in. Keeps their minds off their medical problems."

She didn't comment, and when he glanced her way it

was to see the most smug, knowing expression in her eyes. Almost an I-told-you-so sort of a look, but he couldn't imagine why.

Giving the dog a wide berth, she returned to her seat on the sofa. Humphrey only lowered his head again when she was sitting still. The opening music played, and Thomas sat beside her. He reached into the bowl on the coffee table for a handful of potato chips. Humphrey lifted his head and emitted a soft "Woof."

Janella stiffened.

"He's talking to me," Thomas told her.

She blinked twice, glanced from him to the dog and back again. "What is he saying?"

"He wants a potato chip. He loves the things. Here." Thomas took her hand in his, turned it palm up and placed a chip in it. "Why don't you give it to him?"

"He'll bite my hand off. He hates me." Her eyes widened as Humphrey got to his feet and planted himself in front of her, waiting with his tail wagging a mile a minute. "Make him sit down, Thomas. I cannot see the movie."

"Oh, he won't sit down until he gets a chip. And I'm not going to give him one."

She glared at him, but he only nodded toward the dog. "Go on, try it. I promise, he won't hurt you. You trust me, don't you?"

She nodded, warily, and shifted the chip to her fingertips. Slowly she held her hand out to the dog. Humphrey leaned forward and took it. He crunched it down with relish, staring at Janella. She stared back. Humphrey sighed contentedly, turned around three times and lay down right on top of Janella's feet. She tilted her head, staring down at him as if puzzled.

"You see?" Thomas asked. "Now he's your friend. You gave him his favorite treat and he's grateful."

Biting her lip, Janella reached a wary hand downward and very timidly stroked the dog's head. Humphrey closed his eyes and sighed more loudly than before. She smiled softly, settled back on the sofa, a little closer to Thomas than she'd been before. He tried to focus on the movie, instead of on the way it felt to be sitting in a darkened room with her this way. Sort of intimate, and extremely uncomfortable. The pendant he wore felt warm against his skin.

Janella glanced at the glass of cola on the table, and it levitated, then floated into her waiting hand. She took a sip and returned it in the same manner.

Long after Thomas had gone to his bed, Janella stayed up watching movies. And with every one, she felt she understood a bit more about these people and their ways. Thomas had explained how to operate the VCR before going up, so she could study to her heart's content.

And the revelations were enlightening. The most important of all was that it seemed women were not the rulers of this planet. The males didn't obey them or serve them or even seem to fear them. Odd concept, but one she supposed she could adjust to. In fact, in some of the films, it appeared the women were the ones in subjugation. But in most, the sexes behaved almost as equals. Fascinating.

The other interesting difference was in the mating rituals of these people. Since neither sex was dominant, the choosing of a mate seemed to be a terribly complicated process, consisting of several steps. First, one recognized his or her attraction to the other. Then one agonized while trying to discern if the other felt the same, and went to great lengths to try to attract the other's attention. After that, one spent far too much time, in Janella's opinion, working up the courage to declare his or her feelings to the other. It was all very odd.

Janella had never once considered that she would have to do anything to attract the mate of her choice. At home, she would only have had to choose. It would have been an honor for any of the men to be picked and she couldn't imagine one who would object to it.

Here, things were going to be much more difficult. She realized with a little start that if she wanted Thomas as her own, she would first have to convince him that *he* wanted *her*.

It was such a ludicrous notion she blinked in shock.

And as she recalled the hostile glances of the women in the town, she knew there were plenty of others who'd like to claim him. Fighting for the right to claim him would do little good, for the choice was his.

Oh, dear, this was going to be a terrible effort. From all she'd seen on the screen tonight, there seemed to be an incredible amount of work involved. She would have to dress in satins and learn to apply the face paint as the women in the films did. She would have to learn to...oh, what was that word? Flirt. Yes, that was it. To flutter the eyelashes, and laugh softly, and make veiled, slightly suggestive comments, while making them seem unintentional.

She frowned at the sleeping dog and wriggled her toe from beneath his fur. Then she tiptoed past him, not quite as secure in his friendship now that Thomas had left the room, and inserted a fresh tape into the VCR. She was still confused about several things, and she would study these tapes until everything came clear in her mind.

Thomas found her there in the morning, still in yesterday's clothes, slumped sideways, sound asleep. From the stack of tapes on top of the VCR, it looked as if she'd been up most of the night. He stifled a laugh and moved quietly past her to put on a pot of coffee and see what he could find for breakfast.

When he turned from the sink, with a carafe of water, she was standing in the doorway, watching him.

"Sorry. I didn't mean to wake you. How'd the film festival go?"

She shrugged, scuffing to the table and sinking into a chair. "I enjoyed it very much. But I'm still confused."

Thomas poured the water into the coffeemaker, set the carafe underneath and turned it on. He refused to notice her tousled hair and sleep-hazy eyes. Or to let himself think that she looked almost as if she'd just been thoroughly made love to, instead of just having had a long night on the couch. In fact, he'd pretty much decided it was best not to think about sex at all when Janella was around. It tended to make his jeans too tight.

"I'm not surprised. What are you confused about, Janella? Maybe I can clear it up for you."

"Is it, or is it not acceptable to have sex before one is...um...married?"

Thomas felt his brows shoot up. "Sheesh, you cut to the chase, don't you?" He fished a pair of bowls and spoons from the dishwasher, dropped them on the table and reached into a cupboard for a box of cereal. If his hands were unsteady, it was just because he hadn't had a cup of coffee yet this morning. And he could and would answer what was a perfectly logical question, in a calm and professional manner.

"That's kind of complicated. I guess these days, it's pretty much a matter of personal choice. Some people consider it immoral, some don't." He grabbed the milk from the fridge and sat down across from her to fill his bowl.

"And what is your personal choice?"

Thomas sloshed milk onto the table. He steadied his hand, set the carton down and met her gaze. Damn. She was dead serious about this.

"That's a personal question, Janella. You can't just go around asking people about their sex lives." He reached for a napkin and mopped up his spill.

"I'm not asking just anyone. I'm asking you. How am I supposed to know how to act unless you explain things to me?"

He studied her, wondering just when she'd become so damned interested in knowing about Earth's moral standards concerning sex. "Why the sudden interest, Janella? You considering having sex with someone?"

She lowered her gaze quickly. "I was only curious." She reached for the box, filled her bowl carefully, just as he'd done, and then added milk.

Thomas licked his lips and tried telling himself this was not a wise conversation to be having with her. Not with her sitting there all rumpled, her wild hair tempting him to smooth it with his fingers, her eyes soft and sleepy.

"How did you handle sex back on Krypton?"

She scowled at his name for her planet, but still didn't meet his gaze. "It's forbidden until one's mate is chosen."

His throat went dry. "Did you…have a mate?"

She shook her head. "No. But I have often wondered what coupling would be like. Have you done it, Thomas?"

He almost groaned aloud, suddenly losing interest in his cereal. "Yeah."

"But not with a…a wife?"

Her jet eyes were on him now, searching his face, wide with curiosity.

"No, not with a wife."

"What is it like?"

He shoved his bowl away from him. "It's pleasant, okay? Can we change the subject now?"

"Did you love the woman, Thomas? Or did you do this only to relieve your physical needs?"

"For crying out loud—"

She jerked a little at his tone, eyes widening. "I've made you angry. I'm sorry, Thomas, I only wanted to know—"

"All right, all right. No, I didn't love any of them. Yes, it was only physical, and before you ask, the reason for that is that's the way I want it. That's the *only* way I want it. Now, will you please eat your cereal and get your butt upstairs to shower and dress? We have to be at the clinic by eight.''

She stared at him for a long moment, and he could see the questions in her eyes. She wanted an explanation. But she didn't ask for one. Instead, she finally nodded and focused on her breakfast.

Maybe the movies hadn't been such a great idea after all. Films today were nothing but sex and violence anyway. Good thing he hadn't had a copy of *Rambo* lying around. She'd probably be asking for an Uzi.

Thomas sipped his coffee, glanced across at her, and saw the slightly wounded look she wore. Hell, he'd hurt her feelings, snapping at her that way. But how did she expect him to keep his distance when she sat there talking about sex as if she were thinking of trying it?

''You know, Janella, maybe you ought to read some books. They might give you a much clearer picture of things than the movies can.''

She brightened, nodded hard. ''Books. Yes, that's a good idea. I will…*I'll* do that.''

In the Bear Road Café, three strangers in suits and ties sat at a corner booth, listening to the locals rattle on. So far no one had mentioned a UFO sighting. Seemed they were all up in arms over some local doctor's indiscretions. Still, you never knew what you might pick up on from casual conversation.

Jack Halloway chewed his bagel and pretended to read the morning paper, while the tape recorder in his coat pocket whirred almost silently.

''She's livin' with him!''

''What, all alone out there on the farm?''

''That's right. Pretty thing, too.''

''Rosa's fit to be tied. Had her sights on the doc herself.''

''So I heard. Rosa says she don't know what that girl is, but she's no nurse, that's for—''

"And goin' by the name of Smith. If that isn't the most unlikely—"

"You ladies ever do anything besides gossip?"

The one male voice in the room came from the gangly young man behind the counter. Skip, Halloway had heard him called. The others came from the table just behind his. All female, all married and, apparently, all very upset over the local doc's love life.

"Who do those city girls think they are, anyway? Waltzing in here like they were born and bred, and waltzing right back out again with *our* men."

"Yeah, but *what* city do you think this one's from? Rosa said she talks funny."

"I saw her at The Pink Petunia, hangin' on the doc's arm like she owned him. She was wearing a cast, too."

"Yup. Talk is she was in some kind of accident the other night. Doc Duffy found her and took her home with him."

One of them sniffed indignantly, as if to say taking her home had been the least he'd done with the woman. Halloway pulled a wallet out of his inner pocket. He'd pay up and leave. This was getting them nowhere.

"Musta been some accident. Did you see that light in the sky? Looked like a bomb went off."

Halloway went a little rigid in his seat, his gaze leaping up and meeting that of one of the men across from him. He forced himself to relax, replaced his wallet and took another bite of the bagel.

"I saw it. That couldn't have been her, though. That flash came from the woods out back of Duffy's place. No roads out there."

"Some kind of government test, I bet. And what do those loonies at the paper do but call it a UFO! Hey, Skip, a little more coffee over here."

"Yeah, I'm coming."

"Well, what I saw that night sure looked like nothing

I've seen before. Just a green streak, crossing the sky, and
then that white flash. Scared my socks off, I can tell you.''

"What doesn't, Agnes? You get scared over every thunderstorm.''

"It was no UFO. Likely one of those satellites they got
floatin' around overhead just petered out and came down.
Don't know what everyone's getting so fired up about.''

"You don't suppose that foreign city woman will lure
the doc back to wherever she came from, do you?''

"Wouldn't be surprised. And where would we be then?''

"I just wish Rosa would hog-tie that man and marry
him.''

"Rosa! He's not interested in Rosa. Now, if he'd just
take a second glance at my Becky, I know he'd—''

"Aw, 'Lisbeth, you've done everything but shackle the
man to Becky Jo, and he hasn't so much as blinked.''

Jack Halloway nodded to his two counterparts, rose and
walked to the register to pay for their breakfasts. As he
handed the man his money, he smiled his friendliest smile.
"Say...Skip, isn't it? You couldn't tell me where I might
find a Dr. Duffy, could you?''

The man at the register looked Halloway up and down,
then nodded. "This time of day, he'd be at the clinic. Back
the way you came and turn left. Can't miss it.''

"Thanks, but I didn't want to see him at the clinic. I
was talking about his farm.''

The man frowned. "You a friend of his?''

Halloway nodded. "Yeah, and I've come a long way to
see him. Can you help me out?''

In a corner booth near the windows, a tall man sat, absently rubbing his salt-and-pepper beard and listening.

Janella glanced out through the display window of The
Pink Petunia for the fortieth time and emitted a sigh.

"He's only been gone an hour, hon,'' Eugenia patted her
hand and smiled. "He'll be back soon.''

Janella blinked, a little startled that she'd been so obvious. Thomas had asked her to stay here while he went to the hospital to check on a patient. He hadn't wanted her there because, he said, she might inadvertently be exposed to some illness or other, one against which her body might have no resistance. It made sense. But Janella didn't like it.

"You're sweet on him, aren't you?"

Janella blinked, then frowned. "What do you mean?"

"Thomas. You like him, don't you?" Eugenia filled Janella's teacup as she spoke, then added more steaming liquid to her own.

"Of course I like him." Janella took a sip. She really liked the fragrant tea. Much nicer than that bitter swill Thomas called coffee. "He's been very good to me."

"Come on, Janella. You can tell me." Eugenia winked at her.

"Tell you what?"

Eugenia's lips pursed, and she sighed. "Oh, fine. Be as coy as you want. Just remember, I'm on your side."

"On my side?"

"Yes." She looked down, shook her head slowly. "You know, he used to be so different. Happy and easygoing. Since he came back, he's a different man. Stiff as a board, and so cold it gives most people goose bumps. But he hasn't changed inside, Janella. I think maybe his heart's just taken an extended nap. All he needs is a good woman to shake him right from his head to his toes, and it's gonna wake up again. I guarantee it."

Janella frowned, studying Eugenia's pretty face and trying to understand what she was saying.

"I think you might be that one good woman, Janella. What do you think?"

Janella's jaw dropped. But she thought she understood now. It seemed Eugenia's opinion confirmed her own, the one she'd come to so long ago, when a young boy had rescued her from a hungry-looking dog.

"I think it's like *Beauty and the Beast*," she ventured, speaking slowly, watching Eugenia's face for her reactions. "He's really just a prince in disguise."

The smile that split the other woman's face was nearly blinding. She clapped her hands together, then reached out to clasp Janella's. "I just knew you and I would hit it off," she said. "It took me months to figure Thomas out, and here you've done it in a couple of days. You're a godsend, Janella."

Janella couldn't help but smile back. She was so relieved to know that this woman agreed with her about Thomas. Janella thought something had hurt him, and that he was hiding away, beneath a callous mask, just to keep from being hurt again.

"Eugenia…" She licked her lips and forced herself to go on. "You are my friend now, correct?"

"Absolutely!"

"Then I may ask you a…personal question?"

"You can ask me anything, hon. Go ahead, what is it?"

Janella stiffened her spine, met the other woman's gaze head-on. "How can I make Thomas want me?"

Eugenia lowered her head a bit, a slow smile spreading across her lips. She rubbed her hands together. "You've come to the right place, hon. The doctor isn't gonna know what hit him."

Janella came out as soon as Thomas pulled in. She didn't wait for him to shut the Jeep off or get out. She just climbed in, slung the bag she was carrying into the back and fastened her seat belt.

"What's in the bag?" He shifted into reverse, backing slowly onto the road.

"Books. You said I should read some, so Eugenia loaned me three of her favorites."

Thomas grimaced. "Don't tell me, those love stories she's always devouring."

"What's wrong with love stories?"

"I don't believe in them."

Janella's head tilted to one side, and she studied him. "Why not?"

"They aren't realistic, Janella."

"You've read many of them, then? And you are an expert?"

"Well, no—"

"Oh. Then it must be that you've been in love so many times, you know all about that."

"There's no such thing as love, Janella. Not for me, anyway. I don't need it, don't want it and won't put up with it. Does that explain it clearly enough?"

She nodded. "But Eugenia says it doesn't matter whether you want it or not. She says there is someone for everyone, one special person, and that when that person comes along, you have no choice in the matter."

"And did you check Eugenia's credentials or just buy the whole tale, hook, line and sinker?"

"What do you mean?"

"Well, she's been single all her life, Janella. Hardly an expert on affairs of the heart. She's only telling you what she wishes were true."

"Oh, no, you're wrong about that!"

"Am I?"

Janella nodded hard. "Eugenia saw a man yesterday. A stranger, who stopped outside and just glanced in the window at her. And she said when their eyes met, her stomach twisted and her breath caught in her throat, and her hands began to shake." Janella looked at him and smiled. "You should have seen her when she talked about him, Thomas. It was wonderful to see her eyes shine that way."

"Sounds more like food poisoning."

Thomas had to look away from her, partly because he

was driving, but mostly because of the way *her* eyes sparkled as she talked about it. His attention no longer riveted to those black gems, he frowned, not liking what he'd heard.

"So who is this guy? Where's he from?"

Janella only shrugged, reaching for the bag and pulling out a paperback. There was more in there than books, Thomas noted, glimpsing a scrap of something sheer and black. He shifted in the seat and decided not to ask. He'd probably be better off not knowing about Janella's underwear or whatever the hell that was.

"Come, on, Janella, I asked a question. Who's this guy Eugenia's all overheated about?"

"I don't know, Thomas. She says she's never seen him before." Janella opened the paperback to the first page and began reading.

They'd finished dinner. He was sipping fresh-brewed coffee. Janella had set aside her paperback and helped him clear away the dishes. She used her casted arm as often as the uninjured one, he noticed, so he figured she'd been right about healing in a couple of days. He'd have to take it off and check the arm later.

Now she crouched in front of the dishwasher, studying the buttons. He moved to stand behind her.

"I'll do it."

"No. I should learn to do things, Thomas. I have no servants here, and I can't expect you to care for me forever." She tipped her head back, staring into his eyes and giving him a dazzling smile. "Unless you'd like to volunteer for the job."

Thomas frowned. She looked away before he could decide if she was trying to make a joke or just talking to hear herself talk. Or maybe... Nah.

"No, thanks. I'd make a lousy servant."

She chewed her lip, studying the buttons, her fingers hovering over them. "So would I."

He lowered one hand, pushed her finger down on the right button. "That one."

"Oh." The machine whirred to life.

His hand lingered on the back of hers for a split second longer than necessary before he jerked it away and turned toward the now-spotless table. Spotless except for the stack of cookbooks Janella had piled in its center. "So tonight's going to be a crash course in cuisine?"

"I should prepare the meals from time to time," she told him. "It's only fair." She glanced at the books and sighed. "Besides, I thought I might try to see the appeal of eating animal flesh."

Her nose wrinkled at the idea. Before he thought about it, Thomas was smiling at her. He quickly remedied that and stalked into the living room. "Knock yourself out, Janella. I've got some paperwork to do anyway."

She watched him leave, wondering again if he might want her for his own. She knew she wanted him. For some reason the idea of having sex for the first time was becoming more and more appealing to her. Especially when she read the vivid descriptions of the act in Eugenia's novel. It sounded like something very wonderful. And the notion that she'd like to try it with Thomas just wouldn't leave her alone.

Last night she'd decided the entire thing would be too complicated even to consider, but the way Eugenia had explained it, it couldn't be simpler. All Janella had to do was put on the lacy black bit of clothing Eugenia had given her, walk into Thomas's room during the night, lie down in his bed and kiss him. Janella had been worried about what to do next, but Eugenia assured her Thomas would know exactly how to handle things from there on. He only needed a "nudge" to get him started.

The question was, did Janella really want to go through

with this? She began having second thoughts when she finished with the first novel. It seemed to her that the idea of sex, or *making love,* as the book called it, was more or less a declaration of undying affection. A commitment of sorts. And she still hadn't told Thomas that she wanted him as her lifelong mate. And she had no idea what he might think of the idea. She'd decided long ago that she loved him, but she was no longer so sure. In the book, it had taken a long time for that thing called love to grow between the couple. And while she was fond of Thomas and attracted to him, she wondered if what she felt would last a lifetime. She wasn't even certain she would know love if she felt it. She'd never been in love with a man, and she'd surely never witnessed that kind of tender emotion between men and women at home.

And then there was the whole other side of it. She'd have to make him love her, too. How on earth was she supposed to do that?

Janella studied a big fat cookbook for some time, trying to put thoughts of Thomas and his impending (maybe) seduction out of her mind.

The knock at the door startled her. And she glanced up to see Rosa, the receptionist, standing there. Janella felt her eyes widen. Oh, no! The woman was wearing a dress, and…and face paint. And her hair was not up in a knot as it usually was. It was loose and curly.

She opened the door and poked her head inside. "Is Thomas home?"

Thomas came into the kitchen, looked at the woman standing in the open doorway and swore under his breath.

Janella glanced from him to Rosa and back again, seeing all her plans dissolve before her eyes. If it were as easy as Eugenia had told her to seduce a man, then Rosa was surely going to succeed.

Fury rose to grip Janella, and she had a very strong urge to vent it by sending the woman flying right back through that door. But she knew that would anger Thomas, so she bit her lip and forcibly restrained herself.

She had to do something, though. What? Oh, what on earth was she going to do?

Chapter 6

Thomas blinked twice. He couldn't believe this. He'd never seen Rosa Michaels wearing anything other than jeans. Never! But here she was in a tight-fitting little halter dress that proved once and for all that the woman had a killer body. Her hair twisted and kinked in little curls down to her shoulders, and she wore more makeup than Tammy Faye.

She carried a picnic basket in one hand and a file folder in the other. She'd been wearing a hostile glare when he'd come in, one directed right at Janella. But when she saw him her smile turned sweeter than pure cane sugar.

"I found Shelly Connor's medical records on the counter before I left tonight, Thomas. I figured you'd intended to bring them home and must have forgotten, so I brought them by."

"That wasn't necessary."

Her lashes fluttered, and a hint of uncertainty crept into her eyes. "You know she's due any day now, and there's a lot here."

"Yeah, I know that." He kept his voice cold and flat. There was no way in hell he wanted to give her the slightest hint of encouragement. He did not need this bull. Not now.

"Well, I thought I could help you go over them. I brought some fried chicken and..." Her voice trailed off.

He slid a glance toward Janella. She was rising from her chair, watching the woman who'd somehow become her enemy in the space of the past two days.

"Janella and I just finished dinner."

"Oh." Her gaze fell.

"And I can manage to go over those files by myself. You're obviously dressed to go somewhere. I wouldn't want to keep you."

Rosa frowned, confused maybe. Hadn't he made himself clear enough, then? Finally, she snapped out of it and strode in as though she owned the place, setting the basket on the counter and opening the fridge.

"Well, no sense letting all this good fried chicken go to waste, is there? I'll just leave it for you." She took bowls and platters from the basket, placing them in the fridge as if she did so every day.

"Yes, Thomas," Janella put in. "You know how you love the flesh of feathered birds, especially boiled in bovine fat."

Janella's expression betrayed no hint of it, but Thomas could see the fury in those eyes. They damn near glowed with it. What the hell was her problem anyway?

Rosa met that look with a smug one of her own. "Mmm. That coffee sure smells good."

Thomas thought very seriously about turning around and leaving the room. Let the two of them kill each other if that's what they wanted. Instead, and largely for the sake of keeping a good receptionist alive and kicking, he reached for a mug and filled it. Then handed it to Rosa.

She pirouetted, smiling. "Why, thank you." She accepted the cup and sat beside him at the table. Humphrey snarled softly, and Janella reached down to pat his head and reward him with a bit of the brownie she'd been eating.

Thomas was so shocked to see it that he nearly fell off his chair.

"So, Janella, how is the house hunting going?"

Janella glanced up at Rosa, obviously irritated. "House hunting?"

"You *are* looking for a place to live, aren't you? I mean, I just assumed you wouldn't want to sponge off Thomas for longer than necessary."

"Janella is my guest, Rosa, and you're being rude as hell. You want to tell me why?"

Janella's gaze met Thomas's, softening.

Rosa looked down at her hands, then smiled at Janella. "Did that sound rude? I didn't mean it to. It's just that the whole town is talking about it. I mean, no one knows what to think, Thomas. Everyone knows what a loner you are. And I myself heard you telling Hugh Connor that you'd sooner fly to Mars than see a woman living under this roof with you."

Janella's eyes darkened, and she stared, first at Thomas, then at Rosa.

"Perhaps Thomas was referring to the women he knew then. It *was* before he'd met me. The truth is, he *insists* that I stay here with him."

"Now, just one damned minute—" Thomas began.

"Really, Janella. Don't fool yourself. Thomas would never fall for a city girl like you. I've known him a lot longer than you have, and I know that Thomas—"

"Thomas," he said, calmly setting his cup down and facing them both, "is capable of speaking for himself." He stood. "This conversation is over. Go home, Rosa."

Rosa lowered her head, obviously embarrassed. "I'd better go."

"Yes, you had better," Janella said, her voice low.

As she got to her feet, Janella eyed the filled coffee cup on the edge of the table.

Thomas saw her, gripped her shoulder, squeezed hard. "Don't even think about it."

She pouted like a kid whose candy bar had been stolen, but she restrained herself. Good thing. He hated to think what that coffee would've done to that slinky concoction Rosa wore.

He went to the door, opened it for her. "See you Monday, and we'll forget this ever happened."

Rosa shot a hate-filled glance toward Janella. "I'm sorry, Thomas, but if *she* is going to be working at the clinic, I'm going to have to give notice."

Thomas stiffened. "Giving me an ultimatum, Rosa? You claim to know me...so you ought to know better than that."

Her eyes widened a little.

"You go on home and think it over," he told her. "Then do what you have to do. But Janella stays. Here in my house, and in town at my clinic, for as long as I say."

Rosa huffed, turned and ran out of the house.

"Why do you do that?"

Thomas turned slowly, his skin still prickling with anger. Damn, nothing made him madder than people trying to tell him what to do or manipulate him into doing it.

"Do what?"

"Step into matters that do not concern you." Janella rose, came to stand right in front of him, good arm crossed with the casted one over her chest.

"Why in hell can't you try, just a little bit, to get along with the people here? Can you tell me that? Are you deliberately trying to make Rosa hate you?"

She closed her eyes, shook her head. "Men don't understand these things. I will explain for you. That *receptionist* wants you. She can't claim you because I am in her way. That is the only reason she dislikes me, Thomas."

"*Claim* me?"

Janella sighed hard, pushing one hand through her long dark hair. "Oh, I know it doesn't work that way here. She has to make you want her first. But don't you see, that's what she was trying to do. She doesn't dare to defy me or challenge me for you, so she resorts to this underhanded manner of trying to lure you to her with gifts of food and scanty clothing."

Thomas chewed his lower lip for a moment. Then he nodded thoughtfully. "So you figure Rosa thinks that you plan to…uh…*claim* me for yourself. Is that it?"

She sighed, seemingly relieved that he'd finally caught on. "Yes."

"And do you? Plan to claim me, I mean?"

She tilted her head to one side, looking him up and down. "I might. I haven't decided."

"I see." Thomas paced across the kitchen, picked up his cup from the table and carried it to the sink. As he rinsed it he spoke slowly, evenly. "Well, before you make any plans, Janella, I ought to tell you one thing."

"Yes?"

He turned slowly, slung the cup into the sink and faced her. "No one is going to claim me. Not you. Not Rosa. Nobody. Understand?"

She frowned. "Oh, Thomas, don't be foolish. I didn't say I wanted you forever. Only for sex."

He closed his eyes, gave his head a shake. "You wanna repeat that?"

"Sex," she said again. "I wish to experience it. There's no reason not to. It isn't forbidden here. And you told me yourself it's a matter of personal choice. So, my personal choice is to try it. And I would like to try it with you."

He didn't know whether to roll on the floor laughing or scream bloody murder. "No, Janella."

Her brows drew closer. "But why?"

She took a step closer to him. He took one backward.

"You told me you'd done it before. That you did it only

for physical pleasure. That it didn't matter that you cared so little for the women. So why?''

Good question. Damned good question. Hell, if she was so willing to have meaningless, casual sex with him, why wasn't he jumping at the chance? He'd wanted her from the second he'd laid eyes on her. So what was the problem?

Janella answered his question before he could. Her head lowering, she whispered, ''You do not desire me.''

''Look, it wouldn't be smart, okay? I know how you women are. Sleep with a man once and start thinking he's yours for life. It isn't gonna happen, Janella. If I want sex, I'll get it from a stranger, and if you want some man to *claim,* you'd better look elsewhere.''

She blinked in shock, took an unsteady step backward. Then her face changed. Pure undiluted rage twisted her features, and her eyes just about spat fire. ''I could have you in chains for that.''

''Not here, you couldn't. Hell, it's no wonder you left your planet. What a warped frigging place it must have been.''

She clenched her fists, nails digging into her palms, knuckles whitening. Damn, she was mad enough to kill. Her body trembled as she fought a visible battle for control. The dishes on the table rattled, the table itself vibrating beneath them. She grated her teeth, squeezed her eyes tight. One of the cupboard doors swung open, the dishes inside jostling near the edge of the shelf. The lights flickered.

Finally, she drew a deep breath, held it a long time and released it all at once. Then she turned, slammed out of the house, and the dishes settled down again.

Thomas swore as he watched her stride away from the house, across the lawn, toward the stubbly wheat field. Damn, she had a temper. He shook his head, feeling an odd, disconnected sense of unreality float through his mind. Just what the extent of her powers might be, he had no clue. But he suddenly had a feeling she wouldn't be a good person to cross. If he were anyone other than who he was, he might have thought twice about arousing that anger again. But being Thomas, he didn't.

She should have yelled, vented a little. He thought that as he shoved the dishes back into the cupboard and closed the door. Even though she was dead wrong and needed a good lesson in humility, she should have vented a little.

She sure as all hell didn't take rejection very well. He supposed she was used to getting everything she wanted back up there on Krypton, where she was some kind of princess or something.

He went to the door, thought about going after her, then decided against it. Let her have some time to cool off. He turned back to the kitchen. Maybe he'd try to explain things to her a little more gently when she came back.

If she came back.

He managed to hang tough for two hours. Even when the sun went down and darkness settled in like a shroud. But when the thunder rumbled in the distance and the rain started, he lost his indifference again.

Janella sat at the edge of the charred ground in the woods, and she let the tears of frustration and rage flow freely. Never had she been so utterly alone. And so out of place! No one here understood her. And it seemed they never would. At home, things had been so simple. The men there respected her. She was the daughter of their ruler, the next queen of the planet, after all. They didn't mind their lot in life. It was the natural order of things, the way she saw it. The men were physically stronger and more adept at labor. The women were the ruling class. But they treated their men well, gave them all they needed and even grew fond of them sometimes. Why, Janella's mother had even asked her father's opinion on the running of the world a time or two.

At home, the males had been eager to gain Janella's attention, all of them hoping to be the one she chose as her own. But here, here she was treated no better than that dog Humphrey. And Thomas...he didn't even want her! Eugenia had been wrong about that. And Janella would be hung by her hair before she'd humble herself to ask him again. She could only thank the fates that she had told him she didn't want him forever. It would have hurt ten times as much if she'd offered her heart, told him she was all but certain that she loved him, and he'd rejected what she offered. She'd lied, of course. She did want him forever. Oh, it was all so confusing. No wonder the people in the movies took such a long time before declaring their feelings.

She missed home. She missed her father, had missed him most of her life. He would have understood these feelings. He and no one else. Because he had emotions, too, and refused to erase them from his heart. Janella felt more alone than she ever had, and yet, she was glad to be able to release her roiling emotions here, where no one would condemn her for her weakness. Even when the rains came to cool her heated skin, she didn't move from the spot. She'd die before she'd return to that horrible renegade male and his radical notions.

She lowered her head into the pillow of her arms and let her emotions run free. Better to cleanse herself of them now, and be more in control later.

One thing was certain. Thomas didn't want her. Not in the least. He'd probably only taken care of her, let her stay with him, from some sense of duty. He must not care for her any more than he did for his patients.

And here she'd been thinking he truly did care for them, that his coldness was only a disguise.

But she'd obviously been mistaken about that. He didn't care. Not for anyone, but most especially not for her. And she wouldn't spend one more night in a place where she was so clearly unwanted.

* * *

"Thomas Duffy?"

Thomas gave a sharp nod, eyeing the stranger who stood on his front porch. He was tall, lean. He wore his brown hair long for a man of his age, but it suited the close-cropped, gray speckled beard on his chin. And his warm brown eyes were friendly, despite Thomas's obvious impatience. He'd been on his way to find Janella and bring her in out of the rain. Instead, he'd been waylaid by this stranger.

"I need a word with you, Dr. Duffy. Do you have a moment?"

"No. I was just on my way out."

"I can see that. Believe me this is important. I promise, I'll be brief."

Thomas glanced past him to the cloud-veiled night sky, the pouring rain. He saw lightning flash in the distance. "I really have to go, mister—"

"It's about Janella."

Thomas's attention was caught. "Maybe you'd better tell me who the hell you are."

The man nodded, smiling gently. "My name is Alex Vrooman. And before you get hostile, you should know that I'm on your side in this. But there are some others in Sumac who aren't."

"Look, I really don't know what you're talking about, so—"

"Yes, you do. Dr. Duffy, it's admirable of you to try to protect her, but I'm not the enemy here."

Thomas shook his head and moved to walk past the stranger.

"I know about the ship, Thomas. And the crash. I know you found Janella in the woods beyond this farm. I know where she comes from. I know all of it."

Thomas blinked in shock, refusing to turn and face the man, knowing his expression would betray him.

"They know, too. Or at least, they suspect."

He did turn now. "Who?"

"A man by the name of Halloway. He's with military intelligence. If he gets his hands on Janella, Dr. Duffy, I'm afraid…" He lowered his eyes, shook his head. "It wouldn't be good."

Thomas grabbed the man's arm. "What do you mean, it wouldn't be good."

Alex Vrooman sighed. "Despite our efforts to prevent it, Dr. Duffy, the last extraterrestrial captured by our wonderful government died in captivity. Probably as a result of the constant experiments performed on him. We tried to get to him before Halloway, but—"

"Who the hell are 'we,' Vrooman?"

"ETPN," he said softly. "Extraterrestrial Protective Network."

"For crying out loud." Thomas rolled his eyes, pushed a hand through his hair and turned in a slow circle. "You expect me to *believe* this crap?"

"There's no time to convince you right now, Duffy. I have to know whether there's any evidence of that crash in those woods?"

"There was no crash in those woods, Mr. Vrooman."

"I realize the craft probably appeared to vanish. But there might be ashes, or charred ground, and if Halloway finds—"

"Look, I don't know any Halloway, and if I did, I sure wouldn't let him go traipsing through my woodlot looking for flying saucers, okay? Feel better now?"

Vrooman placed a firm hand on Thomas's shoulder. "He's traipsing through your woodlot right now, Dr. Duffy. Is there anything for him to find?"

The blood rushed to Thomas's feet. He blinked in shock at the man, saw the intensity in those eyes, and swore fluently. "Janella's out there."

"My God."

* * *

She had no idea how long she'd been sitting in the rain, when a hand on her shoulder brought her head up fast. Thomas stood, dripping wet, staring down at her.

"You okay?"

She was glad of the rain, to hide the dampness of tears on her face. She only nodded and looked back toward the burned ground.

"Come back to the house, Janella. It isn't good to sit in the rain. It's cold tonight."

"You made it clear you don't want me there, Thomas. I'll trouble you no longer." She spoke without looking at him, still afraid he'd see signs of her emotional reaction to his rejection. It was only her pride that was wounded. Nothing more.

"I didn't say I didn't want you there."

"Didn't you?"

His hand closed on her arm, and he pulled her to her feet roughly. "You know damn well I didn't. Now, come on, I'm not going to stand here in the pouring rain arguing with you."

She caught her breath as he tugged at her, and jerked her arm free. "You dare—"

"You're damned right I dare." He pulled again, forcing her to walk along at his side.

And again she jerked her arm free of his grasp.

He stared at her, his eyes boring holes through hers, it seemed. And she felt a ripple of fear at the anger she saw there. "Fine. Have it your way." Before she could guess his intent, he'd grabbed her in his unyielding arms. He scooped her up off her feet, flipped her right over his shoulder and, despite her howl of protest or the blows she rained on his back and shoulders, began trudging back through the woods.

Her struggles amounted to nothing. Like battling the wind. So she gave them up. And when she quieted, he lowered her to the ground, but held her upper arms in his hands. "You ready to move under your own steam now, princess?"

"I despise you."

"Yeah, well, it's mutual. So are you walking or riding?"

She glared at him, swiped the wet hair out of her eyes and turned to trudge off toward the house. She would claw his eyes out at the very first opportunity. Why she'd ever thought him a decent man, she couldn't begin to imagine.

He quickly caught up to her, walking along at her side. They'd moved on in utter silence, but for no more than a few steps. She stopped when she heard voices floating through the rain toward them. Glancing at Thomas, she saw that he'd heard them, too. He frowned hard, staring into the distance, and following his gaze, Janella saw the beams of light moving through the trees.

From somewhere a voice called. "Anything?"

"Not a damned thing. Are you sure about the location?"

"This is it. Has to be. The witnesses claim this is where they saw it go down."

The lights moved farther, and Janella stiffened as she watched them pass. Without realizing it, she'd gripped Thomas's arm.

He looked down at her, his face grim. The men were heading toward the charred ground, and if they found it, there would be questions. Janella felt trapped. Who were they? What would happen if they discovered...

"Hold up there!" Thomas's loud, deep voice boomed through the rainy night. The lights stopped moving, turned in their direction. "Stay here," he whispered. With one glance at her, Thomas started forward.

Janella followed.

The men came this way, and only stopped when face-to-face with Thomas. There were three, covered head to toe in dark-blue raincoats. One smiled and nodded at Thomas. "What can I do for you, mister?"

"I ought to be the one asking that, seeing as it's my

property you boys are tromping all over. Who the hell are you and what are you doing out here?''

The men glanced at one another. But it was the same one, the leader, it seemed, who replied. "Look, buddy, we don't want any trouble. We're with the air force. We had a...a satellite crash somewhere in this area, and we have to find it.''

Thomas nodded. "Not tonight, you don't. Hit the road, pal.''

"I'm afraid—''

"Unless you have some kind of search warrant,'' Thomas cut in, "get the hell off my land. Now.''

"We can get one, Duffy. That is who you are, isn't it? I want to get the name right when I file charges.''

Thomas didn't even flinch. "Two f's, one y. Be sure and spell it right.''

The man glared at Thomas for a long moment. But then his gaze shifted, and when it fell on Janella she felt real fear ripple over her spine. He smiled at her, put out a hand. "Special Investigator Jack Halloway, ma'am. And you are...?''

Thomas swung his head around and swore softly. She saw the anger in his eyes. So she was even more perplexed when he reached for her, caught her hand and drew her close to his side. His hand around hers was warm and strong, and she found herself clinging to it, ignoring the one the other man held out to her. The one she felt certain could destroy her.

"None of your business, Halloway,'' Thomas said. And his hand fell away from hers, only to encircle her waist and pull her tight to his side.

"Got something to hide, do you, Duffy? Word around town is, this lady showed up out of nowhere. Same night that...test flight went down, wasn't it, boys?''

"Y-you said it was a satellite,'' Janella whispered. Her voice had deserted her.

"Did I? Well, who knows? *Something* crashed here two nights ago. I'll know for sure what it was when I find the site. And I will find it. Say, were you here when it happened? Did you see anything?"

He knew. It was in his smile. Something wild and frightened broke loose inside her and Janella suddenly wanted to send a tree toppling down to crush this frightening man. Fear made her energy jump and leap inside her mind, and she heard the leaves rustling, the branches overhead twitching in motion, though there was no breeze. She caught herself, forced herself calm. The trees stilled, and she prayed the men hadn't noticed her slip.

"Come on, now, miss. You can tell me. Who are you *really?*"

"I—"

"She's my wife."

Janella blinked in shock at the declaration that seemed to leap from Thomas's lips without his consent.

"I suppose you can prove that?"

Thomas's fingers opened on her waist, exerting gentle pressure. A warning. She was shivering. She hadn't realized it until his warmth seeped into her skin and gradually eased the chill.

"I don't think I have to," Thomas went on, his voice deadly but calm.

"I'm afraid you do."

Thomas's chin lifted. His eyes shot fury. "You want proof, you try finding it. And good luck. We were married on Karicau by the village priest, but no one was really in power at the time, and he was taken out by a sniper. The church has been burned out so many times there's probably not a record left anywhere. It's a mess over there, you know."

"So I've heard."

"I returned six months ago, and Janella was only able to join me recently."

"And I'll just bet she came without a visa. Probably has no birth certificate, either. And it's all a coincidence, right?"

"She's my wife. That makes her a citizen."

Halloway eyed her, doubting, she knew. She called on her years of schooling at home and blurted a string of questions in a perfect Karicau dialect. Halloway blinked in apparent shock, and just a little of the doubt left his eyes. Not all of it, though.

Thomas frowned down at her, but the surprise on his face was quickly concealed. "In English, honey. How many times have I told you?"

"Come on, Duffy. You've got no proof of any of this. And *that* makes her an illegal alien. Maybe I ought to call my buddy at Immigration."

"She'll be legal soon enough."

Halloway smirked. "Planning a wedding, are you?"

Thomas shrugged, hugging her closer. "Hell, it'll be easier than tracking down proof of the first one. Now, if your curiosity is satisfied, would you mind getting the hell out of here before I'm forced to turn my dog loose?"

Halloway fixed his penetrating gaze on Janella, staring so hard she shuddered.

Thomas felt it; she knew he did. "Well? Can I walk you boys to your car?"

"How is it no one in this fly speck of a town knows about their local doctor's new wife?"

"Because that's the way I wanted it. My private life is private, Halloway. I didn't feel the need to post an announcement on the town bulletin board."

"I know you're lying."

"So prove it."

"Oh, don't worry. I will. You have a nice night, Duffy. I'll have a search warrant here in twenty-four hours."

"Well, you just come on back when you do. I might even help you look for your missing...whatever it was."

The man muttered, but turned to those behind him and inclined his head. All three walked behind Thomas and Janella out of the woods. They veered across the wheat field, toward the road where their car was parked, and Thomas stood, waiting until they'd gotten in and driven away, before turning to her once more.

"They know, Thomas. They know about the ship and the crash and...and about *me*."

"They suspect. They don't *know* anything, and they damned well aren't going to."

She stared up into his eyes, confused, and more frightened than she could remember ever having been in her life. "But you told them—"

"Forget what I told them, Janella." He kept his arm around her shoulders as they headed back toward the house. "We've got more important things to worry about, like what we're going to do when they show up tomorrow night with that search warrant."

There was a stranger waiting in the kitchen when they returned. Janella had never seen him before, and she was afraid at first. But Thomas glanced down at her, reassurance in his eyes.

"It's okay, Janella." He looked at the man, who sat at the kitchen table sipping tea, and added, "At least, I'm relatively sure it is."

The man rose slowly. He was very tall, and quite thin. And his brown eyes took her in with something like awe. He smiled at her, lifted a hand. "You wouldn't believe how pleased I am to meet you, Janella."

He came forward slowly. She cringed a little closer to Thomas. Humphrey lunged from under the table to take up a stance at her opposite side. He growled a soft warning to the man, as Janella took the hand the man offered.

"Welcome," the stranger said.

She blinked, frowning at the unlined face, the neat beard and once again at those brown eyes. "Who are you?"

"Alex Vrooman. I'm here to help you."

Janella looked at Thomas, who only shook his head. "We have all night to talk to Mr. Vrooman—"

"'Alex,' please."

"You're soaking wet, Janella. Why don't you go on up-stairs, get into some dry clothes?"

She blinked away some of the fear. "You're as wet as I am, Thomas."

He pushed the hair away from her face. "Go on. I'll be up in a minute."

She nodded and turned to leave them.

Chapter 7

Thomas watched her go, his gut churning. The frigging iron wall he'd been struggling to keep between them had damn near crumbled to dust. It was the fear in her eyes. Fear he knew was justified. Hell, he could be as cold as he wanted when she was arrogant and demanding. Not when she looked like a doe caught in headlights, though. He might as well get used to it, he supposed. He was all she had right now. She needed him, and there was no way around that. His practical mind had deserted him out there in the woods tonight, and his damned emotional side—that impulsive kid inside who thought of himself as her knight in shining armor—had dug him into a pit. He'd have a hell of a time getting out of it.

Facing Vrooman, he squared his shoulders, ready to do battle for the damn damsel upstairs.

"You might as well know up front, Vrooman, if I find out you're lying, if you do anything to hurt her—"

"I only want to help her." Vrooman stepped up to Thomas, clasped his shoulder in a strong grip. "I'm on your side in this, Thomas. Would I have warned you about Halloway and his men if I wasn't?''

"I'm not sure." Thomas took careful stock of the man's face, the kind eyes. He wanted to believe Vrooman was sincere, but he wasn't about to take any chances with Janella's safety. He nodded toward the table, and Vrooman sat, picking up his forgotten tea. "Just what do you think you can do to help us?" Thomas asked, taking the seat across from him.

"I can keep you informed about Halloway and his men. What they're up to, what they suspect, what they plan."

Thomas felt his eyes narrow. "How?"

"ETPN is a large organization, Thomas. We have people keeping tabs on the government. I'm afraid I can't divulge more than that without risking some of my colleagues. Just believe me when I say, we know what we're doing. We've had to do it before."

"*What?*"

Vrooman smiled, carefully setting his cup on the table. "Janella isn't the first. There are others, more than you'd believe. When things settle down and Halloway's attention is diverted, I'll put her in contact with them."

Thomas only stared, feeling as if he'd been struck between the eyes with a two-by-four. "Others?"

"Mmm, many others." Vrooman sipped, licked his lips, replaced the cup. "They all have one thing in common. They're high-strung, highly emotional. It was pure hell for them at home."

"Why's that?"

Thomas turned at the sound of footsteps. Janella stood in the doorway, hair damp and clinging to her neck and shoulders. She wore his blue terry robe, and her eyes were misty.

"There are others?" Her voice was a squeaky whisper.

Vrooman nodded, and Thomas saw her grip the door frame for support.

"Where?" She blinked, but tears shimmered in her eyes all the same.

Dammit. If Vrooman was lying to her Thomas would kill the bastard.

"I can't tell you just yet, Janella. For their protection. Not until Halloway decides you're just another earthling, like Thomas and me." He grinned at her, and she smiled back, nodding hard.

Thomas shook his head. Man, this was getting harder to swallow by the second. "Someone want to explain this to me?" He turned to Janella. "What's so terrible about your planet that it drives people to leave everything and fly off to parts unknown?"

Janella lowered her head. Thomas looked to Vrooman for the answers, but found none.

"It's up to Janella to tell you about that, Thomas. When she's ready. For now, I think I ought to go. You both need some time to digest all of this. We'll talk again tomorrow."

Thomas dragged his gaze away from Janella's face. She looked almost guilty, but he couldn't imagine why. "Vrooman, wait. Halloway will be back tomorrow with a search warrant. What the hell am I supposed to do about that?"

Vrooman nodded thoughtfully, rubbing his chin with one hand. "Wouldn't do to let them find evidence to support their theory. Tell me, does anything remain of the ship?"

"No."

"Good." He nodded, rising from his chair, pacing slowly. "Then you only need to worry about the ground. The topsoil is charred black, isn't it?"

Thomas nodded, certain now that Vrooman hadn't been lying when he'd said he'd dealt with situations like this before. How else could he know about that blackened earth?

"The topsoil ought to be removed, or at least plowed under, as deeply as possible," Vrooman said. "They won't see any sign of the landing, and with luck, their soil samples will show nothing unusual.''

''I hope the hell you're right about that.'' Thomas turned to Janella as she came the rest of the way into the room, walked right up to Vrooman and stared into his eyes. Her own were so intense it seemed she was searching his soul.

''What will they do to me if they find out?'' The fear in her voice was palpable, and it made Thomas want to bundle her into the Jeep and take her as far away from Halloway and Vrooman and all of this bull as he could get her.

Vrooman glanced away from her, toward Thomas. Thomas gave his head a slight shake. *Tell her what you told me and I'll break your jaw.*

Vrooman's slight nod said he'd read the message, loud and clear. He rose, patting Janella's shoulder. ''We aren't going to have to find out, Janella. Don't worry.'' He moved toward the door, pausing with one hand on the knob. ''She needs to be vaccinated against polio, Thomas. Be sure it's an inactive vaccine, and give her a child's dose. It won't hurt her. They seem to be immune to most of our diseases, but that one can be fatal. Also, red meat seems to disagree with them. And watch out for MSGs.''

Thomas nodded. ''What about medications?''

''Hard to say,'' Vrooman said. ''We only found out about the other things by accident. We don't treat them like guinea pigs, you know.'' He tilted his head, looking at Janella for a long moment. ''It's better to avoid anything you're unsure of. Think holistic, Thomas. Don't take any chances with her health.''

''I don't intend to.''

With a sharp nod, Vrooman left, and Thomas turned to find Janella sagging, hands clasping the back of a chair. He caught her shoulders, turned her around, studied her face, and searched within himself for his iron wall.

The damn thing was nowhere in sight.

''You all right?''

She nodded, but he doubted her answer. She looked exhausted, scared, confused and a hundred other things he couldn't put a name to.

"Come on, kid. Upstairs with you. I think a nice hot bath and then straight to bed."

She lifted her head, stared into his eyes. "You told those men I was your wife."

"I told *you* to forget about what I told those men."

"But it isn't true."

"No, it isn't. Hell, Janella, I had to come up with something fast. It was the first thing that popped into my head."

She blinked twice, and he thought if he didn't look away those wide black eyes of hers were going to suck the soul right out of his body and chain it up somewhere inside hers.

He tried, but couldn't.

"What will happen when they find out that you lied to them?"

"They aren't going to find out."

"But—"

"Janella, will you just trust me? I'll take care of this."

She shook her head. "I don't see how you can. You told them we were to be married. When we aren't, they'll know—"

"They aren't going to stick around that long. Hell, Janella, maybe Alex Vrooman will whisk you off to wherever the rest of your people are living. Maybe Halloway will lose interest. You're worrying about things that haven't happened yet."

Her eyes grew even wider, though he hadn't believed it possible. Her lips trembled. "You...you think I should go to them? To the others?" Her voice came out tight, as if her throat had constricted and was squeezing the words.

"I figured you'd want to go to them. You do, don't you?"

Her chin fell to her chest, hair veiling her face as she turned away from him. "With all that's happened, Thomas, our earlier conversation slipped my mind. Foolish of me to forget, wasn't it?''

She started for the stairs. Thomas caught her by her good arm, stopping her. "To forget what, Janella? What are you talking about?"

Without facing him, she shook her head. "Don't concern yourself about me any longer, Thomas. I'll be out of your house, out of your life, just as soon as Alex Vrooman tells me where to go." She tugged her arm free of his grip and tiredly mounted the stairs.

Thomas didn't follow her.

He didn't want her! How had she forgotten that, even for a moment?

Janella fell face first onto the bed, clutching the pillows in her fists. When he'd told those men he would marry her, when he'd pulled her close to his side and held her and called her ''honey'' with so much affection in his voice, she'd actually believed it.

More than believed it. She'd *reveled* in it.

She'd been a fool. A blind, frightened little girl clinging to the false security, the make-believe love of a man who cared less for her than for his dog. Why did it hurt her so much? Why, when she'd known him for such a short time, did it pain her to know he felt nothing for her? He wanted no woman in his life, didn't believe in love at all. He was like the people she'd run away from, emotionless, cold, unfeeling. Why would she even want the affection of a man like him?

But she did. She did want it, and it surprised her to realize just how much. It hadn't been simple anger she'd felt toward Rosa, but jealousy. All her life she'd thought of Thomas as the man who would be her own. Ever since that night when he'd rescued her in the woods, so long ago.

She sat up, sniffling and reaching into the drawer for the small wooden trinket he'd given her then. Lovingly, she

stroked the smooth grain of the wood, her fingers caressing
Thomas's initials. He'd become her ideal that night, and
she'd stupidly spent years longing for his love, his touch.
It had never occurred to her that he wouldn't return her
feelings. The reality of that had only hit her with his cruel
rejection. And it hurt more than she believed possible.

She told herself her feelings for Thomas were false. That
he'd been the only person she'd known since coming here.
That his rescuing of her so long ago had made him a romantic hero in her mind, and that she clung to him now
from a need of security more than from any real caring.

She didn't believe what she was telling herself, however.
And it didn't ease the ache in her heart a bit. She'd spent
her whole life waiting for the day when she could come to
him. Now she had to leave him. It was what he wanted.
He'd made that plain enough. And she knew he wouldn't
change his mind.

Thomas didn't sleep. He couldn't. His pacing and frustration finally led him to his room, which had somehow
become Janella's. He'd been sleeping in Dad's old bedroom
since he'd found her.

She lay still, eyes red and swollen, tear tracks still trace-
able on her cheeks.

Had he caused her tears? Hell, he didn't know. She might
have cried out of fear of discovery, or maybe from the sheer
joy of knowing she wasn't as alone here as she'd thought.

That's right, she wasn't alone. He reminded himself of
that. Before, he'd been all she had. She'd needed him. Now
she knew there were others like her here. And there was
Alex Vrooman and his organization. She could probably
get along just fine without some country doctor's pitiful
help.

Hadn't she told him she wanted to leave?

No. She'd said she would leave because he wanted it.
And she was right. He did want it. The sooner she was out

of his life, the sooner he could repair the damage to his emotion-proof wall and get things back to normal. He didn't like having her here, didn't like the feeling that he was starting to care about her far more than was wise. Hell, she was living proof of what that kind of caring led to. She was walking away, wasn't she?

And he was going to miss her like hell, wasn't he?

He forced his gaze away from her, but it did nothing to ease the ridiculous sting behind his eyes. And looking at the floor only brought to attention the little bag she'd brought home from The Pink Petunia. It lay on its side, books and a black satin strap spilling out. In spite of himself, Thomas reached down, hooked a finger through that strap and pulled the garment out.

The teddy was damn near transparent, with high-cut leg openings and a low-cut neckline.

Thomas dropped it, spun for the door and left the room as fast as was humanly possible. In the hall, he pulled the door shut, leaned back against it, eyes closed, teeth grating.

"Damn, damn, damn."

Drawing an uneven breath, he steeled himself against the images that kept floating through his mind. Images of Janella in that black teddy. Of her hands on his skin, his lips on her mouth.

His first instincts had been correct. The sooner she got the hell out of his life, the better.

The telephone's shrill ring didn't wake him, because he hadn't been asleep. He'd been lying on his back, staring at the ceiling and contemplating what would be so terrible about letting Janella stay right where she was. Stupid thought. She probably didn't even *want* to stay, but the idea kept coming back to him, no matter how he tried to banish it.

He snatched up the cordless, having taken it to bed with him out of habit.

"Thomas? It's Eugenia, hon. You'd better get over here, and I do mean now."

His senses stood alert and he sat up in bed. "What is it, 'Genia. You okay?"

"Well now, Thomas 'Hard-nose' Duffy, is that concern I hear in your voice? You softy, you. I'm fine." Thomas grimaced into the mouthpiece, but she rushed on. "It's Shelly Connor. She was on her way back from visiting Hugh at the hospital, and she went into labor."

"Oh, hell. Well, pop her into your car and I'll meet you back at Saint Luke's."

"I don't think so, Thomas. She's—" A piercing shriek coming from somewhere beyond her interrupted her words.

"Holy crap," Thomas muttered.

"I have to go, Thomas. Get your butt over here, *pronto*."

The receiver clicked in his ear. Thomas hung up, dove into his clothes and ran into the hall. Janella was there, eyes still red, but dry now. He assumed the phone must have jarred her awake. He wished it hadn't. Looking at her fresh from bed, in his rumpled bathrobe, with mussed hair and half-lidded eyes, was only distracting him from the matter at hand.

"Something is wrong," she said softly.

"Shelly's having her baby. Any minute now by the sounds of it. I have to go."

"I want to come with you." She turned and dashed into the bedroom before he could argue. Thomas followed, about to tell her there was no time to wait. Then he wished he hadn't. She shed the robe and stood stark naked in front of an open dresser drawer, pawing through it, yanking out a pair of jeans. He stood behind her, staring like an idiot at her bare legs and the perfect curve of her backside, her slender waist. And when he looked away from that it was only to see the front of her reflected in the mirror. Her eyes met his in the glass, held them for a moment, then tore free.

She bent and stepped into the jeans, yanked them up over

her hips. She dipped back into the drawer for a T-shirt, pulled it over her head. Grabbing her shoes from the floor, she came to him.

He didn't move out of the doorway. She stood there, looking up at him, so tousled and beautiful that for a second he could think of nothing but pulling her into his arms and kissing the living hell out of her.

Damn. What was wrong with him?

"Come on. We'd better hurry." And why was his voice so damned hoarse? He turned away, but not before he was sure she'd seen the desire in his eyes. And he was damned if he hadn't seen the same thing shining right back at him from hers.

She was pretty and young. Small and blond. But her hair clung in straggles to her sweat-dampened face, and her beautiful features contorted in pain.

Janella rushed to the bedside without forethought. She'd never witnessed childbirth, but at home it was done surgically, while the mother lay unconscious and unaware. She was spared the pain of natural birth and the other pain that came later, as those in attendance—representatives of the ruling house—decided whether the child was sound enough to accept, or flawed, in which case its life would end more quickly than it had begun. Those were the only two skills needed by men of medicine on her planet.

Eugenia left her spot at Shelly's side to assist Thomas near the foot of the bed. But Janella was only dimly aware of their presence there. She knew little other than the pain of the woman on the bed, and she focused on nothing other than easing it.

Janella bent over her, placed her hands on either side of Shelly's head, palms absorbing the sticky sweat.

Shelly screamed.

"Dammit," Thomas muttered. "She's not big enough.

We ought to do a C-section, but there isn't time to get her to the hospital.''

"The baby's crowning, Thomas. I don't think Shelly can stand—''

Shelly shrieked in agony, arching off the bed.

Janella leaned in close to her face. "Open your eyes, Shelly. Open them. Look at me. Right into my eyes.''

Shelly's eyes fluttered open, and Janella held her pain-clouded gaze. She searched those eyes, massaging Shelly's temples and chanting in her own tongue, her voice a bare whisper as she sought to draw the pain out of Shelly's body, to ease the woman's suffering.

Another contraction came, and Janella felt its echo in her own abdomen as her mind sought to meld with Shelly's. Her muscles clenched and she caught her breath, but didn't close her eyes. Shelly blinked, panting, her eyes clearing just a little. She started to look away, but Janella held her face.

"Keep looking at me, Shelly. I can help you through this. Don't look away.''

Shelly did, and as another contraction hit her, she gasped, but didn't scream. Janella felt it more strongly this time and again caught her breath, but forced her gaze to remain fixed on Shelly's. Her hands on Shelly's face trembled.

"It's coming," Thomas shouted. "You have to push now, Shelly. Come on, I know it hurts, but—''

Shelly grated her teeth and pushed. Janella felt as if she were being ripped apart from within. She bit her lip to keep from making a sound and probed still deeper into the young woman's mind, sharing her pain, easing it.

Shelly sat up in the bed, her back braced on the head-board, knees bent, feet digging into the mattress. She never looked away from Janella. Janella sat on the bed's edge, hands to Shelly's temples, eyes locked in place. Shelly pushed again, and Janella grated her teeth, sending all of her energies into the young mother, trying to give her strength and endurance. On and on the pains came, until they blended into one unending force. Shelly clung to Janella's shoulders as powerfully as to her gaze, her own tear filled and grateful and confused. She grated her teeth as she pushed, her fingers sinking into Janella's skin. Their faces only inches apart, both women panted in cosmic synchronization, eyes intense, sharing the pain.

And then it eased all of the sudden.

Shelly fell back onto the pillows. Janella slid from the bed, where she'd been sitting, to kneel on the floor, head bowed. She heard the baby's first wheezy cry, and then silence. Her head came up slowly, eyes focused on the unmoving newborn in Thomas's arms.

"Dammit," he muttered, snipping the cord and rubbing the child vigorously. "Come on, dammit!"

Janella pulled herself to her feet; leaning on the bed for support, she moved to the foot of it.

The child's skin was a soft blue beneath the ghostly white film. Shelly sat up again, moaning "No," her gaze pinned to the baby.

Thomas cradled the child with one arm, sweeping a finger into its mouth. Janella drew closer. Please, she begged in silence, please.

"She's not breathing!" Shelly cried. "Thomas, she's not—"

Thomas bent over the still child, covering the baby's mouth and nose with his lips, blowing gentle puffs into the tiny lungs. When he lifted his head, he used two fingers to pump the child's chest, then bent to blow again.

"Come on, sweetheart," he whispered. "Come on, dammit, come on." His eyes were intense as he kept ministering to the infant. He kept working as Shelly's sobs grew louder and she crawled toward the foot of the bed.

"Thomas, please! Please don't let her—"

The baby gurgled. A hoarse sound, like a wheezy gasp, instigated utter silence in the room. Every eye pinned to that child. And then it began to cry like a lamb for its mother.

Shelly doubled over on the bed, sobbing so hard her entire body shook with it. Janella sank onto the mattress, tears filling her eyes. And through the blur of them, she saw Thomas's eyes filling, as well, and a crooked smile tugging at his lips.

Eugenia was bubbling with joy when the siren screamed louder, then warbled to a stop out front. The door burst open and paramedics rushed inside. A medic took the baby from Shelly's arms. Then others transferred Shelly to a gurney and wheeled her out of the room. But as it passed, she reached out to clasp Thomas's hand. She didn't speak, but her eyes gleamed her gratitude.

He gave her hand a squeeze. "See you at the hospital, Shel." Then she was carried past him and out of the house.

Thomas turned to study Janella, still unsure what he'd just witnessed. Somehow, in some weird, damn near scary way, Janella had eased Shelly's pain. He knew it without being told. And he could see the effort it had cost her. Exhaustion was written all over her face.

"Are you all right?"

She nodded, watching the medics as they bundled Shelly and the baby into the back of the ambulance outside.

"Fine, Thomas. But the baby?"

She looked truly worried. "The baby will be okay. Her lungs are a little underdeveloped, and she's small. She'll need intensive care for a while, but I think she'll be fine in a couple of weeks." He put a hand on her face, pushed her hair away, caught the tear that fell.

She shook her head slowly, staring at him with something like wonder in her eyes.

"Janella, I'm not sure what just happened here, but—"

"What happened here was a miracle, Thomas." Her

smile was watery as more tears spilled over. "The baby...
You gave her life. You brought her back. You—"

He closed his eyes to block out the adoration in hers. "I
did what I'm trained to do. That's all."

"You cried when she breathed again. I saw you."

"You're hallucinating. And I wasn't talking about what
I did. I was talking about what you did. You... How the
hell did you—"

The siren's scream made him stop. "We'll talk about it
later. I have to go to the hospital now, Janella. Stay here."
Again he ran his hand over her face. "Rest. You look like
hell. Are you sure you're okay?"

Instead of answering him, she leaned up and pressed her
mouth to his. Her eyes fell closed and her hands crept up
to encircle his neck. Before he thought better of it, Thomas
wrapped his arms around her waist and pulled her against
him, bending to kiss her. God, she tasted good. And when
she drew away, he was shaking. Why the hell was he shaking?

She took in a shuddering breath, released it slowly. "Go.
Go and take care of Shelly and her child." She bit her lip,
lowered her eyes.

Damn but he hated to leave her. She seemed incredibly
vulnerable right now, weak, tired. Kind of soft and pliable
in his arms in a way that made him want to hold her right
there all night long. He glanced over Janella's shoulder at
a smug-looking redhead. "Take care of her, 'Genia. She's
had a rough day."

"So have you by the looks of it, Thomas Duffy. But
don't you worry. It isn't fatal." She winked.

Thomas fastened a forbidding expression on his face,
turned and left on legs that were none too steady.

Chapter 8

"Here, drink this. It'll relax you." Eugenia pressed the tea into Janella's hand.

Janella sipped, let the flavor seep into her tongue before swallowing. The warmth spread down her throat and through her stomach.

"You know I'm your friend, Janella. You *do* know that, don't you?"

Janella met the woman's eyes and smiled. "Yes, I do. I'm grateful to have friends. More than I've ever had before. You, Thomas. Perhaps Shelly now. Even Humphrey."

Eugenia took a seat across from her. "Honey, I saw what happened just now with Thomas."

Janella lifted her gaze, met Eugenia's, prepared herself.

"You don't have to tell me if you don't want to, hon. But I'm gonna burst if you don't."

Janella shook her head. "There is really nothing to tell. I...I was moved by what he did." She spoke slowly, giving her words a lot of thought. She didn't want to lie to her new friend, but she couldn't quite bring herself to tell the truth, either. That she was deeply in love with a man who could never return her feelings. That she'd tried to believe he was as cold and heartless as the people she'd run away from, but that she'd seen undeniable proof tonight that he was just the opposite. "He's a special man, isn't he?"

"Yes, that he is. Though he's too dense to realize it."

Janella shrugged, unsure how to respond.

Eugenia smiled, nodding in quick, sharp movements. "Well, hon, I'll tell you something. I don't have to be a mind reader to see what's going on with you and Thomas."

Janella closed her eyes. She'd kissed him. He'd kissed her back. But she knew it was little more than the over-wrought emotions of what they'd just shared that had caused his reactions.

Her own, well, they were caused by something much deeper. Something bigger and more frightening than anything she'd ever felt in her life. She leaned her head back against the sofa and sighed as she called to mind the feel of his lips on hers. The way his strong arms had run tight over the small of her back. The way his hard body pressed to hers and the feel of his hair tangling around her fingers.

But he wanted her to leave him. How could he kiss her that way if he wanted her to leave him?

"You love him, don't you?"

She felt a warm tear slip over her cheek. But she said nothing. She was so tired. The effort of sharing Shelly's pain and the act of sending her own strength into the other woman's body had left her drained and nearly limp. She lowered her head to the sofa pillow, hugging it to her face, closing her eyes.

Then softness, warmth covered her. Eugenia had taken the blanket from the sofa's back and laid it gently over her.

"That's it, you just rest now. And don't worry, hon. This is all gonna work itself out. You'll see."

Two o'clock in the morning.

Thomas carried Janella upstairs, laid her on the bed,

pulled blankets over her and cursed himself for being a hundred kinds of fool. Damn, he wanted her so much he could barely look at her without getting aroused. And he could have dealt with that if that was *all* there was to it. But it wasn't. Something was happening here, and he did not like it one damn bit.

Fortunately, there was plenty to do to keep him busy for what was left of the night. Good thing, because if he hung around here, he'd probably wind up slipping under those blankets beside her. He'd never sleep anyway. What he needed was physical exertion and lots of it. He thanked the fates that the farmer who rented the land from him kept some of his equipment out in the barn, rather than hauling it back and forth. There was a tractor and a set of four-bottom plows. He hoped the John Deere's headlights were in working order as he headed out of the house.

Halloway had one of his counterparts place the call, since Janella might recognize his voice. He didn't really give a damn whether she was in this country illegally or not, and calling Immigration would be detrimental. If she was what he thought she was, then the last thing he wanted was to reveal her presence to anyone else. And he didn't want another government agency getting tangled up in this. He just wanted to know for sure before he let anything slip. He figured the more he could shake her up, the better the chance she'd reveal something. And she'd probably shake much more easily being called first thing in the morning, before she'd even dressed or eaten. Scaring women's socks off wasn't something Halloway liked doing, but it was necessary in this case. He couldn't really see any other way to get at the truth. So he sat and waited for the call to go through, hoping she'd drop a clue, tell him something.

If there was anything to tell.

Halloway listened on the extension, his lips thinning at

the fear in Janella's voice as Parks—his tone intimidating as hell—identified himself as an officer of the U.S. Department of Immigration and Naturalization and began barking questions.

Thomas not only plowed the secret meadow hidden within the woods, but dragged it, fertilized it and seeded it down with winter millet. And he didn't only do the spot where the ship had disintegrated. That would have been too obvious. He did the entire meadow, which was at least an acre and a half in size.

He returned to the house cold, dirty and exhausted, besides being glad it was Sunday and he had no clinic hours today.

Janella stood in the living room, staring down at the telephone and wringing her hands. She looked as though someone had just dropped a bomb in her backyard. Thomas went to her, forgetting all about his decision not to give a damn.

She glanced up quickly, almost fearfully, relaxing only when she saw who was there. Then she closed her eyes tight.

"What is it? What's happened?"

Biting her lower lip, she faced him. "There was a telephone call...from your Immigration Department."

"Ah, damn—"

"Thomas, the man asked so many questions. He wants to know when we were married, and where, and by whom. And when we will hold the...the *ceremony* here in the United States, and... You never should have told them I was your wife, Thomas." She pushed her hands through her hair, turning in a little circle. "I'm so afraid. What are we going to do?"

Thomas looked at her, the tears streaming over her face and burning holes through his iron wall as if they were made of sulfuric acid. He caught hold of her upper arms and pulled her to him, stroked her back.

A throat cleared and Thomas whirled, still holding her, to see Alex Vrooman standing in the kitchen.

"You have two choices, Janella. Neither is a perfect solution, but both might work."

She lifted her head, stepping away from Thomas to stare at the man. "Tell me what they are," she whispered, eyes seemingly afraid of what she was about to hear.

"One is to come away with me. Right now, today. We'll hole up somewhere safe until Halloway gives up searching for you and then go on to some of your people living here in this country."

Janella blinked twice, glancing up at Thomas as if waiting for him to say something, voice an opinion. But he didn't. Instead he just swallowed hard and asked, "What's the other option?"

Vrooman shrugged. "Fairly obvious, Thomas. Marry her."

He flinched as if he'd been slapped.

Janella stepped farther away from him, head bowed. "Then there's really no choice to be made." She closed her eyes, bit her lip. "I will go upstairs now and gather my things. I can be ready in a few minutes, Mr. Vrooman."

"It's 'Alex,'" he said softly. "Take your time, Janella. I have to make a few phone calls, and—"

"Now, wait just one damned minute here."

Janella froze, her back to him. Alex's brows lifted, and he stopped speaking. The screen door creaked, and Eugenia popped in, smiling at Thomas, then staring in mute surprise at Alex Vrooman. She held a basket of bran muffins in one hand, and the other rose to smooth her hair.

Her confused gaze went to Thomas again. "What's going on? Why's everyone so tense?"

Thomas held up a hand to her for silence, turned to Janella, one hand going to her shoulder. "Look, if you take off with this guy, Halloway will be sure his suspicions about you were right. He'll probably never stop looking for you. You wouldn't have any peace for the rest of your life.''

"Halloway is looking for Janella?" Eugenia cried. "Why didn't someone tell me this? Sakes alive, he was in my shop just the other day asking questions and—''

"'Genia, please.'' Thomas squeezed Janella's shoulder softly. "Look, why don't we just go ahead and do it?''

Janella turned slowly, blinking up at him. "You told me you didn't want a wife, Thomas. You said you would never marry.''

"Exactly. So it isn't as if marrying you would be keeping me from anything. And it would get Halloway and Immigration off your back.''

Her brows drew upward. She shook her head slowly.

"It won't be a big deal, Janella. A quick simple ceremony at the town justice's office. Then you just keep living here like you've been doing. Nothing will change. When Halloway gives up and goes away, you can move on to wherever you want to, and I can—''

Something whacked him in the back of the head and Thomas turned in time to see Eugenia winding up to peg him with another bran muffin from the basket. "Thomas Allan Duffy, I've never in my life known a man as downright *stupid* as you!'' She practically screamed the words at him and let fly with the second muffin. He ducked it, but not by much.

"What the hell is that for?'' Thomas scowled at her. "This is between Janella and me, Eugenia. Why don't you and Alex here step outside for five minutes, huh?''

"It isn't necessary,'' Janella said, her voice rougher than sandpaper.

Thomas looked at her, and the hurt he saw in her eyes almost knocked him over.

"Thank you for your generous offer, Thomas. It's kind to be so self-sacrificing for me, but I think I've put you to enough trouble already.'' She glanced at Vrooman.

"Would it be all right if we left tomorrow night instead of today? I'm very tired right now. And I want a chance to say goodbye to my friends and to see Shelly's little baby girl before I go."

Vrooman smiled kindly at her, nodding. She fled then. Really ran, up the stairs, and Thomas heard the bedroom door slam.

"Well, Einstein, you've got about thirty-six hours to get it right. Think you can figure it out by then?"

Thomas closed his eyes, wondering why the hell he felt like punching someone. Preferably Eugenia.

'Genia faced Alex Vrooman and smiled sweetly. "Eugenia Overton. I don't believe I've had the pleasure."

"Alex Vrooman," he replied, taking her hand and squeezing. "Miss Overton, would you care to join me in town for some breakfast? I do believe our friend here needs some time to himself."

"What our friend needs, Mr. Vrooman, is a mule to kick him in the head. But I don't suppose you have one handy."

Vrooman laughed and, tucking Eugenia's arm through his, led her out of the house.

Thomas shook his head as he watched them go. Then he started up the stairs, intending to talk some sense into Ja-nella. She couldn't just go off with Vrooman. They didn't even know the guy. He could be lying through his teeth, could be working hand in hand with Halloway and his goons, for all they knew. And for that matter, he didn't much like the idea of Eugenia heading out of here with him, either. She was old enough to know better than to take up with a stranger that way.

Thomas reached for the bedroom door, then paused with his hand in midair. Soft sobs, punctuated by an occasional sniffle, came from beyond the door, arrowing straight into his heart. He drew a breath, swallowed hard and tried to still the little spasm in his stomach.

Great job, you big jerk. That ought to be your specialty, making girls cry.

Thomas ignored the boy in his head and stared, unseeing, at the door. Hell, why was she crying? What had he said to make her cry?

Mentally, he went over the conversation that had taken place downstairs, but he couldn't for the life of him figure out what her problem was. He'd offered to marry her, for crying out loud. What more did she want from him?

He balled his hand into a fist, but stopped before knocking, glancing down at his dusty, sweaty clothes and changing his mind. He'd clean up first, give her some time to get over whatever the hell was wrong. Then maybe he could talk to her.

Janella tried not to be angry with Thomas as she wiped away her foolish tears and began emptying the closet of her belongings. She folded each item neatly, made small piles on the bed. She had nothing to put them in, but she'd worry about that later. Her possessions amounted to a pitifully meager display. Some jeans and blouses, a little mound of undergarments, the books Eugenia had given her.

As she lay the little slingshot on top of the clothing on the bed, tears threatened to cloud her vision yet again. She angrily blinked her eyes dry. But the image of Thomas with Shelly's baby returned to haunt her. Seeing him, cradling that tiny child in his strong arms, bending over it to breathe life into it once again, made her heart contract in her chest. He was a special man. A caring man, with a heart full of love.

Just not for her. It wasn't his fault. She couldn't blame him for the way he felt. He didn't want a wife. He'd told her as much. The very act of offering to sacrifice the lifestyle he held so dear only confirmed the extent of his kindness. But she couldn't let him do that for her. She couldn't let him, because she wanted so much more from him than just words on a paper document proclaiming them man and wife. And it wouldn't be fair to let him marry her unless he knew that, understood it. And she couldn't tell him. She suddenly understood the reluctance of the characters in the movies and books. The difficulty of expressing such deep, precious feelings to another. She couldn't do it. Especially knowing already how Thomas felt—or rather, how he *didn't* feel—toward her.

Marrying him would be painful. Uttering vows of love and devotion, knowing she meant every word, would injure her in ways she'd never imagined. Hearing him utter them back, knowing he didn't mean a word he said, would tear her into small, bleeding bits.

She glanced down at the garment in her hand, saw that it was the black scrap of a nightgown, the one Eugenia called a "teddy." She almost laughed at her own idiocy. How had she ever imagined she could win Thomas's heart simply by donning it and going to him. It was ludicrous. He simply didn't want her. It would make little difference what she wore.

He knocked only once, before the door swung open and he stood there, looking at her. She thrust the teddy underneath the nearest pile of clothes, wondering if he'd seen it.

If he had, he seemed to decide not to say anything about it. He came forward, took a seat on the edge of the bed. "Packing?"

She nodded, going back to the closet, knowing there was nothing left there.

"Janella, we have to talk about this."

She kept her back to him. "No, I don't think we do. It's better if I go."

"Better for who?"

She bit her lip, shook her head.

"Come here."

Janella turned slowly, not wanting to go to him, not

wanting even to face him, but supposing she had to convince him the decision she'd made was the right one.

"Right here. Sit down. The least you can do is listen to me." He patted the mattress beside him.

Reluctantly, Janella sat.

"Now, tell me. Better for who, Janella? Not for you, I'm sure of that much. Halloway will be more suspicious than ever if you run away."

She lowered her head. "It won't matter if he can't find me."

"Yeah, but what if he can?"

She only shrugged, not knowing what to say to him.

"Janella, I don't want you to go with Vrooman. How do you know he is who he says he is? How can you be sure he's not in on this whole scheme with Halloway?"

Her head came up fast and she met his eyes. She hadn't even considered that possibility. "Do you think that's likely?"

"It might be."

She knew he wasn't lying to her. He wouldn't deliberately try to frighten her. It wasn't in him to do that.

"Is that a risk you're willing to take?" he asked.

Janella closed her eyes to escape his dark, probing ones. "I don't know."

"Well, it doesn't matter, because it's not a risk *I'm* willing to take. I want you to stay here. You're safe here, Janella."

Pain welled up in her throat, making words difficult. "I can't marry you, Thomas," she managed.

"Why not? I'm not such an ogre, am I?"

He smiled as he said it, and she couldn't help but smile back, right through the pain that clouded her soul. "No, you're not an ogre, whatever one is. You're a wonderful, special man, Thomas. And..." Her words trailed off and she lowered her eyes.

Thomas caught her chin, lifted it, made her look into his eyes. "And what?"

Stiffening her spine, Janella forced herself to answer him. "You think you don't care about people, Thomas, but you do. You have so much love inside you, so much to give, if only you would let yourself. Marrying me would be another way for you to cut yourself off from your own emotions. By marrying a woman you don't care about, you'll ruin any chance of finding a woman you could truly love."

Thomas drew a slow, even breath, closed his eyes, licked his lips. "So who said I didn't care about you? Huh?"

Janella frowned, searching his face when he opened his eyes once again.

"Look, do you think I'd have offered if I didn't give a damn?"

She shook her head slowly, wishing he'd speak clearly and not dangle bits of nothing in front of her like bait. "I don't know what to think."

"Yeah, well, I'll tell you what *I* think. I think you ought to worry about your own problems and let me worry about mine. There's no way in hell I'm going to fall for some other woman, so you can just forget about that. And like I told you downstairs, this doesn't have to be forever. Just until this thing with Halloway blows over. It isn't as if we're swearing to be together for the rest of our lives, for God's sake."

She blinked against a sudden pain in her chest and averted her eyes.

"Janella, I want to help you. Why are you so damned determined not to let me?" He stood, pushing a hand through his hair, turning to face her. His gaze swept the articles piled on the bed and paused on the stack of novels. "Is it those damned books of 'Genia's? Have they got you hoping for some romantic hero to pledge heart and soul to you on bended knee? Is that it?"

Tears filled her eyes, one hand covering the books protectively. "What would be so terrible about that, Thomas? Just because you don't want me, do you think no other man ever will?"

"You think I don't—" He bit his lip, cutting his words off without finishing them. He rolled his eyes, spun in a circle, tipped his head back as if seeking advice from the ceiling and ended up facing her again. "Janella, that crap is fiction. It isn't real. That kind of stuff just doesn't happen in the real world."

His eyes found hers, narrowed. "Ah, hell, don't start crying again. Okay, all right, maybe it does happen for some people. Just not for me." He shook his head, reaching down to brush a tear from her face. The harshness in his own and in his voice softened considerably. "The damned honest truth of it is, you'll probably have a dozen men on their knees before too long. And you probably deserve that kind of romantic bull. Look, if it comes along, I'm not going to stand in the way. Is that it? Are you afraid you'll meet Prince Charming and have to let him go because you're tied to me?"

She sniffed, pulling her face away from his touch. "Eugenia was right, Thomas. You are an idiot."

His face clouded with anger. He bent, reaching past her and scooping up the teddy she'd thought she'd hidden. He held it up in front of him. "Maybe you've already met somebody. Maybe that's why you bought this little number."

She snatched it from his hand, so furious with him she could have hit him. "I bought it for you!" She shrieked the words at him before she could think better of it. Horrified at having said it, she turned her back to him, covered her face with her hands, the teddy still dangling from one of them.

"You…"

She shook her head, not facing him. "Just go. Go away and leave me. I don't want to talk to you any more."

He said nothing. But in a moment, his hands came to rest on her shoulders, lightly, softly. "Janella, I didn't realize—"

"Get out!"

She whirled on him, eyeing the door over his shoulder and flinging it open without touching it.

He looked at her, then at the floor. "I'm sorry. Janella, I—"

She focused her energies, slamming them into his chest with as much force as she could muster. Thomas staggered backward, eyes widening. Janella stayed where she was, sending another mental thrust at him, and succeeded in shoving him out of the room. One more burst of energy slammed the door in his face.

Exhausted, Janella slumped to the bed.

Okay, he'd blown it. He'd more than blown it—he'd nuked it. But how was he supposed to know she'd been thinking—what? Just what the hell had she been thinking? About seducing him, he guessed. About getting him hot and bothered enough to take her to bed. And he supposed he should have known that. She'd told him she was curious about sex and interested in trying it out…with him, no less. But he hadn't really thought it meant anything. Damn, did she really want him? *Him?*

Maybe there was a little more to it than that, though. Must be, or she wouldn't be mad enough to skin him alive right now. Okay, he had to stop and think this through. She wanted him in bed. He'd asked her to marry him, but he'd told her it would only be make-believe. She'd gotten furious.

So it stood to reason that maybe she wanted a marriage that came with all the extras. Sex being one of them. The big question was, what else did she want? Hearts and flowers? Love, for crying out loud?

Thomas closed his eyes and battled the panic that came

with the thought. Hell, he couldn't love her. Despite what she might think, he wasn't capable of it. His emotions had been shut down for too long to just wake up again and produce something that major.

He *liked* her. Hell, he wanted her, too. So badly he could barely close his eyes at night thinking about it. But not enough to want to make her his wife, not enough to give her a lifetime commitment. So what the hell was he supposed to do? March upstairs and tell her he'd be willing to sleep with her?

He had a feeling she'd probably hit him with something large, like maybe the dresser, if he did that.

Nope, he'd blown it. And he didn't have a clue what the hell to do about it. Besides, he didn't really think having sex with Janella would be the smartest move he could make.

He didn't approach her again for a couple of hours. When he did, he found her calmer. Freshly showered and dressed, brushing her damp hair. The cast she'd worn earlier was in shreds in the wastebasket. The arm looked fine, and he decided it would be better not to scold her for taking it off without checking with him first.

He approached with caution, chose his words carefully, kept any hint of emotion from his voice. ''I'm going to the hospital to check on Shelly and the baby. You want to come along?''

She met his eyes, hers hesitant, wary. ''Yes.''

She didn't utter another word. Just walked past him, out of the room, down the stairs. It was the same in the Jeep on the way to Saint Luke's. Stony silence, no eye contact. And she sat as far from him as she could manage without actually riding outside the vehicle.

She only softened up when they were in Shelly's hospital room. There she smiled, hugging Shelly tight. And when a nurse brought the baby in and Shelly instructed her to give it to Janella, she damned near melted.

It was something seeing her like this, her eyes damp and sparkling as she held the child close to her.

"She's beautiful, Shelly," Janella said softly. "Yes, you are, little one. You're beautiful."

"I'm calling her Christine, after Hugh's mother. But her middle name is Janella. Christine Janella Connor."

Janella looked up, blinked rapidly. "Oh, Shelly, that's…" She shook her head. "I'm honored."

"You helped me, Janella. I don't know how—I'm not sure I want to know how. But you did. I don't think I could have gotten through that delivery without you. And we're both grateful."

Janella shook her head. "It was Thomas who gave her life."

"Don't think I'm not aware of that," Shelly said. "First he saves my husband and then my baby."

Thomas looked away from the affection in Shelly's eyes. It made him uncomfortable. Damn, when that baby had stopped breathing, he'd thought for a minute he'd stop, as well. The knot of fear that had gripped him at that instant had been almost crippling. A long way from the distance he prided himself on keeping between himself and his patients.

His iron wall had thinned to a sheer curtain, and even that was worn in places.

"Speaking of Hugh," he said, to change the subject. "I'd better go check on him. I'll leave you two to visit."

He did, and when he returned, it was to find Janella a little less hostile. On the way home, he braved conversation, figuring it was worth a try.

"Did you tell her you were leaving?"

Janella shook her head. "She was so happy. I didn't want to give her a reason to feel sad."

Thomas nodded. "Yeah, well, she won't be the only one to be sorry to see you go. You know that, don't you?"

"Yes. I suppose Eugenia will miss me, as well."

Thomas bit his inner cheek. He didn't suppose it had occurred to her that he might miss her himself, had it? No. Why would it have? She had herself convinced he was completely indifferent to her. And that was the way he wanted it. Wasn't it?

Janella licked her lips, seemed to be working up her courage, and finally, she faced him. "You don't know, do you, how special it is, what you do for people?"

He said nothing, just shrugged and kept driving.

"At home..." She drew a breath. "At home, they would have let little Christine die. Any child born less than perfect is allowed to die...or...or helped to die."

Thomas stared at her so long he nearly drove off the road. He couldn't believe he'd heard her right. He veered onto the shoulder in front of the diner, killed the engine and turned in his seat. "Helped...how?"

She was staring straight ahead, deep in thought. "The old and the sick, anyone deemed a burden are...euthanized. My grandfather..."

"Damn, Janella."

"They decided he was too old to live any longer. He was scheduled for the ritual. The sick are gathered together once a year. But the flawed newborns never live more than an hour. My mother didn't even fight it. But Father did. He refused to let them take his father from him. That's why we were here all those years ago. Father decided to bring Grandfather here and hoped he could live out his days in peace."

So much pain in her eyes. So much loss. Thomas wanted to pull her into his arms, hold her, kiss the pain away.

"And did he?"

Janella shook her head. "No. The trip was too much for

his old heart. He died just before we landed. He's buried in your woods, near a pond. A pine tree is his marker."

Thomas swore again, but Janella went on. "I wasn't supposed to be on the ship. But I sneaked aboard and hid. I couldn't bear the thought of leaving my grandfather here alone after Father had buried him, so I ran into the woods. That's where you found me, lost and alone. Still grieving."

He couldn't stop himself from reaching out, running one hand over her satin hair. She was so beautiful, so hurt.

"I'm glad I came along on that trip, though. That time was the last I spent with my father. He was sentenced to spend the rest of his life in prison for the crime of rescuing Grandfather. I saw him only once more before he was sent away. And he told me to come here as soon as I was grown. He said I didn't belong there, with the cold, unfeeling society of my people. He said Earth was different. That emotions were acceptable here. That no one would condemn me for *feeling*."

He stared at her, shook his head slowly. "No damn wonder you ran away. God, what kind of people *are they?*"

She sniffed, staring into his eyes so deeply it hurt. "I'm not like them, Thomas. I didn't tell you this before because I was afraid you would think I was."

He offered her a smile, cupped her head between his hands. "I know you're not like them. Hell, Janella, I've never seen anyone as emotional as you are. How you ever survived there as long as you did I can't imagine." Her hair under his palms was softly erotic. She felt fragile.

"I didn't tell you this to elicit your pity, Thomas." She gently pulled free of his hands. "I only wanted to make you realize how special you are. How precious your gift of healing is to your people." She took one of his hands in hers, her fingers caressing, tracing its shape. "Here you are free to feel, to care, to be angry or hurt or happy or excited. Yet you don't use that freedom. You close your feelings away in some darkened spot inside you. You refuse to let them out. But don't you see, you can't stop them? You can't help but care about people. It's a part of who you are. You could never stand by and watch my people practice their ritual euthanasia. You would explode in anger, and rightly so. What they are is cold and unfeeling, without emotion. You are as far removed from that as it's possible to be, but you don't realize it."

He sighed hard. Her words cut to the quick. "You're right, Janella. I do have feelings." He looked at her, as she tilted her head to one side and stared back. "And I wouldn't admit it to just anybody. Thing is, I don't *want* to have them. I have to fight them, or…" He shook his head, unwilling to finish.

"Or what, Thomas?"

"Or I'll lose my mind."

"You're wrong. You'll lose your mind if you do fight them. Worse yet, Thomas, you'll lose yourself. You'll battle your emotions until you win, and then you won't be the wonderful man you are anymore. Instead, you'll become the very thing I'm running away from."

He closed his eyes as if it would shield his soul from her probing gaze. She didn't understand. She hadn't seen the suffering, the senseless death that he had. She didn't know how much it hurt to lose patient after patient, especially when you let yourself care.

But he thought he understood finally why she wanted to flee from him. "That's it, isn't it? You're afraid I'm like those people you ran away from." He sighed hard. "Hell, you're probably right."

"No."

He opened his eyes, faced her. "No?"

"No. I know you are not like them, Thomas. You're the one who doesn't know it. Haven't you been listening to me?"

He frowned, searching her face. "Then why won't you marry me?"

She closed her eyes, shook her head.

"You want me. I know that now." Her eyes flew wide, but he caught her, clasping her nape with one hand, keeping her from turning away. "Would it make any difference if I told you I want you, too?"

She shook her head, hair brushing over his knuckles. "No. Because it isn't true."

"The hell it isn't. I've wanted you since I first laid eyes on you, lady. I want you so much I think about it every time I look at you." He couldn't believe he'd just said that. But since he had...

He pulled her closer, lowered his head and took her mouth the way he'd been wanting to take it. Deeply, thoroughly, thinking maybe that if he couldn't convince her of it with words, then he'd have to show her his desire. But it didn't work quite the way he'd planned.

She trembled in his arms, before she sagged against him. It was good. Her lips moist and full, parting as if on their own the minute he touched them. But when he traced their shape, when he dipped inside to taste her, the sweet friction of his tongue rubbing against hers sent a lightning bolt to the tips of his toes. And then her mouth moved under his, her tongue joined in the dance, her fingers slipped through his hair. God, he was dying, drowning in her. And he didn't want to stop.

His arms wound around her, one cupping the back of her head to hold her to him, the other encircling her waist. He pressed closer, bending her back, leaning over her as a hunger like nothing he'd ever known took control of his every cell, his every thought, his every action. All he wanted was more of her, more of her taste, her soft breaths, her passionate responses. She was so small, her soft body fitting against his hard one like a delicate hand slipping into an armored gauntlet. And everything in him screamed to keep her right there, safe from all the pain and danger in the world, safe in his arms.

She moaned into his mouth, and he felt the oddest sensation in his chest. Like something shattering into a thousand glittering fragments.

The shock of that made him draw away, and he could only stare at her in mute wonder. Her wide eyes shimmered. Her tousled hair framed a face that glowed with want, and her lips trembled, pink and wet and slightly swollen. As he watched, she lifted one hand, pressed her fingertips to her lips.

Thomas closed his eyes and slid back behind the wheel. Where he should have remained to begin with. Whatever had just happened, it scared the hell out of him. He did not like it. And he liked it even less that all of a sudden, keeping her here with him had taken on more importance than drawing another breath.

"Thomas," she whispered. Her voice sounding as shaken as his entire being was.

He looked toward her, but she was staring through the windshield, and there was fear slowly eroding the desire and surprise in her eyes.

Following the direction of her gaze, Thomas saw two men sitting on a bench in front of the diner, sipping coffee from white foam cups, talking casually. As if they knew each other, maybe.

The two men were Alex Vrooman and Jack Halloway.

And Thomas felt nothing but sheer relief. What the hell was wrong with him? He ought to be furious, suspicious. Instead he was damn near giddy.

"You can't go with him, Janella."

She met his stare, bit her lower lip. "I know."

Chapter 9

Janella stiffened when they pulled into the curved, gravelly driveway of Thomas's farm. A car was there before them. A dark, four-door boat of a vehicle that seemed designed to intimidate. It looked to Janella like the ultimate harbinger of doom. And she recognized the two men inside, the ones who'd been with Jack Halloway. She saw, too, the reason they hadn't emerged from their vehicle. Humphrey stood beside it, crouched and snarling, looking as if he'd like to make a meal of them both.

Thomas reached across the space between them and closed his hand around hers. "There's nothing left out there for them to find. They can't hurt you, Janella."

She swallowed hard, secretly finding strength in the reassuring grip, the steady voice, the honest gaze. Wasn't it enough to care so much for the man as to hurt when he hurt and laugh when he was happy? Did she have to become dependent on him, as well? Was that a part of this love thing? She wasn't sure, having never experienced it before.

Thomas opened his door and got out. Janella did like-wise, catching up with him, trying to mimic the confidence he exuded as he strode toward the dark car. He called to Humphrey and the dog bounded toward him, and if dogs could smile, Janella felt this one was right now. He looked proud of his day's work.

Thomas snagged hold of his collar, and only then did the two men emerge from the car. Halloway wasn't with them, of course. She *knew* where Halloway was, and with whom he was chatting.

"Well, boys, I assume you've brought your search war-rant with you this time around?"

One of the men stepped forward, wordlessly tugging a folded document from somewhere inside his jacket and thrusting it at Thomas. Humphrey lunged upward, jaws snapping in the air just below the man's hand. He jumped back a little, but Thomas kept hold of the dog.

Thomas unfolded the paper slowly, perusing the words written there as calmly as if he were reading his daily news-paper. Then he shrugged. "Knock yourselves out, then. Where's your fearless leader?"

"He'll be joining us shortly," one of them said. The other remained stone faced and silent.

"Well, I'd offer to help…" Thomas slipped an arm around Janella, pulling her close to his side and dropping an adoring gaze on her face. One she knew was false. "But we have a wedding to plan. Don't we, honey?"

She blinked up at him, unable to force a reply. He turned her toward the house and strolled casually away from the two as if he hadn't a care in the world, pulling an unwilling Humphrey along with them. Janella suddenly felt as if she were carrying a very heavy weight on her back.

Eugenia flipped the pages of the *Autumn Bride Cata-logue,* chattering on and on about the advantages of each gown depicted and telling Janella how beautiful she would look in any of them.

Humphrey sat at Janella's side, tilting his head this way and that, almost as if listening to every word. Janella tried to drum up as much interest as the dog. The dresses were truly lovely. But it seemed so hard to pretend excitement over a ceremony that wasn't going to mean anything at all.

"Oooh, hon, look at this one. All that lace, and the pearls worked into the trim. It's perfect for you."

Janella gazed at the photograph, forced a smile. "It's lovely."

Eugenia frowned at her, shoving the catalogue aside. "You're not very excited about this, are you?" Humphrey looked at Eugenia.

"Of course I am." The dog's head swung back to Janella.

"No, you're not. Don't you lie to me. And who can blame you anyway, with the proposal that fool of a man offered you? Just to get Immigration off your back, wasn't that what he said? I swear, sometimes I wonder how anyone that dense ever made it through medical school." Humphrey barked as if in agreement and lifted one paw to Janella's lap. She stroked his shaggy head.

"Thomas is brilliant, Eugenia. You saw him take care of Shelly's baby—"

"Brilliant about some things. But he's no brighter than a twenty-five-watt bulb about others." Eugenia's hand crept across the table to cover Janella's. "He cares about you, though. It's in his eyes every time he looks at you. He just doesn't realize it yet, or maybe he just won't admit it. Either way, you and I know how he feels. Don't we?"

Janella averted her eyes.

"You do know how he feels, don't you, Janella? Hon, you must, or you wouldn't have agreed to marry him." The woman's eyes narrowed as she perused Janella's face. "For God's sake, girl, I can't believe it. You're as thick skulled as he is.'' She shook her head. ''You two will be the death of me for sure.''

''I like the last dress the best, Eugenia.'' It was a sad attempt at changing the subject, but it was the best Janella could manage at the moment.

''Well, I'll order it, then. And since you have so little interest in this blessed event, I'll take care of the flowers and the reception, as well. Almost like having a daughter of my own, although I daresay if I'd raised you, you'd be a little quicker on the uptake than you are.''

Janella licked her lips. ''All this is going to cost a lot of…'' She searched for the word. ''Money,'' she finally added. ''I don't have—''

''Girl, Thomas is the only MD in fifty miles. He has more money than God, and not one thing to spend it on. Don't you worry about money.''

Janella shook her head. ''I don't think—''

''Spend what you have to, 'Genia.'' Thomas stepped into the kitchen and poured himself a cup of coffee. Humphrey bounded up to him, butting Thomas's leg and making him slosh coffee on his hand. He scowled at the dog, but patted his head. ''Just as long as we can have the wedding within a week.''

''A week?''

Thomas sipped from the steaming mug. ''Sooner if possible.''

''You're both completely insane,'' Eugenia spluttered, scraping her chair away from the table and getting to her feet. ''I better get busy, then. Lord, I don't know what to do with you two.''

She hurried out of the house, still muttering, and Thomas glanced down at Janella and smiled. ''Nervous?''

She tried to meet his eyes, only to find she couldn't hold his gaze. ''This is all happening very quickly, Thomas. I never said I would marry you.''

"You agreed you couldn't take off with Vrooman. I thought marrying me was the only other option."

She felt trapped, and suddenly the thought of just leaving all of them, Vrooman, Thomas, Halloway, this entire town, flitted through her mind like an errant breeze. It was enticing, the idea of being alone, free to do as she chose without worrying about the consequences.

Thomas came closer, took a chair beside her. Humphrey padded over to lie down on top of Thomas's feet. "It's gonna be all right, Janella. I promise. Don't look so afraid."

She couldn't help it. She *was* afraid.

The entire banister was entwined with red roses and baby's breath. More floral arrangements dotted the living room, which had been cleared of all its furniture and filled with folding chairs borrowed from the local grange hall. Lots of frills, and the scent made Thomas want to sneeze, but he figured Janella would like it. And hell, she deserved a nice wedding, even if it wasn't a real one.

She hadn't talked about leaving again. Actually, she hadn't talked about much of anything at all. She'd become quiet, oddly withdrawn, and she avoided him as much as was humanly possible, going to bed early every night, saying she didn't feel like going into the clinic with him days. He hadn't liked leaving her at home alone, but she hadn't given him much choice.

He hadn't kissed her again. She'd shown no indication that she might want him to. And he wasn't sure what to expect after the wedding. Did she still want to sleep with him, or had she changed her mind? He'd have given his eyeteeth to know what was going on in that head of hers. Especially today.

He hadn't seen her at all. Eugenia had shown up at the crack of dawn and kept him away from the bedroom where she and Janella had taken up residence. He'd hoped to talk to her before the main event, to reassure her, to ease her fears, whatever the hell they might be. But he hadn't had the opportunity, and now he didn't really know what to expect.

Half the town had shown up for this thing. The living room was filled to capacity and then some, with Halloway sitting in the back, watching everything with interest. Especially Eugenia. He seemed as fascinated by her as Vrooman. And Thomas got the feeling 'Genia was enjoying every minute of it. Thomas was surprised the guy hadn't given up and gone away by now, having found nothing unusual out in the woods. He'd been half hoping for that, and half dreading it. With Halloway gone, Janella wouldn't be forced to go through with this scam. And for some reason, Thomas wasn't altogether sure that was what he wanted.

Stupid.

Bess Longworth, the church organist, struck up the wedding march on the portable keyboard, and the room went silent. Thomas tugged at the collar of the tux Eugenia had insisted he wear, and looked up to the top of the stairs just as Janella appeared there. And then he couldn't look away.

My God. He blinked and swallowed, and his stomach turned over. His throat clenched as she slowly descended the stairs. She was enough to send every man in the room into immediate cardiac arrest. Her hair all caught up in the back, with ebony ringlets cascading down around her face and brushing her bare shoulders. Her eyes mysterious as ever, more so with the touch of makeup Eugenia had artfully applied. The white gown revealed a hint of cleavage, peeping out from behind pearls and lace. It hugged her waist and slender hips and legs all the way to the floor, where it pooled around her feet.

But her eyes were downcast, and she wasn't smiling. She didn't look at him, just came toward him to a chorus of oohs and ahs and breathy sighs. Thomas figured some of the folks who'd shown up out of sheer curiosity were now glad they'd come. It wasn't every day they got to see a woman like Janella. Decked out the way she was, she looked like some pagan goddess. And damned if every eye that turned toward her didn't have a reverent awe glimmering within.

God almighty, this woman was marrying him. *Him.* Hell, no wonder she'd had second thoughts. She deserved one of those romantic heroes in those damned books of Eugenia's. What the hell was he thinking of, pushing her into this sham? She ought to have more, more than he could ever give her. And why it had taken him this long to realize that was beyond his comprehension.

She stopped beside him and finally looked up. He saw the tears shimmering on her lashes, and felt like the biggest idiot in the universe. He'd taken this whole thing as if it were a game, a little round of cat and mouse with Halloway. But it meant more than that, no matter what he called it. And he thought it had meant more to her right from the start. And *that* was why she'd become so depressed and so distant.

He reached down, took her hands in his and lifted them to his lips. Hell, she was hurting. This damn wedding was tearing her apart. Why couldn't he have seen it earlier?

"We are gathered here today," the Reverend Phelps began, and Thomas knew he ought to look at the man, pay attention to what was being said, but he couldn't take his eyes away from Janella's. They held him like magnets, clung to him as if she were too afraid to look away.

And then he was repeating his vows. Then she was repeating hers, and damned if those tears didn't spill over and splash down onto the backs of his hands, still clinging to hers.

He slipped his ring onto her finger. He hadn't bought her a diamond. She deserved a rock the size of Texas, and he hadn't even thought about it. Damn, if he didn't burn in hell someday—there was no justice in the world. Why'd she have to fall into his backyard? Why couldn't she have landed in the lap of some Prince Charming who could give her what she wanted, instead of a coldhearted snake like him?

"You may kiss the bride."

Thomas drew her close, gently, sensing her fragile state, wanting only to reassure her. He lowered his head and kissed her for the first time in days, and it was as if he'd crossed a desert looking for water, and instead had found champagne. So he drank, and tasted salty tears, and he felt lower than Satan himself.

The room broke into a chorus of raucous cheers. Must have been the tears that did it. First her stunning beauty, her downcast eyes, her palpable uncertainty, and then her tears. They'd worked their magic. Every busybody here suddenly felt a personal stake in her happiness. Even the women who'd shown up with daggers in their eyes were sniffling and dabbing at their cheeks, and smiling those dopey, sugary smiles that women smile at weddings and births.

Eugenia was bawling like a motherless calf. When he lifted his head, Thomas held Janella to his chest, encircling her with his arms, feeling her tremble.

"I'm sorry," he whispered into her hair. It was all he could think of to say, and he knew, too well, that it wasn't enough.

The crowd filtered outside, where a couple of awnings and a half-dozen tables and enough food for the U.S. Cavalry had been set up. Crepe paper and balloons fluttered in the warm autumn breeze. The sky was blue and cloudless, and the air smelled like apples and fresh-cut wheat and new-mown grass. White table cloths, held in place underneath with a little masking tape, billowed in the breeze all the same. A big fat paper bell rolled over and over, traversing the length of one table to plop gently to the ground.

On a small round table in the center of it all rested an

immaculate wedding cake that might have been decorated
by pixies, so tiny and precise were the flowers and the trim.
Someone hustled him toward it, and someone else began
snapping pictures. But Thomas was barely aware of the
bustle around him. He only knew that somehow, he'd managed to hurt this small, exotic woman today. And he knew
that somehow, he had to make it right.

At last they were leaving. Janella hadn't thought they
ever would. A few lagged behind. Eugenia and a pair of
teenagers she'd pressed into service busily covered dishes
with plastic wrap and stashed them in the refrigerator. Janella had changed from the beautiful white gown into a
shorter, more practical dress. She wandered from table to
table, gathering paper plates before the wind could disperse
them. Some had already taken flight. She watched one cart-
wheel across the lawn and thought, that's me. Out of control. Dancing at the whim of an unpredictable wind, with
no idea where I'm going. What comes next?

A hand on her shoulder made her turn. Alex Vrooman
smiled gently down at her, clasped one of her hands in both
of his.

"This has been difficult for you, hasn't it?"

She nodded. It was hard to believe he could be in league
with Halloway when you looked up into those warm eyes.
They seemed so kind.

"I'm sorry. I'm still not certain the choice you made was
the best one, but I wish you happiness. Halloway seemed
a little less sure of himself when he saw you crying at the
altar. I was watching him."

Her fingertips went automatically to her cheeks. She
hadn't wanted her tears to be witnessed by so many. But
holding them back had been impossible.

"I'm going to be around for you, Janella. If you have
any questions, need any help at all." He glanced past her,

to where Thomas stood talking to Eugenia near the house. "Or if you change your mind."

Change her mind? She'd never really made up her mind. She looked at Thomas, and as if sensing her gaze, he glanced up. His brow furrowed and he strode toward them, leaving Eugenia to continue buzzing the lawn like a frantic little bee.

"Anything wrong here?"

"No." She said it softly. Speaking loud seemed to be an effort not worth making.

"I was going to come over and have a word with you, Thomas. I want you to know, I think Halloway was convinced. The ceremony...well, it was moving. He couldn't help but be affected by it."

"You'd know, wouldn't you, Vrooman?"

Alex tilted his head to one side, his face puckering in thought. "Thomas?" No response. Alex frowned harder, his gaze jumping from Thomas's to Janella's. "I get the feeling I've just been accused of something."

"Thomas and I saw you talking to Halloway in town the other day," she told him.

His brows went up. One hand cupped his chin and he nodded. "I see. So you decided I might be working with Halloway. Hence you couldn't leave here with me, leaving you no choice but to marry Thomas." He looked away from her, pinning Thomas with a glare that seemed to darken and throw off sparks. "That was the weakest and possibly the lowest ploy I've ever heard of, Duffy."

"What?"

She thought she might need to step between them when Thomas leaned forward. Instead, she gripped his arm, felt the tension in the bulging muscles, and saw that his hand had become a fist.

"You heard me. Did you even consider coming to me? Asking me about this? No. You used it to plant doubt in Janella's mind, and you used *that* to make her marry you."

"You cocky little bastard, I oughtta—"

"Stop!" She did get between them now, both hands bracing Thomas's shoulders. Twisting her head, she spoke to Alex. "It isn't like that. Thomas didn't *want* to marry me. He only did it because he felt he had no choice!"

"Oh, he had a choice, Janella. You're fooling yourself about that." His eyes glittered as he stared at Thomas. "You got the best of both worlds, didn't you? You get to keep her, without an ounce of emotional risk. Not a word of commitment. Not a hint of feeling. But that's the way you like things, isn't it?"

Thomas's hands rose to close on Janella's shoulders, and gently, but firmly, he moved her aside. "Go inside and help Eugenia."

She shook her head. "No. You mustn't fight over this. It's all just a misunderstanding. Thomas, please, I can't stand any more today. I—" She broke off, blinking, realizing just how close to the emotional limit she'd been pushed. Tired of all of it, she turned away. Let them beat each other bloody, for all she cared. She'd had enough.

"Look at her, Thomas. Look at what you're doing to her."

"*I* didn't do anything to her." But she felt his eyes on her back as she walked away. She tried not to slump so much, tried not to drag her feet over the grass.

"You could have found another way to convince her to stay. You didn't have to make her doubt me."

"Dammit, Vrooman, *I* doubt you. What the hell were you doing with Halloway in the first place?"

"Pumping him for information. And if you'd given it any thought at all, you'd have guessed that on your own."

Janella stopped walking. She sank down onto a folding chair, close enough to still be able to hear them, watch them. She felt badly for having misjudged Alex.

Thomas was shaking his head. "Look, if I jumped to the

wrong conclusions, I'm sorry. But you have to know I couldn't risk her that way.''

''You could have given her the facts and let her make her own decision, though. But I think you didn't want to do it, and I think the only risk you were concerned with was your own risk of losing her.''

''Dammit, Vrooman, you're skating on thin ice.''

''So I am. And so are you. I'm staying in Sumac, Thomas. I'll be here for her if she needs me, and if she decides to leave with me, go to meet others like her, then I'll take her. Don't think I won't.''

Thomas looked toward her and Janella hastily averted her eyes.

Vrooman sighed hard. ''Halloway's half-convinced. Soon he'll give up and go away, and Janella's reason for staying with you will go with him. Personally, I hope she will decide to come with me. It would be the best thing for her, Thomas.''

With that, Vrooman walked past Thomas toward the house, calling for Eugenia. He'd driven her here this morning, then left and come back in time for the ceremony. It looked as if they'd be leaving together, as well.

Janella gathered up the trash bag she'd been filling with paper plates and carried it toward the trash cans behind the house. She didn't look back at Thomas, but she knew he was staring at her. As she removed the lid from one of the cans and stuffed the bag inside, Alex Vrooman's accusations rang in her ears. Alex might think Thomas's alleged deception would make her angry, make her want to leave. But he was wrong. She would have loved to believe it was true. She'd have loved to think that Thomas had wanted her to stay so badly that he'd used Alex's talk with Halloway to influence her decision.

But she didn't believe it. He didn't want her here. Didn't want a wife, especially her.

* * *

The chairs had been removed. Someone, probably Matthew Connor and a few of his brothers, had restored the living room to its original status. Except for the roses. There were still roses all over the damned place. He ought to have knocked Vrooman on his butt for saying the things he had. Would have, if there hadn't been just a grain of truth to them.

Thomas sank onto the sofa, pushed one hand through his hair, closed his eyes. Hell, he supposed he might as well face it. He didn't want Janella to leave. He'd danced around it for days now, but ignoring it and denying it didn't make it go away. He'd gotten attached to her somehow. Gotten used to having her around the house. And he liked it.

So what? It didn't mean a damn thing. Nothing. And he wouldn't let it start to mean anything, either. Because Vrooman was right about something else, too. Halloway was less certain than before. Soon he'd be convinced, and then he'd leave. After that, Thomas imagined Janella would be out of here like a shot. And it wouldn't be long now, either.

So Thomas figured his best course of action was to continue as they'd been this past week. Polite, but separate. No more sitting up all night watching her watch movies, laughing at the pleasure she took in them, feeling as if he were enjoying them more than he ever had. No more singing along to *Beauty and the Beast* and cracking up when he forgot the words and made up his own. No more taking her to the office with him and watching the awe and wonder on her face as he worked with the patients, the damned teary-eyed emotions she felt for every sick kid who came through the clinic door.

And *absolutely* no more slipping into her bedroom at night, to just stand there and watch her sleep. No. No more of that.

She was upstairs now. Maybe asleep already—he didn't know. He'd heard the shower, heard the hair dryer. Her little feet moving back and forth overhead. The gentle creak of the bedsprings as she'd lain down.

He swore softly. The knock on the door sounded as if it were swearing right back at him. Humphrey barked and ran to the door as Thomas got up and headed into the kitchen, wondering who the hell would bother a man on his wedding night.

Yeah. Some wedding night.

Vrooman and Eugenia, who never seemed to leave his side much lately, unless it was to pass the time with Halloway. She was certainly becoming a femme fatale these days.

"Thomas, I need a word."

Nodding, Thomas stood aside and held the screen open.

"Outside, if you don't mind. Here on the porch. It's such a pleasant night for it."

Thomas frowned, but there was an intense look in Vrooman's eyes. Thomas stepped out, Humphrey beside him.

Eugenia went inside. "I'll just go visit with Janella for a few minutes."

"She's in bed," Thomas said, having little hope that it would deter her.

"Don't forget—" Vrooman told her, his eyes lingering on her face. "The radio."

"I won't forget. Sheesh." She released the door as she went in, letting it bang shut behind her.

Vrooman took a seat on the top step. Thomas, wondering what the hell was going on, went to sit beside him, and waited.

The man cleared his throat. "You're…uh…you're going to have to sleep with her."

Thomas surged to his feet as if shot from a cannon. At the same instant, he heard rock music blasting so loudly from the bedroom upstairs the windows rattled.

"What in hell is going on around here?"

Alex looked up at him, smiled a little crookedly. "I've

been thinking about it, checking files on other cases where Halloway's been involved. He's thorough, Thomas.'' Alex patted the step again. Thomas sat down, waiting for him to come to the point.

"We have no way to be certain he didn't plant listening devices in the house while he was here today. With all that was going on, he certainly had opportunities."

Thomas swore. He lowered his head and rubbed his temples with his forefingers.

"He might not have. If not, though, he might be out there somewhere." He glanced toward the fields, the woods beyond them. "Perhaps with a set of high-powered binoculars. All he'd need to see was a hint that two bedrooms were being used rather than one…"

"I get your point."

"His suspicions would be refueled, perhaps stronger than ever. He'd never give up until he had proof of who Janella really is."

"Probably."

"You don't have to *do* anything—"

Thomas shot him a glance that stopped him in midsentence. "What do you think I'm gonna do, force her? Tell her it's all just to convince whoever might be watching and then take advantage? Hell, Vrooman, I'm not a frigging animal."

Vrooman's placid face never altered, nor did his studious gaze waver. "I didn't suggest anything of the sort. You're putting your own interpretations on my words. I only came here as a friend, Thomas. To warn you."

A little of Thomas's anger died. He sighed slowly, his spine relaxing. "I suppose 'Genia's inside filling Janella in on all this?"

Vrooman nodded. "Hence the radio," he said. "In case of bugs."

"Okay, then. Okay." Thomas started to rise, only to

have Vrooman's surprisingly strong hand settle on his shoulder to keep him sitting.

"There's more."

Thomas braced himself, sensing this was no trivial matter. Something big was coming.

"The others...tend to stick together. There's a community in Arizona where all but a few have settled. I...I know them well."

"What are you working up to, Alex? Just spit it out."

"It's going to be hard for you to hear."

He stared into Thomas's eyes with apparent sympathy. The hand on his shoulder exerted a comforting pressure.

"They're good people. They take care of their own, but aren't hesitant to help anyone in need. I think..." He sighed. "Thomas, I think Janella needs to go there, to be with them. She seems to be falling into a state of depression, and it might go on. You're a doctor. You know how dangerous that can be."

Thomas nodded.

"I didn't mean to be so hard on you today. I was angry that my integrity was called into question. But I know you care for her. Want what's best for her."

"And you think leaving Iowa, heading down to Arizona to be with these people, is what's best for her, don't you?"

Vrooman's eyes never left Thomas's face as he nodded.

Thomas shrugged. "Fine. You just let me know when you think Halloway's called off the dogs."

The screen door creaked open, banged shut. Eugenia came behind them, dropped a hand to Vrooman's shoulder. "Ready to leave, Alex?"

Alex rose, using the railing to pull himself to his feet. He offered Thomas his hand. Thomas took it, shook it.

Eugenia snagged Thomas's neck with both arms and hugged him to the point of near asphyxia. Against his ear, she whispered, "Open up that heart of yours, Thomas Duffy. It's time. That girl up there is head over heels—"

He gently set her away, not able, not willing, to hear the end to that sentence. It was bull, anyway. Impossible. Stupid. And not something he wanted. Not something he'd been waiting for all his life. Not something that would fill up the empty pit where his heart used to be. Not something that would bring the hollow Tin Man he'd become back to pulsing, throbbing life. Never that.

Chapter 10

She heard his steps, slow and even, on the stairs. Her heartbeat sped up a little. Her palms dampened. She stood near the window, pretending to look out, but every cell was focused on the sounds of his approach. Traversing the hall. Now stopping outside the door.

It opened. Janella turned.

His eyes were apologetic. "It'll be okay."

She nodded, her gaze slipping inexorably to the bed she was to share with him.

"You look tired. Go ahead, lie down. I still have to shower and…"

His voice trailed off. So that was going to be the way of it. He'd give her a chance to fall asleep before he joined her. She supposed he thought it would be easier on her. How could he know that she wouldn't sleep at all, but only lie there, tense and wide-eyed? Alert to his every movement. Waiting. Wondering what would happen when he came to her.

She flicked off the bedroom light and crawled beneath

the covers. Would he touch her? Kiss her? Hold her in his arms? She wanted him to. Wanted it so much it haunted her thoughts, had all this past week. She loved him. Wanted him. She'd told him the latter. She'd never admit the former, not unless he came to... Ah, but that was foolishness. He'd never...

She turned toward the bathroom when she heard the shower running. Her thoughts strayed to the black teddy in the closet. Should she get up, slip into it and wait for his reaction? Did she dare?

She bit her lip, shook her head. He did not want her. When was she going to accept that as the truth?

He took his time. She heard every movement, almost every breath. It seemed an eternity before he finally emerged. The amulet gleamed against his chest, like a brand proclaiming him hers. Why did he continue wearing it? He wore boxers beneath a short robe hanging open. His hair was wet and curling. He rubbed his head vigorously with a towel before coming to the bed, standing at the side, looking down at her for a long moment.

He sighed, shook his head, tugged back the covers. Shedding the robe, he slid in beside her, his damp body cool against her heated skin.

She sucked air through her teeth. "You're cold!"

"Sorry about that." He lay on his back, not so much as turning to face her. "I thought maybe you were asleep."

"I'm not."

"So I see."

Stupid conversation. Absolutely stupid. A tenseness filled the silence as she waited to see if he'd move closer, or roll toward her and slide his arms around her, or roll away from her and go to sleep, or talk some more.

"About today," he began, still lying on his back.

"What about today?"

A long, slow breath escaped him. "It wasn't exactly the wedding day young girls dream about, was it?"

"I don't know. What do your young girls dream about?"

He shook his head from side to side on his pillow. "Not that. They want to be swept off their feet by some man who can't live without them."

She nodded thoughtfully. "And you most certainly *can* live without me. Is that the point you're trying to make?"

He did turn to face her now, a frown puckering his brows. "Hell, no, that isn't the... Janella, I was trying to apologize. You seemed so melancholy today, and those tears at the altar were not tears of joy. You looked as if your heart was breaking."

She said nothing, only searched his face in the gray darkness, trying to see a sign. But as always his feelings, if he had any, were well hidden.

"The condition of my heart shouldn't be your concern."

He was quiet for a moment, lying back again, pensively staring at the ceiling. Then he said, "You're homesick, aren't you? You miss your own people."

"It's difficult to miss them, Thomas, when you act so much like them."

"What the hell is that supposed to mean?"

She refused to answer, and took her turn at searching the ceiling for the secrets of the universe.

"Alex thinks it would do you a world of good to go to Arizona to see them, be with them."

Janella blinked, a small knot of fear tightening in her stomach. "And what do you think?"

"I agree with him."

She closed her eyes against the flood of tears that burned in them. "When?"

"As soon as Halloway leaves. It won't be long. Alex thinks he's damned near convinced."

Despair was a black, clinging thing that covered your face with ugly hands and made you have to struggle to breathe. Tears spilled, and Janella was glad of the darkness.

He was sending her away. He wanted her away from him this badly. Why? What had she done?

"Of course," Thomas went on, "it will take me at least a week to make arrangements for another doctor to fill in at the clinic. But no longer than that. And there's Humphrey. We'll have to find someone to—"

"Thomas?" She turned on her side, searching his face in the dimness. "You...you would come with me?"

"Yeah. Unless you'd rather—"

He stopped speaking as her arms wound around his neck and she hugged him hard. It was an impulsive act, but he responded, first by gasping in surprise and then by very gently holding her against him. He rolled a little onto his back, one arm beneath her, hand resting against her hair, the other lightly around her waist. Her face was pillowed by his chest, and she felt the thundering strength of his heart beneath her.

The hand around her waist slipped upward, to touch her cheek. "You're crying."

"Because I thought you meant to send me away." She lifted her head, her face close to his, and searched his eyes. He *didn't* want to be rid of her after all. He would come with her if she decided to go. Perhaps he *did* feel something for her after all. Why else would he want to prolong their time together?

She restrained herself from blurting all that and considered again the question at hand. Did she want to go at all, even with Thomas at her side?

She sighed. "I'm still not sure, Thomas. I'm only beginning to become accustomed to Sumac and its people. Traveling to a new place..." She shuddered. "I'm not sure I want to go. Knowing you will be with me, though, will make the decision easier. I won't be as afraid."

He swallowed hard—she felt it the way she was lying on him. He cleared his throat. "Yeah, well, I couldn't very well send you off alone with Vrooman. Only yesterday I thought he might be one of the bad guys. I still have a kernel of doubt.''

She felt her face change. Before, she was sure the love she felt for Thomas had been glowing from her very skin as she gazed into his eyes. Now her face felt frozen, expressionless. So the only reason he'd volunteered to accompany her was his lack of trust in Alex Vrooman.

Slowly she drew away from him. She rolled onto her side, putting her back to him, and huddled beneath the covers as a shiver worked through her from head to toe.

Dammit, he'd hurt her again. Might as well have slapped her as say what he had just said. But what the hell else could he have done? She'd been lying on top of his bare chest, wearing nothing but a whisper-thin nightgown, her hair tumbling down to tickle his skin, her scent tying him up in knots. And the look in her eyes! My God, it had shaken Thomas right to the marrow.

One more second, one more of those hot little breaths wafting over his skin, and he'd have pulled her harder to his chest. He'd have kissed her breath away, and then he'd have rolled her over, covered her body with his own and made her his wife in every sense of the word.

His wife.

The words echoed through his mind like a shot in a canyon. She wasn't his wife. Not really. And he damned well better not start thinking of her as if she were, because he didn't love her. And she deserved to be loved.

Of course, he'd lied about still suspecting Vrooman, and he supposed that if Vrooman knew it, Thomas would probably get a taste of the man's knuckles. Deservedly. Thomas didn't know why the hell he'd suddenly decided to go to Arizona with her. Maybe he was *already* getting a little too attached to her. He knew the idea of just saying adios someday soon and watching her get into Vrooman's car and ride away, not expecting ever to see her again, was more than he could do.

Didn't mean anything, though. Nothing much, anyway. Hell, she was a friend, right? As well as a patient.

Good one, Thomas. Duty to your patient. Excellent excuse and absolute. bull.

All he wanted to do was make sure she got where she was going safely, got settled in, had everything she needed. What was so criminal about that?

And then say adios, and leave her behind. Right?

He closed his eyes. Hell, she might decide not to go at all, and even if she did, maybe she wouldn't want to stay there. She might visit these people and make a few friends and still want to come back to Iowa with him. It was possible, wasn't it?

Why the hell would she want to come back here? For what? What does she have here?

Friends, Thomas reasoned. She has friends, like Eugenia, and Shelly and the new baby. She won't want to leave them.

And you, right, Duffy? Her loving husband and her happy home. Wouldn't want to toss all that aside, would she? Wouldn't want to go out and find herself a real husband and a real life, when she has this perfectly good make-believe one waiting for her.

Shut up, Thomas thought. He thought it loudly, angrily, made it a mental shout. And the voice in his mind quieted. But what it had said lingered all night long.

At least, it did until he slept. And he knew beyond any doubt he had slept, when he woke up to find himself twined around Janella like a some kind of clinging vine. His lower arm pillowed her head. His upper one held her face so tightly to his chest he wondered how she breathed. One of his legs had pinioned her to the bed. As if—okay, he might as well admit it. He wasn't an idiot, and he'd had straight

A's in psychology—as if he were subconsciously trying to keep her from leaving him.

And her lips were touching his chest, her hair rubbing it. He was hard the instant he opened his eyes, or maybe he had been before he'd opened them. There wasn't a part of either of them that wasn't in direct physical contact with a part of the other one. So if she awoke, she'd feel it. And she'd know that he wanted her beyond what was normal, or sane or bearable. He extricated himself carefully, rolled away from her and, since it was still early, tried to go back to sleep.

But apparently his movement had roused her. Because a second later, she was getting out of bed with an economy of motion that said she was trying not to wake him. Good, let her think him asleep. He wasn't quite ready to look into those exotic ebony jewels of hers just yet, anyway.

He heard her pad across the floor. A dresser drawer scraped open. Then the closet door creaked. A coat hanger rattled. More soft steps. She'd gone into the bathroom. Good. But why could he still hear so clearly, and why did each sound produce a vision? Fabric brushing over skin, pooling on the floor. God.

The glass door on the tub slid open. Then closed. Water came on. Thomas rolled to face the bathroom, opening his eyes just to blot out the images dancing through his mind with the sight of the closed door.

Only it wasn't closed. It stood wide. And beyond it, through the frosted-glass tub doors, he saw her. A hazy, flesh-toned, feminine shape. Arms moving with fairylike grace, to reveal the lush mounds of her breasts. Head tipping back, face turned up to the spray. Her movements were a dance, performed behind a silk curtain, for an audience of one.

He groaned and buried his face in his hands. God, what this woman was capable of stirring in him!

To distract himself, he got up, made the bed and reached

into the closet for some fresh clothes of his own. His hand brushed satin, and he went utterly still. Her wedding gown hung there like a royal princess holding court. He remembered the way she'd looked in it. Like a dream. Like a goddess. Untouchable, unattainable, and so far beyond his worth it was like…like two different worlds. He smiled crookedly, but sadly, at the analogy. His hand fell away from the satin and he glanced back to the bathroom once more. He was frighteningly close to walking in there, sliding the doors open and stepping beneath the spray with her.

Dangerous thought.

"Sorry I'm late." Alex Vrooman signaled the red-haired waitress as he settled into the booth opposite Thomas. "Eugenia's kitchen sink was stopped up, and she wasn't about to let me out of there until I'd fulfilled my promise to fix it." He laughed in that understated way he had.

Katie Corrigan pulled a pad from her apron pocket as she approached them. Thomas knew her well. She'd been in his class in junior high.

Vrooman ordered, Katie left them and Thomas continued sipping his coffee.

"You wanted to talk about something," Vrooman began. "I assume it has to do with Janella."

Thomas nodded, setting his cup down. "We talked it over last night. She's not sure she wants to go. But if she does, I'm going with her."

Alex blinked, obviously surprised. "Do you think that's wise, Thomas?"

"I've given it a lot of thought. Seems to me the best possible way to do it. For one thing, it's gonna look strange for a brand-new bride to take a trip without her husband so soon after the wedding. If I go along, no one's gonna raise an eyebrow. Might be a slightly delayed honeymoon for all anyone will know. Besides, there's always a chance Halloway will follow her there."

Vrooman pursed his lips, nodding slowly. His sandwich arrived and he took a bite, not speaking for a long time, just thinking, and Thomas knew he was going to disagree.

"Go on, tell me your objections."

Vrooman swallowed, nodded. "I have only one."

"From the look on your face, I'd say it's a doozer."

He cleared his throat, wiping crumbs from his mouth with a paper napkin. "Thomas, she's going to have a chance to find her own life. She's going to find an entire community of people like her, who understand her, who'll take to her like family. And I think she's going to want to stay with them."

"I'm aware that's a possibility."

"Good. Glad to see you're not blind to it. The thing is, your presence there is likely to influence her decision. She may feel pressured to come back here with you, whether it's what she truly wants or not."

"I won't try to push her."

"You won't have to try. Just being there—"

"There's another point, Vrooman. The most important one, the way I see it."

Vrooman met Thomas's eyes, his own sincere and not a bit hostile. "Go on."

"Janella wants me to go with her."

A sigh escaped Vrooman's lips. "Well, I guess you're right. What she wants has to be our highest priority. So, you'll come along, then."

Thomas relaxed in his seat, his muscles slowly uncurling. He'd expected Vrooman to argue harder than he had. He'd been prepared to argue till he was blue in the face. He hadn't had to.

"But don't get your hopes up, Thomas. It's a close-knit community. She's going to fit right in with them, and I'm convinced she'll want to stay."

"If she wants to stay, Vrooman, then that's what I want for her."

Vrooman nodded, but Thomas could see the doubt in his eyes.

"So prepare me, Vrooman. Tell me a little about these people. What are they like?"

Vrooman leaned back against the vinyl booth seat and smiled. "In a word, they're emotional. Very feeling, caring, loving and a bit highly strung. They're exceptions to the norm on their planet. There the acceptable mode of behavior is coldness. They're taught to be practical and not to allow emotions to enter into their thinking processes."

Thomas nodded. "She told me a little about that." He didn't mention the other things she'd told him. About the ritual euthanasia, the elimination of those deemed unfit or a burden.

"I'm sure such frigidity solves some social problems. Overpopulation, for one, the need to care for the elderly or the infirm."

Thomas's head came up. Vrooman knew about that, then.

"But it's no place for a person with feelings. There's one man in Arizona, Matalin. Good friend of mine. He was sentenced to life in prison for the crime of trying to save his elderly father from execution."

Thomas felt his pulse skip to a stop for a brief space in time. When it thudded once more he could feel it in his temples. "Execution?"

"The old man had outlived his usefulness, according to the ruling house. They get rid of their elderly by lethal injection, I'm told. Matalin, being emotional and a man who happened to love his father, couldn't bear the idea."

Thomas swallowed hard. "What did he do about it?"

Vrooman shrugged. "I don't know all the details. He doesn't like to talk about it. Just that he planned some elaborate rescue, only to have his father die before it could be carried out. Matalin was tried and convicted, but he escaped on the way to prison, stole a ship and came here."

"My God."

"Shocking, isn't it?"

It was shock he felt, but not at the social customs of Janella's people. It was shock at knowing that this man... Matalin...could very well be...

But no. There had to be others who'd tried to rescue loved ones from certain death, only to be forced to flee the consequences of their actions.

That was bull. The details of Matalin's story matched the tale Janella had told him. God almighty, was it possible the man was Janella's father? That he was here, on Earth?

"Is anything wrong, Thomas? You've grown rather pale."

Thomas snapped out of his thoughts, shook his head. "No. I just...I have to go now."

As he slid out of the booth, mindlessly dropping a handful of bills on the table, Thomas knew there was no longer any question. Janella had to go to Arizona. And he'd have to find a way to convince her of it. Even though he was certain now that it would be the same as saying goodbye. And saying goodbye to Janella was going to tear him apart. God, where was his iron wall now? What had happened to his steely heart?

He sighed, long and low. It had softened, that's what. *She* had softened it. And he had a bad feeling she was about to break it.

Chapter 11

The spot where Janella and her father had buried Grandfather so long ago still seemed perfect. The little pond, just inside the edge of the woods. The towering hardwoods, the wild violets dotting the ground like a soft blanket to keep him warm. It had changed little over the years. She'd put off coming here, knowing it would renew an old pain. But now she felt a need to connect…with *family*.

As she sat on the ground beside the invisible grave, two deer picked their way cautiously to the water's edge and paused to drink. A bullfrog droned a monkish chant, and a breeze she could barely feel rippled the pond's surface.

"It's a shame you couldn't have lived here, Grandfather. You'd have loved it. The people…they're different here. They care." She closed her eyes, telling herself that the pain in her heart wasn't homesickness so much as loneliness. She couldn't miss a home she'd hated, or even her mother—its ruler—a woman who personified solid ice. She missed her grandfather. She missed her father, as well, but that pain was an old one. One that had been stamped in thick black ink like a tattoo on her soul a very long time ago. But she couldn't wish Father had acted differently. What he'd done was the only thing he could have done, being the man he was.

She tilted her head, realizing that in the same situation, Thomas would probably take the same course of action her father had, even knowing that it might cost him his freedom. In fact, there were many things about Thomas that reminded her of her father. His moodiness. His refusal—or was it inability?—to take orders. Was that why she'd come to love him so deeply? Because he reminded her of her father?

That might be part of it, she decided, but there was definitely more. She loved him for who he was. She loved the way he looked and the sound of his voice. She loved his touch, his kisses. She loved his talent for helping the sick and injured and the way he cared about them. And she loved his fondness for Humphrey. Another of his traits that reminded her of Matalin. Father had always been closer to animals than to most people.

Except for her. No one had been closer to Matalin than Janella had. Maybe because they were so much alike. Emotional and impulsive. Disgusted by the society in which they lived.

Matalin had been the only person she'd ever loved who'd loved her back. And the way things were going, maybe he'd be the only one who ever would. That knowledge made her miss him all the more. She'd have visited him in the prison colony if such a thing had been allowed. But her people would have been shocked by such a request. After all, she wasn't supposed to care, was supposed to simply forget him. She hadn't, though. And she knew he hadn't forgotten her, either. And she wondered if he thought of her often, if by some cosmic chance he might be thinking of her right now.

The thought warmed her a little, but not nearly enough.

At this moment her absolute loneliness was too much to bear. And she knew why it was eating a hole in her heart, though knowing its cause did nothing to ease the pain.

Thomas wanted her to go. All week long he'd been patiently urging her to do so, and she'd come to some painful conclusions. Even though he would accompany her on this trip, she knew he expected her to stay in Arizona. He would return here without her. And she knew he was eager for that to happen. Why else had he been going on for days about all the reasons she should go? And though the knowledge pained her, she'd finally agreed. If he wanted to be rid of her so badly, she had little choice but to comply. He would unload his burden in Arizona. She felt like an unwanted pet.

The arrangements had been made in record time. Halloway and his men seemed to have melted away beneath the autumn sun. Eugenia was going to take care of Humphrey. A doctor from a neighboring county would handle the clinic. Even now, Thomas was showing him around the little building in town, filling him in on the special needs of each of his patients.

Shelly had brought the baby by today, and they'd shared a tearful goodbye. There was nothing left to do. Tonight she and Thomas and Alex Vrooman would board a plane bound for Arizona.

And at some point in the very near future, Thomas would board an airplane again, alone this time.

God, she didn't want to go.

Through tear-hazy eyes, she saw the larger deer's head come up, ears pricking forward. A second later, the white tail flew upward, as well, and both animals leaped into the woods and vanished from sight. A twig snapped behind her and she looked around to see Thomas picking his way through the trees.

He saw her, smiled, but there was something else in his eyes. Sadness, perhaps. But why? He wanted her gone, and he was getting what he wanted. And suddenly she knew exactly why she'd been thinking about her father and her grandfather so much today. It was because she was about to lose another man whom she loved desperately.

I'm losing her, he thought as he picked his way closer, and the constriction in his chest that came with the idea was becoming all too familiar. Why did it hurt so much?

"Thought I might find you out here."

She rose, and he saw the alarm in her eyes.

"It isn't time to go yet, is it?"

"No. Not yet. We still have over an hour."

"An hour."

It was a whisper, escaping as she lowered her eyes and finally closed them. He moved closer, stopped walking and scanned her beautiful face, hoping to burn it into his mind. She'd probably decide to stay with her father in Arizona. If the man Vrooman had told him about *was* her father. But he had little room for doubt. He was going to lose her, and it wouldn't be long at all now.

"You've been crying again. Been doing a lot of that lately." She had. Homesickness, he figured. And nervousness over the trip. And maybe disappointment in him. Some husband he'd turned out to be, trying every way he could think of to talk her into going away, leaving him. It had been the hardest thing he'd ever done. But he did it for more reasons than one.

All for her, though. First and foremost, there was her father. If the man was safe and sound in Arizona, then he couldn't let Janella go on believing he suffered in prison somewhere. She had to know the truth.

But there was another reason she had to go, leave him, find her own life. She was special, the most wonderful woman he'd ever had the privilege to know. She deserved to be cherished, showered with gifts and affection and... He sighed hard. And love. If he'd been capable of that emotion, he'd have lavished it on her. But he wasn't, and she needed someone who was.

Her eyes flicked open, meeting his. The dark lashes were damp and spiky, and a glistening tear hung, entangled in their sable web.

He clasped her shoulders, drew her to his chest, stroked her hair and her back. "I don't like to see you cry, Janella."

She hugged his waist. Her body seemed to go warm and fluid in his arms. Ah, damn, it was a mistake coming out here, a bigger mistake touching her this way. He'd managed to keep his hands off her this long. So why couldn't he have managed it for one more hour?

Hell, he didn't know why. He only knew it felt good holding her close, and he didn't want to let her go.

But he had to.

His hold on her slackened, but he couldn't quite convince his arms to release her. She tipped her head back, stared up into his eyes. God, she was so beautiful it hurt to look at her. Especially now. Her eyes were wide and maybe a little eager, the message in them as clear as if she'd spoken it aloud. She wanted him to kiss her, and damn him, he wanted it, too.

Maybe it was the knowledge that they had so little time left, or maybe it was just that he'd reached the end of his resistance. He'd been fighting it for so long he would have had to be superhuman to keep it up.

Or maybe it was just the look in her eyes that made him do it.

He lowered his head a little, saw her lips part in anticipation. When he lightly touched them with his, he felt them tremble. Her palms spread on his back, exerting a whisper of pressure. And he gave in to the need that was eating away at his soul. He covered her mouth with his, pressed it open wider, drove his tongue inside to devour and possess the sweetness he'd denied himself for so long. And she welcomed him with a burgeoning passion. An innocent passion, one she couldn't begin to understand. Knowing that, he shouldn't let this madness go on.

But he couldn't stop it.

His fingers tugged the blouse from her jeans, slipped beneath it to trace the shape of her back. His palms ran up the gentle curve of her spine, to her shoulders. No bra barred the way. That knowledge seared him, and he drew one hand around her, between their bodies, beneath the blouse. Her breast filled his hand, fitted it, the pebble-hard nipple poking into his palm. She drew a harsh gasp when he rubbed his rough hand over the sensitive nub. He hadn't thought it possible to want a woman the way he wanted her. But here it was, real and powerful and undeniable. He'd never felt this kind of desire in his life, and it scared him. But he couldn't turn away from it.

Or from her.

When she drew back a little he blinked in shock, letting his hands fall to his sides. Was she frightened? Was he out of line? Would she scorn him now for being a base-driven animal?

No. As he watched in silent mesmerization, her perfect hands rose to the front of the blouse, and one by one, the buttons were freed. It gaped, showing him the flat belly and taut skin he'd been unable to put from his mind. Then she shrugged the garment from her shoulders and it slid silently down her arms to fall on the ground.

Thomas felt an urge to fall on his knees in front of such ethereal beauty. But she came forward again, her nimble fingers going to his buttons this time. And in seconds she was pushing his shirt away, to join hers on the forest floor. She pressed herself against his hair-roughened chest, closed her eyes as she moved. Her hands traveled over his back and shoulders, and her lips touched his neck, his jaw, hesitated near his ear.

"I...don't know what to do..." Her innocent whisper

made him bite back a groan. ''Show me, Thomas. Please, just this once.''

He felt a shudder rock him to the core as he bent to kiss her throat. Then he fell to his knees, ravenous for more of her, and caught one yearning nipple in his mouth. He sucked hard, working the tip with his tongue and teeth, and Janella cried out. Her knees buckled and she sagged until only his arms anchoring her waist to his chest kept her from falling. Her hands clutched his head, fingers kneading there. She was so good, so sweet. Her breasts were a forbidden fruit, her entire body his ultimate temptation. And he relished every taste, every sensation.

Mindless need tore through Thomas as he lowered her to the cushion of pale violets. His fingers shook when he released the button and lowered the zipper of her jeans. He pushed the denim and the panties beneath it down over her hips, bending over her, kissing each bit of flesh as it was revealed to him. His lips followed his hands over her thighs, her knees, her calves, right to her bare little toes. He took his time, realizing dully that he wasn't just making love to this woman. He was worshiping her, and it still didn't seem he gave her all she deserved.

When she was naked, reclining in the green-and-purple bed like a goddess, he could only kneel beside her and stare. If ever there were an illustration of perfect feminine beauty and mind-bending allure, then it was here, right in front of him, right now.

She lifted her hands toward him, and Thomas was hit with the enormity of the gift she offered. She wanted him. *Him.* What had he ever done in his lonely existence to make him worthy of this?

He lowered himself beside her, took her in his arms and kissed her mouth, his hands kneading and pinching her breasts, before slipping lower. He parted her secret folds, felt the dewy moisture they concealed, thought he'd lose his mind here today. Especially when her hands moved between their bodies to open his jeans and her palms skimmed his backside as she eagerly shoved them down.

He rolled to one side long enough to kick free of a tangle of clothing and footwear, suddenly in a hurry to be naked beside her. And when he faced her again, it was to see her gaze roving over his body, pausing on the hardness between his legs, which was so aroused it was almost painful. Timidly, her hand reached for him, fingertips touched, drew away at his harsh gasp, then returned to close around him. She squeezed experimentally, watching his face, her own eyes dark with passion. Her hands were silky soft and strong. And she ran them over him, around and beneath, lifting, squeezing, watching his face as if trying to learn what pleased him by his reactions.

He took her hand in his and moved it gently up and down, feeling the warmth of her palm stroking him. Then, biting his lip, he pulled her hand away, lowered his body gently atop hers. He kissed her again, and their tongues mated, twined and battled. With his fingers he found the core of her desire and worked it mercilessly as her breaths came fast and shallow and her hips rocked off the ground. He licked the inside of her mouth, savoring her taste as he dipped a finger inside her, then two, testing her, hoping he wouldn't hurt her, but knowing he couldn't wait much longer. She was tight, small, but so wet. For him.

Gently, he pressed her thighs open, settled himself between them, felt her juices coating the tip of him where it pressed against her. Exercising more restraint than he'd known he possessed, he nudged inside her. Just a little at a time, pausing at intervals to give her body a moment to adjust to the feel of him filling her. It was heaven and hell and ecstasy and insanity all balled into one hard knot in the pit of his stomach.

She shuddered, but never closed her eyes. They remained open, fixed unblinkingly, sparkling and black, on his. He met with the bit of tissue that offered resistance and pressed deeper. She bit her lip, her nails sinking into his shoulders the only indication she'd felt pain or discomfort.

And then he moved slowly, steadily, sheathing himself inside the damp satin that was her, pulling back, moving forward again. His gaze locked on hers, he saw the pain in her eyes recede, to be gradually replaced by acceptance and then wonder. Her lips parted as her breaths grew rapid and short. He bowed to suckle her breasts, one after the other, and her pleasure increased. He never took his gaze from hers.

He moved faster, thrust deeper, and Janella's hands curved around his backside to urge him on. She began to move with him, rocking beneath him to accept his thrusts, little whimpers of pleasure escaping her parted lips. He was at the brink, and he felt her tightening around him more and more. He took her mouth, his tongue thrusting with like rhythm, swallowing every little cry she uttered. And then she tensed, screaming his name, hands holding him deeply inside her, her body convulsing, milking him. And he held her dark gaze as she drew the essence of his body into hers, drew it from the very tips of his toes, it seemed, and tried to extract still more.

Nothing had ever felt so good. Or so right.

Every one of his muscles melted. His bones themselves turned to water and he lay on top of her thinking he never wanted to move again. A satisfaction like none he'd ever known was the result of this liaison with Janella. A sense of peace, and contentment, and fulfillment. Not to mention that he'd experienced the best damned climax he'd ever had. Shattering.

He slid off her, to the side, gathering her into his arms and wishing he never had to let her go. What was it that made this sex so different from any other? The setting? The time of day? What he'd ingested lately? Was it Janella?

Was this ability to mate with a man's soul as well as his body another of her extraterrestrial abilities?

Her lips pressed to his chest, and Thomas closed his eyes.

"Thank you for that," she whispered.

She was thanking *him?* He stroked her hair, held her closer, bent to kiss her forehead. What the hell was he ever going to do without her?

"There you are. I was beginning to think you'd changed your minds."

Alex Vrooman smiled softly as he held the car door for Thomas and Janella to get in. Thomas had already transferred their luggage from the Jeep to the trunk. Alex slid behind the wheel, and Janella was surprised to see Eugenia get in the passenger side.

She turned, as if reading her mind. "I'm coming along to the airport to drive the car back. And I'll pick you up when you come home again." She blinked a dampness from her eyes and averted them. "And you *are* coming home. Don't you even think about staying with this long-lost friend of yours down in that barren desert of a place. I'll come get you myself if I have to."

Janella smiled, but knew it was a sad smile. She didn't want to leave, and she knew Thomas didn't expect her to come back. He wouldn't have made such sweet love to her in the woods today unless he knew it was safe. That she was leaving. That he wouldn't have to face her much longer and wouldn't have time to discuss what had happened between them.

For just a few moments, Janella had been certain the cold ice he kept packed around his heart had thawed. She'd felt it. He'd let himself love her, if only for those few moments there among the violets. She'd never felt so cherished in all her life, and she wished she could get that feeling back again.

But she couldn't. He'd reverted to his normal self again. If anything, he seemed more distant now than before. He calmly reminded her to fasten her safety belt as Alex pulled the car ahead. She did it, noting that with both belts fastened, they couldn't sit very close to each other. Probably the only reason he wanted them on. She wanted to be next to him, his arm around her, her head nestled in the crook of his neck. She wanted to share whispered secrets and laugh up at him the way the lovers in the movies and the young couples she'd seen in Sumac always seemed to be doing. But apparently it wasn't going to happen.

Though there was *something* different about him. He was pensive, spoke very little. He gazed out his window most of the time, unless she turned to look out hers, in which case, he would stare at her. She could feel his gaze on her, but he always averted it before she could return it. He seemed to be fighting some inner battle. Something was tearing him apart or tying him up in knots of tension. She only wished she knew what.

She knew too well what was raising chaos in her own heart. Her love for him, and now something new and unexpected. Desire. She'd heard it mentioned often in the movies, but hadn't fully understood what it meant until now. Now she could barely look at Thomas without feeling a tightening sensation in the pit of her stomach. It was like hunger, but deeper. She craved him, his body, his touch. It made her uncomfortable and restless and even a bit short-tempered. She wanted to reach for him right now, pull him to her and beg him to make love to her again.

But of course she couldn't do that.

Jack Halloway watched from a distance. A big distance. He hadn't learned a damned thing by following them or pressuring them. So he went to plan B. Give them enough rope... And sure enough, the minute they thought he was gone, they all boarded a plane for Arizona. He'd been right about Janella all along. But Vrooman was still a big question mark. Who was the man? What was his true interest in all this? Whatever his intent, Halloway had a sick feeling in the pit of his stomach that it wasn't good. So he was heading to Arizona. When they got there, he'd be waiting. But not where they could see. He'd be like a shadow.

She'd have laughed at the primitive flying machine if she hadn't been so devastated at the thought of leaving Thomas and frightened at what might lie ahead. Her fears took on a whole new ferocity when she got a look at the place. It seemed little grew in Arizona. It was brown and barren, this little airstrip in the desert. The only things that moved beneath the blistering sun above were wisps of dirty sand spiraling like ghosts and spherical tangles of some sort of weed that appeared dead, rolling at the whim of the wind. There were a few odd-shaped things growing, not trees, but vegetation of some sort, their pale-green skin coated with prickles.

They drove away from the airstrip in a car that had been waiting. Alex must have made arrangements for it. It carried them over a flat, straight ribbon of pavement that shimmered with heat.

And gradually, things became greener. A cluster of buildings rose in the distance, looking a bit more normal. And as they drew closer, she saw that through irrigation, a small city thrived in the midst of this barren land. On its outskirts, lush green lawns grew, sprinklers giving them precious moisture. Some trees and flowers thrived here, and they passed a swimming pool built into the ground, with children splashing in every available bit of water.

The houses were neat and new. Not the old oversized homes of Sumac. One story, for the most part, with open patios and pools in the backyards, and neatly clipped grass, and nice cars in the blacktop driveways. No tractors lumbering up the winding roads or groaning through fields, though. No golden wheat fields dancing in the wind. And no hint of Sumac's cool breezes. She saw the flags some flew in front of their homes hanging limp and lifeless.

"It's really a prosperous town," Alex said softly, looking over his shoulder at her. "There are two shopping malls, a community theater. They even have their own orchestra. The main business is tourism. There are a couple of theme parks nearby, hotels, the works."

Janella shook her head, sliding closer to Thomas without thinking first. So many people. The streets were lined with cars, and bicycles and faces. The houses were closer together now, one after another. And she saw the tops of buildings in the distance, at what must be the small city's center.

Thomas's hand closed on Janella's, and she felt warmed by his touch, despite the frigid stale air that kept the car's interior cool. A tingle of longing crept over her spine, but she fought not to let it show.

"You're not trying to tell me these people are all—"

"Good God, no, Thomas. Most of them are just like you...you and me. Only about two hundred of the residents come from Janella's planet."

She blinked, staring out the side window, wondering if the boy on the bike or the man in the minivan might be her blood brothers. "How will I ever find them?"

"They'll find you, Janella. Don't worry about that. We'll get you and Thomas settled in the hotel, and I'll let word get out to one or two of them. Word will spread like you wouldn't believe, and the next thing you know you'll be overwhelmed with visitors."

She was relieved to hear that, but when she looked at Thomas, he was frowning. She ignored the urge to press her lips to his brow and smooth that frown away.

"What is it?" she whispered.

He shook his head, his mouth drawn tight. "Vrooman, I

thought you knew these people personally. You said you were good friends with some of them.''

"Oh, I am. But, Thomas, it's been a long time since I've been back here. And calling those I know one by one would be tedious at best, assuming I could even reach them. Besides, they tend to be a wary bunch.'' He shook his head, turning the car right, then waiting at a traffic light to turn left. "No, if I were to just announce that Janella was here and invite them over, they'd probably think I was another Halloway, out to trap them. I know the way they think, Thomas. Honestly, it's better just to leak a word or two and let their natural grapevine take over. In a few days, everyone will want to meet Janella.''

He turned again, pulling into the curving driveway of a tall, boxy building surrounded by palm trees and exotic flowers. "Our hotel,'' he announced.

A young man leaned over to open Janella's door. She shot a frightened glance at Thomas.

"It's okay. Go ahead, I'll be right behind you.''

She nodded and got out. Alex joined them after handing his keys to the youth. Janella saw the boy taking their luggage from the trunk. He then handed the keys to another boy, who drove the car away, presumably to park it. Alex went ahead of them to the smiling woman at the desk. "I have a reservation in the name of Vrooman and one in the name of Duffy,'' he told her.

Janella looked around the elegant lobby, thinking it pretty, but rather cold and impersonal. So far removed from Thomas's cozy living room. And there seemed to be strangers everywhere. Several pairs of eyes stared openly at her, and she shifted her feet uncomfortably. Why were they so interested in her? Who were they, anyway? Did they know her secret? Could they see, somehow, a sign that she was not one of them?

In seconds Vrooman had a pair of plastic cards in his

hand. He handed one of them to Thomas. "Why don't you two go on up? I'm going to get things under way."

The people continued watching her, and Janella felt like crawling under the carpet on the floor to escape those knowing eyes.

Thomas took the card in one hand, clasped Janella's hand with his other and led her down a hall and into an elevator. But she felt those strange eyes on her back the whole time. The doors slid closed and she sighed in relief. They were alone.

Too much was happening too fast. An icy finger of dread traced a path over her spine and Janella knew it wasn't just her nervousness. Something was wrong. She could feel it. She glanced up at Thomas, very nearly blurting that she hated it here, that she wanted to go home, now, with him.

But she couldn't do that. He expected her to stay. If she told him how she felt, he'd take her back with him, even though he didn't want her. She couldn't force herself on him that way.

"You're scared, aren't you?" he asked, reading her feelings as if she *had* spoken them after all.

"A little."

"Don't be." He took her hand again, squeezed it gently. "I'm not going to let anything bad happen to you, Janella. I promise."

She tried to smile, but if it looked as forced as it felt, it wouldn't fool him. His reassurance was a weak one, because she knew he'd leave her soon. And then what would she do? Giving in to her fear, she slid her arms around his waist, pressed her face into his shirt.

His strong arms came around her as she'd hoped they would. Oh, if only she could stay right here, protected and safe in his embrace, forever.

But the car stopped and the doors slid open. Thomas stepped away from her, took her hand. "Come on. It'll be all right."

Chapter 12

Thomas had reserved a suite. He'd known somewhere inside him that he probably ought to get them separate rooms, but his mind had balked at the idea. He hadn't stopped to analyze that, partly because he was afraid of what that kind of soul-searching might reveal. He didn't want to figure out his motivations. He just did what felt right, and keeping Janella with him for as long as possible felt more right than anything else he could think of. So he'd booked a suite.

And it was a nice one. Roomy, with a little living room and a kitchenette separated by a hardwood counter. The bedroom was through a door on the right, bath just beyond. There was a tiny cubbyhole of a refrigerator and a little two-burner stove. A sofa and chairs, a wet bar, a TV and VCR.

Janella barely looked around, though. She just walked to the sofa and sank onto it, her eyes wide and glazed. She was scared to death. Of what, Thomas had no idea. She certainly shouldn't be this afraid of meeting some of her own people. People who'd fled their planet for the same reasons she had.

Seconds after he closed the door, someone tapped on it. The bellhop with their luggage. Thomas let him in, tipped him and closed the door behind him when he left. Janella still sat, staring at nothing.

"Try and enjoy this, Janella. Think of it as our honeymoon, okay?"

She blinked and met his eyes, and he thought he detected a glimmer in hers. Tears, maybe. So he'd said the wrong thing again. That was about par for the course, wasn't it?

He ought to tell her, he supposed, that there was a chance her father might be here. Maybe that would cheer her up. But he hesitated. If it turned out he was wrong, her devastation would be worse than ever. No. Better to wait until he was sure.

Meanwhile, he suddenly realized, he had the perfect opportunity to make up for the sham of their wedding day and the pain he'd seen in her eyes.

"So, what do you want to do first?"

She frowned. "Do?"

"Sure. We're not just going to sit here staring at the walls, are we?"

She knew what he was doing. He wanted to keep her too busy to have time to worry or feel afraid. And it worked. Thomas insisted on taking her shopping, helped her pick out a bathing suit, bought her expensive perfume after spending an hour sniffing from various bottles. They walked through the busy streets, browsing in countless shops and finally ending up at the small, but elaborate theater, where they stood in line for tickets. And then he sat beside her through a production of *The Music Man* that had her laughing and crying alternately.

Afterward, arm in arm, they walked slowly back to the hotel. And she felt good. So close to him, closer maybe than ever before. And when she leaned into his side, he didn't pull away, but instead slipped an arm around her shoulders as if it were a natural thing to do. It certainly felt natural to her. Walking at his side, in the cradle of his strong arm, beneath the pale halfmoon in a starry sky.

"Enjoy the play?"

She smiled up at him. "It was wonderful. Did you?"

"Well, it's not Broadway, but it wasn't half-bad." He looked through a window as they passed it and stopped walking. "What do you say to something to eat, hmm? My stomach is empty."

She nodded. She'd have agreed to anything that would prolong this time with him. When would he leave? she wondered. How much longer would she have him near her this way?

He guided her through the doors of a small café, chose a table, even held her chair for her. He really was attentive tonight. She'd noticed that Alex had a room to himself, while she and Thomas shared one. Had Alex made those arrangements? Or had it been Thomas's idea? And if it had been Thomas, then why had he done it? The thought that he might not be averse to making love to her again niggled at her brain nonstop.

A waitress brought them menus, and Thomas excused himself while Janella perused hers, heading toward the pay phone in the back. He was calling to check in with Alex, she knew. And a chill of foreboding crawled over her spine.

"Can he be trusted?"

She stiffened as the deep whisper came from just behind her, near her ear. Turning in her seat, she came face-to-face with a young man whose hair and almond eyes were as dark as her own.

"Can he?" the man repeated.

She blinked and nodded, terror making her throat go dry. "Who is he?"

She wet her lips with her tongue. "My...my husband."

A little of the harshness left the man's face, and he glanced toward Thomas. He nodded and stared hard at her again. "And the other one, the one who came here with you?"

She shook her head, confused and frightened. "I don't understand what you want to know."

Dark eyes narrowed, but the set jaw eased fractionally. "Your father is a hunted man, Janella. Your mother's reach is long, felt even here. We can't be too careful."

She knew her eyes widened, and she fought to breathe. "My father?"

The man nodded, his gaze darting every few seconds to Thomas across the room, his back to them. "If you want to see him, it will have to be alone. I can't be sure of the two men."

"*See* him? I don't under—"

"You must tell no one, Janella. *No one,* do you understand? Your father's life will be in jeopardy if you do."

"My *father* is serving a life sentence in prison." Her fierce whisper drew the waitress's eye. She frowned at them, a little concerned, perhaps.

The man blinked, shock erasing the insistence from his eyes. "You don't know? Honestly, you don't..." He glanced up, and Janella followed his gaze. Thomas had turned in their direction, and while he still held the phone to his ear, she knew by his frown he'd be coming over in seconds. "Your father is here, Janella. I swear it to you. He knows you're here and he wants to see you."

Thomas was hanging up the phone now. He came toward them.

"Tonight," the man said quickly. "Midnight, room 804. And come alone." He turned and hurried away, going through the café's door and out into the night just as Thomas's hand fell on her shoulder.

She jumped, startled.

"What's wrong? You're white as a sheet." He took her

chin in one hand, turned her face to him. "Who was that guy? What did he say to you?"

She blinked, trying to erase the confusion from her mind. Her father? Here? Could it be?

She bit her lip against a flood of hopeful tears and shook her head. "Nothing, Thomas. Just a stranger making small talk." Lies. Lies, told boldly to the man she loved. It sickened her to utter the words. And it seemed senseless. She knew she could trust Thomas, more than anyone in the universe. She'd trust him with her life.

But if she told him, he'd insist on going there with her tonight. And if he did that, she might miss the opportunity to see her father again. She couldn't take that chance. She'd tell Thomas everything, but tomorrow, when she'd learned what this was all about.

She was keeping something from him. Thomas could see it in her eyes. And he could see, too, that she didn't like doing it. For the tenth time since they'd left the café, he wished he'd collared the jerk who'd been talking to her and demanded to know what he'd said. Whatever it was, it had upset her. He didn't like seeing her distressed. And he especially didn't like that she felt she couldn't share it with him.

She was in the bathroom now, getting ready for bed. Thomas had unpacked for both of them after she'd taken what she needed from her suitcase. Then he paced and he wondered. And worried.

Something was happening inside him. Something way down deep was stirring to life, like a big powerful dinosaur that had been asleep for a hundred years. It was coming awake in there, and it was taking control of his every thought. Thomas paced and tried to identify it. He thought it might just be the remnants of the child he'd chased away from his heart. All grown up and ready to take the reins. And though he'd fought it, the kid was winning. He'd already made up his mind to do something he hadn't thought he'd ever do.

He was going to tell Janella that he wouldn't mind if she decided to come back to Iowa with him. He was going to tell her it would be okay with him if she wanted to continue living with him, being his wife. She'd probably turn him down cold, especially if it turned out her father was here. But he couldn't leave without at least offering. Just in case she didn't realize how he felt.

He blinked as that last thought went slinking through his mind like a criminal dodging the police. How he felt. Hell, *he* didn't even know how he felt. Except sort of bereft and black at the thought of going back there without her. Facing that big empty house again, after she'd filled it for so many days with her sunny presence, was not a prospect that appealed to him.

Okay, so he'd make the offer. And whatever she decided, it would be fine by him.

Sure you will, Thomas. You'll make the offer, and you'll put it to her just the way you've planned. But you and I both know what you want to do is ask her—no—beg her to come back home with you. But you won't do that, will you? Because you're just a big, stubborn fool.

It was the kid's voice, with the force of *T. rex* behind it, instead of the timid, soft one he'd heard inside when he'd first come back to Sumac. He mentally ordered it to shut up and leave him alone, but he had a feeling that kid was smiling smugly somewhere in there. He might shut up for the moment, but he'd be back. He'd taunt Thomas to no end if he went back to Sumac alone. Probably for the rest of his life, Thomas would hear that kid telling him what a fool he'd been to let her go.

But what the hell was he supposed to do about it?

He flung himself onto the bed, staring at the ceiling. His feelings were a mess. He didn't know what to call them or how to act on them. It was the first time he'd experienced anything like this, and for someone who'd shut his emotions off entirely for such a long time, it was nothing less than total chaos. He was confused. Where was the guy he used to be? The one who knew exactly what he wanted from life and who let nothing stand in the way of getting it?

The bathroom door opened, but he didn't turn. He couldn't look at her right now. Had to toughen himself up again first, or he'd end up blurting something stupid.

Her footsteps were barely audible as she came into the bedroom, stopped beside the bed.

"Thomas?" It was a quavering whisper.

He turned his head and looked at her, and it seemed every organ in his body stopped functioning—all but one, anyway. She stood there dressed in nothing but that black teddy. His eyes roamed every inch of her body, from her bare feet and perfect legs to the skin visible beyond that sheer black fabric. Flat belly with its dark depression in the center. Firm round breasts he could taste again just by looking at them. The slender column of her throat. And then her face. Lips parted and damp, eyes round and uncertain.

He sat up slowly and reached for her, his hand skimming over her waist until his arm encircled it, and he pulled her down onto the bed beside him. She lay on her back, staring up as if half-afraid. He was on his side, bracing himself up so he could feast his eyes on her. She was every man's fantasy come true. And again he wondered why she would want a man so unworthy of her as he was.

"If you don't want to," she whispered, "it's all right. I'll under—"

"Hush, Janella." She still seemed unsure, so he lowered his head, tasted her lips slowly, languorously, savoring every second of it.

Her fingers twisted and played in his hair as he fed on her mouth. And she kissed him back when she realized he wasn't going to reject her. God, how could she have ever thought he might?

She loved him with every breath she drew, every beat of her heart, with every cell in her body. She loved him. And she couldn't bring herself to tell him, so she showed him instead.

She undressed him, needing him so desperately it made her hands tremble, made her clumsy. When he was naked beside her, she kissed him, his mouth and his jaw, and then his wonderful broad chest. She paused when her lips touched the cool stone of the amulet, and she met his blazing eyes. "You've worn it all this time."

Thomas only nodded.

"Why?"

He shook his head as if to clear it. "I'm not sure."

"I am," she whispered before she resumed kissing his chest. He'd kept the pendant for the same reason she'd cherished the slingshot all these years—because she and Thomas were meant for one another. Somewhere inside him, Thomas must sense that. It was so sad that he'd never admit it. But maybe—tonight—she would convince him.

She worked his nipples with her mouth, remembering the way he'd done so to her and the pleasure that had rippled through her when he had. She wanted to give him that same pleasure. She wanted him to feel for her the way she felt for him.

Her lips skimmed lower, over his belly. She kissed his thighs, and then, gathering her courage, she pressed her lips to the hardness between them. He shuddered, and she knew it pleased him. She parted her lips, took him between them, worked him the same way she'd kissed him, using her tongue and teeth until he gasped her name on a voice that was ragged and hoarse.

His hands clasped her shoulders to draw her upward. She straddled him, her thighs brushing against the soft hair on his. She lay down atop him, and he held her tight, kissed her madly.

It seemed to Janella that Thomas only dropped his coldness and pretense when they made love. As she lowered herself over him, taking him inside her, she felt this was the real man, and the feelings he refused to admit to showed here and now, as they made love.

He must care for her. He must, or he wouldn't move inside her so gently. His hands wouldn't run over her body almost reverently. He wouldn't kiss her as if starved for the taste of her mouth. He wouldn't whisper her name over and over again. She knew he'd been with other women, women he hadn't cared for, but she couldn't believe he'd been this way with them. She felt cherished the way he caressed her and kissed her. Surely it hadn't been this way for him with the others. Janella felt certain no other man could make her feel the way Thomas did. It must be the same for him. It must.

Her thoughts ground to a halt as Thomas drove everything from her with the sensations he was making her feel. Wonder and joy and rapture took a back seat, for a short time, to incredible pleasure. Physical ecstasy swirled through her body like a cyclone, driving her to the pinnacle with remarkable speed.

She clung to him, panting, clutching at his shoulders. His movements slowed, gentled, but didn't stop. And as he began stroking her again, she slowly realized it was starting over.

Gathering her in his arms, Thomas rolled her over, covered her body with his own and continued showing her the wonders of physical love. When she climaxed this time, he was with her, shuddering and whispering her name as he spent himself inside her.

When it was over, he held her close, and she longed to hear him say he loved her. Or that he was fond of her. Or that he was glad they'd made love. Instead, he only kissed her eyelids and said nothing at all.

Damn him for keeping his feelings to himself. He must feel something! Joy, regret, disgust. Something! Why wouldn't he talk to her, tell her what was going through his mind?

But wasn't she doing the same thing? She knew what she felt, and yet she kept silent. Maybe she was wrong to do that. After all, one of the reasons she'd come to this planet was for the freedom to express her feelings without censure. Finding Thomas again had been the biggest reason, of course. But she was being unfair to both motivations if she refused to share what she felt with him.

So she should tell him. Mainly because she couldn't believe in his coldness any longer. She'd seen none of it here. Only tenderness and kindness and caring. And he might think himself incapable of feeling anything for her, but she didn't think he could make love to her the way he had unless he did feel something. Whatever that something was, it was enough. She was going to tell him that she didn't want to stay here. That she wanted to go back to Sumac with him, bring her father, too—if he was really here. And she thought Thomas would probably agree to let her come. He might want her to get a house of her own to live in. And she would take a job helping Eugenia at the shop to pay her rent. But whatever happened, she *knew* that in time he could learn to love her the way she loved him. She would *make him* learn to love her. She'd go to him every night and show him with her body how wonderful it could be between them. And sooner or later, he'd realize what she'd always known. That they were meant to be together. She'd begun to doubt that in the past few days. But this night with him had reaffirmed her earlier conclusion. He was meant for her and she for him. The sooner he came to understand that, the better for both of them.

She smiled as she made her decision. She touched his face with her palm. "Thomas?"

He didn't respond. She rose on one elbow and stared down at his relaxed face, his closed eyes. He was sleeping. And for a moment she just let her eyes drink their fill of his beautiful face. No worry clouding his brow. No tightness in his jaw. She wished he could be so relaxed all the time.

Her smile died as she glanced at the clock beside the bed. With a little jolt she realized it was nearly midnight. Looking at Thomas once more, she wished she didn't have to leave him. But her plan of action could wait until morning. Right now she had an appointment to keep.

Thomas slept soundly as she carefully slipped out of the bed. She retrieved the clothes she'd deliberately left in the bathroom and tiptoed into the living room to put them on. She pulled the jeans right over the teddy. Added the pretty silk blouse and brushed her tousled hair. Carrying her shoes until she got into the hallway, she slipped out. Then paused to put them on.

She was wonderful. She did things to his senses, touched parts of his soul where no one had ever ventured before. He didn't want to lose her. Dammit, he wasn't going to. He'd been dozing in the most contented sleep he could remember, when she'd slipped out of bed. The emptiness was what woke him. Well, whatever she'd got out of bed to do would be done in a second or two. She'd come back and snuggle into his arms, and if it killed him, he was going to ask her to come back to Sumac with him.

A sound made him frown and come more fully awake. Where the hell was she going?

Thomas slid out of the bed when he heard her close the hotel-room door. He yanked on his jeans and went barefoot into the next room, blinking in disbelief. Janella had crept out of here like a thief. Why? What the hell was she keeping from him? He thought immediately of the man he'd seen talking to her at the café earlier, and of how upset she'd seemed afterward. He'd known she'd been keeping things from him then, but hadn't wanted to push her. Maybe he should have.

He went to the door, pulled it open in time to see her stepping into the elevator at the end of the hall. He didn't get it. He just didn't—

"Thomas?"

He turned to see Alex Vrooman standing in the doorway of the room next to theirs. Unlike Thomas, Alex was fully dressed. At midnight? Thomas wondered why, but only briefly. He quickly went to the elevator and watched the indicator light on the outside. It stopped on the eighth floor. He hit the button and waited impatiently. Alex caught up to him just before he stepped into the car.

"What's going on? Where is Janella?"

"Damned if I know. But I'm sure as hell going to find out. You coming?"

Nodding, Vrooman stepped into the car beside him and Thomas let the doors close and thumbed the eight on the panel. It seemed to take forever, though he knew it had only been a few seconds. When the doors slid open he held them with one hand, poked his head out, glanced up and down the halls in time to see the door to a room just swinging closed. He prayed that was where she'd gone. And for a second he wondered why he was so tense and nervous. It wasn't as if she were in any danger. Why was his neck prickling as if all hell were about to break loose?

Thomas started forward. Vrooman caught his arm.

"You can't just go barging into someone's room in the middle of the night. It might not be the place."

Thomas hesitated. Vrooman had a point. But he still couldn't shake the urgent feeling that had consumed him the minute he'd realized she was gone. Adrenaline pumped through him, making him nervous and jittery.

"We can listen at the door, see if we hear her voice," Vrooman suggested.

Thomas nodded, and the two men started down the hall.

Janella stood there, and the young man closed the door behind her. She was afraid, she realized as she glanced around the empty hotel suite, seeing no one. Perhaps this was some kind of a trap. Some kind of...

Jack Halloway stepped out of the bedroom, and her blood slowed to a chilled stop in her veins.

"Hello, Janella. Did you come alone?"

She reached behind her for the doorknob, every cell in her body screaming to run for her life. But she froze when another man emerged behind Halloway. His dark hair was sprinkled with gray, and his face had lines she didn't remember. But his eyes were the same, warm and brown, shining now with moisture.

"F-father?"

He smiled and came forward, arms reaching for her, and she flung herself into them. Shaking so violently she could barely breathe, tears flowing now like waterfalls, she clung to his broad back, buried her face in his neck.

He stroked her hair and held her so hard she thought he'd never let go. "Janella? My girl, is this really you?" He pried her away from his chest, clinging to her shoulders, searching her face as tears spilled over his own. "My God, you're beautiful." He pushed her damp hair away from her face, wiped the tears from her cheeks. "Beautiful. My little girl all grown into a beautiful woman," he whispered fiercely, and hugged her tight to him once more.

"Daddy, I don't understand. How..."

"Ah, but it's a long story, child. And we'll have time, so much time now. You're here, right here where I can hold you. That's all that matters now." A sob tore through his chest, and he clung tighter. "You don't know how much I've missed you, baby. How long I've waited for this moment."

Her shoulders quaked with sobs of absolute joy as she held him. And oddly enough, the main thoughts going through her mind were of Thomas. She wished he were here, to share this moment with her. She wanted him right beside her in this room.

She sniffed as her father's hold slackened, and glanced around again, then went stiff as her gaze met Halloway's. His usual grimace had been replaced by a rather dopey smile, and she frowned, instantly suspicious.

"Why is he here?"

The knock on the door prevented anyone from answering. A gun appeared in Halloway's hand. Janella felt her eyes widen as the young man at the door called, "Who is it?"

"Janella, are you in there?"

"Thomas!" Janella started forward, then paused, glancing again at Halloway.

He nodded once and put the gun away. "It's all right. You can let him in."

The young man opened the door.

Relief was evident on Thomas's face as he stepped inside, and Janella ran into his arms, hugging him tightly. But he set her away from him, searching her face, frowning at the tears he saw there. "Are you all right?"

She nodded, smiling as more tears came. "Thomas, look. My father is here. He's here, and…"

Thomas's gaze rose to look beyond her. The two men stared at each other for a moment, and Thomas nodded. But he was already scanning the room, and when his eyes fell on Halloway, they hardened. Alex had crowded in behind him, and Janella saw him close the door.

"Maybe somebody better explain to me what the hell is going on here," Thomas said, his voice dangerously soft. "Halloway, you want to volunteer?"

She saw Alex's hand lift, and in a blur saw it come down again, hard, across the back of Thomas's head. It wasn't until Thomas crumpled to the floor and Alex stood there with the shiny gun pointing at Halloway that she realized what it was he'd been holding.

She dropped to her knees beside Thomas, sensed the suddenly aborted movements of the others in the room.

"Anyone who moves will die," Alex said in a calm, level tone. "Mr. Halloway, if you would kindly drop your firearm to the floor and kick it toward me, I'd be grateful." He leveled his weapon at the man as he spoke, making the polite request into a command.

Halloway's gaze swept the room, and apparently he found no alternative. He removed the gun with two fingers and let it thud to the floor.

Janella bent over Thomas, her fingers finding the cut on the back of his head as she cradled it. She stroked his face and whispered his name, begging him to wake up. If he died...

Alex had herded her father, Halloway and the younger man, whose name she still didn't know, into a small group at the center of the room. He held the gun on them, not looking away, and ordered Janella to get up and join them there.

She stared at the man she'd thought of as a friend and shook her head, ignoring his instructions. "Why, Alex? Why are you doing this? I don't understand..."

"You don't have to understand," he said, his voice flat and emotionless.

"He's a hit man, Janella."

She blinked in surprise at Halloway's voice as he gently answered her question. She knew what the term meant from the movies she and Thomas had watched together.

"He works for your mother."

She shook her head fiercely, staring in disbelief at Alex, trying to follow what she was being told, but not having much success. Alex glanced down at the gun lying near his feet and frowned in concentration. The weapon rose on its own, coming to rest in his free hand. As he tucked it into the waistband of his trousers, Janella finally understood. Alex Vrooman was one of them, one of her own people.

"So you've managed to track me down at last, Vrooman," her father said, sadness and regret tingeing every word. "I knew my wife had sent one of her henchmen to find me, but I had no way of knowing who. Been in hiding ever since I came here."

"You think I don't know that?" Alex seemed so elated, as if he'd finally reached a long-term goal. "Matalin, I wouldn't have used Janella to flush you out if there'd been any other way."

Matalin nodded in understanding, but Janella didn't understand any of this.

"So, you've won, then," Matalin said tiredly. "I'll surrender to you. You have my word. But you have to let my daughter go. She's not a part of this."

Vrooman nodded grimly. Thomas stirred in Janella's arms, and she saw his eyes open. She ran her palm over his face, knew he was awake now, saw him close his eyes again and lie still, and knew he wanted Vrooman to believe he was still unconscious.

"I would never harm Janella," Vrooman said. "I want nothing but happiness for her. It's the way her mother would want it. Besides, her only crime is defection, and executing her for that would likely stir revolt among the people."

"Not to mention that Shira would have you killed the instant she learned you'd hurt her daughter," Matalin said softly, glancing at Janella. "She doesn't take well to being defied, does she, Vrooman? No matter the reasons, I appreciate your leaving Janella out of this."

"No reason to involve her any further. It's you I was

sent for. But you're mistaken if you think I'm here to bring you back."

He pointed the weapon right at Matalin, and Janella cried out. "Stop! Put it down—what are you doing?"

Thomas squeezed her hand in warning.

"My orders are to eliminate you, Matalin. You're an escaped prisoner. You'll be an example to others who think of fleeing our justice." One hand worked the action of the gun. "Your body will be put on display when I return with it."

"Shira knows you've found me, then? She must be celebrating my death already."

"Shira trusts me implicitly, fool," Vrooman growled. "I was sent here years ago with her instructions. She required no reports on my progress, only my word that I'd return with your body. I'd begun to despair of ever finding you, until I was notified that Janella had fled the planet. I knew you'd come out of hiding if word got out that your daughter was here. And so you did."

Vrooman's finger slid over the trigger. Thomas surged to his feet and charged Alex just as the gun went off with an earsplitting roar.

Janella screamed. Halloway shoved her father to the floor at the same instant the gun went off.

Thomas hit Alex hard, like a rampaging bull, and they both slammed into a wall. They struggled, grappling for the gun. Then Alex got one hand free and plowed his fist into Thomas's face. Thomas staggered backward a few steps.

It all happened in a matter of seconds. The young man had managed to get to the door, and flung it open, fleeing the room. The door stood wide, and Janella's father stood at her side, urging her with his eyes to run, pushing her bodily with his hands.

In slow motion she saw Alex raise the gun and point it at Thomas. She saw his finger closing on the trigger, and she screamed, launching herself between them.

The weapon spat fire. Janella stood shocked into motionlessness by the red heat that seared her chest. She blinked as the room seemed to go silent around her, like a great empty cave. There was a rushing sound in her ears, accompanied by her echoing heartbeat, thudding louder and slower with each second that passed.

She was vaguely aware of her father attacking Alex like an enraged bull, of the gun sounding again as they struggled, of Alex slumping to the floor, his eyes going vacant.

Her knees were melting. Thomas was speaking as he caught her in his arms, his face contorted in agony. She met his eyes as he sank to the floor, holding her, and she saw the blood on his hand when he moved it away from her chest.

She forced her lips to move, forced the words to form, and tried to shout them aloud, even though she couldn't hear them herself. She prayed she could make Thomas hear them, though, before it was too late.

"I...love...you," she mouthed again and again, and as her eyes fell closed and her grip on reality slipped away, she whispered, "my husband."

Chapter 13

Thomas sipped bitter coffee from a foam cup in the emergency room of the tiny hospital. Matalin sat slumped in a hard-backed vinyl chair, looking shell-shocked and saying nothing. He stared, dazed, at the closed door to the treatment room where Janella had just been taken. Nurses and PAs rushed in and out, but Thomas had yet to see anyone with MD printed on a name tag. And he was just about sick of waiting.

"Duffy, are you listening to a word of this?" Jack Halloway stopped his restless pacing and fixed Thomas with a worried gaze.

"Yeah, I hear you. You guys were the ones protecting them all along. I was an idiot, refused to cooperate with you, and thanks to that my wife is lying in there bleeding from a gunshot wound to the chest. That's the gist of it, isn't it?"

Halloway blew an impatient sigh and shook his head. "I should have told you up-front. But I wasn't sure who Janella was or what she wanted here, and I couldn't risk it.

No one outside my agency knows about them, Thomas. And that's the way we want to keep it. They'd never have a minute's peace here if it became public knowledge. And we knew Matalin was a possible target. He told us a long time ago there would probably be someone sent after him. For all I knew, Janella could have been it.''

Thomas didn't care. He'd misjudged Halloway, misjudged Vrooman, screwed up royally, and Janella was paying the price.

''This organization Vrooman claimed to represent is nothing more than a group of diehard UFO watchers. None of them has a clue there are aliens living right here among us.''

Thomas nodded as if he were listening. He wasn't, though. He'd taken to watching that damned door, just as Matalin was doing.

''To us, they're refugees fleeing a hostile government. We take care of them just as we would anyone seeking political asylum. We've even tried to establish diplomatic relations with their planet, but the bastards up there want no part of it.''

Thomas crushed the cup in his hand. ''Where the hell are the doctors in this place?'' He strode to the door, shoved it open and stomped through, leaving Halloway hanging in midsentence.

A nurse hurried to block his path, but he pushed her aside with no gentleness intended.

''Sir, you can't—''

''I'm a doctor, dammit. Apparently the only one on the premises at the moment.'' He snatched the chart from the stainless-steel tray and scanned the notes there. Her vitals were weak, and a glance at the digital dial told him her blood pressure was falling, gradually but steadily. ''Where the hell are her X rays?''

The nurse seemed flustered, but not willing to argue. She pointed to the wall where the dark sheets were mounted, and Thomas went to them, looked at the story they told, and felt his heart plummet.

The door opened, and when he turned it was to see an elderly man in a white coat. His gaze darted to the name tag and he sighed in relief.

"Finally." He extended a hand. "I'm glad you're here, Dr. Kopelson. Looks like she's bleeding internally. That bullet's lodged tight against the heart, and time is the enemy. She needs surgery, STAT. You'd better go scrub and get these people busy prepping her. I—"

The man held up a hand and Thomas's words died away at the grim expression. "I'm not a surgeon, son. Chief of staff and a plain old GP, but not a cutter."

Swallowing hard, Thomas searched the man's face. "So where's the surgeon?"

"Not here, I'm afraid. Dr. Tunner is on call. He's on his way."

"How long?"

Kopelson lowered his eyes. "An hour. Too long, I'm afraid."

Thomas pushed both hands through his hair, chin falling to his chest. He swore under his breath. "This isn't happening. Dammit to hell, this isn't happening."

"You a surgeon, son?"

Thomas's head came up fast, his eyes meeting Kopelson's worried ones. "Not practicing. It's been months—"

"She's not going to make it an hour, Dr. Duffy. If you try, she might have a chance."

"Dammit, she's my *wife!* I can't—"

"There's no one else."

A lump that nearly choked him settled in Thomas's throat. He turned, walked numbly to the table where Janella lay, pale and still. He took her hand in his, felt its unnatural coolness, gazed down at her face. And he knew, right then, that he loved this woman. He had for a while now; he'd only denied it with everything in him. If he lost her, his life would be nothing but a huge, empty hole. He couldn't let her die. He had to try....

He glanced up at the white-haired doctor who stood nearby. "Prep her. Get me the best surgical nurses you've got."

Kopelson nodded and sent a glance toward one of the nurses, who had all of them moving in an instant. "C'mon, I'll show you to the scrub room."

"In a second." Thomas took one last look at Janella, ran his hand over her cool face. There was no iron wall to stand between him and this patient. No way he could be calm and practical and remove himself emotionally. He loved her. She'd become the most important thing in his world, brought him back to life when he'd been no more than a functioning corpse for so long. He couldn't lose her.

Bending over her, he pressed his lips to hers. "It's gonna be all right, baby. I'll take care of you. I swear it."

When he straightened, he saw a nurse blink tears from her eyes. There were a few in his own right now. And his hands were shaking. Dammit, he had to get a grip, had to make this come out right. Janella's life was in his hands.

Turning, he walked quickly back into the waiting room. He knelt in front of Matalin, clasped the man's hands in both of his.

Matalin met his gaze, devastation in his eyes. "Is she—"

"No. But she can't last long the way she is. She needs surgery, and there's no one who can get here fast enough to do it."

Halloway came to stand behind Thomas. "Except you, right Duffy?"

Thomas closed his eyes, nodded once. Halloway swore.

"I need to know if there's been any precedent. Any of your people, Matalin, who've undergone surgery here. Any reactions they might have had to anesthesia—"

"I don't know," Matalin said, sounding as if it were an effort for him to form the words.

"I do."

Thomas straightened, turned to face Halloway. "Tell me then. Anything that might help."

Halloway nodded. "If I'd handled this differently, she might never have been hurt. Dammit, Duffy, you have to know I never wanted to hurt her."

"Look, if anyone mishandled things, it was me. But there's not time for recriminations now. Tell me what you know," Thomas insisted. "Time is of the essence, Jack."

Clearing his throat, Halloway focused, eyes intense as he scanned his mind for the details Thomas needed. "A woman had a C-section two years ago and died on the table. They used a spinal block. Baby's heart stopped, too, but it was revived."

Thomas blinked, fear creeping up on him darker and bigger than any he'd felt in his life.

"Then there was an emergency appendectomy six months ago. Young boy. They used a general anesthesia, and he came through it all right."

Thomas nodded, turned again to Matalin. "I'm asking your permission to operate on her, Matt. I know you don't know me. You've got no reason to trust me, but I swear, I'll do my damnedest to save her."

Matalin looked up, then rose and stood nose to nose with Thomas. "But I do know you, Thomas. You're the young hero my daughter met in the woods such a long time ago. The one who chased off some toothy creature that frightened her, and brought her back to me, safe and sound."

Thomas's head lowered to hide his damn tears from this man. Remembering her then was almost too much to bear.

Matalin lifted his hand and settled it on Thomas's shoulder. "She talked about you all the way home," he said softly. "Told me she'd never marry, no matter how many choices she might be given in the future, because she'd fallen in love that night. And I have to believe that love survived all the years in between. When she came back here, she came to you. And she stayed with you."

Thomas closed his eyes, remembering with a rush of emotion the words Janella had uttered as she lay bleeding in his arms in that hotel room. Still, he couldn't believe they were true. "There were circumstances—"

"I know all about the circumstances of your marriage, young man. Jack filled me in. I also know what I saw in her eyes when you came into that room tonight. If my daughter loves you—and make no mistake, Thomas, she does love you—then you've already earned my trust."

Hell, the guy was going to have Thomas sobbing too hard to think straight if he kept it up. "Thanks for that," he managed, but his voice had gone coarse and gravelly.

"I'll ask you only one question," Matalin went on. "Do *you* love *her*?"

Thomas stared into those deep black eyes, eyes so much like Janella's. "More than I ever imagined possible."

Matalin smiled weakly and nodded. "At home, they'd have just let her die. No heroes like you there, my boy." His eyes narrowed. "Do you have any idea how beautiful it is, what you do?" He shook his head. "No, I don't suppose you do. It's taken for granted here, isn't it? No matter the injury or illness, your people know that somewhere there's a doctor who will do his utmost, give his all, to save them. How lucky they are to have you among them, Thomas."

Thomas felt new tears well up in his eyes.

"And how lucky I am," Matalin added, "to have you as my son."

Son. God, no one had called him that since his father had died. Hell, he couldn't let Matalin down, not now. The older man gripped Thomas in a surprisingly strong embrace, and Thomas automatically hugged him in return.

When Matalin released Thomas, Halloway slapped his shoulder. "I'll go find that chief of staff guy and see if I can help him get whatever clearance you need to operate here. You get busy. Get your butt in gear and save your wife.''

Thomas nodded. ''I'll do my damnedest.''

Sweat coated Thomas's forehead, no matter how often the nurse beside him wiped it away. But his hands were steady. He was amazed that they were. Maybe they understood how important this was. He'd probably shake like a leaf later, but not now. Not with Janella's life in his tenuous grip.

The bullet lay nestled against the heart, perhaps nicking the muscle. He had to remove it without a single slip.

''Let's be ready,'' Thomas said. ''Watch for bleeders.'' The nurses scrambled to obey. Thomas carefully got a grip on the small, misshapen hunk of lead with the forceps. A nurse wiped his brow again, but he felt the sweat stinging his eyes. He glanced at the assistant, who stood across from him. ''Ready?''

The man nodded.

He heard the door to the OR swing open and close again, but was too focused just now to pay attention. Thomas pulled the bullet away, and another tool was slapped into his hand. He used it like a fast gun from the Old West, repairing the damage. It seemed they all held their breath as they watched to see if the bleeding started again. It didn't, and after a moment there was a collective sigh.

''By God, that was the nicest piece of work I've seen in years.''

Thomas glanced up, saw a stranger in scrubs and a surgical mask, with smiling eyes.

''Mark Tanner,'' he said. ''And from the looks of things, I'd say this young lady was fortunate I couldn't get here any sooner. I don't know if I could have pulled that off. Congratulations, Doctor.''

Thomas was rapidly going limp now that the crisis had passed. "Thanks," he croaked.

"You wouldn't like me to close for you or anything, would you?"

The man's eyes were still smiling, and Thomas nodded gratefully.

"Glad to. You go somewhere and sit before you fall down. If I had to perform a surgery like that on my wife, I'd be ready for a month in the mental ward."

Thomas glanced back at Janella, then faced the surgeon. "Take care of her," he said, and then he stumbled through the doors. Leaning back against the wall, he tore the mask from his face and dragged in several shuddering breaths. Someone ran toward him, waving smelling salts under his nose. Someone else shoved a wheelchair up beside him and somehow knocked him into it. Probably with a feather, he thought later. He peeled the bloody gloves from his hands, leaned his head back in the chair, closed his eyes and prayed.

And as he did, he realized that he'd never feel the same way about medicine again. Not if he lived to be a hundred. Not if he saw ten million patients between now and then. The iron wall had melted like butter, and even its remains had evaporated, leaving no trace that it had ever been there.

For the first time in a long time, he felt a little giddy at his talent for healing. Like the way he'd felt the first time he'd played nursemaid to a little bird with a broken wing. The elation that had enveloped him as he'd watched the tiny animal take flight again filled him now. He knew instinctively that Janella was going to be all right. And no matter what else might happen between them, he'd pulled her through, saved her life.

It was as if a light inside him had been extinguished for a very long time. Now it was glowing again, with blinding brilliance. Thank God he'd had the skill to do what he had. Thank God he was here for her. He was thrilled to be a doctor again. And he knew that every day, with every patient he saw from now on, he'd let himself feel that joy.

Janella opened her eyes to see sunlight streaming through the white slats that covered a window. She was in a bed, covered with a stiff white sheet. There were tubes in her arms that led to a plastic bag filled with liquid, high on a pole beside her. There were colored wires running from her chest to a tiny TV screen with funny white lines spiking across it.

And Thomas was standing there, holding her wrist in his hand and gazing intently at his watch. She pulled her wrist through his grip until he held her hand instead, and she turned hers to lace fingers with him.

His gaze found hers, and he smiled. "Sleeping Beauty, I guess my kiss finally woke you."

"You kissed me?"

"Once every fifteen minutes for the past several hours. I guess it would have worked faster if I'd been a prince, but there were none available, so..."

"And I wasn't awake to enjoy it," she said softly, pretending to joke, but feeling real regret at the thought.

He bent over her, brushed his fingers through her hair. "Hey, don't worry. There are plenty more waiting for you."

His tone was light, but his eyes more serious.

"Are there, Thomas?"

He nodded. "If you want them, Janella. I'd like very much to wake you with a kiss every morning for the rest of your life and kiss you to sleep every night. Would that be okay with you?"

She blinked in shock, wondering if he was asking what she hoped he was asking. She tried to sit up, and pain split her chest down the middle. She cried out, and his hands eased her back to the pillows.

"Easy, honey. Don't try to move so much. You're gonna have to be still for a while."

It was difficult to be still when her heart's desire seemed to be on the line, right this minute. And when there were so many questions whirling in her mind. "My father?"

"Matt's fine."

"Matt?" She'd never heard anyone call her father "Matt" before, but she thought he might like it.

"I sent a nurse to let him know you were coming around. Alex is dead. Halloway…" He shook his head. "Believe it or not, Halloway turned out to be one of the good guys."

She closed her eyes and sighed. "Then it's over."

"Oh, no, it isn't, Princess. Not by a long shot."

She frowned at him, about to ask him what he was saying, but she stopped when her father came into the room, all the tension fleeing his face when he saw her. He rushed forward, took her hands in his and kissed the backs of them.

"I'd like to hug your breath away, my girl, but your doctor says I have to be gentle."

"I'm so glad to see you," she told him, tears flooding her eyes the second she saw him.

"Me, too."

Thomas cleared his throat, drawing both gazes. "Actually, Matt, you're just in time. I want to do this right, this time."

Janella tilted her head, confused. Her father sent Thomas a wink. "Go right ahead, my boy. Ask away."

Thomas grinned. "Didn't know you were a mind reader."

"I'm not. Just a good guesser. So spit it out."

"What are you two talking about?" Janella asked, feeling she was missing something important.

"I would like to formally ask your permission to marry your daughter, sir."

Matalin grinned. Janella shook her head. "But we're *already* married." She bit her lip. "I mean, technically—"

"Yeah, well, I don't want to be married *technically*." Thomas glanced at Matalin. Matalin nodded, stepped away from the bed and waved an arm toward it.

Thomas came to the bedside, took Janella's hand in his, and gazed into her eyes. To her utter shock, his own were slightly damp, and his hand was shaking just a little.

"Thomas?"

"Since I came back from the South Pacific I've been a walking dead man, Janella. Or I was until I found you. You brought me back to life again, and if I lose you, it'll be an empty life." He bent closer, kissed her mouth gently, but she could feel the hunger he fought to hold in check.

"I want to marry you all over again. And not because of Halloway or Immigration or what the neighbors might say, I want you to be my wife…because I *love* you. I knew that when I almost lost you, and I don't ever want to feel that way again. I need you in my life, Janella."

She smiled. "Do you mean to tell me I had to be shot before you realized it?"

Thomas blinked as if in shock. "Well…I—"

"I have been in love with you since we first met, when I was just a little girl. And you, Thomas Duffy, have loved me all that time, too. I've been going crazy wondering how to make you see it, and after all of this, I refuse to give you an answer until you admit it."

"I admit it," he said, looking a bit uncertain.

"That won't do. Don't you realize how I pined for you all those years? And then I come back to you, only to have you tell me you had no intention of ever loving any woman. You owe me for that, Thomas." She crossed her arms—carefully—over her chest and waited.

Thomas frowned, then shrugged. "I dreamed about you after you left. Did you know that? It was the first time in my life I'd ever felt that way for a girl. And the last."

She nodded, watching him. "Go on."

He smiled wickedly at her. "And despite my determination to remain a bachelor, you've been driving me crazy
ever since you came back. I think of you my every waking
moment, dream of you every night, crave you when you're
away from me, lust after you every time you draw a breath,
and—"

"All right," she said softly, lifting a finger to his lips to
stop the flow of words.

"All right what?"

"All right, I'll marry you. For real this time. I like your
tradition of the father of the bride walking her down the
aisle to give her over to her husband. Can we do that?"

Thomas nodded, then turned to her father. "You're
gonna love Sumac, Matt."

"I hope so," he replied. "Because I intend to make it
my home." He gripped the door. "Now, I'll go and get a
bite to eat and leave you alone for a while."

He left, and Thomas bent to whisper in Janella's ear,
"I've got a suspicion he and Eugenia might just hit it off."

"You have a conniving mind, Thomas."

"Mmm-hmm. And right now it's conniving creative
ways I might be able to make love to you without hurting
you."

She lifted her eyebrows. "I heal fast, Thomas. And I
have no desire to wait very long."

They both laughed, but Thomas's face sobered, and he
ran a hand over her cheek, cupped her nape, caressed it
with his fingertips. "I can't believe the way I feel about
you, Janella. I can't believe how much I love you, or that
I'm lucky enough to have you love me back. But it's real,
isn't it? It's real. You're mine."

"I've always been yours, Thomas. You're just slow to
catch on." She drew him down to her, and he kissed

deeply, his mouth hot and demanding against hers. Janella reveled in it. And marveled at it. She'd crossed worlds to find this love, and she would never, never let it go.

*   *   *   *   *

**Don't miss
an exciting opportunity
to save on the purchase of
Harlequin and Silhouette books!**

Buy any two Harlequin or
Silhouette books and save
$10.00 off future Harlequin
and Silhouette purchases

OR

buy any three
Harlequin or Silhouette books
and save **$20.00 off** future
Harlequin and Silhouette purchases.

**Watch for details
coming in October 2000!**

PHQ400